THEY SHARED THE SECRETS OF THE HEART

CHARLOTTE—She was too beautiful not to arouse all men's desires and too daring not to play love's most dangerous game.

DOUGLAS—He wanted to show the world's beauty to the daughter he adored, but he couldn't shield her from its cruelty or its hate.

MAX—He would awaken a young girl's first stirrings of passion, and when the world tore him from her arms, her heart would know love's deepest pain.

CAL—He could please a sensual woman with his quick, reckless passion, but his caring went beyond desire and drove him to one last violent act of love.

BLANCHE—She was at the core of Charlotte's strength and goodness. Her ebony beauty reflected the spirit of the land and bore witness to its most terrible contradictions.

**MANY INGENIOUS
LOVELY THINGS**

Many Ingenious Lovely Things

Frederick Young

BANTAM BOOKS

TORONTO · NEW YORK · LONDON · SYDNEY · AUCKLAND

for
Hazel Angie Morton Young
and
Frederic Houston Young
two of
many ingenious lovely things

MANY INGENIOUS LOVELY THINGS
A Bantam Book / August 1984

ISBN 0-553-24187-7

Published simultaneously in the United States and Canada

PRINTED IN THE UNITED STATES OF AMERICA

O   0 9 8 7 6 5 4 3 2 1

Many ingenious lovely things are gone
That seemed sheer miracle to the multitude,
Protected from the circle of the moon
That pitches common things about.

—*Yeats*

1

SHE was blessed and damned in her father.

Years later, memory touched by glamor, she conceived him as all that was fundamentally masculine—intelligent, strong, graceful, and sensitive. She loved him perfectly in every way a woman can love a man, not excepting sexually. When his damnation, his failures, fell on her, she took them to be part of the whole she loved and loved them also, for they were failures of fullness. If he had not casually sold off the sixty-eight Lee Creek acres so that they could spend months rambling in Europe, she would not have been left penniless at eighteen with her illegitimate son to support. But she would never have seen the monastery of Monte Cassino which the Allies demolitioned shortly thereafter in the Italian Campaign.

"Charlotte," he quoted the epigram for the hundredth time, "learn to love luxury, but never become dependent on it."

The night of his funeral, Spencer Fulton, publisher of the *Concordia Herald* and the friend with whom he had moved through the strata of human society, spoke quietly into the palms of his hands, "I don't believe my life would have had any richness if it hadn't been for Douglas Morton."

Later, memory colored by time and loss, it seemed to her that Douglas Morton had had the ambience of Creation. His passions and instincts were Olympian. Given cause, rage or love could consume him. Yet his training and discipline were ordered and rigorous. He worked too hard and played too hard. His focus was too intense. Therefore he was loved or hated by those around him because he was too large for accepted social patterns.

The clash of passion and discipline in him was constant and destructive for he never quite found the vehicle to contain the two. He never really earned a living.

Like his father and grandfather before him, Douglas Morton was a lawyer by training. His great-great-grandfather, a Yadkin River farmer, had been at the Mecklenburg Convention in 1775 and voted to abrogate all "lawes of the crown." Charlotte possessed a sepia edged letter from his grandfather, Edward Morton, to his mother explaining to her that he shared Mr. Lincoln's opinion that preservation of the union was the first consideration, but like Colonel Lee, his heart would not allow him to bear arms against the land which bore him. He died at Chancelorsville, leaving three infant sons, the youngest of whom was named Douglas. This first Douglas Morton read law at the University of North Carolina and became the youngest man elected to the state legislature, a seat which he surrendered at age sixty-two to his son, Douglas, Jr., who, after four terms, returned permanently from the Georgian town house in Raleigh to the Well Street family home in Concordia to sit as judge in the Twelfth District of Kern County. He was still presiding in 1917 when his son, Douglas III, father to Charlotte, fresh from his law studies at the University, was commissioned second lieutenant in the United States Army and sailed to fight the army of the last man who would derive his title from Caesar, the German Kaiser. The judge died in his sleep as his son, the young lieutenant, led his platoon in yet another assault on Belleau Wood.

From 1918 to 1923 two spinster secretaries entered the quietly handsome portico of the little office of *Morton and Morton* on Lawyers Row and manicured their nails, wrote checks for their weekly salaries, and periodically sent bank drafts to their young employer in Paris, Rome, or London.

Douglas Morton III, his father past summoning him home to the family legal tradition, resigned his commission in France and proceeded to discover an Old World. His nature was curious. His education had been classical. He could not resist the geography of that education. At Rheims and Chartres, his spirit soared with the great Gothic arches. In northern Italy, the Romanesque. His letters from France and Italy to his younger sisters, full of sketches and aesthetic theory, make vivid a young man being touched to his final depth. *Today, with my own hand! I tickled the big toe of Donatello's David*, he wrote to Jessica, his younger sister who understood. He wandered the ruins of Greece, crossed the Hellespont to the wreck of Troy which Schliemann had recently excavated— *to get some of Achilles's dust in my sandals*.

And he learned a new world. In *ateliers* and *cafés* he

learned the new Cubism elbow to elbow with the likes of Juan Gris. A copy of Pound's *La Lume e Spento* still rests in his bookcase. Webern, Berg, and Stravinsky were being performed and he listened excitedly. But there was also time for the moody Rachmaninoff and the end of Romanticism.

There were nights too. The saloon pianist and the torch singer were part of his *repertoire*. He could Shimmy and Charleston with the best. *I'm Nobody's Baby, Whispering*, and *April Showers* sung in three languages helped him lift the skirts of girls of four nations.

When Charlotte was twelve she watched him carefully plant the only basil seeds in North Carolina. He told her that basil was his favorite plant because the hotel keeper's daughter on the Greek island of Chios had crushed its leaves on her throat and breasts to make her flesh sweet for him.

In Autumn of 1923, Douglas Morton returned home with fourteen trunks and crates of *mementi* from his six years in Europe. He came because Jessica had begged him to stand for her at her wedding, and she was his friend as well as his sister.

Perhaps part of the reason he came was that the guilt-level built by five years of sister Elizabeth's letters reminding him of his responsibilities to the family, the law firm, and the community had at last begun to bear on even such an instinctive creature as Douglas Morton.

Elizabeth was the 'different' Morton. Born in the year between Douglas and Jessica, she was pious and joyless. She positively *felt* her duty to church, state, and society. She continually threatened Rector Cary himself with damnation, and swore that if the right sort of people were Baptists, she would leave St. Mark's and its loose Episcopalian morality for one more pleasing in the eyes of God. There was no place for passion or humor in her life. To Douglas, Jessica, and later, Charlotte, she was an eternal inconsequence. Actually, she wasn't eternal. She only lived fifty-six years. However, in all that time she was never seen outside her parlor without white gloves.

Douglas instantly liked Chuck Horner, Jessica's fiancé, for two reasons. Chuck nearly beat him each time they played tennis in the days before the wedding, and he matched him drink for drink in the round of parties in celebration.

Jessica and Charles Horner left smiling for Mobile where Chuck would broke cotton, and they would sail and play tennis. Douglas's sense of loss at Jess's departure was tempered when Nelson Summers, the cotton mill scion, after a winter's, and wintry courtship, married Elizabeth eight months later and took her to live in the graceful, old Summers home to accompany Nelson's widowed mother on the journey to death.

Douglas was silently contemptuous of Nelson Summers, because he and Elizabeth were so perfectly matched, and he giggled to himself as the last of Elizabeth's belongings were packed, wondering if Nelson would be able to pry her pious thighs apart. Or if he would even be moved to attempt such a feat.

And so Douglas Morton III, returned from five years in Europe, stood in the splendid old house that had been and would become again, dead center to his being. In it he had grown to manhood, from it he had gone to university, to war, to Europe. To this house he would bring his young wife, then his infant daughter Charlotte. He and they, like the house and all who entered there, came under the care of Blanche Pfeiffer.

When she left, Jessica had hinted that she would like to have Blanche come with her to Mobile. Douglas promptly told her that he would die for her, but that he would kill her before he would allow her to lure Blanche from him. Jessica had glanced up at his face and realized that he meant what he said.

Charlotte Morton's earliest memory was an odor, a clear, sunny friendly odor—wonderful way to begin a life of the senses! Blanche Pfeiffer shed this odor as she held the infant girl whose mother had died bringing her in. It was the odor the child Charlotte would run to in pain and pleasure. It was the odor that she would require to know that all was well even when she was an adult. It was the odor of clothes laundered, then dried in the sun or before a wood burning stove.

Years later, when she told her father of this very first sensation, he solemnly told her that the day would come when she would have to care for Blanche instead of Blanche caring for her, and failing that, she would have failed finally.

Blanche had first come to the great house on Well Street in 1891 at the age of nine to help her mother with the domestic work. Three months after the birth of Jess, Eva Morton, the judge's wife, rounding a curve at a high gallop had ridden her horse straight over the first automobile in the county, John Carleton's Page. She never regained consciousness. So it was that three generations of Mortons learned the heartbeat of human care at the breast of Blanche Pfeiffer.

Blanche's skin came from where midnight is made. It was smooth as still water, fluid as velvet. Her full mouth was like rose satin precisely defined between the round glowing cheeks, chin, and broad nostrils. Her eyes—Charlotte would remember childhood moments when she dropped her play to stare into the surreal world of the brown, depthless, pearl-set eyes. Blanche was profoundly beautiful, even after the wiry, jet hair had become almost white and her natural grace had to carry an unneeded hundred pounds.

Her beauty was involved with her character. Blanche was wise and humorous. She was vaguely educated. She had sat with young Douglas Morton through years of Mr. Klifmuller's Latin lessons. She had poured their tea and she knew—in story, at least—*their* Caesar, Cicero, and Virgil. She had walked the six blocks carrying his portfolio each week to Mrs. Wyatt's weekly art classes. She understood perspective and the color pallette. And she had endured the early piano lessons with the grinding Mr. Schultz who thought McDowell the equal of Beethoven and who made young Douglas get Hanon by heart. An hour each day *she* saw that the boy's *tempi* were correct in each exercise before she would allow him to go on to the next page.

Schultz, endured and despised, had prepared the ten-year-old boy for Miss Katherine French, the plain, slim, bespeckled spinster with the dynamite legs and bosom who taught him that his weight must go to the bottom of each key if his tone was to sing, and that the *Moonlight Sonata* was *not* to be played by any but an accomplished musician. At fifteen he did perform the *Moonlight* at the annual recital of Miss French's pupils. Blanche heard it from the high school balcony where she was permitted to sit that night, and with Miss French and half a dozen others, knew that it was wonderful.

She sat up in the Well Street kitchen until one-thirty that night waiting for him to come home so she could hug him. When the boy came in, embarrassed, and slightly detached from the silence of the sleeping house, Blanche perceived that he had walked Miss French home and that somehow, accidentally and beautifully, the thirty-five year old maiden had held the slim, hard, virgin boy between her arms and thighs. They didn't speak of it, but he was covered with the aura of woman's love. Blanche blessed him and he hugged her good night as though he were embracing all womankind.

At sixteen the beautiful girl Blanche had married Grover Pfeiffer who intermittently worked for the Southern Railway. By the time she was twenty-five she had borne and buried five children, and was raising the two who survived with the three Morton children who were in her charge.

In Charlotte's memory, Blanche had only wavered once, but that was a terrible and valuable experience, for she learned then that there was nothing permanent and unshakable under the sun.

At two A.M. one night when she was eight years old, Charlotte was awakened by her father's voice at the foot of the stairs. She slipped out of bed and ran down the stairs.

Her father put his arm around her shoulder and said, "Come into the kitchen. I want you to hear this. And I might need you. Blanche might need you."

When they entered the kitchen she found Blanche sitting perfectly erect in a straight-backed chair, her black face glittering with sweat and tears, so convulsed with weeping that her massive bulk shuddered. The girl ran from under her father's arm to hug Blanche and learn why. But after a moment of embrace and crying out, she realized that the wall of grief surrounding her old friend was impenetrable and she fell away terrified. She turned to her father and flung herself into his arms.

"Don't be frightened, Precious. Blanche will be all right presently. But she will need our love."

Long, together they stood while the old black woman wept. When at last Blanche's grief began to release her, Douglas Morton gently pressed his daughter away, went to a cupboard and brought two small glasses of bourbon, took one himself, and gave one to Blanche, his hand caressing her heaving shoulders.

They both sipped in silence, then Douglas drew his daughter to him and said quietly to her, "Puss has got Grover again and has beaten him again."

Puss Hoffman was the plainclothes sergeant of the Concordia Police Department. Puss was particularly treasured by the majority of Concordia's population because he 'kept the niggers in line.' Puss was devoted to his work.

The attorney Douglas Morton was constantly surprised at the number of blacks who appeared in shipwrecked condition at court—some would bear scars and ruined noses and toothless gums forever—because they chose to 'resist arrest' and 'attempted to do violence' to the detective sergeant. The young attorney was surprised because of the manifest fear blacks felt for Puss. Whenever two or three or more blacks were gathered together, on the corner of Lee and Cramm Streets, before the Church of the Risen Christ, or in Skeeter's Pool Room, the mere appearance of Sergeant Puss brought profound silence, close inspection of their shoes, and, spoken to, the little shuffling dance which punctuated each servile answer.

Douglas Morton was interested in the policeman because Puss was the only sadist he had ever known personally. This was the sixth time Blanche's Grover had known Puss's authority to put an end to his disorderliness. This time, despite Douglas's efforts, he would go to the chain gang for three years.

"He jus ain't no good, Mista Douglas. Grover jus ain't no good. He won't work. Ever' time I turns muh back he takes money for a jug. He jus ain't no good," Blanche sobbed.

She whimpered on repetitiously until Douglas knelt before her and snapped, "Stop that, Blanche."

He took his handkerchief and sponged her cheeks.

"Blanche, listen to me. Char, you listen too. Blanche, I am a man. Everything in my background and guts tells me that I must be brave and enduring, that I must work for or hunt for the food that will sustain my woman who sustains my children, that I must provide shelter. How well I do these things is my pride. Do you understand? Grover is a man too. His guts tell him the same things. But everything in this society tells him that he cannot. Because his skin is black. He cannot repay his woman's care and his children's love by providing for them, or he does so only by leave of a white man. Providing mere subsistence at that.

"Grover is a man, perhaps sensitive, perhaps ambitious. Was, anyway. But the only thing he can possibly do for the rest of his life is go to the Southern Railway platforms and lift boxes and carry them from one place to another eight hours a day. And that is to be the sum of his work until he is so

7

broken down that he cannot do it any longer. And broken down, that will be his memory of his life. But, Blanche, remember. Remember with me. He was a young man—what? nineteen? twenty? Feeling his strength, when he saw you in your young beauty. And he must have said to himself, if that girl will love me and give me children, I'll kill myself to give her a decent life. And you did. And he thought himself lucky.

"Yes. Yes, Blanche, cry. Cry, because I speak true. But, Blanche, years go by. And he worked every day. But no matter how hard he worked and how dependable he was, there were always eight hours of boxes to be moved, and the babies kept coming, and each day he was dead-tired, and there was just enough money to keep him and you and the kids fed. Right? At the end of each week, it was all gone. Am I right? Even counting the money you brought home. No matter how careful you were. And at the beginning of each week there were another eight hours of boxes to be moved from one place to another. And he was getting tired.

"And that's not all, Blanche. Say he stops by Skeeter's to shoot a game of pool on Friday afternoon. And some of the guys are there and they are laughing and having a beer. Then somebody like Puss stalks in, and just stands and stares, hands on his hips. Just stares, making sure all the boys are behaving themselves. Then Grover and the boys stop laughing, out of respect. And they look down, and Skeeter says, 'Howdy, Mista Puss.' And then the great Puss strolls around the tables, staring everybody down. And if one of the boys dares to meet Puss's eyes, Puss stops and stares and finally says, 'I believe you been drinkin', boy.' Then Puss considers and then he says, 'Hefner'—that foul weasel that rides with Puss—'Hefner, this boy's fallin' down drunk. I think we better take him in and dry him out.' And he does—or doesn't—merely according to how Puss is feeling. Can you see, Blanche?

"And if Grover ever meets me, or even little Charlotte here, on a one way path, he's got to give way. And even if he's seventy and done his forty years of eight hours of boxes a day, and gray and covered with wrinkles, he's got to answer to 'Boy'. And say, 'Yassuh' to the likes of Puss. Think, Blanche, and you too, Char, what that can do to a man. So, Grover, your man, started by buying a jug on Saturday nights. Then it became Friday and Saturday nights, because with the jug there was no past or future. Then he started the weekend

8

early, on Thursday nights, and couldn't make it to the boxes on Friday. And so it went until he got laid off. Blanche, it isn't new. Historically, men have drunk wine and worse to escape life when it seemed unbearable.

"Blanche, listen, I am a man. If I was black, I believe I would either be a drunk or dead, because I don't think I could endure the daily assault on my manhood and pride that your men live with all their lives. Hell, Blanche, Grover's drunkenness may be a measure of his manhood. He is a drunk because he *is* a man and can't bear to be less. Can you understand that? Now, Blanche, I will do all I can for him at court, you know that. But you must remember him as the young man you married. And if he is sent away, you must have clean clothes, food, and tobacco for him when each week you, Charlotte, and I will drive out to the prison to visit him."

Blanche stopped weeping. She sat erect, breathing heavily, clasping Douglas Morton's hand to her cheek, looking deeply into his eyes.

"Blanche, you must understand. Grover and Charlotte and I depend on it. Especially poor Grover."

"Yes, I knows. I always knowed it. It's jus that sometimes it's so hard that I lets it slip away. Yes, I know."

Douglas Morton embraced her for a long moment, then gave her to Charlotte. He stood and refilled the two glasses, and gave one to Blanche.

He tossed his drink back and, when Blanche had emptied hers, he filled the glasses once more, hoping to get Blanche tipsy enough to sleep through her troubles. She did get tipsy, so tipsy that after saying good night to Douglas and Charlotte, she slipped and twisted her ankle when she got out of the Packard in front of her house. They helped her into her tiny clapboard house and Morton promised to drive down to pick her up in the morning, in case the ankle was swollen.

The next morning, bringing the beautiful brass-topped cane which had belonged to his grandfather, he called for Blanche. The ankle was swollen, clearly sprained. He drove her to the police station where Grover was being held, helped her in and told Whitcomb, the desk sergeant, that she wanted to see the prisoner Pfeiffer. Puss, lounging there, avoided looking at the two.

He left her there and went down Lee Street and told Billy

9

Kinston, who owned and operated the Negro taxi in the town, to go to the police station and wait for Blanche and bring her to the Well Street house, help her in, and collect his fare.

When Douglas Morton returned from the Country Club tennis courts at two-thirty, an anxious Charlotte met him at the door.

"Daddy, Blanche is hurt. Billy brought her home at two o'clock and had to carry her in. She can't walk. Billy said they waited till one o'clock to see Grover, and finally Blanche asked when she could see him, and asked if she could sit down because her ankle was swollen. Billy says Puss just came over to Blanche and stomped on top of her foot and she fell down. So Billy brought her home."

"My God."

He followed Charlotte into the parlor where Blanche was sitting on the love seat, her foot soaking.

"That animal!"

He gave Blanche's hand a squeeze and went to the telephone and called the Drs. Cleland, father and son, old family friends. Tom, Jr., his own age, promised to come by in half an hour to check on the ankle.

He did. The ankle wasn't broken but it was badly sprained. Douglas, Dr. Tom, and Charlotte helped Blanche out to the Packard and drove her home. Douglas Morton went next door to Blanche's friend Elvira and made arrangements for her to feed and care for her for a few days.

Then he said goodbye to Blanche, promising to come the next day to check on her, and to do what he could for Grover. He hugged her and promised to explain to Grover why she had not visited him.

Douglas Morton did not speak on the way home. Charlotte felt his fury and noticed that his fingers were white along the knuckles, so tightly did he grip the wheel of the Packard.

She huddled beside her father in the enormous car, vaguely aware that forces were at work that she had never encountered and did not understand. She was frightened.

"He did it because I brought her there. Puss just can't bear quality."

At home, Douglas Morton turned the car into the drive. But suddenly, he slammed on brakes, flung it into reverse with such ferocity that Charlotte was thrown from the seat to the floor beneath the dash.

Morton shot the car back onto the street and drove furiously through the town, directly to the police station. He screeched to a halt in front and blared the horn. He sat on the horn.

Officer Hefner's weasel face popped out of the screen door.

"Hefner, is Puss in there or on the road?"

"He's in here."

"Tell him to get out here," Morton roared.

"Puss, that lawyer Morton wants you," Hefner squealed.

Charlotte peeped across her father and saw Puss's bulk appear at the door, pause, and then slowly and deliberately saunter toward the car. She had seen Puss many times before, but now that she knew her father was going against him, he seemed enormous. Puss was big, six-feet-two-inches tall and weighed two hundred forty pounds. He was a powerful man and only recently had some of the weight begun to settle at his waist. He approached the car, squinting with piggy eyes beneath dark shaggy eyebrows. He was wearing the only suit Charlotte had ever seen him in, a light seersucker with sweat stains at the armpits.

"Get in," Morton snapped.

Puss studied him.

"What . . . ?"

"Get in this car."

Puss glanced over his shoulder to Hefner at the door.

"I'm on duty. What . . . ?"

"You get in this goddam car," Morton roared.

Puss glanced again at Hefner, then opened the rear door of the sedan and heaved his bulk in and Morton shot away.

The great machine careened through the small town and broke into the open country of the Rock Quarry Road.

Twice during the eight minute ride Puss spoke.

"Wh—where're we goin'?"

Morton ignored him.

Crumpled in the front seat Charlotte was terrified. Her child's mind knew only that the powerful engine was carrying her to a crucial time.

At the little dirt road beneath Kit's Mountain, the Packard slowed, skidded, fishtailed, dust-plowed half a mile and then came to a slurred halt before the magnificent abandoned quarry. The quarry was a huge hole in the earth, two hundred yards across and sixty feet straight down. It had been mined for granite for years until the dynamite had opened a spring that was too industrious to be pumped. The granite

11

company had abandoned it and the spring had filled it with sweet clear water. It was an incredibly beautiful, masculine vista, sheer walls of granite that plunged sixty feet through limpid ice cold water. Though posted, each summer it claimed the life of at least one swimmer who misjudged his dive from one of the precipices and eviscerated himself on a ledge below.

Morton ground to a halt before the burned out company shack. He got out of the car, took off his jacket and tie, and flung them on the seat.

"Get out," he snapped.

Puss opened the door and got out.

"What are we gonna do here?" he drawled.

Morton fixed him with a stare. "Puss, at last you are going to have to hit a man whose arms are not pinned behind him by Hefner or another of those skunks you work with."

"Looka here, Mista Morton..." Puss began, eyes shifting from place to place, any place but the lawyer's blazing eyes.

"Take off your coat."

"Now, just what is...?"

"Puss, you're going to fight. There's no choice. Take off your coat."

Puss finally looked into his eyes. He saw there was no choice. He slowly peeled off his jacket.

"Throw your gun in the car."

Puss unbuckled his holster and tossed the heavy pistol harness on the back seat.

Morton nodded and Puss followed his lead out to a flat space twenty feet from the Packard.

When they squared off, Morton took a handkerchief from his hip pocket and carefully wound his right hand with it.

"This is the way you do it, isn't it, Sergeant? You can beat 'em to a pulp and not break up your knuckles. Right?"

It was a decoy. Morton closed, fired two quick left jabs. They weren't hard, but they were crisp enough to perfectly ruin Puss's nose and begin a gusher of blood that lasted throughout the fight.

Charlotte could not have told how long it lasted. She was so frightened that she could not get enough oxygen to her lungs and tears streamed down her face. She leaped out of the car and danced around the snarling, stumbling, swinging, cursing, rolling, groveling fighters.

Her father's agility was his weapon. He tried to dance,

strike, move out of range. He went under, over, twisted, tried to flank, took jarring glancing blows, any of which, if solidly landed, could have ended the fight.

Puss was a brute. Twice he managed to grasp Morton around the rib cage. Charlotte feared he would crush the life out of her father. He didn't. Morton squirmed and pounded his way to freedom, trying always not to close again. Several times, scrambling for advantage, he did what he did not want to do, went down. Once, a rollicking tumble luckily left him squatting on Puss's chest and he still had the strength to batter and batter the face of the heaving detective.

Once the flailing, panting two rolled perilously close to the edge of the quarry, but death did not want them just then and combat jerked them away.

Charlotte covered her face when she saw her father's shirt shredded and his back cross-hatched with lacerations from the rough terrain the fight covered. Both his kneecaps were exposed and bleeding.

Finally, progressively, movement slurred to slow motion. When their muscles locked, they strained, trembled, gave. Attacks became aimless, lurching, broadsides. Taking the next breath became all the fight.

When it ended Douglas Morton was scattered on his back. Puss lay face down across his knees. Neither man could move.

Charlotte stood over them, sobbing, looking into her father's face, not knowing what to do, then kneeling, stroking her father's hair.

Finally, through swollen, blood-clotted lips, he whispered to her, "Water."

She dashed about, found a rusty tin can and climbed down to water level and filled it. She scampered up the rocks and knelt over her father. He managed to shake his head once and she gently poured it over his face.

After a moment, he whispered, "Puss."

She repeated the trip and poured the full can of water over Puss's battered head.

After another five minutes, with Charlotte's help, Puss managed to roll down Morton's legs and off him.

Ten minutes later, Charlotte helped her limp father to his knees, and at last, tugging him forward, to his feet. After many minutes the two helped Puss struggle to his knees, then feet, and the three of them, joined for support, lurched to the Packard.

Charlotte, still whimpering, propped them against the car and opened the doors. Puss fell head first across the back seat. Douglas Morton crawled under the wheel. Charlotte shoved Puss's feet in and closed both doors.

Fifteen heavily breathed minutes later, Morton started the car and began the arduous drive home. Four minutes later, he was still in second gear.

As they neared the police station, Douglas felt a tentative tap on his shoulder and heard Puss's hoarse whisper, "Round back, please, suh. To muh car."

When the car crept beside Puss's old Ford, Charlotte jumped out and opened the door and helped him out. Puss lounged against the door and whispered, "Thuh girl. Round front 'n tell 'em I can't ride tonight. Sick."

Douglas nodded to Charlotte and she ran to tell the desk officer that Sergeant Puss was sick. Then she ran out, leaving the Concordia Police Department with a great mystery.

As the Packard nosed out of the parking lot, Douglas mumbled with great effort, "Precious, don't let me hit anything. My eyes are closing fast."

If Blanche had been home to see the angle at which he left the car, cock-eyed, hanging out in the street, she would have said that Mistah Douglas was drunk again.

Douglas Morton sprawled on the couch in the parlor with ice packs on both his eyes, a three-finger bourbon clasped in both hands, devoutly wishing for the gentle hands of Blanche Pfeiffer. But his agony alternated with exultation. Though he had not won the fight, he had surely taught Puss that hitting a man whose arms are free was a different matter from punishing one whose arms are pinned. But best, Puss now knew that a bookish, piano and tennis playing Country Club snob just *could* beat the shit out of a man.

As Douglas Morton forced the stinging salutary drops of cold bourbon past his swollen lips, Spencer Fulton walked in, made his customary dive for the decanter and ice and poured his usual three fingers in a tumbler. It must have been exactly ten minutes after five. He didn't look at his friend for he always found him sprawled on the couch after his daily three sets of tennis on summer afternoons.

Today, Spence was excited.

"Jeeezus," he said as he poured. "The god of justice liveth and flourisheth. I just ran into Dr. Tom. He says somebody finally got hold of Puss. Says his wife just hauled him into the Emergency Room looking like he fell asleep in front of a steamroller. Says his nose is flat as a three cent postage stamp and the bastard'll be eating soup for a week. God, it's time. I thought Puss would never get his. Doug, I swear, when I find out who did it, I'll buy that man a bottle of bourbon. I drink to the avenger, whoever he is." He turned to lift his glass.

When he saw Douglas Morton's wrecked face he froze in shock. It was a full minute before he realized and concluded.

"Why, Doug! Doug, was it . . . ? Doug, it was *you*? Doug!"

He burst into laughter. He laughed and laughed and sputtered as he tried to drink. Charlotte rushed in to see how such merriment could follow such disaster. She found her father contorted in the agony laughing caused. He rolled off the couch without spilling a drop of bourbon, sat crossed-legged on the floor, bloody back bare. Spence joined him, roaring.

"Doug, I love you. Puss! God, I can't believe it! Pussy cat. Got his ass stomped. And by lawyer Morton. Every nigger in the county is gonna be drinking your health tonight. Charlotte, your father is a prince. Listen. How in hell . . ."

He straightened. "How can I get this in the paper without somebody wanting charges pressed. How did it happen? How in hell . . . ?"

Morton motioned to his deformed mouth, and then to Charlotte.

Now that she saw her father laughing, she realized that the shock would pass, and she told. Animatedly and proudly.

Spence was in rapture. When she finished he reached over to slap his friend on the back and it was then that he realized Douglas Morton had paid a heavy price for glory.

"My God, Doug. You've got to see a doctor. Let me see that eye. Jesus, that's got to have stitches."

He went to the telephone, gave a number. "Hello, Mary, is Dr. Tom there? Tom. Listen, I know who wore Puss out. It was Doug. Right. But listen. He's pretty beat up too."

Spencer Fulton drove them to Dr. Cleland's office where Charlotte held the drink the doctor gave her father and watched him groan, wince, swear while Doctor Tom cleansed and disinfected his raw back, bandaged his knees and hands, and used four clamps to close the deep wound at the corner of his right eye. He wore the small scar on his handsome face until the day he died.

That night Charlotte came to *his* bed to kiss him good night. He took her hand. "Precious, I've been thinking about what you saw today. I guess it's not too early for you to learn that there are men like Puss in the world. And that even men like me can act like fools some of the time. But you've got to love us—in spite of all the evil, meanness, and stupidity. All right, dear. Now, go to bed. Tomorrow night you can play the new sonatina for me and read me about Rikki Tikki Tavi, the smartest mongoose in all of India. O.K.?"

2

WHEN the ex-soldier and ex-patriot Douglas Morton returned to Concordia, North Carolina in 1923, the town was already over one hundred and seventy-five years old. It was centrally located on the main line of the Southern Railway between Richmond and Atlanta and was the location of the great steam engine repair shops and freight transfer sheds. Four miles north of the town was the main channel of the Yadkin River, a ready power supply for five cotton mills. The railroad and these mills provided a respectable living for most of the seventeen thousand people who lived in the town and its environs.

The town boasted two small liberal arts colleges, one for whites and one for blacks. There were three hotels, one respectable if not grand, with a graceful dining room where Judge Morton and his son and two daughters frequently dined; the other two were for railroad trainmen and travelers with less means. The latter two had resident prostitutes.

On the night before he left the town to fight in France, Lieutenant Douglas Morton and his family had seen the great Charlie Chaplin in person as he toured selling Liberty Bonds at the Iris, one of the town's three movie theatres.

At that time, as when he died, Douglas Morton was one inch above six feet and carried one hundred eighty pounds on his lean frame; he was a perfectly formed man, long legs, thin torso, and shoulders broad enough to bear the fluid muscles that his amateur gymnast father had taught him to define on the parallel bars. At sixteen he won the Country Club tennis championship which he held (excepting the years in Europe) until he was forty-two when he happily surrendered it in the third set to Ed Chambers's eighteen-year-old son, whom he had taught.

He was an excellent horseman and he showed promise as a golfer until one day—after driving his first ball from the tee clear across the Creek which cut the fairway of the first Country Club hole—when he declared that he would never again spend hours hitting and chasing an insignificant little ball whose entry into a hole was a matter of indifference to him. He thereafter antagonized Club golf Ardents by calling it the lawyer's game and saying that if they considered that exercise he wondered that they dare mount their wives each Saturday night for fear of heart exhaustion.

Douglas Morton was extremely handsome. His face was finely and classically modeled, full sensual mouth, straight chin, high cheekbones, high forehead which was always partially hidden by the dark waves of his willful hair. The waywardness of his hair gave him a slightly unkempt and boyish look even after it began to gray. He returned from Europe wearing a moustache which, though it changed shape periodically, was with him when he died. His smile was brilliant and always at ready.

Years later when she was an adult with a child of her own Charlotte would remember a hundred evenings when from his room she had heard his rich voice intoning

> When the weather's hot and sultry
> That's no time to commit adultery.
> But when the frost is on the pumpkin,
> That's the time for peter dunkin'.

When the little girl entered she would find him knotting an Italian silk tie and sweeping back his moustache.

"What's that song, Daddy?" she demanded the first ten times.

"Hum," he would reply, clearing his throat. "Actually, Char, it's a verse from a cantata by J.S. Bach honoring a certain St. Peter. It was composed in the autumn of the year between the birth of his thirteenth and fourteenth children.

However, my dear, you are not quite ready for that cantata yet. One day you will be."

"This all means that you won't be home for dinner, I suppose."

"Yes, it does, Precious. But Blanche has a fried chicken all ready for the two of you."

A few years later, when Charlotte understood that particular cantata, she understood that it meant that several dinners might pass before her slightly rumpled, smiling father returned.

For women, all women, dames to adolescents, found him irresistible—and he them.

Douglas Morton was astonished at the overwhelming love he found he held for the old house on Well Street when he returned after five years of war and Europe. He spent much of the time before Jessica's wedding walking about the house, touching, remembering, loving, rehearsing the past.

His boyhood had witnessed remarkable changes in the human condition, and these changes made him, with the majority of his generation, a devout believer in technology. He was four when the first telephones came to Concordia. He kept memories of the merry tinkle of the bell, and later, he still laughed at some of the party line conversations he had eavesdropped on.

He would never forget the miraculous night that became as day. He had been ten years old and the judge had taken him and his sisters to the Square to be with the rest of the town to watch the electric lamps defeat the darkness. A few months later, electricians, the men who understood the wonderful new power, wired the beautiful brass gas lamps in all the rooms of the house.

Well Street was a scant three blocks from the Square, commercial heart of the town. But the magnificent oaks which formed the arch above it and the lovely homes which lined it were firm in their contention that Well Street would remain residential. It did so even through the boom years following World War II, though the population of the town nearly doubled. *Things must be either beautiful or strong to become old*, his journal noted.

The Morton house and lawns shared a large city block with five other houses. It was located on the corner made by Jackson Street, so named because four blocks to the north was the tiny square clapboard office where Andrew Jackson had read law years before.

The house itself rested fifty feet back from Well Street. A square two-storied structure, with wide galleries on both floors across the front and along one side. It was made graceful and light by the perfect proportion of the columns supporting the galleries, and by the tall shuttered windows. Balance was maintained on the side without a gallery by the large bay window in the music parlor. The entire property was surrounded by six feet of dense hedge. There was a rose garden, which, when Charlotte was left to tend it, was seventy-five years old. There were two magnificent oaks and three elms which Douglas Morton said 'went to heaven.' The far corner to the rear, bordering Jackson Street, was the only flat, cleared space. Before 1918, it had been a carefully manicured grass tennis court. Later it would become a clay court, and, in the 1930's, a vegetable garden. Diagonally across the property from the 'tennis court' was a stand of four of the long leaf pines for which North Carolina is famous. Generations of Mortons gathered the perfect eight inch cones and sunburst sprays of eighteen inch needles for interior decoration.

At the far corner of the property was a small lattice-work summer house. Ivy and honeysuckle took it, as they did the gallery along the side of the house.

Rising in the mornings was easy for the girl Charlotte and her father, if his hangover was of human proportions. In robes they would meet on the gallery outside their bedrooms to breathe the honeysuckle, see the air fluent with birds, the ground comic with squirrels. Then Blanche would appear with a tray of steaming coffee and juice.

As children, Douglas, and, twenty-five years later, his daughter, Charlotte, used the columns supporting the gallery off their bedroom to escape after they had been sent to bed.

The boy Douglas had used them to go to Miss French. He had nearly choked with excitement as he padded along the gallery, swung his lean body over the rail and shinnied down, using inch-thick ivy stems for hold. Silent as an Indian, except for his heart which seemed to jar the whole night, he would track across the lawns, each bush known by heart for nights when the moon gave no help, strike the long easy stride down the newly laid sidewalks the six blocks to the little comfortable house where he would scratch the screens on her bedroom window. Many times she would be sitting at the window waiting. Without speaking she would open the back door and he would slip soundlessly into her arms and she could not hold him close enough, and kiss his body enough, and her little moans as he lay hard as an arrow between her thighs taught him that women too got pleasure that could shake them to the core of their being.

Twenty-five years later these same ivy-tangled columns were for his daughter Charlotte a path to sensual revelation. One night during her eighth year as she churned her pillows, furious at her father for his command that she go to bed, she decided to use the columns for the first time at night. She had used them many times during the day for a short cut, and for pure excitement. Tonight her fury drove her. It was unfair. The old grouch! The *reprobate*!—her newest word.

For an hour she had heard his piano and Mrs. Woods's violin playing over and over a Mozart sonata, stopping to perfect certain phrases, as they rehearsed to perform for the *Pro Musica*. It was ridiculous for her to be in bed.

And unusual. Normally her father told her to come down if a rehearsal, or an impromptu gathering occurred—Spence would drop by with his French horn, or Sid Jacobson, the shoe merchant, with his cello, or Miss French, or Dr. and Mrs. Neidlinger from the college, or any of the *Pro Musica* group. And he would allow her to stay until the session was over, no matter how late.

Sometimes she would already be in bed and he would call her saying, "Char, we are working on the Brahm's trio. Come and listen."

And she would join them in her nightgown, reading the score over her father's shoulder. He would always take time to explain phrasing problems or other intricacies. Sometimes he would waken her when he was working on a piece alone.

"Precious," he would whisper in her ear, "wake up. Come down. I just discovered something."

She would slip her hand into his gigantic, tennis-calloused hand and dance beside him to the music parlor. They would sit side by side at the piano and he would push the score before her.

"Now," he would say, "listen to the bass line."

And he would play. And finished they would both be pensive.

"See," he would say, "isn't that how it should be?"

And excitement would take them. It would develop into a lesson for her. Soon Clementi and Mozart sonatas ran from under her skillful fingers, for she had learned to read music symbols as she had learned to read language symbols and years later she realized how natural it was for a child to learn both symbols for sound concomitantly.

On such nights there was no bedtime deadline. She went when the fun or learning was over.

That night, biting her pouted lip in anger, she monkeyed down the column, nightgown catching on the ivy spurs, two stories to the ground, padded around the house, and climbed the rose lattice beneath the bay window of the music parlor. The night was soft, and the Mozart, despite repetitions of practice, irresistible. Her father was an ogre, a Grendel, a *reprobate*. Bed, indeed! She should be *there*!

So she *was* there, perched on the lattice, peeking through the vine growth into the parlor.

Her father was at the piano. Mrs. Woods was standing beside him with her violin. They were playing the second movement and he was cajoling her, "Make it sing, Eleanore. Must sing. Right. Make love. Like making love."

When they finished the movement, he sat erect and said, "All right. Lovely."

"Oh, Doug, we *can* do it. That's divine. That movement *is* like making love."

He took her hand. "Almost."

She leaned over his shoulder so closely that she nearly touched him, peering at the score. Charlotte saw her father lean forward and press his mouth against Mrs. Woods's breast.

"Oh, Douglas, stop that. Stop that now." But even Charlotte knew that Mrs. Woods was not angry. She wasn't sure Mrs. Woods even meant it.

"Let's take it from here one more time," she said smiling.

"From here?" her father leaned again toward her breast.

She placed her hand over his mouth as if to push him away, but stayed for the kiss.

"You! You're evil," she said softly. "Come on. Let's take it from there."

Charlotte listened as the piano and violin lines once again played gently against each other and then came together for the last sweet statement.

When they finished, they both sighed. Then Douglas

Morton took her hand and kissed it, and again pressed his mouth to Mrs. Woods's bosom.

"Douglas," she murmured finally, "behave. Stop that and give me another glass of sherry."

He sighed, whispered, "Witch!" stood and filled her glass and made himself a bourbon. When he brought the drinks, she was leaning over the piano, perhaps studying the score. Charlotte saw her father walk behind her, place the sherry on the piano, then lean, lift her hair and kiss the back of her neck.

"For you. The kiss and the sherry."

Mrs. Woods did not move and Charlotte saw her father encircle her tiny waist with his big hands. Mrs. Woods still did not move. Charlotte saw her father's hands move up and up and firmly cup Mrs. Woods's breasts. Then his hands moved down Mrs. Woods's waist and across her hip flare and around her bottom and all the way down her thighs and then back to her bottom, then her breasts. Mrs. Woods still did not move. Then Charlotte saw her father press his lean body to Mrs. Woods and hold. Mrs. Woods did not move, but after long silence, she murmured, "Oh, Doug. No. No. No, please."

Then her father turned Mrs. Woods firmly to him and kissed her mouth and held her close. Charlotte saw Mrs. Woods's arms close around her father's neck and they kissed a long time and her father's hands tenderly moved over the body he held. Charlotte could hear them breathing as they kissed.

The little girl now vaguely realized why she had been sent to bed. She was witnessing something *adult*. It was *very interesting*.

When the two adults stopped kissing, Mrs. Woods leaned her head into her father's chest and seemed to sob. Her father kept whispering into her hair.

Charlotte was breathless. She knew Mr. Woods too. She did not understand. But it was very secret, and exciting, and *very very interesting*.

Then her father moved and turned out all the lights except the tiny cranberry lamp on the desk, led Mrs. Woods to the lounge near the window and raised her dress over her head, then her slip, then her bra. Charlotte had never seen an adult woman's breasts before and her eyes nearly popped their lids when she saw how large Mrs. Woods's were, and how her father knelt and sucked them a long time. *Both of them!* But there were more and bigger surprises. When her father took Mrs. Woods's underpants off—why would he do that!—she thought how white and full and smooth Mrs. Woods's flesh was and she was startled at how Mrs. Woods's pan was a nest of dark hair. And she saw her father bury his face in Mrs. Woods's pan and Mrs. Woods flung her head back and closed her eyes and murmured, "No. No," over and over again.

Very strange! And very *interesting*. And very secret.

But more surprises.

When her father took off his clothes she was *Astonished*. She had seen her father naked many times. They often took long hikes on the river, and would stop, strip and swim out to the tiny wooded islands to sunbathe or nap. She had seen him naked many times and *that* was how he was. But this! His winky was—well, enormous now. And standing up. And looked positively gigantic and very stiff and proud! Mrs. Woods seemed astonished also, but very pleased, and she tenderly caressed his winky while she said over and over, "No."

Then Mrs. Woods said softly, "No," when Charlotte's father pressed her back on the couch and she said, "No," when she opened her arms and thighs and took him to her.

Well, *what on earth are they doing?* Charlotte was very excited and felt the secrecy. For a moment in the demi-cranberry light, her father's lean, muscle-plated body seemed like a giant insect bent on injecting venom into the soft, white, splayed body of a victim.

At first Charlotte was terrified. Would her father hurt pretty Mrs. Woods? They were locked together and every muscle in Douglas Morton's body was coiled. And Mrs. Woods's white legs moved to encircle him. It was strange and frightening to the little eavesdropper. Her father kept thrusting himself slowly but firmly to Mrs. Woods. And then Charlotte noticed that Mrs. Woods was arching herself to meet her father as he thrust. It was fearful to watch. But *very interesting*.

When they had done that for a while, Mrs. Woods began weeping, and it was then that Charlotte began to think that the two clasped together were very beautiful. Her father's lean body seemed a shaft which Mrs. Woods took to her and arced her own body to accommodate. And her hands moved over his back as if his body were the dearest thing in earth. And then she realized that the moans and sobs they were making were not of pain, but of nameless, powerful pleasure and she realized that this pleasure did not seem so different from pain.

When at last the two clasped, and held and held and shuddered together and went limp in each other's arms, breathing, the little girl thought that they had made a secret between them that they would keep forever.

She remained frozen as the two slowly fell apart as if it were a hard, regrettable thing to have to do, and held each other and stroked each other and nuzzled each other and spoke softly to each other. She watched as her father tenderly helped Mrs. Woods dress. Her own breath came more slowly as she saw with relief that they had not damaged each other. She was happy to see that his winky was back as it should be. Charlotte thought that she had never seen Mrs. Woods more beautiful.

When at last the two left the parlor, her father carrying the violin case, Charlotte skittered down the trellis, scampered around the house, and squirreled up the column. She slipped in bed, but dawn would come before sleep could stop her racing mind.

Sometime later her father stopped in to see that she was all right before he went to bed. She played sleep. She longed to embrace him but there were too many impressions and she did not trust herself. Nothing was as it had been.

For weeks she could think of nothing but what she had seen that night. She forgave her father for sending her to bed. Whenever Mrs. Woods was in the house she stole glances at her but somehow could not look her in the eye. She would look at Mrs. Woods's bosom and think how big her nipples were. And she was a frightened rabbit whenever Marshall Woods, the husband and owner of the biggest cotton mill in town, was present.

For weeks she longed to ask Blanche who knew everything, something—anything—about it. But she could not. There was a secrecy about what she had seen that she could not violate, even with Blanche.

So for weeks she walked to and fro in the great parlor, thinking, her first steps on the long way to discovery.

Many years before, her father, Douglas Morton, had walked to and fro in the same parlor, running his hand over the lounge and pianos and desk, thinking, rehearsing his love for this vast room. Six years of war and Europe had separated him from his home.

This had been a place for music. There were two pianos, a

concert grand and an upright. In the storage room above the staircase were thirty curved-back oak chairs which had been hauled down and set up in this room for the weekly *musicales*. In his father's time, people had made their own music, and the cello which stood in the corner had been the judge's instrument. Douglas Morton remembered the flurry of excitement each Friday as preparation for the evening began. He forgot the discomfort of the stiff starched collar Blanche helped him with, as he thought of the good music he had heard, for music was the one thing without which he could not imagine life.

Beyond the great parlor was his father's study, now his, a ponderous comfortable room full of books, busts, etchings, and engravings of Napoleon, on whom his father had been an authority. It was a place for scholarship and meditation.

Douglas Morton wandered, thinking. The hall with its giant beveled mirrors and forest of coat trees and brass umbrella stands. Then to the family parlor, comfortably arranged around the huge fireplace. Then to the loveliest room in the house, the dining room. A formal wedgewood blue beneath the chair rail, silk paper in quiet taste above, also formed around a white marble fireplace, a room heavy with the oiled wood table, Jackson Press, and serving tables.

It was the room in which young Douglas Morton had presented himself, washed, combed, and gleaming, promptly at six-thirty each evening. Sometimes he had to dart into the room with his hands folded for grace as though he were diving instead of dining, for the judge would tolerate no tardiness at dinner.

From there he stepped through the pantry into the vast kitchen over which Blanche reigned. He leaned on the chopping block table and vaguely remembered the old black woodstove where the gas range now stood, the icebox which had been replaced with a refrigerator. It seemed that by concentrating, he could actually hear the brass bell from the ice wagon as old Henry and his dead-tired nag hauled ice daily up and down the streets. He and Blanche would run out to stop Henry, and watch his cruel icepick cut glittering diamonds from the chunks of ice. Then he would help Blanche back to the icebox, running to keep from dripping all over her sparkling floor. When they got the refrigerator, Blanche had converted the beautiful wood icebox into a cupboard. It still stood in the kitchen.

He could almost hear other bells and sing song chants. The knife and scissor sharpener. But best of all, the dozens of old black dirt farmers whose mule carts carried fruit, corn, blackeyed peas, collards—oh all the brilliant greens!—beans and sunburst tomatoes and all good and beautiful things.

Food, he thought, is the most consistent pleasure this world offers.

On the second night after his return from Europe, Douglas Morton and his boyhood friend, Spencer Fulton, whose father owned the *Concordia Herald*, walked the six blocks through the town, talking, reaffirming their friendship. As they surveyed the streets with yet several old barroom fronts boarded up, Douglas Morton said, "Spence, I simply cannot understand how a civilized nation can punish itself by prohibiting likker."

Spencer was so dejected by Prohibition all he could do was mutter repeatedly, "Goddamit. Goddamit."

"Why, hell," Douglas went on. "Don't they know that man has traditionally needed escape from this vale of tears by one means or another, drugs, wine, likker. Why wine is older than history. Don't they realize that without an occasional flight from reality, man will go mad."

"God*damn*it!" Spence growled.

"It's those goddam Puritans. Damn them. Spence, if I could have one wish for this country, it would be that the Puritans had stayed home and let the Italians or the French settle America. Anyone but them. God, they have cast a long shadow across this land. If an American doesn't feel guilty, he gets light-headed. No wonder. Joyless, self-righteous fools."

"Goddamit. Goddamit!" intoned Spence.

One of Douglas Morton's first actions on his return was to establish good relations with several of the county's most reputable bootleggers. A great deal of a man's substance lay with his bootlegger. Spencer paved the way with introductions.

They had turned north on Main Street, walked a block and stood before the rundown old Hotel Vanderford, across from the Kern County Court House where Washington had spoken, not slept.

Douglas leaned against one of the slim Corinthian columns of the hotel portico. *That column!* Memory leapt between the two friends. A bond sealed anew.

"Do you remember . . . ?" Douglas began.

"Huh," said Spencer and their eyes met, memories fusing across nearly two decades.

The year was 1904. Midsummer. Dead air. Heat that had mass. Nine-thirty at night. The two twelve-year-old boys adventuring through the streets which were alive with open stores and the still novel electric street lights. They were rambling, looking into the hardware windows, watching for drunks being ejected from the bars, stroking the noses of the horses tied outside. Boys, they somehow didn't notice the steady, purposeful drift of people past them, headed for the Square and beyond, not even when they saw every man vacate one of the largest saloons and move in mass, buzzing, pushing, waving bottles, breaking into a half trot.

But quietly and insistently a presence in that night pressed itself on their consciousnesses. A hum trilled in the air. As the boys stopped to identify the source of the persistent noise, several volleys of gunshot split the air from the direction of the courthouse and the hum rose to a roar. Douglas Morton's nerves jigged. The Presence in that night was violent. It was Death.

The boys broke into a dead run for the Square. As they topped the hill that gave to the street below, they saw a mob gathered before the courthouse. From here the roar was deafening. Torches flared. The night was split sporadically by the spitting flame and crack of gunshot. The street was a swaying log jam of humanity. A semi-circle seventy-five yards in circumference clustered and pressed toward the great, columned, Graeco-Roman courthouse.

"Jeesus," muttered Spence.

"What . . . ?"

Center was unapproachable. And fearful. Douglas grabbed his friend's shoulder and ran for the alley at mid-block. They moved in near darkness behind the stores, stumbling on the piled refuse of the day's business. Several men ran before them.

"What's happening?" one asked.

"Sheriff Homan's done got them three niggers that chopped the Kirks."

"Wadda ya mean?"

The boys did not hear the explanation. They burst into the light of Liberty Street. They still could see nothing but the backs of the mob. Douglas leading, they wriggled their way

27

to the Liberty Street entrance of the Vanderford Hotel. The lobby was mobbed.

Conversation was loud and irrational. Bits reached the boys.

"What the hell's the matter with Homan?"

"They oughta string him up with 'em."

"Them bastuds used an axe on all four Kirks."

As the boys pushed toward the Main Street entrance, one greasy drunk laid hands on both of them.

"Stick around, boys. Ya gonna see three niggers with very long necks 'fore long."

Douglas Morton was frightened, but excitement compelled him. Spencer grabbed his belt and hung on as he groveled his way out the Main Street entrance. The hotel portico was solid humanity, stinking of sweat and liquor. Douglas's eyes went up. The columns! Three of the slim poles were occupied. He made for the fourth, Spence hanging on. A man gave him a boost, but he was twelve and could shinny with the best. Spencer clawed at the bottom.

Douglas could see the great khaki-clad bulk of Sheriff Homan standing directly between the two central columns of the courthouse. He was astride a crude barricade of courtroom benches. He had both his hands raised above the shouting mob. He took his broad brimmed hat and began to wave it.

A chant rose.

"Lynch 'em. Lynch 'em."

The two-beat rhythm swelled, nearly drowning the occasional gunfire.

The boy saw the sheriff suddenly whip out a huge revolver and fire three times in rapid succession over his head.

Sudden silence followed his shots.

He bellowed, his voice filling the building-lined street.

"Break this up. Them niggers is in a cell and they'll be in court tomorrow standin' trial for murder. The law'll take care of them. Now break this up. Clear this street."

"We want 'em," a voice screeched. Others rose with it.

"The law's got 'em. It'll take care of 'em."

"Give them bastuds to us, you nigger lover."

"I ain't no nigger lover and you boys know it. Every man of you out there knows me. But they's in a cell and they's staying there till the law deals with 'em. Now break this up 'fore you do somethin' shameful. Go home."

"Maybe we'll do you too, Homan, if'n you don't move."

The chant rose again. "Lynch 'em. Lynch 'em."

Again the sheriff fired twice into the air.

The chant muted.

"Listen to me, you boys. You're standin' in front of your own courthouse. This is where you come fer justice ya'selves. Don't do nuthin' to disgrace it."

"Hangin' them three black-ass butchers ain't gonna disgrace it."

"You listen to me, you fools. You know me. I been your sheriff for twelve years. I'm tellin' ya there ain't gonna be no lynchin' less'n ya git by me and ya know goddam well somebody's gonna git hurt bad doin' that. Now break this up. Go home."

Suddenly a voice from the edge of the crowd screeched, "I got the string. Let's do it."

Douglas looked and saw a man standing in the bed of a two-horse wagon at the edge of the crowd holding a torch in one hand and a coil of rope in the other.

The tide carried. A roar rose. Douglas saw the barricade and the massive sheriff disappear. Torches blazing, a flood of men poured into the huge doors of the courthouse. Moments later they burst back out of the door pressing before them three crouched figures—the only black men present.

As if by signal, the crowd parted and let the two-horse wagon through to the courthouse walk. The three Negroes were mauled and manhandled to the wagon and thrown like bales on it. Four men mounted.

"Gosney Woods," someone shouted.

The team was turned, the crowd giving way, and headed down Liberty Street directly below Douglas's perch. The narrow street pared the mass to a column ten or twelve abreast. At the head of the procession was a cordon of torch bearers, shotgun wielding men in overalls, and several falling-down drunks, one of whom was half-led and half-supported by the horses.

They passed two feet below the boy locked around the column, fingers tearing at the acanthus leaves of the narrow Corinthian capital. He saw many faces that were familiar to him, now horribly transformed. He saw Coy Trexler, the sixteen-year-old apprentice carpenter who had, with his father, repaired the summer house in the Morton backyard. Trexler's white shirt was plastered by sweat to his shoulder

29

and collar bones beneath the suspenders of his overalls. His hair was sweat-plastered to his freckled forehead, and gnarled in curls on his thin neck. His eyes glittered under the rust brows and the pointed nose gleamed above the aimless, sleek, thin lips, careless of their hold on the Camel dangling there. Light magnified the clustered brown freckles spotting his face beneath the day's grease and the night's sweat. Douglas saw that Coy was supremely happy. God and this night and three foolish black men had given vehicle for his hatred for all creation.

The wagon drew abreast and the boy's eyes fixed on it. To his dying day Douglas Morton could close his eyes and form that tableau. The shining backs of the horses. Four white men standing, three with shotguns artfully balanced over their shoulders, one with the coil of rope slung over his shoulder. They stared straight ahead, as though they were the guardians of destiny, untouched by the crowd which boiled about their barge.

In the center of the wagon were three black men. One was on his knees weeping uncontrollably, his whole body shuddering, his hands clasped across the top of his head. Another, standing, mindlessly shifting his weight from one foot to the other, eyes wide, screeching, "I never done it. I never done one thing. He done. He done it. Lawd, I never done it." He was hysterically pointing to the crouched figure. Once he pounced on the weeping man and began battering him across the shoulders. A shotgun butt in his kidney returned him to his wailing.

The third man was a handsome black youth who stood erect with his hands hanging loosely at his sides. To young Douglas he seemed neither frightened nor resigned, but merely curious. He slowly turned his head to and fro, gazing down at the faces that pressed about him, as if he were trying to understand. As he drew abreast of the hotel portico, the black youth turned his gaze fully on the face of the young white boy who hung from the column. For a long moment their eyes met and held. Douglas remembered forever the black eyes set in pearl, staring at him without hatred or fear. The next day he would see these same eyes protruding from their sockets, staring down at him again without hatred or fear.

"Dougy, boy," he heard from below him. He looked down

into the moon face of young Marshall Woods, the son of the mill owner who lived only a block down Well Street from him. Marsh was wearing a rumpled white linen suit, a straw hat pushed back on his head. His collar was loose, gold button gleaming, tie undrawn. His right hand was loosely tracing the turn of the wagon wheel, his left holding the neck of a whiskey bottle, and he winked broadly as he snatched the cigarette from his thick lips and turned the bottle up.

Douglas's eyes flashed from Marsh's face to the profile of the black youth. He did not understand what on earth one man could have done that would cause another so casually to usher him to death.

As the wagon passed beneath him a sullen purposeful quiet fell over the crowd. The boy suddenly felt a violent tug at one of his ankles which dislodged him. As he slid to the ground he heard his father's voice roar, "What the hell are you two boys doing here? You could get killed."

He turned and looked into his father's face. The judge was in his shirt sleeves. He was sweating, flushed, wild-haired and wild-eyed.

He seized the two boys and shouldered his way through the hotel lobby and to the desk. The clerk was kneeling on top of the counter watching the procession pass.

"Where's the Skipper?"

"Oh, Judge Morton. He's there in the broom closet. Back there. Probably shittin' in his pants."

The judge, carrying his burden, wheeled and pressed through a curtained alcove.

"Skipper," he roared.

A black, wide-eyed head topped with the round green and gold bellboy's cap appeared.

"Skipper, I want you to take these two boys home. Don't turn loose of their hands until they are inside my house. Do you understand?"

"Lawzee, Mista Judge Morton, I don't dare go out there."

The judge's face tightened. Yes, it was true. Some drunken fool might catch a glimpse of the scarecrow bellboy and casually take a shot at him. Skipper was too humorous to lose, not to mention the boys.

"Yes, you're right," he said. He looked out into the lobby. "Skipper, keep them in here with you for five minutes."

Then he knelt before the boys. Douglas had never seen his

31

father like this before, no collar, his moustache askew, eyes burning, "Now, listen to me, you two. You stay here with Skipper until this crowd is gone. Gone, you understand? Then I want you to run home as hard as you can go. Now is that clear? I've got to go and see if there is anything I can do to stop this madness."

With that he clasped both their shoulders and left.

For eternity the two boys stood in the demi-light beside Skipper who was breathing heavily and muttering, "Lawzee. Lawzee," repeatedly.

At last there was no noise beyond the velvet curtain and the two boys stepped out.

"You be careful now. You hear me. You git straight home," Skipper ordered.

The boys stepped out on Liberty Street. It was still. One drunk about half a block away sidled along the building fronts. Douglas Morton started after the crowd.

"Where . . . ?" Spencer began.

He caught up to Douglas's dogtrot, fell in with him, and they broke into a sprint. They ran up the middle of the street, three blocks to the railroad tracks, crossed into the darkness where the street lights ended. Now the air hummed with the presence which had drawn them in the first place. They could see torch light and turned from the street to cross the lumber yard which bordered Gosney Woods.

The crowd was knotted and swaying beneath a gigantic oak. Light from the torches flickered. Astraddle a huge limb about twenty-five feet above the ground the boys saw Coy Trexler. His skinny arms were winding ropes about the limb. The noosed ends danced neck high above the wagon on which stood the four white men and the three blacks.

"That's about right, Coy," someone yelled authoritatively. "It'll fit."

"Wait'll I git down," Coy croaked.

Two of the white men on the wagon slipped the nooses around the necks of the two standing blacks. They had to lift the third from his knees and hold him as another hand noosed him. He was still weeping uncontrollably.

The one continued howling, "I ain't done none of this. Please, boss, I ain't done nuthin'. Tell 'em, Luther. You done it. Tell."

A sharp, shotgun butt stroke across the face closed him. He never spoke again.

Douglas, atop a pile of logs, saw a ripple of movement among the heads of the mob near the wagon. Then he saw his father's flying hair, white shirt, and one raised arm, as he attempted to mount the wheel of the wagon. Then half a dozen hands clutched his shoulders and back down he came and disappeared from view.

"That 'uz Judge Morton," someone said nearby.

"Yeah. Wal, tell 'im he's done missed his chance at them niggers."

"Got them rope ends, fellers?" one of the men on the wagon yelled.

"Hey, let young Trexler do it. He arned it."

Coy Trexler's slight body was hoisted up to the wagon.

"Ahhhhll raight," he screamed. "Let's do it."

One of the men placed the reins in his hands. He struck the tall, stoic, black boy across the shoulder with the ends, wheeled him around. "Ahll raight, boy," he spat in the Negro's face. "This here's yore goodbye."

The young black still looked about him as if he was carefully remembering and would be around tomorrow to describe the curious things he was seeing.

Coy walked to the front of the wagon and waved one hand to clear a path. He gave a rebel yell which broke as he tried to hold it too long. Then he lifted the reins and let them fall across the horses. The wagon lurched forward.

The three black men, held from heaven by the ropes about their necks, took three or four capering steps, keeping their balance, as they walked, pacing the ground which moved out from under them, from under their anchor point. At last the end was reached. The ground on which they depended broke off. They didn't fall. They were anchored from heaven.

They twitched and jerked as though surprised to find that their necks had caught on something, a snag, which prevented them from joining all those around them on the wonderful ground. How they twitched and jerked!

Silence came over their fellows below until the silly puppet paroxysm ended and they hung, heads askew, hands behind their backs in an attitude of infinite patience.

"Heist 'em up, boys. So's all kin see," Coy's screech from the wagon broke the silence.

The three patient bodies gradually made unearthly ascension as the ropes were drawn from the ground.

"Yippee," howled Coy.

That broke the silence. The mob exploded. Dozens of gunshots ripped the night. Smoke billowed to the haze of the burning burlap. Again the patient bodies resumed their twitching. They turned slowly, then jerked before the blasts of the shotguns fired at ten foot range. At last they were so minced that only their shredded clothes held them together.

Douglas Morton knelt at the edge of the logs and vomited. When he had finished, his pale friend touched his shoulder and whispered, "Let's go home."

They did. Without speaking.

Young Douglas sat motionless in the leather chair opposite his father's desk in the study, waiting. He had witnessed a thing which had shaken his whole being. Death. Death willfully caused by men. Why had they done that? His father would explain.

His father returned shortly after he did. The judge looked permanently defeated. Hair, moustache disheveled. Distance in his eyes. His collarless shirt shredded.

He walked directly to his son, embraced him.

"I can't say anything now, boy. I just don't have anything to say."

"But why? Why did they do it?"

"Did you come to the woods?"

"Yes sir. I couldn't help it."

"Of course." The judge splashed himself a drink. "Come with me."

They walked into the kitchen. There the judge silently made his son a cup of hot chocolate. The milk took a long time to heat.

They returned to the study.

"Douglas," the judge cleared his throat, ordered his thoughts. "Those three Negroes were accused of murdering Hanson Kirk, his wife, his daughter, and his son. With an axe."

"But . . . Why?"

"I was there this afternoon when Homan brought them in. I heard their statements. Everett, the one who was so hysterical tonight, claimed that Kirk sold him a sick mule yesterday. Died this morning. Dead when he went out to feed him. He and the one—can't remember his name now—the one who was screaming that he didn't do it, went to Kirk to demand his money back. Says there was a quarrel and Kirk came at him with an axe. Says it was self-defense. The son and daughter got into it. I guess he got crazy with fear and

34

went in the house after the wife. God, horrible. The tall young one is Marvin's son, the boy who delivers papers around town. Goes—went—to the college. He claims, claimed, he was just walking by on his way home from the river fishing and heard the fight. He claims it was all over when he walked up to the house. I don't know, son. And I guess I never will. There's nothing more mindless than a mob. I was frightened when I saw you. They were blood-mad. Why, boy, one of those fools could have shot you from that column for the fun of it, like a partridge."

The judge sighed heavily. "All this horror over a dead mule."

The boy began crying quietly. He could not forget the calm of the handsome black youth, the frenzy of Coy, the bloated luxurious smile of young Marsh Woods. And he thought of the axe. He had watched his father's strong arms heft the axe at the river house as he cut firewood. How neatly and cruelly the blade sheared the pine logs. He looked down at his own thin legs.

"There was only one axe," the judge mused. "I think that two totally innocent men are hanging out there right now. God help us. All the years. The struggles, the books, all the great men. Fifteen minutes of madness and we might as well be wearing loin cloths in front of caves."

The judge rose and stood in front of his son.

"Douglas, justice is a web a few fine men spin over a society. It won't bear much weight. It exists, and always has, only in the minds of noble men. Nowhere else. Not in nature. Certainly not in most men. And those fools who remember this night at all will remember it as the night we hung them three niggers. May God forgive us."

He sighed. He was drained.

"Now, boy, go up to bed. Try to get some sleep."

At that moment, there was a loud knock at the door. A battered Sheriff Homan slumped against the door jamb. He wanted to know if there was anything to do. Should he attempt to arrest anyone?

"Hell, no, Ed. You could get killed tonight. I'll call Raleigh. No, don't do anything tonight. Go home and have Martha fix you up. Oh, Ed, I want you to know I think you are a damned good man. Tomorrow I think a lot of people are going to be ashamed to face you. No, go home and get that cut cleaned and bandaged and get some rest."

Nearly twenty years later the two friends, reunited after the great war, mused on that night. Douglas thought of his father, now dead. It occurred to him that he had not known him well enough.

"Coy Trexler's still around. Married, kids," Spence offered. "When I close my eyes I can still see him perched on that limb."

"Yes," said Douglas. "Yes. And Marsh Woods. I remember his face. Clearly. What is he doing?"

"Oh, he has an office out at the mill. Mostly he's on the golf course or at the Club bar. But, well, you'll see him. He's engaged to Eleanore Swanson. You remember her? I can't understand that."

They strolled on, damning the Puritans, lamenting the closed bars, remembering that night. Douglas remembered scampering to Spencer's house the next morning. The two boys returned to Gosney Woods. As they passed through town, the sun seemed killer, not life-giver. The streets were lifeless. Heat heavy. The few faces they met avoided their eyes.

The shredded corpses still hung, banners of guilt and defeat. Douglas could not stop staring at the young black, hands at his sides, head gently tilted to the left, who still seemed infinitely patient with a universe which had not even acknowledged his presence.

"This way," Douglas said. Soft, insubstantial rain began to fall. They cut right at the Square and walked the block to the statue to the Glorious Confederate Dead. Douglas whimsically doubted if there was a town below the Mason-Dixon line which could not point to such a statue. Concordia's stood, wet and shining, caught by the street lights. It was a bronze, romanticized angel, her left arm extended as if to declare a cessation of all suffering. Her right arm supported a beautiful, wounded youth, a shattered musket cradled in his arms, who was slumped against her. The rain fine-lined the features of both figures and lent an aura to the great wings. The statue, heroic in size, stood on the grass plot which began here and proceeded for two blocks down Bridge Street in boulevard effect. On both sides Bridge was bordered by huge oak trees which extended their branches across the wide street. The angel and her pitiful charge presided over the entrance to this green canopied drive. Douglas thought it beautiful this night.

When they parted, Douglas embraced his friend. "Good night, Spence. It's good again."

"Right. Right. Damned glad to have you back."

"Tomorrow you'll tell me about the girls."

"That I shall do."

And Spence did. Douglas listened. And foraged for himself. Luckily, as always.

And he flung himself into the law. The two secretaries found themselves without time to have lunch, much less coif their hair and polish their nails. Research and briefs were their lot. Both fell in love with their employer and vied with each other in performance.

His charm, mastery of language, and absolute obsession with thoroughness made him a superb legal craftsman. He liked being trusted, and he *would* be worthy of that trust. Never in his professional career was he reprimanded or set aside for lack of preparation. The attorneys he went against knew that a single detail could lose them a decision. He enjoyed their respect and the tribute the court room loungers paid him by staying awake when he summed up. He knew he had done well whenever Pappy Starns, who had not missed a day in court in twenty-eight years, muttered from his shady bench in the courtyard after adjournment, "Wal, Mista Douglas, you shore skinned that cat."

A year after he returned he pled the first case of Eminent Domain heard in the state. He represented a group of farmers opposing a Yadkin River dam project. His opposition was the gigantic power company. He won. The company got its dam, but eight miles upstream and with water release provisions. Besides the farmers, he was fighting for his beloved river. Later, he turned his researches into a monograph which was published in the *Southern Law Review* and which is cited to this day.

He loved it when a case hung on wits and rhetoric, for he loved language. He was a duelist and language was a slippery weapon.

To his dying day he would grin like a Cheshire beneath his moustache whenever he recalled that day in his second year of practice when he had beaten both members of Link and

Kern. He had walked out into the blazing summer sun, looked up into the blinding sky and said to himself, *All right, now you can go against the best*.

Then he sauntered over behind Pappy's bench under the broad oak and whispered very softly, "Pappy, yippee."

Without turning, Pappy considered a moment, zinged a brown bullet of tobacco juice eight feet, and finally nodded once and said, "Uh-huh," with the accent on the last syllable.

Douglas had turned to go when Hal Link's silky voice cut the heat, "Doug, you sonavabitch, where in hell did you get that, 'Your honor, as we all know from the *State of South Carolina versus Hale*.' Where the hell did you get that shit?"

Douglas had turned with his broadest smile, speaking from the peaks of condescension, "Well, Hal, you know. Why that one cost the taxpayers of South Carolina dearly. Pappy knows that one. When was that, Pappy, nineteen-fourteen, fifteen?"

Pappy had sat for a moment, then pivoted his ancient rickety frame around on his bench—his neck had long since lost mobility—and faced Douglas. He squinted at the young lawyer for fully sixty seconds, then, "Twas in the spring of fourteen. Aright arter thet long rainy spell." And wheeled around to resume target practice.

"Shit," said Hal, who with his partner Giles Kern, had the reputation of being the most formidable, greediest counsel in the county. "Time I get back to the Row, there're gonna be three unemployed legal secretaries, I promise. You can bet their hair is in better condition than my research. Bitches."

When he was out of hearing, Douglas helped Pappy to his feet.

"Pap, c'mon over to the Row and I'll pour a shot of bourbon. This one deserves a drink."

Inside his office, feet on his desk, Pappy stiffly before him, he poured. Pappy sloshed it for a minute, allowed Douglas to lean and touch his glass, and threw it back.

"Mista Douglas," he rasped and whistled at last, talking as he had drunk, around his chaw, "*South Carolina versus Hale?*"

Douglas grinned, leaned very close to Pappy's cross-hatched toothless mug, and tapped his forehead with his forefinger. Then both men crumpled in great gut laughter until the old man finally struggled to his uncertain legs, tapped his jaw to indicate he had to go because he had to spit, and waddled out.

Like all intelligent lawyers, Douglas was interested in defining the law by pressing it to its farthest limits and he found the English common law system rigid enough to structure human society, flexible enough to grow. And in the Eminent Domain case, he felt he had approached one of those limits.

But mostly, he found himself dealing with deeds, making wills and sorting the debris of old men's commonplace lives, defending drunken drivers, organizing bundles of dull and aimless adulteries.

He began to find it harder and more interesting to perfect his overhead tennis shot, or finalize the interpretation of a piano score than to sift the thousands of papers of legal trivia that came through the little office on Lawyer's Row.

Sybil Schraeder with whom he had grown up and who lived down the block from him could lure him from the office for a cross country ride three or four times a week. Sybil was an excellent horsewoman, a witty confidante, and the only woman with whom he shared friendship without romantic involvement.

He began to lie to Miss White, his secretary, who was diligent, but would invent excuses for his frequent absences from the office.

And there *were* the girls. It *was* the twenties. And he was young and strong and handsome. And woman's flesh could have drawn him over the rim of the earth. He became a skirt-lifter because he could not be other. These other people, these with the rolling, swaying gait, slim wrists, thighs whiter than split almonds, these persons with nothing, *nothing* between their legs—*vacancy!*—to be filled, *interested* him.

Douglas Morton's first divorce plea suggested, if not a pattern, at least a possibility for many to come. She was Wilda Sumner, wife of Lee Walter Sumner, a cotton broker. She had selected the young lawyer only six weeks after he returned from Europe.

One afternoon she sat in her bathing suit on the Club terrace sipping lemonade, chatting with Sybil Schraeder, watching him play tennis on the near court. Suddenly, she was surprised to discover that lust had risen in her to a point which caused her to wish to lick the sweat from his lean body. Sybil did indeed know who he was.

Two weeks later, Wilda Sumner was sitting across his desk, her hair demure, but her bust plumping out above her dress line, asking if he could muster grounds for divorce from the fact that "Lee Walter now loves only God and profit." As the conference progressed, Wilda found confidence in the handsome face with its gray, gently empathizing eyes, stopped her pacing and wringing of hands, stared at the *Legal Code of North Carolina* on his book shelves and blurted that since Lee Walter had broked his first million dollars' worth of cotton he seemed guilt-ridden, prayed too much, gave up movies, proposed giving up the frivolous Club membership, caused them to kneel side by side each night before commending themselves to God's care in sleep, and culminated with, "Hell, I haven't been kissed in four years."

She went tearfully on to say that she hadn't been touched since he had inseminated her with their second child who was now in the first grade.

Douglas Morton kissed her. Her mouth, her throat, her ears, her nipples, lifted her skirt, and splayed her on the couch in his office with such vigor that she could not walk from his office for forty-five minutes which made her late for her book club meeting. Thus did Wilda Sumner get loved and divorced for the single fee.

Women invented problems without even marginal legal implications to bring to him. They exaggerated gaiety in his presence. When he was at a party, the Charleston became pure frenzy. Daring was expanded to overt seduction. No husband was at ease when Doug Morton was there, or scheduled to arrive.

Miss Amelia White, the fortyish legal secretary and irreplaceable asset to Morton and Morton, was visibly shaken, outraged, then jealous when she opened a parcel addressed to him and found that it contained a delicate pair of lace-trimmed, satin panties. He roared—and had no idea which of five likely ladies had sent them.

A small but persistent legend grew about him. He demurred with, "If I got half that people say I get, I'd be a happy, exhausted man."

The great Hutch would have been jealous when he sat at

the piano at a party. He respected the saloon pianist's art and he gained a style himself.

It was all beautiful and careless. The Country Club ballroom, adrift with taffeta gowns like purposeful clouds. The speakeasies and roadhouses with their aura of conspiracy. The bootleggers with the possibility of danger. The house parties at South River. Charleston weekends. And Mobile. The great Packard with its dignity and speed. It was a life. Working hard, playing hard.

3

THE giant killer was five-feet-six, slender as a river reed, if you except the woman's bust and hip flare, with an oval face framed by a waterfall of black hair which she would not cut despite the new fashion. Yet she was the first to appear in the Country Club ballroom wearing the new short, fringed dress.

Her name was Ann-Charlotte Hayden and she had been roommate to Mary Anne Heitman at Salem College. She was a twenty-four-year-old widow and she was visiting Bobby and Mary Anne Heitman at their new home. Her architect husband had died of influenza after a year of marriage. She had just returned from a six month tour of Europe with her doctor father and her mother.

Douglas Morton was already seated at Mary Anne's piano with a bourbon before him and Norma Woods, Marsh's baby sister, beside him, when Mary Anne brought her guest in for introduction to Concordia society.

Marsh, whose engagement to Eleanore Swanson was off again, was to be her date and was first to greet her. Douglas stood at the piano behind Marsh.

"Marsh," Mary Anne was saying, "Ann-Charlotte dances a mean Charleston and has just returned from blazing a trail of Latin lovers in the capitals of Europe."

She smiled brilliantly at Marsh and gave him her hand. After greetings, her eyes skipped past Marsh's face and squarely into the face of Douglas Morton. They held for a

41

moment and the smile gave way to intent. Douglas too was suddenly intent. Two beautiful people passed acknowledgement of beauty. A moment's moment.

Then Mary Anne, spitefully Douglas always thought, took her and Marsh away to meet the room full of others. When at last they returned, Douglas stood again and acknowledged the beauty of the smiling girl before him.

"And this is Douglas Morton, brilliant lawyer, divine piano player, and tennis star. He's evil, evil, evil."

Douglas smiled and nodded. His eyes could not leave the marvelous face.

"Doug," Mary Anne went on, "Ann-Charlotte is my dearest friend and old roomy. She's from New Bern. She will be here for a couple of weeks. She will be at Patsy's party. Now, do you think you can make it?"

"I will be there even if I am scheduled to plead before the Supreme Court."

Later that night at the Club he could arrange to dance with her only twice, for Norma sensed and became possessive, and Marsh's eyes glittered with lust. When he first held her, he knew she fitted. They talked of Europe, the law, music, and, at last, he talked of her beauty. When he looked down into her face, he found her eyes—eyes almost too big, certainly too dark and deep to be believed—always firmly on his. Before the dance was over he said to himself, *if I don't kiss this red mouth before sunrise, I'll cut my own throat.*

The second time they danced was late in the evening. Slow tempo. He was possessed. He had watched her all night, unable to do other. Had seen her turn her lovely head on the long slim throat. Had seen her move in dance so that the woman's breasts turned on her supple waist away from her hips as in a life of their own. Had seen the short fringed skirt splash up her white thighs that narrowed to needles at the ankles. Had seen the luxurious hair wash back over her white shoulders. Had met the too large, too dark eyes over the shoulders of dancing partners. Had met and held. There was not enough bourbon in the Club to keep Douglas Morton from the knowledge that this was *she.*

Dancing, he spoke through her hair to her ear.

"I can't stop myself from looking at you."

"I look at you too."

42

"I think it's out of my hands now. I don't think I can ever let you go. You will die here in my arms on the floor of the Concordia Country Club."

"I may scream. You're evil. Mary Anne said so."

"If you do I'll close your mouth with a kiss."

"Marsh will step over a bourbon bottle to protect me."

"Listen. Shhhh. I just gave your ear a little kiss through your hair. Did you get it?"

"Wait. I'll check. Yes. Uh-huh. But it was so small. Could you repeat it?"

He could.

He turned her in the dance—he could circle her waist with his hands—guided her past the open French doors that gave onto the gallery. The number one fairway, gone magic in moonlight. Tall, long leaf pines, moonbursts of needles. Other couples talking softly.

At the railing, he lifted her straight chin with his hand and kissed her full on the mouth. When he stopped, he saw that her eyes were not closed, but were studying him.

"No way not to," he said. "Sweet mouth."

Those eyes never left his.

"Listen," he whispered, "I *have* to have you."

Norma Woods's voice, thick with drink, cut through. "Oh, there they are."

She and brother Marsh lurched out on a tide of music.

"Mary Anne has just discovered another bottle of champagne. We're to share it. Come on."

Norma took his arm and towed.

Marsh was dragging Ann-Charlotte toward the door. But she broke away for a moment and tiptoed up to his ear.

"*Get* me," she dared, and turned away laughing.

For Douglas Morton the next two weeks were agony perfected. And for Miss White, who could not juggle his schedule to suit him. For Blanche who could not prepare food that he would eat, or have proper shirts for him to wear.

For Spence who could not console him.

"Heitman is a bitch," he railed. "Every hour of every day is scheduled so that the girl is never free. She is dated up with every single bastard in this town. Why not me?"

"Because of Norma, Dummy," Spence would say.

"Spence, do something. She'll be gone in a few days."

"I shall give a luncheon and invite everyone who is anyone," offered Sybil Schraeder, whose social stature would not permit refusal. "At my home. You will be seated beside her. How's that?"

Sybil Schraeder, friend and confidante, lived in the handsomest house in the town, a huge elegant mansion, airy light because, instead of columns, it had New-Orleans-style wrought-iron supporting the galleries across the front of the house. The only child of her late parents—millionairess to a huge granite supply firm—Sybil now lived alone in the gorgeous house with three Negro servants.

Sybil Schraeder's name was much on the lips of Concordia society, not for what she did, but for what she did not do. She had been pursued by the finest men in town, including such seasoned womanizers as Douglas Morton and Marshall Woods. She had beauty, wealth, and unassailable status. All failed. Marsh, after years of unsuccessful effort, claimed that old J.C. Schraeder had welded a chastity belt on the girl during puberty. But he never boasted of having touched it. Douglas Morton did cartwheels of charm intermittently over the years in an effort to pry her thighs. He never got beyond a good night kiss. He finally gave up and happily settled, like the rest of Concordia society, for her wit, her grace, and an arms-length friendship with this remarkable woman. Sybil dined at the Morton home once or twice a month all her life, and often had drinks with Douglas and Spence in the late afternoon.

This time her social weight was of no avail. Mary Anne Heitman had indeed scheduled every moment for her guest.

So Douglas dashed off to the Club every day for lunch— just in case. Twice he saw her there across the room, a million miles away, surrounded by people. One day about four as he toweled off between sets with Hal Gregory, a colleague, he turned to see her and Mary Anne lounging at the fence beside the courts watching him. Hal suddenly found himself facing a demon. Douglas drilled or hooked his serve, nearly beat it to the net, and pumped volleys at impossible angles. Finally, poor Hal realized that Douglas wasn't angry. He was showing off for the striking girl standing by Mary Anne Heitman.

She smiled brilliantly at him as he approached. "You *are* a tennis star!"

"Hi. I'd begun to wonder if I had dreamed you. Where have you been?" He glanced at Mary Anne. "All right, never

44

mind. But come to the clubhouse and have something cold with me at least."

As they sat on the gallery, he learned that her visit was drawing to a close indeed, that Mary Anne had promised her for several parties, and had arranged dates for her. After all, wasn't Douglas presently occupied?

"No, dammit. No. There was never anything serious between Norma and me, and what there was had been riding on habit for months. And last night my indifference concluded that episode by getting me a glass of bourbon in the face."

But Ann-Charlotte continued to be maddeningly diffident. At parties, she smiled at him, danced a couple of times with him, was unwilling to exclude her dates, and would not allow herself to be 'stolen.' There were long glances, when she seemed to be studying him. But for all the world and sleepless nights, Douglas could not decide whether or not she considered him like 'all the rest.'

It *had* to be Patsy's house party. The girls convened on a Wednesday. Douglas could not be free of legal duties until Friday. And damned as he felt himself to be, the Packard had a flat on the way out to South River and he actually sprained a toe kicking the car. Spence, coming along after, found him sipping a pint of bourbon and longing for death. Together, they changed the tire and arrived with, Douglas thought, nothing to lose.

There were nine girls and twelve men, if you counted Marsh. They canoed, picnicked, swam, played croquet, gathered around the piano and sang, danced. And she did kiss him good night late Friday evening.

Their time came late Saturday night. He had just laid his head on his pillow when he heard a scratching on the screen of the little maid's room to which he had been assigned.

"Hey, Douglas Morton, it's warm enough for a swim. Come and protect me from moccasins and moon stroke."

In two minutes they were running hand in hand across the lawn heading for the landing. They swam out into the sweet, cool river, in the moon path. And back. He spread boat cushions near the canoe rack beside the summer house. They kissed and held each other hungrily.

"Why have you . . . ?"

"Hush," she said brushing his mouth with her own. "What could I do? Mary Anne is my hostess. Besides there's now."

45

They moved close together. Couldn't get close enough together.

"You don't think any other drunks are going to want to swim under our moon, do you?" Her breath was hard got.

"I don't think so. We own this night. We won't permit it."

She pulled away, edged to the water and slipped in. He sat and watched her cut a moon-traced path out thirty feet, then back. Ten feet out, she whispered, "Want me?"

"Yes."

She stroked in, stood silver naked, bathing suit in her hand. Her wonderful, lean white body began curving and never stopped. He started to rise and help her out.

"Stay."

She glided out of the water, flung her suit, and stood before him. She took a towel and turning and turning, dried herself. He watched and thought her perfectly desirable.

She knelt into his arms, turned and offered. He moved slowly, gently between her gleaming arms and thighs, and they were at last close enough. They lay long without moving. He lifted his face above hers. She gave him her wonderful smile. Gave him her most wonderful smile.

"Man, you are burning me up inside."

"You're so . . . so very beautiful. I think we belong."

"Oh yes, oh God, yes."

"I think I'm in love with you."

"Oh, make it so."

Dawn chased them back to their rooms. It was hard to part at the staircase.

Both of them were foolish all day. They missed conversation. They smiled, just smiled. Sometimes they yawned at the same time.

On Sunday evening, he stayed behind Bobby and Mary Anne in the car caravan back into town. She looked back. She blew a kiss.

On Monday morning Miss White announced Miss Ann-Charlotte Hayden.

"Mary Anne is outside in the car with my things. I'm taking the noon train."

He held her. God, how to hold her close enough?

"Your bags are outside?"

"Yes."

"We could put them in the Packard, drive to South Carolina and get married."

"Yes, we could."

"I'll get your things."

"Wait." She was still in his arms. "Listen. If you are going to be my man, listen. I've got terms. Douglas Morton, I want a rich life. Do you understand? I don't mean riches. I don't mean things. I mean rich living. I mean various and vivid. I want to see and do and feel."

"I promise it."

They got her bags, kissed Mary Anne, who wasn't surprised. They put the luggage in the Packard. He told Miss White to cancel everything for ten days. They stopped by the Well Street house and in fifteen minutes he was packed. He walked her through the house. She loved it. She could live here with her man. When Blanche returned from shopping, he gave his woman to her arms. Blanche wept and blessed them.

They drove. She telephoned her parents from Keanston. They were married the next afternoon in Charleston.

For ten days they roamed the old city, dining, dancing, walking the Battery, shopping, hand in hand. Charleston loved them back—restauranteurs, shop owners, waiters, speakeasy musicians let him sit in, cabbies, hansomes—for they were what a man and woman could be.

When they returned to Concordia, they were properly celebrated, with envy and genuine affection. She fitted. Spencer became as a brother, Sybil a sister, and the five o'clock ritual remained intact. She avoided clubs, luncheons, bridge parties, and book clubs. She was at his side for all musical events. They joined the community theatre. They read together.

In six months she was one of the best woman tennis players in town. She could hit a ball. He pulled her game up. She *could* concentrate and she would practice. They were a tough doubles team. He admired her grace as she moved along the base lines, and her stamina as she continued to move.

He admired her grace as she made their house and table a delight. He was delighted when she and Blanche, instant 'old friends the most,' conspired redecoration schemes in the family parlor and their bedroom. And when she and Blanche collaborated for special dishes, and that Blanche willingly added some of her mistresses's delicacy to her own splendid, hearty *repertoire*. And that the two women, the one old and fine and black, the other, young and fine and white, could bend side by side for hours at the flower beds. That they could shop together for vegetables, could make private jokes about him.

He was pleased when Sybil Schraeder leaned out of her accustomed aloofness to her. They were a striking pair, the tall, fair Sybil and the dark fluent beauty of Ann-Charlotte, shopping, lunching or riding at the Schraeder Meadows stables. Douglas was astonished that Sybil's warmth went to his wife with an intensity she offered to only one other person, himself.

Astonished and happy.

She could drink with him. They were brilliant at the Riverview Lodge, dancing. They were brilliant at the Country Club, dancing. At Lenny's, at South River Fish Camp, at Winston's Roadhouse, wherever there was music. People watched them. This was what could be between a man and a woman.

Blanche would wake them softly with coffee and chide them gently when she came to the house on Saturday or Sunday mornings and found them sleeping like innocents fully dressed on pillows before the fireplace in the family parlor, or in the hammock on the side gallery, where they had fallen drunk and happy. But she would fuss like an old wet hen when the Packard was parked wopsidedly, half on the sidewalk. "What will the neighbors think?" she would murmur as she assuaged their hangovers with cool juice.

Douglas Morton was working harder and playing harder than ever before. Yet everywhere he went was to or from her. She was dead center. She was endlessly *interesting*. And interested. She was one of those rare people who listen when others are talking. She involved herself in each of his cases. She listened to his long rhetorical speeches on anything that possessed him. But she could shoot him down when his passion outran his reason. For she had reason.

He pondered her when she was not beside him. Meeting her, he was always slightly surprised at his good luck that this beautiful woman was coming to him, smiling. Sometimes he would study her, at table, or in a movie, or when she was dancing with Spence, or sleeping. Her face fascinated him. It had fineness, but such fluency that it could change from glittering intent to outrageous gaiety in a moment. Her body could drop from a sensuous slink to a broad mime of the great Chaplin.

She was his mate sexually. She was incalculable, inventive, deviate. He never knew whether his bed would hold a nymph demanding meticulous seduction, or a lusty bitch with her hands on her hips above black clocked stockings, daring.

But he loved to think how all nights ended with her curved against him, warm, breathing softly, smooth, forever safe. Douglas Morton was supremely happy.

They were planning a four month trip to Europe when she announced that she was pregnant. There was time for Europe. There was world enough and time.

It was sweet planning for the child. Sometimes Ann-Charlotte became detached and secretive. At times she and Blanche became conspirators. Douglas Morton was curious, proud, and astonished. If she was very private sometimes, each night she became his *confidante*. In bed, they talked for hours. He touched her, carefully, excitedly. She led his hand.

"It feels like a slithery eel," she said. "What if I have an eel? Or a monkey?"

"No monkey," he laughed. "Definitely a swimmer. And Douglas Morton Eel has an unlikely sound. Besides, Tom Cleland would probably refuse to deliver it."

They selected names. He was too astonished to prefer a sex. He wanted the Biblical Mariamne if it was a girl for the sound. "Sid Jacobson would think he had not argued all those hours in vain. He'd probably let her be Chosen also."

She wanted "Joanne of Arc Morton. She's restless enough to be a warrior."

But in the end, and time began to make their considerations serious, they settled, and Blanche confirmed, on Charlotte or Douglas Cadet Morton IV.

The child born under full September moon was Charlotte.

Old Dr. Cleland brought the bundle out at dawn and placed it in the arms of disheveled, weary, pacing Douglas Morton. At last, in the hospital hall, the astonishment of Douglas Morton was perfected.

"Well," he looked up into the face of the man who had

delivered him also, "Doctor Cleland, is this Charlotte, or Douglas?"

"Doug, this is Charlotte. Charlotte Morton, perfectly made and healthy," the old man said.

"Well, hello, Charlotte. Hello, Charlotte Morton. She has hair. Hello, Charlotte. Welcome. Welcome to the world. She does have hair. Has—has she seen her? Has she seen how well she did?"

"No. No, she hasn't. Listen, Doug, let me take her now. Tom will be out in a minute."

"Can I see her, Dr. Cleland? Can I . . . ?"

But he couldn't stop looking at his new daughter. He carefully swayed with her—their first dance.

He almost couldn't surrender her to the old doctor, but at last he did.

"Tom will be right out, Doug. Let me take care of her now."

Tom Cleland in his baggy whites came out in a moment to find Douglas Morton doing a buck-and-wing down the corridor. He turned to his old friend.

"Tom, did you see her? Did you see all that hair? Tom, I'm a parent. A father. She's great."

"Yes, Doug, she is. She certainly is."

"It's a whole new world, Tom. A whole new world. Hey, Ann-Charlotte? Has she seen her yet? Hey, when can I see the mother of that great child?"

"Doug," he put his hand on the new father's shoulder. "Step in here with me."

He led into a small desk and chair office. He leaned back against the door.

"Sit down, Doug."

But Douglas was using the whole office to pace. He was popping his fist into his palm.

"She has beautiful hair already. Black, like Ann-Charlotte's. When can I see her? Hey, has she seen the baby yet?"

"No, Doug. No, she didn't. Doug, I . . ."

"Well, when you guys . . ." Then the tense of the verb struck Douglas. He looked at his friend.

And he knew.

"No, Tom. No. Please, Tom. Tom, please."

"Oh Doug. Oh God, Doug."

Douglas Morton went slack. Nothing in his life had prepared him for this, not his own motherless childhood, nor months in the trenches in France, nor his own carefully considered philosophy that man was an accidental, flawed, ephemeral species which the earth would probably be better without.

Douglas Morton the lucky. The blessed.

"Tom . . ."

"I'm sorry, Doug. Oh God, I am so sorry. We . . . There was nothing we could do. It was a massive hemorrhage. I . . . Oh Christ. Doug, I loved her too. And, God knows, Dad loved her. She just slipped away."

"Tom, are you sure? I mean . . . There's no poss . . . ?"

The doctor pulled his friend to him.

"Doug, I can't tell you . . ."

Douglas turned from his friend and set his forehead against the wall. He felt his center slipping. He stood on sand.

"I have to see her, Tom."

The doctor took his arm and led out of the office, down the corridor into the day's first sun which flamed against the window, into the operating room.

She lay covered in white. Tenderly Tom Cleland turned back the covering.

Her face was so calm. The splendid black hair was swept away from the broad forehead. Her eyes were closed in profound sleep. When he realized that she had no concern with him any more, Douglas Morton began to weep quietly. Called to a hundred times, for love, for music, for laughter, she would not answer. She had no interest. It hurt his heart that she was so beautiful. That she could not care.

At last he clamped his eyes and nodded once. Old Doctor Cleland put his arm around his shoulder while his son drew up the sheet. It was over.

Douglas Morton turned abruptly and walked out of the room.

He was desolated. He could not look at the infant Charlotte, and so for a week, Blanche spent her days in the hospital and Charlotte had her first care from her.

Douglas Morton wandered aimlessly through the house. He held Ann-Charlotte's clothes. Her scent was still in them. The black clocked stockings. *I'll get my figure back soon so we can play again.* He toyed with the little, silver purse flask he had given her and from which the two had secretly nipped so often. He touched the wallpaper and curtains she and

Blanche designed for their bedroom. He clenched the tiny rubber mouse she had once playfully put on his pillow. He swung her tennis racquet.

He wandered the river house and property. They had risen before dawn here to watch the birds and squirrels.

He did these things. But he did not weep. Douglas Morton was oddly detached. He simply did not know these things and places anymore.

Not even Jessica who came up from Mobile could reach him. "Jess," he searched for words. "I'm not going to die, or anything. It's just that everything is plain and gray now. Bear with me."

"But, Doug, the baby. You haven't seen her. She's so dear. Ann-Charlotte would fuss at you if she were here."

"I know. I will come to that as soon as I can."

His natural grace carried him through receiving her parents, the gentle old Doctor Hayden and his wife, whom he had grown to love. And through the funeral. His sister Elizabeth and Nelson Summers arranged the service—a task suited to their lugubrious natures.

Even the durable Blanche began to look drained, so Jessica arranged nurses for Charlotte.

The night before she returned to Mobile, she and he drank and talked late.

"Doug, darling, listen. Blanche and I are frightened for you. You don't eat or sleep or talk. You haven't even looked at the baby. Brother, you must bury your dead. Mourn her, but don't let it consume you. That child is her legacy. If ever a human loved life, it was Ann-Charlotte. I doubt if she would have much patience with you. Please, darling, get hold and let time take care of your loss."

"Ah, Jess, I can't even feel anymore. That girl—the whole universe . . . I can't find place or plan. Jess, ten times in France I was ten feet or ten seconds from death. It is absolute whimsy that I am here now. Look, we idly step on an ant. Why *that* ant? A life. Each life is absolutely singular, never, never another like it. She was so beautiful, so quick, so intelligent. Is Nature so wasteful that it can squander the likes of Ann-Charlotte?"

"Oh, Doug, I don't know such answers."

"Goddam indifferent Nature. For thousands of years men have searched for a plan. Is there plan? She came to me in a flash, an accident as incidental as a South River party. Now in a flash she is gone. They couldn't stop her from bleeding. Christ, she drew from me, invented in me, such love as I never even imagined. God, I don't know whether to rage or weep. Hell, rage at whom?"

When they parted, he promised his sister that he would write weekly.

But it was Blanche who wrote.

Three weeks later, suddenly he slept again in the master bedroom. The next morning she found him standing in the new nursery over the crib. He was holding one tiny foot in his huge hand. The owner of the foot was goo-ing amiably.

"Blanche," he said, "do you really believe my foot was ever this small?"

"Yassuh, Mista Douglas. I knows it. I saw it with these old eyes."

They both laughed. She helped him move the crib into his bedroom and she terminated the night nurse. And that day Blanche wrote Jessica a letter.

It said that Douglas Morton was in love again.

And so he was. For though she couldn't dance, or play tennis, she could flirt.

Blanche came to expect to find the two on the gallery, the big man pointing squirrels and birds to the infant in his arms, when she came to work each morning and she brought coffee to one, and warm milk to the other. Spencer expected to find the two in the parlor at five o'clock each evening, the big man playing a Mozart sonata, the infant buried in pillows on the couch, the one drinking bourbon, the other, warm milk. Everyone came to expect long dissertations on the latest theories of child care, backed by page and author wherever they met him, on the tennis courts or over bourbon.

After a year or so, Charlotte began to know woman's—or women's—care and love beyond that of Blanche. Douglas Morton was too involved with life to mourn it away.

The long succession of visitors to his bed began with Gloria, who was a waitress at the Pullman Cafe in the railway station. Platinum blonde, tall, full-breasted, slim-waisted and with an ass which could have caught his attention in the midst of a murder summary, Gloria was a natural. She was twenty-one, had been abandoned by her husband whom she had married when she was sixteen. She was part of the great, tough, common heart which offers casual sympathy, has no outlandish hopes, less ambition, and makes no unreasonable emotional demands. She asked only small consideration and occasional sensual pleasure. For she was involved with the small daily comforts of food, warmth, and humor.

A couple of late nights a week, she became accustomed to the presence, book in hand, of the widowed lawyer Morton. For six weeks she smiled and answered his, "Hi, Gloria," served his coffee, and after a couple of cursory conversations, told her life and offered him sympathy when he cared to talk.

Then came the night when it rained as she was leaving work. He offered a lift. She accepted, and let it be known candidly that life was slow and he was handsome. She considered that they both were lonely. What was more friendly than that they share a drink? She loved the Packard and his house.

Blanche concealed her astonishment, but not her approval when she had to bring coffee for two and warm milk for one the next morning. She felt that she could count Mista Douglas cured now.

Gloria was rare and lucky. She and Douglas remained friends and lovers until he died. When she remarried, she told him, "Oh, Doug, he's nice and he'll take care of me and the kid. Oh, I'll see you sometimes. Oh yeah. Couldn't live without that."

Douglas counted himself blessed in her. Her body excited him, pleased him, and carried him to the edge of sleep. He respected her healthy sensuality and felt genuine affection for her simple willingness to please and be pleased.

And he knew that she had come to him at the right moment.

A long succession of lovers came and went, but his true love remained the little girl who slept in his bedroom each night, and whose arms were always open to him—except when the rag doll of Winnie the Pooh occupied them.

The mornings on the gallery with the squirrels and birds were wonderful, and were never the same because her perceptions changed so rapidly. It seemed but a day to him before she was able to support herself by clinging to the wooden poles of the balustrade and peer through them. Her delight was goo-ful when a couple of friendly squirrels began coming up on the gallery rail for some easy food. Their names were Harrison and Hedrick. The two became part of their Circle. Soon the little girl was waking her father early so as not to miss breakfast with their friends.

He passed up business and social luncheons to rush home at midday to lunch with the dark-haired, long-lashed girl. Sometimes she would sit in her collapsible stroller under the tall pines and watch him play tennis. And afterwards, she would sit in his arms in the Club bar and try to steal his bourbon and ice. He wasn't above giving her a sip now and then. She liked it, which confirmed his faith in the quality of her genes.

Spence couldn't decide if it was the bourbon or the charmer which caused Douglas Morton to rush home each day at four-thirty. For lately he would find the man and the girl at the piano, she sometimes punctuating whatever he was playing with exuberant rhythms and chords. And it was not long before Spence was treated to her halting rendition of *Twinkle, Twinkle Litte Star*. Soon these sessions grew into regular lessons. She was being readied for Katherine French to perfect. From the beginning Douglas Morton was careful that the girl understand correct time. Using a metronome, he concocted outrageous gyrations somewhere between dance and spasm to make his little one 'feel' time and rhythm. It made Spencer feel amusement which sent him into stitches of laughter.

Not many years later, Spence would hear, "Goddamit, Charlotte, I can't hear the bass line. It is one big smudge. You have got to hear every note. Every, single, particular note. It's fast but it's got to be perfect *legato*, or it's a mess. Now tomorrow I want you to play it slowly twenty times, feel the bottom of every note, release and sound the next one at the same moment. Keep your foot off the pedal so you can hear it."

Before she was nine, the crisp bell-like tones of Clementi sonatinas became a pleasure Spence anticipated.

They all would remember her first snowfall. North Carolina was treated to six wonderful inches. Charlotte, Blanche, and her father built a Mickey Mouse snowman, but her father could not make the ears stay on. Two days later, the whiteness was gone. The little girl wept. She ran to Blanche for comfort. And comforted, she was allowed to hold the Wesson oil can tilted to the steady needle stream needed for absolutely creamy—snow like!—mayonnaise. Her sorrow dissolved into the maelstrom of Blanche's whisk. She tried to track the swirls as they sank into the smooth miasma which she would spread on her sandwiches, her hair, her nose, and her dress.

Douglas never tired of reading to her, and quickly, she to him. Winnie and his circle were friends. Most vivid were *The Red Cross Knight* and *Don Quixote* rendered by the Bookhouse, read with extravagant flourish. Not long after came the *Once and Future King*. Merlyn magicked the Round Table and these two. It was years later that she finally distinguished between her father and each of the knights. And more years later that she again merged her father with the Don. Neither of them had ever met a stranger who was not a gentleman— though, later, too many of them revealed that they were not.

Girl to young woman she was fascinated with his moustache, slightly jealous of the affection he drew from women, loved the masculine feel and scent of his wet tennis shirt as she hugged him after a match.

She was a classically beautiful child. She had taken her mother's hair, large dark eyes, and broad full mouth. And her carriage, child to girl to young woman, always seemed to her father like Ann-Charlotte's purposeful but stately gait. She came early to an awareness of her womanness. Once, when she was nine, her father took her along to a business lunch of great importance. He was the guest of the president and two vice-presidents of the power company.

He carefully instructed her. "Smile. Look directly into their eyes. Ask about the schools their children attend. Ask if they have gardens like yours. Tell them about your school. But, and listen carefully, if the talk turns to business, be silent and eat your lunch. We'll tell them that your nurse is sick, and there was no one to leave you with."

She followed instructions perfectly. She was absolutely winning. The talk remained social. The president was so taken by her that when they left the restaurant, he stepped into a florist down the block and presented her with a little bouquet.

Though she tried, her charm somehow did not work on Blanche and her father when she sought to avoid punishment for some monumental crime. Many times she bore the red imprint of an adult hand on her bottom.

"Justice is not susceptible to huge smiles, blinking of the eyes, and little cunning kisses," her lawyer told her.

Blanche was more to the point. "Wickedness, git up to your room. *Now.*"

Nor was her charm of any benefit through the long dreary dinners she and her father had to attend with Aunt Elizabeth and Uncle Nelson, where she had to endure Nelson's six-minute grace before she could begin eating, and Aunt Elizabeth's dinner-long interpretation of ways to gain damnation. She learned the possibilities and limitations of femininity.

She felt her womanness when she grew tall enough to dine with her father at the Country Club—sometimes with his current flame—but some lovely times with him alone. On those evenings she could dance with him as much as she wished, at least when he was not being rushed by bored wives and unattached daughters. They danced like young lovers, for the bodies of both were slim and agile and incapable of graceless movement. It was clear that they adored each other. Spence, deep in his cups, declared them Olympians—returned so that mortals could again glimpse the Golden Age.

By the time she was twelve she could drive the Packard. Her father had taught her to shift gears on the river property. Spence began to slightly fear her on the night that she firmly announced to him, Florence his wife, and her father, as they lurched down the curving Club drive, "You are all drunk as goats. Fall into the car and I'll drive you home." She did.

Charlotte went to school, but her real education was with her father. They read together each day of her childhood. From the beginning he had spoken to her in both French and English. Latin came when she gained vocabulary. From the time she was four he had insisted that she draw one picture a day and write one page a day in the journals he bought her.

"Listen, little one. We think in terms of words and pictures. So the better we use words, the better we think. Do you understand? The same goes for pictures. The truer your lines become, the better you will see things. So every day, one picture and one page. OK?"

They both laughed later at her first journal entry. *My Dairy, by Charlotte Morton. I am fore yeers old. My name is Charlotte Morton. My hose is in Well Street. I am a puella. Harrison and Hedrick are my frends. Blanche is my frend. She is a puella to.*

The daily entry into her journal became a lifelong habit.

And those first trees that looked like green lollypops were the parents of the elegant botanical pictures which came later.

She would remember her first drawing lesson. He took her and her lollypop tree drawing out into the middle of Jackson Street. "Char, look at the sky in your drawing. Now, look at the sky down the street. Where does the sky end?"

And she realized that the sky went all the way down to the horizon. But when she colored the blue all the way down to the ground, she could hardly make out her tree, and thereby, learned about shading.

When she was ten and they were reading children's versions of the *Odyssey, Iliad,* and *Aeneid,* he came home with a three foot roll of brown wrapping paper and they began a huge black crayon chronological table of historical dates which they hung from the walls of the room that became her 'office.' Through the years the table grew until it covered three walls. It pleased her to have the history of the world marked out year by year as wall paper in her 'office'. At a glance she could tell that Troy fell in 1197 B.C., that Homer lived *circa* 800 B.C., that Caesar died in 44 B.C., that Charlemagne was crowned in 800 A.D., and that Shakespeare and Cervantes died in 1616. She added to that vast chronology to the end of her life. She and her son would smile to note that Charlotte Morton was born in 1927. That particular date was entered in very large letters and bore an enormous star in the margin to indicate its importance.

"Neither of David nor of Christ," her father said.

The two Mortons dined at least twice a month with Katherine French, his first lover. Miss French had been delighted when Douglas Morton married Ann-Charlotte and she instantly loved the infant Charlotte. Douglas saw that her interest in his daughter was particular, that the child fulfilled a fantasy which in life she had never realized.

Miss French had retired from teaching several years before but she gladly agreed to teach Charlotte when she became five. Charlotte returned her affection wholly. They baked, went to movies, worked in Miss French's garden, played duets together. Shortly before her death when Charlotte was ten, they had been working on a concerto by Mozart.

Death had begun its zigzag graph across the life line of Charlotte Morton at her birth. This second slash which carried off the treasured Miss French happened when she was old enough to know loss. Only two days before, the teacher and Charlotte had performed the Mozart for Douglas in the big music parlor as he sipped tea and ate from the platter of cookies that the girl and woman had made that afternoon.

Forty hours later father and daughter cried as they stood side by side and looked at the dear dead face.

"No, darling, no," he comforted. "Don't cry. Rejoice that we were lucky enough to know her, because she was so rare."

Home, he made tea for them.

"But I'd like you to understand what she meant to this whole miserable town. You see, Char, she was a delicate and sensitive spirit. Yet she was also tough in the sense that she demanded the best and that she gently nudged this town into a recognition of excellence. Char, we live in a town that worships athletes and money. Sweat and greed. Most people live on a purely physical plane. Feeding and watering and working and sleeping. She was different. She was like our conscience. She tried to tell us how to live. That the difference between us and animals is mind. That we can contemplate and feel things beyond food and shelter and physical stimuli. And even if people did not listen to her, they had the subtle feeling that they ought to. You know, she infuriated half the town by dropping their little darlings from her lessons because they wouldn't practice. And, of course, many dropped *her* because she demanded too much, wouldn't spend her time teaching ricky ticky hotel music.

"But you saw the mob at her funeral. They didn't love her, but they knew they should have. Some of them anyway." He was talking to himself as much as to his daughter. He and this woman had been first lovers to each other, she in middle age, he an adolescent. He would never stop giving thanks that she, sensitive and tender, had been his first, that she made it sweet, and exciting, and shameless.

With Blanche, the two went frequently to her grave with flowers. Not for her, but for themselves.

He searched for another teacher, but he found none who could offer what he wanted his daughter to have, so he and she worked together. There was never enough Mozart and Bach, but he continually ordered new scores, sought contemporary composers. The little girl, her fresh sensibility wide open, began to play the little pieces of Bartok and Stravinsky without realizing that atonality was to be feared.

Throughout her childhood he took her to New York for two weeks in the fall and spring to attend concerts, see pictures, and the theatre. Charlotte was astonished the first time she heard the young Horowitz at Carnegie Hall. She simply did not know that a piano could sound like that. She did not know that clarity was possible with such speed. She did not know that great chords could materialize and hang in the air about her. She had never heard such tone. Her father had to pay scalpers' prices to get tickets to the next three performances.

Then she heard Rubinstein, marveled at his singing tones and absolute joy in making music.

But they took the A train also, she in make-up, sophisticated dress, anything to make her look older. She heard Duke Ellington and Billie Holiday. And other standards were set.

And the museums. As a toddler, she loved the Natural History. All the dinosaurs were named Harrison and Hedrick. Later, it was the ravishing Metropolitan. Before El Greco's *Toldeo* she learned that terror could invest a landscape . . . and the sweetness of the Italian madonnas.

She learned that the Plaza was another kind of standard. For elegance. And that much of her life was controlled within the steel and granite, grotesque and handsome facades of the Wall Street banking houses.

Her father talked much of architecture. He was readying her for Europe. He was preparing her to become a magnificent woman.

4

CHARLOTTE Morton always loved school. She loved the teachers. She loved the other children. She loved the books, pictures, the singing, the games. And she loved to talk about school. Neither Blanche nor her father could feign enough interest in all that she had to tell each evening at dinner. And neither of them could keep track of Amy Winston's birthday, Billy Weant's broken toe, Miss Thompson's victories and defeats in her perpetual war against chewing gum, or whether it was Whitlow Manson, or James Manson who had brought his great grandfather's Civil War musket to school. But they were both visibly embarrassed for Lucy Rodgers who had tinkled in her pants while reciting *Snowbound* in front of the class. And they hated Coy Trexler, Jr. for saying loudly during the concluding stanza that it should have been entitled *Rainbound*.

Blanche learned quickly that there must be a ready supply of cookies and grape drink each day at two o'clock for she never knew whether there would be four or a dozen freckled faces beaming about the house. It seemed that every mother within two miles had to come to the Well Street house to collect her offspring at five o'clock.

The house was adazzle with crayon drawings and finger paintings of never-never flowers, suns that would have blinded and scorched had they truly risen, and dogs that actually said *Bow Wow* in black and white. And each day there were dozens of notes, written beneath a few lines of practice Palmer method swirls.

Dear Dad, Have a good lunch. My dearest Blanche, Amy will be staying over tonight. To Whom It May Concern: Miss Charlotte will be out for the evening. She is attending a pajama party at the home of Miss Louise Whitley.

Charlotte took school as her responsibility. Though she had become social in a new way, she always put assignments and projects first. Her father had his work, Blanche hers, and school became hers.

The school loved her. She was bright, polite, and cooperative. She was able to read and write when she entered. By fourth grade she could take over the piano when the class had music lessons and could provide majestic renditions of *Pomp and Circumstance* and the grand march from *Aida* when there was an assembly. Always she could be counted on for a performance in talent shows, and she always had the lead in plays. Early on, teachers allowed her to 'free read,' and Mrs. Donaldson, the librarian, helped her select books.

If Blanche and Douglas could not keep up with the birthdays, broken toes, and the battle of the chewing gum, there were two figures in her world throughout school with which they were perfectly familiar. The first was Maxwell Compton, only son of the straight-laced Mr. and Mrs. Compton who lived down the block from them. Max was a handsome dark-haired boy with clear sensitive features which promised a handsome man. He was one of the quickest pupils in her class, which meant that he finished everything that was assigned before most, and therefore had time to make the largest trouble. He was The Terror of Goodson School. Max was neither sneaky nor malicious. He was merely completely alive. He never lied. When confronted with one of his crimes, even by Miss Cash, the principal, he simply turned his blue eyes on his inquisitor and admitted his deed, promised not to do it again, and proceeded to spend each day for the appointed period after school with the best will possible under the circumstances. At least once a week Charlotte would say at the dinner table, "Do you know what Max Compton did today?"

Upon which Blanche and her father braced themselves for the blackest of deeds.

"He tied a chair with a blind cord and lowered it out the window. Miss Thompson was in a State for half an hour before she found the chair. Max is in jail for a month for that."

Or, "Max Compton stole twenty-eight valve caps last Saturday."

Or, "Max got caught writing *Miss Swicegood is a blimp* on his desk."

Another person who was constantly in Charlotte's reports was the one she called Ratface, with good reason. His name, which caused Douglas Morton to wince, was Coy Trexler, Jr. Throughout early school years fate placed him in the seat directly behind or beside Charlotte. At first the ugly boy with the perpetually greasy red hair plastered on the forehead of the half-starved face merely pulled her hair, or tied her waist bows in forty knots, or snitched her pens. Later came the malicious notes, distinguished by their original spelling, still later came the vile phone calls.

Early Coy began to grow into his destined meanness. He lived on the edge of the Mill Hill with his parents who devoutly hated the entire world, each other, and their spawn. Laughter was so alien to the Trexler clan that unless it was laced with cynicism, it was regarded as weakness or a paroxysm which seized the stupid. Early on he hated niggers, Jews, and the snotty Country Club crowd. The thing that distinguished Coy's meanness was its cleverness. His cruelties were inventions of warped ingenuity, as the time he buried up to their necks six little chicks belonging to a neighbor and ran over them with a lawnmower. The neighbor, Frank Manson, father to Whitlow Manson, fueled Coy's hatred for the world by beating his bony bottom with a split shingle and then by breaking his father's nose when he attempted to intervene.

Charlotte could not conjure a picture of Coy without his most characteristic gesture, that of forming his little finger into a fishhook and vigorously digging into his ear while squenching his liver-like lips and slit eyes.

Sometimes he would come to the Well Street house with his father, a mill worker who was also a handyman, to hold a ladder while his father performed some carpenter task. When Blanche would bring cold drinks to the laboring father and son, Coy, Jr. would take his without thanks and sit in the truck to drink.

Once, after tennis, twelve-year-old Charlotte bounded naked out of the shower and into her bedroom to dress. She was horrified to find Coy, Jr. peering in from the gallery screen door. She froze. She was silent and simply stared him down and away from the door. Coy Trexler was the first male, except her father, to see her naked body.

For weeks after, all the boys in her class looked at her strangely. At last Amy Winston told her that Coy had told everybody about her bush and titties.

Charlotte grew up in the company of adults. With her father she went places that no other girl her age had been: the Club bar, Clint's dark smoky poolroom where she was given a soda and taught to climb up in the tall straight chairs which lined the walls.

Some nights she would not be put to bed, and so became familiar with all-night diners where she came under Gloria's affectionate eye. Many times she had her hair combed while she ate a banana split at one A.M. in the Pullman Cafe.

Many dawns found her pouring bourbon or helping make ham and eggs or sitting cross-legged in the study or music parlor as her father argued Isolationism with old Ed Duncan, champion fisherman, bourbon drinker, and the only registered Republican in Kern County; Spence, of course; Ed Kinder, who had the best men's shop in town; and any of his patrons.

Sometimes Sid Jacobson was there, flourishing the latest issue of *New Republic* to support his left-of-liberal views. A special relationship existed between Sid and Douglas Morton. The Jacobsons were one of three Jewish families in the town. All of them were merchants. Sid owned the best shoe store in town.

Sid and his family had come to the town shortly after the Great War. He was the only one of the Jews to establish any social intercourse with the Gentile population. Douglas Morton cherished Sid for his lively, informed mind, his gutsy wit, and his ability to play a passable cello.

To Sid, Douglas Morton provided the only place he could go outside his family for true talk—without the ubiquitous haunting feeling of condescension which pervaded all his contacts with the town where he made his living and raised his family.

Their friendship had begun at one of the American Legion dinners when both were young veterans. Sid had casually mentioned that he could play cello and Douglas immediately insisted that he come to the next chamber music session at his home. Sid had hesitated for he had accustomed himself to the isolation in which he and his family lived. But when he looked into Douglas Morton's eyes, he saw genuine welcome.

Sid loved the girl Charlotte and personally fitted her shoes and gave her three lollypops each time she visited his store. Douglas saw in Sid a chance for his daughter to learn. He was at great pains to explain to Charlotte the historical reason for the Jewish financial and mercantile tradition.

"Charlotte, in Medieval times, you know, knights, the Crusades, the Don, there were only three occupations: priest, crusading soldier, peasant. Clearly a Jew could not become the first two, and he did not want to be a peasant. That is why many Jews became bankers and financiers and merchants. Besides, money was the only protection the Jews had against an intolerant society. I want you to understand that before you begin to hear all the ugly, bigoted talk that is in this town."

Many evenings after the music had ended, Sid lingered over coffee, sometimes with Judith, his vivid wife who had come to listen. At Douglas's request, with Charlotte sitting at his feet, Sid would talk of Jewish tradition and theology. Charlotte loved Sid's head with its lion's mane of curly graying hair and bushy eyebrows.

When excited, Sid's words came in torrents and his full lips churned above the sagging jowls. He was scholarly enough to use the language with precision and rich metaphor.

And other. It was at these sessions that Charlotte learned that cursing was a minor art and began to get the *repertoire* of curses which later gained her local fame.

"English is the language of Shakespeare," her father said, "but its curses are merely coarse. Now the Italian and Yiddish languages raise cursing to a fine art." He gave her a sampling from the Italian beginning with *figlio di buona donna* and Sid supplied a collection of Yiddish damnations.

One of her fondest school memories was the day she wheeled on Coy Trexler, Jr. and said as if in litany, "May all your teeth fall out—except one. And may it rot."

Amy Winston, Max, and the new boy, Cal Hendricks, who were standing by, then burst out laughing.

Autumn moved to a gorgeous Indian Summer in Charlotte's thirteenth year. She, Blanche, and her father were leaving to spend the weekend preparing the river house and property for winter, when she delivered her most exciting report on Max Compton. It came just weeks after she had duly reported the arrival of the new boy Calvin Hendricks.

"Oh, yes," her father had said. "I met Mr. Hendricks. He's the new agent out at the railroad transfer sheds."

"They have vanished," Charlotte said excitedly. "Max and Cal have vanished from earth. They were captured this morning smoking in the boys' room. Then they escaped. And they haven't been seen since. I know. I went by Max's house right after school and his mother is *In A State*."

This had to be considered serious. Though America was recovering from the Depression, there were still numbers of drifters and hoboes, enough to make the town uneasy.

That morning, Mr. Quincy, a math teacher, had found the two imps puffing away on Luckies in the second floor boys' room. Whit Manson, who had been set on watch outside, had been busy watching a girls' gym class outside the window, and had been caught unawares. Mr. Quincy marched the two criminals down to Miss Cash's office, plopped them side-by-side on the wooden bench outside, and gone inside to report their crime.

The two had already become friends in this very place, and

65

they both knew they were going to get a paddle when they got home.

As soon as Quincy had disappeared into the principal's office, Cal said, "Let's get out of here."

They moved as one, ducked behind the receptionist's desk counter in the outer office, streaked down the halls, out the side door, to the bicycle racks.

It was before lunch so they both had money. They pedaled, most of the time using no hands, out to The Track Barbecue and had hot dogs and Cheerwine soda.

Leaving, Cal checked the pay phone slot. Empty. Then he juggled the bubble gum machine, but it was impregnable. So they were on the road without a dime in their jeans.

"I got it," Max said. "Follow me."

They pedaled the half mile to the college campus, cut past the lovely pine strewn lawns, past the tennis courts, down to the football stadium and baseball field where the class D professional Giants played.

"We're lucky the Giants made the play-offs. It just ended last week."

They parked their bikes.

"Did you see the last game?"

"No."

"They won. Schimer hit a triple with two on in the ninth."

"Let's cruise the fence and look for homeruns and batting practice balls. It hasn't rained all week so they won't be water soaked. We'll keep the best and sell the rest for a dime each."

They fanned out and walked slowly, eyes glued to the stubble and vine-covered ground. They found five balls. Two looked brand new, another fair, and the other two looked as if they had been there since early spring. They put the three good ones in Max's saddlebag.

Then they slithered under the gates of the football stadium.

"They played Elon here first game last Saturday. Charlie Watson returned a punt eighty-five yards. There's bound to be money under these stands."

"Right," said Cal. "Hell, I bet you could make a living combing these stands after a ball game. All the drunks buying chasers and hotdogs. Sheee-it. Let's go."

They got down on all fours about five feet apart beneath the bleachers and began at the goal line. Immediately, run-

'ning his hands along the stubble and weeds, Max turned up a dime.

"Hell, we'll be rich by the time we reach the fifty."

On the fifteen yard line he found a condom.

"Wow! What a load!" Cal whistled as Max held it on a twig.

"You said it."

By the fifty they had three dimes and two nickels.

"Hey, Cal, can you cum yet?"

"Yeah. Sure."

"I can't, goddamit. I got hair, but no wet ones yet."

Then Cal found their first quarter. They were on their way.

"Watch out for spiders. That bastard was just waiting for me."

"Right."

By the time they reached the other goal line they had eighty cents, two combs, a set of keys, and had resurrected an even dozen condoms.

"Jesus, those college girls really put out," Cal observed. "We oughta hang around here."

"You ever been laid?"

"Sure. A few times."

"Yeah?"

"Yeah. It was easy down in Atlanta."

They were walking the track around to the other bleachers.

"What's it like?"

"It ain't *like* nuthin', man. It's all by itself."

They were at the goal line under the other bleachers.

"How many times have you been laid?"

"Well, actually I've only been laid once, but I had a couple of blow jobs."

"Yeah? What were they like?"

"Great. Just great. Grrrreat!"

Then Cal found a pen knife. There was no rust on it.

"Might come in handy," he said and put it in his pocket.

By the time they had reached the other goal line, they had a dollar and sixteen cents.

Rich, they hundred-yard-dashed, lay panting under the goal post.

"How's about Lee Creek?" asked Max.

"Where is it?"

"Follow me. It's great."

Cal nodded. They rode. About six blocks past the college was Lee Creek bridge. A cut-off road that led to the remains of the old bridge ended within twenty yards of the creek. They dismounted and half carried their bikes over the rocky terrain. When they reached the steep bank, they decided to hide their bikes under some of the trees that bordered the creek. Max stripped back a large canopy of vines and they shoved the bikes under and then laid the vines on top of them. They stood on the steep, ten-foot, tree-lined, root-gnarled bank.

Lee Creek was an amiable, gushing, boy-sized creek which changed character every hundred yards. At its widest it was about thirty feet across. Beneath the bridge was a rapid made of huge stones, forming miniature falls and whirlpools, plunging into a waist deep pool. The high Southern sun broke through the bordering trees and quicksilvered the ripples. It was irresistible. Cal and Max were naked and in at just about the time Mr. Compton and Mrs. Hendricks entered Mrs. Cash's office.

They swam laps, splashed, climbed the rapids beneath the bridge, dug out some pure gray clay and formed a woman's torso with never-never breasts on one of the rocks. Then they stretched out and sunned on the dun sand which massed on one side of the pool beneath the rapids. There were several condoms here also. It seemed that sex was everywhere.

"You really have got a big prick," Max said and regarded his own with displeasure.

"You oughta see it hard."

"What's pussy like?"

"Strange. It's hard to find. You know, exactly. It's very hot. Just thinking about it makes me want some."

"Yeah. And women really like it, huh?"

"Oh, yeah. That one I had just went crazy."

"How'd she act?"

"Crazy. Moaning and all."

"How'd you get it? I mean where and who was she?"

"OK. It was like this. She was our nigger maid in Atlanta."

"Nigger?"

"Yeah. Well, high yellow. They're supposed to be best. It happened a couple of days before we moved here. Well, actually, I screwed her the last day we were there. But for three days before that she gave me a blow job."

"Yeah. Where? At your house?"

"Yeah. Mom was out—you know, shipping stuff and things.

Sue, that was her name. She was nineteen. Biggest tits I ever saw. Like grapefruit."

"Well, how'd it happen? What if your mother had come in?"

"Oh shit. Don't even think of it!"

Cal came as close to being pensive as Max would ever see him.

"Well, I came in from swimming at the pool in the park near our house. Hey, that was the greatest pool. There was this guy Gary who was lifeguard and he taught me how to dive. I was just learning the front 'one and a half' when we had to move."

"Well, Mike out at the Club teaches diving. Are you members of the Club?"

"No. Not yet anyway. How do you join?"

"I don't know exactly. I'll ask Dad. OK. So you had just come in from swimming."

"Yeah. Sue had some sandwiches ready for lunch. Said Mom wouldn't be back until four and that I was not to unpack any of my junk. I ate and jumped into the shower. I had a towel around me. Everything was packed and I couldn't find any shorts, so I called Sue. She came in and dug out some shorts and pants and a shirt. She told me to comb my hair before it dried and got rats' nests in it. And she walked up behind me and snatched the towel from around my ass and started drying my hair. And she turned me around and was drying and then I felt her give me a squeak on the prick and she said you've really got something there, haven't you? Then she gave me the comb and she started drying the hair around my prick."

"Wow."

"Yeah. Of course, I got hard as hell. She said looks like I've started something. I said yeah. And she said want me to make you feel good? I said yeah. She said will you tell your mother if I make you feel good? I said no. So she started giving me a blow job. I didn't last two minutes. We both laughed and she cleaned me up with the towel and told me to dress before my mother came in. I was on the porch when Sue left. She whispered did I like it? I said hell yeah. And she said she'd do it again tomorrow."

"Hey, great. I wish we had Sue instead of that fat Martha who snitches on me all the time."

"Yeah. Shit, I get hard just thinking about it."

"Did she do it the next day?"

"Bastard!" Cal swatted a horse fly on his leg.

He went on, "No. Didn't get a chance. Mom was home all day. But she kept winking at me. But the next day Mom spent all day in the garage getting things together, and she told me to go up to my room and get everything straight. Sue came up, unzipped me and did it again."

"Jesus. With your mother in the house?"

"Yeah, well, she was out in the garage."

"And did you screw her?"

"Yep. Wow, thinking about it makes me stiff. Look at this thing."

"Cha-rist. How big is a pussy anyway?"

"That's hard to say. I'll tell you it's a little hard to find. It seems to hide. Sue put it in and she had a little trouble."

"Well, when it's in what exactly do you do? I mean . . ."

"You'll know. It comes naturally."

"But . . ."

"Well, here's how it happened. Mom was going out to lunch for the last time with some of her friends. I was supposed to help Sue pack the towels and stuff. We were in the towel closet with a box and she kept brushing those big tits against me, so I asked her to let me see 'em. She said let's finish this first. She stood on the bottom shelf to reach some sheets and junk and she told me not to let her fall so I put my hand on her ass and held her but it was—it felt so nice that I started playing around. She said uh-*huh*, you're getting me all worked up. So I put my hand up her dress and between her legs. And she just stood there and kinda wiggled and gurgled. Then she said let me down 'fore you drive me crazy."

"What did it feel like?"

"Well, her panties were wet and it was a very warm place. Friendly."

"What happened then?"

"She grabbed an old towel and we went into my room. She said do you want to see me? And she took off her dress and her bra and her panties and just stood there. Hell, my prick was so hard I looked like a mobile telephone pole. Then she came over and unzipped me and she just put her tits in my face and I really sucked them. Jeeee-sus, did she have a big set! Wow, Max, it's really hard to think about it without going nuts. Then she said come on and laid down and pulled me between her legs and started kissing me."

"She kissed you?"

"Yep. Hell, I liked it. Then she said take it easy and she reached down and put it in. And . . . well, skyrockets."

"Wow."

They both lay back to think about it. Soon Cal was pacing.

"I wish we had some butts."

"Yeah."

"Why don't we follow the creek down a ways? See what we can find."

"OK."

They put on their pants, rolled them up, tied their shoes together and hung them around their necks.

Just beyond the rapids the trees closed over the creek. It was smooth, running water, cool, dark. They moved out, wading. Max had been down the creek many times, but the creek was always changing. There were times when it seemed like a cavern, so dense was the vernal canopy. At other times, where a farmer had cleared close to the bank, the sun broke through brilliantly.

At times it was eerie and dark. Max was forever seeing something that he had to investigate—a flight of tadpoles in a serene shallow, stones that showed mica in a sun burst, crawfish, squirrel chatter, bird calls. There were places where the water was still as a mirror, and his feet raised cyclones of sand on the bottom. Gliders raced before his invasion. Dragonflies buzzed him. There were times when the vines draped down over the creek and he had to brush them away with his arm. Roots of huge elms convoluted out of the banks like gnomes about to spring from the earth. Every step was excitement for him. There were moments when he sensed the powerful fertile life on the creek and its creatures as an organism, alive and about its business—completely indifferent to his tiny space and disturbance. Max felt very small then. Here he did not matter. This creek and its life had been here before he was born and would be here after him.

Investigating things, he continually fell behind Cal.

Cal was in love with motion. On and on he moved. Each new sight, each new bend in the creek drove him. He ran up the bank at a gentle slope to scout. Then plunged back in, churning forward.

A knife of sun fell on a gleaming object. He turned to summon his friend. His friend was not in sight. He called. Silence.

He crouched to guard his find. At last Max rounded a

bend, a four-inch crawfish clamped between his fingers—
carefully.

"Hey, Max, come here. Look at this monster."

"Jeee-sus."

Cal pointed to an enormous spider sunning itself on a flat
stone. The spider was emerald under the shaft of sun, flecked
with spangles of scarlet and gray. Its legs were thick and
armor-like.

Max gasped. "It's beautiful."

Cal grasped a stone.

"No," Max said. "No. He's just sunbathing. God, he's like a
great jewel."

"Yeah," Cal agreed, dropping the stone. He was already
looking over his shoulder downstream.

"Look at Harrison here," Max held out the crayfish. "He's
a real Harrison. My friend Charlotte calls everything Harrison
or Hedrick. Yeah, you know Charlotte. You know, Morton."

He dropped the crayfish.

"Go back home, Harrison," he called.

They moved out, Cal ahead. Max dropped back to exchange whistles with a towhee, then to skip a flat rock back
up stream.

Suddenly he heard Cal shout, "Moccasin. Hey, Max, water
moccasin."

Max broke into a run. "Which way?"

He rounded a bend to see Cal firing a barrage of rocks that
didn't seem to disturb the serene glide of a bullet head
cruising downstream ahead of them. They gave chase, but
even in shallow water they were ducks on land compared
with the skillful water creature. At last, they sat down and
rested.

"That was a big mother," Cal said.

"Yeah. Glad I didn't walk up on him. Where was he?"

"On that big flat rock sticking out back there. See? That
one. I guess he was napping. And I came along like a
nightmare."

"Yeah."

"Hell, I wish I had my .22."

"You got a .22?"

"Yeah. Just got it six weeks ago. For my birthday. After this
I won't have it. Shit. I just can't stay straight."

"Shit, me either."

They moved on, staying together in case of other snakes. Gradually the trees began to change and the creek widened.

"We're getting near where she joins the river," Max said.

The banks opened out and the vines fell back. The trees now were scrub pine. They climbed the bank, cut on land for fifty yards, and saw the river.

They put on their shoes and dashed down to the banks. Here the river was about a quarter of a mile wide. They could look upstream and see the great railway bridge, green banks and a dozen tiny, wooded islands. The sun was beginning to fling long tree shadows out onto the quietly running river.

They struck out upstream.

"Shit, wish we had some butts," Cal said. "The rifle and some butts."

"Yeah. We got money but there isn't a store for miles. It's crazy. Most of the time there's stores and no money."

Cal leading, they rounded a point that gave on a quiet cut reaching into the pines about fifty feet. It was a dark silent reflecting pool. On the bank leaning back against a pine was an ancient black man holding a homemade fishing pole. He was napping beneath a worn felt hat, but their approach warned him and he regarded them with glittering eyes beneath bushy, gray eyebrows.

"Howdy," said Cal.

"Howdy," followed Max.

"Howdy."

"Any luck?"

"Well, done got a couple of sun perch and one 'bout two pound cat."

"That's all right."

"Good luck," said Max as they passed under his gaze.

Ten feet down, Cal stopped and turned.

"Hey, Pap. We got money. Can you sell us a couple of butts?"

"I ain't got no ready rolls, but I got makin's. Can you roll?"

Neither could.

"Well, c'mon, we'll see." The old man reached into the chest pocket and brought out a little white cloth tobacco bag with draw strings and the paper pasted to its side.

"Ain't you boys a leetle bit young to be puffin'?"

"Pap, I been smoking a year now. So's he."

"Well, we'll see." He quickly rolled a splendid cigarette up to the lick. He held it out to Cal. "Reckon you want to do your own lickin'. I'd prefer it."

Cal licked and the ancient man made a neat final fold and handed him the cigarette. Then he did the same for Max.

Cal offered money but the old man just shook his head. He made himself one and the three smokers sat by the cove and talked.

He said he came here to this spot almost daily now. "Ma boy takes care of me now. See, ah stays with him and his fambly. Back ovah that a piece. I try to add a few fish to the table now and then. My son works for the Southern, so I work an acre and a half back there—few vegetables and things. That's ovah fer now, so's I fish mostly."

They told him they were rambling.

"Done a heap of that myself," the old man cackled. "You boys done been to Boone's cave?"

No, they hadn't.

"It's a piece up yonder ways. Too fur fer today. Good place though."

He clearly understood the essential goodness and badness of rambling places.

Cal stood and started pacing. It was time to move. They thanked the old man.

He had the great good grace to offer them a cigarette apiece for later. They accepted, wished him luck, and walked.

"Hey, young 'uns."

They stopped and went back to him.

"Ah ain't stickin' in your business, but up thar a spell is a place where's usually a gang of hoboes' camps. Might not be bad to avoid it. Least, take a look 'fore you walk in on it."

"Right. Thanks, Pap. Good luck."

Around the bed they passed a boat landing with a canoe and skiff heaved up. There was a little summer house by a path that led back into the pines. No house was visible. Cal wanted to hook the canoe.

"No, man," Max said. "That'll put 'em on our trail for sure."

The river was quiet in the deepening light, the islands like dream places that could be defended, lived on.

Cal forged ahead. Max tried to spot an early hoot owl. Suddenly he heard running footsteps. He wheeled and saw Cal cutting through trees like a broken field runner.

"Hey, Max, around the bend? The hobo camp."

They ran like Indians tracking. A quarter of a mile and they could smell the rich wood smoke. Cal dropped to a crouch. Max followed. They moved from tree to tree.

There were five of them lounging around a fire. Periodically, they passed a huge jar, each taking a slug, then wiping their stubble chins, then seized and shaken by coughing so violent that it seemed it would eviscerate them. As the boys watched, one took a big hunting knife and began to portion whatever it was they were cooking.

The boys back-tracked for a conference.

"It's getting dark. We gotta start thinking about a camp."

"Right."

"Probably better put some distance between us and that bunch."

"Right. Dammit, I wish I had that rifle."

Max turned and faced the river.

"Hey, Cal," and he pointed to an island about a hundred yards down stream and about seventy-five feet off shore. It was the largest island they had seen, thickly wooded with scrub pine which rose to a pyramid in the center. It looked serene and friendly.

"Perfect," said Cal, and began taking off his shoes. Then he stopped. "Hell, I'm starved."

"Yeah. Right. Me too."

"It's too late to start fishing. We shoulda bought the old man's catch."

"Never mind. I got it," Cal said. "There was fenced property about a mile back. Remember?"

"Yeah."

"OK. Fences mean houses. Right. Why don't we go back and see if we can hook something. Or buy it."

"OK. Sounds good."

"Wait a minute. You a good swimmer, Max?"

"Yeah. Sure."

"I mean out to the island?"

"Yeah. Sure."

"OK. You go out there and set up a camp and get a fire going and I'll go see if I can round up some rations."

"You want to go alone?"

"Yeah. Sure. There's still plenty of sun. Make a fire though so's I can see in case things get sticky and I run late."

"OK. Oh hell, Cal. Matches."

Cal reached in his shirt pocket. "I hooked the old man's."

"Wow. Good thinking. He probably had extra anyway."

"How am I gonna keep them dry? I don't know about swimming with one arm out of the water."

"Oh, yeah."

Max's eyes scanned the shore. "I'll float 'em on a log or something."

"Right."

They started foraging. They would need two rafts. Fifty feet downstream they found a fallen pine about ten feet high.

"Perfect," said Max. "I'll strip and hang my clothes on the branches. Just kick my way out to the island. Now something for the rations if you get some."

A little farther down, at water's edge they found a three foot piece of two-by-twelve.

Cal carried the plank to the nearest point to the island and leaned it against a stump. Max stripped.

"Should be easy. The river's smooth as silk."

"OK, baby. Have a fire going. Wait. Here. Take my shirt too."

"Good luck, man. Hey, don't get caught."

Cal set off at an easy dog-trot through the pines. Max pushed the tree out into the stream and started kicking gently. The floating clothes tree oozed soundlessly, an arrow head moving slowly toward the island.

Max touched bottom. He waded around in front of the raft and pulled it ashore, snatched the clothes, and beached the tree in case they needed it again. He turned and began his inspection of the island.

Immediately his eye caught a weathered piece of plank nailed to a tree. Freehand painted in faded white elegant letters were the words ISOLA BELLA—PRIVATE—KEEP OFF.

"Huh?" muttered Max. He moved with caution as he began his tour.

The island was lovely. It was about fifty feet long and thirty feet wide and shaped like a ship. It had clearly been built up by river silt and at the upstream side the shore was rounded and cleanly gnawed away. Downstream it tapered off to a red clay and sand point. There was a slight rise in the middle and there were a half dozen pines about fifteen feet tall. There was almost no underbrush under them and years had made a deep carpet of pine needles. Around the shores there was short, thick, leafy foliage, seeds that had blown or floated and taken hold.

Max rambled the entire circumference of the island, finishing at the downstream pointed beach. When he turned around he saw, tucked back in the foliage away from the beach, a lean-to. He approached it cautiously. It was so well hidden that he had walked around it without noticing it. The roof spar of the lean-to was a single two-by-four securely roped to two living trees. Its sloping roof was made of old planks and foliage had been trained to completely hide the planks from the wooded side. Before the entrance was a fireplace blackened with use, precisely made of native stone with three iron bars fitted for a grill.

Max dropped to a crouch and entered the shadowy shelter. Its floor was soft with a cushion of pine needles. Back in the corner was a tin-covered wood box, two by two feet. Max knelt before it and started to lift the lid. Then he changed his mind and went outside and found a stick. He went back in and with the stick lifted the lid. His caution was unnecessary. Inside he found four cans of pork and beans, three cans of sardines, two tin plates, two sauce pans, and two long slender cloth bags. The cloth bags held a hunting knife, can opener, and two knives, forks and spoons, and a big serving spoon. Beneath them was a Prince Albert tobacco tin full of matches. The two oil skin packets held a blanket and two towels. Tucked away in the towels was a thin little book entitled *Renascence* by Edna St. Vincent Millay.

"Wow," Max muttered. "Terrific."

He immediately began gathering brush for a fire. He considered that he had better wait a bit to light it so it wouldn't be consumed before Cal needed the landmark.

He covered the island again. On a flat stone at the upstream side, where the water lapped at the gnawed foot-deep drop-off, he found three six-inch clay figurines facing the river. Two were clearly meant to represent Indians. The other was a bust of a girl with long hair swept from under a helmet. It was much smoother and finely modeled. Max liked it very much. Fired and glazed it would have been beautiful. The three figures seemed totems. It was a nice place to sit and watch the sun set. He did just that. When the top rim of the fireball was beneath the pines upstream, he went back to the lean-to and took out one sauce pan and a can of pork and beans and the can opener. He was starving. He opened the beans and dumped them into the pan. He took a spoonful.

Jeee-sus, he was hungry. He wished for Cal. He walked down to the shore side of the island and sat against a tree to wait.

After five minutes of sitting and five of pacing he saw Cal emerge from the trees, wave, hold something up in his hand. He waved and watched Cal strip, place his clothes and his prize on the plank and wade out. Cal kicked slowly, taking care not to splash the plank which he nudged ahead of him.

Max knelt at water's edge and received the tiny raft.

"How would you like a fresh baked apple pie, man?" Cal gurgled.

"Terrific." Max shook the raider's hand. "Hey, it's still warm. But have I got things to show you. C'mon."

Cal slipped into his shoes, grabbed his clothes, and followed Max.

"See. No place like home. And, sir, I can offer you a three course meal. Shall we begin with sardines, then pork and beans, then apple pie?"

"Wow, this is grrrrrreat. Where'd you get all this stuff?"

Max explained.

Then Cal said, "I cut up through a cornfield and ended up right near a big old house that belonged to the landing we passed. I was just lying there casing the joint when a big black woman stepped out of the back door and set this pie on the railing to cool. It was easy. I'll bet she's wondering where in the hell her pie went. It's still warm. Feel."

Soon the fire was crackling and both tins of sardines had disappeared. They ate the warm pork and beans like pioneers.

"How does it feel to cum," Max asked, still consumed with curiosity about this wonder which must soon happen to him as it had to all men before him.

Cal pondered a moment.

"Max, I just can't tell you. It comes from way down. It's the best thrill I've ever had and it's impossible to think of anything else for a couple of weeks afterward. I remember that when it happened I felt so good, but I was afraid it would never happen again. So every day I'd rush home after school and jack off just to be sure. It just takes hold of you, man."

They ate. Max thought of something else to ask.

"How much do you cum?"

"Hmmmm," Cal was trying for accuracy. "I'd say about a spoonful. Not much, I guess. It's just that everything stands still when it's happening."

They ate some more.

"It's not much but when it comes it's like everything in you is trying to get out that little hole in your prick. It's really great."

They had gotten to the apple pie which Max had set near the fire so it would stay warm. He cut two slices that together made half the pie. It was dark now and the night noises joined the shurring fire. A hoot owl got above everything else. At least a dozen whip-o-wills joined in. It was a cosmic symphony.

"Did it feel better with Sue than by yourself?"

Cal pondered again.

"That's hard to say. The feeling? I'd say the same. But it was better with Sue. You know, it's funny but I never can remember exactly how it is. Like I close my eyes and try to remember, really think and concentrate, and I can never quite track it down. Exactly. You know what I mean? I remember that it's the greatest feeling in the world and I want it all the time but you can't place it exactly. I know that Sue was very warm—it actually seems to burn. Not the way fire would burn. But burn. It's like peppers burn your tongue, but wouldn't burn paper. You know what I mean? Anyway, it's so good you don't want to do anything else the whole rest of your life. Just cum."

"Well, I sure wish I would hurry and do it. How old are you, Cal?"

"Jeeee-sus, this pie's good. That old black woman sure can cook. Fourteen."

"Ummmm. I'm only thirteen."

"You got a lot of hair. You'll cum soon. Then you'll see."

"Do girls feel it that good?"

"Well, Sue just about went crazy. I was scared for a minute. Yep, I think so. Anyway, for sure, they love it as much as we do. Hell, down in Atlanta, I put my finger in old Nancy Spruance, just my finger, and she went up in smoke."

"That's good," said Max.

"Yeah, that's really good."

Max pointed at a shooting star. "You know, that blanket and those towels are gonna come in handy. It's getting a little chilly."

"Right. We'd better keep that fire going. That's one problem with an island. There isn't too much firewood."

"Yeah. Let's get in some."

They poked around the pines and gathered some dead

limbs and cones. Then they walked down to the river and pissed together.

"Tomorrow we'll have to dig a latrine," Max said.

"Right," Cal yawned.

They went back to the lean-to, made the towels into pillows and spread the blanket.

"'Night. Don't think about Sue too much."

"Yep, there sure ain't no Sue on this island."

They were silent.

"Jeez, I'll bet my parents are mad as hell."

"Oh man, don't think of it. This is the third time I've run away. My old man will beat my ass until my nose bleeds. Wow."

"Three times. Jeee-sus. Why?"

"Well, the first time was when I flunked fifth grade. Shee-it. I wasn't about to go home after that."

"Where'd you go?"

"I went to the Atlanta train station. I was gonna hide out in a train, but it's harder than you think to get on a train. I wound up just hanging around the station. Finally fell asleep in the waiting room and the cops woke me up and hauled my ass home."

"Hmmmmm. Wonder what my folks are doing now? Well, I'll never know. Hey, Cal, tomorrow we gotta make a plan."

"Right."

They slept like pioneers.

5

WHEN Max woke Cal was gone. He sat up, scratched, admired the clear September morning. The sun was above the tree line, but the river mist still hung in near the banks.

He got up, walked to the water's edge. He saw Cal, nearly a hundred yards away, on the far bank. They waved and Cal gave an echoing cow whistle.

Max stripped and waded in and began the slow distance pace. Cal was sitting on the bank beaming.

"Wow," Max said as he waded ashore. "What a way to begin a day."

"Beats old lady Thompson and her bubble gum guff."

"It's Saturday. We should have waited until Monday."

They laughed. They lounged, rested, poked around the shore, talked about pussy some more.

"Hell, I'm hungry."

"Me, too. What'll it be—apple pie, sardines, or pork and beans?"

"Or all three?"

"Hey, Cal. Did you ever think of the pioneers? Or the Indians? Man, there were no roads then. Look at those pines. That's all there was. No houses to hook apple pies from."

"Look, there's that landing and boats. Think we ought to stop in and thank them for the pie?"

"Yeah. In a pig's ass. Last one back has to wash dishes and dig a latrine."

They swam. Cal won by five feet.

They rationed the pie so that there was a quarter left—two girl slices. Max did dishes, then they both dug the latrine, using the hunting knife and one of the sauce pans.

Suddenly Cal saw something and hit the dirt.

"Get down."

Max did.

"Look."

Max saw a swimmer approaching from the near shore. The white bathing cap told them it was a woman. The stroke was sure. When she neared and stood to wade ashore, Max clutched Cal's shoulder.

"Hey, it's Morton. It's Charlotte."

"Yeah. It is."

"Hey, Morton. Hey, Charlotte."

She stopped knee-deep in water. She frowned and squinted. She brushed the water from her eyes, unsnapped the cap, removed it and shook out her long hair. Then she burst out laughing.

"Maxwell Compton. Cal Hendricks!"

She ran into the arms of both boys and they did a triple war dance, clinging to each other.

At last they fell apart.

"Well, tell me," she said.

They locked arms and walked to the fireplace. Suddenly Charlotte stopped short.

"Why, you bandits! You bastards. It was you!"

Her eyes had fallen on the apple pie tin lying beside the fireplace.

"My father nearly got his gun and headed for the hobo camp. Blanche was completely screwed out. And it was you!"

She collapsed laughing on a stone beside the hearth until she could speak. "That apple pie. That blessed apple pie. They were MacIntoshes. My father brought them all the way from New York last week. We waited all week for that pie."

"You mean that's your house up there?"

"Yes, you creeps." And she continued her gutsy laugh.

Max and Cal sat down and joined her.

"Well, at least, I get the pie tin back."

Then her eyes fell on the sardine tins and the cans. She pointed.

"You damned cattle rustlers. You'll eat me out of house and home."

"And this is your island?"

"Well, I took squatters' rights. This mansion is mine. It's my secret place. Mine and my father's."

"Jeee-sus. How about that. The whole world to ramble and we wind up on Morton's doorstep."

"We coulda done worse," Cal said. "Those sardines and beans saved us from starvation."

"And the blanket. We woulda frozen last night."

"Oh, you found my whole cache. But how? Where in hell have you been? The whole town's worried. Max, your mother's on the edge of a breakdown. Hey, Spence, Mr. Fulton, the editor of the *Herald*, was just speaking to my father on the phone. You guys are going to make the headlines in this afternoon's paper. The sheriff and the state patrol are looking for you."

Max looked at Cal, Cal at Max. Obviously neither was averse to fame.

"Sheee-it." And all three burst out laughing again.

Finally, they collected themselves and the two fugitives explained.

"Well, at least, you could tell me the pie was good."

"It was great. Cal even got it here before it had cooled."

"Oh God, wait till Blanche hears this."

"Did you make the lean-to? And those statues on the point?"

"Sure. Well, my father made the one of me. Didn't you recognize me?"

They scrambled out to the bow of the island, as Charlotte called it. They bent over the three totems.

"Yeah. Right. I can see it. It does look like you."

"It does, doesn't it? This one is the Great Father. This one is Coyote, a great spirit. You know about Coyote. He's the cleverest of the spirits. This is the way he looked—you know, tall and handsome, when he fooled the Indian maiden and married her. You know that story? Anyway, imagine her surprise when she woke up and found herself on a mat with a fuzzy flea-ridden coyote. Probably grinning from ear to ear. Dad says there's a lesson for all girls in that."

The boys laughed.

"Hey, watch out for that Max. He's got a real tail in his pants."

"Right," she said. "Coyote's tail. *Right!* Do you know why all the animals sniff each other—you know, sniff? Well, Coyote again. He was born with no tail. He was so jealous that he called a meeting of all the animals—*but* before any of them could enter, they had to leave their tails outside. When they were all assembled, Coyote slithered out, picked the most gorgeous tail and took off, and mixed the others up. What a mess when the animals went out to claim their tails. Everybody was all screwed out. That's why animals sniff each other. They're looking for their own tail."

Cal snapped his fingers. "I always wondered. Right."

"And me. Well, my father says this is me as Pallas Athene, the most wonderful Goddess man ever invented. Remember last year? She was the one who helped Odysseus."

"Right. Right," said Max regarding the girl who knelt beside him. "Yeah, I can see both. Yeah, hell, your nose and chin—and, and cheeks—your whole face is . . ." Max stared at her clean features as she looked down the river, and for the very first time in his life, he thought a girl beautiful.

She turned her dark eyes directly on his. She was smiling under the still-young sun. "Well, you're . . . you're very pretty, Charlotte."

He immediately dropped his eyes.

She smiled brilliantly and looked at the other boy, who was now rolling a handy stone on the ground before him.

"Yeah?" she said.

"It's . . . ah, true . . . yeah. Morton, you're damned pretty," Cal said, mainly looking at her neat round bottom as she knelt.

It was so quiet they could hear the river breathing. For a long uneasy time. They were all testing.

"Hey, have you guys seen Harrison the catfish?" she broke it.

"Who?"

"He comes here to this rock all the time. We feed him. God, he'll eat anything from peanut butter sandwiches to beans."

"Who?"

"Harrison the Catfish. Jeee-sus, he's this long. Dad says he would go forty pounds. He has broken three of my father's lines. Dad says he deserves to live. So he quit trying to catch him and now we feed him almost every day in summer. He actually comes here to dine sometimes. I swear."

"How do you know he's Harrison?" asked Cal.

"Some things you just know. Some things are just clearly Harrisons. It's something you just know."

"I told you so. I told you she calls everything Harrison."

"I guess you just know," said Cal. They all laughed and were glad to be together.

"It's a beautiful place. You put up that sign, didn't you?"

"Yep. Isola Bella means beautiful island. In Italian. My father and I named it and settled it. When the river's up, it's a lot smaller. C'mon."

She stood and they followed her through the trees. Max suddenly found himself paralyzed by the way her bottom moved as she took each step, sometimes dancing aside to avoid a pine branch. He turned and looked at Cal who was following. Cal looked at him, shrugged yes, and licked his lips.

"This tree is called Lookout. It's like the crow's-nest on a ship. You can climb and get a good overview. Here. It's easy. Look."

And she started to climb, easy step to step from branch to branch. She was panting as she climbed, because an intimation had crystallized in her mind. *Cal and Max are looking at my bottom and I'm climbing this silly tree because I can't stop liking them looking at my bottom.*

"See?"

Neither Cal nor Max could move their eyes from the little

purse where her thighs met. It looked wonderful, soft and friendly. Jeee-sus, this was Morton from school.

She came down, making exaggerated movements because she couldn't help it. She was exquisitely aware of her body. It took her, made her giddy, dancy, talky.

She pointed.

"That's Isola Piccola—little island. Want to swim there?"

"Sure."

"Hey, we haven't got swim suits."

"We could wear our shorts. Char?"

She nodded. Turned away as they took off their pants. Then looked.

"It's harder going than coming. Against the current."

They swam. It was only seventy-five yards and their feet touched twenty feet out.

"There isn't much here," she said. There wasn't. But it was a place to go and going was good.

There were four large flat rocks that were ideal for sunning. They lay out for a while. The island's three pines kept it from desolation.

"Well, what are you guys gonna do? I mean, sooner or later somebody's gonna think of the river and everybody in town will be down here looking for you. Besides, my father will probably come down for a swim this afternoon. He's not creepy, but if he sees you he will just have to tell your parents to keep them from worrying. You know what I mean?"

"Yeah," Max said. "He knows my mother and father."

"Well, we're gonna get our asses beat anyway, so's we might just as well stay till we run out of money and food. Hell, I'd just as soon head up the river and just keep going."

"Me too. 'Cept my family is going to New York for Thanksgiving."

"Hmmm. Well, let's see how things go."

"Right."

"Well, look," Charlotte said. "I'll show you something secret when we get back to Isola Bella. That is, if you won't ever tell anybody. If you don't use it. OK?"

"OK." Cal was on his feet. "I can keep my mouth shut. Let's go."

The swim back was easy and fun. They sprinted the last thirty yards.

Cal turned head down ten yards out and hand walked in.

Max lay back in a float and watched. Charlotte sat by the three totems and watched the boys come ashore. Cal already had clear muscle definition. He was sleek and brown and grinning as he waded in. Max was thin and wiry and fleet. Their fine bodies glistened as the sun caught and held the rivulets running from them. Charlotte was fascinated as the water caused their cotton shorts to cling to their bodies, fascinated by the way their bodies narrowed at the hips, the way they had almost no bottoms.

"Nobody, now. You swear. You'll tell nobody."

"Right. Nobody."

"Right."

"Even if you don't use it. OK?"

She led toward the water's edge nearest the mainland. She turned and sighted from the Lookout.

"See? On a line from the Lookout."

There were two flat rocks with a third placed on top. She lifted the top rock. It was the smallest. The other two were about a foot and a half across. She knelt and, straining, spun one of them. Max dropped and spun the other. His brown shoulder and arm pressed against hers, warm and smooth. Their eyes met as their arms did. They smiled shyly and looked down at the little metal box they had uncovered. Charlotte scratched the soil and needles away from it and lifted it.

"You know," she said shyly, "I guess it's not so much. When I'm here alone—well, it's like a treasure, or it was, when I was a kid. I'm embarrassed now. But anyway, here it is, in case you need it."

The three of them knelt so close that the thighs of both boys were touching hers. She could feel Cal's warm breath feathering her shoulder.

She opened the little box. There were two little cloth tobacco bags. She gave one to Cal and one to Max.

"Yes," she said.

Cal unstrung his and poured into his hand eight silver dollars.

"OK, Morton," he said. "Wow. It is a treasure."

"Where'd you get these?" Max asked.

"Well, sometimes Dad gives me one—you know, birthdays and things. It's not much money. But, you know, if you need it. It's always been my secret treasure. Dad says a woman must have mad money. This is mine."

She nodded to Max and he poured his bag into his hand. Out fell five perfect flint arrowheads.

"Jee-sus."

"Yeah," she said. "Not money, but they are so perfect. Look. Each one. There are lots of them along the river. We, Dad and I, have found at least a hundred. Mostly, he gives them to Old Clint—you know, the guy that writes the history column in the *Herald* on Sundays. But these were so perfect that he said I should keep them and give them to my grandchildren. Aren't they great?"

Cal and Max passed them hand to hand.

To Max they had the feel and sing of flight.

"Dad says that maybe they were all done by the same man—or from the same camp anyway. I love them."

Cal was fascinated. "You mean that there are lots of them around here?"

"Sure," Max verified. "I've found a couple on scout hikes. None as perfect as these."

"Hey, we oughta look for some," Cal said.

"OK. We'll keep our eyes out."

"Take one, Cal. For keeps. Max, you too. Go ahead. Pick."

"Naw, these are yours. Maybe we'll find some."

But Charlotte took two of the flint masterpieces and pressed them into the hands of the boys.

"Gee, thanks."

"Morton, this is great," Cal said.

"OK. Now you know about my treasure and if you need it, you know where it is."

They replaced the treasure and the boys replaced the stones.

"We've got some money," Cal said. "We looted the football stadium before we came."

They ambled back to the lean-to.

"Anybody hungry?" Cal said.

"Yeah, it must be noon," Max said. "Judging by the sun."

"Listen, you guys, I've got to get back. I promised that I'd come back for lunch. I've got to help Blanche clean and store the barbecue equipment this afternoon. We're kinda getting the house ready for winter."

They went to the box and took out the last tin of sardines and last can of pork and beans.

"Well, we've got to go ashore before tonight, that's for sure," Max said.

"Yeah, or catch Harrison," Cal grinned. "I still want to see that big mother."

"Don't you dare. He's like a pet now. Sunrise and sunset are good times to look for him. But don't hurt him. He's my friend. My father says he's a gallant foe and deserves respect."

"OK. OK. But I'd like to see him anyway," Cal said.

"OK. So listen. I'll try to get some food and bring it this afternoon. How's that?"

"Terrific."

"OK. It'll be later, after I've done my chores. Now listen, if Dad and I come for a swim this afternoon, I'll make a lot of noise from the bank. Now you guys keep an ear open, and have this place cleaned up so he won't know that anybody's been here. Aw, he'd think they were fishermen anyway probably. But if you hear me squealing, take off for the other side and wait till we've gone. OK?"

"Right."

"Listen, I'm gonna take this back," she said, lifting the pie tin.

"Wait a minute," Max said. He took a piece of firewood charred at the end and wrote inside the tin *Please refill*.

"Why don't you sneak it right back to the porch. Old Blanche will be screwed out."

Cal and Charlotte roared.

"Hey, Char," Cal said. "Could you hook a pack of cigs? We'll pay for them."

"Gee, Dad smokes a pipe."

"How's about some tobacco and papers?"

"OK, I'll try. Yeah, I think there are some papers in his smoking stand."

"Why don't you take that plank as a raft for the provisions. We used it."

"Yeah, good. Now, listen, keep your ears open for my warning in case Dad and I come swimming. Gee, I hate to keep this from Dad. He'd love it. Being an adult is too much responsibility."

She pushed the plank out and slipped into the river after it. The water chilled after the sun, and the hotter-than-the-sun-lust of the boys.

The two boys sat before the beans and sardines.

"Morton is OK," Max said.

"She's great. Hey man, what a pair of tits!"

"Yeah. In fact, she is damned good-looking."

"Right you are, man. She is just all around OK. I'd really like to get some of that."

"Hey, do you think she would?"

"Who knows. She's a gamy little woman."

They ate and lounged. Cal fell asleep. Max dozed, then went to see if Harrison the catfish had arrived. He hadn't. He looked for arrowheads on the way back to the lean-to. Halfway back he saw Cal in the middle of the river, blowing spouts of water, floating, lolling. He jumped in. They revisited Isola Piccola. They lounged, looked for arrowheads, made red clay statues which were failures. Cal formed a single enormous tit which was a success. They raced back, finished in a dead heat.

And dead tired. They lay down behind some shore scrub to watch for Morton. Cal imagined that she had nipples the size of silver dollars. "Coy said she had big tits and a full bush. For once I don't think Trex was lying."

"Yeah," Max agreed. "Wow, would I like to see her naked! Would I like to see her naked!"

Cal got a hard on just imagining and remembering her climbing that tree.

"Jeee-sus," Max said. "What a prick!"

"Yep. Old everready." Cal's pride in his appointment was well-placed. Max was all envy and admiration.

"I'd really like to see old Morton nude. Do you think she would let us?"

"Well, we could ask her. I don't think she'd get mad."

"OK. Let's just kinda lead up to it slowly. I like her. I don't want her mad at us."

"Naw, she won't get mad. Maybe I'll just show her this and she will jump out of her clothes." Cal leered.

"Who knows? I don't understand girls anyway."

"Me either."

They waited.

And waited.

At last, Charlotte appeared on the mainland shore. She waved and blew kisses and held up a big bag—food! She balanced the bag on the plank raft, and pushed off. They both jumped in and swam to meet her.

"Tobacco. Hey, Blanche is in a State. 'Some nerve,' she screeched. Dad and I nearly died laughing. Hey, you know, I think Dad suspects that you two are the Great Apple Pie

Thieves. He's not coming swimming. He's out screwing around with the tractor. But I think he suspects and didn't want to give you away." She giggled as they swam in.

There were six peanut butter sandwiches, four country ham sandwiches, a jar of Blanche's own canned peaches, and a quart of milk.

"She'll sure miss some of this, especially the milk. But I've got lies on my lips," Charlotte teased.

Max and Cal did a war dance. She couldn't stop looking at the way their penises jiggled and at the dark outline of their hair beneath the wet cotton pants. Then, she thought, I guess I jiggle too when I move.

When the boys saw the bag of tobacco, she got two cheek kisses, and Cal held on and gave her one on the mouth. She felt his chest against her breasts.

They decided to celebrate with a peanut butter jelly sandwich each, a slug of milk, and a fat whop-sided cigarette rolled by Cal.

They practiced inhaling and, though each would have denied it, got dizzy.

They went back to Harrison's landing, Charlotte bearing bread, and sprawled face down beside the three totems. They talked about school. About who was in love with whom, which girls were becoming Sweater Girls.

"Amy Winston is definitely the biggest," Max said with authority.

"With Morton a close second," Cal observed. "In fact, Morton may be the most." A little flattery couldn't hurt their cause, he reasoned.

Charlotte smiled. They were all dreamy now with the heavy afternoon sun. This day! the river! the dazzling sun! The swimming and running through the woods! Her body in motion. The boys' eyes glittering with desire! The river slowly cruising past them! The sun! The sun! Falling warm on her skin! This day wonderful things were being said to her by the whole universe!

She pressed the cushion her breasts made beneath her.

Not more than five weeks ago she had lain on this spot sunning with her father, with whom she shared tenantship of Isola Bella. They lay exhausted after a long swim straight upstream. As was customary, their clothes lay on the mainland bank, dropped where the impulse to swim

90

had taken them. He had dozed but suddenly opened his eyes to find her intently studying that which made him male.

"Well, Char," he finally said with humor. "Guess the time has come when we better start wearing bathing suits."

She had smiled and said, "I guess so."

He sat up and looked at her, stirred by the beautiful young woman who lay nude beside him, but stricken by the loss of his rambling friend.

"Yep, you're a woman now."

She nodded, pride welling in her.

"You've menstruated, stained, of course?"

"Oh yes. About a year ago."

"Hmmm," he pondered. "I had meant to tell you about that so you wouldn't be surprised. What I know, that is. Funny. I didn't track your progress from girl to woman. Couldn't think that way. Was it hard for you?"

"Blanche told me. It was OK."

"Good, good. I almost feel I owe you an apology. Good old Blanche."

"It was really OK. Very interesting. I guess being a woman is a little complicated."

"Yeah. Man too though."

"I guess."

"Anything I can tell you?"

"Sometimes I want to know what it means. But now I'm finding out what it is. I've had some feelings—wow, really good feelings. I think I'm a little scared."

"Yeah, sure," he smiled. "I'm prejudiced. I admit that. But you are a wonderful young woman, and after about eight minutes of clumsiness, some giggling and maybe a little embarrassment, it will work out. You will hold your man. I sure hope he will know how lucky he is. Don't worry. When the time comes help him. Help each other. I want it to be beautiful for you. Don't worry. Anyway, you'll probably be compelled beyond worry."

"OK. I won't worry. You told me and you know everything. Right?"

"Wrong. But I know that. Ah—say, Char, did Blanche mention getting pregnant?"

"Yep. I think she said it all. Including a long litany about sin and damnation."

"Yes, darling, there is that. I'm not religious, as you know. I've taken pains, and pleasure, to read the Bible with you, to see that you understand what Christianity is, and why it is. And we have had good lectures from Sid on Judaism."

He paused.

"My point is this, Char, you must be true to yourself, but at the same time you must always remember that you live in a society where people are to be cherished and their opinions are to be regarded, if not held. Society has its rules—and stupid as it seems—good and evil are largely defined in sexual terms. A man may exploit in business, lie, cheat, and still be respected. But let him have a love affair, or surrender to lust, surrender to his natural impulses, and he is condemned. Socially, at least. I've always believed that society envied far beyond its condemnation. But it does condemn. You heard Aunt Elizabeth castigate poor, unlucky Alice Wilkes at dinner last Thursday. It does condemn. I want you to understand that. For sure."

"Yeah. Aunt Elizabeth was really vicious. I understand."

"For sure?"

"For sure."

They both thought a while.

She said, "Sex is terrific, isn't it, Dad?"

"It is. There's no use in my trying to tell you how it feels. I'm a man, anyway. You'll like it, Precious."

"Hummmm, I think so."

"There's something else that's important. It isn't dirty. It's an impulse mysteriously locked in all of us. I'd like for you to think of it as the best pleasure a man can give a woman and a woman a man. That is enough to make it holy. Don't be deceived by that holiness of marriage cant either. Actually, Char, marriage or an affair, or merely sex, can be made holy only by the two people involved."

"I know that, Dad. I've seen enough to know that merely being married doesn't make for holiness, or happiness, or anything else."

"Yes. Right. Anyway, don't let it become a burden. It's got to be a joy. If that isn't, not much else will be because the body has a set of demands entirely separate from anything else. And it will torture you in imperceptible ways if the demands are not met."

"All right. I seem to be seeing something new every day. It's very mysterious and exciting."

"As it should be. Hey, if I can help, ask. In fact, promise."

"Sure. I promise."

That had been five weeks ago and the excitement and mystery were becoming more intense each day.

"Well, Harrison isn't coming," Cal said. He stood. It was impossible for him to be still for long.

Max yawned and stood. Then Charlotte.

"What are you guys gonna do?"

Cal was nonplussed. He was then as he remained, absolutely incapable of contemplation, a creature of impulse.

"I sure don't want to miss that trip to New York my family is planning," said Max who had been pondering the situation when he wasn't pondering Morton's sleek smooth body. "Wadda you think, Cal? Should we just amble in tomorrow and ask how everything has been? Hell, they are probably so worried by now that they'll forgive us anything. Besides how far can you get on four peanut butter sandwiches and eight bucks? Even if we were willing to take Morton's treasure. What do you think, Cal?"

"Suits me, I guess. But man, think about going back to that damned school."

It hung there until Charlotte announced that she had to go home for dinner.

"But, listen, you're gonna be here tonight, right?"

"Yeah. I guess."

"Yes. Listen, Dad and Blanche are going to work again tomorrow. Which means that they will be going to bed soon. Maybe I could slip out after they've gone to bed."

"Hey, great," Max said. "We'll have a last-night-on-the-island party."

Cal did a war dance around Charlotte, snatching at her long hair to pull her to him, and kissing her cheek.

"Keep a big fire going," Charlotte said, pulling away and heading for the river.

"OK. Island Princess," Max yelled.

"A big one," Cal yelled. Then to Max, "I'll keep a big one for her."

The moon was foolish—so much brightness for only one night—as Charlotte carefully closed the back door of the house, ran barefooted across the lawn and followed the foot path to the summer house and landing.

"Dammit," she muttered once as a pine needle stood up to nick her summer-calloused foot.

The fire was blazing as she reached the river bank. Indeed, it looked like the whole island was on fire. She smiled.

She waded out at the landing, tested the current, found it easy and cool, and struck out downstream and out toward the island, into the moon's silver way across the water. It was silent, the river going about its business soundlessly. As she moved out, the water became cold and vivid. Once she turned on her back to take the moon, the stars—the millions of stars! She gasped and fell into the illusion that she was swaying in a star river.

It required effort to turn again and concentrate on making the glow of the fire her true path. She swam strongly. She would never be tired.

She was surprised at how quickly her hand touched the soft, sand bottom. She stood and waded ashore.

She gave a soft cow whistle. Then, "Halloo."

She saw Max and Cal stand and turn toward her, the fire blaze lighting their features. She bounded into the camp site for hugs.

"Wooosh, that fire feels good. Give me a towel. No wait. Hey, it's so beautiful and calm and mystical, let's go for a swim out to the middle, and then come back and get all warm and dry. I mean, look at that moon."

"Coming, Mother," said Max. And the boys went down to their shorts again.

"Close your eyes, Morton," Cal said. "I'm skinny-dipping."

"Me, too," said Max. "Nothing worse than wet pants."

"Hey, Flashers, let me in," she said and ran to the water and struck out. She turned ten feet out and watched the two naked silver boys come in.

They came along side and the three swam slowly toward midstream. There she said, "Turn and float. Look up. Oh God."

They turned.

"It's like floating in the sky. Look!"

"You know, I can't tell which way is up and down. Almost."

Then they lay, long, not knowing heaven from earth, a river of stars all around them.

It was the restless Cal who broke the spell, swimming in circles around the two, full of the night.

"We're drifting downstream," he yelled.

Max couldn't turn from his back, spellbound, until the other two were well on their way back. Reluctantly, he turned and headed for the fire light.

Charlotte and Cal scampered ashore and to the fire.

Charlotte laughed at his nakedness, snatched the blanket, flung it about herself, and opened for him to come in. The fire tingled up their wet, cool legs. Her arm under the blanket was around his neck. He circled her waist. They came close, held, faced each other and kissed. Her eyes were closed and she seemed to sway. She felt his lean, cool body against her and she couldn't breathe, but she was drawing his hot tongue into her mouth. Then they both couldn't breathe and broke panting. They turned and opened the blanket to Max, wet and shivering. She put her blanket arm around Max, held him and then kissed him on the mouth. He was surprised and stiffened for a moment, then came to her warmth, kissed back and she took his tongue. It was first and wonderful for them all.

"Brrrrr."

"Wow, give me a towel," Charlotte shivered.

Both boys, naked under the moon, scrambled for a towel to give this girl whose kiss had made them and herself dizzy.

She flung off her cap, shook free her long, dark hair. Both boys began drying her back and legs. Cal's toweled hand went between her thighs.

"Calvin," she said without anger.

She was facing the fire, her long legs and breasts and face aglow. He was kneeling before her. He lifted his eyes and smiled, "I can't help it, Morton."

She smiled down at him and didn't move. Then she lifted her arms and Max dried her throat and breasts and could not stop toweling her breasts. She turned over her shoulder and kissed his mouth. All three were dizzy with the moon, the river, the swim, with affection and the compelling sexual trill singing through their young bodies. She and Max nearly tumbled on top of Cal.

They laughed. Then she took the towels from them and spread them on pine needles before the fire. She plopped down and they sat beside her, huddling under the tent of the blanket. The fire transfixed them. They stared dreamily, thigh to thigh, the boys' hands on her listlessly, where they should not have been, but where they could not help but be.

"Calvin. Maxwell, roll some cigarettes," she murmured.

Charlotte held the blanket over their shoulders while their trembling fingers fumbled, spilled, but finally rolled two ridiculous cigarettes. They lighted up one and passed it between them. They were silent and stared into the fire. Their thighs touched and it was hard to think of things to say.

While Max was taking a drag, Cal turned to her. She was smiling at him and he leaned and kissed her because he thought it would feel good. Then, he took her pliant hand and led it between his thighs because he thought that would make him feel good. She held him, long and hard and male. Cal found it did feel good. For her it was a wonder. How it pulsed, a warm vivid thing—a life.

When the cigarette came back to Cal, she turned and smiled at Max. She swept his wavy hair back from his face. She kissed him and then moved her hand over his thigh. She held him.

"Nice?" she whispered when they could no longer kiss and breathe at the same time.

"Huh," was all Max could manage.

When the cigarette was finished, they had a long discussion about inhaling the smoke. They all claimed they could do it. Cal lit the other cigarette and they all tried. Max and Charlotte coughed a lot. Cal did it like a pro. Then they watched the fire until Cal thought of something else that he thought would feel good, or rather, look good.

"Hey, Morton, Max and I were talking about how nice you looked. Let us see you without your bathing suit. Besides we could dry it out for you."

"Oh no," she said. "Do you think I want you two guys running your mouths about me around school. Like that bastard Coy Trexler did."

"Trex is a slimy bastard," Max said.

"I wouldn't do that," said Cal, "and neither would my buddy Max."

"Yeah. That's what you say now. My father says that the major failing of the male ego is that it forces man to brag about his conquests."

"We wouldn't do that," Max said. "After you have fed us and shown us your treasure and all. I swear."

They stared at the fire.

Then Charlotte said, "Do you swear?"

"I swear on a stack of Bibles," said Cal.

"Me too," said Max.

"No touching," Charlotte said.

"No touching," both boys croaked.

She kissed them both, shook off the blanket, and stood. She walked around the fire.

"You look like two monkeys," and she flung her hair back and laughed her great, throaty laugh. "Ready?"

They didn't speak. Their eyes were fixed on her. She felt power in her slightest gesture. The fire heat licked up her thighs. River mist chilled her back. She dropped the straps across her shoulders, then she lifted her head to the stars and pulled the suit down to her waist. Her young breasts glowed. The slim throat, slight shoulders, tiny, taut waist, at once held the breasts, and seemed apart from them. They were an integral part of the lean form, but seemed under the moon and searing firelight, to have a life of their own. She lifted her arms slowly and turned, the moon her axis. The slim waist should have bent or broken, but her axis was sure and fixed. She seemed suspended, not standing. She turned all the way around but the slim ankles did not cross. Turning was like swimming. She lost sense of up and down. She seemed in free flight. Her breath came easy now. Her smile streamed across her face, teeth flashed and trailed light arcs under her cheeks.

The world and she were old as the oak by the gallery at her bedroom, and new as the silver platelet the moon lay on each ripple of the river. She leaned left and right, then flung her head forward, hair coasting across her face, supple spring bending like a willow. She caught her thumbs in the suit and arced out of it, laughing like a witch free at midnight, and spun to face the fire and her court. She raised her arms and wove on the long legs, caught the fire flare and laughed her witch's laugh.

Neither Max nor Cal had breathed since she had risen. Both had deep, primitive knowledge that they were seeing woman as beautiful and stirring as any man had ever seen. Cal the restless was transfixed. Desire and awe brought a tear surge to Max's eyes.

But she broke it with a laugh, scampered around the fire,

and under the blanket between them. No one spoke. They held each other and stared into the fire.

Seventy-five yards away, Douglas Morton turned away from the pine against which he had leaned to watch his daughter's first sexual ritual. He too was stirred at the beauty her slender frame had described, a girl, a woman—The Woman— Virgin, illumined by fire light, an island in soft, flowing water, moon, millions of stars. The tableau was primeval. How many times that ritual, old moon?

He had seen her scamper across the lawn and dash toward the river. He had shrugged, then thought of the hobo camp, and followed her.

"So that's where those two rogues are," he muttered to himself. Then, "Oh, little lady, have the luck your beauty deserves."

Then, "Little bastards, you'd better deserve what you just saw."

Then he laughed aloud. "Rogues," he muttered. He knew rogues had the best of it. He was a rogue himself.

Back at the house, he took a short bourbon and went to his bed to remember the marvel of being a rogue.

On the island in primitive firelight the three huddled silently staring into the fire. Their thighs touched and burned, and they kissed and stroked each other. Charlotte amazed with her smooth body, was amazed by taut maleness.

"Morton, it was..." Max whispered. "Morton—Charlotte, you're wonderful."

She felt so tender toward him. She kissed and held him.

Then she felt an enormous need to be alone, to swim. She slipped from between them and moved to the water. They watched her all the way into darkness. They laughed. Cal stirred, threw rocks, plunged in, swam. Max sat and smiled. And looked at Morton from school. This night! He had never seen a girl's body before.

Later, in her room she arced out of the suit and stood before her mirror. She smiled her witch's smile, climbed into bed and slept.

Max walked out under the moon. My God, he thought, I understand.

When he lay down beside Cal, he said, "Morton's wonderful."

"Yeah."

"I'll never mention this to anyone."

"Me, either."

And they didn't.

At breakfast, Douglas Morton archly remarked four times that he hoped the hoboes had taste enough to enjoy the pie, and that he had a certain respect for the gallantry which had moved them to return the tin with the smart alecky message.

At last Charlotte said, "All right. All right, wise one, what do you know?"

"I know that if two missing rogues don't turn up at their homes by dinner time tonight, concern for motherhood will force me to report them to said mothers."

"They are going home today. Promise. How did you know?"

Blanche wheeled from the stove and said with exaggerated anger, "Was that Maxwell Compton who stole my pie?"

"And the new boy, Calvin Hendricks," Douglas added.

"Those imps. Wait'll I get hold of them. I'll cover them with sin-punishment. Worryin' their mothers to death, stealin' pies. That Max will wind up in the pen." By now she was smiling broadly. "Those two would break out though."

"But how did you know?" Charlotte pressed her father.

"Well, when the pie tin came back, I guessed. Also I heard you go out last night. Then the hoboes came to me and I had to follow. I didn't mean to spy. It was honest concern. When I was sure I came home."

"What did you see? I mean . . ."

"Just enough to be stricken with admiration for my beautiful daughter. Relax. You're still answerable to me. I guess you were answerable to something stronger last night. I do admire you."

She took his hand.

"Listen. I'm going to go down and help them break camp and be sure they leave our island in good shape. OK?"

"OK. Give the bandits my regards. But tell them when they come to the house again, they had better beware the Black Avenger over there."

"That's right," Blanche grinned. "Those two Evils had better watch out for my rolling pin."

Immediately upon pedaling home and asking how things had been, Maxwell Compton was smothered with hysterical kisses, covered with guilt, and sentenced to one month 'in jail' by his jittery mother and insensitive father who was baffled by this free spirit he had sired.

Cal also was smothered with kisses, then taken to the garage and made to know his father's belt across his bottom, pain which he endured without a whimper thus driving his father to actually raise welts. He had to stand or lie on his belly for three days. He also lost his .22 for six months.

They were famous throughout the school. Charlotte's complicity was guessed by 'the company she kept.' Amy Winston and her set were dying of curiosity, but the three were vague in talking of the past weekend.

School was the time for great conspiracies. Max had only fifteen minutes after dismissal from school to return home to jail, his room. Supplies had to be gotten to him. Cal stole a long length of fishing line from his father's gear and Charlotte swiped a net laundry bag. On Friday and Saturday nights, Cal would bike over and they would sneak across the lawns that separated Max's house from hers. The laundry bag would be dangling from Max's second floor window and they would whistle and place in it the bottle of beer Cal had stolen from home, the half-empty pack of cigarettes, and some candy bars hooked anywhere security was slack. Charlotte would add a piece of Blanche's baking, with the Black Avenger's blessing, and sometimes a book—her father's pirate Paris edition of *Lady Chatterley's Lover*, Louys's *Aphrodite*, Suetonius's *Twelve Caesars*, something called *Dark Passion*, anything vaguely suggesting sex. It was these clandestine books that began the literary aspect of Charlotte's relationship with Max. Cal could never leave off movement long enough to read a book through, though he would read purple passages pointed out to him.

The school conspiracies were so intense that young Mr. Caddell, the English teacher, called them the Terrible Trio, partly out of respect. Stella Meese, the civics teacher, who hated all children, and them especially for their pure joy in being alive, treated them with contempt which carried over on to their report cards.

The first Saturday night after Charlotte and Cal had made Max's delivery, he caught her around the waist as they entered her yard through the cave in the thick hedge. She pulled away from him, laughing, took his hand and led to the summer house. The great cushions had been stacked for winter removal to the house. She leaned back on them and whispered, "What do you want? To play island?"

He kissed her hungrily.

She held him close, felt his body which seemed to depend on her for its next movement. She felt him hard, pressing. If she withdrew, turned, arched, he followed. I'm impulse, she thought.

But her own vision was narrowing. His hands were over her body beneath the cotton dress. She turned her back on him. He moved his hands from her waist to cup her breasts. She breathed deeply, felt them swell against the contour of his hands. His breath was in her hair. She was mad for him to hold her. It was hard to breathe. She turned her head over her shoulder and the sweet intimacy of the island swept over her. She kissed, and kissed, and kissed.

Then panting, she thought how she liked Max's way of kissing too. She had kissed two men. And all her body was screaming in her ears. She lost balance. Cal held her. She sucked his mouth like a leech. This boy wanted her. God, this boy wanted her.

But in the end she spun away. Discovery was a long journey, wonders were many.

When she had kissed the breathless Cal good night, she stood naked before her mirror and was pleased by the witch she saw. And knew that Cal's imagination was fixed on this body as he pedaled home. Again she thought of Max's way of kissing, how it pleased her.

What if I have two lovers, she thought. She thought of Catherine the Great, the insatiable, and Cleopatra, whose lovers had owned the world. Her nipples tightened as she considered her sex. It cried out in her. She thought, if a boy gored me, I could move from the center and possess him. I could turn on his axis.

When her father came in at midnight, she was sitting at the piano furiously playing the *Revolutionary Etude* with her foot off the pedal. He read her, but she couldn't talk. And the good night buss was worrisome.

Max's jail term wore out. With two boys in her life, there was much kissing and rubbing and fondling. She could not concentrate on studies or the piano. Her diary was a jumble. Her answers to the simplest questions were laced with pretentiousness or sarcasm. She walked out on Mr. Caddell's Great Books Club, even though she had a wild crush on him. Her voice became shrill as her sweaters became tight. She cried easily and for four days each month she was like a squirrel hiding nuts.

Cal was the one. Max and Charlotte found in him the perfect vehicle for the energy that possessed them. He had received a set of barbells for his birthday, and each day the boys, with Charlotte in tow, biked to his garage for the daily workout. Cal was constantly trying to lift her skirt. He did it with such good humor that all three enjoyed it, and she promised that when she did, they would be the ones. Max was quieter but his desire was more focused because he could concentrate. His baffling, thrilling dream had come on him.

Douglas Morton, who had already begun his slow surrender to whiskey, despaired of ever understanding his daughter, never mind the world.

"Blanche, nothing is more erratic, mercurial, or incalculable than an adolescent girl. God, she spends two hours dressing and combing for school. Then goes to the garden and kicks sod to properly scuff a new pair of saddle oxfords. How long will this last? She has a fine mind, but these days she won't go near the piano and she doesn't read an hour a week. Christ, her curiosity used to drive me mad. Now she can't sit at a task for five minutes."

"Mista Douglas, it lasts until it ends. It's just the price we pay for making a woman."

"Well, it's a heavy price, indeed," he grumbled.

Other confusions came. Charlotte had seen the sadism of Puss Hoffman and the malice of Coy Trexler. But she had been surrounded by people who genuinely loved life. In the eighth grade she met the first hostility to be directed toward her simply because she was the being she was.

Stella Meese had gone to college. She even became a teacher, the highest social position ever reached by a member of her rural family. And she married a city dweller named Harold who was in the insurance business. Harold Meese had done well. They lived in a comfortable house in a completely respectable neighborhood. They had no children.

Mrs. Meese was forty-one when Charlotte Morton sat before her in civics class. Mrs. Meese had plain features, sharp, and weapon-like. Genuinely associating joy with sin, the corners of her eyes and nose formed firm lines against her mouth to shut off the smallest temptation to smile.

Stella Messe's degrees were in education, therefore she had spent years learning how to teach a subject of which she knew nothing and in which she had no interest. When confronted by the massive curiosity and incipient scholarship of Charlotte Morton she felt threatened. Instead of confronting the problem professionally, she retaliated. The knowledge that Charlotte was one of those Country Club snobs strengthened her will to injure.

From the first, Mrs. Meese's defensive belief that all men were created equal caused her to inform the young girl that 'privilege' had no place in the public schools, and that those who lived on the Mill Hill were equal to those who lived at the Country Club or on the venerable Well Street. This constitutional exposition was delivered because Charlotte's placement in the alphabet had landed her in a seat at the rear of the room and she had asked if something closer could be arranged. From that point on, Mrs. Meese systematically ignored Charlotte's efforts to question or recite.

In its wisdom the North Carolina Education Department had decreed that, even in the face of the whole scope of human history, one full year of public school education should be spent learning the history of the state. The eighth grade was designated as the year. This narrow area of study was particularly suited to Mrs. Meese's intellect. She *knew* where the state capital was and all about the Lost Colony. To Charlotte, who with her father had surveyed and chronologically charted the history and literature of mankind, the study did not challenge.

Individual incidents brought out Mrs. Meese's contempt in supremely surpressed form. Early in the year, Charlotte pointed out that the County Court House and the Post Office were poor copies of Graeco-Roman temples. Mrs. Meese sniffed at this unpatriotic news. But when Charlotte went on to assert that the same was true of many buildings in Washington and some were appalling failures because the columns and facades of the buildings were disproportional and created a stunted or brittle effect, she was frightened at the controlled violence of Mrs. Meese's jingoism. Charlotte quickly regretted that she was the only child in the class who could translate North Carolina's Latin motto.

Charlotte could not comprehend Mrs. Meese's attitude toward her. She had never met anyone who found her contemptible before. At first, she thought that she had encountered a higher standard and tried harder. Gradually she began to realize that effort and courtesy could count for nothing here.

She discussed it with her father.

"I could have you transferred from her class. But I'm not. Neither am I going to speak to Stella Meese. Your grade may suffer, but you are going to meet people like that from now on. You stay, and you work. If things get bad and grades are low, you will take pleasure in doing a good job and in the things that you learn. Can you do that?"

She said yes. And she did.

For her research project under Mrs. Meese, she chose the old German graveyard at the Findstone Evangelical Church. The church had been built five miles out in the county in the late 1790's by the growing German immigrant population. For years this ancient church had been a favorite rambling ground for Charlotte and her father. It was boxy and architecturally naive, and, at first glance, ugly, despite the green lawns and the oak, pine, and elm setting. It was made of free form ochre and blue native stone, handsomely and skillfully planned. Rooted and innocent, it seemed a simple challenge to eternity, and it was the simplicity and the rolling countryside which won the Mortons. Here was such sturdy lack of sophistication that it seemed not even to know of Time's threat.

The Findstone interior was perfectly anticipated. White plaster walls protected the ancient pews and turned-wood barrier surrounding the altar. Above the single door entrance was a small gallery which had been hung for slaves, that they too might worship the austere Protestant God. The interior was a simple statement of peace.

Charlotte concentrated her research on the tombstones surrounding the old church. They too made their claim against Time. Most of them were simple benedictions, and many of them were in German. The white, weathered granite had come from the quarry where her father had battled Puss Hoffman.

For his project, Max had chosen the legend of the school teacher, Peter Stuart Ney, who according to fable was really Michel Ney, Marshall of France and Napoleon's general. Myth had it that in 1815, he had escaped a firing squad formed of his own troops and slipped away to Bordeaux. There he was put on board a ship bound for Charleston and made his way to the obscurity of the local one room log schoolhouse out in the county where he died in 1846, carrying final knowledge of his past to the grave with him.

Cal, of course, chose not to do a research paper, and thus bitched his way through summer school to make up the failure, a pattern which he followed throughout his dismal academic career. He did agree to suspend the daily weight-lifting sessions to join the two historians as they put decades of miles on their bikes riding out to Findstone to copy the German inscriptions and out to the old school where the Marshal of France had taught. But he skipped the long afternoons in the record rooms of the Public Library and the county courthouse and the newspaper morgue which Spence made available to the scholars.

When the six weeks were over Charlotte had produced a thesis of twenty-three typed pages plus an appendix which attempted an aesthetic evaluation of the art of the stone sculptors by comparing them with the New England sculptors from the same period and earlier. She and her father had visited the Granary Burial Grounds in Boston and admired the work of Lamsden and the like. Charlotte had the rubbings they had made in the New England cemeteries and a monograph to refresh her memory.

The young girl, already depressed—two days before, she had had her first real quarrel with her father—waited breathlessly for the return of the paper. This had been her first truly scholarly effort and she had been absorbed by it. In fact, there had been whole hours when she did not think of boys during its accomplishment. She was pleased with the product and her father had admired it as he and Sid Jacobson had translated the German inscriptions for her. She had been taught that excellence could expect recognition. She could not think that Mrs. Meese would deny her in this. Besides a good mark on this major effort might be the very vehicle for making peace with her father.

She *knew* the moment that the teacher started around the room returning the papers. Mrs. Meese sniffed and fairly trembled with pleasure as she handed Charlotte her paper. Charlotte placed the paper on her desk without looking at it. *You will take pleasure in doing a good job and in the things that you learn*, her father had said. Tears were welling. He was angry with her now, and she feared the teacher's judgment of this work on which she had worked so hard. *It is good*, she thought. *I learned in the doing. That is enough.* She crossed her hands in her lap and raised her chin for a moment. Then she looked. The grade was 70. Beneath in the teacher's pinched script was the comment: *A dreary, dreary paper. One cannot imagine what could make a child write at such length on tombstones—in view of the rich history of this county. However, the form is correct with the exception of those footnotes marked. Incidentally, your preference for the New England stones is merely a matter of taste.*

Charlotte fixed her eyes on Mrs. Meese as she droned on about the Azalea Festival in Wilmington. From that moment the teacher became enormously *interesting*. Here was a person whose hatred for her was unreasonable and intractable. Charlotte's very *being* was cause for contempt.

Suddenly she raised her hand to her left cheek in revelation. Two evenings ago, her father had slapped her across the cheek in an act of pure rage. It had stung and reeled her and caused her ears to ring. It was the first time he had ever struck her in anger. He had risen and walked from the house and she had not seen him for two days. And she was crushed. Now, suddenly, before Mrs. Meese she understood the cold fury in his gray eyes.

She had come to him after dinner as he was reading in his study.

"Mister Douglas Morton. Miss Charlotte Morton announces that she will attend a sleep-over at Miss Amy Winston's house on Friday night and therefore will not be home until sometime Saturday," she had said with perfect smart-aleckyness.

He had been drinking—he was always drinking after five these days. What he came to call his Cosmic Depression had its teeth in him and drink was his defense. He had smiled at her pretentiousness. "Well, I can't think of any reason to interdict Miss Charlotte Morton's social calendar at the moment. But I suggest that she check with Mrs. Blanche Pfeiffer before she makes the engagement final."

"Oh why?" Charlotte became shrill. "She'll just go into one of her hot-dog-nigger moves and invent reasons why I shouldn't go."

She had seen her father's face move from slightly drunken amiability to stone. The gray eyes filled with distance. He closed his book, stood, and struck her full in the face so hard that she reeled. Then he had taken his jacket from across the chair and stalked out of the house without a word.

Never, never before. Charlotte had knotted her pillow, wept, listened hour on hour for the sound of his return. He never came. That night she realized that childhood was at an end and that *all* would not be forgiven any longer.

Now, sitting before Mrs. Meese's contemptuous gaze, she realized why he had struck her, that her mindless remark about Blanche—not Blanche personally—betrayed the presence in her mind of what was to her father a humanistic sin, and that the remark placed her squarely on a level with Mrs. Meese.

When the bell rang ending the period she ran from the school though it was only eleven o'clock. She went straight to the bicycle racks and pedaled as hard as she could to Lawyers Row, parked against the building and flung open his office door.

"Miss White, is he in?" she gasped.

He was.

She ran to his door and threw it open. He was sitting at his desk with papers before him. She threw herself into his arms, sobbing.

"Oh, Daddy, Daddy. I love you. I love you so much."

He opened to her.

Finally he pried her loose from his throat and looked intently into the stained face of his woman/child.

He folded her to him again, whispering, "Listen, I'll take you to lunch, and we'll talk. I love you too."

"I'm so ashamed. So very, very ashamed."

She fastened her arms around his neck again. She was not happy, for an enormous groundswell of dread had risen in her. She knew how passionately her father, and her grandfather before him, had felt about racism. She feared that her momentary meanness might taint his love for her forever.

They sat across from each other in the manorial dining room of the hotel. As soon as they had ordered lunch, she reached across the table and held his hand. Her eyes were glistening.

"Oh, Daddy, I'm so ashamed. I don't truly feel that way . . ."

"I love you, Char, darling. I have been in hell since the other night. I just didn't know how . . ."

"Oh, if you still love me, I don't care. I don't care for anything else."

She released after long tension, smiled crazily through

steady tears, full of the pleasure that follows pain. Then she reached into her book bag and handed him the paper.

He read Mrs. Meese's remarks. "Why that girdle-brained, old..."

"No. No, Daddy, it's all right. Really, it's OK. You see. I'm doing what you said to do. I enjoyed doing the paper, and learned a lot. So it's OK. Besides, if you still love me, nothing else matters. Daddy, you do love me?"

He sighed. Then he smiled. "Precious, I not only love you, I'm proud of you. You know, if you weren't my daughter, we would be friends. But it's a shame Stella Meese is what she is."

"But don't you see. That's why I'm here now. When she returned the paper I realized that she truly hated me. And for no reason. You know, she doesn't have to like me. That would be OK. But she really hates me. And I knew that when I saw the grade. Suddenly I knew why you hated me the other night—just for a second—when I said that dumb awful thing."

"I didn't hate you. But I surely hated what you said."

"No. You hated me. And you should have. See, Mrs. Meese hates me because of what I am. You hated me because you know where I come from and because there is no excuse for that remark. Now, am I right? That's different from... say, staying out too late, or not being at dinner on time. Those things upset you. But they don't cause hate. This was different. Right?"

He nodded. "Right, Char, right. There are so many people in this world who go about hating people because they are different. Or because they believe differently. It's as stupid as hating all redheads. I lost my temper. But, yes. You have thought it out perfectly."

"I'll never be that stupid again, Daddy. I'll never think it or say it. Cross my heart."

"I'll never hit you again either, Precious. I can't believe I hit that sweet face. Never again. Cross my heart."

"Say you love me again. Once more."

"I do. With all my heart."

"I love you too, Daddy. Let's never quarrel again. 'Cause I can't sleep."

"Me either. Never again."

And they held hands across the table.

"Hummmm. It looks like my presence would be an interruption."

Spence was standing beside the table.

"No. Hi, Spence," Douglas said. "No. Even the best friends must smooth out rough spots once in a while. But we have kissed and made up. Sit down, Spence."

6

CHARLOTTE's eighth school year was mercurial.

Throughout she was alternately baffled and pleased by the prodigious swell of her breasts. Dressing was a continual tizzy. She could never decide whether to accent her bust or sublimate it. The coming of down had given her sex softness and definition, but it also made it secret. Suddenly, riding her bicycle became more thrilling and her knuckles sometimes went white from gripping the handlebars and she realized that it was not merely the feel of speed. But sometimes the bicycle seemed childish. She loved dancing and motion and she was delighted by the fluidity of her hips. And God! What to make of the exquisite excitement the hands of Max and Cal caused? She realized that she was beautiful, and it both pleased and embarrassed her.

Toward spring she was frazzled with motion and vagary. She began to define things in terms of absolutes. There was no middle ground. She was hard on herself. She became furious when she could not master a piano piece, read a book, draw and paint, and translate a Cicero speech all in the same day.

She began to find Amy Winston's ceaseless chatter about clothes, jewelry, hairstyles, and diets unbearable. The relative cuteness of boys and their attraction to her was without pattern. Her father and Blanche exchanged glances when one night at dinner she announced, "I am myself. I refuse to value myself according to the whims of a bunch of ballplaying, nickel-matching, silly boys another moment. And if Amy Winston doesn't want to be seen with me in pigtails, so be it."

It didn't work on any level. Nothing was pure. Cal was absolutely irresistible. Dickens was dull and dreary for long passages. Sex was exciting, but scary. Even she could not fail to notice her worshipped father falling deeper into drunkenness. Then Billy Ennis destroyed Absolutism forever.

One day in early fall, having left the lunch room mating ritual early as had been her habit since the advent of Absolutism, she walked the corridor of the school basement where there were three piano practice rooms. As she opened the exit door into the practice area, piano tones sounded. Immediately she recognized the long rolling base line of the Chopin C *Sharp Minor Nocturne*, on which she had lovingly worked with her father. The reading was incredibly slow, yet carried with authority. When the melody line came, it came with a sweetness of tone which caused her to think it must be a recording. The gorgeous theme seemed merely to materialize above the base.

She ran to the door of the room and paused to listen. It was not a recording. She could not imagine who was playing. Surely not the mechanical music teacher, Miss Bassett. She listened a moment, breathless. Then she cracked the door and peeped in. The skeletal figure of Billy Ennis was warped over the keyboard. Charlotte slipped in and took the desk closest to the door. When the final note of the *Nocturne* was released, she sighed, released herself.

She spoke. "Oh, Billy, that was magical."

Ennis's long frame jerked like a worm tortured by a pin prick.

Charlotte walked to the piano.

"I'm sorry. I didn't mean to break in. I was just passing. It was wonderful, Billy. I didn't know that you . . ."

She involuntarily took his hand which was resting on the edge of the keyboard. Again he recoiled, pulling away as though bitten.

Both of them were embarrassed.

"Thanks," he squeaked. His voice was just working its way toward the bass register. After deciding who was speaking to him, his eyes darted to his hands.

Billy Ennis was a mess. He was not an *absolute* mess. However, in a building thickly populated with adolescent messes, Billy Ennis was a runaway for the Most Mess.

Beyond mere appearance, Billy Ennis was a mess. But his

appearance, acting as both cause and symptom, guaranteed the result. He was already six feet tall, and none of the expanse synchronized. All this was mounted by a head which looked like its maker had had a momentary impulse toward a human face, but had lost interest. Thick lips hung slack over his chin. His head was round and centered by an equally round nose. He may have had eyes, but they were hidden by glasses so thick that under sun he was in danger of first degree burns. An apprentice thatcher had slapped mud-colored swatches of lustreless straw haphazardly on his globular head. It defied comb and brush. The doughy face was a pimple garden.

Each day Billy Ennis hauled his disgusting being to school in dark pants, freshly starched shirt, and a tie which had been laid out the night before by his mother, Mrs. Carleton Ennis. It was her hand which plied the comb and brush daily to no avail. By the time Billy arrived at school his clothes had given up the charade and joined the general mess—tie akimbo, shirt drooping inches above his belt, and pants slid so far over his missing hips that decency was threatened.

But none of this mattered, because no one saw Billy Ennis. In all his fourteen years no one had seen him—with three exceptions: Carleton Ennis, his father and director of the YMCA, saw him and winced each time. His mother saw him, cuddled him, and, in her retreat from her husband's brainless masculinity, ruined him. The third person who had seen him was Miss French, who just before her death had excepted her retirement for him as she had for Charlotte and taught him for two years. It was from her that he gained the direction to piano and musical theory that he possessed.

Billy spent most of his life avoiding contact with his fellow humans, for not even his ego had adjusted to being found contemptible by the entire race, including his father who avoided him in public and ridiculed him at home.

For Billy to have had a father who made a career of hitting balls, lifting weights, and spouting platitudes about fitness and manhood was a twist of biology. Billy assumed that the whole universe ordered itself for his discomfort—he knew he wasn't important enough for the universe to devote itself to his destruction.

Throughout his school career, Billy had entered each classroom, curled like a caterpillar under attack into a desk and not been seen or heard. He was a miserable student. He borderlined every subject which he did not have to repeat in summer school.

Every teacher told the obsessively interested mother the same thing, intelligence seemed native; interest, scholarship, and confidence were absent.

But Billy Ennis understood music as if it were his native language. Just as the alphabet symbolized sounds made by the tongue, notes symbolized tones which are not words. And he could read those notes, could think in terms of them, and express himself in their terms. It began as a retreat, the nervous mother teaching him rudiments. The boy found that he spoke this language, could read it, could formulate his thought in it.

After his mother's continual pleas, Miss French had agreed to hear him play, then agreed to teach him. She found him nearly photographic as a sight reader. Indeed, it occurred to her that this boy so keenly understood the logic of music that he followed its argument and almost anticipated each phrase. He was inexhaustible in pursuit of technique. When he entered seventh grade he began violin lessons with the school orchestra and was already first chair and beginning to investigate the cello. He also was the only accountable trombonist in the band. It seemed that he only needed to know where the notes were located and spend two weeks learning an instrument's limitations and possibilities to begin making recognizable music with it.

So the Billy Ennis with whom Charlotte shared a long moment of embarrassed silence following her outburst of praise. A dull monotone from the rear of the room broke their stand-off.

"Play the new piece for her, Billy."

Charlotte turned and saw another boy seated in the back of the room.

"Play the new piece for Charlotte, Billy."

"Oh, Jennings, I didn't see you. I'm sorry. The music was so great that I . . ." She turned on Billy again. "What new piece?"

Billy inspected his hands. "No, it's not ready. . . . I . . ."

"Play it, Billy," Jennings urged.

"What piece?"

"Well, Billy composes. The last thing you wrote, Billy. Play it."

"It's not ready. . . . I can't remember all . . . I don't have the music with . . . the bell's going to . . ."

Billy also never seemed able to finish a sentence. His eyes darted around the room.

"He calls it a sort of *scherzo*. Come on, Billy, play it for Charlotte."

He doodled some keys. Then, mercifully the bell did ring. Parting, Charlotte told him again how much she had enjoyed the Chopin.

Throughout that afternoon Charlotte considered Billy Ennis at the piano. He would be zero on Amy Winston's list of social acceptables. But this Mess became organized and effective before a keyboard. Oh, how he did! *He is better than I am,* she thought.

Thus with Billy Ennis, died her devotion to Absolutism.

After school she headed for her bike and spotted him lurching toward the street, looking at his feet, listening to Jennings Hall who strode beside him.

"Hey, Billy," she yelled. "Wait a minute."

They turned, expecting that the voice called another of the many Billys in the school.

She ran to them.

"Hi, Billy. Hi, Jennings. Billy, listen, how's about playing the *scherzo* for me tomorrow?"

Ennis was too overcome by the fact that this beautiful much-courted girl had spoken to him *in public* to answer.

"I . . . Well, maybe if . . ." He looked at his shoes.

"Sure, he will. Won't you, Billy? I don't really know anything about music, Charlotte, but it sounds great to me."

"Please, Billy, I'd really love to hear it. Is it written down? Bring me the music too. I can play. I'd like to try it."

Ennis hemmed and hawed, inspected his shoes, evasively refused until Charlotte, feeling his embarrassment, left it with, "If you can remember, I'd really like to hear it."

He didn't, of course. He couldn't believe anyone could possibly be interested in anything about him, especially anyone of Charlotte's stature in school society. He could not believe that she was not trying to set up another of the cruel jokes so often made of him.

Meantime, Charlotte thought of him, of Amy and her set. *I cannot lose,* she thought. *I choose him. Besides the rest will follow.* Billy Ennis became her project. It took her five weeks.

She began joining him and Jennings, his shadow for different but equally passionate reasons, at their far corner customary lunchroom seats. She began by bringing whatever piece of music she was working on at the time and asking questions about her reading of it, dropping her father's comments on it, and once in a while luring Billy down to the practice rooms to hear and to play. She realized that her motives were not entirely unselfish. This boy was marvelously adept with a new score and so interested in any new music that he sometimes took what she was working on from her, "just overnight, I promise." She began lending him things from her father's large music library. Over a score or at the piano Ennis was in focus, animated, and out of himself. She learned from him.

Max and Cal were insanely jealous when she abandoned the 'in' table at lunch to sit with the 'outest of the out' but as the weeks wore on, they began to drift over to the table where the two musicians pored over a score. Some days, Max, sensitive to Charlotte's purpose, would accompany them to the practice room and sit and listen.

Amy Winston's small meanness glittered through her basic frivolity. She became shrill. She referred to Billy as the thing. She mounted to a frenzy when she realized that Charlotte did not care what she thought. Not to be noticed was the only thing Amy could not bear.

Billy would squirm and writhe before Max and Cal. They were reflections of his failure, were what he was not, could not be. But worse, someone else began to *see* Billy Ennis, see him in the glare of the light Charlotte's friendship brought to bear on him. Coy Trexler could not pass up such a target for torture. He corkscrewed his little finger in his ear and shrieked, "Quair Ennis" every time Billy came on his horizon. This was followed by, "C'mere, Punching Bag. I haven't rattled your bones all day." Then Coy would begin throwing rapid-fire lefts and rights into Billy's rib cage and skinny arms.

One day, Charlotte, Max, and Cal rounded a corner in the school and found Billy crumpled in a corner being Coy's punching bag. His glasses popped off and landed on the floor, just as the three came in sight. Coy immediately lifted his foot and crushed them. "How do you like that, you quair fruitcake?" he shrieked with frenzied malice.

Cal was baffled and annoyed by Charlotte's attention to

Ennis, but he understood that she was serious. He reacted like a good sheep dog. In two bounds he reached Coy and delivered a round house right that sent Trex bounding off the wall to crumple on the floor.

"Trex, you'd better evaporate," Cal roared. "Now."

Coy began crawling like a game dog on threes, holding the red sea his nose had become.

Charlotte and Jennings led Billy home that day.

Five weeks after she had begun the campaign to engage Billy, she won.

After a practice room session, exasperated by his disorientation, she grabbed him by the bird-like arm.

"Billy, dammit, bring me that *scherzo* tomorrow. I've loaned you enough music to put you in debt," she snapped. "Dammit, look me in the eye, I'm talking to you. Listen, I really want to see it. Don't be a fool, Ennis. You and I can help each other. Now, that *scherzo* Jennings keeps talking about. Tomorrow. Or I'll never speak to you again. And I'll throw rocks at you every time I see you. Promise."

Even Jennings was startled by her ferocity.

It worked. The next morning as they passed in the hall he handed her a sheaf of ragged, dog-eared, but clearly marked music sheets.

She couldn't find him at lunch time.

"I don't know where he is," Jennings said. "Could he have gotten sick?"

She and her father read through the three short compositions that night—certain passages many times. The techniques were not naive. Her father was excited that a boy that age could produce music so clearly articulated. When Charlotte ran to Billy the next morning she was at last sure that her messianic impulse rested on solid ground and that the Mess was conceivably the most valuable person in the school.

She found Billy and Jennings before the day's session began, sitting in the corner of Mrs. Meese's room. She skipped into the room and mortified Billy by throwing her arms around his neck and kissing the pimples which armored his cheek. Then she dropped to her knees before him.

"Oh, Billy, they're wonderful. We played them all last night. My father and I. They're wonderful. Just wonderful. My father liked all of them. Billy, look at me, I'm talking to you. My father wants to meet you. So listen, you're to come to dinner tonight. Jennings, you're to come too. You're to be at my house at seven. My father says so. If you need a ride you're to call us and my father will pick you up. Billy, you're not looking at me."

It wasn't an invitation, it was a command. Billy's eyes were on the run. He was curled tighter than a tapeworm. Everybody was staring. Charlotte Morton had just kissed Billy Ennis on the face. It was very hard to be invisible when that had happened. Ennis was sweating and his agile fingers were continually checking that his tie was properly askew. Charlotte captured his right hand and held it.

"Listen, you'll like my father. He speaks your language. And he loved them. Truly. Seven, Billy. It'll be great," she ordered.

She carefully prepped her father and Blanche.

"Billy is very shy. So we must be careful. Very careful. It's as though he considered himself a flaw in the universe. Really. It's that bad. So, Dad, don't praise the pieces too much. He'll see that as insincerity. He's sensitive and he's so warped he'll actually be looking for that. I mean, you thought them smushy, but promising. So tell him that. And, Blanche, just let your smile loose. In other words, just be glad to see him and show it. 'Cause, boy, it's gonna be a tense evening if he starts twitching. That's the reason I wanted Jennings. Maybe that block can be some help."

At exactly seven, the two boys appeared at the front door, scrubbed, polished, and so stiff that the slightest movement threatened to snap them. Billy was choking six roses from his mother's garden and Jennings bore a box of candy. Both were thrust in Charlotte's face with such suddenness that they could have been weapons.

Douglas Morton set aside his paper and bourbon to greet his guests.

"Jennings, you're welcome. Your father is the wholesaler? Yes, I thought so. And Billy Ennis. You are especially welcome because of the pleasure you've already given us. Did Charlotte tell you that both of us read through your music last night? In fact, a couple of times. Come in. Sit down."

Douglas felt their unease, and carried the conversation. He told the shoe-watching Billy how lucky it was that Charlotte had heard him playing that day in school, and that he was famous in this house because Charlotte had spoken of him so often. He spoke of the music, walked to the piano, apologized to the composer, and played passages from the *scherzo*, asked questions.

"Billy, you will play them for us after dinner so we can know exactly how they should sound."

Blanche appeared beaming, bearing a tray of cheese, crackers and stuffed celery.

"How are you, Jennings? It's nice to have you. And lawzy, Billy—I heard such beautiful music last night. And it was yours? Charlotte told us it was beautiful. And it sure was. Now, Billy and Jennings, I hope you both like fried chicken and spoon bread 'cause that's what I've fixed. Will that be all right? Good. Mista Douglas, in ten minutes?"

Dinner was pleasant. Douglas loosened them up by beginning a long discussion of the sonata form. Billy began to ask questions, his interest out-distancing his compulsion to vanish.

"Billy," Douglas said, seemingly casually, "in many ways this small Southern town is a good place to live and grow up. But in many ways it is not. Some people need music, art, and so forth. If we don't have those things, part of us shrivels. And those things are not here. Most of our town is preoccupied with sports. I'm not knocking sports. I'm a compulsive tennis player myself. But surely a man, a whole man, should think of something besides hitting or kicking a ball."

Douglas knew that he was chipping away at the boy's inferiority created by his muscle-minded father. Billy knew it too and sensed an ally.

After dinner Billy played his compositions. Douglas admired, but was firm in saying that he found them too broadly romantic and suggested that Billy study some of the devices of development. He also invited him to bring anything else he worked on. Then the two went to the shelves of Douglas's music library. They talked more easily now. For Billy, there was no question of this man's sincerity. He even looked into the man's eyes fleetingly.

Jennings remained an amiable block throughout.

The evening ended at ten-fifteen when Mrs. Ennis called to ask if Billy was truly there. Douglas drove the boys home.

When he returned, Charlotte hugged him. She had already hugged Blanche.

"Thank you, Daddy."

"Don't thank me. I loved it. Ennis is very interesting. And gifted."

"I think he really enjoyed you. Wow, we're making him near human."

"Listen, be careful not to accept gratitude from him. After all, he gave us more than we gave him. You are right. He is valuable. And a Mess."

"Yes. Dad, do you think he's queer? Some of the kids are saying it."

Douglas frowned. "I don't know. Surely his father will be offended if he is not. And Martha Ennis will not have done her job as she sees it if he is not. I don't know. I doubt if his body has made that decision yet. What's he? Fourteen?"

"Yeah. Dad, can that be changed? I mean . . ."

"I know what you mean. I don't know. I don't think anyone does. Anyway, does that diminish his value?"

"OK. No, it doesn't."

Gradually, Billy found a niche. Charlotte and her house had been the focal point for many of the kids on Friday and Saturday nights. Cal and Max always began weekend nights there. Then it began that once in a while, they would arrive to find Billy and Charlotte playing piano together. Then off on bicycles to the hang-out drug store for sodas, or The Track for a barbecue, hanging around, and dancing in the parking lot.

Cal and Max, hovering on manhood, were derring-do. They stole cigarettes, led the way to the Country Club pool for late night skinny-dipping, and with Charlotte as accomplice, sometimes swiped Mr. Morton's opened bottles of Jack and got hopelessly, throwing-up, falling-down drunk.

At first Billy hung back, still trying to be part of the furniture. Gradually, he began to display a wry wit with fast one-liners, followed by a quick inspection of his shoes. When he found that he could have Max and Cal in laughing stitches, and Charlotte screeching, "Ennis, if you do that again, I'm gonna lie down and die," he loosened up and his one-liners became monologues.

As often as not he played on his own daffy eccentricities, then he found that Cal could take and encourage jokes on himself. He called them the unlikely foursome: the epogee and the downogee of school society—the two smartest, Max and Charlotte; and the two dumbest, Cal and he. He always clocked the race between Cal and him to see who could score lowest on Clam Meese's tests. And it was close. Ennis, momentarily brazen, would rise and walk across the room each time the teacher returned a paper, to collect or pay a dime.

"What do you mean getting out of your seat during class, William Ennis?" Mrs. Meese would enunciate with the razor clarity only perfect hatred could attain.

"Cal owes me a dime!" Billy would simper, still unaccustomed to attention.

"What?"

"We had a bet on test scores. Cal made a fifty. I only made a forty. He owes me a dime."

And he began to share the hard bench outside the principal's office with them.

At first Cal and Max were confused at Billy's entry into their circle. They began by tolerating Billy because Charlotte wished it. But tolerance was touch and go with what they considered territorial prerogative.

The conflict peaked on a Friday night when nine-thirty still found Charlotte and Billy absorbed at the piano.

Max sat brooding, for he too was in a manic period of intermittent frenzy and silence: crazed physical activity mixed with concentrated memorization of every major historical date so he could baffle Charlotte with questions like—"What were the dates of the Punic Wars?" and, "When was the Children's Crusade?"

Cal was pacing. He had gone in the kitchen to joke with Blanche and dry the mountains of dishes that she washed after dinner. He had carried her parcels out to the Packard when Mister Douglas had driven her home. Then he had sneaked a shot of Jack from a bottle, sponged the top, and, belly burning, walked behind the piano and goosed Charlotte, leapt at Max, grabbed both his legs and drew him from the couch, bottom first. Then he snapped nervously, "Hey, Char, c'mon. How long are you gonna sit there with that fag plunking that long hair stuff?"

Billy, still insecure, still searching for reasons to find himself abominable, stiffened. His eyes welled and he licked his pursed lips.

He stood suddenly, whimpered, "I'm going," and dove for the door.

Charlotte, fleet and agile, intercepted him. "Wait, Billy. I've got four dollars. We're going to The Track. I'm treating."

"No," Billy screeched and wrenched away and made for

119

the door. They heard his oversized feet clapping the porch steps.

Charlotte wheeled on Cal. "Dumb ape."

She advanced, leading with straight chin and pointed tits, hands clenched by her sides. She backed him over the piano.

"Big man. Stupid. Do you feel better now? Did that make your muscles bigger? What's the point? So he's a fag. Does that change your sex life? God, if brains were dynamite, you couldn't blow your nose. Ape, that's what you are. Half a brain and you'd be dangerous. Never speak to me again. Never touch me again. Animal!" She bit off each individual syllable so that it sounded like it was from Above and Forever.

Cal, squirming, bent backwards away from her fire-touched tongue, searched for and found a plan. Suddenly, he lifted her aside, and dove for the door. Max and Charlotte heard one bound across the porch, but he never touched the steps. They heard his bike spin on the moss-covered brick walk.

Eight minutes later they heard four feet cross the porch, the door slammed and Cal with Billy in tow strode into the room. Billy was puffy with tears. Cal was absolutely stoic. He fixed his handsome face on the mantel and mumbled, "I'm sorry."

Silence. Billy sniffed.

Then loudly, clearly. "I'm sorry. Billy, I apologize. I'm dumb. I like the music. Billy, I like to hear you play. I like you. I'm sorry. I didn't think."

Long silence. Billy looked at his shoes. Cal stared at the mantel.

Charlotte broke it by throwing her arms around both of them, then reaching for Max's hand. They hugged. Billy made tears, but nobody noticed.

Max turned them toward the door. "Last one to The Track *is* an animal. Morton's got bucks."

Ennis was, of course, last, but no one labeled him.

Charlotte pulled Cal aside when they parked their bikes. She drew his marvelous head close and whispered, "Ape. I love you. Later on I'll give you two handfuls."

Cal's splendid, mindless grin filled her eyes. He hugged and lifted her.

"How about a mouthful?"

"And yours just may be big enough."

They had two sodas each. Cal got someone to buy them a

beer. They heard *Two O'clock Jump* eight times. Ennis did his ridiculous, double-jointed jitterbug with Charlotte in the parking lot and half the cats there applauded.

Thereafter, Cal took Billy as his personal responsibility, defending, waiting for, saving a seat for. Coy Trexler lost a front tooth to that defense in a squabble over a seat in study hall.

Jennings Hall became a problem for Billy. He owed Jennings, for Jennings had single-handedly maintained him as a member of the human race for several years. But in order to be with Charlotte and the boys, Billy began to break his habit of going to Baptist Youth Group meetings every Friday night with Jennings. It was better to play piano and laugh with Charlotte and the boys than to bump through hymns, pray, and sip lemonade with the Baptist youth. Indeed, he confided to Charlotte, there was no occasion which did not cause Jennings to propose prayer, and he was a little sick of piety.

Several times, out of loyalty, and with Charlotte's permission, he brought Jennings along when the four were scrambling through a Saturday night. Max and Cal were horrified. Jennings was even more horrified. On their second outing together, he saw Cal and Max take surreptitious drinks, soul kiss with Charlotte, heard all four curse eloquently, and witnessed Cal lean forward and lick Charlotte's left breast through her sweater. He remained a school companion to Billy, remained polite to Max and Cal, but declined Billy's insincere invitations thereafter.

Jennings Hall was grim in appearance. He was already tall, nearly six feet in junior high school, and in manhood, concluded at six-feet-five. He already advertised the joyless man he would become. He had a plain face, fronted with glasses. He had already begun the slope his shoulders would perfect, and finally bring into harmony with the stern, straight lines his eyebrows described.

He was distinctive only when he spoke, not for what he said, but for the great effort which went into each utterance. It seemed that Jennings could not utter even such trivia as *thank you*, without great concentration and a great summoning up of effort which formed creases above his eyebrows and at the corners of his mouth. Everyone who talked to him was uncomfortable with the urge to yell, 'Spit it out, Jennings.'

Jennings Hall was considered brilliant. He was always at

the very top of his class throughout his academic career. He was not brilliant. He could not create. He could not *imagine*. But he could summarize, and he had a disciplined memory. And he had the ability to concentrate, to sit before a piece of work until he had mastered it. This was taken for brilliance because nothing pleases most teachers so much as to have their wisdom repeated *verbatim*.

Billy could not abandon Jennings because he thought him to be genuinely good. Billy thought that Jennings had cultivated him, not out of affection, but out of mercy. He was right. Jennings Hall was good. He was good out of passionate determination to be good. In a society bent on being cute, sexy, desirable, Jennings Hall consciously chose to be good. He was a religious fanatic.

The son of a Baptist grocery wholesaler and his dull devoted wife, Jennings had for many summers gone away to religious camps. A child, he had learned to love the One who died for him. He wanted Grace terribly, so terribly that this desire was his only act of passion. The lesson of the Cross gave him the belief that Grace was not given, but earned. From childhood he devoted himself to its attainment.

He swore that in every act he would attempt to 'bear witness.' In prayer, Jennings Hall could approach ecstasy.

He conceptualized Evil in order to attack it. And he didn't have to search to find sin. He glimpsed Eternity in terms of Hell. Like most, he was never able to crystallize a vision of Eternal Bliss.

Jennings quite early considered beauty, joy, physical love, popularity, and games incidental when confronted by Eternity. This isolated him from the world. He was a loner.

But he did bear witness. Billy always knew that Jennings chose to be his friend because he was the Mess. He could not say that Jennings liked him, but he knew that Jennings was genuinely interested in his soul. He was right. Jennings had chosen this miserable one precisely because of his misery.

Early in life Jennings determined to bring his devotion to preaching or medicine. He realized in time that he was not a dynamic speaker and so he chose medicine. As in all things he directed fierce unwavering concentration to that end.

Jennings Hall had determined to be good. By any assessment, he was close to his conception of his goal. But it is in the definition of the lure Good that the hook is found.

7

THE girl Charlotte lay with her two boys early in their freshman year of high school, and she was as lucky as her father had wished her to be.

She was indeed a young woman. No one spoke of her as pretty any longer. She was beautiful. Her body was long and angular, but informed with the clear promise of fullness. Her face was straight lines and hard angles. Angry, it could become as sharp as a carefully honed hatchet. Except the mouth. Except the mouth, which was made of full curves. And this above the chin which right-angled from the long slender throat.

Charlotte Morton was involved in life. She could wait no longer for the dead center, pivotal act of life.

Late October Indian Summer Saturday night. Cool, but windows still open. Door of her room still open to the gallery. Her father gone with Spence to the fiddlers' convention in Flat Rock; gone and to be drunk for two days.

Charlotte met Max at The Track. He had bucks, he boasted. Enough for hamburgers and juke box. They danced in the parking lot beneath the orange moon to Dorsey, James, Miller, and Ellington.

Two of the high school senior footballers, lounging against their fathers' Chevys, passed at her, but she let them know she was spoken for. Their wanting was sexual. So was the moon, and her moon memory of Max's naked body before a camp fire—oh, years ago.

They drove off Amy Winston and other 'cutes' with recitals of the twelve Caesars, the dates of the Persian Wars, the Punic Wars. The moon was talking to them.

They danced again. He swung her out, and she hated it, but coming back was all lovely, his hip moving against hers.

"Max, the moon. Hey, the creek? Now?"

He doubled her on his bike the six blocks to the bridge,

skittered down the embankment. He shoved the bike behind some trees and they walked, hand in hand, knelt to the creek. He leaned and took a handful of water. He touched her cheek.

"Cold."

They sprawled across a huge flat rock, listening to the creek and night sounds, looking at the moon through the trees which hung over the water. They felt clean and cool. They touched hands. He leaned over and kissed her mouth and she breathed his breath and took him in and knew it was tonight. When he put his hand under her sweater, she whispered, "No. Let's go home and find it all."

When they entered the dark house, she said, "Steal us a Jack. I'm . . . Max, I'm . . . I love you. Max, I'm nervous. Max, make a drink and come up."

She ran upstairs to her room. Across the bed lay the beautiful white gown Sybil Schraeder had brought her from New York.

She slipped into the gown, stood in front of the mirror. *I am beautiful*, she thought. *But Max. Will he not come before I jump out of my skin?*

She ran to the head of the stair.

"Max," she called.

"Yes."

"Come on."

She went back into her room and cut off the lights. She paced, then turned and stepped out on the gallery. *I can't breathe.*

"I'm out here," she called, when she heard him enter her room.

He came to her.

She took his hand. "Look. Look, Max, look."

The moon, gone cream from orange, had made a halfway house of one of the limbs of the giant oak beside the summer house—the one that her father said 'went to heaven.'

Neither spoke. It was so silent that the late cicadas were deafening. She took the drink from his hand, trembled the ice tinkling against the glass, and clicked it against her teeth. It burned and burned, all the way to her belly.

His arm circled her. She went into him. He was gasping into her hair.

They walked clumsily together into her room. The boy trembled in the thrill of undressing his first girl. He could not believe that his friend and love, Charlotte, could be so warm and not burst into flame.

The girl turned and twisted in the thrill of being undressed by her first boy. She turned and twisted to show all her treasures. But she helped him too.

They both giggled out loud at how tricky, slippery, and intricate a thing it was to merge. *This cannot be done!* But how impossible not to!

She forgot the flicker of pain a thing so large and hot and male caused in her. It became part of her and sent electrical points all over her body.

They lay motionless long, receiving the messages each tissue was screaming to them. The woodsy smell of her hair was over both of them.

Then it seemed to Charlotte that they were suspended in space, turning and tumbling in slow motion, but she was pierced and hung on him. Then suddenly it was over before they could remember it, capture it. They lay together, perfectly entangled, given over. When the messages came less frequently, she rolled her head aside. His arm lay on top of hers, outflung, hand clasping hers above her head. Charlotte seemed for a moment strangely to leave herself and mystically hover above them. She could look down on the two lovers, the lean boy lying like a shaft across the girl's body which closed like a wound around it. *I will kiss them both*, she thought from her mystical vantage. She kissed the arm her mouth was against and was surprised to feel her lips on her own flesh.

Bless you, she thought.

When they parted she sighed that something that had become a part of her was taken away. For days, in flashes, she felt him still there and was disappointed that it was not so. She knew she must, soon, again and again, until she could know how it really was.

Max tried to remember too, but it hid behind a vague veil of pleasure, an aura so indefinite, but so strong that he went into frenzies of crazed action. Meeting Charlotte at school, he could not stand close enough to her. When she spoke, he leaned because he wanted her warm breath.

She understood so much now. She caught herself staring at her father because she understood why he spent so many nights out. She remembered Eleanore Woods, and Gloria, and all the rest. Now, she pondered the unmarried Sybil Schraeder in a different way.

God, the world was different. Did her teachers do this wonderful thing? Did Amy Winston? And the others? She wanted to try this with Cal too.

Max came Thursday and she was alone in the house. They could not get their clothes off fast enough. Oh, it was better. She slept one hour that night. Nineteen times she had to get up and go on the gallery to be sure that the moon was still there, and to touch herself to be sure—yes, it was still there, but not *it*!

Loving Cal was vital, enormously good humored, almost comic—being tossed, caught, treasured, knowing an undercurrent of violence. She intimated *Yes*, he took her, did it to her, pierced her, gored her, talking, kidding, laughing. She loved it.

She pondered her two lovers. With Max it was a coming together, silent, ritualistic. He touched her tenderly, held her gently, but, oh, with such firmness that though she wriggled like a fish, she could not escape. When he left her she felt empty and wanted to clasp him and keep him forever.

With Cal it was high spirited surrender. He left her exhausted.

She loved them both. Knew she was the luckiest girl in the world. My two boys. My lovers! None like them under the sun! What else in the world!

When she fantasized, she thought of Max. But when Cal touched her, resistance was silly.

But not even the profound experience of love, or the excitement of organized learning, could shield her from the bitter realization that she was slowly losing her father.

Douglas Morton had never thought of money. Money had simply always been there and, if he thought of it at all, he thought it would always be there. Even in the early thirties, when he began to receive home-cured hams, a handsome old saddle, a mint condition Confederate pistol, boxes of tomatoes, and the like in lieu of payment for legal services, he did not think of money. He casually instructed an outraged Miss White, who was Baptist and 'paid her bills,' to issue paid in full receipts to farmers who shyly delivered a bushel of corn as testament to their good faith. He never moved to evict anyone from the real estate holdings his father and grandfather had accumulated.

"But, Mr. Morton, old Al Weaver hasn't paid his rent in five months. The old drunkard hasn't even had the courtesy to communicate with us. You can bet he finds money enough to lie drunk every night. Why don't we get rid of him?"

"Now, Amelia. You know how hard times are for folks. I know he drinks. But he does have a woman and five kids."

He and his tiny daughter Charlotte had been surprised one morning on the gallery by a ladder placed against the railing, followed by the head of Frank Manson.

When he discovered he was intruding he quickly raised his old shapeless painter's hat. "Oh, I'm sorry, Mista Douglas. I figgered you to be at the river what with fine weather 'n all."

"What the hell are you doing, Frank?" asked the astonished Douglas.

"Well, suh. I been owing you a long spell. And you know how things are. I wuz by here a day or so ago and noticed some peeling up under the eaves. Well, I had twenty gallon of white lead that I had ordered for the Strand Theatre. Wuz supposed to paint it—then, you know, it closed. Well, anyway, I figger'd I'd come by and slap a coat on your house. You know, just to keep my hand in, and to let you know I ain't forgot what I owed. I'm sorry to break in on you like this. Howdy, Miss Charlotte."

Douglas rose and walked to the railing. "Frank, save that paint. A job might come along and you'll need it."

"Naw, Mista Douglas, ain't no use. Likely I'll forget how to spend eight hours on a ladder 'fore a job comes along. Nobody's got money enough to paint no more."

"Frank..."

"Mista Douglas, I wanna do it," Frank said with finality.

"Well, all right, Frank. It'll more than take care of the debt." He leaned over the rail and called, "Blanche, can we have coffee for Mr. Manson?"

In five days the house was shimmering white, and Frank Manson slept better.

* * *

The Great Depression permanently and irrevocably took toll from the Morton family in March of 1935. Jessica telephoned from Mobile crying, "Oh, Doug, Chuck's gone. I thought he had gone to the office. He left just as usual. But he went straight to the yacht club, took the boat and just sailed...out. There was a big storm last night. No, he *couldn't* have made it. Besides that boat needs at least two for crew...Oh, Doug...he didn't *want* to!"

The brilliant and amiable Chuck Horner had taken over the Morton family's financial management when he had married Jessica. The conservative Elizabeth had withheld her share and saw much of it go the way of several banks which failed. Frequently Douglas would receive accounts which bore out Chuck's acumen. He had filed those accounts with the indifference he gave all financial considerations.

However, Jessica and Chuck had visited him several weeks before Chuck set sail for eternity to explain and account for the bankruptcy of the estate. Jessica, Douglas, and Charlotte had listened patiently as Chuck, sipping steadily on bourbon, sweating profusely, and offering heartfelt apologies, went over the details of the loss. Near the end of the disastrous recitation, Chuck's voice began to break. Douglas had stopped him. He placed his hands on Chuck's shoulders and looked him in the eye.

"Chuck, stop it. Listen, Chuck, let's forget it. There's no accusation here. We know and love you and we know that your intention was right. And your skill. It's a tidal wave. You couldn't stop it. But stop this now. First of all, nothing is settled yet. Wait until things calm down a bit and the damage can be truly assessed. And even reasoning with the worst, we won't starve. My god, we own a quarter of this county. I'm still collecting some fees.

"And look. Everybody should have known this had to stop somewhere. Sooner or later things had to burst. Somewhere down under, there had to be something solid to support the structure. My God, we have been blowing up a bubble since the war. All right, the bubble burst. Maybe in six months or so, you can start again. That'll be the real test—bouncing back."

After Jessica and Chuck returned to Mobile to learn if there was anything left to assess, Douglas found that he had to comfort his young daughter. She had never seen a man cry before.

Aunt Jess and Uncle Chuck had been unapproachable: tension and sadness veiled them. The drinking had always been there, but now it had a frantic, dark purpose. Jessica and Chuck did not take her shopping, or to the river, or crazy driving, or for a wonderful dinner at the Club. Aunt Jess could not be interested in Harrison the squirrel, or in Blanche's wonderful table.

Douglas was at pains to explain that men cry, and probably should do a lot more of it than they do. "Darling, Uncle Chuck thinks that he has failed all of us. He is blaming himself for things which he could not control. Men do cry. Our arms are stronger than those of women, but I don't think our hearts are. I hope it doesn't happen, but someday you may well see me cry. It is part of life to have pain and loss. You wouldn't want people to be so insensitive that they couldn't cry, anymore than not to laugh when there is a reason. Remember, if they can't feel pain and loss, they won't feel joy and beauty deeply either."

Three weeks later, Chuck Horner sailed out of this life. Neither the boat nor the body were ever found. Douglas and the girl Charlotte went to Mobile for the memorial service. They returned alone for Jessica and her two daughters elected to stay, at least for a while.

A long letter from Jessica closed with:

If living well is the best revenge, I have had some revenge, and come out of it knowing that living is best. For now anyway.

Oh God, Doug, I loved Chuck. Life with him glittered. He was handsome, charming, and the wittiest man I have ever known. And he loved me. But he was boyish and soft at center—I've known this all along. He needed me—at least partially as a proxy mother. So it's ended. I'm not depressed. In a perverse way, I'm looking forward to finding if there is something else to life besides gin and frocks and motion that is not real action. I'll let you know when I find out. Doug, let us remain as close as ever. Brother, you wrote wonderful letters to me from a trench in France. I didn't say happy, I said wonderful. Do it again.

Life would be different for the nation from then on. King Edward VIII romantically forsook England's throne in

1936 for the love of Baltimore-born Wallis Warfield Simpson, giving America dreams. WPA and the Social Security Act gave promise. But one day as he was driving out past the great railway shops, Douglas was astonished to see a large tent standing beneath the oaks and elms of Railroad Park. There was a block long line of men standing, waiting for entry into the tent. He drove past the park and stopped. He took off his tie, unsprung his collar, and turned up the lapels of his coat to avoid stares, and walked back along the line to the tent.

His preparations were unnecessary. As he walked down the line of men not one man raised eyes to meet his. They stood silently, close behind each other, looking down—at nothing. Most of them had their collars turned up against a brisk autumn breeze. Some wore crumpled felt hats pulled down. As he passed one man turned and handed a smoking cigarette butt to the man behind him.

"Thanks, brother," he heard.

Inside the tent, Douglas saw three old codgers ladling out cups of stew and a slice of bread to those who passed. The only sound inside was an occasional cough, the click of the ladles against the huge steaming pots, the shuffling of feet. It was so silent he could hear the sodden splash of the stew. Speech would have been violation. Occasionally, one who took a filled cup nodded to the one who handed it to him.

Over the tent exit was a crude, hand-scrawled sign which read *This Brotherhood Sticks Together*.

Douglas drove on.

Down by the river, the nights blazed with the campfires of hoboes, the luckless who followed the rails to some promised land where there were jobs, food, shelter. Somewhere. Anywhere.

There were massive lay-offs in the mills and the railway. The courtroom loungers increased in numbers. Railway police had to drive away unofficial porters. Hardly a day went by without a Bible salesman approaching him. One night as he had coffee and chatted with Gloria, a pretty girl from the Mill Hill who could not have been more than thirteen promised him everything for fifty cents. He bought her eggs and bacon and gave her a dollar.

Neil Foster, an old friend who had owned the Olds agency in town, broke down and cried in Douglas's office. "God,

Doug, I'm trying to sell insurance. Insurance! Now. When people can't buy bread. Oh God, Doug, I can't make a dime."

It seemed that everyone was looking down.

Or touched with frenzy.

Three men whom he knew in passing died horribly of drinking poisoned whiskey. One summer night, Elsa Hunter, who had been a perfectly docile lap dog of a Country Club wife and mother, did a striptease on the bar of the Club and was carried woozily to the locker room where, she was told the next day, she had six men in rapid succession.

It went deeper.

Two Saturday nights after Elsa went under, Douglas came in late from the river house and decided to dine at the Club. When he entered the dining room, Sugar Lady Duncan, gown flying out behind her like scarlet wings, snatched him from the *maitre d'hotel* Harris.

"Doug, darling, we can't have you dining alone on a Saturday night."

She took his arm and led to her table. Her quietly fair face glittered with the gaiety got by too much drink.

"As you can see Howard is lively as usual. And I need a handsome man to dance with."

His old friend Howard was face down on the table, his customary posture in the last several months. Douglas knew that like most of the country, the Duncans were in financial trouble. He had loaned Howard a thousand dollars several months ago to meet the rent and payroll on the finest jewelry store in the town. And he had seen the signs of disintegration early. Recently he had watched the lapse into hopelessness—Howard's listless drinking, Sugar Lady's move from quiet sweetness to shrill frenzy.

Douglas Morton had always counted the many evenings with the Duncans among his pleasures. Howard was a chess expert. It was his obsession. Even in the jewelry store Howard poured over chess books, dueled set boards, while his clerks obliged customers. He sustained eight telephone chess games with opponents as far away as Pittsburgh. Evenings began at Sugar Lady's graceful table, then the long grueling chess contests. Douglas Morton, a fair player, had never once beaten Howard.

The Duncans were in every way an advertisement for small town American life. Financially comfortable, beautiful, charming, charitable people with three handsome children. Sugar

Lady had been sought after. She was graceful, lively, could play competitive golf, and was from a substantial old Concordia family. The same could be said of Howard. They had been off and on high school sweethearts, on sweethearts in college, and he had married her immediately after his return from the war. Spence Fulton had been Howard's best man, Sybil a bridesmaid.

The young couple had moved effortlessly through the pleasant business and social life of the community. They had no enemies and even those who envied them could find nothing to justify malice.

Until the Depression.

Howard simply could not understand why the elegant little store which his father had successfully operated for thirty years should suddenly be running in the red, why month after month he had to increase the surprising debt to keep it open. And he had begun to drink more than he played chess.

It was this crumpled, insensible Howard that Douglas joined that Saturday night, as he had for consecutive Saturday nights. And it was this Howard who had met him the last several months when he had gone to dinner and a night of chess. By nine o'clock, he was immobile on the couch.

And it was this Sugar Lady who had spent the evening reciting her sorrows. There was no money. She did not know how to manage without Liza, the maid who had been passed to them from her mother and whose salary they could no longer pay. She hadn't bought a thing in months. Sometimes she would walk Douglas to his car. The tears would go on. She was sick of the continual hangover, the vomit, the money problems, the lack of attention. She hadn't been touched in months. "God, he can't get it up anymore." Sometimes she would lean on him, press too close. The good night kisses were too long, too deeply given.

Then this night.

Douglas tried to rouse Howard. No use.

"Want to try to get him out to the car?"

"Oh, what's the difference. He can sleep here or at home. Have your dinner and then dance with me."

He ate and she chattered. She didn't seem embarrassed. She was accustomed to it.

They danced. With *Chicago*, Sugar moved. But she came close for *I Cried for You*, very close. They had another drink. She sang along in his ear *I'm Nobody's Baby.*

"You're beginning to make me feel like a woman, man."

He was uncomfortable. She was so soft and warm and she was forbidden.

Then, "Doug, help me get him home. I'll give you a nightcap." She clasped his hand.

When he tried to lift Howard, he realized that he too was drunk. *You poor bastard*, he blessed Howard, *but I'm like a dog in heat. And this beautiful bitch is in her time.*

The three of them swayed down the Club drive. Sugar produced a bottle of bourbon she had snatched from a table. They stopped to fortify themselves at the base of the impish marble Cupid. They propped the unconscious Howard against the pedestal.

Sugar raised the bottle. "To that horny little bastard who has a spell over us all."

She drank. And handed to Douglas.

Just then a sedan, lights blinding, stopped in front of them.

"Yes, thank you, I will join you," came a husky voice from the car.

"Marsh Woods, how come you are spying on this innocent man and me?"

Sugar took the bottle and skipped to the driver's side. Marsh's red face loomed from the window. He took the bottle and drank.

"Hell, I thought you two were dancing." He flicked up the radio.

"I *am* dancing, Marsh," and Sugar began to improvise. She danced into the flood of the car lights.

Marsh got out and leaned on the car fender. "Oh God, look at that sweet meat. Oh, how it bounces. Go, Sug, go."

She went.

Douglas sat on the statue base, raised the bottle and snapped his fingers.

Sugar whirled her skirt above the garter belt, up to the laced panties.

"What legs. How'd you like to get those apart. Doug, baby?"

"Marshall, in matters of lust, you are never wrong."

Suddenly Sugar was curling with laughter. She pulled Douglas to the front of the statue.

"Look. His little prick is just like Howard's. He can't get it up anymore. He just can't cut the mustard anymore. He just drinks. And he's got all this woman to take care of. But he just can't do it anymore. Poor Howard. He's missing all this good stuff."

Douglas straightened. This was knowledge of his friend that he did not want. And he knew she lashed Howard with it repeatedly.

"Shut up, Sugar. I don't want that."

She turned into him.

"Oh, you're hard already. I can feel you, baby. C'mon, baby. What you need is in my panties. Like old Eleanore Woods and all the rest."

He straightened again. How in hell did she know about Eleanore?

"C'mon." She was stroking him.

But after they had hauled Howard up to a bedroom, Douglas left.

He walked back to the Club for his own car, thinking. Thinking how she needed it to stay a woman, how Howard probably had no insides left, how they were all members of the saddest species.

The collapse of Chuck's investment plan—not Chuck's, the world's—left Douglas Morton with little except land. There were still a few fees. But there was little current work. He still went to the office for an hour or so a day, but had no stomach for the small work there was. Amid the universe of human hopelessness, a deed or a foreclosure did not seem worth the trouble, or the sadness. Douglas had always been able to afford the luxury of contemplating the human condition. This consideration was too large and engaging to allow him to fall back into an interest in merely earning a living.

He repeatedly said to his daughter, "Charlotte, the principal difference between man and animals is in the skull cavity. All of us need food, shelter. Man is unique in that he contemplates the universe and his place in it. That is, when he has cared for those first wants, food and shelter. But only then. And perhaps that is the only justification for the study of economics. For when the failure of an economic system forces men to think only of food and shelter, men are the saddest of creatures."

He was sickened by the glittering greed and malice of bankers and landlords anxious to foreclose or repossess on men whose earnest will was to pay their way through life, but who now found it impossible to earn a dime. It sickened him to see old Mr. Craver, a skilled furniture maker, an artisan in the ancient and grand sense, listlessly knocking together packing cases for the railroad the few days a week there was work.

Roosevelt's fireside chats and legislative action spawned hope, but he was sickened to watch daily closing of another shop in the downtown area. Another store front boarded up. By 1938, town streets were ghostly—rust, broken windows and peeling paint. The poolrooms were crowded as never before. There were more hustlers, the migrant pool shark who hit towns, shot the local sharks, and moved on from dingy town to dingy town. He saw men whose dimes and quarters should be going for a quart of milk, buying chances on tip boards and shooting craps.

He hated the change he observed in people he had known all his life. Men like Howard, once erect, thoughtful, cheerful, now unable to take their eyes off their shoes, eyes that were full of failure. Their wives, once graceful, pleasant, gone shrill and carping, because they could not, or would not, understand that their men had not failed out of will or cleverness or diligence. Bootleggers flourished for frenzy and escape and Prohibition (now enforced by Fundamentalist local authorities) had spawned a whole underground industry— the manufacture of clear-as-diamonds white whiskey that might kill—or thrill with its oily, smooth, fiery journey to the nerve center.

The countryside, on his frequent trips to the river, wrenched him. The lovely, rolling green hills of Piedmont, North Carolina, had been paced with wonderful little farms. Now the houses were in disrepair, roofs like molting insects. Men sitting on sinking porches at almost any hour. Fences collapsing, fields overgrown, plows going to rust.

Black farm shacks and the Negro sections of town were a shambles, a people caught in a world they never made and never wanted. Blanche could buy their vegetables for pennies, their yard labor for dimes.

These images contributed to what he began to call his Cosmic Depression.

He was entering middle age and he began to mark the differences with perverse pleasure. A natural athlete, he joyed in physical competition, but he began to find that he could not hone his body to instant and powerful response. At forty-two he had gracefully, but sadly, surrendered the Club tennis championship to old Ed Chambers's eighteen year old son, whom he had taught.

With the imminent failure of his body, he returned more often to the meaning of mortality. And to all Western man, this meant consideration of religion. Douglas Morton had been raised in the high church Episcopalian tradition. At twelve, he was an acolyte and he loved the one hundred and fifty year old St. Mark's, its ancient woody smell, the brilliant naive stained glass, lovely carved wood pews and gorgeous ritual.

At sixteen, he had become rebellious and independently thoughtful and he began to set himself first against his father, then society. After weeks of testy argument, including great nit-picking, like—"Well, did Adam and Eve have navels or not? And if so where did they get them?"—his father agreed with him that perhaps he should drop out of the church temporarily.

Douglas Morton had always held a lively interest in science and technology. He followed the universe that science was inventing almost daily. He knew about the Relativity Theories. He knew about Kepler. He pondered the terrifying implications of Galileo. He actually shuddered trying to 'know' what Galileo knew when he took earth from the center of the universe, out as 'apple of God's eye,' and reduced it to an incidental planet in an insignificant solar system. When he walked out to star gaze, he shivered in the knowledge that the star he saw tonight might have been a dead cinder for two thousand years and that the light he saw tonight was cast before Christ was born and was only this night reaching earth. He knew that our planet's life was Hart Crane's 'wink of eternity.' And he knew in his guts that there was no personal god to beg small favors of. He knew that he was merely one of the innumerable organisms to stir for a span, then pass.

It was in the music parlor that the girl Charlotte grew up on cosmic speculation. Theology and religious doctrine were, with art, the hard core matter whenever Sid Jacobson, Spence, and the amiable Father John Cary of St. Mark's, along with any of half a dozen other bourbon drinkers, assembled without musical instruments.

"Everything that predicates Judiasm and Christianity offends either my senses or my intelligence. I know that men don't rise from the dead. I know bushes don't burst into flame in the absence of lightning which I won't allow as some petty god's anger. Furthermore, I suspect any doctrine which is so hard on fornication, the species' second most powerful urge and the instrument for its perpetuation. And I second Paine's old objection: revelation is revelation for *one* man at *one* time only. Thereafter it is what he *said* was revelation. And, Father John, I've known a few fanatics, a lot of fools, and numberless liars in my time."

Father Cary, tinkling his bourbon and ice, would glance anxiously in Charlotte's direction, and Douglas would say, "I want her to hear and think about it. You can have her—if you can get her. But it won't be through indoctrination."

"But, Douglas," the patient priest would counter, "you believe history merely because you read it. It's what someone *says* is history. Follow your logic and could you believe Caesar crossed the Rubicon merely because someone said it. Was Alexander at Caronea just because some ancient historian says so? If so, why not the Bible? Why not God's Ten Commandment etching on the tablets? Why not the pillar of salt. The Resurrection? Where do you draw the line between belief and disbelief in history, the Bible—in all printed words?"

"No analogy, Padre. Armies cross rivers. Done it myself. I can believe that. Men fight battles. Every decade or so. This I know. It's possible. Probable. Natural. But everything my brains and senses tell me says that men don't rise from the dead. That is supernatural—and I'm not taking anybody's word for it. It's an act of faith, and faith cannot be founded on desire."

Always after the others had left, Douglas would mutter to Charlotte, "It's good to question the beginning and meaning of life, but because you don't know the answer doesn't give you license to invent one. That is, if you have regard for truth."

"And," he shrugged, "if all flesh is grass, there are worse things. For instance, perpetual Baptist hymns."

Nevertheless, death was the surrender of perception. He could not imagine nothingness. He tried. His ego prevented. The longer he struggled with that ultimate question, the deeper he sank into his Cosmic Depression. Drink could carry him to a place where he could think of it with cynical humor, or not think of it at all. This argued for the use of drink.

By 1938 the Nazi legions were poised. He and Sid Jacobson, they of the radical journals, seemed the only men in town who knew what was coming. Spence had moments of optimism and pessimism. He could not believe men would do that again. Man could not go back to war.

"Man can do anything, anything he wishes. Trouble is, he always seems to want the wrong thing," replied Douglas.

The impending disaster was partly the reason Douglas sold the Lee Street acres and took Charlotte out of school and to Europe—"before there is no Europe."

8

IN April of 1939, after a long wrangle with the city school system whose vision was 'localized,' he took his fourteen-year-old out of school and the two sailed for Europe. He knew that seeing the Parthenon and Chartres were more valuable than half a year of high school algebra and history.

It seemed to Charlotte that Europe realized a part of her imagination in which she and her father had lived for a long time. They had read history, literature, and myth since she was old enough to walk. They had looked at pictures, studied architectural styles.

At Salisbury and Rheims the young girl gasped as the Gothic arch swept her senses into the soaring vaults. In Florence from their hotel on the Arno she could see the graceful curves of the *Ponte Santo Spirito*, with the great dome of Bruneleschi hovering over all.

Before the *David*, she dared not blink for fear it would move. It was a boy. No. A man. No. In a split second it would move from youth to manhood. The great white Apollo calmly in repose before action. But no. Every muscle drawn taut, balance perfect for action.

She was lucky in her guide, for her father already knew the cities and the monuments, and he had old acquaintances wherever they went. Her diary was full of breathless superlatives. There were sketches—a column in *Santo Spirito* with the *dado,* the tiny block between capital and arch, clearly indicated by an arrow to show how Bruneleschi gave his arches their flight.

In Rome, before the *Moses*, her father whispered, "That man *has* heard the voice of God."

"Yes," she gasped.

The youthful *Pietà* drew her tears. Then exaltation. The husk of a body draped across the Virgin's knees seemed utterly looted of life. But the face was serene in light sleep. The beautiful mother was stricken with grief. But, no. The raised arm signed that he only slept. That he would waken. Then the face sweetened with mother's care.

"Dad, I can't tell."

"It is both, Precious. Both are there. Death and the promise of life. There is nothing in the world like it."

He was talking to himself, and to her.

And at last, she saw Donatello, Giotto, Cimabue, and on and on.

She sent Max a photo of herself on the Capitoline overlooking the Forum. *Tonight Augustus and I will give a grand dinner party—exotic birds and Greek dancers. Horace will be there and will recite.* It was signed *Livia.*

South. Naples, Pompeii, Capri.

In Athens there was the temple of Athene—the most beautiful building Charlotte had ever seen. Athene had long been her favorite deity, the gray-eyed goddess of wisdom—through her care for Odysseus, her favorite man, on his voyage home from Troy, the goddess's hand by his, on oar, sword, or woman's couch. This was her temple. She told mankind what it could be.

They took a miserable island steamer to Delos and watched French archaeologists carefully removing two thousand years of debris from a gorgeous mosaic. Then to the Hellespont to be the only guests at the two room hotel in Cannakle and roam the plain and ruins of Troy. Max read and re-read the letter which ended:

This evening I stand on the wall by the Scaean Gate from which my beloved Paris shot the arrow which killed Achilles. It is sunset. I can see from here the Greek ships drawn up on the beach, and beyond, the island Tenedos. For days now the Greeks have been hammering and hammering, building some colossal con-

struction of wood, which has begun to look like a horse....

The letter was signed —*Affectionately, Helen (called of Troy)*.

She was almost devotional as she filled a little Turkish jar with sand from the plain of Troy, half for herself, half for Max. *Perhaps some sand that ground through the sandals of Achilles* her diary ran. She bought Billy a little skin covered, rococo Turkish drum and Cal a meerschaum cigarette holder. She bargained in the bazaar at Izmir for silver Alexander the Great coins and an Athenian owl.

She wrote to Cal about climbing the Acrokorinth, belly dancers, wines, food and swimming at Cape Sounion. She didn't tell him that his body was like the *David*.

The trip was leisurely. Douglas and Charlotte stayed in each place as long as they wished, until they had learned enough or loved it enough.

For her it was the happiest of times. He had determined to drink nothing but wine. Thus she had her father, for the last time in her life, her real father, the teacher, the friend, the clown, not the one who was cynical or clever with drink. It was all lovely. It shone. He talked and talked and talked—history, food, art, wine. Charlotte could listen. She reached for the 'feel.' She loved the stick men drawn two thousand years ago on the walls of Pompeii and seeing *M. Agrippa fecit* cut on the Pantheon. They ate well, wandered the Left Bank, swam Nice, saw the bulls in Madrid, danced in a *taverna* on Mikynos. An interesting couple, the beautiful girl/woman, the handsome middle aged man.

For him it was a sunburst of joy. The old places he had loved so much, old friends, some new lovers, the boiling energy of art seen again through the freshness of Charlotte's delight. An old old world with roots and monuments which drew him to the sense of a hugh plan which had little to do with him personally, but of which he was a part. These monuments signaled purpose, grace, and movement for mankind—which was enough, even against a backdrop of nothingness.

And how he loved the girl/woman who was beside him. He knew that he had done well by her when she clasped his hand and held it in the quiet cells of San Marco Monastery across the Piazza from *the massive David*; when she spent part of her allowance on a leather bound edition of Dante and attempted the difficult, thrilling move from modern Italian to the medieval.

She thrilled him almost painfully as he sat in the chaise in their Parisian hotel watching her applying kohl to make herself look older and sophisticated so that they might go from *café* to *café* on Montmartre. It pleased him to observe the glances they drew from waiters and habitués. He delighted to imagine their perverse admiration. Dining with her was a pleasure because she talked with as much charm as anyone he had known, was interested in everything, quickly adopted European table customs, and enjoyed the adventure of new dishes. And she was a tough traveler, taking the plumbing of Southern Italy, Greece, and Turkey with a shrug. "Yep," he had cracked, "every time I start feeling romantic about American pioneers, I say aloud to myself, 'toilet paper'."

She would be, like him, a consummate sensualist, good books, good food, good music and art—and she was clearly sexual.

But if the trip replenished, it alarmed also. He was skeptical as the amiable Sandro, his art dealer in Florence, told him that Italy was on her way back to greatness, and that greatness demanded sacrifices. He was momentarily thrilled at the elegant uniforms, at the crowds in *Piazza Venezia* screaming, "*Duce! Duce! Duce!*" For a moment he conjured visions of new Roman legions grinding the bricks which still bore the engraving SPQR. But the sacrifices were too great. The Ethiopian debacle ended the fleeting vision. He knew what was ahead. And it would be hellish.

They returned to Concordia, glowing. He renewed, Charlotte completely without horizons, all boundaries destroyed—and anxious to get on to the business of living.

For three days the house was a hub of comings and goings. They told the same stories over and over again. They explained that *Eye*-talians were not strange; that the French drank wine but were not alcoholics; that the Catholic Church was not a beehive of perversions.

And the gift giving. "Here, Spence," he said, "learn the taste of pure light. It is like drinking silk," as he gave the editor two bottles of vintage Medoc. He and Sid pored with a magnifying glass over twenty Piranesi etchings. Sid and Spence were to choose two each as gifts, and for each a Juan Gris lithograph. "This man may be the finest cubist after all is said and done." Sid took, understanding.

Charlotte was nervous as she called Sybil Schraeder out of the noisy room into the family parlor to give her two exquisite cameos from Florence. To Charlotte, it always seemed that the elegant Sybil was mounted on a horse, so erect was her carriage at table, at bridge, strolling her lawn, and even here. Horses *were* Sybil's life. She spent most of her waking hours at Schraeder Meadows on the old Ferry Road. Her father had built the stable for her when she was a child. She had expanded it and now rented horses, gave lessons, and, for pleasure, rode herself.

Mounted, Sybil was a thing of beauty, the only *dressage* rider in the county. She had taught Charlotte. Clearly, in her distant manner, Sybil adored Charlotte. The girl admired Sybil, but, even after years of riding together, could not quite cross the line into affection.

Sybil was moved by the beauty of the cameos. "Thank you, my dear. They are so lovely. Oh, Charlotte, you are so dear."

Still holding the brooches, she embraced Charlotte and kissed her cheek.

Charlotte was oddly relieved when she heard her father's voice interrupting, "Char, here's a handsome young man to see you."

Douglas was standing in the foyer with his arm on Max's shoulder. Charlotte turned, stood. She was shocked. Max was taller. His shoulders and chest had broadened, but had not kept stride with his height. He was lean and angular. And he was smiling.

They both stood and looked at each other. To be sure. Then smiling—oh, smiling!—they came into each other's arms. To hold, then shyly fall away, then again hold.

How slender he was in her arms. And how dear. "Oh, Max."

For the next two hours, past the constant flow of people through the house, the talk, the laughter, their eyes and hands kept meeting.

The little rosy-cheeked Father Cary and his wife arrived. "Douglas, welcome back." The priest reached up to take the tall man's shoulders. Then he turned and embraced Charlotte.

"Padre," Douglas said. "We thought of you as we walked Luther's one hundred steps. Is it true, Char?"

"Douglas, the altar of St. Mark's has received daily prayer for your safety and happiness, and prayers that in God's mercy, you would not be able to buy Jack Daniel's in Europe."

Everyone roared.

"Padre, for six months nothing stronger than wine has passed my lips. Look," he lifted his glass, "sherry. Charlotte, do I lie?"

She beamed. "Can we give it to him now?" she said, releasing Max's hand. She danced to the desk and returned with a dog-eared cardboard box.

"Sit down, Father Cary," she ordered and placed the box in his hands. "Come, Max, and see."

Everyone gathered around and the little priest opened the box. From it a small madonna and child with piercing eyes looked up at him.

"Father," Douglas spoke quietly, "I am not certain, but I believe—and Sandro, my Florentine art expert bears me out—that this icon is older than Luther and your whole Protestant movement. We bought it on the island of Tinos."

In the hush, the little priest gasped. His heart was won by the simple candor of the Virgin's eyes which looked directly to him from the oval, mantled face, slightly tilted over the child in her arms. The figures were flat, two dimensional, stylized, but the eyes looked out with piercing humanity.

"My friend Sandro wanted to clean it, but Charlotte and I thought you would take pleasure in the film that the many candles burnt before it have left. Sometime you may want to have it cleaned so that the golds and blues gleam. But, for now . . ."

Tears came to the little priest's eyes. "Douglas, you dreadful atheist, I take this now without a word. In a few days I will think of some way to thank you. And you, Charlotte."

The steady stream of visitors continued. They were kissed and hugged by dozens who had missed them. The girl and her father attempted to use words to describe the multitudes of feelings for places, people, food, art.

"Oh, Max, my Max. I have literally millions of things to

tell. It will take weeks and weeks. And pictures to show," she leaned and whispered to her boy.

He reached and touched her shimmering hair, as if he couldn't believe. "I'll listen. I'm so glad you're back. So glad, Char."

"And Cal? Tell me. He never answered a single letter, the rat."

Cal was fine. He had gotten to the state wrestling semi-finals in the one hundred forty-five pound class. He had failed every single subject except gym, shop, and math. He had gone to summer school and eked by. He now worked nights as car hop at The Track. They threatened to make him wear overalls with the pockets sewed closed because he knocked down so much money. He would be sixteen in October and his father had promised him two hundred dollars on a car if he would match it. Cal was working and stealing his way toward that sum. He was laying Amy Winston and a couple of others. They'd go out to The Track later and see the bum.

Charlotte threw her head back and laughed. Cal was Cal.

"And Billy? But I know about him. He wrote every week. Hey, he says he's written a piano suite called *Charlotte's Letters*. Isn't that great?"

Finally, she took his hand and drew him into the parlor. He took the tiny box from her hand. He reached and stroked her hair. He couldn't keep his hands off of her.

"Charlotte, you're so beautiful. Sooooooo beautiful."

"Oh, Max. Wonderful. Wonderful."

When he opened the box, she said, "It's Alexander the Great, Max. That coin probably bought a barbecue twenty-two hundred years ago."

It gleamed in his hand. He turned it. He looked at the girl from whose hand he had taken it. Then he turned his back on her and leaned before the lamp. It was him, the golden king, dead at thirty-three with the world in his palm. The coin took life in his hand.

"Charlotte, I . . ."

"I know. Isn't it wonderful?"

"Yes."

"I have one for Billy too. And I have something just as dear for you when we're alone. And look, this is for Cal. Perfect?"

It was a little silver winged cock and balls from Pompeii. Max bent with laughter.

"Perfect. Perfect. I can't wait for him to see it. We'll have to go to The Track. We'll call Billy to meet us."

"Right. Oh, right."

About eight-thirty, Douglas herded the adults out the door, bound for dinner at the Club. Charlotte helped Blanche with the glasses and plates to the kitchen and with a special hug and kiss, wished her good night at the door.

Blanche, hovering, told her of the flowers and vegetables as if reporting on persons. She tweaked Charlotte's cheek. "The lilies-of-the-valley were mos' as fresh as you. I took me some home every day to sniff when I woke up. And the crepe myrtles were waiting for you like they were planning a party, specially on the front walk. Wish they could have waited for you to walk through. And the tomatoes and collards! Oh, Chile."

And they had held hands and laughed and laughed.

When she left, Charlotte turned to Max, kissed him lightly and said, "Excuse."

She went upstairs to her room. She took out the little Turkish jar containing the Trojan sand and placed it on her bedside table. She slipped out of her clothes and into the gown Sybil had given her. How beautiful it was. How lovely to slip into it again. She had worn it her first night of love.

She called, "Max, come up."

He stood at the door, tentative, looking at the tall, slim, white gowned beauty who stood before him. They came together and kissed.

Outside the gallery door, the cicadas sang, and for all she knew, Harrison and Hedrick cracked the last nuts of the day. But her breathing, and his, was deafening.

"Oh, Max, I ache. I ache."

She broke for him.

"But wait. Sit here on the bed."

She took the little jar and carefully poured its contents into a pin tray.

"Max, touch it. It's from the plain of Troy. Half of it is for you. Half for me. To keep," she whispered. "Maybe it's some of Achilles's dust."

He ran some through his fingers. He was dizzy. He was hard and flooding at the groin. Achilles's dust! This girl.

"Wonderful?"

He nodded. She poured half the sand back into the little

145

jar and capped it. She pressed it into his hand. Then smiled, and took it back and placed it on the table.

"You'll need your hands. I ache, Max."

She turned off the light and stood before him, and dropped the gown.

He held her and they kissed and kissed and kissed and lay back on her bed and did not speak until her clock said ten-thirty. Then they quickly dressed each other and headed for The Track and Cal and Billy.

The Track parking lot was a medallion of light under deep purple. Cars flashed and honked to summon car hops. Duke Ellington's *A Train* blared from the speakers. In the open pit glowing coals cast a halo over the spitted haunch of a pig. The odor was what starving men dream. Barbecue—a Southern institution, flourishing again in the healing land.

As Charlotte and Max came into the circle of light, the service door was kicked open and Cal, tall, lithe, broad shouldered, wisp-hipped, blond curls in flight, spun out bearing two trays loaded with cokes and beer.

He saw them, stopped, executed a knee-bend, placed the two trays on the concrete, rose, ran into her open arms, lifted her feather like, did three merry-go-rounds, both laughing, stood her on her feet and fell in with *A Train* and they danced their brains out all the way to Harlem. Laughing. Looking at each other. Oh, laughing. Stopped, he held her away by both hands, looked, and howled, "Morton, what a pair of boobs."

"Ape," she said, "Ape, I love you."

They hugged again. Close up, she whispered, "Cal, I'm so glad. Cal."

And he, "Me too, Morton. Me too."

Horns blew and lights flickered. "Service. Service."

"Hey, Hendricks, you're a car hop not a floor show," a voice boomed from the service door.

"I'm hoppin', boss. I'm hoppin'." And to Max and the beaming girl, "You'll stick around until I get off?"

"Sure, Ape, sure."

Others gathered around. Hugging and kissing the traveler. Amy Winston gushed. Charlotte said wonderful, wonderful, wonderful ninety times.

Then over a shoulder, Charlotte caught a glimpse of a tall, skinny, bespeckled scarecrow standing back, waiting.

She made the word *Billy* soundlessly with her mouth. She

smiled. She pushed through the crowd and walked to him, stopped three feet from him and smiled. His eyes bopped from the ground to her radiant face fourteen rapid-fire times. His smile was so broad and uncontrolled that his loose lips nearly flipped his face inside out.

Then they came together. Billy's eyes glistened. His true friend had returned.

"I have so much to tell you," she said.

He gurgled.

Then she noticed the bespeckled, slack-jawed face of Jennings Hall. She reached out and took his hand behind Billy's back. In a momentary lapse into earthly joy, Jennings gave his hand and oozed a considerable smile.

When Billy was at last able to release her, she made to embrace Jennings, but sensed in him a flickering impulse to withdraw and settled for squeezing his hands.

That night ended at three o'clock in the music parlor, twenty voices talking at once, Charlotte trying to describe all that she had seen and which is itself the only description, her eyes moving from face to face, astonished that they had changed so much in six months, but mostly relishing the faces of Max, Cal, and Billy.

9

CHARLOTTE returned to school with purpose. She obtained textbooks and read them, and in three weeks had passed the examinations missed while in Europe. She was not a prodigy, but she could concentrate on whatever was before her. Max helped her with the math.

High school was not a world of wonders after Europe, but a world to learn. Language credits were required of those tracked for collge prep. French and Latin were offered and there were two teachers: one amiable drone—and Edna Graham.

To most people in the town, Edna Graham's life was cut from the devoted, underpaid, old maid, firm but human, stereotype teacher pattern as surely as the saints are cut from the iron patterns of hagiography.

The teacher Edna Graham was in the Presbyterian Church each Sunday. She lived in the modest, but eminently respectable rooming house of the widowed Mrs. Thompson, where she had a room and took her meals with half-a-dozen colleagues. She was seldom seen after sunset.

But Edna Graham overreached the pattern. She *lived* in her classroom, and she was absolute mistress of her craft.

She was a taskmaster, but not a martinet. She had a sense of humor and was willing to laugh as long as it did not interfere with instruction. And she never confused busy-ness with instruction.

Edna Graham was not erect and plain. She was stooped and ugly. This grieved her because she passionately wished to love and take love. And she had wished for children. She had wished to be touched, but no man's hand had touched her shoulder, much less the grieving flesh inside her thigh. Since her days at Converse College when she had been ignored or considered with mere politeness by young men she had studiously sublimated these desires. She lustily wished that men listened to Ben Franklin when he advised that all cats look gray in the dark. But they did not listen, and she knew they would not. She recognized soon in herself a tendency to become bitter, and she saw that this was the way to misery. Instead, she chose to become a master teacher. For indeed, Edna Graham had quality.

In her early years she saved from her miserable salary to pay for summer courses at the University of North Carolina which got her a master's degree. Thereafter, she saved so that she might spend summers traveling in France to perfect her command of idiom, and to indulge her almost lasciviously sensual delight in French art and culture.

Edna Graham knew that her students in this small parochial town took French for two reasons: because colleges required a language; and so that the few who might travel to Canada would be able to read a menu and locate a toilet. Edna Graham also knew that the only true reason for studying a language was to read the great thinkers and poets of that language.

Therefore, Edna Graham led a secret life while practicing her craft. She waited and watched. She waited and watched for a student with whom she could rise from master teacher to teacher as artist. In her thirty-three years of teaching, she had had seven such students. Sometimes six or eight years separated their coming, sometimes they had come one after another. But now, there had not been one in seven years—the last had been young Thomas Eason, son of Dr. Eason. He was now at Harvard, a Ph.D. candidate in biology. They still corresponded in French.

When Miss Graham received her class lists the day before school opened she noticed that Charlotte Morton was enrolled in French. She had heard of the uproar her father caused when he took the girl out of school for a European trip. She knew that the lawyer Morton was said to be a drunkard and a seducer. But she had also heard him play the piano several times at *Pro Musica*, and she knew that he was a small scale art collector.

When French class convened the first day, Edna Graham placed herself at the door, her head and shoulders stooped, her hands clasped in front of her, looking for all the world like a bird of prey, owl-eyed behind thick glasses, made more grotesque by the smile her heavy lips formed around her buck teeth. Murmuring good morning, she considered the young people with whom she would be spending the next year: boys swaggering in anticipation of manhood; girls sedate or snickering under the weight of newly formed breasts.

She recognized Charlotte Morton approaching between a tall handsome boy and that animal spirit, Calvin Hendricks, whom she knew by reputation. The girl had grown tall and beautiful, Miss Graham noted as the dark eyes above the candid smile met hers. She admitted relief when Charlotte and one boy turned into her class and Calvin went prancing by. He *did* have a reputation.

When the bell rang Miss Graham stalked to the center of the class.

"Good morning. I am *Mademoiselle* Graham. Let me add my welcome to those you have already received. I hope each of you had a pleasant summer," she smiled her gargoyle smile.

"I hope also that none of you is more unhappy than I am that summer is ended and we find ourselves back in school. If so, you are miserable indeed. However, summer *is* ended and we *are* back in school. Let's see what pleasure and profit we can make of it. I shall begin by calling the roll."

She moved to her desk and began calling names. The tall boy was Maxwell Compton, the banker's son. She recognized several other names and sometimes paused to ask if the here-sayer were brother to so and so.

Charlotte Morton answered her crisply and met her gaze.

The roll completed, Miss Graham walked to the center of the room and again clasped her hands and assumed her bird of prey attitude.

"There are many beginnings for you today. Today you begin a new school year. You begin with new teachers and you will meet new friends. Most important, you begin with a new freedom, that of selecting some of your courses.

"As always, freedom demands responsibility. You sit in this French class because you choose to, and I stand in front of you because I choose to. Having exercised freedom, we have taken on responsibility to each other and to the very great subject which we will be studying together.

"I think that you and I should have a short heart-to-heart talk now, so that from the very beginning, we may know what we can expect of each other. I urge you to listen carefully to the things I say now because these things will apply from now to the end of the school year. I shall speak truly, I promise. But, if you doubt any of the things I say, you may ask anyone who has studied under me in the past—or you may test me for yourself as time goes on.

"I—my salary—costs your parents money in the form of taxes. Therefore, they have a right to expect a great deal from me. And since your parents pay for my services, I shall expect certain things of you in order to meet my obligation to them. Let us at the beginning understand what we shall expect of each other.

"First, those things which you may expect of me. They are two. I promise that I will be as good a French teacher as my brains, talent, and training allow me to be each day that we meet. Secondly, I promise to be just in assessing your progress at the end of each marking period. Those two. You will notice please that I did not say I would be an easy teacher, or a funny teacher, or even an entertaining one. I said good. I am paid my salary to see that in June you know first-year French. No one with half a brain ever thought that becoming educated is easy. And I am not an entertainer. If I were I would be on the stage, or radio, or in a night club."

Here Miss Graham smiled broadly. The thought of her appearance in a night club seemed to amuse her.

"I am a teacher. I shall make no apology for boring you at times or for working you very hard at times. Your parents do not pay my salary for me to be a playmate or companion to you. They pay me to teach you French, and I can do that if you cooperate.

"My second promise to you was justice in marking your progress. Marking is the worst part of my job. I do not like it and I doubt if any numerical scale can properly assess what any student has gotten from a course of study. However, I am required to mark you, and I shall. At the end of each quarter you will have received ten grades on your work. I shall, without even looking at the name that is beside the column, add up these ten marks and divide by ten and the result will appear on your report card. If the average is 25, that will appear on your card. If the average is 99, that will appear on your card. I will be as stone about this. I may love you like a son or daughter, but I will never give you a single point beyond what your average shows. Please understand that and do not embarrass either of us by asking."

Miss Graham paused to allow all the class lawyers to digest her remarks.

"Now, ladies and gentlemen, those are the things which you have a right to expect of me throughout the year. Are there any questions?"

She paused.

"Now I must tell you the things which I shall expect of you. We all believe that democracy is the best political system man has yet devised. However, a classroom is not a political situation. I shall be in charge of this classroom. I alone shall decide what and how we shall perform each day's activity. And, again, I say, I make no apology for boring you on occasion. If I judge that boredom is necessary to your mastering a problem I intend to bore you."

Charlotte smiled and glanced at Max, but he was too terrorized to know humor at that moment. Her eyes skipped to Billy who was concentrating on being invisible. Charlotte returned to the front of the room and found her eyes squarely fixed by Miss Graham's. She continued her smile, but it moved to the wry.

"These things are required of you if we are to have a successful year. Each day when the bell rings to commence class you will be in your seat, your mouth will be closed, and you will have before you a textbook, paper, and a writing implement. You will have these every day or there will be consequences. There will be no acceptable excuse. And on no account will you be tardy to this class.

"In no occupation can a successful practitioner be late or without his tools. Imagine a surgeon appearing to operate and turning to the patient and saying, 'Gee, I forgot my scalpel!' Is my point taken?"

Her logic was unassailable.

"There will be no trips to the boys' or girls' rooms during class period. Do not ask. There will be no trips to the water fountain. Do not ask. If you have something to say in class I insist that you raise your hand and obtain permission to speak. Students, this is a matter of common sense. There are thirty of us in this room. If we all speak at once nothing will be accomplished. I am chairman of our meetings. Therefore, you will raise your hand if you need to speak. This is a rule I will enforce without deviation. And is it not sensible?"

Again, her logic was well founded.

"However, do not misunderstand me. I have no intentions of suppressing your personalities. You are bright, interesting young people or you would not be studying language. I want to know what you think. I expect to learn from you. I certainly want to answer your questions if I can. But you will receive permission before you speak. I have no intention of wasting time saying such things as 'quiet,' or 'calm down'."

Several students began to squirm. Edna Graham smiled slightly. There were always transfers from her classes early in the year.

"There will be homework in French five days a week. That homework will come in on the day it is due, or not at all. I will accept no paper late. I have no intention of becoming a filing clerk. Furthermore, it should be clear that languages are learned day by day. No one can miss or skip lessons and expect to be successful."

Charlotte glanced at Jennings Hall. He was bent—she could never remember seeing Jennings when he wasn't bent—over his desk taking notes. Her glance turned his eyes for a moment. They exchanged shrugs.

"Now, students, I offer proof of my humanity, which, by now, you may have begun to doubt. I know, and I want you to know that I know, that French is not the most important thing in your life. It should not be. I understand that things will come up—a dance, a party, or a special movie. But you will have old lady Graham's everlasting French assignment. What to do? My answer would be go to the movie, or the dance, or the party. And you may do that three times each quarter without hurting your mark. But—and listen closely to this—on the fourth time that you fail to hand in an assignment, it will cost you five points from your average. The fifth incompleted assignment will cost you another five points, and so on. Have I made myself clear in this? You may miss three assignments without damaging your average. For each thereafter, five points will be deducted. I hope that it is clear because I will not discuss it with you when reports are issued."

She paused. There was more squirming. A hand went up. "Yes?"

"But, Miss Graham . . ."

"Who is speaking, please?"

"Amy Winston," Amy said putting on her best churlish, too-polite voice. "Miss Graham, but suppose—well, let's say that you have already missed three assignments and something really important comes up that you couldn't possibly miss. I mean really important."

"Miss Winston," Miss Graham replied, having read Amy's attitude immediately, "the answer is very simple. If you couldn't possibly miss it, don't miss it. Then be prepared to find your average five points lower when you receive your report card. Are there any other questions?"

There were none, as Miss Graham knew there would not be.

"Now, students, lest I have sounded too grim, I will tell you something which I will of course have to prove. I believe that this class can be fun. Yes, fun. For learning can be exciting. Also, I am a serious teacher, but serious does not necessarily mean miserable. Believe it or not I like to laugh. I like to joke. I understand that after what I have said, this will have to be proven. And I must warn you, laughing and joking will never take place here when instruction should be taking place.

"Further, both you and I are human. There are things and people that we like and dislike. As time goes on, you and I may learn to like, or possibly dislike each other. But always, let's keep our purpose firmly in mind. Likes and dislikes have nothing to do with why we are here. None of us is here to win a popularity contest. We are here to learn and teach French."

"That is all I have for you today. Thank you." Then she called, "Charlotte Morton."

Charlotte perked, raised her hand and said, "Here, Miss Graham."

"I understand that you have just returned from a European trip."

"Yes. Yes, I have."

"Did you enjoy it?"

"Oh," Charlotte gasped, searching for words. "Oh, Miss Graham, it was . . . well, it was the most wonderful thing that has ever happened to me."

"Yes, I can imagine. What countries did you visit?"

"We were in France. And Italy and Greece and Spain and England and Turkey. We passed through Switzerland, but we didn't stay long, because my father says that the Swiss have the Alps, but that all they do is finance war, and that their sole gift to Western Civilization is the Coo-coo clock."

Miss Graham paused, considered, then burst out laughing. It was certainly one way to look at it. Charlotte smiled too, breaking her intensity.

"And which country did you like best, young lady?"

Charlotte touched her forehead with her forefinger.

"Well . . . all in all, I think . . . but no. I can't choose. Sometimes I can close my eyes and picture wonderful things in all the countries." She shook her head and smiled brightly. "I couldn't possibly choose."

"Sometime, Miss Morton, you must tell us of your travels. How long were you in France?"

"A little over two months."

"And did you pick up any French?"

"*Oui, Mademoiselle*." And speaking in French, Charlotte went on to explain that her father had lived five years in France and that from the beginning he had taught her that language. Still in French, she told Miss Graham that she also knew Latin.

Miss Graham, step by step, had come beside her desk. Her face was aglow.

"*Bien*. Good, *Mademoiselle* Morton. We must talk more. I think that we must make an adjustment in your schedule. Surely you don't belong in a first year class. We will see what can be done."

When the bell rang, she walked back to her desk. *Perhaps*, she thought, *perhaps one more had indeed come*.

Outside class, out of earshot of anyone who looked adult, they clustered.

"Gawd-dam. Whew!" murmured Billy.

"What a bitch!" snarled Claire Lynn.

Now that they were in high school it was *de rigeur* to curse at every opportunity. Everything forbidden to childhood was delicious.

"Just who the hell does she think she is? I mean, who the hell does she think she is?" shrilled Amy, hands on hips, breasts in firing position.

"I think she *knoooooooows* who she is," Charlotte said. "Miss Schraeder, Miss Sybil, had her when she was in school. She told me about her. Yep, I think she knows who she is...."

Indeed, Edna Graham did know who she was. She was a teacher.

The next day Amy Winston and Claire Lynn withered under a fifteen second stream of clipped, rapid-fire rhetoric— without benefit of curse—delivered by Miss Graham when they, deciding to test early, entered the class moments after the bell sounded. Amy had the girls' room excuse poised on her tongue, but she never got off a single syllable. And she was never ever tardy to French again.

"Now, students, I shall ask you at the beginning to perform that act which all mankind seems to find most difficult: I shall ask you to think. I propose a deceptively simple question. What do you consider the most important invention—indeed, idea—conceived during the whole scope of human history? Think for a moment, then raise your hand."

Several hands went up. Several more tentatively joined them. Answers came. The wheel. Control of fire. Electricity. Telephone. The internal combustion engine.

Not so.

Charlotte knew what she was after, but Max beat her to it.

"Maxwell Compton. Language, Miss Graham?"

"I think you are correct, Maxwell. Class, consider for a moment and see if you can agree. There could be no civilized social order, no communication, no questions asked or answered without language. It is so basic that we take it for granted.

But there are deeper aspects of the importance of language, students, which I am not learned enough to explain. Let me suggest a few, however. For instance, humans think in terms of words and images—pictures. Have a thought. Does it not occur in your brain as a word or a picture? One wonders if we could really think anything beyond the most basic needs—pain, hunger, pleasure—if we did not have language to shape thought."

Click! went Charlotte's brain. My father said that.

"Another simple example indicates its importance to the thought process. There are primitive tribes still living on earth whose language is so simple that it only utilizes a present tense. No past or future tense. So, if language is an instrument of thought, these peoples, having no past tense, can have virtually no memory. No future tense, no capacity to plan ahead. Can you see? Language is indeed the instrument of memory and possibility. Do you follow?"

She paused.

"Class, I am neither historian nor psychologist so I cannot amplify these ideas. What I am trying to do now as we begin the study of the great French language is try to give you a respect for our subject. I would like you to have some feeling of the importance of our study—beyond merely meeting college requirements, because meeting requirements may be done by simply sitting in class two years memorizing a certain amount without touching on the essence."

Miss Graham smiled her grotesque smile at Max, then at Charlotte. Engagement was in the eyes of the two young people. *Perhaps,* she thought to herself.

"Let's continue thinking about language in general before we actually open our French books. What is this thing called language, that I am now using as I speak to you? Let's define in a single simple sentence. Let's say that language is a form of communication using sound and written symbols. Sound and symbol. Sound is easy."

Charlotte saw that Jennings had it in his notebook.

"I am opening my mouth and making sounds at this moment. All music is sound, though certainly all sound is not music. We will speak of sound again shortly. Symbol? A very profound concept which we use constantly, almost without thinking of it. But here's an easy example."

Miss Graham walked to the corner of the room and touched the American flag.

"This, class, is a piece of cloth with other pieces of cloth colored red and blue arranged on it. We call it a flag. But whenever we see this piece of colored cloth we think of our country, do we not? This is a symbol for America. A symbol, then, is a thing which stands for and suggests another thing. Take these."

She wrote with chalk on the blackboard 1, 2, 3.

"These are symbols for quantity. So you see that each time you make a mathematical calculation, you are working with symbols. You are thinking symbolically."

Then she wrote beneath the numbers, A, B, C.

"These too are symbols, are they not? They are symbols for sounds which we combine into words, sound units which are symbols used in communication."

She turned again to the board and quickly drew a musical staff, put a treble clef, and a series of notes.

"More symbols. Your Benny Goodman uses these very well. They too are symbols for sound. Organized correctly they could be *Two O'Clock Jump* or Beethoven's Fifth Symphony. Do you see?"

Charlotte glanced over her shoulder at Billy. He raised his eyebrows, nodded and smiled.

The old teacher returned to the board and wrote I, II, III over the 1, 2, 3.

"These too are symbols which . . ."

Suddenly, with surprising agility, she wheeled, and fairly leaped to the second row of seats to crouch like a lioness over Amy and Claire.

Then speaking softly, but with a slight hiss underpinning, "*Mademoiselles* Winston and Lynn. I, your teacher, am now giving you, my students, an order. This is not to be taken as a request. Follow it carefully. Both of you place your lower lip against your upper lip. Now, press. If either of you disobeys this order henceforth, you will find yourselves registered on the next day for study hall, or"—she pronounced the next with careful syllabic precision—"Home Ec-o-nom-ics."

Her arrowed stare moved from one face to the other. Then back to the board: ". . . the Romans used for numbers. But you know those already."

She wrote three separate sets of squiggles side by side.

"Perhaps these will help you see the symbolic and miraculous quality of language. This is the word for *God* written in Greek, Hebrew, and Arabic. I won't mislead you. I only know the rudiments of these languages. But what I want you to see is that there are many different symbols for sounds, and that though we speak English, it is not the only language in the world and its alphabet is not the only one. Indeed, many more people in the world do *not* use English than do.

"Now listen closely. I am going to make some strange noises. *Ferme la fenetra. Ferme la fenetra.* Can anyone—except you, *Mademoiselle* Morton—get meaning out of the noises I have just made? No. Well, there is meaning there. Charlotte, if I had made those noises to a group of French students, what would they have done?"

"You said, 'close the window'."

"A perfectly logical statement, but the noises that I made with my mouth had no meaning for you. Notice—and I hope you will be full of wonder."

She went to the board and wrote *fenetre, fenestra, window.*

"French, Italian, English. Window." She walked to the window and placed her hand on it. "Now. Is there anything *intrinsically* in this glass and wood which is *equal* to the sound *window*. Or *fenetra*? Or *fenestra*? Why is this *desk*?" She placed her hand on a desk. "Why do we not call this, say—bicycle?" She paused, and pointed. "Why is that *la porta* to the Italians, *la porte* to the French, and *door* to us?" She wheeled again to the board. "And further, why do these sets of squiggles mean *door* to us, the Italians, and the French?"

"Why not this, for instance." And she made a series of circles, dots, lines, crosses, and curlicues.

"What can be the reason that we chose *this*—using the word *chose* imprecisely, of course—instead of *this*?"

She paused. She had them, even Amy and Claire.

"Of course, I don't know," the old teacher continued. "Indeed, no one knows. We do not even know what was the first language used, nor the first which was written, using heaven knows what kind of symbols for the sounds. Now, class, do you begin to understand a little of the miracle that language is? For the fact that I can utter sounds with my voice, and make strange marks that you can understand is indeed a miracle of the very first order. Do you get a little feeling of the miraculous?"

Her eyes went to the Compton boy and the Morton girl. The boy's brow was furrowed and he was biting his nails. The girl's lips were parted and her eyes were on her desk. Were they . . . ?

Perhaps.

"Sometimes it's fun for me when I read articles in some of my philological journals—philology is the study of words—to try to imagine the first expression a man made which was understood by another man. Surely it was an expression of pain, or pleasure, or hunger. Maybe it happened—try to imagine a cave man, like Alley Oop in the comics who stubbed his toe on a rock. Maybe he yelled, 'Ouch!' to his friend or mate. And 'Ouch' became the very first *word* man ever used."

The class tittered.

"If that is so, *that* man was greater than that very great inventor who hitched up his loincloth, cursed the load he was carrying, and conceived of—the wheel. Wonderful to imagine. Well, that's all I have for you today. Tomorrow we will begin to learn some of the strange noises and squiggles that make up the French language."

Thus did Edna Graham leave her first 'mind-print' on a few.

Classes weren't all.

"Only three things count on this field," Coach Joe Hudson had told the seventy some candidates for the high school football team who sat around him in the massive heat of that August morning before classes began. "Those three are conditioning, blocking, and tackling. No team can win without them. This week we'll put the finishing touches on the first. You'd better be in fair condition already. If you're not, this is going to be the most painful week in your life. Next week, when we put on pads, you're goin' to run head-on into each other four hours a day until tackling will feel just as soft as those little girls that hang out at the drug store and The Track. So let's go. Form a circle around Pete and let's loosen up. Pete! Side straddle hop."

Pete McCanless, the tail back in Hudson's single wing, led the calisthenics.

Joe Hudson had been coach of the high school for fourteen years. Since his second year, he had always had better than fifty percent seasons, despite the small town population. He never had, and knew he never would have, a state championship team. He simply did not have the depth to draw on. But every coach on their schedule, even the larger cities who were perpetually championship contenders, knew that Concordia was always capable of an upset, and that Hudson's team would be hitting them as crisply in the fourth quarter as they had on the opening kick-off.

Hudson drove them like animals. As promised, they ran head-on hour after hour. "Head-on tackling," he would bark. The two lines would form. Hudson would flick the ball to one line, and the first man caught it and ran straight ahead as hard as he could. The first man in the other line hit him as hard as he could. "Tackle the ball!" Hudson would yell. "Tackle the ball."

Cal loved it. It was physical. It was all motion. He was now one hundred sixty pounds. The whack of the shoulder pads sang in him exactly as did the feel of Amy Winston's breasts. Do it. Do it, hard, deep, fast. He was a beautiful animal. He reacted to stimuli perfectly. If food was before him, he ate. If Amy's thighs were white beneath him, he screwed. If a ball carrier was before him, he knocked him down.

Cal had been under Hudson's eye since he had made a name for himself wrestling while still in eighth grade, for the coach knew a natural athlete when he saw one. Hudson had seen the semi-finals, where Cal's God-given skill had taken him, but where his youth and inexperience had got him in four pin positions without collapsing beneath the man who won the championship. Hudson had exulted as he watched this boy who did not yet have the skills to win, but who did not have a heart that would allow himself to be pinned.

Sure, Cal would try out for football. He was ready for the next event in life. But after only six weeks of practice, the first of many clashes between Cal and the coach took place. It had been six weeks of drilling, hitting, then sitting on the grass watching the varsity scrimmage. Enough for Cal.

"I want to carry the ball," he told Hudson for the tenth straight day.

When he wasn't called, he stood up, spun his helmet thirty yards across the field, and headed for the gym.

"Where do you think you're going?" Hudson roared, nonplussed.

"I'm playing—or leaving." Cal yelled over his shoulder and kept walking.

"Somebody lick the chocolate off your cherry?" sneered Hamilton Beard, Rufe Edmond's colleague at tackle.

Cal whirled and went for him. Hudson's whistle blew.

"All right. Defensive drill. Asters on defense. Begonias on offense," Hudson shouted. *All right,* he thought, *we'll see.*

A in asters was for the first string. B in begonias was the second string.

"Hendricks, run fullback on offense. We will see if wantin' and carryin' are the same things."

He yelled to Tommy Johnson, the second-string blocking back who called signals.

"I want you to run 14, 15, and 16 over and over again until I tell you to stop." These were straight ahead strongside or weakside power plays with the fullback carrying.

"Tell me what to do," Cal said to Tommy. "I don't know the plays."

"*I'll* tell you what to do," snapped Hudson. "You get five yards every carry, if you want to carry. Edmond, Beard," he called the two huge first-string tackles. "Hendricks is coming at you. Knock him down."

Six plays later, Hudson knew that he had found his varsity fullback for next year and the two years after. The first string piled up each play, but Cal did not know that six stacked bodies meant that you did not get yardage. He went straight ahead like a young bull, knees high, or over, twisting free of the stack, or—and Hudson's eyes glittered when he saw it—he went to the hole, and if it wasn't there, he slid along the line, picked an opening, or opened a narrow crack, and went for it. In every play, the linebackers had to be the tacklers to stop this young fool who wanted to carry the ball. On two plays Cal broke loose, and Hudson realized that one tackler was never going to be enough to stop him.

"Hendricks," Hudson called Cal to him, popped the top of his helmet. "You're gonna carry the ball. Pete, Mark Allen, C'mon'ere."

Mark Allen Smith was the varsity fullback.

"I want you two to start workin' with Hendricks here on ball handlin', fakin', handin' off. Try to give him a little finesse. Now, baby ape, are you happy?"

Cal grinned. Hudson did not regret.

The first six weeks were bad days for Max whose chemistry was balancing between boy and manhood. He dreaded reaching the head of the tackling lines. He would eye the other line when he was fourth or fifth. He would count. It was random. He sighed relief when little Whit Manson came up to face him. But next time it could be Rufe Edmond, the enormous senior tackle, whose kneecaps seemed on eye-level to him. When the ball was tossed Max would move forward, pause, then fall back and Rufe would roar over him.

Next came blocking. Same story. "Fists between your pads!" was Hudson's cry. "Head up. How can you block a man when you can't see him?"

Max feared. Trembling seized him. The few times he was called into scrimmages at the end of the practice day, he tried to disappear in the maze of play. But worst, oh worst, were the punt return drills.

Past all reason, somehow, of the nameless kids who hung on after the dropouts had cut the squad to around fifty, he and little Whit Manson were selected day after day to return the punts. Up field, Pete McCanless, Mark Allen Smith, the two team punters, and later Cal, would take the ball from center and kick, sometimes practicing high hangers, distance bullets, or corner shots. The rest of the squad were lined up in the end positions to come down under the punts and hit the returner.

"Manson and Compton," Hudson would shout. "Cannon fodder."

Then Max and Whit would go down and try to bring the ball back. Everyone noticed that these two were always cannon fodder, but no one knew why. Maybe it was because most of the other backs were tired and they, at one hundred ten pounds each, had not been used and were fresh. Maybe it was because Max was the son of Maxwell Compton of the bank and the Country Club and Hudson wanted to see if such a boy could take it. And Whit Manson was from the Mill Hill and didn't matter. Both boys were slight, but both did have speed. Maybe that was it.

Max stood alone waiting. It seemed like a mile to where the center snapped and Rufe Edmond and Ham Beard heaved their two hundred pound bodies like juggernauts down field toward him. Then thud, and the punt was soaring. Max spotted it and began to track it, but his fear was so great that he could not keep from constantly glancing at the two masses hurtling down on him, intent on knocking his head loose from his body. Sometimes, tracking both the ball and the tacklers, he completely misjudged the ball. Sometimes he fumbled. When he got it, he was so scared he relied on speed, but when contact was imminent, he would cut back and lose yardage.

"Hey, Compton," Hudson yelled after the whistle. "You're supposed to return it this way, not score a safety for the other team."

Max hated the shower room, where he had to reveal his skinny body among all the huge hairy bodies of the seniors. Proud in their new manhood, they loafed and soaped and strutted. Max slid in and out as fast as possible.

Nights became horrible. Dinner with his parents was needles. He spoke in monosyllables. He couldn't care about his mother's flowers or his father's bank. Manhood, masculinity, to hit and be hit gracefully obsessed him. He couldn't concentrate on his homework. He couldn't sleep. Pillow gnarled, he would turn on the light and look at himself. It was all somehow related to his prick. Where the hell was the hair? He had nothing but fuzz. There was no line of it going up his belly like the rest of the guys. He felt his nipples. They were hard and sore. The goddam shoulder pads rubbed them raw. There was fuzz under his arms. His upper lip promised a moustache. His mother complained, proudly, that he grew out of his pants "every two months." A lot of crap. He was still a shrimp. *I'm a squirt*, he thought.

He looked at his prick. It wasn't so little. He got it hard. Geez, it looked bigger than last night. Yeah, it did. He went to his desk and took his ruler. He could cum. He had cum with Morton. He actually trembled as he tried to recapture the times—the night Charlotte had mystically seemed to hover over she and me, saying to herself, bless us.

He measured. But wait. From under his desk blotter he took the pictures of Carole Landis in a tight sweater and Marie 'the Body' MacDonald. Movie stars. Carole Landis had the biggest tits in Hollywood. She was a sweater girl. Oh God, he'd like to get his hands on them. He looked at them and stroked himself. Things started going. Oh shit, he had to stop. He had forgotten to measure himself.

He jacked off with Carole Landis as inspiration. When it came he just felt. He could concentrate on nothing. Not even those tits. He looked at his oil. Billions of little swimming sperms, his biology book told him. OK. He could cum. *He was a man*. Christ, that felt good. He thought of Morton.

Then he looked in the mirror. It went away.

"But you are yellow," he whispered. "Jesus, am I really a

163

coward?" He choked. "I'd rather be dead. I would really rather be dead."

He fell across the bed, thinking of little Whit Manson, the other cannon fodder. The punts came too fast. Didn't that bastard Hudson realize there were only two of them?

But Whit wasn't a coward. He stood there. He waited for that ball to be in his arms. Rufe and Ham could be breathing in his face, but Whit—little skinny Whit—caught that ball first, then took his beating. He really admired Whit. Yep, Whit was great. And he wasn't yellow. Whit was a man.

Max clawed the sheets. *Why me?* Of all the guys on the football team. *Why me?* That ancient question.

He could quit. Hell, thirty guys had quit after the first week. *Why not?* Even Tom Kinder, whose father owned the men's shop where Hudson and all the jocks hung around shooting the shit about sports—*he* quit.

He rolled over. *No. I can't. I'm a coward, but I can't quit. Why can't I quit? I'm a yellow belly, but I can't quit. Jesus, I can't quit.*

God, I'm going crazy. Maybe I jack off too much. They say that makes you crazy. Fuck it. Who cares? If you're a coward, who cares if you're crazy. Oh God, I don't want to be a coward.

He thought of Cal. Days he watched Cal. Cal wasn't afraid of anything. Cal was a man.

Max writhed and stared at the ceiling. He was so goddam scared that he couldn't even catch a punt. *I didn't used to be scared. I would do anything. There was no dare I wouldn't take.* It all seemed to come with the sex thing.

I'd really rather be dead than be a coward, he thought. *That's the truth.*

OK. That was the worst thing that could happen. He could get killed. And that was better than going on like this. Like a yellow belly.

OK. So tomorrow will be different. Let Rufe and Ham come. *I am going to stand there and catch that ball and, by God, I am going to come up the middle as hard as I can. I don't give a fuck what happens.*

But he didn't. He misjudged. He fumbled. His hands were sweating and he simply could not stop watching as the huge tackles bore down on him.

Things went straight down. It gnawed at him until he almost stopped being himself. He swaggered and strutted.

He cursed in every sentence. He affected the foolish, obvious veneer of masculinity. A couple of times he made petty remarks to Billy about Classical music being for sissies. He sassed poor old Miss Greer before the class. She was hurt. He was ashamed. He wised off to Miss Graham. But she let him have it right back, humiliating him. And he really loved Big Edna. In a way she was a female version of what he wanted to be, and could not. She was hard and true and straight. There was no bluffing her. She assigned, you studied and delivered, and there was a relationship of such sweet respect that it became love. But if you didn't deliver, everything was bad.

Finally his posturing and pretensions to masculinity led him to do something that shamed him deeply. He picked at little, four-eyed Blaine Watkins. First he cut him out of the lunch line. Blaine offered weak objections and Max knocked his books out of his hand. Little Blaine. Everybody knew he couldn't fight his way out of a wet paper bag.

Coy Trexler was close at hand and joined in. "Atta boy, Max, kill that creep. Smear his nose all over his fat face."

It ended with Coy torturing Blaine all through lunch and then finally giving him a bloody nose on the way out of the lunch room.

Max was so profoundly ashamed that he vomited his dinner that night. *Well,* he thought, *this is really the end. You are such a coward that you have to pick on poor little Blaine. Boy, you are the lowest of the low.* And to make things worse, he had become an ally to that snake Trex. And poor Blaine had to take the consequence of that alliance. Max churned in bed. No matter how bad things were, he didn't want to be associated with Trex. He dug his nails into his arm. *Shit, I'll never be a man. Amy Winston's got more muscle in her left tit than I have in my arm. Oh God, whatta you do?*

He got up and looked at Carole Landis and Marie 'the Body' MacDonald.

It didn't help. *I don't care if I squirt cum all over the world I am never gonna be a man.*

Hudson crowned his misery, brought it out in the open, raised it like a flag. It was not an act of malice; Hudson had a whole team to think of. If he had had time he might have found the sensibility to realize that Max was going through what all boys go through sooner or later in a society which measures manhood in purely physical terms.

165

It was punt return drill. Max backed off and got under the first kick and waited. But the boiling action before him distracted. He was so nervous his brain seemed detached from his body, and he fumbled.

He scooped up the ball, but his fear of being hit drove him into a crazy dance, five yards, then ten, backward.

The whistle blew. "What's the matter with you, Compton? Your goal is that way, not back there. Hey, Compton. What is it with you? Are you afraid to get hit? Are you afraid somebody's gonna scratch those rosy cheeks? Get over there and sit in the shade and find a daisy. Mark Allen, kick a few. Pete, you come and bring a few back."

Max was perfectly humiliated. Tears came. He choked. It was The End.

When the drill ended, little Whit shambled over, helmet in hand, dead tired from having been hit and hit and hit. He flopped beside Max and lay back, panting still from the last return.

"Jesus," he whistled. That was all.

Max knew that now Whit knew absolutely. Little Whit, little, but with bravery equal to any. Max looked down the western end of the field. It was sunset.

This is The Sunset, he thought.

It ended.

Max didn't shower. He dressed and slipped out. The night and the next day were unrelenting agony. Neither Cal nor Billy, nor his Charlotte, could make him laugh. Friday, game day—the first game of the season—Charlotte purposefully leaned over him before Latin class, but not even her sweet breath, nor round breasts against his shoulder could stir him. He was numb.

That night, sitting on the bench beside Cal, he could not share in the joy as they took a three-touchdown lead. He seemed outside himself, watching himself, indifferently watching his team. He couldn't laugh as majorette Amy Winston cavorted and twirled, and Cal quipped that she was a helicopter with tits.

The game was in hand, but they were both surprised when during the fourth quarter Hudson yelled, "Hendricks!"

Cal ran to him, helmet in hand. Max saw Hudson talk intently to Cal and Cal nod his head. Then the coach slapped him on the back and Cal went in for Mark Allen.

And they ran him. He went straight ahead, hard, getting a couple of yards per carry. But they stalled and punted, Cal blocking as Pete kicked.

After another exchange Pete marched them down to the Thomaston twelve in the last minutes of the game. He called 14, fullback straight ahead. Cal took and drove. There was no hole. Without stopping, Cal slid along the line, saw an opening behind Rufe and Ham and barreled through, cut outside, and carrying three defensive backs with him went over the goal line. Hudson was right. Past the line of scrimmage, no one tackler was going to bring this fool down.

Cal had scored his first touchdown.

Max's generosity of spirit overcame his personal grief. He was happy for his friend. He met Cal as he trotted off the field, his handsome face aglow. "Cal, baby, beautiful."

But his own misery now touched his whole life.

After the game they rallied at The Track. It was carnival. Cal was able to arrange with the car hops for some beer concealed in paper cups. They drifted around the parked cars, danced outside in the crisp October night under a harvest moon.

Everybody circled and clapped when scarecrow Billy and Charlotte moved their saddle oxfords to *Two O'Clock Jump*.

Amy 'hadn't had time' to change out of the scarlet, satin, skin-tight majorette costume, and had flung her coat over her shoulders. Cal, full of success, danced her around until every male in the vicinity shared his lust.

It was clear and crisp and they had won the game and the moon was full and it was good to be young on that Friday night.

"Dad's down at the river house tonight," Charlotte whispered to Max.

It was what they dreamed of. Friday night. The whole empty house. Max didn't have to be home until 12:30.

But when they were alone, Max was detached. From her and from himself. It was like he was watching himself. And her. He felt her hair, its fineness, its richness. Her mouth was full and warm and sought his. And her breath was sweet.

He sat on the edge of the bed and watched her take off her bra, offering. How round and full her breasts were. And the large luxurious nipples. He touched her. She turned and his hands moved over the fine body. *How beautiful*, he thought, as he watched himself touch her.

She knew her boy and felt his detachment. "What is it, Max?"

"What do you mean?"

"I mean . . . what . . ?"

He didn't speak. How could he hide from Charlotte?

"Max, you aren't jealous of Cal, are you?"

"No! No. God, no. He's great. He was so great tonight."

She believed because she knew her boy was not small.

But he couldn't do her. Crouching above her open, waiting, wanting body, lying on her, feeling her warmth, her desire, he could not become hard. She played, caressed. He was humiliated. She offered forgetfulness, release, an untying of knots, and he couldn't take it. He was unable to take it.

They lay side by side, her arms about him. He was choking. This was Charlotte. Live a million years, he knew he would not lie with a woman more beautiful. This is Charlotte. What . . . ? But he knew.

Finally, he could bear it no longer. He wheeled away from her and sat on the edge of the bed, face clamped in his hands, naked, and chilled. He sobbed.

She curled around him. "Max. Maxie, what is it?"

He didn't answer.

Then she stood and knelt before him.

"Tell."

He sighed and shuddered.

Finally, she brushed his hands aside and cupped his face between her hands.

"Max. Oh, Max. I'm Charlotte. I love you. I have to know."

His eyes moved to hers for a moment. Then he lowered them.

"Char, I . . ." He couldn't say, I *am*. "I think I'm a coward."

She didn't say anything for a moment. It didn't make any sense to her. Max, her beautiful boy, Max, the dare-devil. She had to wait a moment to comprehend its importance. To him, therefore to her. Her hand slipped to his shoulders, hard with the coming of muscle definition. This body, and Cal's, were different and exciting to her. Suddenly she was swept with the realization that their bodies were very different and that it went farther than nakedness, and lying beneath them, and holding them in her arms. There were different uses and different tests for them. And these tests

168

she must now take seriously, even if they were incomprehensible to her, or at least, unimportant.

She embraced him, held him tight. To draw it from him.

"Char, I think I'm a coward."

She pulled him even closer. She did not say you are not. That would have been simple.

"Why, Max, do you say this? What has happened?"

He choked again. Broke free of her grasp, stood and walked, slumped against the door.

"I just know. I'm different from Cal. From Whit. From everybody. Christ, I'm yellow!"

She knelt on the floor and looked at him and thought how fine his body was and how desolated he was. She waited.

"I can't tell you . . . Oh, it's football. I . . . I'm just scared. I can't make myself do it. I get so scared I can't think. I can't be . . ."

She said nothing. His hands were clenched around the door. She knew better than to say it wasn't true. Max was near panic.

He turned around and faced her. He dropped his hands. He looked down at himself. He glanced at her.

"I can't help it. I try. I swear every time . . . I'm sorry."

"Max, listen. Come here. Sit. Wait a minute."

She ran downstairs to the kitchen and made tea. She splashed a little Jack Daniels in each one. She was filled to choking with pity and love for him. *But, go slow,* she thought. *This is serious.*

She put his tea on the bedside table and sat at his feet. Still naked.

"Drink this," she whispered. She pressed her cheek to his thigh.

She sipped in silence. Twice he tried to speak. He couldn't meet her eyes.

When the tea was gone, the silence became terrible. She stood in front of him and drew his head to her belly.

"Max, listen, I love you. Are you listening? Now this is not over yet. Do you hear?" she whispered. "I promise. I love you and want you. OK? Just remember, it's not over yet."

He held her so tightly that it almost hurt her.

"Godamighty, Charlotte, I love you so much I . . ." he sobbed.

He dressed in silence. She helped him with his shirt.

On the porch, she held him again. She couldn't release

him, let him go like this. She felt him tremble. *What are men?* she wondered. *I must think. I must ask my father. Oh!* She lifted and kissed him, almost frantically.

"Max, remember. This is not over. That's all. Just ride for a while. I'm with you. Remember that. I love you. I love you a lot. Whatever happens. Max, can you remember that?"

On the way home in the middle of the street, beneath the great arch of elms and oaks, under the harvest moon, he kept saying, *I gotta do something. Everything would be perfect if I . . . Jesus, she loves me. She's so great. I've gotta . . . just for her if no other reason. I've gotta do something. . . .*

"Hendricks! *Calvin Miles Hendricks! Touchdown* Hendricks! Get up! Your fans want you. Cal, you *ape*, get up!"

He had a hangover. He stirred. Yep, he was home. It was ten forty-five. Cal brushed the curly blond mop out of his face. He rolled to the window.

"Morton. Wow! Hi! Wha—?"

"Listen, I gotta talk to you."

He yawned. "Wait a minute." He yawned again. "OK. Talk."

"I mean *talk*. This is serious."

Cal turned toward the bedroom door and yelled, "Mom?" There was no answer.

"Yeah, it is serious. You sure have got on your boobs this morning." He looked her up and down, leered, and whispered, "Nobody's home. C'mon in and give me some of that good stuff."

"*C'mon* ape! I said it was serious."

Thought twisted his wonderful face. "OK. Gimme eight minutes."

"OK. I'll be on the porch."

He appeared combed and gleaming in corduroys and sweat shirt. They went in the kitchen where he drank a quart of orange juice, ate four eggs with bacon that Charlotte fixed while he toasted four slices of bread.

They talked as he gorged.

"It's Max," she said.

He ate.

"Cal. Something's really at him."

"Yeah, what?"

"Well, have you noticed anything? Recently. You know—is he acting funny?"

"No. Well, for the last couple of days, he hasn't waited for me after practice." He smiled. "I figured that was because you're wearing sweaters these days."

"C'mon. I mean—say, at practice."

Cal chewed and pondered. "Nope. Not that I noticed. But I've really been working on getting the backfield moves down. Hey, how'd you like that touchdown?" He leered and walked his fingers across the table and gently touched her breast. "Don't I get a little reward for that?"

She smiled and pressed his hand to her breast.

"Yeah. One feel. Now, you happy? But be serious, because I'm worried."

"OK. OK. Serious Hendricks—that's what they call me."

"Cal, this is strictly between you and me, right? I don't want even Billy to know. OK?"

He frowned. "Sure. Sure." She *was* serious!

"OK. Now listen. Is Max yellow? I mean, a coward?"

"A coward? Naw. *Max?*" It clearly had never occurred to him, but many things did not occur to Cal. He thought. "Maxie? Naw, why hell! After all the scrapes we've been through together?"

"He thinks he is."

"Why do you say that?"

"He told me last night. Cal, he cried. Cal, he couldn't get a hard-on last night. Cal, if you ever tell anybody this..."

He waved his hand. Now he was sitting upright. Then he smiled.

"Did you show him your wares?"

"Cal—"

"Well, sometimes that happens. One time I..."

"Cal, listen, he's really upset. He thinks he's a coward and he's obsessed with it. Didn't you see that mess between him and Blaine and Trex the other day? That's not like Max, acting like he had to prove something."

"Yeah. I guess it was funny—funny *odd*, I mean. Yeah, 'cause Max never wants to hurt anything."

"Yeah. It's bad, Cal. It is really in his head."

Cal turned his milk glass bottoms-up.

"Wanta doughnut?" he asked.

Charlotte shook her head.

Cal stood and walked to the cabinet. Then he turned.

"Hell, Max ain't a coward. Listen, you remember that day out at the quarry? Nobody would dive off that highest cliff.

Nobody. You remember? Over by those pines. Everybody was daring each other. You know who did it first. Max. Then me. And we were the only two. Hell, Max wasn't a coward then. That's sure."

"Look, Cal. I know that and you know that, but Max doesn't. I'm telling you. It's in his head and it's changing him."

"Well, let's get it out of his head."

"Terrific, Calvin. Very astute," Charlotte said, giggling at his foolish face and simple answer. "Just what I'd expect from you. Now I await your plan—for implementation of your solution."

"Well, we'll just..." He was talking around half a doughnut.

"Just tell him he's not yellow. Very good, Calvin. I'm impressed with your solution. And your sensibility. I don't know why I was so concerned."

"Morton, I'll turn you over my knee," he growled. "And don't forget I scored a touchdown last night. I'm tough."

"You *were* great, Cal," she was serious again. "OK. Now listen. Think. And I'll think. Because this isn't simple. And I believe things could get worse. And I want Max back. Like Max."

"Right. Yeah, you're right. OK."

She was leaving.

"Hey, Cal, don't forget. This is strictly between me and you. Gotta be. It would kill Max if he knew I'd told you."

"Right."

And wonderful! Cal remembered to watch his friend. At practice the next week he noticed that Max shied away from body contact. That he fumbled during punt return drills. That Hudson sent him to the daisies. And that Max was sullen, that he no longer waited for Cal after practice. That Max, in fact, was no longer Max.

On Wednesday, Cal caught Charlotte by the arm.

"I gotta plan," he said. "About Max. Meet me at the gym door four minutes after school closes. Hey, you got a jacket today?"

"Yeah," she looked puzzled.

"Bring it. OK? Right after school. Be there."

She was there. The gym door popped open and Cal handed her his windbreaker, which he gripped at all corners like a bag.

"Take it. Yeah, under yours. Get outta here."

"Hendricks. Hendricks." Coach Hudson popped out of the door right after Cal.

Cal froze and looked guilty of murder.

"Where are you going with those? Hello, Charlotte. What are you two up to?"

Charlotte was nonplussed. She didn't even know what was in the ballooned windbreaker.

"Look," Hudson said. "I saw you sneak them. What is this, Hendricks?"

Cal looked him straight in the eye.

"Coach, I'm just borrowing them. Listen, I really really need these for just a coupla days. I was gonna bring them back, I swear."

Hudson took the windbreaker bag from Charlotte. "Charlotte Morton, your father is a lawyer. Cal," he said, "this is school property. Don't you realize that—"

"Look, Coach," Cal had on his most appealing hang-dog expression. "Listen. I'm gonna ask you a favor. I need these for—till Monday. I swear I'll bring them back Monday. I was just borrowing them. Nobody's using them. And I really need them. And I swear I'll bring them back Monday."

"What do you want them for?" Hudson opened the windbreaker and Charlotte saw for the first time what she had been accomplice in trying to steal. Boxing gloves.

"Uh, I can't tell. But, please, Coach, I'm asking you to trust me."

"Look, Cal. These are school property. If someone got hurt with these, do you realize the mess there would be?"

"Coach, I promise you, nobody'll get hurt. I swear it. You can break my neck if anybody gets hurt. Or if they're not back in your hands on Monday."

"Why can't I know why you need them?"

Cal took the coach by the arm and pulled him away from Charlotte.

"Listen, coach. Man-to-man, I just can't tell you," sincerity was dripping from Cal's tongue and he knew that Hudson would never be able to resist the man-to-man pitch. "I just can't tell you now. But it's important. To me and to another guy on the team. Look, if it works I'll tell you. Coach, please."

Hudson looked past Cal to Charlotte.

"I'll make him bring them back, Mr. Hudson."

Hudson shrugged. "If anybody gets hurt, Cal—all right. Keep them covered until you're home."

"Hey, Coach. You're a jewel," Cal piped. "Hey, if you put me in the game Friday night, I'll go fifty yards for another T.D."

Hudson grimaced at him and went back into the gym. Cal winked at Charlotte and followed him.

10

CAL'S left was always in his face. He was not actually hitting, but the big, sixteen-ounce glove was tapping him on the forehead, or incessantly pushing, or slapping him across the cheeks.

"Hey, lay off, what are you trying to do?" Max was backpedaling, stumbling over a bicycle, the barbells, around Cal's garage.

Cal had grabbed him after Thursday's light equipment drill, a loosen-up, pass, punt, extra point, no-contact drill before Friday night's game.

"C'mon home with me. I wanta show you something."

"Naw. I'd better get on home. Big Edna gave us a goddam book to write by tomorrow."

"It won't take long. I hooked something. I want you to see."

"What?"

"Come on and see. It won't take long."

"Maybe Saturday," Max said.

"Max, you'll be home in fifteen minutes. Don't be a creep. Mommy can wait."

Max came. 'Mommy can wait.' That always worked with boy/men.

Home, Cal took him out to the garage, barred the door with such furtiveness that Max thought he had hooked a carton of cigarettes or a whole bottle of whiskey.

"Boxing gloves?" he said.

"Yeah. Put 'em on and let's spar a little."

Max turned to go. "You big ape, you'll kill me."

"Naw. Just spar a minute. I wanta see how to move."

Max wouldn't, but Cal was already annoying with his left and clearly not listening. In a moment, Max realized that he had to. Cal wasn't listening. He was jumping around and beginning to use him as a punching bag.

"Jesus. Wait a minute. Lemme get 'em on."

In a moment, he was backpedaling, covering his face.

"C'mon, you're too big."

He could hardly talk for Cal's big left, perpetually just in his face. Not really hitting—just there.

"What are you trying to do?" Max yelled, covering and backing off.

Then it began to come. Not in the face. But on the shoulders, hard, and in the chest. Hard and fast. Max backed off, stumbled, was driven into the wall.

"Hey, Cal."

Max glanced at his friend's face over the gloves. Cal wasn't smiling. What was happening? He moved fast enough to glove one glancing off his forehead. But a powerful right struck him squarely on the shoulder and jarred his insides, drove him into the garage wall.

His eyes flickered to Cal's face. And he feared. Cal was not playing. Whack! again across the shoulder.

Max felt the cold snail of fear sliming the hair on the back of his neck. Cal's crazy. He's gonna kill me. He looked up again. Cal's right was coming. It was exactly like punt return drill. It was coming. He tried to run but there was no place to go. Whack! Full into the shoulder joint. He was rammed into the wall again. The big left into his chest. His hands were sweaty inside the gloves. He couldn't breathe. No sooner had one blow landed and jarred, than the next came.

"Cal!"

No answer. Just one jarring blow after another. He squirmed and covered. Tears were starting. Jesus. He clasped his head. He moved toward the door. Cal cut him off. He dropped to his knees, gloved hands over his head. Cal didn't stop. Across his shoulders, hammering his own gloves into his head. Max was crying.

Suddenly he was flinching for nothing. Cal had stopped.

"Get up."

"Whatta you trying to do?"

"Get up."

"Fuck you, you bastard," Max sobbed. "Quit it."

"Get up. If you don't get up, I'll kill you."

Max sat sobbing, covered, head between his knees.

"By three," Cal said.

"No."

"One. Two."

"No. Whatta you trying to do?" Max was sobbing openly.

"Three. You gonna get up?"

"No. You bastard."

"Here it comes."

It came. Cal bent over him. Not hard, but steadily. Across the shoulders. Across his gloved head.

Max was blubbering. "Quit it. Quit it."

Cal paused. "Get up."

"No."

"Here it comes."

Max rolled back. Cal leaned and whopped him across the chest with the big glove.

"All right. All right," Max slobbered. "Lay off, will ya? Gimme time."

He struggled to his feet. He didn't have time to get set. It came. It was hard. It jolted. Into the shoulders. The chest. Into the shoulders so hard he was driven backwards. Into the chest hard. He was bawling and covering and cringing. A combination. A left into his chest bounced him against the wall. A right roundhouse into the shoulder drove him into a spin, and literally over Cal's bicycle on the floor.

He crumpled, absolutely bawling. Panting, flinching, waiting for the next blow. It didn't come. He peeked through his gloves. Cal's big feet were right before him. He flinched again, sobbing. Nothing happened.

"It didn't hurt."

He didn't move.

"It didn't hurt," Cal repeated.

He peeked again through his gloves. He could tell from Cal's shoes that the bastard was squatting in front of him.

Hesitantly, he looked up, still through his gloves. Cal was smiling. He met Cal's clear, blue eyes for a moment, then covered.

"Maxwell, it didn't *hurt*!"

He blinked. Sniffed.

Cal grabbed his gloves and pulled them away from his face.

"It didn't hurt. Move your shoulders. Right? It'll jar your guts. It'll knock you down. 'Cause I'm bigger and heavier. But it *didn't* hurt. Move your shoulders."

Max looked up into the handsome smiling face. He held his glove in front and slowly moved both shoulders. It didn't hurt. He had been knocked on his ass—but *it didn't hurt*.

Cal was smiling. "Does it hurt?"

Every province of Max's being was swept with a flood tide of realization. Cal knew. He was transfixed by Cal's eyes. Cal *knew*. Cal, the dummy, the brave, great, bawling dummy, *knew*!

"Did it hurt?"

Cal's voice came to him over great distance, from beyond the two huge mountains of awesome, gorgeous, life-giving realization—*It didn't hurt*. And—*Cal knew!*

"If you don't answer me, I'm gonna stand up and kick you in the face."

Max managed to shake his head.

"Right. OK. Now get up. Max, if you don't get up I'm gonna beat the shit out of you there."

He leaned and grabbed Max by the shoulder, heaved him up.

They stared at each other for a moment.

"Get ready. Here it comes."

Cal lifted his gloves and closed in. It came to the shoulders and chest, hard. Max backed off and covered. Whack! He was jolted backward. Whump into his chest and he was rammed into the wall. It kept coming.

It doesn't hurt, Max's brain flashed the beautiful new message. It knocks you down, but it doesn't hurt. At least, not now.

He lifted his eyes. Jesus, he could actually see it coming, each blow. He reacted. His left actually stopped Cal's right and glanced it off.

But that left was coming. He was looking and could see it coming. He whipped and took it on the shoulder. Watching still, he whirled left and got off the wall. Cal's right caught him solidly before he was ready and literally jolted him over that goddam bicycle again. But he got up and covered before

Cal could get to him. He kept watching. That was it. He was fast. All he had to do was look and he could avoid. Cal kept closing. Cal's right skidded off his shoulder and before he realized it, he reacted. He threw his own right. It caught Cal's shoulder. He had hit back. All he had to do was watch. And get in when there was a chance.

They sparred around the full garage. He steadily back-pedaled, but his eyes were open and he was beginning to catch most of Cal's blows on his gloves.

Then Cal threw a combination with such power that even though he took the right on his shoulder, he was driven against the wall. But he was watching, and without knowing or thinking he bounced off the wall and threw his own right. It had motion behind it and skidded off Cal's shoulder and caught him solidly on the side of the head. Cal's head popped back and he found Max's left in his belly.

Cal jumped back and dropped his hands.

"Maxie, baby! Attaway to go!"

Then he bored in again. Max got knocked over that bitch bicycle twice. But he was up and covering and throwing instantly. After another four minutes of steady pounding, neither of them could hold his arms up. Cal slumped against the door and Max eased himself down on the barbells. Both were panting, hoping for enough oxygen for the next breath.

So they sat until, "Calvin. Calvin. Come and wash up for supper. Calvin, right this minute!"

"Coming, Mom," Cal managed. He walked to Max and held out his right glove.

"Hold," he said. And pulled his hand out of the glove. He untied the other and pulled it out. Then he helped Max.

"You wantta eat with us?"

"Gotta get home," Max gasped. He looked up at his friend's face. Cal was smiling as he took Max's hand and heaved him up from the bar.

Cal lurched his weight against the garage door which popped open and they wobbled out. Halfway to the house, Max felt his friend's bulk against him as Cal leaned on his shoulder. At the door Cal slapped him across the back and went in.

Walking home, Max was careful. *Very* careful. Maybe, he kept saying. Just *maybe*.

Once, abetted by the brilliant, October sunset and the

Autumn's gorgeous, golden shroud wound around the trees, he skipped, flipped Big Edna's French book in the air and yelled, "Maybe."

Dinner was unreal for Max. He was self-involved, full of wonder. He was an initiate. The vows were known, but their implications were endless. He was so silent that his mother excused him from the table when Martha brought coffee.

He ripped haphazardly through the math homework. Then skim-read twenty pages of *Silas Marner.*

Then he paced for minutes. He was saying over and over to himself, Maybe. Maybe. He took off his shirt and stood in front of the mirror. He was getting muscle definition. Some veins in his arm were in relief. In fact, his chest looked A-OK. But then he saw his left shoulder. It was absolutely blue. He raised his arm. Jesus. It *did* hurt. It had hurt. But, he thought, I kept my eyes open. I hit back. I really did. I'm sure I did. He tried to reconstruct it in his mind. He tried to make that one right to Cal's head concrete in his memory. Cal's head had popped. Yep, I really did, he thought.

He walked back to the desk. Fuck French, he murmured. Fuck you, Big Edna, you red hot sweetheart, you.

He took out Carole Landis's tits. I would lick those, he thought. Twenty minutes each. God, I'd lick them. God, she's got *two* of them. I'd bury my face between them and blow bubbles.

His prick got very hard. He thought for a minute. There was some relationship, vague but true, between his new knowledge and his prick. Prick. That was kind of a creepy word for such a fine strong handsome being. Prick. Sounds like an insignificance. Practically an insult. Cock. That was better. It had some strut to it. Charlotte, I have a hard cock for you. Hell, her tits were as good as Carole Landis's any day. Almost.

He went back to the mirror. Be careful, he thought. You're still not sure. Be very careful. Maybe. Just maybe. Hot damn. *Maybe!*

He had an idea.

"Mom," he called downstairs. "I left my French book over at Cal's this afternoon after practice. Can I run over there and get it?"

"All right," she called.

He telephoned Cal. "Hey, Cal. Max. Can I come over for five minutes?"

"Oh, Maxwell, out on a week night. Mrs. Compton's little boy? Sure, c'mon."

"Hey, I'll tap your window. OK?"

"Right."

Ten minutes later, Cal leaned out.

"C'mon out to the garage."

Cal came out and they put on the lights.

"Five minutes. Just five minutes, Cal, OK? I wantta see something," Max said, smiling shyly.

Cal grinned and put on the gloves.

Three minutes later Max could not hold his arms up. His left shoulder was truly throbbing. But he had kept his eyes open *all* the time and he had thrown punches back.

Cal put his arm around him on the way back to the house.

"Two T.D.'s tomorrow night, Cal?"

"Right, baby. If Hudson lets me play."

"Thanks, Cal. Later on."

Cal slapped him on the back.

"Right. Later on."

On the way home Max kept saying, It's gonna be OK. It's gonna be A-OK. Calvin, I love you. Morton, I love you and I'm gonna fill you with a million little squiggly sperms and blow bubbles between your gorgeous tits. Morton, I really love you and it's gonna be perfect from now on. Calvin, you big ape, score a million touchdowns. It's gonna be OK!

Charlotte was answering the phone at that moment.

"This is your old Uncle Calvin. Morton, everything is A-OK."

"What?"

"Maxwell just hit me with four rights and three lefts. It's OK."

"Oh, Cal. Oh, Cal, Cal."

"Yeah. See you tomorrow, Boobs."

"Yeah. Yeah. I love you, Calvin, you ape."

"You gotta prove it."

"I will. Oh, I will. Two feels at least. Oh, Cal, anything. Anything. Tomorrow."

She took a deep breath.

She dialed Max.

"Hi, Max. Char. Whatcha doing? French?"

She heard him gasp. "Oh, Char. Yeah. Yeah."

"I was just thinking of you. I thought I'd call."

"I was thinking of you too," he said.

"Good things?"

"Oh yeah. All good things. The best things. Glorious, charming, wiggly things."

He's OK, she thought. He's OK.

"Terrific. Study hard. Big Edna's probably straining her brains now to make the test impossible. Good night, Max."

"Good night, Char. Hey, Char. Yeah, good night. Hey, Char, thanks."

The weekend was intolerable for Max, but now for different reasons. He had to test it. All weekend he kept saying, this is it. Man, this is it. If it's true, OK. But if it isn't. Oh shit. No. No. My eyes were open and I *did* hit back.

On the bench during the Friday game, he wasn't sure, but he *thought* he actually wished to get in the game. To hit just once. Or get hit. To test.

Cal played in three quarters. He now handled the ball with grace. He could spin from the single wing fullback, hand off, or fake, and he could run. They lost to the powerful Greenburg team by two touchdowns, but it was clear to Hudson that this boy needed only a couple more games to become fearsome.

From the bench Max could tell too. What a guy was his friend Cal. He wanted Charlotte too. Tonight. But there was no chance. Mister Douglas was offering drink and dinner that night and the house was full of his cronies, Mr. Fulton, Mr. Jacobson, Miss Sybil, the Cleland doctors, Sugar Lady and Howard, *etc*.

Monday came. He was tense all day because it now seemed to him that his whole life would go on the line this afternoon at football practice. He was sure if he did not perform well today, he never would. Changing to the practice uniform, his mouth was dry. He kept saying, imitating Cal, *It didn't hurt*. He moved his left shoulder. It *did* hurt. It hurts and I love it.

They scrimmaged most of the day, Hudson working on mistakes, making them hold blocks until the whistle. Then he told them his scouting report on Wynnsboro, next Friday's opponent. They were light, fast, took chances, ran inside and out, and threw. Talbot, their tailback, could pass, and would if they got behind. Greaves, their fullback, weighed two hundred and could go straight ahead. He was also the best punter in the conference. So work on returns.

The team formed two lines.

"He kicks them high so that the coverage has plenty of time to get down. Let's run through a few, then we'll put some blockers down there too. Cannon fodder."

Whit met Max's eyes. They both snapped their helmets and moved out.

"Manson and..." Hudson paused. "Manson and Pawling."

Oh Christ, Max thought. *I gotta have this.* All the other times it was me.

In desperation, he turned. "Me too, Coach?" His voice cracked, he was so intense.

Before Hudson could answer Cal jumped to the head of the end position line.

"Get that creep down there," he bawled out. "I owe him. He hit me with a right hook yesterday. I'm gonna wrap him up."

Hudson nodded. Neither Cal nor Max ever knew whether he understood.

Downfield, he said to Whit, "I'll take the first one."

"Well, God bless you," Whit registered disbelief.

Upfield Cal bellowed, "I'll be there the same time the ball is, Maxwell. I'm gonna smear you."

Up there, a mile away, Hudson was talking to them. OK, baby, this is it. Watch that ball. Get that ball before you do anything. It didn't hurt.

The punt and Cal were off. Max moved ten yards over to get under it. It was a high hanger. He glanced once at the coverage thundering toward him and then fixed his eyes on the ball and waited for it. *Get that ball.* The last thing he thought was *It didn't hurt.* He caught it. He caught it and gripped it like it was life itself. Cal hit him at the same time. But he *caught* that fucking ball.

Cal grinned down in his face, slapped the ball which was clamped to his chest, and said, "It didn't hurt."

It hurt his heart. His heart was so big it honestly hurt. He got up grinning and grinning, and threw the ball up field.

Whit took the next one. Max watched. Get that ball. He could not wait. It's OK. It's A-OK.

Max returned twenty-five punts that day. It was all over. He had tears. It was truly all over. He fumbled once, only once, when the coverage hit him at the same time the ball did. It's all over, he kept singing. He actually wanted the next one and the next one. By the tenth, he was in love with it. Catching the ball was only the first part. That he could do now. Every time. By the fifteenth, he had moved on to returning. He felt a glory if he had a few yards' running space because he had the ball in his arms and he could actually try his skill and speed against the monsters who were coming after him.

One time he pushed Whit aside and took two in a row. He did it because Rufe and Ham were at head of the lines. Fuck them, he thought. It didn't hurt. They're big but they're slow. I'm gonna catch the ball and run them. He did.

He was on his way to the shower after the last whistle before he realized that he was battered, that every bone had its own particular special complaint.

"*Some* day," Whit said to him on the way in. Max knew Whit meant a lot more.

"Yeah, Whit. Right you are."

He showered. It was long and hot and sweet. Afterwards he flipped Cal for a coke at the pharmacy and lost smiling. He treated Whit. Everything was sweet.

At dinner, he talked incessantly, ridiculously.

After dinner, he called Charlotte just to say, "Whatcha doing?"

He skim studied. That stuff wasn't really important on balance with manhood. At least, tonight.

Carole Landis and Marie 'the Body' MacDonald were gloriously violated before he finally laid his weary, happy, man's body to sleep that night.

Before many weeks of school, Miss Graham was firmly and finally Big Edna, and she knew it and took pride in it. She was secretly pleased to watch the several transfers from her class which inevitably followed her opening day statement, students who were not willing to enter even a pretense of excellence. But primarily she was intent on watching the Morton girl. At fifty-eight, at the close of a career largely spent teaching that which she loved to the thousands who ignorantly memorized, she wished devoutly for one more fellow spirit with whom to share her special beauty.

Edna Graham had passed most of her fifty-eight years alone. It was not that there wasn't Angie Severance, the English teacher who roomed down the hall and with whom she shared dinner and the movies and student gossip. And Alice Pierce, the home economics teacher who kept them supplied with sweets and frivolous laughter.

But there was a deep passion in Edna Graham which in most humans is tapped sexually or in domestic affection and business. This passion had been channeled to her beloved study. But ultimately, there was never anyone there if she were to say—'Listen to this.' Or—'Look at that.'

Therefore did she watch the Morton girl.

Each day for the first week she carefully set aside a few minutes of the class for conversation with the girl. And was pleased. Their little chats about what Charlotte had seen in Europe, that the girl could understand the intent of Gothic architecture, comprehend the static majesty of Romanesque sculpture, and that she would read a poem for its sense *and* for its craft, thrilled the teacher.

Though she had the beginning work in hand, Charlotte Morton, for her part, realized from the conduct of the class and the little French asides addressed to her alone, that in Edna Graham she had indeed encountered a new standard. She had never sat before a teacher who demanded such absolute precision of performance from a class, and who so clearly loved her subject matter. This woman wanted desperately to communicate her own enthusiasm. Daily she sprinkled the lessons with little intellectual hooks from French culture: "How can a people who have invented so many cheeses be anything but interesting?"

One day she quickly retold the story of *Chanson de Roland*. Another, she read a stanza from Villon in English and in Old French and then told how the poet claimed that it grew so cold in his attic that the ink froze as he wrote. She teased them with the fact that had Charles Martel failed at the Battle of Tours, they might all be Moslems now.

She was pleased when Charlotte Morton brought her father's editions of the *Chanson* and Villon to school for her to see. And best, relying on the footnotes, the girl was trying to read them.

And the two women were delighted to discover in each other a lively sense of humor.

Alice Whitener's parents had taken her out of school for two weeks for a trip to Montreal and Alice reported that she could read parts of a menu and had used, *'Ou est le toilette?'* effectively.

Miss Graham had piped, *"Avec bidet, eh, Mademoiselle Morton."*

On Monday of the second week of school she asked Charlotte to drop by her room after school for a moment.

"Mademoiselle Morton, the powers that legislate some of the value and much of the stupidity in public education have decided that in order for you to receive language credit you must sit in this class for at least two years. That goes for Latin also. Clearly, you do not need first and second year French and Latin.

"This leaves us with two possible courses of action. You can choose to come and sit one hour each day and twiddle your thumbs, score well on all tests, and make an A on the course. Or, I would take pleasure in preparing a reading list for you to pursue throughout the year. I would require of you a paper, short at first, each week, based on the reading. You may feel free to use the class time for your reading and writing. Then each Monday we could meet and discuss your paper and the reading that you have done. I would then base your mark on these weekly papers and our discussions."

"Oh, Miss Graham, of course. I would love that. Not only me, but my father. He'll probably do the reading with me. That sounds great."

"Now, *Mademoiselle,* let me warn you at the outset. I will not be easy. I will keep you reading and writing an hour or so a day. And I will be exacting with your papers."

Charlotte looked directly into her eyes.

"I know that, *Mademoiselle.* I can tell. And you know, you *do* have a reputation. I am not brilliant, *Mademoiselle,* but I can work. I would like the reading list, and I promise to be diligent. But, do *you* mind? Surely it will be extra work for you."

Miss Graham smiled. She thought, *Beautiful child, you do not know what this will mean to me.*

"Not at all, Charlotte. I will enjoy it. Now, I have a small library of my own from which I will loan you books. However, *Mademoiselle,* I shall wring your pretty neck if you return them scuffed or dog-eared, or if you lose them."

"Oh no," the girl smiled. "I will care for them. I'd have to answer to my father if I damaged a book."

They ended the conference by deciding that Charlotte would follow the class when grammar instruction was given if she felt she needed it, then she could proceed with the reading. She agreed to submit a written paper each Friday and confer with Miss Graham each Monday.

"Who knows," said Miss Graham as they walked down the hall, "in a year or so you may be reading Villon in the original."

"Oh, I hope so. Thank you. I'll work. I promise."

Thereafter, almost daily Charlotte was in the teacher's room after the last bell. Sometimes their meetings were academic, discussions on questions which Charlotte would raise. Sometimes these questions were knotty or interpretative so that the teacher would require some research of herself and the girl. But sometimes the visits were social, serious as when Charlotte told her fear of losing her marvelous father to drink—this became an ongoing topic—or, merely delightful as when Blanche prepared a bouquet of late October flowers or a tin of cookies for the girl to bring to her friend. Or humorous as when they discussed the latest antics of the school clowns—Max, Cal and Billie.

The two women reached out to each other. Edna Graham again had someone who would gladly, 'Look at this picture,' or, 'Listen to the rhythms in this stanza.' And Charlotte Morton had a *confidante* whose views she could balance with those of her father and Blanche.

It was not long before Edna Graham realized that this girl brought other superficial but delightful gifts to her life. First it was the day that she dropped her unzipped briefcase in the hall and Calvin Hendricks—in her eyes The Son of Attila— broke from a knot of students, galloped down the hall, and flashing his sunrise smile, knelt, pawed the scattered papers together and with a mock-heroic bow, handed them to her.

Then there was the day when she walked out of school toward home and noticed a mob of kids around an old but newly waxed Pontiac with a fox tail attached to the insignia.

"Hey, Big Edna, come and take a look." It was of course The Son of Attila, braying across the lawn.

She came, a huge, mock frown on her face. Cal had scored his third touchdown last Friday night and his father had added another hundred to the promised sum for a car. Cal had saved one hundred dollars and Max threw in twenty-five.

The result was the gleaming machine before Miss Graham.

Cal rushed to the teacher, took her hand and impulsively led her around the shimmering jewel.

"C'mon, you guys. Clear away so Miss Graham can see. It's mine. It's really mine. Now, is that reality?"

Her frown lost its purpose. She smiled and ooooh-ed and aaaaah-ed and touched gently. She admired as he opened the door, held her ears as Harry James's trumpet blared on the radio.

Then she backed away and truly smiled. "That," she said, "is reeee-al-i-teeee."

She walked to him, grasped his golden curls, pulled him down, and bussed him on the cheek. "It's absolutely beautiful, Cal. Enjoy it. Enjoy it."

Then she jerked his head straight up and hissed, "I am no wrestler, but if you ever call me Big Edna again within earshot of others, I shall with tooth and nail do horrible violence to your person."

"Yessum," the sobered Cal said.

Her smile returned. "Now, drive me around the block in reality."

He did.

At the Harvest Dance for which she was impressed as chaperone, a continuous stream of tall, skinny, stiff, uncomfortable boys, choking on their neckties, approached and formally asked her to dance. Maxwell Compton, William Ennis, the unlikely Jennings Hall, and, of course, The Son of Attila. She knew that they did not want to dance with her, but they did it. And she knew that they did it at the command of the stirring girl with whom she now shared the things that she loved most.

These frivolous events added immense pleasure to the old teacher's circumscribed existence. She knew that Charlotte Morton had put out the word that Big Edna was A-OK.

Of course, it had all depended on the hours that Max and Charlotte spent drilling into his handsome head the preparatory manual so that he could pass the driver's test.

"It was so easy, even a dummy could pass it," then laughed when he realized what he had said.

But they were now mobile. Cal's car added dimension to their lives. They could go down to the river at will, or when finances allowed a couple of gallons of gas. It meant that they could go to Kernston to car races, to drive-in movies, could collect their whole crowd at The Track—the most they ever got into the car at once was fourteen. It meant that early

Saturday mornings, twice in their sophomore year, more often later, they could load up and drive to Chapel Hill for football games. And it meant that when they received their bi-weekly invitations to the dances at the Country Club or hotel ballroom with 'Your date is ——————,' Cal could pick them all up and, with luck, deliver them before the car coughed to a stop after running two blocks on fumes.

And it meant the evenings when Cal would say, "Hell, here it is eight o'clock and I haven't been laid yet." And he and Max would cruise the Mill Hill for girls.

But most exciting, it meant that they could get out to Rabbit Harelson's on their own. None of them ever saw or talked to Rabbit. He was legendary, numinous, perhaps non-existent. He was a bootlegger. Since the fall of Prohibition, wine and beer were sold in the county, but the Fundamentalists had their way with hard whiskey. Hence the stature of Rabbit Harelson. Everybody in the county, including the sheriff's office, knew exactly where Rabbit's place was, exactly how much he charged for a pint of bottle in bond (the gorgeous white likker was now regarded by most as untrustworthy since, during Prohibition, several drinkers had 'got sick unto death'). This was tacit knowledge on Lawyer's Row, the rectory of St. Mark's, the County Court House and the sedate homes on Well Street. Periodically, certain virtuous sources in the community put such pressure on the law enforcement agencies that one of the deputies would have to call Rabbit's establishment and hint that shotgun armed deputies would be out that night. Rabbit would be put to the trouble of shifting his merchandise to another backwoods location until the heat dissipated. In any event, the raids on the bootlegger rarely produced any contraband. Society needed Rabbit as it needed its doctors, its clergy, its grocers, though it was a long time before it would legalize this need.

If Max, Cal, Billy, Tom Kinder and any of the others needed to 'wet their whistles' for one of the dances, for a football game, or for the hell of it, they had to do this: they had to take the Ferry Road two miles out into the country, make a left at Klutz Road and go one hundred yards past the steel county bridge, there to turn off on a narrow, nameless gravel road. After two curves, one left and one right, they would come to a gate in the barbed wire fence which tracked the road. One of the gate posts was a tall, slim, loblolly pine. There they must get out and in the pitch darkness feel the hinter side of the loblolly pine until they found a doorbell button. They could hear the ring from several yards in the pine filled darkness. Then a voice from nowhere, "Yeah."

Whereupon Cal or Max or Billy or whoever would stage whisper, "Pint of bourbon."

In sixteen seconds, a tall lean shadowy figure in pulled down felt hat would materialize.

"Five bucks."

"Right."

A bottle and bill would exchange hands with, "G'night," and, "Later on."

And it was done. And it was then that some of them began to associate fun and excitement with drink, as many of their elders exampled them. And learned to their discomfort that more drink did not necessarily mean more fun. And some never learned that because you possessed a pint did not mean that you had to drink a pint.

For many, it meant weeks in 'jail' because they had thrown up after midnight in their mother's immaculate houses, or had been brought home by Puss, or had got black eyes because they thought whiskey made them tough enough to handle a couple of rednecks at the weekly square dances in the outlying grange halls.

And later, in their senior year, it meant profound mourning as they gave their hearts to the Watkins family when the luckless Blaine, having passed his crisis long after Max, had come to a reckless young manhood, failed to make the curve at the steel bridge, and had totaled his father's car and his own small life.

For Cal, Max and Billy, Rabbit's meant many hours of straightening fenders, touching up the paint, scouring junk yards for Pontiac bumpers, until they finally gave up and began calling it The Wreck, labeling its battle scars after those responsible—Ennis's Folly, Charlotte's Rear End, and Cal's Falling Down Drunk Right Head Light.

To their elders, to Douglas Morton and Blanche and the mothers Compton, Hendricks, Ennis, Winston, Kinder, *et al.*, high school meant motion. It seemed that they had spawned a breed of bug, indeed, properly called 'jitter.' Dancing was as natural as eating. Everywhere, anywhere, any time. The Club, the hotel ballroom, the Morton parlor, between classes in the halls.

It was lovely. It was release. It was sexual. Lounging

outside the drugstore after school, puffing weeds, Ennis would mimic the reeds in *String of Pearls,* Morton would come in with the trombones, Cal with the trumpets, Amy, Tom and anyone else who was around filled out the choruses, and their dah, dah, dah, was loud, balanced, on beat, sharp enough to compel dance—there in the sidewalks, or in all creation.

Sometimes they would retire down the backroads, especially the old Lee Creek road whose pavement dead-ended where the old bridge had been demolitioned. The concrete was still smooth, the creek babbled in the background, and the southern moon rested on the spumes of loblolly needles. Cal would pull up amid the other two or three neckers' cars, turn the radio full, and Smokey, the local DJ, would fill the night with Miller, Goodman, The Dorseys, Ellington—and on the concrete, sleek, lithe bodies would fill it with motion.

It was a great place. After Rabbit's bottle had been passed and passed and at last bottomed up and thrown to the loblollies, and chased with cokes, cigarettes, and coughs, and grimaces, they would take the standard equipment blanket out of the trunk, split up and get down to some serious smooching. The woods were filled with whispers.

"I gave you my Hi-Y pin. Doesn't that *prove* I love you."

"I'm yours from the waist up."

"Listen, I'll bring you my letter sweater, if you'll wear it."

"Not tonight. I've got my friend."

"God, honey, it's so big."

"How in the hell do you get that bra on by yourself?"

"Louise, I really love you. I really really love you."

"Of course, I wouldn't go out with anyone else. Oh, Rich, I was just talking to him. It was nothing. Really. I love *you.*"

"Wait. I've got a Kleenex in my pocketbook."

For a period of six weeks, Cal was stricken in the nervous system by Harry James's *Two O'Clock Jump.* He had to dance. If he were driving, he merely slammed on brakes, flipped the volume, got out, and danced.

Sometimes it came at inopportune times. One night about one-thirty as they returned from Lee Creek he was seized at the stoplight before the town's monument to the glorious Confederate dead. *Two O'Clock Jump* rocked up the town's deserted streets as Cal leaped from The Wreck, knee-walking drunk, dragged Charlotte with him and swung out. Billy, Max, Amy, Louise, Patsy Whitman and Tom Kinder and two others joined, dancing a bacchanal beneath the bronze angel and her beautiful wounded youth. When *Jump* ended, out came the remains of the bottle from under the car seat. It was passed in toast to the angel.

Max considered that the wounded soldier had the look of a man who needed a drink. In two minutes he and Cal boosted Billy up the pedestal where he cradled the empty bourbon bottle between the soldier's musket barrel and the angel's ample breast.

"Give her a small feel while you're there, Billy-O. What a pair of knockers. Heaven isn't going to be so bad if all angels have a set like that."

Billy placed his hand over the heroic sized bosom.

"It's cold and hard, Cal."

"No way to get those steel robes up anyway," said Max.

Just as Billy's feet touched concrete, as Fate would have it—now one of Charlotte's favorite phrases—auto lights passed over the rise at the Square, quickly these lights were augmented by a spot, a rev of engine, and the police car glared at them like a dragon beneath the violated angel.

"What's goin' on here?"

It was Puss and Hefner.

Charlotte, hands on hips, saucy with drink and contempt for the two rednecks, replied, "A harmless revel, officers."

"We'll see about that. Hey, Hendricks, is that you? What are you doing out at this time of night? If Hudson hears about this there's heck to pay. Hey, you kids been drinkin?"

Cal, having scored three touchdowns, was a minor celebrity among those townspeople who regarded last night's score as the only really important thing under the sun. And those who knew, knew that this boy, barring injury, was going to be one of the great running backs in the high school's history. Therefore, they were willing to grant him boyish pranks.

"Naw, we ain't been drinking. You know I wouldn't drink, Puss," Cal, aware of the edge of fame, fell into the easy man-to-man camaraderie the officers would appreciate. "We're just fooling around. Naw, I wouldn't drink. I'm in training. We're just on our way home. Hey, Puss, how do you like the car? It's mine. The old man loosened up. How're you doing, Hefner? Hey, Puss, I sure wouldn't want Hudson to know I was out at this hour. You know how he is about curfew? And we got Jameston next Friday."

"I know you have. Listen, Hendricks, don't get cocky just

because you got loose a couple of times. You got talent, kid. Don't waste it."

Puss fell into the clean-living sermon he would deliver to Cal and Max twenty times in the next three years.

Properly admonished, they did go home.

The angel cradled her bottle for three days, amusing sinners, outraging saints, before the city workers removed it.

"My invitation says your date is Maxwell Compton," Charlotte loved to say when the dance or party invitations arrived every other week. "Hummmm. I wonder what he's like."

"Mine says Charlotte Morton. She's probably some four-eyed, bucktoothed, freckle-faced, chocolate-covered-cherry-eater with a figure like a watermelon."

Then they would clasp hands. Friday night was taken care of.

There began the telephone conversations with Amy, Louise, Patsy, and others about who was going to wear what. Blanche, of course, was in on it. And when the invitations came so rapidly, Sybil Schraeder shared her elegant wardrobe with the excited girl. She even allowed Blanche to hem her gowns the inch or so that was required.

"Why, my beauty," Sybil exclaimed at last one day. "This dress is absolutely perfect. You have grown. Wonderful. Blanche, I don't think anything could be done to make it fit more perfectly."

Sybil would leave Douglas, Spence, Phil and the others in the study with their drink to join Charlotte in her room for the fitting each Friday. If it were a special dance she would take Max's corsage from the refrigerator and bring it to pin on the girl's breast.

"Charlotte, clearly you can no longer wear my sweaters. You'll stretch them all out of shape. You have indeed become a woman."

It was all lovely, dream-like, graceful, or—driven by a jump beat—frenzied. The girls were beautiful, shimmering like underwater hangings as they bent over the arms of the boys, beneath lights filtered through colored balloons from the medallioned ceiling of the old hotel ballroom. Or the Country Club, where light seemed to materialize without source, shadowing the motion out on the wide gallery in spring and fall when the long line of French doors were open to the green and the moon.

Dancing was in her. Music—it was irresistible. She loved when Max, or Cal, or the wonderfully fluid Billy sent her out to turn, to invent, to feel the *feel* of her hips moving contrary to her breasts, her head arced, the lift of her long hair lightly against her cheek, then recalling her to them with the slightest pull of a finger, returning to their arms, merging, turning, depending on those arms.

Charlotte could not stop glancing down at her bosom in the low cut gowns. *I have beautiful breasts*, she thought. She loved to press them against her partners. She could not stop herself. *They want me*, she thought.

She pressed against Cal. She couldn't help it. The strong arm around her caused it. Max she came to, kept coming to, even when the music stopped. He would whisper, "Get away, witch. Everybody will know. I won't be able to walk."

And she would laugh and press closer.

She even did it to Jennings Hall. She knew she could cause him to desire. She could feel it. His chest heaved. She could hear him struggle for breath. She knew that Jennings's conscience would torture him later. *But he can't resist,* she thought deliciously.

Later, tracking disaster in her memory, she would recall the night that she had heard loud singing and clapping from the bar downstairs and how she had skipped down the steps to find the cause of joy. She would remember that Jennings had stopped her at the entrance. He caught her hand. "Charlotte," he said, "come and dance with me."

"What's going on?" she asked, pressing toward the door.

"No," Jennings said, and barred the way. "Come and dance."

Charlotte tried to brush past him. "In a minute. Let me see what's going on."

Jennings, strangely, insisted. He caught both her hands. "No," he said. "Not now. One dance. Then . . ."

She tried to pull away. This wasn't like Jennings. She tried to turn out of his grasp. He pulled her to him. The bodies met. He became taut and held.

"No! Please, Charlotte. I . . ."

She did not understand. The singing and clapping and laughter from the bar became wild. What possessed Jennings? She could not get free of him. For a moment she was frightened. *Did I go too far with him?* Then a flash of anger.

"Jennings, let me go." she spoke evenly.

He straightened and dropped his hands to his sides. She brushed past him and entered the bar. And instantly she understood.

It was the time when her father's drunkenness had begun to move to the outrageous. Everyone in the packed bar was singing, clapping to the beat.

It's me, it's me, it's me
Oh Lord
Standing in the need of prayer

In the middle of the bar floor, surrounded by a circle of wild-eyed drunks, her father and beet-faced Marsh Woods were doing a mock tribal dance to the primitive beat of the clapping. They had already flung off their jackets and were stamping them to the drumming rhythm. With the next chorus off came their ties to be flung on the floor. With the next, they began unbuttoning their shirts. Marsh lifted his head to the ceiling and ripped his open and tore it off. Just as Douglas Morton was about to follow suit, his eyes met his daughter's just outside the circle of singers. He froze a moment. Then he rebuttoned his shirt, smiled across the hands and heads to her, and was content merely to clap and sing and urge Marsh to madness.

Charlotte felt a hand on her shoulder. She looked up into Sybil Schraeder's beautiful, expressionless face.

"Come, Charlotte, let's see what's doing upstairs."

The girl allowed herself to be led up to the ballroom.

"Don't worry, dear. I'll drive him home. He's really in his cups tonight."

"Oh, thanks, Sybil. Thanks a lot."

"You look beautiful. Do dance. Have a good time."

Charlotte leaned against the huge mantel. Pensive. *I'm losing him*, she thought, *and I can't stop it*.

Desperately she sought Jennings. She found him standing with Billy. She walked to him. She took both his hands and reached to kiss his cheek. He recoiled. She was uneasy for a moment, but she held his hands. She looked up into his pained face.

"Oh, Jennings, I'm sorry. Thank you so much. That was sweet of you."

He was flustered. "Charlotte, I . . ." He trailed off. "It's all right. I'd like to dance now. If you would."

He held her at arm's length as they danced. But Charlotte liked that dance with the gloomy boy who had tried to protect her from embarrassment, and who, she knew, respected her father.

11

IT wasn't all dance.

"*On Self-Discipline by Maxwell Compton, Miss Severance, English, Period 3.*"

Max was reading an English essay to them for suggestions before laboriously typing the final draft. The class had read several Emerson essays and had been assigned a five page imitative effort. Max cleared his throat and commenced.

"*Self-discipline consists in the denial of the senses.*"

"*Consists in!* Tsk-tsk," interrupted Charlotte. "Uncle Calvin, Bishop Billy-O, Friar Jennings, methinks yon youth Maxwell doth begin most pretentiously. Think ye not so?"

"Yclept and welladay," spouted Billy, who had just scored 32 on an exam which covered Beowulf, Chaucer, and Shakespeare.

"Odds bodkins and codpieces," said Cal, who had scored 26 on the same test.

"However, it hath a transcendental ring," groaned Jennings. His score had been 98.

"Further. Please note 'denial of senses.' Is not sexual also sensual. And should not we, as yon youth's comrades, aid him in his noble search for discipline. And, therefore, should we not discontinue such temptations as kisses, feels, playful gooses? All for his edification, of course?" Charlotte persisted.

"Oh, shut up will you? This thing is due tomorrow. I'll be up till dawn typing it."

It was also the time of playful intellectual pretension, a time of fatuous precision in dates. A time of knowing that the Children's Crusade occurred in 1212, that Shakespeare and

Cervantes died in 1616, and that Lincoln delivered himself of the Emancipation Proclamation . . . when he did.

It was a time of ept and inept quotation, as when Billy announced that his parents were back from Boston, spoke "of the *wo* that is in marriage."

Or Max of Coach Hudson, "He hears no music."

Whoever did something daring was immediately "the noblest Roman of them all." They were forever coming "to bury someone, not to praise him." And when it rained on a spring weekend Charlotte announced that "April is the cruelest month."

Cal managed to stay even with them by quoting old obscenities, as "If she is old enough to bleed, she is old enough to butcher."

It was also the time of The Great Vocabulary Enlightment. Max carried around a little notebook of new words with which to stymie them.

Romantically, he whispered in Charlotte's shell-pink ear that she *ensorcelled* him.

He was furious when after several trips to the library he had to ask Charlotte how to spell *apnoea*, after she had, with studied carelessness, thrown off, "Compton, if you do that again, I shall commit apnoea."

Max took consolation in informing her that apnoea was medically impossible.

Everyone knew that old lady Severance was a *virago*, that Amy Winston was *hypermamarous*, and that Charlotte Morton was *callipygion*. And everyone, but everyone, knew all about *fellatio, cohabitation, fornication, adultery, incest, cunnilingus*.

Charlotte became the acknowledged Queen of Philology when she ferreted out the word *stercoraceous* from her father's Oxford. It was the jewel which crested her coronal. She used her weapon with enormous grace. She even had Cal ignorantly walking around for three days proclaiming that he was the most stercoraceous cat around. When Max finally told him that it meant having the quality of dung, he actually turned Charlotte over his knee in The Track parking lot.

However, it was the most useful word they learned in high school. It concluded any argument. As Cal put it, "Wow, you can tell anybody they're full of shit and all they do is give you a thousand yard stare. It's great."

Lounging at the drugstore, or on the courthouse benches on Lawyer's Row, or anywhere, a new game developed which rivaled their renditions of jump tunes: giving character to passersby.

"Here comes old Clyde Knob, in town to git the latest copy of *Grit*," Billy said as a farmer plodded by. Thereafter, all rural persons were Clydes.

Or Charlotte would say, "Here comes Amelia Wasp searching for something disagreeable." It was only ancient Mrs. Catherine Whitcomb Julian, widow of the late senator, High Episcopalian, early Daughter of the Confederacy who acknowledged no existence north of Richmond or south of Savannah, tentatively creeping under the burden of years, her straw hat, heavy plaster of rouge and ghastly powder, white gloves, parasol and ropes of pearls. As she finally drew abreast of them, they chorused, "Good morning, Miz Catherine."

She stopped, steadied, worked her head around on its gossamer neck and cheered, "Good morning, young persons."

Moments later, she again achieved motion. Charlotte claimed that she was the town's only true Vestigial Remain, and therefore a respected monument.

She was barely out of sight when came "Hazel Heavytits hurrying to the drugstore to replenish her supply of chocolate-covered cherries." Cal's characters were always graphic.

And there were also Bonnie Loveshoes shopping for the latest tangerine lipstick, and Lance Moonlight, checking to see that Brylcreme impeccably maintained his hair.

There was an endless supply of material, so they played the game all through high school. Indeed, Charlotte played it privately all her life.

There were seasons, even in high school.

Summer. It was South. Sometimes heat had mass. Like walking in warm water. Throat deep. Movement was effort. Or frenzy. But you could plunge into the clear icy water of the spring fed quarry. You could go as deep as you could go and still see forty feet straight down. And you could swim two hundred yards toward the sun. Or the moon. To a sheer granite wall. And truly, if it was the moon you swam toward, you could turn on your back and forget which way was up. And if your head and heart were right, you could swim in stars.

If you walked out in the garden with Charlotte at night, you could have seen her catch a rosebud at precisely the right moment—with a real tear of dew in its heart. You could have seen that, if you were lucky and the timing was just right. And the honeysuckle which was both parasite and paramour to the hedge along the 'tennis court' filled the night air, for honeysuckle is no myth. Neither are the mosquitoes. Some nights, they actually tugged your leg.

The river had rich, bull tallow banks, a deep red found nowhere else in the world. Collards were a modest dull green, spinach and turnip greens vivid, young limas pale, and tomatoes big as faces and red as lust. Some corn was white as girl's flesh on the inside of the thigh, sweeter than a Hershey, and crisper. Spilled, blackeyed peas scatter. You could never find them all. Summer was so lazy and good it died hard. Some people wore shorts too long and caught cold.

Autumn became official on the day that Charlotte ate her breakfast with her school books stacked beside her on the table and the kitchen air was heavy, laden with the rich musk of pumpkin pie. She would have skipped into the warm room and plopped down—to *no* good morning from Blanche, who played a waiting game. It would come to her slowly, leaving a smile in wake of realization. She would rise, put her hands behind her and mince up beside Blanche who was studiously ignoring her. She would lean over the great bulk of shining black woman and kiss a gleaming cheek.

"What fo' you wastin' time, chile. You gonna be late fo' school."

Then the great black eyes would meet hers and they would exchange twinkles.

Then, "Why don' you get Maxwell and Calvin and Billy over heah fo dinnah tonight?"

Or it was official when Blanche met her at the walk with *two* rakes in her hands. The dry, rich, rusty smell of the leaves and the rough, itchy, burlap bags used to make the mountain of the leaves at the edge of the tennis court. Harrison and Hedrick and all their kith and kin worried about just out of reach of the rakes, deploring the fact that perfectly good acorns were going into burlap bags and they would be put to the trouble of attacking and sorting the edges of the leaf mountain.

And the *crepitation*—how Charlotte loved that word!—of the second leaf fall beneath her feet.

But a moment in her sophomore year which she would remember forever because there was living testimony in the yard. She was near the summer house raking when, "Precious! Precious, come here. Quick, girl."

And Blanche came trundling to her, took her hand and led. "Look."

They both dropped to their knees. Beneath the pocked, leprous trunks of their long leaf pines, where only a few leaves had blown, Blanche's rake had uncovered a tiny, waxen, green with cream striations, leaf of a Trailing Arbutus. Tiny, tiny, secretive.

"Oh, honey, I haven't seen one in ten years. They're so rare."

Charlotte had never seen one.

"Oh, look. Here's another. Look! How they hide. Look, honey."

Then another revealed itself. And another, and another. On their knees, the two women found twelve.

"Just you wait 'til spring, chile. Just you wait. You'll see the most delicate little flowers. And you'll just stay on your knees sniffing. They just won't let you leave."

They got ten sticks to mark them off so Mr. Jimmy, the rickety old husk of a yard man, wouldn't step on them.

And the day they had stood hand in hand, perfectly still at sunset, just before going in for dinner, and breathed quietly the last sweet dying gasp of the Ella Agnes. Then checked the dozens of Nandinas for their brilliant scarlet sprays of berries—especially if the perfectly conical Holly Tree was in off year. There must be red berries for Christmas.

And it was also the time to hang the gallery bannisters with winter sweaters for the autumn air to cleanse them of acrid mothballs. And at last, the first fire in the study to dream before. Perfect place to pretend to be studying. She counted the rings on logs—wound up estimating, of course—and pondered all the years and years the flame consumed in so short a time.

Each year there was a real honest to goodness hayride. Sybil Schraeder arranged it. Mr. Jimmy, who, by night's end had snuck and sipped until he was drunk as a goat, drove the horses, also supplied by Miz S. This one was in their sophomore year too. Halloween night, the Saturday after Cal had scored his fourth touchdown. It was Indian Summer. The moon magicked. They sang *Down by the Old Mill Stream*, *Whispering*, *Carolina Moon*, *Standing in the Need of Prayer*,

On Top of Old Smokey. And all night. Billy brought his banjo. Billy could play anything.

It was a 'life-print' night for Charlotte. After the singing, she had flopped over on her belly, swept some tricky twigs from her tickly nose, and drowsed to the sway of the wagon. She was sleepy. That afternoon her father had taken her to the Club courts to work on her serve. The afternoon before they had very nearly lost a doubles match to young Dr. Helms and his wife Stella. It was partially because Douglas Morton had a massive hangover, but also because they had decided to serve to the doctor's backhand in both courts and Charlotte's serve had been so erratic and had such an arc that he was able many times to run around and take it with his really tough forehand before Charlotte could get to the net. So this afternoon her father had laid a hand towel in the backhand corner and Charlotte took target practice. It was the day of the Praying Mantis also.

He had crept out of the chill grass to the warm sun on the clay. Crisp autumn had slowed his metabolism so that he was run down, brittle, and creaky. As they moved around him, he could hardly cause his neck to turn his emerald eyes with their movement.

"Our great-great-great-great-grandfather needs help to safety," her father had said, and the insect did not resist the man's enormous thumb and forefinger and seemed content with relocation against the fence.

Then Charlotte had served 'forty-leven' balls until she was raising chalk with some regularity.

Lousy serve, she mumbled to herself as she gave up to sleep on the undulating hay. Body warmth against her right hip drew her back from the reaches of sleep. Nice. Comfortable. She pressed against it. It pressed back. Then . . . a hand, slowly, an inch an hour, open palm, over the moon of her bottom. Warm. Wonderful. That Cal! Sneaky. He would lift a hand from his deathbed for a feel. Hummmmm. Nice. The big palm was slowly warming her other moon, firmly but gently. She felt its movement, and seconds later the warmth penetrated her wool slacks. Not Cal, she thought. Too subtle. Too exquisite for that savage. Max. Maxwell must be moon-struck. He's wicked as I, she smiled into the fragrant hay. Then over her full thighs to trace her panty line. She began to tingle through the urge to drowse. Then single—almost tickling—finger going where no moonlight could go. She opened and moved to meet, so slightly, so slowly. She couldn't help it. Between sleep and waking she felt her honeycomb begin to give honey. And it was sweet drowsy pleasure.

Then the caressing hand left. She lay moments wishing for its return. She shuffled toward its warmth on the hay. It was gone.

Then she heard Max's voice. "It's a coon, Mr. Jimmy."

"I hopes him ain't no skunk," Mr. Jimmy cackled.

Then it wasn't Max. He was up front with Mr. Jimmy. Cal was with them. She heard him too.

She lay a moment. Then who?

Charlotte sat suddenly and looked around. Nobody was within a yard of her. That is, except Jennings who was resting on his back looking at the moon. Jennings wouldn't, she knew.

She looked around again. Nobody. Now who? Bemused, she lay back. Then she chuckled to herself. She chuckled again before dozing. Funny how her body had received pleasure signals from an unknown touch. She half pondered. Perhaps the body has its own set of terms, completely detached from any other consideration. She had been touched in a sensitive area. That was all her body cared. She could not feel violated. She had enjoyed it. She had to look again. Max and Cal definitely not in sight. Neither was anyone else.

She never knew who. And never knew that Jennings Hall spent four hours that night praying for deliverance from the sin of lust.

And it would not have been autumn if she had not sat the next day, an apron hammocked between her knees for the shells, cracking the pestiferous pecans, walnuts, hazel nuts, Brazil nuts—Niggertoes, Blanche called them—for the six fruit cakes Blanche would soon be baking, storing in tins swaddled in wine-soaked cheesecloth. In fact, every Saturday, she would have to remind Blanche—or Blanche would pretend that she had to be reminded—to open each one, sniff the gorgeous cake musk, and then splash the cheesecloth with the heavy sweet wine so that they could cure properly over the weeks until Christmas.

They talked as they shelled nuts.

"I just don't understand men," Charlotte said, pondering last night, changing the subject from the vegetables Blanche had canned for winter.

Amid giggles, a warning or two, and some eyelash fluttering,

Blanche allowed that men wanted "to get possession of our weensies."

It was all very interesting to Charlotte, this older woman's appraisal, and she was both confused and delighted when Blanche closed with, "Actually, honey. they wants the same thing we does—'cept much faster and for a shorter time, the rascals."

If they were lucky, in winter everyone had to rummage through attics and basements for the little used antique sleds for three or four days of sledding in Wilhelm's pasture on the outskirts of town. Frost flagging their breath, cherry-cheeked, muffled and sniffling, bulky in unaccustomed clothing, they doubled and tripled up on the sleds. Night didn't stop them. It was South. Snow wouldn't last. It must be used before it vanished. All heaving, they pushed The Wreck, skidding and slithering, to the crest of the knoll, turned on the lights, divided into camps and built fires, zipped the hill and fought snowball battles of Trojan dimensions.

Springs dizzied, always have, always will. From every compass point Charlotte's senses were titillated. Rich, earthy odors crowded her. Flat on her face, palms to earth, it seemed that she could feel the urge and press of impulse, of the Coming. Birds were dotty, zinging haphazard song everywhere, a scattershot that demolitioned reason and symmetry.

"Too early!" Charlotte croaked into her pillow, wakened by the shrill urgency. "I hope every worm stays home in bed, dim-wits."

She cried easily, at least once a day. Cal comforted when the two came upon a dead robin. "Easy, Boobs, in six weeks there'll be millions of them."

Despite its wasteful profusion, the brilliant clarity of spring made it easy to think each life singular and irreplaceable. She cried.

And cried when Harrison blobbed his bulk up to the bow of Isola Bella, having wintered well in the Floridas of catfish.

"Oh, you're back, you're back," she bawled, leaning down as if to embrace him—and the whole jeweled river. "I was so worried about you. You're so old and fat. Oh, you're back."

And that first day on her island, feeling naked, had to become naked, sprawled in the dun sand, legs spread and extended into the surface water, already warm beneath the sun that seemed to singe through the still crisp air, so bright that she had to squench her eyes, but so bright that floating mystical spangles crept through her lids and she had to concentrate on one to finalize its shape and follow its drifting path before it vanished and another exploded in its place. It was sexual, the tips of her nipples burning, burning; warm surface water between her thighs, but her heels freezing in the river's remembrance of winter.

Her buried treasure was safe. Childishly, even when a woman, she would check it with miserly greed each time she was there. But the little clay images at Harrison's landing, Coyote and Charlotte as Pallas Athene, had gone into the seasonal drift.

Spring dizzied. Billy planned massive symphonies. Max took his self-discipline paper seriously. He was back to memorizing every major date in human history—this time *seriously*. Returning football punts had secured his manhood. But it had taught him something else: that he was fast. And he had stamina. In spring, Cal turned to track and field events, the javelin, shotput and discus. The mile was the classic track event. Max began to research mile records, thinking. Coach Hudson's record book told him that the North Carolina high school standing record for the mile was 4:17. He began his assault on it as a sophomore, rising each morning before dawn to run five miles. And then at track practice, five more.

He bored everybody to death discussing and practicing his new 'walk,' which he tried to carry over into running. It was a ridiculous little kick as the forward foot went down.

"But if I can just get one extra thirty-second of an inch with each stride, can you imagine how much I would gain in a mile?"

Nobody could.

"Besides you look like an ostrich in saddle oxfords," Charlotte told him.

But in the final meet that year he clocked 4:20.

His new regimen annoyed Charlotte. He wanted to be in bed by ten, even on weekends. Her annoyance became so strong that she slowed down enough to let Pete McCanless, the Biggest Man on Campus, who had begun to follow her around, catch up. This older boy mildly interested her. Max was nearly suicidal when she went to the movies with Pete, when she let him hold her hand after school, and even took his YMCA pin for a few weeks.

"You smooch with him, don't you?" Max accused.

"None of your business. Go run around the track," she retorted.

Pete was her first real date. Movies were nice. It was fun being envied by senior girls. And frat parties at UNC next fall were a real carrot.

Amy, whom spring had driven to buy bras which bunched her breasts into sharp pyramids so that she looked like an armed torpedo boat, was wild.

"Pete McCanless. Wow. What's he like? Ummmm. He must be tasty."

"Hum," Charlotte was noncommittal.

Actually, Pete considered that his role was to overpower a woman physically, kiss with such vigor that front teeth were in jeopardy, and to be a loud 'good ole boy' jock.

After three weeks, Charlotte was disenchanted with the fame he brought her, returned his Hi-Y pin, and gently told him that she meant to keep her panties on.

Max was so happy that he agreed to forget training on Friday and Saturday nights.

This spring, Blanche lost all her clothespins to a brown wren. She left them hanging on the line in the little canvas bag. By evening the next day, a nest was taking form. She and Charlotte could not dispossess the family.

Spring had no visible effect on Cal. He simply went on reacting to whatever moved him. He ran cross country with Max, threw javelin, shot, and hammer with the best in track meets. Maybe spring edged his crotch-craziness a jot on whatever scale measures such things. Warm and wet were quite enough for him. But then, they always were.

"You deserve Venus's disease, you ape," Charlotte told him.

But as Blanche always said, "God takes care of drunks, fools, and little children."

Cal qualified for divine protection on all three counts, and the deity was diligent. He didn't get killed or syphilis.

Time moved, even in high school. One crisp winter Sunday afternoon in their third high school year, Charlotte returned home from a bright afternoon in the woods where she and the others had been scouting for mistletoe, that lovely random parasite which lived at the tops of trees and dared the brave to collect it for Christmas decoration. They had spotted three clumps, she had been roundly kissed under it, and they had marked in their memories the trees which held the treasure. They would be back.

The big parlor was mobbed with people. Two radios were blaring. Charlotte ran in to tell of the mistletoe find and promise sprigs to all. But one look at the faces in the room and she took disaster.

Sybil Schraeder was crying. Sid Jacobson was crumpled on the floor in front of the radio, his face in his hands. Spence and her father were pouring over an atlas spread on the desk. The others milled around, speaking in half-whispers.

Sybil went to her and put her arms around her. "Oh, darling we are in war."

It was December 7, 1941.

Senator Taft and the Isolationists had had their limb cut from beneath them. Not even the numinous Roosevelt could comfort.

Sid and her father looked like tired old men. They had known. Not when. But what. It was written.

Her father showed her where Pearl Harbor was. As she looked, she was told it was flames.

"It's so dumb, I find it hard to think," Sid said over and over again. "What do they think they are going to do? Get on a line and march from California to the East Coast? It's all so dumb. Maybe that's what I really hate about it. It's just so damned dumb."

There came the predictable heroics from Tom Kinder, in whose men's shop the meeting would have taken place had it not been Sunday.

"Well, damn them, we'll beat the hell out of them. We did it before and, by God, we'll do it again."

"Yes, Tom, perhaps we will," said Douglas Morton glumly, "but at a cost so staggering that we cannot even imagine it. It may even cost your young Tommy."

Later, alone in her room Charlotte was filled with a fear and loathing that went to the roots of her being. She apprehended, without comprehending, that something had happened which would alter her life, her world, over which she—and not even her father—had the least control. Walking the chill, bare December gallery alone, it seemed that a huge, crushing, malevolent force inhabited the oaks and skies around her which at will could, in a single, gratuitous gesture, crack the planet in half and demolish all that was beautiful and dear.

The doomsday tension pervaded her high school years. But gradually, like any condition, long duration causes assimilation. This was the way life was. It generated such things as a Victory Corps to which all the students belonged. Its purpose remained nebulous but it gave cause to otherwise idle hours. Both Charlotte and Blanche agreed that their garden was now a victory garden, but the greens and tomatoes seemed, as ever, concerned only in their own brilliant, luscious victories.

For a while, under the enormous canopy of civilian defense, they rehearsed blackouts. The great railway shops and transfer sheds were declared strategic because their destruction would paralyze the entire Southeast. Early in the war there was large talk of Fifth Columns and saboteurs. A small detachment of soldiers was sent to guard the river bridges. A USO club was opened, and a few soldiers from not-too-distant army camps, began to discover the pleasant little town. Once in a while there was outrageous conduct to be forgiven, but mostly the GIs wanted forgetfulness, rest, and the comforts of woman's flesh.

There was the draft. There was gas rationing, though Cal always seemed to wrangle enough gas coupons to keep The Wreck mobile. Charlotte couldn't decide whether or not this was unpatriotic.

Everything was organized. Years later, Americans would look back in disbelief at the effort, singlemindedness, and sacrifice of which the nation had been capable. There were, of course, a few draft dodgers and profiteers. Ernestine Holmes, whose husband owned a small optical factory in town, remarked at the Club one night that if the war lasted long enough, they would be millionaires. But, generally, the nation was marshaled, and the struggle became a matter of time and suffering.

The real cost struck the town only later when stars began to appear in nearly every house window, and when the casualty rolls began to appear. It was then that Douglas's prophesy became reality: victory would cost young men—the brilliant, the stupid, the cruel, the idle, the industrious, the sensitive, the brave, the tender—each holding his singular hopes and dreams, with an indifference so blank and enormous that it denied consideration.

But as the war years wore by, the nation maintained the effort through an abiding belief that to fail would be a final failure. It was not until after the war, when the concentration camps were revealed, that they realized how final the failure would have been.

Periodically and dangerously, it occurred to Max, Cal, Billy, Jennings, and the rest that it didn't matter whether they learned Latin or math or anything else if one was going to be ground into blood and bone mire within a year or so. The pervasive day-to-day living that soldiers must learn had infected them. It was then that men like Douglas Morton were valuable: he could tell them that poems and sonatas and vaccines outlast armies, and that—even in victory—there must be those left who could give it meaning, and that those must have knowledge. They would be the ones who would protect what was truly human in us.

"The only thing that makes our species worth a cosmic damn is art. Politics is a historical disaster. The military, devoted to perfecting murder and destruction, is the sink of stupidity. Art, and I include science under that heading, is the only thing that endures."

Then he would laugh and say, "The river will outlast even that."

In his persistent insistence that victory was not the sole aim of the nation, Douglas Morton had an ally in Edna Graham.

Edna knew that in any argument between a rational man and a brute, the brute would take initial gain because he would resort to out-shouting and then violence, courses not open to the rational person, who would be considering cause and effect. Therefore she was flung into enormous frustration by the war. She saw in her mind the image of her beloved French culture as a flower beneath a lout's boot. She suffered visibly with each day's news. When Paris fell she wept openly before the class. She was like the person in the classical nightmare who knows, but is powerless to speak. She bravely bought her pitiful share of war bonds, and, in small defiance, vowed to teach and teach and teach her gifted few that the mind's candle not be extinguished in her insignificant corner of the planet.

Big Edna was plodding down the halls in the music wing one spring day burdened by the daily news of the steady collapse of Western Civilization, when she heard the tones of one of the monuments of that civilization, Chopin's *Revolu-*

tionary Etude. It broke off suddenly and she heard Charlotte, shrill in praise.

"Zing. Terrific, Billy-O! Right, Maxwell? Right, guys?"

She stood and listened as the piano sounded the long arpeggio runs again—then again. She walked to the door window and looked in. Maxwell and The Son of Attila were lounged against the piano. Charlotte and Jennings were sitting in a student desk pouring over the score. Billy Ennis was at the piano.

She opened the door and stepped in as quietly as possible.

"Hi, *Mademoiselle*," Charlotte called. "Come and listen."

"*Bone jeor*, Big Edna," Cal grinned and grabbed his head as he said it.

"Go on," said the teacher, sitting in the back of the room. Billy stared at his hands.

"Play it for *Mademoiselle*," Charlotte said to Ennis, who grabbed his tie. "He's trying to get perfect *legato* in the runs, you know. And dynamics, like a whisper, then an expolosion. It's hard, because you have to hear every single note and it's so damn fast—oh, I'm sorry. But you understand."

"I understand. Please play, William."

Ennis fired her a moment's glance and grabbed his tie again.

"Come on," said Charlotte.

Billy clamped his lounging lips, sat straight, proving that his curved shoulders were mobile. Cal stuck out his tongue at him. They exchanged smiles. And William Ennis played.

Before her eyes Edna Graham saw the boy she had known for the six months he had sat before her as a psychically wounded, self-committed failure delivering a powerful statement in an idiom over which he was clearly master. Hers was the same revelation as Charlotte's had been.

Charlotte had pled Billy's case to her many times. He was sensitive, intelligent, and gifted the girl had said. It was not exaggeration. The old teacher listened as Billy's fingers filled the room with sound, building tone on tone, releasing before they blurred, trumpeting a figure, whispering the reply, the bass line supporting, moving lightly, or roaring, but always undeniable.

Even Cal's fundamental sensitivity was moved when the last great chords formed, hung, ended. Properly delivered, the warhorse showpiece never failed.

When it was over, Billy shot Big Edna a glance and slumped. She came to him not smiling, but radiant.

"Oh, William, William, wonderful. How absolutely wonderful. Charlotte has told me what you could do. But I didn't dream this."

"Thanks," Billy slurped.

"Play. Play some more."

"*Campanille*," said Charlotte. "Play Liszt's *Campanille*. You've got that in your fingers."

"Oh yes," Miss Graham said. "Yes. Do." And she turned and took a seat again. Charlotte and Max joined her. And Billy made bells, little bells ring clearly around the room.

As the last little bell tinkled, three huge thumps jarred the door, broke the lovely attitude, and Coy Trexler's face, gantried on his vulture's throat, thrust into the room. "Watcha doin', quaar? Playin' Bee-toe-vun?" he croaked with subhuman malice.

Then he swung his glance around the room and met the cold stone of Big Edna's eyes. He was held for a moment. Then vanished.

Edna Graham dismissed him: "We are always waiting for the barbarians." Then, "Well, William Ennis, you have given me much pleasure. At *last*," she smiled. "And I am grateful for it."

She turned to Charlotte. "Do you do this often? Come here and play, I mean?"

"Yes. Three or four days a week. Miss Eller leaves the door open for us."

They assured her that she would be welcome to join them anytime.

Going, she turned again to Billy.

"William, you have indeed given me much pleasure. But you have gotten yourself into a genuine predicament. You have consistently failed my course. Now that you have revealed that you have a brain and talent hidden in your indifferent self, I will not permit failure another moment. You be in my classroom directly after school today. I have horrible plans for you."

"Uh, *Mademoiselle*, I have a dental appointment this afternoon."

"You be in classroom," she said with finality. "It won't take long. The dentist is only going to straighten your teeth. I mean to straighten your brains." She smiled. "Besides, the dentist won't hurt at all after what I'm going to do to you. Charlotte, Maxwell, Calvin, Jennings, deposit him at my classroom at the end of the day."

"Yessum," they chorused.

They did. Jennings and Cal escorted Billy-O, with Max and Charlotte in rear guard, and sat him full of fear and trembling before Big Edna's desk that afternoon.

Miss Graham turned Billy round that afternoon.

"William Ennis, I have checked your records since we talked. You have succeeded in failing every single subject every single quarter since you have been in high school. I should conclude that you are a ninny, or have set out to establish some sort of new record for this institution. Within the last four hours I have discovered that you are not a ninny. Therefore I must conclude that the second alternative is correct. There must be private reasons for *trying* to fail more often and more miserably than anyone in the history of the school. Look at me. I am talking to you. And it is just as well that your friends are here to hear it all. They like you, therefore, there is no reason to be embarrassed."

Billy Ennis squirmed. He perspired. Miss Graham's eyes were a firing squad.

"I will now proceed to ask a series of rhetorical questions which I shall aim at your mind. I do not expect an answer, except in your mind. *Look* at me! Do you think that you gain a comic kind of popularity by failing? If so, I can assure you that it will be temporary, and will change to scorn when your life becomes as dismal as your school record.

"Or, are you merely lazy? Indeed so lazy that you are willing to spend sixty years clownishly rather than one hour a day industriously, as all your friends do. Of course, with the notable exception of Calvin here."

She focused her beacons on Cal.

"Or, are you so disorganized that you are unwilling to keep something like this"—she tossed a small spiral assignment pad across the desk at Billy—"and write each day's work down, then in the evening spend the twenty minutes required to do each assignment, then make a neat check by it. Or write *This stinks* beside it? Or tear each page into four hundred and thirty-two tiny pieces when you have done it?

"Or"—here the teacher paused—"is there some private reason for seeking revenge on your parents and you have chosen failure as the means?"

Her voice had gone soft as she spoke. She waited. The things Charlotte had told her about Billy in the past had been assimilated.

She allowed the silence to hang. Billy was motionless. Then he began to twitch. She knew she had scored, had said what Billy had not permitted himself to think, much less verbalize.

She allowed him to suffer for a moment, regarding the miserable youth with such pity that she felt tears forming behind her firm glance.

"I don't expect an answer," she broke the perilous silence.

Then, "Look at me, Billy. Look. I am an ugly, old woman. No," she held up a quieting hand, "I am. And, Billy, I was an ugly, *young* woman. And, Billy, when I was a girl, do you know whom I wanted to be like? Norma Talmadge—have you ever heard of her? She was a movie star then. Imagine. I wanted to look like, and be like, Norma Talmadge. At the very least, I wanted to be married and have children. It did not happen. And it would have been easy to blame Nature and my parents for not making me sexy."

She said *sexy*, thought Cal and Max. She actually said *sexy*.

"But that would have been the way to become bitter and wasteful of any possibility of joy. So I looked about and found that Nature or my parents had given me brains. My brains told me that the sounds of French and Latin intrigued me. I opened myself to that intrigue. I won a scholarship to college. So, while Norma Talmadge might dance with John Gilbert— he was another movie star—hummmm—very handsome, almost as handsome as Calvin—I could begin to read and hear Racine and Corneille—and, later, actually *feel* with Villon. For most women, I'm sure, it would be a poor exchange."

She chuckled, and looked out the window. Then went on. Still looking out the window. The five students before her now knew that she was sharing her most secret heart with them. Even Cal felt the tension of being honored.

"Later, when I had to earn a living, I learned that I could teach. Though you will find it hard to believe, with its many difficulties and disappointments, teaching has been a great delight throughout my life."

Here again, she paused, still looking out the window.

"And young people, believe it or not, from this vantage, I am not at all sure I would exchange my life for that of Norma

Talmadge. For though it has been less exciting, I am not at all sure that it has been less rewarding."

She sniffed, turned to face them.

"So, William, we must all do what we can, and not waste ourselves for whatever mean reasons we might invent to justify failure."

She looked from face to face.

"Now, I could *not* teach Calvin. But this does not mean that Calvin does not excel. Billy, have you ever seen him wrestle? You have seen him on a football field. And he is wonderful to watch. He can just...*do* it. With grace and power. *And,* William Ennis, he does not do it by inventing excuses."

Cal was embarrassed, and pleased to be so. For the first time in his life, a teacher was not deprecating him. He loved her madly.

"Who knows what Jennings will do, with his methodical, thorough mind? And Maxwell? And Charlotte, with all her gifts?"

Now she became deadly, frowning serious and turned to Billy.

"And you, William Ennis, will begin being a student tomorrow. I have considered approaches to revising the mess you have made of yourself thus far. For heaven's sake, look at me. It's not easy, but, for a moment, it's important." She smiled. Ennis looked.

"You are going to become a student tomorrow—not just in French, but in all subjects. Because everyone who is truly worthwhile is interested in all creation. Einstein, our greatest scientist, writes like an angel and plays Beethoven quartets for pleasure. Galileo claimed that his theory would be believed because it was so beautiful. *Beautiful,* of all things. Leonardo knew and did everything. Beginning tomorrow, you are going to be a student in French, English, science, history—and, God help you, shop."

Billy was squirming like crazy. He loved her but he'd be damned if he was going to study. He was wrong.

"I have devised a scheme which is going to be a combination of games and fear. I will explain the games in a moment. The fear is coming from me. Beginning tomorrow, if you fail to hand in an assignment, or to recite when I call on you, as I will every day from now on, I shall pour such a torrent of abuse on your head that you will wish to evaporate. If that doesn't work I have a very muscular friend on whom I shall call." She winked at Cal. He growled appropriately.

Billy tried to smile, but it didn't work.

"Now the games. You, I perceive, are interested in sound. I saw that this morning. You are more keenly aware of sound than any of us. From bird songs, to the horrible sounds Calvin makes when he scratches off in The Wreck, to the sounds of irritation in my voice. All of these carry meaning, and, as I say, for you, probably more keenly than for any of us. Correct? Now language is sound, carrying meaning, and having rhythms and pitches, just as does music. And language has symbols for those sounds. Just as musical sounds are symbolized by notes, so language sounds are symbolized by the alphabet. In combination, notes make a chord, or a phrase. In combination, letters make a word. Billy, do you, by any chance, recall the little talk I made on symbols the first week of class?"

"Yessum."

"Don't lie to me. You haven't heard a word I have said in class since September."

"No, *Mademoiselle*, I do remember." Billy was looking at her and clearly telling the truth. "That was interesting."

"Ah, good. Very well, combined with the game of checking off each assignment in that little book, I want you to make a game of the sounds of French words. When we make French sentences, I wish for you to listen closely for the rhythms, for each tongue has its own musical personality, and your ear will be sensitive to that. Now, you will begin by memorizing the sounds of French—though you have probably already picked that up merely by being in class. Then you are going to read aloud each day in class and at home. Just read French sentences for sound. Soon, you will not be able to bear not knowing the meanings of the symbols which you are sounding. And you will learn French. Your assignment for tomorrow is on the board. Copy it instantly. Tomorrow I shall examine that book to see that it is checked off. Then I shall call on you to recite. If you cannot recite, you had better have a strong ego indeed. Because I shall yell at you so long and so hard that you will wish to crawl under your desk. Is that clear?"

"Yessum."

"I also notice that you failed history. Some questions. Why was the Beethoven *Third Symphony* called the *Eroica*? For what English king did Handel compose the *Water Music*? Do you know these things?"

"Well, Napoleon, I think. Uh, I . . ."

"Hummmm. Well, how did the *Archduke Trio* get its name? When did Bach live? Who was on the thrones of England, France, and Spain and what wars were being fought then? Ah, why was the *Revolutionary Etude* so called? What were Vivaldi's dates? And Scarlatti's? And what was going on in the world when they lived? What centuries encompass the Baroque Period? Do you know that?"

"No, mam."

"You see. You are ignorant about that which you are most interested. Now does the game I have in mind become clear?"

"Yessum."

"Yes. And it makes sense, doesn't it. You can begin with music, your central interest. And from there, you can go to the events, the kings, the wars which relate to it. A tide of history caused Beethoven and the Romantic Movement to appear—if I may say it that way. And the Romantic movement affected literature. In music and literature, the Classical Period gave way to the Romantic Period. Now you see. From music, you can go to history and to English. Now, I suggest you start something like the chronological tables that Charlotte tells me she and her father keep. Has she told you of them?"

"Yes," Billy allowed. "I've seen them."

"Sure, Billy," Charlotte said. "That's what we'll do. I'll help. Won't we, Max? Ennis, you're gonna pass, in spite of yourself."

It wasn't easy. Schedules were set. Charlotte and Max determined that each evening from 8:00 to 9:30 Ennis would be seated at his desk—at first, to be seated was enough. They alternated nights calling. "Are you studying?" they would ask. "If you're lying, Cal will give you knots tomorrow."

Each day in class, *Mademoiselle* would snatch his assignment book and check it. Any deviations, omissions, derelictions would indeed bring a merciless torrent of abuse from her. Each day she would make him read and recite. It was awful at first. But she patiently spooned, actually put words on his tongue, until he began to gain grasp and confidence.

Each night he would sit fretfully at his desk, at first doodling, twisting his fingers, sweating. At last, giving up he would open his books. Gradually he began to marshal his attention, ten minutes a night, then twenty, and finally he could go through most of the assignments.

"Very good, Billy," *Mademoiselle* would murmur. Then make him read French aloud.

Max and Charlotte fired French at him at lunch, after school, dancing—all the time.

Gradually, Billy's brain began to take over. His native curiosity began to supplant his cultivated laziness. And anyway, he preferred to study rather than face that wild Graham woman when he hadn't.

The music game worked. He memorized composer's dates, linked them to historical dates, learned of new composers, wished to hear their music. He researched the development of the piano. What he did spilled over into history and English.

There were frequent lapses at first. One does not gain discipline overnight when one has spent years developing excuses for doing nothing. Frequently, *Mademoiselle* reduced him to tears with sheer rhetoric. Sometimes Cal was called upon to give him knots. Once when he busted a ten minute vocabulary quiz, Charlotte ignored him for three days. One night in rage and frustration he scrawled across a page in his assignment book *Big Edna is a witch* and forgot to tear it out of the notebook. The next day she snatched it as usual and saw. She was barely able to keep from bursting out laughing as she turned to the next page and scrawled *Billy-O is a Mickey Mouse*.

For the first time in his life, Ennis squeaked by every course. His mother's fawning joy was nearly indecent.

Billy was pleased. He felt himself becoming part of the world, not a curiosity. His success was partly due to desperately clinging to the schedule demanded of him by Max and Charlotte, partly to the fact that his curious mind had been forced to crack, then spring open to possibility. And largely to that good and true woman, *Mademoiselle* Graham, before whom no one wished to be unworthy.

By the time he graduated, Billy was an 85 student in all areas except shop. And this small success and small gain in self regard helped Billy through deeper pain.

High school is a time for the first pairing of male and female, beginning with kissing games, dancing close so that one's breath comes hard. Billy's friends were occupied by the ineluctable thrill of undressing their first girl, of the first awesome touch of woman's flesh. The difference was consuming. These girls with a thin layer of silken fat beneath skin more smooth than powder. Their heady scent. The enormous power of an impulse that could cause Amy Winston to mar Cal's back with her nails, could cause Jane Lea to cry out and go unconscious for a moment.

On the Lee Creek nights Billy soon found himself unaccountably alone with the moon, listening to the crickets and the giggles and sighs.

When he walked behind Charlotte and Cal he perceived that he preferred Cal's long stride and flat bottom to Charlotte's swaying, rounded, ample bottom. He listened with wonder as boys reported the astonishment of dreams which left them tingling and wet with their own first sperm and caused them to make their own beds quickly in the mornings to avoid embarrassment. These dreams did not happen to him. He worried. He was different.

He was the best dancer in the school. He preferred the jump tunes where he moved free of his partner. His fellows wanted what they called belly rubbing, free tit, and when the girl got excited, triangle to triangle. Billy shuddered when he was with Amy Winston and a slow one came up. He found that he must hold away from her sweaty bosom. Walking arms across with Charlotte and Max, he could affectionately lay his arm across Charlotte's slim frame, but Max's hard shoulder set longing through him.

Charlotte was sensitive to this difference. Several times in moments of triumph or joy she had leaned to kiss his mouth, and had felt him stiffen and withdraw involuntarily. Then give his cheek. She understood that he could not kiss her friend on the mouth. It was not lack of affection for her, she understood.

The only time he came to her arms, came willingly, out of sheer need, was the most horrible night of her young life. It was the night after he had decided to tell his feelings to a fellow, to acknowledge to another human being that he too had need of love, of physical contact, of the new-found joy of touching flesh to flesh.

He could not have chosen worse, for he chose the one who was least equipped to give sympathy. He chose Jennings Hall.

12

JENNINGS Hall always was the most enigmatic figure in Charlotte's circle. She could not say that she liked him. Nor could Billy, Max, and Cal. But no one could say that they did not like him. He had come to them with Billy, as extra baggage. Somehow Jennings was always simply there, as was earth and sky. Perhaps it was his absolute dependability which accounted for it. Charlotte decided that he had never been truly a child.

Everyone acknowledged Jennings's scholarship. Every year throughout his academic career, which carried all the way through medical school, Jennings was first, or within a point or two of first, in his class in every subject. This too was enigmatic to Charlotte and Max, also pursuing excellence.

Jennings was not brilliant. At times he seemed dull. His speech patterns were slow, as if even the simplest decision—whether or not to have a soda—required consideration. Certainly he lacked boldness of thought. Unlike Max, he could never attain that free-flight of the mind which could leap to large concepts, accruing every possible shading and tone that was suggested. But Jennings controlled his mind absolutely. Confronted with a problem or assignment, he pursued it until each detail was mastered and each question followed to its farthest, final conclusion.

Physically, Jennings grew and grew and grew. He finally stopped at six feet three inches, but he remained long and stringy and never in his life reached two hundred pounds. To everyone's surprise, he had privately approached Coach Joe Hudson four weeks into the freshman football season, and asked permission to join the team. Hudson, who believed that every boy should be given a chance to grow into his conception of manhood, gave the boy the equipment, expecting him to drop out in a day or so.

But it was not in Jennings's nature to drop out of anything. For the first two years Jennings drifted from position to position. His height suggested an end, but he was not a natural athlete and he wasn't fast. At last, after Hall had

217

become too big to sit on the bench of any high school team, Hudson tried him at center and Jennings, with customary tenacity, set himself to become the best center his body would allow. It was one of the luckiest choices Hudson ever made.

In the eighteen games Jennings played during his last two years in high school he only made four bad passes from center, and three of them were to the long punt formation. But he brought more. He could pass the ball and then set his blocking assignment better than any center Hudson had ever coached. He did it with such efficiency that he became no longer a post for a double team block, he became the *only* blocker, an achievement almost unknown in high school football. In doing so he freed a guard for another assignment, which as much as anything else, accounted for Hudson's successful running game those two years.

Everyone who knew Jennings at all knew that he was a religious fanatic. This fervor had led him to Billy initially. He did not know how to press, for to press was offensive. But he did persist. He perpetually suggested that Max, Cal and Charlotte bike with him to every single church function, youth meeting, and evangelical rally. He kept a Bible in his school locker, and he read it. He persuaded Coach Hudson to allow him to lead the team in the minute of prayer before each game. He begged Charlotte to help him organize a Bible study group in school.

He did not anger them with his obsession. He never argued, and he never pouted at their automatic no thank yous. But he always pointed the Way for them, just in case.

Jennings actively pursued the Hound of Heaven. He came from a strict Baptist family. But at the age of thirteen, he came under the spell of Reverend Kirby Frye of the Church of Christ Four Square. He fell in with that small fundamentalist sect when one of his colleagues in the Youth for Christ told of having attended a Church of Christ Four Square service and swore that he had actually heard a member of the congregation speak in Strange Tongues. Jennings had to see. If God revealed Himself in such a clear way in Concordia, North Carolina, that revelation would not escape him. He went on his bike the following Sunday morning.

He heard no strange tongues that first Sunday. But he

heard Reverend Kirby Frye. For three hours. There was no reversal.

Nobody knew how old Kirby Frye was at that time, probably not even Frye himself. He was a tiny, fragile man. His clothes seemed strung on a frame of single strand wire, and strung on perfectly straight lines and angles. But it was his coloring that struck viewers first, and continued to strike. Kirby Frye was orange, a deep pumpkin color orange which went rust around the edges, no matter from which angle he was taken. And that orange hue possessed a numinous, translucent quality. It seemed that the source of that light burned inside his bulbous, hairless head and hands and that it passed through the membrane which was his skin. His skin, except on the dome of his skull and the linear bridge of his nose, was cross hatched with trillions of perfectly straight needle lines as if his Maker had shaped a three dimensional dry point etching of a bull tallow clay. His eyes were flickers of light between the slits that were his lids. Search though one might, one never quite fixed the eyeballs that caused that flicker and was never sure whether they were in constant darting shift or whether they looked out from a darkness which one could not look into.

Kirby Frye had been a dirt farmer on the banks of the Yadkin River all his life—however long that had been—until that dead-tired, heat-heavy day in mid-August when the heavens had cracked open and God had driven sun shafts like eagle's claws into his skull with such force that he could not move until sunset, until he had taken his Call into every tissue. People said that Kirby Frye had not spoken above twenty words in his whole life before that day.

People who heard him speak thereafter never forgot it. Charlotte Morton was one of those people.

Charlotte Morton was the ambush in the path of Jennings Hall's journey to salvation. She vaguely perceived that Jennings was drawn to her in some way that went beyond their mutual affection for Billy Ennis. She never confronted that perception, but it played about her consciousness when they were together. She assumed as he did, that it was concern for her soul.

During the summer after her freshman year, she agreed to go with him to a service one Sunday when she was so angry at Cal and Max she declared hatred for them both: they had departed on a no-girls-allowed canoe trip down to Kinston

Dam with Whitlow Manson. Jennings asked her for the forty-sixth time to come with him to a service and hear a certain Reverend Kirby Frye. He had told her many times how he had begged Frye to truly baptize him, to give him the rite of re-birth, and that Frye had steadfastly refused for a period of six months, a testing period in which the boy had proven his devotion. And she remembered the day when the solemn boy told her that 'It had happened': he had been baptized at the old quarry under the hand of Reverend Frye. He had spoken of the event with such gravity that she perceived her stoic friend was capable of passion, but that its nature was different from any she had known before. Thereafter, when she argued religion with him, as they did often, she never did it lightly. And never playfully referred to him as Friar Hall again.

That Sunday, lured by the intriguing possibility of hearing Strange Tongues, she biked with him the six miles to the little, white, four-square church that stood on an unpaved, county road. Hard and rooted the church glared among the loblolly pine stumps where the forest had been cleared for fifty yards on every side. Jennings explained that this congregation was new, that Reverend Frye was a prime mover, a true evangelist. This was his fourth founding. Once a congregation was formed, he moved on, so hungry he was for souls. If he spoke first to a new congregation of two in a dirt farmer's home, the next time he preached there were twenty. The following Sunday, there would be fifty, and so on until ground was cleared and broken and another four-square house of God plumbed and planted.

They parked their bikes and walked through the little clusters of the congregation waiting for the signal to enter and worship. Jennings exchanged "Good morning, brother" with many. Charlotte realized that she was being inspected by the congregation, as a stranger, she thought. She learned that she was wrong when one of the brothers called Jennings aside and whispered with him, and Jennings returned, and begged her to wear his jacket over her little cotton dress even though it would be uncomfortable. It was then that Charlotte crystallized her awareness of otherworldliness in the congregation. The women's dresses were quaintly old fashioned. All had long sleeves and the skirts came almost to their ankles. And she noticed that not a single woman wore make-up or any other ornament. She quietly removed the silver barrette that held back her own hair.

An aura of expectancy hung in the hard morning sunlight. When they spoke at all, the people spoke in low voices, and their eyes constantly drifted from the church door to the tall loblolly pine ten yards inside the clearing at the rear of the church. Beneath it stood a tiny singular figure. He was dressed in black pants and a white shirt, buttoned up to the neck and down to the wrists. He stood unnaturally straight, feet six inches apart, hands down the seams of his pants, unmoving, indeed, totem-like. Charlotte was struck by the deep almost orange color of his small round head, which seemed to take and return the brilliant sun.

"That's Reverend Frye," Jennings whispered. "He doesn't like to mix with the people before the service. I think he is preparing, receiving."

After another spellbound five minutes, Charlotte saw the small white shirted figure stir and begin slowly walking toward the church. His stride was mechanical, his face straight ahead, and he did not swing his arms. His hands remained fixed at his sides.

The church door swung open a moment after Reverend Frye began his approach, and the congregation swiftly entered. Jennings nodding frequently to others, seated them three benches from the front and they sat in the stillness, waiting. The interior was perfectly austere. New wood smell, unpainted beams, unpainted benches with crude backs, six unpainted chairs on the small raised platform at the front of the auditorium, and an old black upright piano against the wall at front completed the house of worship. Three darkly-clad men sat near the piano. One held a trombone, another a guitar. The third sat with his hands folded.

She was astonished when she noticed Reverend Frye seated in another straight-backed chair on the opposite wall. She had not seen him enter. He had materialized. He sat rigidly, hands dangling from his apparently immobile arms. His gaze was straight ahead.

A plain fat woman in a gray tent of a dress scuttled up to the front, mounted the platform, and seated herself at the piano. Then the man who had been sitting with his hands folded rose, walked to the center of the platform and led them in brief prayer, asking Jesus to allow his servants to receive the message this day. The fat woman threw her weight into the piano, the trombonist raised his shining cone, the guitarist found the rhythm, and for fifteen minutes singing, clapping, and praising God rocked the sturdy little church in such extremity of volume that when it still stood after the near hysteria was over, Charlotte allowed that this church might be eternal.

Then silence.

After the silence had begun to bear on the nerves of the congregation, Reverend Frye rose mechanically and strode to the center of the platform and stood as he had stood beneath the pine outside, feet apart, hands at his sides, chin raised so that his gaze went over the heads of his congregation to some point of contact near the roof. So he stood in the perfect silence of the church for fully five minutes. Above such silence, high in the beams, the business of a wasp or a stray horsefly became known to the host below. No human stirred. And Charlotte realized that she was attending the arrival of a word, some word, perhaps The Word.

At last the little orange faced man broke his trance-like pose and, beginning at the back of the room, began to traverse his eyes up and down each row of stalls, giving the impression that he was looking into every face before him individually. Charlotte felt herself stiffen to receive his gaze as his traverse approached the row in which she sat. She found herself entering a semi-trance, her eyes guiding her brain into a study of the small man-like creature who so perfectly commanded attention. Her mind followed the instruction of her eyes and formed an image of a monstrous homo-botanical mutation. It was a root vegetable shaped like a man, an organism which had turned and burrowed its tap beneath the earth, down down into the dead bull tallow, tenacious in its search for sustenance—a turnip or radish or, no, carrot, yes, a carrot for the color won out. Ring on ring the vegetable had spiraled down—water! water! water!—earth giving before its dogged single-minded thrust. Then must have come the lure of the sun, and the freakish growth matured, rounded, orange, finely etched by the needle edged filaments of the soil which slowly gave before the impulse. Perhaps in pounding rain the organism emerged, teetered, its gleaming top surprised to find member arms and legs, struggled for and took perilous, hesitant motion, and as it stood before her, still struggled for mastery of unfamiliar motion in arm and leg.

She formed her image when she faced him directly, his traverse of the row coming at last to her place. She faced him candidly as she did all beings. They regarded each other for a long moment. At last the face snapped the wire between them and he moved to Jennings. She thought, was not sure, that he returned to her for a moment before crossing the aisle in his mechanical traverse.

At last, the tiny mutant faced those who attended him. He straightened and again fixed the slits that were his eyes on the wall at the rear of the building, above the heads of those spellbound before him.

He spoke.

The voice pained Charlotte. It was a child's—no, it was an imperfectly developed mechanism. Not weak. Not unclear. Crystal clear. Brittle unto shattering. Resilient, never to shatter. And pitched from just inside the razor thin lips, or hung deep in the bird-thin rib cage.

The matter did not register. The manner was all. Afterward Charlotte could barely remember a word spoken. She realized that with slight idiomatic differences—she had to follow closely to determine that 'Devil's Pasteboards' were playing cards—she was listening to precisely the same imprecations against the same sins that were being delivered in the same clichés in thousands of look-alike churches throughout the South in that moment. The tiny talking vegetable began with gambling, moved to sloth, to drinking, greed and money worship, to dancing, to the painting of faces, and climactically, to carnal sin. Trivia, worn out cliché after cliché, childish rote, each documented by book, chapter, and verse. She no longer doubted Jennings's claim that Frye had the entire Bible by heart.

Yet Charlotte sat entranced by the torrent of trivia. The manner was all. At first she thought it was the voice quality, the waiting to hear it shatter like broken crystal, or vanish in cobwebs of the narrow chest. Not so. Though the thirteen year old girl could not have said it, she apprehended that she was listening to a man, who, though he demolished the grammar of English, could marshal every persuasive device of the language. Reverend Kirby Frye was one of those natural rhetorical geniuses who are the bedrock foundation of fundamental religious ecstasy.

Frye went to the rhythms of English as naturally as a calf moves to the teat on the banks of the Yadkin River. He was

223

master of *tempo*, machinegun syllables fired from tongue's tip, then paced so slowly, so firmly, that the words yearned to fulfillment. He could stretch a period out like a snake . . . then snap it with three syllables. When he wished speed of delivery, he naturally fell into the present participle form and i-n-g verbs would zing through the air. And Charlotte's knowledge of Latin marked this clearly—Frye could pile up tri-colon after tri-colon, clauses, phrases, neatly, cleanly, one after another until the brain was dazzled to find that he had suspended his verb until the very last word. This was especially effective when the verb was one of pain—"*. . . and there, brothers and sisters, eternally you will b . . .*" the first consonant impulse, then a ten, twenty second beat pause, the voice lowered to a whisper but pitched in treble, ". . . burn" or ". . . sizzle."

After Frye had held his listeners for above an hour—Charlotte glanced at her watch—he suddenly fell silent. In the middle of a sentence he bit off a word, and stood, his eyes still fixed on his point above them.

In a moment the silence became a presence. Charlotte perked in her seat, expectantly. She felt Jennings stiffen next to her. The silence bore on. Wasp or horsefly paused. She shifted her eyes to the bare windows where the sun poured through in shafts, shimmering in the imperfect glass. The distant pines took no motion from the clear blue beyond. For a moment she imagined that the entire planet attended a gasp in the universe, waiting for the next cosmic breath to resume life.

Charlotte became aware of movement to her right. She turned and looked past Jennings. An old relic of a man in the row just in front of where they sat began to twist his rawboned head on the slack-skinned neck which supported it. Finally the head, bald except for a thin dead-straw coronal around his ears and above his red wrinkled neck, rolled across the bench back and the mouth opened and he uttered a gutteral "Aghhhhhhh."

Then he rose, head still hung backward loosely, eyes clamped, and spoke the Strange Tongues.

Awful, Charlotte, ears tense to ringing, strained to hear. It was language. It clearly had rhythm, a syntax, breath signs, but it had no meaning. He spoke in periods, paused, and went on. The sounds were distinct—but gave no meaning! Chilled, she grasped Jennings's hand.

Another voice rang out to the left and rear of where she sat. Shocked, she turned and saw another rawboned man was standing, eyes clamped, erect, speaking. He spoke English. She heard. She understood.

He spoke four sentences.

"Mind your lives. God's wrath beneath palm trees. The Chosen People shall suffer unto death. They shall return home."

He stopped and stood.

Then the first speaker resumed, again in Strange Tongues. More sentences. Charlotte snapped her head back to him. He stopped, seated himself, head still lolled back.

The second voice resumed. Charlotte understood. He interpreted.

"The Chosen People shall return home. Mind your lives. Judgment is at hand. Mind your lives."

He stood for a moment, then slumped back, disappeared among the heads across the room.

Charlotte snapped her eyes back to Reverend Frye. He was motionless, exactly as she had left him. The deep silence hung for a moment, then the wasp or horsefly in the ceiling resumed tentatively.

She slumped in her seat, released. Reverend Frye's voice drew her back. He continued the sentence which had been interrupted and went on with his message. It was the final phase of the sermon.

Ultimately, the sermon was a sexual experience. Frye had hoarded carnal sin until last, and Charlotte had never heard women's flesh evoked so sensually. The preacher's images, pauses, tone qualities graced the temptation to lust with an almost tactile quality. Charlotte felt the syllables from Frye's tongue slither between her bra and nipples, play delicately about the edges of her cotton panties, and the girl felt sexual oils join the dampness of perspiration. The sins so deliciously extolled could not be canceled by the preacher's promise of damnation and Charlotte imagined that many of the plain women present would undress slowly before their husbands that day as they changed into their cooking clothes.

Throughout the sermon little moans and cries and mutterings issued from the congregation. Once, during the lust passage a woman behind her screamed so suddenly and pitiously that Charlotte started. But there were no more Strange Tongues. Now she would never deny Jennings's account of involuntary incantations rising from a member of the congregation at some moment when all passions converged.

When Reverend Frye released them at last, Charlotte went limp. He had wrung them out. An Altar Time was called but she was barely aware when individual members of the congregation rose and walked up beneath the plain, black cross to reinstate commitment or beg forgiveness.

When at last Jennings took her arm and led her to the door where she was stunned by the brilliant sunlight, she was electrified by a violent, crushing seizure of her hand. Her eyes dropped to her hand whose bones were being ground together and saw the orange fingers which grasped hers were smaller than a child's. Her eyes leapt back to his face, expressionless, expressing all, as he regarded her from the slits which were his eyes. Neither spoke.

The bike ride home was dream-like.

Thereafter, she would find herself studying Jennings Hall, this slightly repulsive being with whom she had shared obsessive moments. What was the nature of this boy who sat beside her bent over a French book, or who, helmet in hand, dragged his stooped frame from the field after forty-eight minutes of bruising headlong contact? This was the Jennings who had pronounced the dear, defenseless Billy an 'abomination on earth.'

Billy had crumpled in Charlotte's arms the night Jennings had broken him, confused by the difference he now knew existed in himself, baffled by the fact that what everyone on every side told him was exquisite pleasure was repellent in some inexplicable way to him. He now saw that nearly every act humans commit was predicated on the attraction of male to female. How could he act, or exist in this world?

He and Charlotte had talked around this before. He knew that Max and Cal intuited his difference, and tacitly avoided anything that brought it to realization. He knew that they treasured him for other reasons, largely brought out by Charlotte. But suddenly he was overwhelmed by the massive sexuality of the world which surrounded him, cut him off, and aside from the sensitive few, despised him.

For three hours Charlotte held him, comforted him, reassured him of his worth, of her love for him.

She brought it out into the open finally and clearly.

"Billy, you are queer, aren't you?"

"I—I think so," he sobbed into her shoulder.

"So?" she whispered.

He sniffled.

"Billy, could you change?" she asked naively.

He could not answer.

"Billy, Billy, change—or don't change," and she held him. And, "Billy, you can try with me anytime, anytime."

Her candid offer touched his core. But his mother's bony, dry smothering breast, giving a haze of sickly sweet powders, came to him. And repelled.

"I told Jennings." His whole body shuddered.

"He said that the Bible said I was an abomination on earth."

He left her that night skewered, writhing in pain, but certain of her care, clinging to her reassurance that somewhere in his abominable being there was value.

The next day she sought Jennings. He came. He too was suffering.

After school they sat, or paced as they had done before in the wide music parlor.

"Oh Jennings, Jennings, it's Billy. Our Billy."

He was on the wrack. He knew—had grappled with, had prayed against, hour by hour—her argument that revelation was revelation for one man at one time only. And her demands for better proof and for mercy.

Now the two young people were on other ground. The dear, comic, talented, pitiful person of Billy Ennis.

At last, he turned from her to gaze out the window. His trembling as he stood, hands clenched at his sides, drew her sympathy. Never had she seen Jennings so passionate. She could actually hear him struggling for breath.

"Charlotte," his voice broke as he spoke her name, *"I will do God's will*. I have sworn. *I will do God's will.*" He was gasping.

She gasped herself, frightened. He was swaying before her.

She walked behind him and put her hands on his shoulders. She was silent for a moment, then she cut him down like a reed.

"Jennings," she spoke softly. "Of course. In so far as you can determine that will."

He stiffened, then went limp. She had hit the mark. She had gone to the very heart of his obsession. *In so far as I can determine that will*.

She walked beside him and took his hand and led him close to the window.

"Look out," she whispered. "It's so big, and creation is so various. Oh. Look, that spider, here on the sill. And that ridiculous squirrel. Your God can tolerate them in his creation. Not someone as dear as Billy?"

"They cannot think," Jennings sobbed. "Billy knows. Billy can choose."

"That too is God-given. Thought is God-given. Isn't it all God-given in your view. And Billy's—thing. God-given too, isn't it? Would he choose that? Would he purposely cling to it? It's killing him. You should have seen him last night. Did we, you and I, choose?"

Tears were running down Jennings's cheek.

"I must go, Charlotte."

He turned and walked out of the room.

"Jennings," Charlotte called. "Have mercy. Think, Billy is very dear."

Just after six that evening, the telephone rang. Charlotte answered.

"Hello, Charlotte, this is Mrs. Hall. My dear, is Jennings there by any chance?"

"No, Mrs. Hall, he isn't. He was here for about fifteen minutes after school, but he left."

"That's very strange. He hasn't come home. His father and I are beginning to worry. This isn't like him. Do you have any idea where he can be?"

"No, I don't, Mrs. Hall. We had talked. I think he was slightly upset with me when he left. But I can't imagine where he went."

"Oh," the mother said. "Charlotte, I'm sorry to hear that. He's very fond of you, I know. Charlotte, I don't want to pry or intrude, truly I don't. But would you tell me this much? Was your quarrel concerned with religion? I don't really want to intrude."

"Oh, it's all right, Mrs. Hall. But, yes, it was religious, in a way. Yes, I think so. But it was more a discussion. We didn't really quarrel."

"Oh, my dear, I thought so. Charlotte, Mr. Hall and I are devout people. And, of course, we want Jennings to be. But, Charlotte, I wish you wouldn't mention this, but we are beginning to be concerned with Jennings. Has he spoken to you of a Reverend Frye? Since he began attending that church, well...it's reached a point where he could damage his health. He literally spends half the night praying. And...but I don't want to trouble you with this. Please, Charlotte, call if you hear from him, or from anyone who knows where he is."

Charlotte promised, wondering.

At ten-thirty, the door bell rang.

"It's Jennings, Precious. Can you come down? He says it's important."

When she skipped downstairs in her robe, her father, drink in hand, said, "He wouldn't come in. He looks terrible. Let me know if there is anything wrong."

She stepped out on the porch.

He came to her looking drawn and weary.

"I've been talking to Reverend Frye. Charlotte, he told me to look into my heart and God would put the answer there. I love Billy too. I'll...well, I'll try to explain to him tomorrow."

She knew that he had been on his knees for hours with Reverend Frye, without dinner.

"Charlotte, thanks. I...well, I'd better go. My folks are going to kill me."

"Oh, Jennings, bless you. And bless Reverend Frye too. Hey, listen, your parents are wired. Is it OK if I call them and say that you are on your way? Hey, my father will drive you."

"No. I've got my bike. Yeah, call them please. I'll be there in ten minutes."

"Right. Thanks again, Jennings. See you tomorrow."

"Thanks, Charlotte."

She called Mrs. Hall. At Charlotte's delicate suggestion, the anxious mother promised to feed him and warn him never to do that again, and let it go at that.

God-given. The chance in biology. Charlotte pondered the gifts and blights of people she knew. Pleasant contemplation for one who was tall, slim, beautiful, intelligent, and sought after.

I am lucky, she thought.

"You are like your mother in many ways," her father said, drawn into the contemplation. "There's some of me in you too. But I think you are more opinionated than either of us. God-given? Yes, I suppose, in a way, whatever God means. Does it create a debt? Of course. But the only way I know to pay that luckiest debt is to live richly. Live fully. Be excellent in what you do. Yes, great gifts create great responsibility. It's a hard question worth a lot of thought."

Clearly certain persons were born with gifts and circumstances that no amount of hard work or virtue could attain. *Justice exists only in the minds of men*. She pondered selection, or election. The blind luck of it all. Her beautiful Max, becoming all a man could wish to be. Cal, the lucky, the happy in merely being. Amy, friendly, open, happy, boring, desiring only to be desired. *Mademoiselle* Graham, altogether lovely, but partially unrealized because of her striking physical ugliness. But dear Billy, the marred. What could have changed him? Nothing, she knew. Nothing in the world. Coy Trexler, Jr., who never had a decent impulse, whose only pleasure derived from another's pain. Jennings baffled her. Something in him required a God who would seize him and shake him like a rag doll.

She always played Devil's Advocate with him.

"Jennings," she would say, "you are becoming a fanatic."

"I hope so," he replied. "One cannot be too fanatic in performing God's will."

She could not be cynical with him after the day he had bicycled six miles to spend hours on his knees with that preacher in his concern for Billy.

She knew he was forever lost to God on that February Sunday that Reverend Frye allowed him to assist in baptism. It had happened on the day after Cal had suffered his worst shoulder separation. During a wrestling match. Cal, going into a takedown, the arm full out and taut, had gone down squarely on the shoulder, and had howled in pain as he writhed on the mat. He was taken to the hospital, had it popped back in, and spent his first Saturday night at home. The arm became a painful joke. Thereafter, it jumped out in football games and Max would have to run over, set his foot in Cal's armpit, and tug the arm back in. Even Charlotte learned how to do it, just in case.

"I'll look up your dress while you do it," Cal would laugh.

It could happen twice in the same week, or once during a whole school year.

Ecstatically, Jennings had told Charlotte that night that he was going to bed early, for tomorrow he would bike out to the quarry to assist Reverend Frye in his very first ceremonial service to his stern God.

"Bike to the quarry?"

"Well, my parents are in Atlanta this weekend," Jennings said. "Besides, I don't care for them to know about it. You know."

When Charlotte woke next morning, she saw ice on the birdbath beneath the gallery. Jennings's God had caused the temperature to plummet abnormally that night.

In her role as Mother-to-them-all, she called him, "It'll be postponed."

"Oh no. You know Reverend Frye."

"For Christsakes, Jennings, it's twenty-eight degrees outside. The birdbath is frozen."

"Baptism is a thing which can't be put off, Charlotte. Things can happen."

"Well, you can't bike out there. You'll catch pneumonia."

He was, he said.

She immediately called Cal who said that his shoulder felt lousy, but that she and Max could use The Wreck. She wondered if Jennings would be corrupted out of Grace by riding in that chariot of sin.

But Max picked up the car, then Charlotte, then the grateful and genuinely touched Jennings. "If only you could see your way to join us," he said.

That day Charlotte and Max sat in the car parked at vantage on the stone rim of the great quarry and watched as a congregation of forty or fifty souls knelt on the glacial rock slabs in prayer before Reverend Kirby Frye. After the prayer Frye and Jennings, hand-in-hand, stepped down, granite slab after slab into the freezing crystal water and began receiving initiates. Jennings steadied, and handed them over the treacherous rocks to Frye who performed the immersion and blessing.

Neither she nor Max would ever forget what they saw that day. Their stoic friend stood chest deep in icy water and aided each devotee to his baptism, then aided their return to the open armed congregation. They were young and old. Jennings actually lifted an old grandmother from the platform rock and gave her to the chest-deep little preacher who tenderly immersed the gray head. He took and held small children as their blessing was pronounced. The initiates, seized with paroxysms of shivering after immersion, gathered arm-in-arm to watch the washing of their fellows.

And it went on and on. And the little preacher and the unflinching youth stood in the icy water.

After ten minutes, Charlotte lunged across the seat to the door.

"I'm going to get him," she cried. "He'll be frozen!"

Max held her. "I don't know," he said. "Charlotte, I don't know."

After twenty minutes, he had to restrain her.

"Max, he's God-eaten! He'll kill himself!"

"Listen, that little old man is in that water too."

Charlotte fixed on the glowing head of Reverend Kirby Frye. Could he feel? Was the mutation complete with nerves? But yes. Look into your heart, he had told Jennings. Twice she was sure that the strange head screwed round on its neck and gazed up the precipice where she sat. Expressionless.

Fools! Fools! Fools! her brain screamed.

In another ten minutes it was over. After a final prayer, much embracing, the crowd ascended the irregular slabs of marble.

Charlotte leaped from the car, taking off her coat as she ran towards Jennings. She flung the coat over the stooped shoulders and, hugging him, walked toward the car.

They put him, dripping wet, between them. He didn't speak. His face was serene. Charlotte noticed a gleaming disc of ice on one lens of his glasses. A splashed drop had frozen.

She was rubbing him and crying, "Oh, Jennings, Jennings."

At last he was able to say, "I'm all right. I'm fine."

"To my house," Charlotte ordered. "As fast as this crate will go."

Home she marched the tall, soaking wet boy in, upstairs to her room, ran out and returned with her father's robe.

"Get out of those clothes quickly. Max, run a hot tub."

She bounded downstairs and made hot tea.

And she burst into the steamy bathroom, where Jennings, his parts covered, looked for all the world like an eastern monarch, a king of the rainy country, at his ceremonial bath.

"Drink this." She handed him the steaming cup.

He looked at her for a moment.

"Drink. It'll warm your insides."

"How are you feeling?" Max asked.

Hall considered a long moment, as usual. Then, "Charlotte, Max, thanks a lot. For everything. But don't worry. I'm fine. In fact, I've probably never been so fine before in my life. I am so fine," he said, staring into the steam.

They believed him.

*   *   *

Thereafter Jennings was drawn by stronger currents to Charlotte. She had shared vital moments of his young life.

They remembered often the Strange Tongues, the prophecy they had witnessed. Jennings told her that some of these—he would not allow the word *possessions*—Strange Tongues had been recorded, had been studied by philologists, and that they remained inexplicable.

Though religion brought Jennings Hall the only ecstasy he would know, it also brought him the most profound pain. For Jennings Hall confronted problems squarely, and even as a boy, he faced spiritual crises. Charlotte, his Devil's Advocate, was his testing ground. He worried about trivia, such as drinking milk which had been delivered on the Sabbath and gambling as redistribution of wealth.

But his most tortuous crisis, one which never left him, was the oldest problem, the one faced by every devotee—the Nun's sin, pride. His efforts to rise to a rarer spirituality demanded that he periodically stop to take stock, to ask if he was, indeed, purifying himself in some kind of measurable calibration. If he found, as he did periodically, that he was wrong, that he was directing poor, human intelligence on the divine and that error had diverted his course, he tried to make correction.

But this is to make assessment. If assessment was promising, if progress was calculated, he took pride. And pride is sin.

"I can't seem to avoid it, Charlotte. If I believe that I am perfecting myself, I am proud. I can't seem to separate my joy from pride, no matter how hard I try. Then I become arrogant. Forgive me, Charlotte, I try to fight it. I sometimes feel that I am superior in my holiness. I just can't . . ."

She could not help him. The problem was part of the process, indistinguishable, inseparable.

Charlotte realized that Jennings truly suffered as he sought his answers. She could not know how much the boy who vowed to do God's will would struggle with that vow throughout his life—or how profoundly it would affect hers.

13

IN a broken field, under a punt or a kick-off, cutting back through a hip-wide opening in the defensive line, Maxwell Compton had become a thing of beauty. He had a marvelous gift for gauging the relationship between space and motion. He had speed, poise, and change of pace—a 'dancer's gift,' Douglas Morton called it. Max brought an edge of excitement to high school games of their third and fourth years because each time he laid hands on the ball he *could* get away and, given half a step lead, nobody in high school football was going to catch him.

Maxwell Compton had fought his short, crucial battle for self-confidence and he had won. He was so grateful for that victory and so confident of his own resources that he grew into a beautiful, generous spirit. This generosity carried over into every area of his life.

In huddle he would say, "Uncle Calvin, our beloved alma mater hath need of four yards for a first down. If you don't get them for her, I'll let the air out of The Wreck's tires. Jennings, supply an opening for yon ape. Fourteen on three."

And Cal would get the four.

Max loved the feeling of comaraderie among those who hit and were hit together, between those who counted on each other's strength and guts for achievement, even in a silly game.

If one man says to another, I want you to get knocked down to give us four yards, and that man does it, regard grows. Charlotte was aware of this, and it was mysterious to her. It was not a part of the female ambience. Physically she and Amy competed, not cooperated. She knew that Max and Cal shared a bond from which she was excluded. She had tasted it playing tennis doubles. But where it involved hard, bruising body contact it gained another dimension. This small but persistent aspect of life was unavailable to her. Girls, of course, had different bonds. They shared the mystery of menstruation. And the danger and promise of pregnancy. Both more profound, but both, ultimately, individual encounters. Charlotte gained a low-level jealousy of masculine fraternity.

That canoe trip, for instance, annoyed her. Afterwards, she would not have exchanged her visit to Jennings's church for anything, but she snapped her resentment at exclusion. And she knew, knew! *knew!* that whore-hopping Calvin Hendricks and Maxwell Compton spent many Friday nights cruising Mill Hill getting laid.

Well, she wasn't *sure*.

No, she *was* sure, damn them.

They were.

The exquisite mystery of woman's flesh possessed Cal and Max as Jennings's God possessed him. What would she be like? This one? That one? And what does a woman think, look at, when she's mounted? What? What are they really like? It drove them. And that *feeling!*

Cocksters, Cal said. That's what they were. Out from under the seat would come a pint bottle. After two drinks, they *were* cocksters, for all they knew.

Most of the time, late night found them drunken *potential* cocksters, considering themselves lucky if they had gotten conversation, receiving saltines and chili and coffee from Gloria at the Pullman Cafe.

But sometimes they scored. After all they were locally famous. Almost every Saturday a picture of one of them was in the paper during football season. They were handsome. They were fun. Cal had native boldness, delivered with such charm that it disarmed. Max, courtly, more reserved, had wit and gallantry.

The girls would usually agree, if they agreed at all, just for a ride. The rest came easily.

First they always tried the bus station. The mill shifts didn't change until eleven. Twice the bus station was lucky. Once there were two girls from Virginia returning to a Mobile war plant after a trip home. They had four hours to wait before spending the long night on a bus. Sure, they would take a drink with these kids.

"Now, how old are you?" Max's girl said to him as they sat on a blanket down by the Steel Bridge, passing the bottle and smoking cigarettes.

When he told her, she said, "You're cute. C'mon."

That night they swapped off and both had both. Then they had a dip in the river.

The second time was near the end of their senior year. They had checked the bus station. No luck. Had hurried to be at the mill for the release of the second shift. No luck. In fact, had been told to go home and get their diapers changed. They had hung around The Track. Cal even hopped a few cars to help out in the rush. On the way home they checked the bus terminal again and arrived just when a bus did. The station was mobbed. All chairs and benches were littered with sleeping service men. A pretty girl in a dark blue dress struggled with two small bags and her purse. Max took one and held the door for her. There was nowhere to put it down and he followed her around as she pitifully scanned the hopeless, garish station.

"Thank you. I guess just here," she said shyly. They stood in the middle of the station. She glanced momentarily up at him from large dark eyes. The dark hair surrounding her sweet face was in disarray. He was touched by her helplessness.

"How long do you have to wait?"

"I suppose I'll have to check. You never know these days." Again her glance met his for a moment only.

"Go ahead. I'll watch your bags. The ladies' room is over there if you wanted to know."

She smiled faintly, without looking at him.

"Hey," he said. "I'll get coffee. Sugar and cream?"

She smiled again, over her shoulder. Her mouth made thank you.

Cal stood with the bags and he took her coffee as she stood in the line.

"Thank you. You're very kind," she murmured.

At last, she learned that her departure time was six-thirty-five. It was now one-thirty. She slumped. She had been on a bus for eighteen hours.

Max and she stood and chatted for a while. Her name was Joan. She was on her way to meet her husband, a soldier at Fort Jackson, South Carolina. She had been married eight months ago, just four days before he was drafted. She lived with her parents in a small town in Ohio and was a junior in college.

Max offered the car, just to sit in. And a drink.

No, thank you. And she didn't drink.

236

But she followed him to the wall where they could lean when a space came empty.

She was going to be a teacher. She hated the war. Max told her he was seventeen.

You'll soon be in it too, she sighed.

At last, she accepted the seat in the car outside. She looked as though she had to. He carried her bags. She didn't want to keep him up all night. Weren't his parents worried?

No, he was staying the night with Cal, whose father was a railroad official and was in Atlanta for a week. His mother too.

She sat between him and the yawning Cal, who had kept out of this one because he sensed that Max was touched by the girl.

At two-thirty Cal snored.

After glancing at the bus terminal, at the soldiers lounging outside, she said all right. She would ride with him to take Cal home. But didn't he want to go to bed himself?

At Cal's house she relented and went in. Cal went to bed and they made coffee.

Yes, Ohio was nice. But the war was over everything.

Finally, she couldn't keep her eyes open any longer, and she faded away against his shoulder on the couch. Max didn't breathe for fear of disturbing this—this lost child.

She slept quietly for half an hour and then stirred. He leaned and kissed her on the forehead. He couldn't help it.

Her eyes closed. She raised her face. He softly kissed her mouth. She raised to meet him. They kissed again. She opened her eyes and for the first time looked steadily at him.

He got up, went to the kitchen and heated the coffee. He was surprised when she came behind him and put her arms around his waist.

"You want to make love to me, don't you?"

"Yes."

She sipped some hot coffee in the silence.

Then, she took his hand and they kissed. He led to the bedroom Cal had assigned him. They held each other again, and then began to undress each other.

"I've never done this with anyone but Paul. We did it six times before we were married. We had four days before he left."

She lay down across the bed artlessly.

They were very clumsy. She helped, but he had more experience than she.

They loved briefly. And then held each other for an hour. She napped peacefully twice. Max listened to her breathe. Wondering.

Then, as dawn began to feel its way, they dressed. Max thought how soft she was without clothes.

Sitting to put on her shoes, she whispered. Aloud, but to herself, "I'm crazy. What have I done? Tomorrow night I'll sleep with Paul."

She looked up at him, clasping a shoe, "You'll all be dead in a year anyway."

She was crying. "I'm sorry. I don't know . . ."

They held each other before they left the house.

"Oh, Max. Maxie—do they call you Maxie?—I can't be sorry it happened."

On the way, through the dark, silent streets, she said again, "Tomorrow night I'll sleep with Paul. I'm crazy. You're nice, Max."

You'll all be dead in a year anyway, Max thought as he drove. Tonight he *knew* the war.

At the terminal she took his name and address and number. She would be coming back in a week. She would call him.

She didn't.

If she was the one who lasted longest in Max's memory, Geraldina Lowder was the one he and Cal most frequently hunted out. She educated them. They met her through Whit. When they drove him home from school one afternoon, she stepped out of her house to go on the second shift.

Cal was driving slowly down Whit's street simply because he could never remember precisely which house was Whit's. On the Mill Hill, all the houses looked exactly alike, white clapboard on some blocks, two story on others, set ten feet back from the streets. The mill had built them in the days when the mill had its store, extended credit at outrageous terms, and literally held the workers in bondage. Those days were over now, but the hum of machines still stung the air twenty-four hours a day, and though conditions had improved, many of the older men—the lint heads—still died coughing, their lungs too clogged with cotton frize to get enough air to keep alive.

The houses declared life a dullness. Declared universal sameness. There were the inevitable suspended swings and straight-backed rocking chairs on the porches. There were huge, hard-packed, red clay patches around the wooden steps and in the small yards—for grass lost the battle here. Children were stepping stones, six or eight with barely a year separating their ages. But there were always geraniums, that brave blaze on the spindly stalk, nonchalantly stuck in a coffee can. The plants gave the impression of dying from the bottom up. But how the flowers shone. Some of the porches were fired as if their scarlet were the last color in earth.

Geraldina, lunch in hand, had eyed The Wreck inquisitively as Cal slowly cruised the street, hoping that Whit would indicate the house without his having to ask.

"Whitlow," she sang out smiling.

"Miz Lowder," Whit said.

She was twenty-seven or eight, tall and slim, with mouse colored hair and forgettable fair features. Geraldina was all-in-all undistinguished. Even her breasts under the T-shirt could be forgotten, and she did not have the mighty hip flare that Cal so admired.

Cal came to a stop. Whit had signaled that his was the next house. "Where're ya goin'?" she asked leaning on the car.

"Just coming from school. Going to work?"

"Yeah. Where else?" She leaned in and looked at Max and Cal. "Hi."

"This is Cal, and Max, friends of mine. We were on the team together. This is Geraldina. She lives next door."

"They're cuties. Oh yeah, Max and Cal. The stars. Listen, I gotta run. It's five of three." She pushed off from the car.

"Hey, we'll drop her," Cal said to Whit. "Hey, we'll drop you. We can go right by the mill."

Whit stepped out and she slid in beside Cal.

"Real service." She looked Cal over, then turned and inspected Max in the back seat. "Hey, I haven't been in a car with two such cuties since the flood."

"Keep talking and we'll be by every day," Cal said.

"Yeah. Well, it's around 'leven that I need two cuties."

"Two cuties and a pint?" Cal asked.

"That sounds like the way to end the second shift," she reached over and put her hand on Cal's knee. "My old man's in the Navy. Ain't seen him in nine months and don't have no idea when. Couple of young 'uns like you could turn my head."

Cal said, "We'll be there at eleven sharp. With a pint."

She laughed. She laughed easily. "Listen, honey, I'd probably tear you two up, it's been so long. And, I am married. I can't let none of these people round here get to talkin'. My old man'd swim the Atlantic to tear me up."

"We could park a ways off."

She turned and smiled at Max. "Think we could give each other some good stuff?"

"Yeah."

She cocked her eyes at Cal. "Listen, if you want, be here at eleven. Listen. Park over yonder under them trees. Now, listen, honey, if some others are tagging along, I can't come with you. 'Cause, like I said, I can't get in no trouble. So don't get mad now if I just walk away. But if I'm alone, I'll come and jump in and we'll sail away. OK?"

She jumped out. "Thanks. Maybe I'll pay you back tonight?"

"We'll be here."

And they were. She skipped across the street. Max jumped out and opened the door and she slipped in. Cal drove.

"Whooooee," she said. "How're you doin'? I was thinkin' all through the shift, I hope them two do come. I'd like to strap pleasure all around them skinny young 'uns tonight. And here you are."

"Right," Cal said. Both of them had had erections since three o'clock. Nothing could have kept them away.

"Drink?" Max offered, reaching under the seat.

"Oh yeah, boy."

"Want a chaser? Coke or something?"

"Wait a minute. Just let me light a cigarette."

Max lit one for her. Then one for Cal.

Max watched her as she turned the bottle up, dragged the cigarette, then shivered.

They passed the bottle. Cal smoked, drank, drove, and tried to look at her.

Twice they passed the bottle, it burned going down, glowed in their stomachs.

"How old are you guys, anyway? Are you Whitlow's age? Oh, listen, Whitlow don't need to know about this. He knows my old man and all the family. OK?"

"Scout word of honor," Cal said.

She laughed again. A good gutsy laugh. They would hear it often. And it was always good to hear.

"God, let's see what old Geraldina's got here." She put her

hand in their laps. Both at once. She laughed again. "Two real good bulges here. Ooooh, they feel nice."

Laughing all the while, she unzipped them both and freed them. Then she truly laughed, as the car lunged down the highway. "I swear I never had two things more alike in my hands before. God, I been tossing in my sleep for nine months. And here I am with two pricks at the same time. Don't worry either of you. I'll take care of you both."

She began to pet, fondle, and laugh.

Suddenly she really laughed as Cal had to jerk The Wreck back on the highway. "What did you do all over my hands? I think you wuz ready as me."

All three roared.

"You're Max? Max, you're gonna be first so's he can get his giz up again. This is what I like, young, dumb, and fulla cum."

She was wonderful for them. Gutsy, earthy, laughing, simple, enjoying their young hard bodies perfectly. She did need. She did them both twice, three times a night. She had no regrets, no sense of sin.

At least once a week for two years, she would skip into the car, drink, prepare them, deliver them. It was so utterly simple.

They were lucky in Geraldina.

But neither of them would forget that night that they were parked near the phone booth at Clint's Drive-In pouring liquor in their cokes.

"Huh-uh," Cal said.

Max followed his glance to the phone booth. Two young black girls were faking a call, glancing out of dark eyes, inventing movements, giggling.

"Need some change?" Cal called.

One of them sidled over to the car. "Whadcha say?" she giggled.

"Well, we thought we'd pull down the street about half a block. Why don't you stroll down? Course, after you made your phone call."

She looked around to see if anyone was noticing. "Well, we'll see."

Cal pulled out and slipped down the block and parked. Both of them were scared. "Jeez, what if somebody saw us?"

Both knew that neither whites nor blacks would take kindly to such a sight.

The girls were just as anxious.

"Where ya want us?" one whispered.

"In the back seat. Hey, stay down, huh, 'til we get out of town."

Neither of the girls wanted a drink. Max was wondering if they were younger than they had thought. He asked.

Both were fifteen. They were Erma and Alice. They hadn't done anything like this before either.

"Ain't you outa town yet?" Alice asked from down under.

"Yeah," Cal said. "OK. If we get a follower, duck down again."

Max turned and looked at the girls. They were both pretty high school girls.

"We's just on the way home from Youth Meetin'," Erma ran on.

"Won't your parents be expecting you?"

"Naw. Not right away. We told 'em we's gonna stop off at Court Street for sumpin' to drink."

"Who's gonna be with who?" Alice asked shyly.

"Let us see something. Then we can decide," Cal said. He flicked on the ceiling light.

"Whatcha wanna see?" Erma asked. She was clearly the instigator.

"Whatcha got?"

"You ever see a black tittie?"

"No," said Max.

"OK," said Erma, who had on a button blouse. She showed. Cal drove with difficulty.

Erma was pretty. She had very pointed nipples.

Alice had on a pullover dress so she couldn't.

"I'm not ridin' around naked," she said.

"Let's see your pussy," Cal said.

All four were feeling very sexy. It was forbidden and exciting.

Alice was bashful. She quickly upped and downed her dress. Her thighs were full and smooth. Little, white, cotton panties kept Max from seeing all, but he had seen enough.

"Alice, OK for me and you?"

"I guess so," she said. They held hands over the seat.

Erma was bolder. She leaned over. "Hey, driver, I want to see your white swan. I ain't never seen one of them."

Cal and Max roared with laughter.

"Calvin, I didn't know you had a white swan."

Cal pulled off on a country road, then into a lane under tall pines between two fields.

"Oughta be OK," he said. "Erma, baby, I'll give you a white swan for two titties."

Max and Alice had the car. Alice, shy still, finally slipped out of her white dress and Max laid it with care across the seat. He took off his shirt and pants. They talked. About school. About the war. They touched each other and made friends.

"I sure hope you like me," Alice said.

And she asked it over and over again as they made love. He liked her and told her.

All the way home she asked, "Did you like it?"

After they dropped the girls a few blocks from their home, Max and Cal reflected.

They were drinking coffee from Gloria's bar in the Pullman Cafe.

"You know something. I think they did that just because Erma wanted to see a white swan. She just kept playing with it and rubbing my belly in the moonlight."

"Godamighty. I'm still nervous, Cal, do you realize what would have happened if we'd gotten caught. By some redneck out there in the country?"

"Yeah. I sure do. Hell, I'm glad old Puss and Hefner didn't see us. You know, they're always stopping me anyhow just to shoot the shit."

"Oh shit. I can't even think about it. Can you imagine what he'd have done to those little girls?"

"Yeah. Well, how was Alice?"

"Good. Shy. Scared. It was pitiful how she kept asking me if I liked her. Hell, I don't think she enjoyed it at all, for worrying."

"Well, Erma had a good time. She doesn't give a shit. So did I."

"Cal, I liked the way Alice looked. She was OK. It's too bad she couldn't relax."

"So?"

"Well, she said, 'I ain't never gonna see you again, am I?' Cal, I'm still shaking. I am not going through that nervous wreck business again. No matter how horny I get."

"Me, either. Goddam. What if Puss had come around the corner just as they got in? Whew. Hey, you don't think we got burnt, do you?"

"Hell, I don't know. No. Alice was too shy to be spreading much. Hell, that Alice was sweet as a woman can be. Little white panties. She was so smooth. Cal, hey, was Erma as good as that Sue? In Atlanta?"

"Nobody is as good as Sue. But, Maxwell, Sue didn't tell me I had a white swan."

"Right. And everybody ought to be told that once in their life. Right?"

"Right."

Nobody in school ever understood why Max periodically called Cal the White Swan and why Calvin Hendricks blushed when he did.

Max wished Alice well, but he never wanted to see her again. He was too scared.

Thus did Charlotte, denied *macho* fraternity, fume and feel neglected, excluded, put upon and lightly regarded.

14

"HE *is* like the David," Charlotte thought of Max when she saw him walk from the water to the bank at the river, or in demi-light in those times when she waited to take him in love. At seventeen, Max was poised at the Michelangelic moment between youth and manhood. A flicker of movement, running, lifting the canoe from the water, leaning toward Edna Graham with a question on a French construction and Charlotte thought, *he has become a man*. But licking an ice cream cone at the pharmacy, or writing on the light panel backstage at the high school auditorium, "Calvin Hendricks is really Mickey Mouse badly disguised," she would think, *he's a bad little boy*.

Max was moving, learning, searching, making mistakes. He was a senior. Decisions loomed. He was as disciplined as Jennings Hall, but he was open to more options which made him a butterfly in a luscious garden. He must choose a profession. He must decide what to do with his life—*in case he wasn't dead in a year*. Joan's words echoed in his mind.

During the last six months of high school, Max chose, finally and definitely, eight occupations. First, he decided on forestry. He would be a ranger. After all he could not walk down Lee Creek without investigating every bush, tree, and tadpole encountered. Next he decided on architecture. Immediately, at Douglas Morton's insistence, he began to study Alberti, Bramante, Bruneleschi, Wren, and he became the only person in the town, with the exception of Charlotte, who knew Frank Lloyd Wright.

Then he had his Hemingway and T. S. Eliot period. Even his themes were bad imitations of Hemingway or eclectic as if he were trying to draw everything he had ever heard or read into a two-page English theme on Milton.

But then history seized him. After all, didn't he know every major date in Greek and Roman history. And he had made a good beginning in Latin. That was it, at last. He would be a Classical historian. He started looking at the Greek alphabet. This led him to consider archaeology.

From there he turned to medicine. Charlotte killed that. "What do you wanta do? Spend a year cutting up old dead bodies?"

He was learning, searching, making mistakes.

And all this under the canopy of war—and the sentence that Joan had whispered.

Douglas Morton was his *confidant* and adviser but he was no help in this. "Max, I've lived half a century and the only thing I know is that I don't know a damned thing. Especially about people."

Max pondered people. Mr. Morton, for instance. In a town which valued money and last night's score above all, how did this man happen? Coming from a small, jingoist, middle-American town, Douglas Morton was completely sophisticated, in the broadest sense. He rejoiced in diversity, embraced all men, all *ways*. He was an aesthete—Billy the musician adored him—yet he had been one of the best tennis players in the state, and his fistfight with Puss Hoffman was legendary. His mind went everywhere. Every topic Max ever brought up, Mr. Morton knew something about, or, at least knew where to tell him to go to learn about it.

And yet this man, this complete man, had been sinking

into alcoholism for years. He could understand it in someone as empty as that useless Mr. Marshall Woods. But Mr. Morton?

Sometimes Douglas Morton spoke of a Cosmic Depression. Max didn't understand. Here was a man with every attainment Max could imagine. Yet it did not protect him from an addiction that was going to destroy him. Perhaps, Max intuited, it was the cause.

Max compared him with his father. Driven to choose, he would choose Douglas Morton every time. His father was a solid, successful, pious man who ran a bank, could be kind, could be hard, was a community leader. But he was joyless in a sense Max found hard to define. Douglas Morton, for all his failings, had known and caused intense joy. And at his cynical, drunken worst, he still communicated a vital life force, a sense of awe, which Max apprehended, without quite comprehending.

> "Here's to rape, riot, and revolution,
>   Vice, crime, and the eradication of virtue.
>   May prostitution prosper,
>   Son of a bitch become a household term,
>   And fornication be taught in the public schools."

It was the great rolling voice of Douglas Morton, his glass raised above the constellation of glasses about him in the Club bar only last night. He and Charlotte had joined the laughter Mr. Morton's toast had caused.

A half an hour later, they had sat with the entire Club bar, spellbound and listening.

"And on August 31, in the year of grace 1862, on the command of General Robert E. Lee, attacking at dawn from the vantage of the woods in the left flank, Longstreet hurled the gallant Confederate forces into the fray, outflanked, outfought, and overwhelmed the witless Yankee commander and his numerically superior rabble. And in a battle of a mere six hours' duration concluded a complete rout of the barbarian forces. On that day the Army of Virginia took an unprecedented number of prisoners: seven thousand, according to the archives of the Confederacy now lodged in Richmond, twenty thousand rifles, thirty field pieces, and so much booty in the form of food stuffs, ammunition, and clothing that the transport of the victorious general could not bear it all and much had to be put to the torch."

Douglas Morton's scholarship and rhetorical skill were such that he could deliver a succinct and hyperbolically comic history of the Civil War to any gathering of drunks in twenty-eight minutes, citing sources, commenting on strategy, pausing only to swill an occasional two fingers of Jack, and never losing a single listener to boredom or the bathroom. He had done it many times, sometimes playing to the same audience.

Max pondered Mr. Morton. He *did* have every attainment. He *did* have a fierce aliveness about him. And a sense of awe. But he was surrendering it all to alcohol. Max listened and considered. His father could never do this. Yet, Mr. Morton...? So he pondered.

Max was the most popular boy in their class. Charlotte decided that it was partially because when someone spoke to him, he had the gift of looking at the speaker and truly listening. He did not fidget, look past, turn to move on. He gave his attention, and thereby gave compliment to the speaker. He did not betray confidences. He did not join in that perilous adolescent game of gossip which wounded so many.

Max was interested in people. It seemed at times as though the world was populated merely to provide him with fascination.

"You know who he is most like? From literature, that is," Max was talking about Cal to Charlotte and her father—Cal who was a continual source of interest because he was incalculable. "He's like Achilles."

"Precisely," Douglas leaned forward. "Precisely. Cal is not brainless, but he *is* thoughtless. He is entirely a creature of impulse. Right. Achilles. He reacts exactly to whatever stimulus is present."

"Yes, sir," Max said. "He is a natural athlete like Achilles. He cannot make a wrong move. He simply reacts perfectly. And, you know, I've seen him go from fury to laughter in thirty seconds."

"Yes, he's wonderful. I don't suppose I've ever known anyone quite like Cal," Douglas said. "He is completely consumed in being right now. He has, in a sense, no past and no future."

"That's what makes him so wonderful," said Charlotte.

"When he's around, you have the feeling that something is going to happen. You know. Sometimes it doesn't happen, but you always know that it could."

Max was perpetually studying Billy, who could be so free and funny, but always with that deadly undercurrent of sadness. Max worried about him because Billy was so fragile. Or Jennings, whose devotion had his respect because it was so passionate. Since that freezing day of the baptism, for there was a nobility about him.

Max would even talk to Coy Trexler, Jr. Coy fascinated him. He would shoot pool with him, watch Coy cheat raking the line, losing to him just to watch. Charlotte would remember bitterly the time Max laid hands on Coy, seemingly possessed, not with anger but by curiosity. She had turned the corridor corner at school and Max had Coy against the wall.

"Why? I want to know why you did that? Tell me. I want to know why."

When Coy didn't answer, Max slammed him back against the wall. His fingers moved up to Coy's skinny throat. Charlotte had looked at Max's face and been frightened. He was not out of control. He was absolutely calm and icy in purpose.

"Why? Why?" he demanded.

"Lemme go," Coy whined. "Lemme go. I'll tell you. Jesus, gimme a chance."

Max released his throat, but kept him in tow by the arm. "Tell me. Just why?"

Coy was holding his throat and whining, his rusty hair awry, eyes darting. His finger corkscrewed his ear.

"Why?"

"Well, I just wanted to see what the critter'd do. That's all. It's only a cat. Wadda ya so excited about, Max?"

"But why? Where'd you get the fluid?"

"Hooked it at the pharmacy."

"Yeah, but how did you happen to do that to the cat? I wanta know why?"

"Wadda ya mean? He was always pissing around. That's all. It's only a cat, Max. What the hell?"

"How did you think of it? How did you think to do that? Tell me!"

"Nothin' was doin', Max. That's all. A little action. That's all."

Charlotte watched as Max released Coy, who sauntered off, muttering, "Jeeeuss, a lousy cat."

Max didn't move. He stood staring at the wall where he had pinned Coy.

"What is it, Max?" asked Charlotte. "What did the bastard do now?"

Whit had told Max that Coy had doused Geraldina Lowder's cat with lighter fluid and set the cat afire. Nobody could catch the pain-crazed beast to put it out and it had burned nearly to death. Whit's father had ended the agony with an axe when the animal finally stopped running, and lay smoking and twitching. Trex lived just around the corner from Whit and Geraldina. That Saturday morning, when Geraldina had heard what had happened, she had lit out for Trexler's with a kitchen knife. Whit had seen her and chased her, begging her not to do anything crazy.

Old Man Trexler intercepted her on the porch. He knocked her clean down the steps.

"Ain't no crazy bitch gonna punish a kid of mine over a goddam cat."

"What are they like, Whit? The Trexlers?" Max had asked.

"Max, I don't know. I can't tell you. I just don't understand them. That's the weirdest family I ever heard tell of." Whit looked out of his clear, blue eyes, searching for words.

"No, but I mean—you know, what's his mother like? His father? Has he got brothers and sisters?"

"There are seven kids. Coy's in the middle. We've been living there nine years and I've never seen his mother. Not once. But she's a punching bag, I promise. Lotsa times we hear her screaming. All the neighbors. Some of the people around there keep saying they're gonna call the cops. But you know. You're scared to get into a thing like that. I don't know Max. I just don't know."

Max couldn't get it off of his mind. For weeks he pondered it, caused Charlotte to ponder it.

"Just why?" he said over and over again.

"Well, you remember a long time ago what he did to those little chicks. Max, Trex loves pain. There's something missing in Coy Trexler."

"God, yes."

After his night with Alice, Max became aware that Blanche was black. *Really* aware. Alice's pitiful wonder if she pleased him also nagged at Max. She was a girl lying down for a boy. Why shouldn't she please him? It was that she was black, he knew.

He hung around the kitchen, drying dishes for Blanche, talking. Asking questions. How did she meet Grover? What was their courtship like? How was Prince School—the high school her kids went to? What were they doing? Did her boy play football? Max realized for the first time that for someone born with black skin life was a totally different proposition.

Blanche, who understood all, understood that this sensitive white boy had suddenly noticed her color. She talked candidly, answering his questions, not glossing the hardness, but assuring him that she had some joy, maybe some the likes of which he would never have. "And some of it comes right here in this house, Maxwell. That glass is Waterford, Maxwell. If you drop that you'll have to deal with the whole house, and I sho' won't be the softest."

Blanche loved him, he knew. But what was it like?

At least part of Max's sexual drive was simply interest. All the girls he knew behaved differently when they gave. All different. It was essentially the same act. But it was at the same time, essentially a matter of personality. The nights with Charlotte, when they had the whole house to themselves, were the most stirring times of his young life. She was different, too. Sometimes. Each time. He would stare at her the next day, in class or wherever. So tall, proud, confident, doing well whatever she had to do. So unspeakably beautiful. Walking as if she had purpose. But with that gently swaying gait. Sometimes he just wanted to put his hand on her ass as she walked. Not lecherously. It was just a wonder. How did it work? Exactly? Not sexually. Well, sexually, too. When she wore slacks, he looked at her little puffy, soft place, her non-bulge. My God, what is she?

A kitten sometimes. Soft, saying, Oh Maxie. Sometimes pulling at him. Tugging, saying, come on. Oh Max, come on. Sometimes standing naked, enjoying being naked before him, moving slowly, angling her hips, raising her hands to toss her hair. Sometimes, undressing him, she would murmur, God, I love a man's body.

A man's body! Why didn't she say, *your* body? Oh hell, he didn't know.

She loved him. He was sure. And, Oh, godamighty, he loved her. But that Pete McCanless thing had bothered him.

Sometimes he thought of her and Cal. He just couldn't think of that. But did they really?

Oh shit!

The other girls. Some did him a favor. He hated that. He took it, but he hated that.

He and Cal and Geraldina had a pact. They used each other. What did she think? He asked questions. She interested him.

"When I was sixteen, my old man said, 'Well, girl, it's time you got your feet out from under my table.' He'd done that with the boys. But I was a girl. I didn't think he'd do that to me."

She'd married a guy twenty-two, a mill hand. They lived with his folks. She still did. She couldn't have babies. He was gone. Fucking war. I just love it, she said. I need it. Gotta have it. Why had Joan gone to bed with him, when in another day she would have been with her husband?

All in all things were slippery, without center, like walking on sand. Max granted Mr. Douglas his case. *I don't know anything. Especially about people.*

Max tried to center himself. Be accountable to himself. I'm going to get that mile record.

For two years Maxwell Compton had clocked fifteen miles a day. It was not all work. Max loved to run. He felt free. Sometimes Cal would run with him, to train, or just to be with him. Max didn't like that. He liked Cal, loved him, liked to be with him. But he wanted to run alone.

Nobody knew where he ran. Only Charlotte and Cal knew that he was doing fifteen miles a day. His parents knew nothing of his purposes. He left before breakfast, but was in his place for grace. Summer nights, he was just gone.

He liked cross country the best. He could go where he wanted to, where cars couldn't. Through woods. He could jump rabbits. Snakes. He could splash down Lee Creek. Not even a bicycle could go where he could go.

In the spring of his junior year, Max finally went for it. Early in practice he clocked himself at around 4:19. Cal, between throwing the shot and hammer and javelin, would take over the watch, angle across the corners and keep him posted on the time. Max felt that he had lengthened his stride all he could. He stopped cross country running and stayed on the quarter mile track to get the feel of laps. He wanted them to come as naturally as breath.

In the first two meets he ran under 4:18. In the next he was under 4:17. *Now,* he thought. He told Cal the next one was it. He knew that it was going to be a matter of a split second. He practiced starts all week.

On the Friday of the meet, a considerable crowd gathered because the paper had given play to the fact that the young runner had come within two seconds of the mile record in the last meet.

The field events and the dashes were over. Cal, as usual, had taken three events. Max warmed up and was sprawled on the grass in a sweatsuit watching the clouds roll overhead, thinking, *I've got to get the feeling of skimming right away. Half of it is in my head. Gotta get that.*

Armed with a stop watch, Cal flopped beside him.

"How do you feel?"

"Good!" Max said. "Perfect. Perfect weather. Perfect everything."

"I'll let you know how you're doing."

"Right."

They called the mile at four-thirty. Max was ready, sweating, loose.

As he walked to the line he kept his head down. *Within ten paces,* he said to himself, *I've got to have that feeling of skimming—just skimming—right away. If I can get that right away, I'll do it.*

He practice started and went forty yards. *Yeah. It's out there waiting for me,* he thought. *I'm coming, you mother!*

He turned to Cal.

"Listen, Cal, don't tell me anything. I got a fix. I don't want to know. OK?"

"Right. Do it, baby. Hey, Max. It didn't hurt!"

He met Charlotte's eyes at the line, but he didn't nod. His mind was where he wanted it.

He got his good start. In eight paces he was skimming. He let his mind go. He left the rest of the field by the turn. They didn't matter. The watch didn't matter. He was loose, free. If he had had to stop running, he felt he would die.

Cal was sitting with Charlotte, the watch ticking. Charlotte peering with him at the murderous instrument.

Max cruised by.

"Good first quarter," Cal muttered. "Solid. Solid."

Charlotte watched Max lean around the first curve. He was so beautiful. It looked so effortless. *She* had the illusion that he was skimming through the far turn. Then drifting down the straightaway. *He is beautiful.*

He passed the second time.

"Good," Cal said. "They are the hardest for him. He's got to gain some in this one."

Max's face was serene when he passed the third time.

"Great. Great. Great," Cal said. "He picked up four seconds."

Charlotte's eyes jumped from the clock to Max. Christ, that watch moved.

To Max.

To the clock.

Goddam that watch!

He was in the far turn. The watch was moving—like hell.

"He's got kick. He's got kick. He's flying. He *can* do it. He just might...Char, he could really *do* it."

Cal jumped from the bench and tore for the far end. He didn't speak when Max approached. He swung both arms around, as if he were trying to fly.

Then he angled a dash across the field and grabbed the watch from Charlotte. The hand passed the four minute mark as Max hit the turn.

"Jesus. Jesus."

"Oh, Max. Come! Please, come."

He came.

When he hit the tape, Cal snapped the watch, cupped it in his hand and blew on it.

"I can't look. Here. You tell me, Char. What does it say?"

She took it. Looked down field where her beautiful boy had broken to a trot.

She opened her hand.

"Oh, Cal. Oh, Cal. It says 4:14."

"Sonofabitch. Sonofabitch. He did it. Come on." He grabbed her hand and dashed, dragging her, to the official table.

"What have you got?" he roared. "We got 4:14. What have you got?"

"We got 4:14. It's a record!"

Cal leaned. "He did it. Hey, gimme that watch. For him. OK? For him!"

They looked for him. Max had not turned up field yet. He was walking in a wide circle, hands on hips.

Cal turned to the stands. "Hey, Mr. Compton," he bellowed. "4:14. He did it."

Then, Charlotte in tow, he scrambled toward Max.

"Max. OK. 4:14. 4:14, baby."

He dropped Charlotte's hand and ran ahead. Max opened his arms to him, whirled and then opened them to Charlotte. Then took Cal in. Then came Billy. Whit. Then Jennings. And in one gigantic embrace they headed for the judge's desk.

"Here, baby," Cal said. "Don't ever touch this." He handed Max the official watch.

Max broke loose from all but Charlotte and met his parents. He gave his mother the watch, with instructions not to touch the buttons.

Then his eyes caught a tall, slim figure behind his parents. It was Douglas Morton. He ran to him, towing Charlotte. Cal ran to join them.

"Live forever, Maxwell," Douglas said. "I'm so proud of you."

"I didn't know you were here. Wasn't it wonderful?" Charlotte snuggled in.

"Did you think I would miss this? Here's Spence. Max, running, you are truly a thing of beauty."

That night there was a victory celebration in Charlotte's parlor. Early in the evening, Douglas Morton and Sybil Schraeder entered with a bottle of sherry and glasses.

"Let Miss Schraeder and I intrude for just a moment, please, young people, before you begin to enjoy yourselves properly. We would like to join you in a toast to Maxwell over there, who this day achieved something memorable."

Sybil splashed sherry in the glasses and helped pass it around.

"I do hope none of you will go home and tell your parents that Old Man Morton is feeding you booze. But this is a special occasion."

Then, "Oh come, Jennings. Just this once. To celebrate Max."

"No, Mr. Morton, I won't drink, but I will join the toast with all my heart."

"Good enough, Jennings. Good enough. Sybil, some Coke for Jennings."

All were ready.

"Now, young friends, let's raise our glasses to our friend

here. But first, I'd like us to think for just one moment of what we saw this afternoon. We saw a young man do something which was absolutely singular. There has never been anything like it before. We saw Maxwell run a mile better than anyone in our state has ever done it. And that is a splendid thing. It is always splendid to see a man push back the boundaries of excellence. We all become a little better, a little more noble by it. So, to Maxwell, who gave us that gift this afternoon."

"To Maxwell!"

After the party was over and they were alone, Max took Charlotte's hands and cupped them in his.

"Take this," he said. "Because I love you."

She opened her hands. It was the stopwatch.

For the rest of her life that watch read 4:14.

Early in their senior year, Charlotte Morton, always extraordinary, did that which set her firmly apart—from classmates, indeed, from the town. She shamed them deeply. And she did it by deliberately violating propriety.

The student council decided to stage a variety show to raise funds for the USO. They presented their plan to the principal who approved and appointed Edna Graham as advisor. Big Edna in turn asked Charlotte and Max if they would enlist talent and be student coordinators.

"I always wanted to be a big time producer," said Max, and by that afternoon they had a list of exhibitionists and prima donnas.

A band was easy. Charlotte could play piano, Billy could drive them on bass, then give it to somebody else and take sax solos. Tommy Kinder played a respectable trumpet. They could fill in from the school band. With Billy and Charlotte to steer, a band could be whipped into shape.

Amy had been taking dancing lessons all her life. She would do a number. A tap solo—"Don't wear a bra," Cal advised—then she and Billy would work up a duo to *Me and My Shadow.* Jane Lea and Louise Whitley and a couple of others would sing pop songs.

Big Edna suggested that both Billy and Charlotte play piano solos. And Martha Hunt, who had sung at several assemblies, could do an operatic aria.

"Then there will be two distinct parts," said Miss Graham. "One pop. One classical."

"Terrific," said Billy. "Why not make the first part a night club scene—then intermission, and the classical part?"

"One problem," said Amy. "Do you think *these* kids are going to sit and listen to classical music?"

"Well," said Big Edna, "I know what you mean. But surely there will be many parents here."

"What we do," said Max, "is stage the classical section, then close with the dance band. You know. Leave 'em live."

"Sounds good," said Big Edna. "Also, let's not jump to conclusions. Give people a chance."

That was it. Open with a night club scene. Band at back. Few tables out front off center, for verisimilitude. The acts under spots in the center.

Then intermission. A piano before the short curtain so that the bandstand would not have to be moved. The classical section. It over, draw the short curtain and there was the bandstand. And the finale.

Max took charge of the first section. Trumpet in hand he was the band leader and M.C. He nagged them into discipline, insisted that they begin when he announced it.

"If there is going to be a lot of flip flopping around we'll lose the audience. One follows the other. After the last note of one act, the first note of the next. Right?"

He got hold of Whit. "Whit, do me one favor. Learn that light board and operate for this show. We just got to have precision."

"OK."

Cal agreed to set the recorded music on Whit's cue.

Miss Eller volunteered a violin solo by her star pupil Ann Marie Hansell. Miss Eller herself would accompany.

Charlotte and Billy couldn't decide what they would play. They talked to her father.

"I'd like to play Mozart, but I think it had better be something Romantic and fairly well-known. What do you think?"

Her father agreed. "You're right, I guess. *C Sharp Minor Prelude*. *Military Polonaise*. Something like that. But on the other hand, Billy, it would be nice for you to play something of your own. You would get a hearing. It would be valuable experience."

Billy scratched his head.

"Maybe you are right. Hey, Billy, why not? Premiere performance, and all that. Listen, why not? Dad's right. You would have a performance of your own composition before an audience."

"Yeah, but those kids . . . You know, Charlotte."

"Billy," Douglas Morton reminded, "there will be other people there. I'll be there. Sybil. Miss Graham. Mr. Fulton. Your parents."

"Uggh."

"Listen, Sid and Judith Jacobson will come. Gladly. Dr. Hansom from the college. In fact, you could get some pretty good criticism from such a performance."

He was swaying.

"What about one section from *Charlotte's Letters*. Say 'Florence.' It has a lovely melody. It's romantic. The theme is transparent."

"Right," said Charlotte. "That section is beautiful. Do it, Billy. Do it."

They talked him into it.

Charlotte selected Schumann's *Traumarie*. Then she listened to Horowitz's recording and decided against it. She settled on a Schubert *Impromptu*.

They rehearsed and rehearsed. Each his own act. Then for the night club ensemble. Max insisted on precision.

"Amy, get out here. Your music's on. The spot is moving. C'mon, will ya? We're not Broadway stuff. If we don't keep it moving, we're gonna flop so bad we'll be ashamed to come to school for a week."

When they had run through the first section, they drew the short curtain on the night club scene and rolled the baby grand to center stage.

"Go play, Billy. Max and I want to wander around and check the acoustics."

They were fine. So was Billy's tone.

"Oh God, Max, I hope the audience is civilized. Ann Marie's fiddle sounds terrible. Well, let's hope."

Two final rehearsals and they were as ready as they could be.

Charlotte peeked at the audience on performance night.

"Well, Max, it's full. And there are a lot of parents. I guess about a third are adults. Look."

"Yep. I see Mayor Hurst. See. On the aisle. With Dr. and Mrs. Council. Wow, I hope it goes OK."

Five minutes before the curtain, Miss Graham rushed back-stage with the news that there were no more seats.

"Oh gosh, did you see my father and Blanche with Miss Schraeder?"

"Yes. And we chatted. They are up in the balcony."

Max gave the downbeat. They raised the curtain with Ellington's *Take the A Train*, Charlotte on piano intro. Billy and Tommy Andrews on drums kept them crisp and they were off to a good start.

Then M.C. Max said, "It's show time at Club Groovy. At great expense to the management we proudly present a galaxy of stars of stage, screen, and radio. First, welcome please, Miss Bubbles Winston, straight from Broadway and Las Vegas. Everyone, Bubbles!"

Bubbles was welcome. On cue Whit dampened the light on the band, and Cal grooved the needle. Bubbles too was on cue and just long-legged right in skin-tight, green, satin costume.

It clicked along. Max was genial, charming, and witty. Cal and Whit were with it. Amy and Billy won with *Me and My Shadow*. The pop singers were passable and the band remained credible. It worked right up to the last curtain-closing chord of the theme, *A Train*. Part one was OK.

"Well, we're ahead," Max said backstage.

"It was great! It was great!" yelled Jennings who had rushed backstage to report.

Fifteen minutes later, Max walked onto a stage holding only the piano.

The audience was silent.

"Ladies and gentlemen, no longer the Club Groovy. Here"—he swept his hand—"we have a concert hall. We will hear first Fritz Kreisler's *Caprice Vennoise*. The violinist is Ann Marie Hansell. Miss Eller will accompany."

She got through it. But the audience almost didn't. If she didn't squeak, she laid it flat and lifeless. And Miss Eller set a tempo Kreisler himself couldn't have sustained. It seemed four hours long. Halfway through the audience restlessness was audible to Charlotte standing in the wings.

She looked at Max. He shrugged.

"Now we will hear the aria *Cara Nome* from Verdi's *Rigoletto*. Our soprano is Martha Ann Hunt. Miss Eller will again accompany."

There was minimal welcoming applause, and from the

wings, Charlotte could see the fidget begin, hear the whispering, and some outright laughter. Martha Ann did well enough and bravely enough. But there was a bare ripple of applause from the now noisy listeners.

Billy was next. He didn't have a chance.

Max walked to the microphone but had to wait fully a minute to gain attention.

Charlotte took Billy's hand. It felt like wet Kleenex. He glanced at her. She forced a smile. He would have been better off in front of a firing squad.

Jesus, she thought, *have mercy.*

"Our next offering is a special one. Our pianist is also the composer. We will hear a section of a piano suite by the composer based on letters he received from a friend traveling in Europe. The section we will hear is called 'Florence' after the Italian city. The composer and pianist is our own William Ennis."

There was no applause. A heavy current of conversation. Charlotte clearly heard one voice, "Christ, that creep Ennis."

"Play for me," she whispered to Billy.

Max touched his arm on the way offstage.

Billy walked out, bowed to the disorder, and sat down quickly. He waited a few moments, but the noise increased. Charlotte saw him clenching his fingers beside him, waiting for the noise to subside. It didn't. Desperately he began to play.

The noise grew. There was a whistle. Then a hiss. Louder. Louder.

Midway through, someone shouted, "Billy, baby, you sound like Bay-toe-van."

That gave other humans courage.

"Groovy, you queer."

"Hey, quair. Quair Ennis."

There were shouts of "Quiet. Shhh. Quiet."

But the barbarians won. The piano was barely audible.

Charlotte buried her head on Max's shoulder. "This will kill him," she said. Then hissed, "Bastards! Bastards! *Bastards!*"

"Oh Charlotte," Jennings said.

"Damn them," she snarled. "Damn them. God damn them. I hate every one of them!"

Max felt her nails on his wrist.

Miss Graham put her hand on Charlotte's shoulder. The girl's whole frame was trembling. Max held her.

259

"Please, Charlotte." Max was frightened, for Billy and for her.

At last, mercifully, it ended. Nobody had heard it.

As he hit the last chord, Billy dove for the curtain. Charlotte moved to him, but he hurtled past her and straight out the stage door. She ran after him but the door slammed. She pressed her forehead against it. She was sobbing. Max stood behind her. He put his hands on her shoulders. She was slack. But in a moment, he felt her stiffen. Every nerve drew guy-wire taut. She whirled out of his arms, faced him squarely. He didn't know her. Her face was absolutely expressionless. She looked through him. She walked toward the stage. Then she stopped, and still looking straight ahead, said, "Cal, go find Billy."

Behind her, Max saw her shoulders heave to brace, her head snap back, lifting that chin. Then she strode onto the stage.

Beside the piano, she wheeled and stood, arms at her sides, chin still high. The flood fell across her shining, black hair, across her beautiful icy face, across the white shoulders framed by the black gown. She did not move.

Gradually, the audience became aware of the presence facing them and a hush fell. She stood. The hush diminished to silence, that silence which chimes with silence. She did not move. Sixty seconds of unbearable silence passed. She did not move.

Max pressed the wall. In the balcony, Douglas Morton took Blanche's hand and leaned forward. Sybil Schraeder's fingers went white, so tightly did she grip her arms across her breasts.

The motionless vision commanded.

And ignored. Chin forward, carrying a dare, eyes cast beyond the balcony, beyond walls, beyond beyond, where no audience could be, she stood. And stood. And stood. Expressionless, solitary ice queen, she acknowledged no presence before her. Her terrible, blank gaze held center. Her terrible stillness held all.

And so she stood. And stood.

At last, decisively, she turned and sat at the piano. And sat. Erect, chin forward, still daring. The silence became mass. Then she raised her hands and struck the shattering initial chords and torrential progression of the *Revolutionary Etude*.

Beneath her assault, slender fingers arced like claws, the piano roared.

The bass figure marauded beneath the trumpet call of the treble. Then, over a fuming, snarling bass, came the whispered answering figure. Then the roar, the trumpets, each note singular, each phrase whole, statement of her livid, controlled, perfected fury.

"Jesus Christ," Douglas Morton involuntarily murmured as he watched a daughter he had never known lift her whole frame from the bench and drive it to the bottom of each chord. Sybil had not moved since this shaft of fury walked on the stage.

Max was a statue, awful, terrified before the purity of her rage.

At last, the Fury at the piano flung herself into the last thunderous chords, hung them in the air for their span, and released them to the silence.

She dropped her hands into her lap and sat erect, staring straight ahead.

After a long moment, tentative applause began in the stunned audience. Once begun, it rose to thunder. It had been a stirring performance of a stirring piece and had driven reaction into the dullest. People began to stand, clapping and whistling.

Still the Fury sat. Sat until the applause became oceanic.

Then with perfect calm she rose and walked to the center of the stage and stood, unmoving as before, expressionless as before, a deadly, beautiful, white bust bathed in the flood, framed by the shimmering jet hair. Just so, she stood. And stood. And stood.

Gradually the applause began to fade, erratically, as though everyone had been caught doing something shameful. The silence that chimes with silence again gripped the auditorium.

And still she stood. And stood. The chin forward as though daring one hand to strike another again.

Then in a voice at conversational level, but with such precise enunciation that it was clearly understood in the farthest seat, she spoke one simple sentence. And she spoke it very slowly so that there could be no misunderstanding. And she clearly defined each *D* in the words that she chose so that the sentence sounded like it was from Above and Forever.

She said, "I don't want your GoD DamneD applause."

Then she stood as before. And stood longer. Daring.

At last, having covered them with her contempt, she strode off the stage.

Max took her in his arms, in fear, as though touching her flesh might be lethal.

She went limp.

"Billy?" she sobbed.

"I don't know."

She moved out of his arms to the door. He followed. Miss Graham took her hand and kissed it before she went out.

Cal had Billy in The Wreck outside. He was a slobbering, wiped-out Mess. Charlotte slipped beside him and cradled him, covered him with her hair.

Then Edna Graham did a wonderful thing.

"William Ennis, come here," she commanded. She was standing like a gargoyle beside the open car door.

Billy, Max, Cal and Charlotte thought her mad. They were immobile.

"Did you hear me?" Miss Graham snapped.

Charlotte got out. She pulled Billy. What else?

Big Edna grabbed Billy's arm and headed for the stage door. Charlotte, Max, and Cal followed. Edna marched Billy through the door, past the lighting board, out to the center of the stage, and sat him at the piano.

Four or five students loitered at the rear of the auditorium. "Get out," she snapped to them.

"Whitlow, the flood over the piano, please," she said over her shoulder. The flood bathed them.

"Now play 'Florence' for me."

In the back of the auditorium Douglas, Sid and Judith, Sybil, and Blanche stood silently.

Billy collapsed in tears over the keyboard.

"Stop that. Instantly," Edna snapped. "Play. I will not be deprived of a beautiful piece of music by a bunch of lobotomized barbarians. Do you hear me? Play."

Then her voice softened. "Oh, Billy. Listen. There are always those. So many of them. But you do not compose or play for them. You play for people like Charlotte and Max and Cal and Jennings and Whit. And for people like me. Oh Billy, people like us depend for part of our lives on people like you. Please play it for me now."

"Play," Charlotte whispered.

He straightened. He nodded.

Edna Graham motioned and they followed her down the

stage steps and took seats. Douglas, Blanche, Sybil, and the others came down and joined them.

"Billy," Miss Graham called softly.

Billy played.

When it was over, they applauded.

"Thank you, Billy. Thank you. I loved it. I truly loved it," Miss Graham said softly. "And now, good night."

She took Charlotte's hand, drew her near. Then she turned and started up the long aisle. Douglas Morton stopped her, and kissed her cheek as she passed.

Once again Billy Ennis had been narrowly saved from destruction. Thereafter, Charlotte and Max regarded him as a dear moment which could never be relived. And it seemed inevitable that a crisis would come when there would be no Charlotte or Cal or Edna Graham to salvage him.

"Well, tonight at least demonstrates clearly the level of love on which most of our species operates. God, if mankind survives, my sense of justice will be outraged," Douglas had thrown back several Jacks and quickly gained his cynical height. "It's their obscene, gratuitous, bad manners which is frightening. Every time I hear that mindless rhapsody about 'expressing myself,' and being an 'individual,' I thank heaven for manners and custom. They at least provide fools with patterns of behavior. But after tonight, how can you hope?"

He seized the neck of the bottle, a tumbler, and lurched for the staircase, leaving Max and Charlotte to find comfort in each other.

But in a moment, he reappeared in the doorway. "Sorry, I . . . There is a way. Learn to expect nothing. But try . . . try to stay prepared for joy. Just in case. Good night my children."

Next day, lunching at the Club after golf, Sybil heard the gist of town opinion from the table next to her.

"Louise, were you at the high school show last night? Wasn't Tommy in it? Didn't he play drums, or something?"

"Oooooh, you mean the Morton girl? I certainly was."

"Tell us. Is it possible that what I have heard is true?"

"It is. The worst you heard is true. Charlotte Morton performed some classical piece, and beautifully, I must say. When she finished the audience gave her a tremendous ovation, the largest ovation of the entire evening. And she walked to the center of the stage like The Queen Bee, mind you, and announced—and this is verbatim, I'll never forget it as long as I live—'I don't want your G. D. applause,' and pranced off the stage."

"She didn't."

"She did. I assure you. Except she didn't use letters. She said it. Very emphatically."

"Horrible. Before all those young people. And in the school. But Doris, why? Why would she do something like that? I understand that she is a very bright child. And very pretty."

"I think she was angry because the audience was not very polite while Billy Ennis played. You know Billy. Howard Ennis's son. The YMCA?"

"Yes," with arched eyebrows. "I've *heard* about him."

"Well, I must say that the audience *was* very rude while the boy played. I am sure that's why the Morton girl did what she did, though that certainly doesn't excuse it."

"It certainly doesn't. It's absolutely horrible. Though, actually, one must feel sorry for the girl. Her mother is dead, and I understand that her father is a bedrock alcoholic—after years of chasing every woman, married or unmarried, who would put up with him. I don't suppose that she has a chance of growing up like a lady."

"That's true. This, however, is inexcusable."

"Excuse me. Hello, Louise." Sybil turned around in her chair. "I didn't mean to eavesdrop. But I couldn't help it. I was there last night too. And I must say that I thought she was magnificent and gave *that* audience exactly what they deserved."

"Sybil, she took the Lord's name in vain, before an auditorium full of youngsters."

"Not in vain," Sybil said crisply. "In that case, not in vain."

Sybil wheeled in her seat, thus closing the conversation. Well, her Charlotte was now famous. No, notorious.

School was different. Several teachers no longer greeted her. Mrs. Godwin, the history teacher, did not return her 'good morning.' She was a new presence to her fellow students. She had shamed them, those who were capable of shame. They had mistreated one who was helpless. It was cowardly. She had told them so. She had spoken words before faculty, administration, and parents which none of them would have dreamed of uttering in public, and she had done so from the vantage of what she believed to be justice and they knew that she did not regret it, and they knew that she would do it again.

Charlotte realized the deference which was now hers. She had told them that she did not need their approval. She became aware that it was so. She became aware of the fact that she could rely on herself, that Amy and the popular set had almost nothing to do with her essential life. She had the respect and affection of the few who truly mattered: Miss Graham, Max, Cal, Billy.

"I am myself," she told her mirror.

15

THE feeling of doom which had crushed her that Sunday afternoon, December 7, 1941, persisted. Younger she had felt it as a huge malevolent force marauding the earth, capable of formless devastation that could blot her loves from the planet. With time, the blight had changed from a generalized to a personalized terror.

She had learned to live with the war as an impersonal horror. The daily papers, the nightly news broadcasts were facts of life, to be accommodated. Her father's rage and fear as he tracked the losses on his atlas were part of daily routine. There was gas and food rationing, and her father could not buy a new tire for the Packard and was forced to drive slowly, when he drove at all.

Now she knew that the generalized attitude toward the war was over. She knew that it was going to hurt her very own heart.

The casualty lists began to be reported. It was not long before she recognized some of the faces in the paper.

Tommy Summersett was the first. The Summersetts lived across the street. Tommy was the only boy of three children. They were all older than Charlotte but she knew them well. Tommy was an accountant who had joined his father's firm for that year between college graduation and the draft. Now he was dead.

She looked at Tommy's fine face in the paper and could not believe that he would never come home again. She tried to touch his cheek. She had seen him just five months ago—handsome in his lieutenant's uniform.

Each day there were pictures of servicemen, some of whom she recognized, some she knew, who were wounded, killed, transferred, commissioned. She read how Pete McCanless had received his wings and commission as an Air Force pilot. She had actually dated him. Had kissed him. He was not much older than she. Than Max. Not much older than Cal.

It was going to happen. They too would be going into this organized insanity. And they were hers. The insanity was massive and impersonal, yet it threatened her small, personal love.

The day came. Max told her that Cal was thinking of enlisting. He was failing too many courses to graduate in spring anyway. Besides, the war was where the action was. It was the ultimate stimulus. He wouldn't have been Cal if it had not drawn him.

"I'll finish school after it's over," he grinned without the slightest regret.

Max and Charlotte knew it would be the Marines. It was their reputation. Amid romanticized publicity, they had begun their long, bloody, island-by-island march across the Pacific. Max was envious: the masculine bond became tighter, more exclusive. She felt shut out and could not be consoled.

Cal enlisted in February. Three weeks later he had to report to Parris Island.

He gave Max The Wreck. Five months later, it would be Charlotte's.

Half the school was at the bus station that night to see Cal off. He got many kisses. Before he gave his parents the last embrace, Charlotte pulled him behind the bus.

"I'm not going to cry, you ape," she said. She cupped his handsome, grinning face between her hands and looked deeply into his eyes. "Look. Do what you have to do. But don't do anything stupid. Promise. Because I really really love you."

"Hey, Morton, how about one little feel before I go to no-woman's land?"

"Jesus," she said. "I don't know why I even think of you."

He kissed his mother and was gone.

He and Max nodded to each other as he stepped on the bus.

Two months later, boot camp over, he was home for ten days. It was as though he had never left. *That* was the Marines. *This* was here. Then he went to Camp Pendleton, California.

Six weeks later, his address was Fleet Post Office, San Francisco. Charlotte wrote him two letters a week the entire time he was gone. Billy and Max wrote. Amy wrote every day for two weeks. None of them ever got a single line from him. His mother got infrequent illiteracies five or six sentences long. Mrs. Hendricks and Charlotte talked on the phone and Charlotte kept everyone posted on his address. The FPO address was good for a long time.

There were the last spring days at the river, the last dances. The last days of sitting at Big Edna's feet. Happy, precious days touched with the sadness of imminent partings.

Charlotte had enrolled in Salem College for September. Harold Preston, a piano teacher of reputation, was there, and the college had an excellent reputation. She didn't like the idea of a woman's college, but her mother had spent four years of her brief life there. Her father was pleased.

Billy enrolled in Davidson College which had an excellent music department, hoping to get through a year before the draft caught him.

Max enrolled in North Carolina State College. He guessed that architecture would be the course of study. But his moods were becoming more and more mercurial. This war was part of his generation's environment. He needed to go. He began to feel that great tides of experience were flowing past him.

Jennings was investigating a Naval program whereby, in exchange for service, they would put him through medical school. He spent an inordinate amount of time on his knees. One of his turn of mind could not be sure that this was not Armaggedon. No one could.

Whit had chosen the Marine Corps too. He enlisted on provision that they would not call him until after graduation. Max stood by him when he took the oath, as he had done for Cal.

"Max," Charlotte asked one day. "Because Cal is like Achilles, will he die young too?"

"Char, Cal has heels of steel. I know. I have felt them."
Charlotte knew that Max too would go.

It seemed the earth got uglier and uglier. People sought pleasure frantically. Charlotte had seen drunkenness aplenty, but she had never seen it on such a scale, and with such purpose. A single weekend could reveal a town debauched. Mr. Phillips, the real estate man, slumped senseless across a table at the Club. Harriet Holman, young and beautiful and married to George, who was in the army, dancing like Charlotte knew she shouldn't with a soldier at Granite Inn. Later, when Charlotte and Max went to The Wreck in the parking lot, they passed a car and clearly saw Harriet's legs across the front seat. Between them was the soldier. George had been gone too long. Old stupid Harold Clure came to blows with Marsh Woods in the Club bar. Gorman Neill, a lawyer contemporary with her father, seated himself at her table in the Club bar, talking drunkenly about soft, young things and before she knew it had his hand up her dress. She was stunned. Gorman Neill! She simply dropped her eyes to her lap and then fixed their cold, blue steel on his. How dare he? But how dare Richmond Grimes, city councilman, and Dr. David Poe stretch themselves across the Club drive so that no one could leave the party?

Other ugliness appeared. The papers told of hoarding, black marketing, shorting government contracts. Three local service stations were closed for violating rationing regulations. The small electrical supply company was placed under indictment for shipping materials under government specification.

And there were some draft dodgers—like Mark Allen Smith, the ex-fullback, comfortable at the University, while his former teammates were playing games with death.

But somehow the nation launched a ship a day, supplied armies all over the globe, bought war bonds. England held on. The tide slowly turned and the Allies went on the offensive.

Charlotte Morton would rehearse in her mind a thousand times the events of that last spring.

Cal's absence touched everything, caused her and Max to cling to each other, made Billy try harder at his brand of comedy, drew dear, silent Whit solidly to them. Impending disaster was close enough to give each moment an aura of intensity.

Slow dancing to Harry James's *I Cried for You*, Max would suddenly want to see her face and raise her chin with his hand. She would be crying quietly.

"Don't," he would say.

"Well then, Max, live a thousand years. Because I'm never going to love anyone as I love you now."

"Char. Char."

There were moments of free flight. She'd had three bourbons. Billy and Max two more than enough. Ellington, Goodman, or Dorsey music. Or Krupa's hard, driving beat. And she could move. She loved it. Flying out from Billy. From Max. No thing, no bird, no gorgeous hound loose in a field ever loved motion more than she. Her hair lifting out, whipping back across her face, her breasts twisting counter to her hips. It was all gorgeous. It was flying. It was delicious.

A rush of power filled her when in the last six weeks of school she began to write out *her very own* translation of Book VI of the *Aeneid*, Dido's book. Miss Graham praised it. Yes, Charlotte Morton would get the Latin medal at graduation.

And the piano sessions with Billy, music for four hands; he at the grand, she at the upright. They could 'feel' each other and the music. Little audiences, Whit listening intently, her father and Sybil or Sugar Lady, who had buried the luckless Howard, dear Sid and Judith, Spence and Florence, sometimes Amy and Louise (if they absolutely promised not to talk), Tommy Kinder, anyone.

And, of course, Max. Sometimes they invited Big Edna. Her father always fought to stay sober when she was there.

In May, Mr. Compton relented and Max enlisted in the Marines. Besides his father, Whit was there. Charlotte, too. Six other men were sworn in at the same time. He was the tallest, straightest, handsomest of them all. She thought of the oath he took: *But he's mine. He's mine. No matter where you take him*.

Their lovemaking that spring haunted her ever after. They learned each other's bodies perfectly that spring. Nights on the river, after swimming to Isola Bella, Max kneeling between her thighs as she offered.

"You!" he would say. "Oh God, Charlotte, I can't believe you're true—and mine."

"I am," she vowed. "Come."

269

He entered her slowly and they always looked, one into the other's eyes, as he did. Then they would not move for so long. They lay looking at each other, memorizing. Then they would kiss and every inch of him would be touching her and they felt merged and inseparable. Then he would move, searching her core, center, heart. His touch when they discovered the moment. . . . His hand would grasp her hair and pull her head back to catch her gasp in his mouth.

Later, much later, a thousand, a million times she would try to recreate these moments in her mind. Max's hold: secure, yet oh so delicate! She could have wriggled like a sun perch and never escaped—but never have been crushed either.

Her body was young. Every sense stood on tiptoe, leaning to this beautiful boy who loved her and who was mortgaged to forces so vast and impersonal that they could never know what a fine thing might be ignorantly destroyed.

Her gown was blue. Sybil pinned Max's orchids on her shoulder. He was handsome in his evening clothes. Their Senior Prom was in the hotel ballroom. It was all lovely, subtly lit, festooned with balloons. They loved in her bed after.

Jennings Hall was first in their class. Charlotte was third. Max fifth. Whit ninth—funny, she had never noticed how skilled he was. She did win the Latin Medal. And it was over.

There was the Marine Corps bus. Whit was with Max. She hugged Whit. "Have luck," she whispered, "dear Whit."

She and Max looked carefully at each other's faces.

"I love you. That's all," she said.

"That's all there is," he said.

And it was over. So much was over.

She had feared that she was pregnant for three weeks. When she missed her period, she told Blanche.

"Tell your father, honey."

She did and he held her.

"I'll arrange an appointment with Dr. Tom tomorrow. No use worrying until we are sure."

In three days they were sure.

"Max?" he asked quietly.

She nodded.

"Well, what are you thinking?"

"I don't know. He doesn't know."

"Perhaps you should tell him, darling."

"I don't know. Yes, perhaps. But he was upset. So much change and all that."

"I mentioned abortion to Tom. He can arrange something."

"Oh, I hate that word." It had become one of her favorite curse words—as in, "Coy Trexler is *truly* an abortion!"

"Yes. It is ugly."

"Let's think for a few days, Dad. Max will be home for ten days after boot camp. Oh, I don't know."

"OK. But, remember, you don't have too long. At this point, there is very little danger. If you wait too long, it gets more complicated, according to Tom."

"Yes. I've done some reading."

She sat in Miss Graham's room for an hour that afternoon. Ultimately the old teacher had no advice: abortion was alien to her thinking—yet, how horrible the war was!

Mademoiselle was entirely sympathetic. "My dearest Charlotte, whatever you decide, weigh it carefully. You will soon be eighteen. You cannot realize how short life is. You are on the very edge of adulthood. I can say this without you accusing me of flattery. You are a remarkable person. You are intelligent. You are gifted in every way a person can be gifted. And you have a quality of beauty which causes everyone to admire you. Certainly you have that extra characteristic which is rare enough and which is perhaps your most lovely quality—your compassion. I do not say that all people love you—but you are certainly not a person whom they can ignore. You have a force of character that causes them to be aware of your presence."

The teacher paused—and sighed. "That is why your decision is so important. I believe that you could do something in this world. I do not say that your decision will destroy that possibility, but it can certainly affect it. So please think carefully. And, my dear, I assure you, I am always here and prepared to do whatever I can."

"Thank you, Miss Graham. That is the loveliest thing anyone has ever said to me. Oh, thank you."

They embraced. But no decision had been made.

* * *

She was sleepless. She twisted her pillow, ground her nails into the mattress, felt her belly, her breasts. She paced the gallery. God!—to talk to Max!

She traversed the usual metaphysical arguments. There was life in her belly. Her father had always said to love life—*all* of life. All life probably came from the same cell anyway. *See that lizard,* he would say. *Our brother. From the same cell—only he took a different evolutionary route.*

The oils from Max's body were in her body. A baby. Is it really woman's first reason?

Practical thoughts were somehow easier. Salem College would be a wonderful experience. If she could get assigned to Preston as tutor, he would bring her to her potential as a musician—if not concert calibre, at least a competence which would be a joy as long as she lived. But that could wait. And she would not have to backslide. She could practice, learn. Her father would help.

If only she could talk to Max. Max was wise. He was wise in a way her father and *Mademoiselle* would recognize. It was the wisdom of that love her father praised, called so rare. That broad, splendid kind of love.

She told her father that she wanted to go out to the river for a few days alone. He offered to drive her. No, she had The Wreck.

The day she left she had a letter from Max. He had no hair. But he had her picture. He had green underwear. His shoes were shined. He drilled eight hours a day in sand. A steel helmet becomes an oven under the South Carolina sun. It wasn't too hard physically, but he missed her. To say 'I love you' wasn't enough. There were no words. He and Whit were in different companies. He hadn't seen him. He had been hit with a swagger stick by his drill instructor. He didn't like that. He told her he wanted to kiss her mouth more than anything else in the world.

She had an address. She wrote. She called Mr. Manson. Then she wrote Max of Whit's company in case there was a way for them to get together. She told him how she wished for him. She too found that there were no words. She told him of Blanche, her father, Billy, The Wreck. That Jennings was in the Naval program which would make him a doctor in four years. She told him of Big Edna. And that she could tell him nothing of Cal. That she was reading all of Shakespeare's plays. That she was doing a water color portrait of him from a photograph—and memory. He must promise not to laugh. That she and Billy were working on a piano suite by Bela Bartok. That he should listen to the "Dancing Bear."

She told him that she wanted to kiss his mouth too. But she did not tell him that he was alive in her.

She went to the river house with a basket of groceries, a pie from Blanche's hand, and Shakespeare. She walked and swam, jumped rabbits in fields, startled frogs—"Hello, brother!" —from the landing. She slept on Isola Bella. Harrison came —she was sure she glimpsed his bulk beneath the shimmering surface—a good omen. It's always good to see old friends. She counted her treasure. I may need this. Before the lean-to, she thought, *I lay here for him, with him, under him. See. My bottom still fits the sand. His knees were here. The sky swam with stars. I could see that. He couldn't. His face was in my hair. We swam after. I thought it was close enough to my period. What could I have done anyway? Said no? But it was here. I'm sure. The sky did swim with stars.*

She swam. Against the current. Half a mile. She felt her strength. Once she almost wanted to look to see if he was behind her. *Silly. He's wearing a steel helmet, learning to hurt people.* She swam on and on. *I am strong. I could swim forever.* She turned, now with the current. Beautiful. Easy. She could wait forever between strokes and still glide.

She cut, angling the current to land at Isola Bella. She waded ashore. Her body shone in the moonlight. *I could do it again. I am strong.*

"I am strong," she said out loud. *What a baby I will have! It's our mix. Strong, and intelligent, and handsome. It'll have the longest legs in the Western Hemisphere. Max and mine.*

Stupid. Sentimental.

What every woman thinks.

Right. So what. It's earned.

All right.

But—*Oh moon, what a baby I'll have!*

She was at the piano when her father, Spence, and Sybil simultaneously arrived at five o'clock. Douglas walked at once to the piano and looked at her across the keyboard.

She smiled at him.

"I'm going to have the baby."

He looked closely at her for a moment, and he knew she meant it. He walked around and embraced her.

"What baby?" said Sybil softly.

"Miss Sybil, I'm pregnant."

"Oh Charlotte."

Spence was quiet. Douglas had told him. Charlotte had said to ask what he thought.

Sybil seemed serene as ever, though a ragged note in her voice indicated her shock. "Have you thought this through? It's Max, I assume."

"Yes."

"Oh, *why* did he have to go just now?"

"Or *ever*, Miss Sybil."

"Yes. What do you plan?"

"Nothing beyond having the baby. He will marry me."

"Oh Charlotte, you're so young. And I love Max dearly, but something could happen. In this time..."

"I know. It won't. It can't."

"Charlotte. Douglas. Spence." Sybil seemed suddenly frail as she turned to each of them—appealing— "Something else is possible."

"No, Miss Sybil. *No*. I've decided."

"It will be very hard for you, dear. Hard in ways that don't even occur to you."

"I know. I have thought. The other way would be harder, I think."

"No, I'm thinking of people."

"Yes. I understand."

"And *I* think of the girl that I see before me," said Douglas, speaking both to Sybil and to Charlotte. "She is so much. She will *be* so much more. I don't want that girl hurt or restricted in any way."

"Precisely," said Sybil. "Charlotte, do you realize what this town is going to say about you. Do you realize what that congregation at St. Mark's is going to do to you?"

"I know."

"My dear, I don't think you do. You know, there are those who still feel you owe them an apology for your conduct at the variety show. They will eat you alive for this. You know that you will be ostracized? Absolutely ostracized."

"Will you ostracize me, Miss Sybil?"

Sybil rose and put her arms around the girl and kissed her cheek. "Of course not."

Sybil thought to herself: *In a sense, in a real sense, this girl became a woman on the night she stood on that stage and damned this town. And . . . In a sense, perhaps I too became a woman that night. Strange. Before that night, would I have made a pledge to her that might cause my own ostracism—at least, criticism? And just this moment, I made such a pledge to this girl. And I meant it.*

"Neither will Spence forsake me," Charlotte continued. "You see, Miss Sybil? Neither will Billy. Nor Cal. Nobody who really counts will. *Really* counts."

She reached for Sybil's hand. Sybil gave it gladly.

"Oh," said Charlotte. "Blanche! Blanche, come!"

"You call?" Blanche came trundling in.

Charlotte ran into her arms. "Blanche, you're going to be a grandmother."

"Oh, child." They held each other.

"See, Miss Sybil?"

Sybil came to her. "Yes, I do. I truly do."

"Oh, I know that I won't be able to go to the Club. I'll lose Amy and Jane Lea and Louise and Patsy and Claire Lynn. Their mothers won't want them with me anymore. I know that. And I'll miss them. But I will have those I truly need. Those who are really valuable. Oh God, what will *Jennings* say?"

"You will stay here, then?"

"Well, one thing at a time. Max will be here in a couple of months—for ten days! We'll see. Then all this talk of ostracism may be useless. But this isn't the only place in the world, I guess. Right now, Dad, I keep remembering what you said to Max and me. And I've got to keep remembering it. Expect nothing. Be prepared for joy. I guess the last is going to be hardest."

When she spoke those words, she thought she had Max's ten-day leave in the bank, that bravery would be a place of last resort.

It was difficult to prepare for joy when ten days later she learned that Max and Whit were on a troop train bound for San Diego. The Marine Corps had found it logistically convenient to give this group of trainees boot training on the West Coast, then after ten-day leave (hopeless to try to get home!) infantry train them at Camp Pendleton on the Pacific, where they could begin to replace the torn divisions from Guadalcanal, the Marianas and Marshalls.

Charlotte was stunned. Ostracism became a genuine possibility. She examined the idea of traveling to California to be with Max on his leave. But research showed that marriage would be legally impossible in California in so short a period of time. Both her father and Sybil discouraged the trip.

Her heart was broken. Again abortion appeared as an alternative. But she had formed her mind, had felt the ineluctable glow of maternity seep into her consciousness. It would be surrender to a dream. *What a child I'm going to have*. Get prepared for joy!

Very well, she had months. Salem was out—for now anyway.

One evening, Spence said that the public library was trying to organize its records, nearly two hundred years of deeds, marriages, death, old court records, which the county had ruled inoperative and presented to the library archives. He could get Charlotte the job classifying if she wanted it. It would be temporary, perhaps a couple of months. She said yes. It would pass the time. She could earn some money, and it interested the antiquarian in her.

She went to see Mrs. Daniel, the librarian, who had known her since she was a toddler. She was hired and assigned to Mrs. Godfrey, the assistant in charge of the project.

It was interesting. Some of the records were dated in the early 1800's. She read that horses were stolen; that the ferry across the Yadkin was suspended during a freeze; and that her great-great-grandfather had married, had served as bandmaster to General Kirby Smith in the Civil War. She was surprised at the number of times the name Morton appeared in the records.

"Hum," said Mrs. Godfrey, "You come from a very old family."

"Yes," said Charlotte. "My father's ancestors came from England in 1616 aboard the H.M.S. *George*. The same year that Shakespeare and Cervantes died."

"Really!" said Mrs. Godfrey.

She was a fat, pleasant woman, diligent but willing to stop and read interesting entries, and share her homemade pies with Charlotte at lunch time.

So passed the last days of summer.

Nightly she wrote to Max. To Cal. To Whit. Then the piano, reading. Billy was her companion. Sometimes they went out to The Track in The Wreck. A couple of times they went to one of the roadhouses, drank too much and danced their brains out. Jennings was already at the university, wearing a Naval uniform, taking the cram courses that would make him a doctor. He was studying, drilling, praying.

One night when she was truly detached, Billy pressed her, consoling for the absence of Max—and she told him.

He comforted, swore devotion through any crisis. She knew he meant it, with all his limited means.

"Write Max," he urged. "Please write Max and tell him. He'd get here some way. You could get married."

"Thanks, Billy. We'll see."

Sometimes she took a couple of hours for tennis, with her father, and others. And there were nights with Amy and the girls who were busily selecting wardrobes for college and wondering if there would be any boys left in school by next year.

After those nights, Charlotte murmured to herself, "It's OK. What a child I'm going to have."

She and her father went through the joyless weekly ritual of dining with Aunt Elizabeth and Nelson Summers. Her father bravely maintained sobriety until he was safely away from Aunt Elizabeth's table.

"Sooner or later, she's got to know, Charlotte. I'm damned if I don't dread that. What an outpouring of pompous platitudes that is going to occasion."

"Me too," Charlotte joined his wry laughter.

She followed the news, read how, step-by-step, island by bloody island the Marines were carrying the war toward Japan—Guadalcanal, Kwajalein, a spit of sand called Tarawa where the air was filled with steel. She read that, there, to stand erect was to be fragmented. The Marines advanced on all fours, as beasts advance. Oh Cal!

She watched her belly. It was there all right. And twice she had the famous morning sickness. Blanche was ever solicitous, ever gentle. They talked of baby clothes. Of what breast feeding might do to her figure. Of the small bedroom which would be the nursery.

There were terrible times too.

At night in bed she wondered what this organism in her belly was like. Why had it come? And it's in me, like cancer, like death. I carry it with me every day. There's no running away. And it's growing.

She remembered when Alice Wilkes had become pregnant in their junior year. Despite all the precaution money could buy, everyone knew. Everyone also knew that she had had an abortion in Kernston; that there had been complications, because no doctor wants an abortion patient hanging around his office. Alice had hemorrhaged and spent six days in the local hospital. God knows how much money it had cost Mr. Wilkes to prevent an investigation.

Charlotte recalled the almost hysterical gaiety Alice affected on returning to school. It had happened. Since it was never acknowledged publicly, it was almost never discussed. But it had happened. And it had not happened.

Charlotte knew that, with her, the evidence would be permanent—growing, and vocal.

Just as the classification of the documents at the library came to its conclusion, she noticed that Mrs. Godfrey became aloof, began to work in haste, clearly preferred not to chat.

Charlotte glanced at her belly beneath the cotton dress and knew that anathema was to begin.

At last the afternoon came when Aunt Elizabeth summoned her to tea.

"Come alone, my dear. Don't bring Douglas. Let's just you and I have a chat."

Elizabeth had heard whispers from one of her bridge club members that Douglas Morton's daughter was pregnant.

Charlotte looked her straight in the eyes—I will *do this each time*, she vowed.

"Yes, it's true, Aunt Elizabeth."

"Well, my dear Charlotte, you have sinned dreadfully. And, Charlotte, I shall never speak to you again."

"Aunt, you have never spoken to me anyway. I have always simply been an object toward which you addressed religious platitudes, warned against sin, urged to virtue. We have never talked. You don't know me. I don't know you. Aunt Elizabeth—I have always wondered if you were ever young. How you would look if you smiled? And your virtue? What *good* is it?

"I shall never forget your lecture for what I did at the school variety show. I thought to myself then—*She doesn't care that the audience was cruel to Billy*. Perhaps they could have driven that boy to suicide. My father and I tried to make

278

you understand why I did it...that I was not being gratuitously mean or evil or arrogant. But you were only interested in the fact that I spoke two words—words forbidden by your kind —by all of you who are interested only in form, appearance, how you *look*! Are you human? Can you feel, or care, or love? You've never shown me the slightest warmth. We have been desperately polite to each other. Never..."

"Good afternoon, Charlotte."

She told her father that she guessed she had effectively ended the weekly dinner ordeal.

"Well," he said, "perhaps that's not all bad. In fact, I should kiss you for saving me so much pain. The food was bad, the conversation dull, and really nothing was going to cause her and Nelson to regard us anyway."

Of course, she had written Aunt Jessica in Mobile. Jessica immediately suggested abortion, offered Mobile as a haven, sent love and support, and promised to visit soon. Jessica loved her and nothing could change that.

Sybil Schraeder, whom Charlotte had never quite understood, was as loyal as she had promised to be. Charlotte was surprised and began to feel genuine affection for her. And Sybil proved invaluable to her in her hardest moments. Sybil reported to Douglas the gossip as it began to emerge. No doubt about it, Charlotte's plight delighted the town. What a delicious target was this too beautiful, too gifted, too arrogant Morton girl. She had splayed her legs to every boy on the football team. Indeed, any boy who would take her. Who was the father anyway? Huh, who could guess? So, she hadn't needed their applause. *Huh!*

Sybil never told Charlotte any of this, until Charlotte said she would really like to know. They had long intimate talks when Sybil took her to Kernston to buy maternity clothes. Shopping became an excuse for the trip and long lunches. Charlotte perceived in this elegant woman a warmth and personality which had always been boxed with charm and social presence. Sybil was no longer form without feeling. It came slowly, but Charlotte felt honored. She came to see Sybil more clearly than had her father or anyone else in the town, and Charlotte sensed that Sybil actually envied her in some strange way. She sensed that she and her predicament caused Sybil to learn—gladly learn—of human intimacy. Sybil was childish in the delightful discovery. An open laugh supplanted the cold formal smile on the erect, handsome woman.

Hoping for even more, Charlotte was at pains to tell her how much her loyalty meant, to find excuses to depend on her.

The afternoon that Charlotte knew that Amy knew, she could hardly keep from laughing. Amy and Claire and Louise had dropped by. They sat in the summer house. Charlotte and Blanche brought cokes and cookies. Charlotte felt their eyes fastened on her belly. She made up her mind not to say a word. If they really wanted to hear it, by God, they would have to ask. She also made no effort to pull in her stomach.

They talked idly about the coming of college, news of the boys. Amy had disclaimed Cal, since he had not written a line. Charlotte said that she had not had a single letter from him either. But she still wrote once a week. Cal was Cal.

When the other two left, Amy hung around. Charlotte told her that she had decided to postpone college for a couple of years. She was going to study on her own, and really work at the piano. Also, she hinted, she had some other plans which she wanted to launch before she began college.

Amy didn't ask. Charlotte let her go consumed with curiosity.

When the library job ended, Spence gave her proofreading for the newspaper. She told him she would take it until she became cumbersome. He told her that she did not have to come to the office, just get it there for deadlines. Watch style, he said, and perhaps she could write a few stories later. She did. And she wrote a story on the old documents she had filed, and it drew some reader comment from those who had seen their family names or had an antiquarian's interest.

Amelia White, her father's legal secretary, retired at the end of the summer. For years now, she had promptly opened the little office and sat out her eight hours with nothing to do. No one could explain why Douglas Morton would not close the office. He had not actively handled a case in years. But somehow, he *could* not close the office. Perhaps it was simply that the century-old firm was a town institution. Several times he had considered taking a younger partner simply to maintain the practice. Each time the negotiations broke off because of his inability to remain sober long enough to bring them to conclusion. His reputation was tattered. Brilliance was not enough, nor past performance. But he lacked the will for sustained effort.

Charlotte was beginning to show, when she assumed Amelia White's post in the office. On her morning walk to the office she would stop by the newspaper office and pick up a sheaf of proofs to be done. Spence would send a messenger for it later. The proofreading filled empty time in the office, for there was little else to do. Miss White had shown her all the records and explained the files and accounts. Sometimes Charlotte would amuse herself by examining the century of legal work the firm had done.

On first looking over the account books, she saw that the office was providing no income at all. She was astonished, however, when a cursory examination showed the number and amounts of receivables which no effort had been made to collect. Some of them stretched as far back as the Depression. She decided to ask her father if he wished for her to begin a billing process.

Aside from the proofreading and these casual researches, Charlotte spent her days in the office reading, sketching, writing the daily letters to Max, Cal, and Whit. She also had to write to Billy and Jennings when September came and college resumed session.

Amy Winston came several other times during the summer. On her last visit before leaving for college, she and Charlotte at last talked candidly. Amy sympathized, but Charlotte would have none of it.

"Well, Amy, some of us took our chances. I lost. Or gained. Who can say at this point?"

"Oh, Char, you could have had an abortion. You-know-who had one."

"Yes, I could, I suppose. I'd be lying if I said that I didn't consider it. I had some horrible days. But I decided against it—for reasons that I'm not sure I can explain. It's a bad time for this to happen. You know, the guys leaving and no real chance to discuss it."

"Oh, Char, you should be going to college. I mean, you're so brilliant and all."

"Oh, that's not over. There's plenty of time for that."

"It was Max, wasn't it? I mean, I know that he'll marry you."

"Look, Amy, I'm not unhappy. Don't think that. There's going to be a lot of gossip. There's going to be a lot of unpleasantness. You know that won't bother me. And there is compensation. I've got a glow inside me now—sort of a compact with Creation. I hope that will stay—no, I will make it stay! I . . . well, everything's OK so far."

"Listen, does Max know? Have you written him?"

"Actually, the only people I've told, not that it needs telling at this point, are Dad, Miss Schraeder, Billy, Aunt Elizabeth—now *that* was an unpleasantness—and now you, Amy."

"I won't tell."

"I don't ask that, Amy. Look. This is here. To look is to know. Soon it will be heard." Charlotte smiled.

"Does Mrs. Compton know?"

"I don't know. She will though."

When Amy prepared to leave, she promised to write.

"Do, Amy. I'll write back. Promise. Don't I write Max and Cal—and now Billy? That bastard Cal never writes. Hardly to his mother!"

"I know. Isn't he a bastard?"

Aunt Jessica's visits were godsends to Charlotte. They came when she was powerless to snap depression, or nervous with the fears which beset all expectant mothers.

Jessica, beneath her elegance and charm, remained that beautiful, intelligent, gutsy, stirring woman that the South somehow produces in limited edition each generation. Now in late middle age, she was slim, agile, spirited, and beautifully presented.

Economically, she and the nation had recovered together. With a friend, she had opened *Jessica Horner*, the shop which by relying on exquisite taste alone, had gradually become Mobile's final arbiter of *haute couture*. Jess and her partner, placing their hopes entirely on the value of snob appeal, resisted all temptation to expand. Their hopes were realized. They became modestly wealthy.

Luckily Jessica was there when the gratuitous meanness began. First there were the telephone calls, usually late at night. Charlotte would answer and hear the likes of, "Hey, Morton, since you're screwing everyone, there are a couple of us who'll drop by and put it to you." Or, "I've got a big hard prick for you." Or, "How's the whoring trade these days, you bitch?" Sometimes the caller would only breathe. Twice it was a woman's voice. She could not guess who the callers were.

Charlotte was shaken each time. She was profoundly saddened that another human would take the trouble to provide her with misery. She had never, in her memory, hurt anyone purposely.

Douglas raged. "Because you are what you are—that's why. They cannot bear quality. They cannot bear anyone who does not need their goddam approval."

Worse came. Several times, usually on Friday and Saturday nights, cars would screech to a halt outside the house and catcalls would echo down the quiet oak-arched street. "Whore Morton!" And "Morton sucks prick." Followed by rebel yells, tires snarling. Then the silence that condemns. One night, after the yelling, a beer bottle caromed off the side of the house. Another night a beer bottle shattered a pane from the large window just beside the piano.

Douglas came galloping down the stairs drunkenly, robe flying, waving a huge, black pistol.

Jessica was standing in the parlor in her dressing gown.

"Oh, put that away, silly. Don't dignify that obscenity by getting angry."

She calmly poured three bourbons and told them to sit.

"Charlotte, I have a great plan. Listen, become a de Staehl, a George Sand, Catherine the Great, an Emma Hamilton, a Cleopatra. Take dozens of lovers, each grander than the last. Intellect, charm and sex shall be your weapons. I shall dress you myself. *Blaze* in the capitals of Europe. That is, if there *is* any Europe after this wretched paperhanger's war. You, Pallas Athena incarnate, to cause men to be what they can be."

She glanced at the broken window.

"Ugh. Persons who drink this beverage cannot rise even to the level of vulgarity." Jessica tipped the beer bottle with her slippered toe.

"But I can see it now. *Charlotte regina.* The consummate woman. Crowned heads shall bow before your salon gate to be received—or disdained."

Jess beckoned Charlotte to rise, took her hand, and led the beautiful pregnant girl in a circle figure.

"Turbaned janassaries shall guard the gates to the salon. Batteries of arbiters shall screen prospective devotees. And you shall lend your jeweled lobes only to the great and near-great, your repartee only to the witty, pungent, and cosmic in scope. It shall be bruited abroad: Queen Charlotte's war on platitude, baseness, and inconsequence. Queen

Charlotte's reign over the new Golden Age of grace, wit, and beauty. God save the Queen."

Douglas and the shaken girl forgot the intruders, as they were engaged by this imaginary Olympian Charlotte. "I can see her now," Douglas said, "gliding past the likes of Eisenhower, Rockefeller and Gable to give her hand to Einstein, Pound, or Horowitz. *Bravo!*"

"After the attainment of great wealth, of course. Ah, but beware, my dear. You must have it *here*," she touched Charlotte's bosom, "or you will shatter like crystal."

"How does one get it *here*?"

"I think it is granted, not gotten," said Jessica. "Perhaps you have been elected. If so, it will begin to show very soon. I have observed preliminary signs."

"Dad, was there a comet shower when I was born?"

"No," he sighed, and walked to embrace her. "But it cost a lot to bring you in."

"Then it's settled. Charlotte," said Jessica. "One sweet Mozart movement and then we'll sleep again, having provided the unwashed their amusement."

They did.

Those summer months, in the time of indecision, then decision, Max's letters sustained her. They were newsy— swagger sticks, bad chow, no privacy, green underwear. He fired expertly at the rifle range—and the one comically poignant revelation that he was still her Max: *I don't like sharing a bathroom with eighty people.*

But there was nothing the Marine Corps could demand of his body that he could not perform.

The letters always concluded with a telling of his love. His thought and phrasing were so simple and deeply felt that his sentences sang in her heart for days. She said them over and over. *I want to kiss your mouth—now. I can see you running toward me, your hair flying, the day I broke the mile record. I never admired you so much as that night you beat down poor Cal when he had hurt Billy. In my dream last night we lay across your bed and I actually smelled—truly smelled— your hair across my face—it was there when I woke!*

Sometimes he naughtily told her of her breasts and bottom and thighs, and where her thighs met and how he longed. He had seen Whit twice, their boot leaves corresponded. They went to Tijuana for five days, then Los Angeles. He called her twice during the leave. They were awkward, tender conversations, ending each time with the slightly dramatic, "Charlotte, whatever comes, I love you."

She was crying each time she hung up the phone. She knew that he was too. Whit yelled hello. And they sent hairless, stern, mugface automatic photographs.

After leave, they reported to Camp Pendleton for infantry and landing force training. Having survived boot camp, they were now human again and had a few weekends free. He always called.

And he wrote of his fear of landing force operations, which, even in practice, always claimed casualties. Descending the side of a ship onto the landing craft would be difficult on a smooth lake, but the swells of the ocean made it gamey indeed. He had seen a landing craft swing out, crest so that the net sagged between it and the ship's side, then crash against the ship and crush one of his fellows. "But don't worry, I'm agile."

In six weeks he too sent her the Fleet Post Office address. He had followed Cal beyond the telephone, beyond the daily letters. Not beyond her love.

Charlotte sometimes met Mrs. Compton in the streets. They had never been friends. The Comptons were a conservative, pious couple who had married late in life. Max was their only child. Charlotte had rarely been in their home; her own home had always been the rallying place for the young people. For several months after Max left, she and Mrs. Compton greeted each other and chatted for a moment, comparing the news each had received from their Marine.

Lately, Charlotte noticed that Mrs. Compton's greeting had become cool. Then merely a nod.

She knows, the girl thought. *Does she not know that it is Max?*

Finally Mrs. Compton actually avoided her and Charlotte knew that this woman was choosing not to admit the reality which was, in her eyes, the ultimate embarrassment. Perhaps even mortal sin.

The FPO letter from Max for which she would have laid down her life arrived just before Christmas. She took it to her room and closed the door. He knew that she was pregnant. He loved her. So much. His mother had written him. Charlotte gathered that it had been a one-sentence piece of news—*Charlotte Morton is pregnant.*

Well, he loved her. Three times he asked the question that she could not answer: Why, darling, didn't you tell me? We must marry. We would have anyway. Did she think that he was going to let *her* slip away? If only this horrible war would end. But we will do it all together. It will be wonderful. We will go to college together, learn, grow together. Write to me every day. And, Charlotte, I love you perfectly. Remember it always. P. S. What will we name him? Or—gosh, *her?*

When she read the letter the first time, she held it to herself, lifted her chin, and closed her eyes. And sat quietly.

"Merry Christmas," she whispered to herself and her unborn child. "Merry Christmas."

She reached blindly to her bedside table drawer and took the felt bag which held the stop watch. She pressed it to her cheek. 4:14. Her Max had done that.

She went to Blanche in the kitchen. She walked to her and simply held her. Her tears ran to Blanche's cheeks. Then Charlotte read her the letter.

"I knew, Precious, I knew all the time."

She met her father at the walk when he came in. He embraced her and said, "Of course. Of course."

And Sybil, who began planning the birth and the wedding instantly.

It was a happy Christmas.

Jessica came, since her two daughters were married—one in California and one in Texas—and could not be with her. She informed them that she was having a serious affair with a Naval Commander which could develop into something permanent. She, too, was happier than Charlotte had seen her since Chuck's death.

Billy was home and spent most of the holiday with her. Aside from the absence of Max and Cal, one other failure caused her pain.

Jennings Hall was home from the university for a short stay, his first since he had reported after high school graduation. Billy had prepared him for Charlotte's condition. He said that when he had told him Jennings had become almost catatonic. He made no comment whatever. Then after five minutes of distracted conversation—mostly Billy's—about work and the war, Jennings had said that he had to go. Billy had not been able to reach him by telephone since. When

Jennings did not come and did not call, Charlotte called him two days after Christmas.

"Jennings, Merry Christmas. This is Charlotte. When am I going to see you in your uniform?"

She heard him gasp. Then clearly unable to summon his bearing, fumbling, hesitating, he pled family and church commitments. Finally, the agony ended as they wished each other a happy holiday, and good luck.

It was the most painful sixty-second conversation that Charlotte had ever had.

She sat by the telephone table after they had disconnected, thinking of the brave, fanatical, possessed boy whom she had seen stand in that icy water for half an hour at the bidding of his God. He was now a young man and his possession had grown with him.

She could not let him leave like this. She dialed him.

He had not moved from the telephone either. He answered immediately.

"Please, Jennings. This is Charlotte. Please. There has been too much—Oh, Jennings, I don't want this."

He couldn't speak. She heard his ragged struggle to breathe.

"Jennings, listen. Very well. I know that in your eyes I have done wrong. I have sinned. Horribly. But Jennings, we have been through things together. You know me. You cannot believe me intentionally evil. Oh, Jennings, I don't want us to be this way."

She heard him take a breath.

Finally, hoarsely, "I'm sorry, Charlotte."

"Jennings, please—"

"Charlotte, I *am* sorry. I am so sorry for you."

"Jennings, for what we were to each other, please forgive me. Jennings, this is Christmas. The season—Jennings, Christ forgave. Your Christ forgave."

He could say nothing but "I'm sorry."

Tears streaming, "Oh, Jennings, this breaks my heart. Jennings, if you can ever forgive—If you can, I'll be here. I'll be hoping."

There was silence.

She whispered, "Goodbye, Jennings. I will hope."

When they were in school, she had sometimes turned suddenly to find his gaze fixed upon her. Embarrassed, he would flick his eyes away, redden, retreat.

Jennings Hall's attraction for Charlotte Morton had grown into obsession. It coupled love, hate, self-contempt, the addict's meditation on the drug which destroys him. She was so much, so much. But she had a wildness that frightened, a willingness to track life wherever it went.

Nowhere did life throb more insistently than in sexual expression. And Jennings, an aberration of the sternest Judaic-Christian ethic, equated sex with sin. Still, Charlotte drew him into that powerful, primitive sphere which he could find no way to exclude.

That night of the hayride when her body had carelessly touched his, he had learned perfectly the depth of his weakness. He had sinned as surely as if he had murdered. If she had turned to him offering, he could not for his soul have turned away.

His mother had to exercise command and plea to end his fasts each time he fell from devotion into desire for this girl. His father had to order him inside the house one sub-freezing night as he stood in shirt sleeves, statue-like, on the porch of their home, exorcising the desire Charlotte Morton had called from him by playfully sitting on his lap before Latin class that day. He had been standing two hours when his father ordered him into the house.

Now, she was pregnant. He *must* rid himself of this obsession. Billy was helpless in his abomination. Charlotte had chosen hers.

Jennings left the telephone. He went upstairs to his room and took out his photo album. There were dozens of pictures of Charlotte. With Max and Cal and Billy. And himself. He took them all out and laid them on his desk. He took his high school year book. She was there—six times. On the candid pages under the heading "The Big Seven," she was with Max, Cal, Billy, Big Edna. And himself. Her stirring beauty survived the mug shot photography of her formal portrait. She could have been a saint. But, no, the directness of her gaze. There was too much pride there.

He rose and went into the bathroom and returned with a razor blade. He carefully excised her picture from the year book wherever she appeared.

Carrying the pictures, he went down into the basement. Placing a metal pail between his knees, he struck one match after another and burned each picture of Charlotte Morton to ashes.

Several days later when he returned to the rigor of the Naval unit at the university, he was certain that he had purged himself.

16

LIFE grew in her daily. "Here, Sybil. Right here. Feel." Or, "Blanche, he's kicking. It *must* be a he. A football player. Or a chorus line."

It was Life!

But Death was gaining. The casualty lists grew in the evening paper. Daily. The news broadcasts were filled with bombings, assaults, demolitions, cities in flame. Horror on horror. One could not isolate, personalize, such volume of pain. It seemed that all life on the planet was bent on destroying all life on the planet.

Death slipped around war's giant panorama and came to the Morton home simply. Skipper Henshaw, bell boy at the hotel died at the age of eighty-eight. He fell asleep on duty in a chair in the broom closet off the lobby, where he had shielded the boy Douglas Morton all those years ago from the dangers of the lynch mob. The man Douglas Morton cried like a baby.

Skipper had been panderer extraordinaire, facilitating the frivolous, necessary sins of the flesh. Skipper always kept several bottles of bootleg whiskey on hand for special clients in emergency. It was Skipper who was alert to late night signals through the lobby windows, who would casually saunter to the most deserted side entrance of the hotel. "Well, this week, they's a blonde. Very big up hyar, but too big down hyar. And they's a brown head, young and skinny, but they tells that she's very active."

Charlotte would miss this little stick of a man who had always greeted her like a princess when she and her father walked through the lobby on the way to the dining room. She had approached him several times in emergency herself, when Cal, or Max or Billy, had guzzled the whole pint too soon at a dance in the ballroom. He always obliged. "Now, Miss Charlotte, don' you dare say nuthin' to Mr. Douglas 'bout this. You hyar?"

Skipper took enough secrets with him to the grave to damn most of St. Mark's Parish. Douglas Morton saw Skipper's passing as the end of an era of honor, of sin with style, of his own vision of the way 'the way of the world' should be.

Death moved on. Edna Graham suffered a massive heart attack in front of her class two weeks after Skipper had gone, and she died where she had lived.

There was no definition to Charlotte's sorrow at this loss. She knew that she was as much as she was because of this woman. The old teacher had changed her perception of the world.

The beloved was gone, but the perception remained.

So Charlotte entered a mourning which would accompany her the rest of her life, though gradually it would change from a dark absence to exultation. Big Edna's death was a consequence of her life—a quiet, abiding glory.

Letters of tribute appeared in the paper, some lovely and perceptive. Spence, knowing Charlotte's grief, asked if she would try a short eulogy for the editorial column.

Charlotte began her process of transforming her grief over *Mademoiselle*'s death into exultation for her life by the writing.

She had short words for the teacher's dedication and scholarship. They were taken for granted. She accented the breadth of character, the willingness to accommodate all of Creation, the refusal to countenance meanness in any form. Charlotte closed with *She could not teach this town regard for excellence. But she taught it that there are still a few places where nothing less will do.*

Writing the eulogy helped channel her grief towards creation—an act Big Edna would have approved. Spence reported that many had asked who wrote it and were shocked to learn that it was the work of the degenerate Charlotte Morton.

Charlotte moved away from saturnine grief. But she still cried when she thumbed through her diaries and relived the discovery that *Mademoiselle* had provided.

Death moved on.

Having flicked Skipper like a bug from the branch of life

and paused to fold the noble Edna Graham into quiet earth, Death went mad.

He went into a crazed jig. He found little spits of sand and disks of coral in the vast Pacific and zigzagged from one to another like a giant insect over the great water which cared nothing for him. These little wisps of waste were useless—except to land aircraft. They had silly names. Names like Tarawa, Kwajalein, Saipan, Eniwetok, Tinian. Silly. Why did so many men want to stand on them? He would teach them.

Like a great winged spider, he zoomed down on them, these ash and rock disks, clamped his six legs at their edges, and injected the very air with his venom. He would teach them.

How he glittered! The whole air about these islands was full of shining. That way it didn't take long. Sometimes only a day or two. Sometimes a week or two. It was nothing. Legs clamped, he squatted, spraying bursts of venom until the air was lethal, until there was so much death there wasn't room for life. Then he zoomed on to the next. There were many of them, these little nothing sand spits. He zoomed. To light again. Inject again. He was obsessed. A crazed jig. Zig zag over water wastes. Clamp legs. Inject. Crazy.

Charlotte Morton held her breath. Cal. Now, Whit. And her beloved Max.

Never had the papers and newscasts been so vital to her. Her Marines were all in staging areas when last she had news of them.

Now almost daily she spoke with Mrs. Hendricks on the phone. When they had nothing to say, it was worst. She could feel the mother's desolation, her thanks for a kindred spirit with knowledge of desolation. Cal always tacked little messages to Charlotte to his mother's notes. To write another whole letter was a task which somehow he could not bring himself to do. But weeks separated those beloved illiteracies.

Then one day Mrs. Hendricks said to Charlotte after they had discussed the mounting casualty tolls, "Charlotte, dear Charlotte, I—well, it's none of my business, but—I heard several weeks ago that you—that you . . ."

"That I was pregnant, Mrs. Hendricks. Yes, it is true. I am. In fact, I'm due anytime."

"Oh yes. Charlotte, believe me, I bring this up simply to say that if there is anything I can do to help—well, anything at all. . . ."

"Thank you, Mrs. Hendricks. Thank you so much. I had bad luck, I guess. Or good. It's all right. Everything seems fine. I'm healthy and strong and I'm going to have a beautiful baby."

"Oh, you sound wonderful. Promise to call if there is anything I can do. You are a brave girl. Promise? I may have lost my touch with babies, but I'd love to get it back."

"Yes, I will. Oh, I will. I'll keep you posted. And you'll be the first to know whether I have a boy or girl—or twins."

Charlotte thought of Mrs. Compton. She must be dying to know if I have news of Max. Why can't she call? Or speak? Mrs. Hendricks had no reputation to protect. Her husband was a railroad executive. And she was only a human being.

At four-thirty, on a crisp February morning she shook her father out of deep sleep.

"Hi. A friend is coming in. I thought you'd like to get up and meet him—or her."

Douglas Morton shook off his drunken haze. He jumped up and took both her hands.

"How do you feel? I would like to meet him indeed."

He went down the hall and called Jessica, who was staying until the baby came, and the house was settled. He telephoned Dr. Tom. Jess helped the unwieldy, panting Charlotte while he went down and warmed up the Packard.

He left the two women at the hospital with Dr. Tom who had beaten them there and went for Blanche. She had made him promise that he would.

At dawn it happened. It was easy. The pain was clear and sharp and clean. It was earned. He was strong and healthy as she. Eight pounds. Male.

Blanche wanted him. Jessica's smile rivaled that sunrise. Douglas held him, quietly remembering another dawn in the old hospital, another baby, eighteen years ago. And a loss.

That day four letters arrived from Max and one from Whit. They had been on no island that shone with Death's glitter.

Post-natal depression lasted two hours. The letters and the boy took care of that. She held her baby. It cried. No, he. *He!* She sank into a dream of fair skies and warm sunshine where caring was all there was.

She looked at him all the time that they would let her have him. She had one lingering fear—that he would get mixed up with another baby. She memorized him.

But, "Why are his hands so tiny? *So* tiny."

Then, "Never grow," she whispered to him. "Never. You are so . . . so right. You are so right in my arms. You are as right as the sky and the trees and the sun."

She was home in four days. In full charge in six. She was strong.

The house was full of advisers. Everybody knew all about babies. When he squeaked, Sybil was at the crib.

Blanche knew best.

"Precious, if he cries, go and look. If he is not wet, and it's not feeding time, let him cry some. That way in a few days he'll sleep through the night."

Sybil was a nervous wreck. Jessica hovered. Douglas was baffled. But Blanche was right.

He was a boy. Nobody knew what to do about his name. Dr. Tom pestered about the birth certificate. He became Morton Male in the county records. It could be changed.

In one of his letters, Max had—jokingly?—suggested Alexander the Great Compton. Soon it began to sound right, in spite of the fact that Max had also suggested Helen of Troy Compton.

She wrote to him. And wrote. And wrote. March passed. Spring stirred earth. Then in the first week of April she got five letters. Yes, he wrote, Alexander *was* great. Alexander Compton. He liked it. How was she? How was his darling? His mother had written foolish letters. She would come round, he was sure. He was trained to the hilt, he said. They moved from one staging area to another, but he was ready. His outfit was ready. He would be careful and he would be lucky.

She was happy. She rolled and carried her fine son to the office with her. She talked to him. She played Mozart for him. She sang to him. She cared nothing for what the town thought. She had her son. She would have her man. If only this ghastly war would ever end.

Mrs. Hendricks did come. She brought blue linens. And she brought news that as Charlotte was delivering her son, Cal was assaulting a sand spit in the Pacific called Eniwetok. He sent his love. The two mothers held each other as though they could merge their hopes and strengths.

And Mrs. Hendricks pointed to the newspaper. Didn't Cal and Max know this young man? A smirk leered from the page. Not even a uniform could ennoble that face. She read

293

that Seaman Coy Trexler, Jr. had reported to Norfolk and to sea duty.

I wish him luck, Charlotte thought. *I wish them all luck.*

Jessica urged exercise. She hated to go to the Club. The cool nods. The askant glances. But she seriously began trying to get her tennis game back. Sometimes she could pick up a game, and sometimes she would make her father play with her. She was strong and her natural grace remained. In tennis you hit a ball. *She* could hit a ball. And she could move like a cat. It came back.

Nights she stood before her mirror and studied her body. It looks the same. To me. It looks the same. Yes, it *was* the same. She had her dark, soft, fur triangle back. She considered that she looked like a 'good piece of plunder,' as Cal used to say.

She longed for Max. She wanted to test. She was a woman. She had brought in a splendid baby. She wanted her man.

In spring, William Ennis was inducted into the army. Charlotte did not know whether to laugh or cry. *We must be losing if they need him,* she thought wryly.

Alexander Morton Compton's first spring—she thought that would be his name, or maybe Maxwell instead of the Morton—Alex's first spring in the world was soft, bright, vintage Southern.

There were the gentle early rains. He and his mother watched the splash on the gallery bannisters. Green became greenest. Dogwoods, pink and white, millions. Wisteria. Lilacs. Little Stars-of-Bethlehem corrupting the lawns with beauty. And oh, the cowslips, so orderly, so green and yellow.

Harrison and Hedrick, or their great-great-grandsons, were there. Alex reached for them. They preferred nuts. He didn't mind.

And the birds, too sudden for his reactions. Ah, but the song.

Buttercups, Blanche's were gold for him. She put several fresh ones on his bedside table each day—"They's sweet as you, Precious."

He lay and kicked in a veritable grove of Trailing Arbutus, whose perilous survival his mother and Blanche had protected for years. They showed their gratitude.

There *were* days! "These goddam diapers are driving me crazy," Charlotte screeched.

Or, "I'm not ready to get up yet, loud mouth."

Or, Blanche would say, "You gotta feed Alexander, honey. I got a mess of collards to clean."

And he slid off the bed. And he ate a button. And he drooled on nineteen of his mother's blouses.

But he smiled. And he said 'goo' clearly. And he lay like a *putti* in her arms. And the arms of Blanche. And Sybil nearly had to be physically subdued before she would give him up. She begged Charlotte to go out so she could baby sit, since despite good intentions, her father was becoming more unaccountable. On rare weekends when Billy came home she sometimes did. But Sybil would come anytime, when Charlotte could get a tennis game, when there was a good movie she could walk to. Anytime.

Then summer. They sat by the river, and paddled in a sandy spot, him naked. Him in a bassinet, while his mother swam. Her stomach was flat. She would keep it that way. Him in a carriage while she practiced her serve.

He perceived the other woman—as his mother had—by her marvelous clean-clothes odor. Then the ample bosom, the great glistening black cheeks, the smile that sun-rose in its brightness, the sweet warm breath. But she was of other odors, too. Baking, the strong smell of greens as they boiled, coffee in fresh morning, and bacon. And sounds. Spoons ringing against pots, vivid sizzling grease, the clacking of dishes together, the tinkling of silver, the furious fuming of running water. Sound. The lovely contralto voice singing hymns and lullabies. They were comfortable sounds and odors and feels.

As they walked by the river under the loblollies and squished the bull tallow in toes and fingers—her toes, his toes and fingers—Cal was wading ashore on an island called Saipan cursing the pack which made him deformed and unwieldy, dropping it after with a growled 'fuck you' that could not be heard even by himself. Other people were trying so hard to kill him that he had to lie in the same spot for hours—perhaps, except for sleeping, the longest time he had ever been still in his life. He compensated by yelling rapid-fire 'fuck you's. He was actually relieved when he was ordered to run zigzag ten yards straight ahead to a place exactly like the one he left, and then put out as much cover fire as he could so someone behind him could make the same zigzag run. Some did not make the full ten yards. Cal did not like any of this. If he had had common attitudes he would have been scared. Being Cal, he resumed his 'fuck you's. There were too many stimuli for reaction. Stimuli were all over his tiny space on the planet.

In September the two mothers again clasped each other to merge strength. Mrs. Hendricks had heard that he had been on Saipan. He had been on another island called Tinian too. He told his mother that he was tired. But he wasn't too tired to kiss Charlotte's kid and Charlotte. And dance with her. Where was Max?

"That's three," his mother said. "Surely they won't send him in again. Oh, Charlotte, he's been so lucky."

"Sometimes your father acts like he was got in a cotton patch and raised on a flat car," Jessica sputtered.

She could not decide whether to be furious or cry. She swept back and forth in the parlor swinging the make-shift cat tail attached to her black tights. She flung off the mask cowl with the pointed ears and plucked her whiskers.

"A Halloween ball is a marvelous excuse to get drunk as a goat. Tomorrow he'll say, 'Well, it only comes once a year.' And we all know he *only* gets drunk once a year. Huh, once a day. Oh, Char, he even drinks in the morning. Is this how it is all the time?"

"Yes, Jess," Charlotte sighed. "I'm afraid so."

"He's killing himself."

Charlotte nodded.

"And that gross Marsh Woods. Why does your father team with him. And Sugar. She's nearly as bad. First, your father went through his Civil War routine again. Then Sugar got on the table and did her almost-but-not-quite-but-too-damn-far strip tease. Nothing is more disgusting than an over-the-hill bag showing her stretch marks.

"Then His Grossness Marsh began his catalog of hangover woes. Have you heard it? You know, it begins with the cat stomping its big feet around the house. Witty? Then the slimy bastard started on my tail. This tail. Not this one. Incidentally, speaking of Sugar and tails, are you sure that I can still get away with wearing something like this?"

Charlotte laughed. "Aunt Jessica, sex-eee. How old are you anyway?"

"Are you sure? Why I am on the threshold of middle age. The threshold, mind you. Incidentally, Sybil was absolutely smashing as the Fairy Queen. All in silver, and that great, cold, Nordic face."

"She's so great. Oh, Jess, she has been so great to me and Alex. And she isn't so cold. She has warmed to me."

"Oh? Too bad nobody's been able to crack her armor. I grew up with her but never really felt that I knew her. She was always on a horse."

Her father was always *in* a bottle. And she *needed* him.

Douglas Morton was the classic type of alcoholic the South produces in such quantity—intelligent, cultured, charming, with a rhetorical gift which is approximately Gaelic. Perhaps they are Southern because the South paces life so as to gift these gifted men with time to contemplate the human condition and other final questions. Thus, though they remain nominally WASPs, they no longer believe the precepts on which the tradition is founded. They drink. They become cynical, though not entirely separated from the joy of life.

For as long as he could remember, Douglas Morton had been sipping bourbon from the judge's decanter, which had once belonged to Andrew Jackson. Bourbon was a condition of the gentle Southern household.

But there was the other too. Secret, cabalistic, illegal.

Each autumn since he had returned from his war, he and Spence had been invited to the village of Slant Rock in the Smokies for a night. They would drive up, register at the only hotel in Slant Rock, have a hearty dinner, and drive nine miles back into the hills over a series of perilous mountain roads, the last leg of which dwindled to a path that only two goats walking in tandem could manage. They always joked about who was going to drive back later that night.

They would pull up to a cabin at road's end and nose between the several trucks and cars parked among the pines. They would knock at the door in darkness, and identify themselves as "Doug Morton and Spence Fulton of Concordia."

The door would be opened by a man in a black hat with a shotgun cradled on one arm. He would nod and they would walk in. A dozen or so silent men would be standing around inside. When the newcomers were recognized, quiet greetings were exchanged.

Some of the men wore business suits as did Spence and Douglas. Most of them wore overalls and wide-brimmed felt hats.

"Hello, Jessie."

"Mr. Douglas, it's been a coon's age."

"Howdy, Locke."

"Howdy, Mr. Fulton."

"How're the kids, Alvin?"

"Fine. Mr. Douglas. Fine."

"Well, Cody. Your five."

And so on.

Formal.

Quiet.

Some of the men in the business suits spoke of cotton broking, the law, the pharmacy, the mill.

There were several other knocks, entrances, greetings, after Spence and Douglas were assimilated.

Then without ceremony, they stood to the business at hand—the tasting of the new batch of white liquor eight of the finest whiskey makers in North Carolina had produced.

In the center of the single room cabin was a rough hewn, pine-slat table. Directly over it was the sole source of light, a kerosene lamp suspended from a stud running below the peaked ceiling of the tin roof. Its glazed white shade flung a fierce arc of light down on the table which held, lined as if in formation, eight fruit jars containing liquid as clear and cold as diamonds. A tin cup was before each. By the cups was a bucket of icy well water with a tin dipper in it.

The eight producers grouped near the end of the table. Seven were mountain men, clad in overalls, some with shirts under them, two with buttoned up, long john tops, baggy at the elbows, ingrained dirt around the sleeve ends and neck lines. They all wore broad-brimmed felt hats which drooped over their faces. The eighth producer, Wiley Cruikshank, clad in a seersucker suit, mussed shirt, and a clearly uncomfortable tie, was from the sandy pine barrens near the coast. He was a good ole boy who made the trip each year "so's these heah ridge-runners don' git to thinkin' they're the only ones who can sear a goat's insides."

The mountaineers were all lean, feral-eyed, raw-boned. Wiley was plump, red-faced. He would be loquacious and friendly in any other environment. Here, he stood silently by his colleagues.

"Well, Mr. Hannah, you be the first according to age," said Cody Jamison, their host.

Mr. Hannah, an ancient gentleman farmer clad in a gray suit and dark tie, stepped to the table. Cody splashed one finger from the first fruit jar into a cup and extended it to Mr. Hannah.

Mr. Hannah turned to the gathering, raised the cup, sniffed, sipped and swished, and swallowed. An expression of profound satisfaction oozed, wrinkle by wrinkle, over Mr. Hannah's aged face. His next breath came quickly. He held the cup high and turned to one of the weasel-faced mountaineers.

"George, congratulations," he croaked.

The other tasters, including Spence and Douglas, followed Mr. Hannah's suit.

"Slips down real easy, George."

"George, nice belly fire. Warms real well."

And so on.

George smiled a slack weasel smile.

Cody then gave Mr. Hannah a dipper of well water. He swizzled and swallowed. Then he took another swallow, and passed the dipper to those who followed him.

Cody splashed a finger from the next fruit jar into the next cup. Mr. Hannah's face again succumbed to profound satisfaction. He raised the cup to Locke Swicegood and murmured his congratulations.

The others followed.

After the fourth fruit jar had been sampled, cigarettes came out, and the men chatted for a spell. The conversation became animated and relaxed.

After the spell, Cody beckoned Mr. Hannah to sample the contents of the fifth fruit jar. Mr. Hannah gladly, if unsteadily, responded.

And so on until all had one-fingered from each of the eight fruit jars, and offered commendations to the producer.

This done, it fell to Mr. Hannah to offer congratulations to the eight producers *en masse* for having kept alive one of the finest traditions two thousand years of civilization had developed. He ended by exhorting them all to live forever.

Then as was the custom and privilege, each of the tasters purchased a quart from each of the producers. The jars were stored in motor oil boxes which Cody had had the foresight to stack in the corner of the cabin.

"Now, Gentlemen, I will ask that you leave at five minute intervals. The woods are crawling with revenue agents this year."

He turned to Mr. Hannah.

"Mr. Hannah, as in all things, you may go first. Do you feel able to reach your car? I know that once there, you will manage all right."

"I do, Cody. Gentlemen, again I thank you and commend you."

With that, he aimed and lurched for the door, missed, was set right by the man with the shotgun, and disappeared into the night.

So with the others.

Spence drove, since Douglas could not even find the car when their time came to depart.

Once back home, another tasting ceremony was arranged for the gentlemen of the town. Each of them had his special 'debts' of affection to pay.

Douglas always presented one of the coveted fruit jars to old Ed Duncan, respected political enemy, captor of a thirty-eight pound catfish, weighed and verified, and the only registered Republican in the county. One had always gone to Skipper the bellboy for clandestine services and for silence. Of course, one to Dr. Tom, and one, shyly, to Father Cary. Which left him four jars to be sparingly sipped when illness or adversity became particularly cantankerous.

The Slant Rock trips were a thirty-year annual pilgrimage. The personnel changed over the years. Death, the marauder, had thinned ranks, caused replacements, and occasioned an extra cup to be lifted in memory of the deceased in certain years.

First to go had been the venerable Mr. Hannah who passed on at the age of ninety-two, Cody reported, holding his cup high beneath the kerosene lamp. "Strong drink finally caught up to him, ifin Dr. Elkins is to be trusted."

Then, cups high, "To Locke Swicegood, may the lord give rest to him who give so much pleasure to his fellow creatures. And special thanks to the deceased for having the thoughtfulness and mercy to teach his son his skill that the remainder of our journey be lightened."

And so on through the years.

* * *

Another landmark in the path of addiction for Douglas was the night 'Jack came over the mountain.' Charlotte remembered that occasion because in the ensuing three days the police were at the house five times at the behest of the neighbors.

Spence had just returned from the annual Conference of Southern Press Writers, which by a loving kiss of Fate, had been held that year across the Smokies in Knoxville. One night during the conference a fellow editor from a small South Carolina paper had beckoned Spence into his room at the conference hotel, handed him a glass, and told him to "Sip this and tell if it is not of extraordinary quality."

Spencer's trained palate instantly told him that God in His Mercy had given His children an additional aid in bearing the slings and arrows of outrageous fortune.

He seized the bottle from his friend's hand. He memorized the label. He asked where in earth this could be purchased. He skipped the meeting scheduled for that hour and repeating over and over to himself, 'Jack Daniels, a Tennessee sour mash whiskey,' searched out a bellboy called Ransome Stevens and arranged for a case of the said Jack Daniels to be delivered to his room, all the while delivering a silent obloquy against Tennesseans for having kept this ambrosia to themselves for so long.

When Spence arrived in his home county two days later, he stopped by his farm and filled three one gallon jugs with sweet, clear well water and drove directly to Douglas Morton's home. He spent thirty minutes on the telephone and at five o'clock some dozen of the town's most discriminating drinkers were gathered in the Morton parlor.

That afternoon lives were changed.

No tasters from the Medoc, or the Rhone Valley, or exuberant Tuscany were more grateful to the good earth and sun and rain than were these several Southern gentlemen. And they manifested their gratitude by becoming falling down drunk and staying that way for nearly seventy-two hours. Whenever they became worn down by lack of sleep, they would take two fingers more. "I'll have two fingers in a silo," Marsh Woods gurgled repeatedly.

Or two fingers to perk them up and get them on the road. Somehow the two additional fingers caused a loss of interest in getting on the road.

"Charlotte, my child," cooed old Ed Duncan, him of the

thirty-eight pound catfish, "if you could find in the goodness of your unblemished heart and steadiness of your young hand to pour me about two fingers in this glass, I think I could find the strength to defend right-headed Republican economic policies to this witless assembly of New Dealers who are so benighted by..." and there he trailed off, attending to the replenished tumbler of Jack and well water.

The police came and were put off by promises of subdued conduct.

At three A.M. in the second night after Jack came over the mountain, it occurred to Marsh Woods and Douglas Morton that they should renew their efforts to get into Sybil Schraeder's panties by serenading her. With five others, they maneuvered the two hundred yards to Sybil's house and tuned themselves beneath her bedroom window.

> "*Violate me*
> *in the violet time*
> *in the vilest way that you know.*
> *Ruin me*
> *ravage me*
> *brutally savage me*
> *on me no mercy show.*"

rang down oak-arbored, sedate Well Street.

Sergeant Puss and Officer Hefner made the fifth call at the Morton house. But what could they do? Judge Richmond Hartline was asleep on the couch. Mayor Billy Pritchard was glassy-eyed in a chair. Dr. Tom Cleland and Lawyer Morton and Spencer Fulton begged them to just taste this ambrosia. One little taste. Just one little taste.

They reported back to headquarters that they thought the party was winding down and that it might be better to just let it die of its own weight than take any official action.

There were many justifications a man like Douglas might make for drinking, but pleasure was not the least.

17

ALEX crawled to the Christmas tree. Its brightness attracted, its tangy smell. He tried to eat a decoration. His mouth wasn't big enough. He got his hand slapped. He got even. He bawled for eight minutes.

The biggest person in his life unsteadily sang *God Rest Ye Merry Gentlemen* to him and the small revenge was distracted by moustaches moved playfully in song. Then, perhaps, the bourbon-rich breath soothed the young anger because Alexander fell asleep and did not hear the clatter of reindeer hoofs on the roof.

He crawled to mischief. He was a missing person for eight minutes. His mother was frantic. Sybil weeping. Blanche fuming. The big man with the moustache found him beneath the bedspread in a guest room.

He crawled to danger. Head first and down two stairs. He tasted his own blood. For the first time. He had cut his lip.

One morning Harrison's and Hedrick's world was pure white. White was in the air. The world was new, waiting a colorist. The big man with the moustache found a sled in the attic which once even he couldn't lift. Now he could lift it and even pull the excited small person along with the one whose heartbeat, breasts, warmth, odor, and dark great-to-pull hair was home to the small person.

William Ennis, Private, United States Army, got home for a couple of days each month. Charlotte considered that he looked even more ridiculous as a soldier. Before he was a Mess. Now he was The Uniformed Mess. She loved him.

After the obscenity of basic training, for which he was constitutionally unfit, the vast impersonal army, perhaps somehow realizing that he would be a liability anywhere else, had issued him the luckiest possible assignment, the base band at Fort Jackson, South Carolina. It was truly a good band, Billy said. The commanding officer was a major formerly of the music department of the University of Michigan. Billy's talent attracted the major immediately. Best of all, the military band supplied the personnel for the base dance band and he was tapped for the dance and jazz bands.

Billy had had a successful year at college. He had begun to penetrate musical theory at an academic level. He was probably the only man in the nation to whom the army became a blessing. The reasons were several.

Most important was the transfer to the band at about the same time of Sergeant Bucky Stafford. Stafford was in his late twenties, a draftee who in the early part of the war had gone the way of most draftees, into the infantry. He had been badly wounded in North Africa and was no longer fit for combat. Before the war, Bucky Stafford had been a side man for three of the most popular big bands in the nation. Now stateside, after two and a half years in line companies, Bucky Stafford could not get his mouth to a tenor sax quick enough, and having got his lip in shape and his fingers limbered up, he could not be made to put it down. Billy Ennis could sit at a piano or ride a bass as long as Stafford could blow, and in a few weeks with Stafford's horn at his ear, he could follow, then add to, then create improvisations that made Bucky's transparent. The two came to *know* and *feel* each other musically.

There were plenty of good musicians around the band barracks all the time. Others started sitting in, a sharp piano man, trumpet, trombone, drums, other rhythm.

Everybody wanted to jam with Bucky because of his invention, the ease with which he set them up, followed them. Then they wanted to jam with Bucky *and* Billy for the same reasons. Guard duties, mess duties, and inspections were kept at a minimum by the major who was interested in musical results. Therefore at almost any time of the day, a jam session or rehearsal was in progress. Sometimes a standard would go on for several hours with complete changes in personnel before it had wrung out. Billy was in heaven. Bucky was back in shape. Billy was growing, learning, fitting into a milieu as he never had before. It seemed to him that here, in the army of all places, musical ideas by the thousands were floating around him.

He began doing arrangements for the jazz band. He and Bucky wrote tunes, arranged them, and played them at base dances on Friday and Saturday nights. *Cool Drive*, the jump tune that was recorded by two big bands in the late Forties and that every American danced to, was a Bucky Stafford number which grew out of a riff that he and Billy felt their way into during one of the jam sessions.

Bucky and Billy spent hours at the base library listening rooms with records of Benny Goodman sextet, quartet, and trio, Louis Armstrong, Lionel Hampton, Teddy Wilson. They listened to the great singers, Billy Holiday, Lee Wiley, and best, Bessie Smith. They knew all there was to know about phrasing.

"Hey, listen," Billy would shout, "she's behind the beat. Bessie's behind the beat on that. Listen."

"Yeah," Bucky would say. "She knows, man. That's blues. Wow, that's heart-hurtin' blues."

On three-day passes they would ride all night with someone going to New York to hit the jazz spots, and Bucky knew where to go to sit in till dawn when everybody was playing for themselves. Billy could go with anyone on bass. He had found his place.

Several times Bucky came home with Billy and they would spend all night in the music parlor leading Charlotte in circles as she tried to fill in on the piano. She couldn't go where they went, but she became aware of the beautiful interaction and invention of the two. Sometimes they made her sing, backing so beautifully that she sent her husky voice to places of feeling that she hadn't known about. After *Body and Soul*, *I'm Beginning to See the Light*, or some other torch standards a hush would fall over the drifters and drunks who had come to the Morton parlor when the roadhouses and Club closed.

"Too true, Char," Bucky would coax. "Go blue. Right between the notes. Listen."

She listened. She could do it.

"I'm believing every word you say, Baby," Bucky would murmur. The final compliment.

Billy had wandered into his true path. He and Bucky began to talk about after the war. Bucky had connections. They would try a small group. After the everlasting war.

In February, Alex showed impulse toward his first step.

And in that same February the Marines made the bloody, penultimate step in the long march across the Pacific to an island which was to become the most celebrated symbol of the Pacific War. It was called Iwo Jima.

All reports said that it was worse than Tarawa. Every family in the town that had a blood or love interest in the Marine Corps held its breath.

From Iwo Jima's airstrip, the war would be brought to Japan by American bombers. The entire nation leaned forward for five weeks. Iwo was eight square miles. The Marines would win. Nobody doubted that. But, please God, not at cost of my son's life, my husband's, my lover's.

Ten days after the landing was made. Charlotte had letters from Max and Whit. She knew they were there. The letters both said we're moving out. Whit said, wish me luck.

Max closed with a lovely, simple, I love you.

She was mad for news. Devoured the daily newspaper. She traced the island in the atlas. Eight miles. My boy could run it in less than an hour. Why is it taking so long?

The photographs were ghastly, hazy, netherworld scenes. So many men in so small a place. How can either side miss? her father wondered. Shoot in any direction and someone will scream. No one will hear.

Two weeks. Three weeks. The pictures. Is this he? Sprawled, dead, hit, or just taking cover? Charlotte paced. She could not eat. Alex was an annoyance. Then her only comfort. She ignored him. Then smothered him with kisses.

Cal was not there, Mrs. Hendricks had a letter. He was training hard. Oh God, for the next damnable island. Let them *keep* them, for God's sake. But, oh, he was not on this most horrible one.

Four weeks. One afternoon, she rounded the corner from Main Street on to Lawyer's Row. She ran squarely into Mrs. Compton.

"Hello, Mrs. Compton."

"Oh, I'm sorry. Oh hello, Charlotte."

She passed quickly, erect.

Charlotte stood for a moment. *She looks ninety years old*, she thought. *A very erect, brave ninety.* She walked on slowly. Then she stopped and ran back. *I must speak to her. She knows Max is there. And she knows. Has she news?*

When she rounded the corner, she found Mrs. Compton no longer erect. She was slumped against the bank building, her face in her hands, her whole body trembling, sobbing.

Charlotte put her arm around her, and whispered, "He'll come out of it all right. I'm sure. I'm sure of it."

Mrs. Compton was unable to speak. She allowed herself to be led into the bank. One of the tellers ran to Mr. Compton's office and he came and took her from Charlotte. He led her away without a word.

Charlotte went to her office. She cried.

The very next day Max's face stared at her from the newspaper. It was a copy of the one he and Whit had sent her after their boot leave. The article simply stated that the Navy Department had reported Private Maxwell Compton, son of Mr. and Mrs. Maxwell Compton of Well Street, had been wounded in action.

Spence telephoned her five minutes after she had read it.

"I just noticed it myself. I would have called," he said. "Now, take it easy. He may have cut himself shaving. Stranger wounds have been reported. I talked to Maxwell, Sr. They don't know anything either, but he had called Senator Dunham and if anything can be learned, he will learn it. Don't fall apart, Char. I guess from what Maxwell said, Elsa Compton is in shock."

"Spence," she said evenly. "I will not fall apart."

"No," he said. "You won't. And I'll keep you posted, when and if there is anything to know. Maybe he'll have luck, Char. I'm with you. And him with all my heart."

"Thanks, Spence."

She thought of her beautiful boy. She thought of him running. She thought of his wonderful body which she had watched grow into manhood—lean as an Indian. Running, waiting under a punt in a broken field, dancing, kneeling over her. Where was it marred? How dare they, *how dare* anyone or thing mar that dear body?

Goddamn this war. This sea of stupidity. Goddamn it. Goddamn them. Goddamn. Goddamn.

At last there was the photograph of the flag raising on Mount Surabachi, Iwo Jima had fallen. Charlotte stared at it, the flag tricking in the breeze, the men leaning against it. The huddled, indefinite figures, crouching, almost unlike humans. What did it mean? Here was victory. Victory.

She wrote daily to Max and Whit. Please write, she pleaded. Please let me hear from you.

She called Whit's house. Mr. Manson, defeated by the Depression, by life, spoke drunkenly of victory. "Like we did in the first war." No. They had had no mail from Whit. But he was sure both boys were all right.

A week after the island was secured she had a note from Whit. He was OK. He still observed censorship rules. He had been in combat and the assault was over and they had won. Funny, he could not remember a thing which had happened to him over the past weeks. It had all come so fast. He hadn't seen Max and he hadn't been able to find Max's outfit since he was still restricted to his own area. All he did was nap between work details. He felt good. Just tired, dead tired. He had forgotten how to be tired these past weeks. Now it had caught up with him.

She immediately wrote Whit—thank God, dear Whit, that you are safe—to please try to find out about Max.

The very next day she had another note from Whit. He had seen some of the guys from Max's outfit. Max had been hit. He didn't know where or how badly. He heard that Max's outfit had been in the third wave and that he had not even made it ashore. As always, Whit explained, the Japs had let the first two waves in, hoping to isolate them on the beach by preventing the other waves from landing. They had really ripped the third wave and those that came after. Max's landing craft had been hit off-shore. Nobody here knew anything beyond that. He would try to get more information from the central medical unit here when he could.

She thought she would go mad. She dialed the Compton's home several times but simply could not cause herself to wait for the hello. Her father followed her about, hovering, watching, his heart leaning out to help. There was no help. Sometimes he found her door closed. He understood. And, over bourbon, patiently awaited her return to human sympathy.

Spence was dear and tenderly solicitous. He came by every day, and sometimes called her at the office with his 'no news.' She finally gave up calling Frank Manson. The endless stream of simplistic, patriotic stupidities annoyed, then enraged her.

God, she thought, you are talking about the possible sacrifice of your own son. She thought of the horrible organization of this huge, ugly war: the gorgeous deadly lines of the planes, bombs, ships, the massive energy, the truly wondrous effort the nation was expending. For this ... this war. Sid

Jacobson and her father were right. War gives purpose to the dull and useless.

Alex was now walking. Everywhere. Into the street, the garden, neighbors' yards seeking new things to touch, new friends. New! New! New! The world was all new. Must be touched, investigated. Learned. Hot must burn. Cold chill. Fuzz tickle. Dirt must be put on. To be washed off. Immediately put back on. He walked into the river. Into the pool room. Into a machine shop. Always into the street. She and Blanche performed harrowing rescues daily. He saved her sanity. She could concentrate on nothing. His harum scarum patternless impulses occupied her.

On April Fool's Day, Spence walked around to the office on Lawyer's Row. She read his face. He had news.

"He's in Hawaii," he said. "Senator Dunham got the information. Maxwell just called me. He's in a hospital. Charlotte, it's a head wound."

She gasped. He took her hand.

"That's all we know now. Listen, dear, wait. We don't know anything else just now. Let's not assume the worst."

She sat erect, her eyes on his.

"Jesus Christ, Spence," she spat out. "I am consumed with this insane war."

"There's more," he said softly.

She pressed her shoulders back.

"The Marines began an assault on an island called Okinawa this morning. Do you know where Cal is?"

"He was staging—training and reforming—when last Mrs. Hendricks heard. She guesses New Zealand."

"Maybe not, then."

"But maybe."

"I looked on the map this morning. This has to be the last one. Then Japan itself. It can't be much longer, Char."

"There is still a lot to lose."

"I know. Why don't they surrender? I don't know why they don't surrender. They can't win. I guess that men find power the hardest thing in the world to surrender."

"I guess."

He stood. She went to his arms.

"Thank you, Spence."

There would be no more sweet sleep. The long nights

pacing the gallery began. Sometimes her father's hand on her shoulder. But he knew that she preferred to be alone.

She knew the stars. They *were* cold and ignorant. They *were* unconcerned. They saw. They witnessed a piece of steel fired by a man who did not know the men he was shooting at, did not know their hopes and fears and dreams. Neither did the steel. It went where it was aimed. When it struck something solid it exploded, as it was so precisely made to do. It flung jagged pieces of smaller steel in all directions, in all trajectories. If something, a man, a boat, a hand, a *head!* were in its path, it tore. Why, stars, why? Why that precise path? Why the head, the dear head of a man? Why that conjunction in that split second?

My man was chosen.

And that beautiful, beloved head was where a piece of steel had to go. In that moment, he did not lower his head to scratch his chin, or sweep a speck from his eye. Or he *did!* The trajectory and head met in perfect geometry. And chance!

The brain? No. No. That she could not prepare for. No. She had seen some of those faces. The thousand-yard stare, the foolish smile. No. Not the final damnation. Not that brain. So agile, so curious. No. That she could not imagine.

Scars. Oh, yes. I will kiss them. The handsome face, perhaps scarred, made more handsome, more dear. Yes, scars, she would accept. Not the other.

She did not know what she was granting.

"Char," it was Spence's voice on the phone, "Elsa and Maxwell have gone to San Francisco. Apparently Max has been transferred to the Naval Hospital at Terminal Island. In San Francisco."

"When? Spence, when?"

"They left this morning. Senator Dunham arranged for them to get on an Air Force plane out of Fort Bragg."

"Well, is there any news? Why doesn't she call me, Spence? She knows Alex is Max's child. He told her. I know he did."

"I don't know, Char. You know how formal Elsa is. Hell, she'll probably be wearing little white gloves on her death bed."

"How long will they be gone? Is there anything about Max's wound?"

"No. Hey, Char, what are you doing for lunch? Where's Alex?"

"He's with Blanche today."

"I'll walk by and we'll go to the hotel. How's that?"

"All right, Spence. That'll be nice."

The editor took her hand across the table.

"It is serious Charlotte. I think that you had better prepare for the worst. I don't know anything. And I may be wrong. Neither does Maxwell. Nothing really. But the fact that they hustled him back to the States makes me uneasy. You have heard absolutely nothing from him?"

"No. Nothing."

"That's hardest, isn't it?"

"Yes. Oh Spence, I think of the brain."

"Yes. That's occurred to me too, I confess."

"Oh Spence."

"Yes. Well, let's not jump to conclusions."

"When will the Comptons be back?"

"I don't know. But, at least, when they return, we will know. Try to be patient, dear."

She nodded, knowing that it was impossible. Spence guessed that just Naval Hospital, Terminal Island, California would be address enough.

She wrote every day. There was no reply. Each night she walked past the Compton house to see if lights told of the Comptons' return. She called Martha, the maid, twice and extracted a promise of a call when they did return.

She had never known how powerful anxiety could be. She lost weight.

"Darling," Sybil said, "you must rest. You are becoming drawn."

She tried to tire herself physically so that she would be exhausted at day's end. Alex helped. She played tennis. She and Sybil rode the only two horses Sybil still kept.

Twice Charlotte sat late with her father drinking, hoping for oblivion. The next day's hangover made everything worse.

She snapped at her beloved Blanche, then collapsed in tears on the old woman's breast. The sun-drenched aura of Blanche's embrace conjured up a long-ago time when that aroma had meant all's well. She cried anew. It had been so simple then.

Finally Martha called. It had been over two weeks.

"They'll be back tomorrow. No, mam. They didn't tell me nothin'. It was one uh them telegrams."

Spence came to the little office at three the next afternoon. She stiffened in her chair. He didn't sit.

"Char, close up and let's go home and have a drink."

"Tell me."

"Char, I—"

"Now."

He sat.

"Yes. It's been long enough. I just left Maxwell in his office." He reached for her hand. She withdrew.

"Dear God, Spencer, tell me."

"It's as bad as we could have imagined. It's the face. The lower jaw. It, ah, is gone. The whole right side."

Her hands were in her lap. She closed her eyes. Spencer rose and went behind her and took her shoulders when she began a slow, mindless rocking.

"Listen, there will be plastic surgery. They can do wonders. Maxwell says . . ."

He went on to say that Max had refused to see his parents, steadfastly refused for the entire two weeks. Because of this, Mr. Compton thought that the mind had been damaged.

"But, listen, dear. It isn't. I believe that Max's mind is all right. Listen. Here's why. Let me tell you exactly what Maxwell said. He can't talk, of course. But when they tried to see him he wrote—and the doctors say it is the very first communication he has made—he wrote, *Tell them I am dead*."

She stiffened.

"No, listen. It was the first communication, according to the doctors. Charlotte, it means that his mind is OK. He's depressed. Christ, he's probably in shock. But don't you see? It means that he's thinking, reacting."

She rose and turned into his arms. He held her tight.

"Now, can you see? His mind is all right. Now, sit down. Listen, Maxwell tells me that they will begin plastic surgery immediately."

He went on to say that a psychiatrist was working with Max. It was horrible. But at least the note was one positive indication. The *first* communication Max had attempted, Spence kept repeating. If plastic surgery was successful, or even partially successful, it might not be as bad as it seemed. The Comptons did not seem to realize this.

"Both of them are almost irrational. Understandably so. Maxwell broke down completely. I just left him. They are terribly hurt because Max wouldn't see them. I've never seen him like that. He was crying and trembling. He says Elsa spends most of her time in bed. She won't eat. Won't see anybody. Started this in San Francisco. She is on the verge of a breakdown. The thing about it is that they have always been so formal and cold. I guess that—well, you know how Max worshipped Doug—I guess that this horrible thing coming into their formal world, forcing emotion and a caring that they had never considered before, is absolutely shattering them."

She had not moved.

"Charlotte."

"I'm all right, Spence. Oh, Spence, those people. Those poor people."

"Yes. I feel for them. They were there two weeks, trying every day to see this son of whom they were so proud, and yet so ignorant. I know that Elsa is wishing that she had held him and kissed him a little, and given him some warmth—at least, I guess that's what she's thinking. Funny, I can't decide what Maxwell is thinking. Maybe they are both simply and superficially thinking only that he refused to see them and merely feeling sorry for themselves. I never really knew either one of them well."

"Spence, will you take me home?"

"Of course."

On the way, she said, "He wants me to consider him dead, too?"

"Perhaps now. But he's going to need you, Charlotte. Oh, he is going to need you."

"He is not dead, Spence. I love him."

Home, she held Alex, who pulled her nose and her hair, and wanted to run, and not to be held. She held him, studying his face. She covered his chin with her hand.

She released him. He toddled away. She went to her photographs. Maxwell Compton was a handsome man, had been a handsome boy. She studied close-ups. Laughing. Stern graduation pictures. The cheap mug shot he and Whit had sent from California. She covered the mouth and chin.

Others. Football pictures. The broad padded shoulders, the slim hips. Always the ready smile. By The Wreck, with Cal and Billy and herself. Smiling. By the river. In the tank suit. Lifting the canoe. Gleaming with sun-caught streams of water. Clowning with Cal, head back laughing, the clear young man's muscle definition, the proud bulge of his penis beneath the suit, a half turn so the taut stomach and thigh muscles coiled.

She covered the lower face. She cried. *All I know,* she thought, *is I love you. Love for you is all I know.*

Her father's hand was on her shoulder. She went to him. "Spence told me."

They held until she stopped trembling.

She fed Alex. Sang him away to sleep. Wrote to Max.

Every night. She did not know how to refer to the wound. Suddenly she thought of eating. Oh, my God, she thought. *Eating!* That simplest, loveliest pleasure. She nearly gave over again. But she thought of him. She did not speak of the wound. *I love you, darling, as your heart beats,* she closed the letter.

There were no replies. Ever.

Tell them I am dead.

Busy Death had skimmed over Max. It dropped its dark mantle over Sid Jacobson. Suddenly. A freak spring cold. To pneumonia. The gentle, radical, cello playing Jew died because there wasn't enough air to breathe.

Charlotte was jolted from her private, controlled grief by the loss of this man who had so often tripped her racing mind and heart, then picked her up, laughing, and pointed a whole new way to run. Sid had been one of her testing grounds for ways to feel and think, and this meant uncommon trust. Sid was irreplaceable.

She was jolted by the fierce Mediterranean grief of the plump, sweetly simple Judith Jacobson and her daughters. Dark shimmering hair flying like pennants of death, they fell upon each other and on Charlotte and Douglas and Spence, wailing their grief openly, without shame or restraint. Sometimes their cries unnerved Charlotte, so grief-ridden was the timbre that there were moments when Charlotte heard them as the translation into sound of the final loss.

Yet within a week Judith had straightened, begun negotiations with Hal Link Enterprises for the sale of the store and the house. It was as if in that week she had spent all the grief her emotions could hold and cried every tear her body could make. She had four children. She must go on. She had talked to her only son, stationed now in Germany, who had been in law school before the army had called. They decided to return to New York where her family lived.

Three weeks later, in Douglas's arms at the train station, she said, "Well, Douglas Morton, there is no use trying to say what you have meant to us."

He put his hand over her mouth. There was no use.

There was huge vacancy in the lives of the Mortons and Spence. And loss was marring Douglas.

Nothing came from Max. Nothing. Sid's death briefly diverted her. From grief to grief.

She was concerned for Alex. Instinctively, she knew that no child should grow in an atmosphere of gloom. She forced herself to song and sometimes lost herself in the melody. She spent part of each day with him on her lap at the piano. He was fascinated at the movement of her skillful fingers. And there were books, her childhood books, carefully shelved in the room—her room where the walls were covered with the giant chronological tables of human history. And there were the colorful crayons with which she and now Alex made their squiggles. He delighted in color and sound, at all things bright and mobile.

She still walked by Compton's house at night. Usually the house was dark and sullen by ten o'clock. Sometimes there would be a single light in the study to the rear of the house. Sometimes she would walk early, just after dark.

It was so cruel. If they had information, why not tell her? They knew that she and Max loved. Loved. Some people, some mind sets seemed not to recognize love and its implications. These minds relied for conduct guides, on social mores, custom, manners. There was no room for emotion. What were the Comptons like? Seen at St. Mark's, in the hotel dining room, they looked like—what they were. A banker and his wife.

Max had spent more of his waking hours in her house with her and her father than he had in this house. Perhaps loneliness accounted for much in him, the distance running, the self discipline, his ardor for her, his affection for Billy the outcast, for Cal the prodigal. *But*, she thought, *perhaps it stands him in good stead now*.

She stood at nine o'clock one evening before the house. Bright moon through the Well Street elms and oaks sheened the formal, noble house, its coiffed lawns and boxwoods. It, like its owner, seemed to be wearing a dark suit, white shirt, and dark tie. Always.

A light shone in the study. That single light. What do they know? An illegitimate child is not the end of the world. Good God, do they think I and Hester Prynne are the only women in the world who have lain beneath a man before marriage?

Perhaps they do. Perhaps their world can't include Amy Winston, Jane Lea, the rest, *in flesh and blood*. Only when they sit in St. Mark's, hands folded in their laps, looking cherubic.

Oh God, I have to know what they know. She started up the walk. She stopped, brushed back her hair, buttoned her blouse to the throat. Walked to the porch, lifted the knocker—once only.

The parlor lights went on, then the hall chandelier, the blinding porch light. The door opened. Mr. Compton stood in pajamas and robe.

"Yes?"

"It's Charlotte Morton, Mr. Compton. Please tell me what you know of Max."

"Oh, Charlotte. Yes." He looked over his shoulder back into the house.

"I beg you, Mr. Compton."

He hesitated. Looked again over his shoulder. Then he opened the door.

"Yes, Charlotte. Please be quiet. Mrs. Compton is already in bed. Come with me."

He led through the formal parlor into the study. He closed the door behind them. He clearly did not want his wife to know that Charlotte was there.

He drew a chair for her to the desk. They sat. He looked straight ahead. He seemed to begin several times before he spoke.

"He wouldn't even see us."

Before he reached the word *see* his voice cracked. He covered his face with his hands. She did not know what to do.

He looked eighty. He was sobbing.

"It's all right, Mr. Compton," she said softly, "I love him too."

He sniffed, took a handkerchief and pressed his eyes.

"Yes, Charlotte. Thank you."

Then he reached into the drawer and handed her a slip of paper. It was Max's script. *Tell them I am dead*.

"We were there two weeks. Every day. He wouldn't even see us. Elsa . . . I . . . I don't know what to do."

"It's because of the wound, Mr. Compton. He loves you. He doesn't want you to see him that way."

"He is my son. I . . ."

"Of course. But he is proud. I am sure that he is acting this way out of love for you."

"Do you think so, Charlotte? Doesn't he know how he's hurting his mother? Doesn't he know that we would take him anyway? Do you think that is why?"

She reached across and took his hand.

"I'm sure of it. Max is very gentle and considerate. I'm sure of it. We must be patient."

The old man talked easier after that. He told her that the wound was perhaps as dreadful as a wound could be. The doctors had been very kind. They had explained carefully. He brightened as he spoke of the possibilities of plastic surgery. If only Max had been ashore. But to be hit in a boat that had gone adrift under that hail of fire. Perhaps if he could have been lifted carefully onto a litter. But it must have been awful, under bombardment to get him from one boat to another, then aboard the hospital ship in his condition.

Charlotte, speaking softly, holding Max's note in her hand, told of Spence's conclusion that this terse communication was indeed a hopeful sign. She said that it clearly indicated that Max's mind was not damaged. She said that we must be patient. She said that surely Max was in shock. She begged him to take the hope that the fact of the note offered, to look beyond its face value.

The old man brightened. She took his hand again. It was true. He was clumsy in responding to kindness.

Now he told her how he feared for his wife. She had simply given up, could no longer find reason to live. Charlotte thought, *I could give her reason to live if she wasn't so simplistically moral*. Suddenly, she asked herself, has it occurred to this defeated old man that I have borne his grandson? *Yes*, she thought. *He knows I have had an illegitimate child, but he simply has not realized that it was Max's son. My God, I'll bet he and Mrs. Compton have never discussed it.* Charlotte Morton had had a bastard. That was all.

When they parted, he thanked her. He seemed encouraged by her attitude about the note.

She begged him to please call her if there was any news. He promised, glancing over his shoulder up the stairs. And she told him that if he ever felt like simply talking, he would be welcome at her house.

"I have a splendid new son. I would like you to see him."

"Oh yes. Thank you, Charlotte. Thank you so much."

She left him standing at the door.

18

THE first pictures of the concentration camps began appearing. Spence brought some that the paper had received over the wires. And the stories.

"Can this be?" he asked Douglas.

"My God!"

"Such efficiency," Spence whispered. "Read this. Read some of this. Such hellish precision."

"That men could do this to other men. There's no hope when men can do this."

"I'm glad Sid did not know of this."

Douglas ground his teeth. "Is this the same people that produced Beethoven and Mozart and Freud? My God, can there be any hope?"

But there was hope.

Bedlam from every point in the town announced, proclaimed it. From every point in the nation! On May sixth. Horns, shouts, sirens raking the air, bells of every church, music, the skirl of whistles.

Germany had collapsed. Victory! sweetest word.

Astonished, Charlotte tried to place it in her mind. It didn't fit. There had always been war. Always. Always young men going, being wounded, fearing to go, planning to, always the goodbyes, separation, the waiting, *oh God, the waiting*. She could not accommodate the possibility.

Two blaring radios in the parlor gainsaid her. Times Square, they told, was carnival. Blanche came speechless to her, shuddering, clinging desperately.

Cars darted Well and Jackson like fleet, frantic hornets, staccato horns a distant fret, then a frenzied burst, then receding, merging in a general roar. Hand in hand, her father tugged them up the stairs, out onto the gallery.

Sybil, waving both arms, skipped up the walk below them. Spence came running. Horizon to horizon the air throbbed, diastole and systole, the pump and breath of ecstasy. The firehouse alarm, fearful at midnight, was a humourous barnyard quack beneath whistle, horn and church bell clang and resonant chime. They became infected, drawn to the heart of the vast aural cone. The Square.

Running, skipping, holding hands, threading the log-jammed cars, darting, laughing, crying people, they pressed into the swaying, jubilant mass of humanity. Music blared from jury-rigged speakers. It was bacchanal. Bottles were raised and shared. A hundred hundred arms reached out to embrace. Farmer, shopkeeper, lawyer, worker, shopgirl, service men, uniforms in disarray—all, all. To be a girl was to be kissed. Charlotte laughed to see Sybil seized by a soldier, held, kissed, Sybil laughing. Charlotte was kissed and kissed. She was passed from arm to arm. There was dancing.

She became infected. It was release. A bottle was thrust at her. She took and turned it up. Yes. Why not? It was victory! Two soldiers lifted her, beautiful and glowing, to their shoulders. Lurching, swaying, they carried her above a landscape of faces. Other girls at her height, waved and blew kisses. She waved and kissed her hand to all. Father Cary's face glowed beneath her. She came plunging down. He struggled to her, hair awry, a red cheeked cherub in a Roman carnival. "Oh Charlotte, Charlotte," he sobbed in her ear.

Again, she rose on shoulders, laughing, kissing her hand. Another bottle rose to her. She turned it up. But there was more kissing to be done. Down she came. Into waiting arms. Soldiers bent her over for kisses. They pressed against her.

All right. She was kissed by one, fondled by another. All right. All right.

"It's over."

"We won."

Arm to arm.

"Oh baby, never nothing so soft."

A swirl of uniform color, shining buttons against her, battle ribbons, insignia. She was log jammed against a soldier, a freckled faced boy, weeping openly, speaking, his mouth making words, over and over, intent on her understanding. She leaned her cheek to his. "I'm going back to Kansas. I'm going back to Kansas," he repeated earnestly.

"Yes. Oh yes, boy," she shouted. Yes, he must know.

Suddenly she went flying into the arms of a sailor. Laughing, she prepared to kiss and looked into the face of Coy Trexler. His hat was awry. He was drunk.

"Coy!" she cried.

"Hello, Charlotte. C'mon 'ere."

He kissed her hard. Pulled her against him. Bent her. Pressed into her.

Then she was taken by a soldier. He lifted her for his kiss, smiling and laughing. But she felt a hand over her bottom, then up her dress, where her legs met, hard, too hard, vicious. Hurting.

She turned her head. Coy was behind her.

The soldier turned her into an opening. Music. And suddenly she was dancing. Partners changed, arm to arm. She danced, freely, laughing, moving. Released. Victory! Then she was captured, held, turned and Coy's glittering face pressed against her again. The kiss was hard. She felt her teeth click against his and tasted his sweat across her lips. His hand over her skirt, hard, too hard. He clutched at her.

Another sailor pulled her from his grasp. Again Coy's hands gouging from behind. *God, he's trying to burrow into me!*

She broke and turned on him.

"Cut it, Coy."

She was back in his grasp. His ugly thin lips mashed against hers. His hands were all over her, clutching her flesh beneath her clothes.

"C'mon, Morton. You been laying around making babies. C'mon," he spewed in her face.

His hands were kneading her, hurting her. She felt violated.

320

A cold chill. A stand-still moment of repulsion. But she was saved by an army lieutenant, merry and wanting a kiss. Again, from behind, clinging like a leech in running water, Coy's fingers trying to pierce her clothing.

At last she caught sight of Sybil and her father. They clasped hands over heads and joined. They all hugged. Spence squeezed in.

"It's over. It's over."

Holding hands they snaked through the crowd toward home, spasmodically stopped for more kisses. Again and again she felt that hand through the press like a vile mole, burrowing, burrowing.

Then they broke clear of bodies.

She turned. He had followed.

"Coy, welcome home. But, my God!"

"I'll git ya later, Morton," he snarled and plunged back into the crowd.

"How are you doing?" Sybil panted.

"OK. It's really over, isn't it?"

"It's over," yelled Spence. "Hey, let's go out to the Club."

Home, Charlotte said. She had not been to the Club since her disgrace, except to the tennis courts. Spence argued. Her father joined him. She didn't know. She was rumpled, manhandled. They had forgotten to eat. And there was Alex.

"C'mon. This is truly one night in a million."

Blanche agreed to stay on with Alex.

Spence drove, careening and drinking straight from the bottle that her father had grabbed on the way out. Even she and Sybil nipped—straight. They were both crumpled and kissed out. But released. Happy. Exhilarated.

The bar was a mob scene. She and Sybil were roundly kissed again. It seemed that the whole room was drunk. There were uniforms here also. Noise was deafening. Singing, rebel yells, frenzy, squeals from women who had not had their sex acknowledged in years. Charlotte felt a sexual ecstasy—an almost orgiastic timbre in the jubilation. The nation had lived under pall so long that it was as if it were unaccustomed to joy, needed to test its limits for definition, to purge itself with pleasure.

"Doug, baby," Marsh Woods rasped across the room.

Sugar, in a too tight, too short dress flung herself into his arms. They were swept into the crowded room, drinks were thrust into their hands.

Charlotte felt an arm circle her close under her breasts.

"Honey, where have you been? I haven't seen you in a coon's age."

The slack face of the lawyer Gorman Neil leered down at her.

"Give us a kiss for victory."

He pulled her to him and kissed her hard, holding her against him obscenely.

"Where ya been? Prettiest piece in town."

He knew very well where she had been. She put her fists into his chest. Looked into his leer.

"I've been having a baby."

"Good, that's what you were made for. Let's go make another one."

Sybil's hand took hers and pulled her toward where Marsh, Spence, and her father were crushed together at the end of the bar. Charlotte felt the eyes of all on her as she passed, sometimes leaning over the tables because of the crowd. Not even V for victory could blur her scarlet letter. She had been the subject at their bridge tables, over their drinks, in their cabals too long. She, like war, had given purpose. She saw one woman pull a man's shoulder and point at her. Victory was no cause for forgiveness. She lifted her chin, squared her shoulders, letting her breasts press against her blouse.

Marsh drew her into the crowd, bussed her cheek. The room was heavy with smoke and noise. Release was electric here as it had been on the Square. Custom, purpose accomplished, gave way to carnival after a long Lent. Charlotte found it hard to assimilate. She could swing into a chorus of whatever song Marsh and her father were singing, feel free, then suddenly catch the hard eyes of a woman on her face, her breasts, her belly. Or a man's eye—the old ones were the worst, Gorman's—searching her body. *I'm a little drunk,* she thought. *I want to rejoice.* Never in her lifetime was there such universal cause for joy. She sang.

Turning she met the eyes of a handsome Marine lieutenant. He was leaning toward the bar trying to get a drink. His eyes passed, then came back, acknowledging her beauty. He looked at her deeply for a moment, his smile fading as if distracted, then returning.

"Hello, beautiful girl," he said.

"Hello, handsome Marine," she smiled. His face was clear and clean and straight. She noticed his beribboned chest.

322

"My gosh," he said. "You *are* beautiful. Do you need a drink? Or anything else in the whole wide world?"

She leaned and kissed him on a sudden impulse. He looked sweet and healthy and happy.

When she had given her kiss, he dropped his eyes.

"Thank you. That almost made the war worthwhile."

She looked at his ribbons.

"Were you at Iwo?" she involuntarily asked.

He turned his left shoulder, and pointed his division insignia.

"Yes. Third Division."

"My Marine was there too," she said.

"What outfit?"

She told him. Then, "Mine was in the third wave. He was hit before he even got ashore."

"I'm sorry." He pointed to his Purple Heart ribbon. "I've still got a piece of steel in my thigh. I got hit the second day. That's why I'm home. How's your boy?"

"It's bad. He's at Terminal Island Naval Hospital now."

"I was there for a while. They're good. He'll be OK."

"Oh, I hope."

"He will. He will. He's got to be for you. I'm Bob Wilkins."

"Hello, Bob. I'm Charlotte Morton."

The bartender filled his drink.

"Happy Victory, Charlotte."

"Happy Victory, Bob."

"Charlotte, you *are* very beautiful. Your boy will be all right."

She watched him go. My boy will be all right. My boy has stood here, in this spot with me, holding my hand a hundred times before. Maybe. Maybe.

She turned back. Her eyes met those of an army lieutenant across the room. It was Pete McCanless. He waved. She smiled at him. He was more handsome than ever. The young warrior athlete, sharp, handsome features, careless smile, stance touched with swagger. He moved out from under his father's arm and worked his way toward her.

"Charlotte Morton!"

He embraced her and drew her to him all the way to the knees. They kissed.

"Pete. Welcome home. I'm so glad to see you."

He held her away. "Godamighty, look at her. Whatta woman. C'mon, tell me everything. I been out of circulation." He pulled her back. "Wow, you were worth fighting for. How are you doing? Some woman."

They had backed against the wall. Pete, pulling her, slid along the wall, reached the door, and turned her outside onto the lower terrace.

There were a dozen couples in various states of drunkenness, embrace, celebration. He led her to the end of the porch, stepped down, stumbled drunkenly, caught himself on a pine trunk, stumbled on, still holding her hand.

"Hey, I hear Max Compton and Cal Hendricks and Whit what's-his-name really carried on the old football tradition. The folks sent me clippings."

"Where are we going? Yes, they did. Where are we going, Pete?"

"I don't know. Just out of there."

The night was clear. The cool air refreshed after the packed Square and crowded bar. They came to the pine-ringed first tee of the golf course and Pete flopped on the wrought iron bench.

"Where the hell is Mark Allen? I hear that he beat the draft. Is he at Chapel Hill?"

"I think so. That's where he was the last I heard."

"Goddam draft dodger."

"How do you know? C'mon. You were friends. Maybe he had something wrong with him. What about you? How've you been?" She was still standing.

"Oh bullshit. Well, I don't blame him, I guess. I'm fine. You know me."

He reached out and took her hand, circled her waist and began fondling.

"Charlotte, you were the damned best looking cat in school and you haven't lost a thing. In fact, things have gotten better."

He pulled her closer and leaned forward as if to kiss her breast. She withdrew.

He laughed easily. "What have you been doing with yourself?"

"Oh, I hang around Dad's office. Not much. I have a baby, a son."

"Yeah," Pete said. "Yeah, I heard. How's motherhood?"

"I like it. A lot."

He drew her closer. He sat upright and circled her waist with both arms.

"Yeah, well, you're some baby-making machine."

His hands slid down across her bottom. He pressed his face into her bosom. She pulled away, but he held her.

"C'mon, sit," he pulled her to the bench beside him. "Give us a kiss for victory."

He too kissed hard, like it was an act of violence, and tried to enter her mouth.

She turned. "C'mon, Pete. Let's go back."

He was kissing her neck, panting, and his hands were over her breasts.

"Hummmm, sweet meat. Wow, those are really a couple of handfuls."

"Pete, enough now. Let's go back."

"Back hell," he slobbered. "I missed this in school. I want some of this." He jammed his hands between her thighs, then tried to go up her dress. Her hand caught his but Pete McCanless was strong.

"Pete, enough. Stop, will you? C'mon. Pete. Enough."

"What's the matter with you? Five minutes. All I want to do is play around in your panties. Relax, Charlotte."

He took her hand and put it on his crotch. She pulled away.

"Pete, dammit." She didn't want this unpleasantness. For a few hours this night she had plunged into joy. She didn't want this mess. She knew what he was. A strong, good athlete with low average intelligence, but so handsome that his ego could not acknowledge rejection. She was revolted.

"Stop it, Pete. I'm not a bean bag."

"No, you are not, honey. You are some piece. C'mon," he growled.

She tried to wrench free. He clasped her face, jerked it to him.

"Listen, Morton. For two years I been over there getting my ass shot at while you were here spreading for everybody."

She didn't speak. She looked into the beautiful cold eyes. He was drunk, a combat veteran, owed by the world, desired by the world. Her silence and gaze wore on him.

"I shoulda pumped you back in school. I figgered you were a little young. Well, you been laying it out while I was sweatin' it out. Now, little lady, I want in your pants."

She continued to stare into his eyes.

"No," she said evenly.

He tightened his clasp around her face.

"Everybody knows you've screwed half the town and most

of the soldiers at Fort Bragg. Now spread those legs and I'll give you something worth having."

Oh, God, she thought. *This revolting bastard.* She tried to turn. He was strong. He shoved his hand up her dress, caught the top of her panties and pulled. She caught and held. They tested a moment. He laughed.

Then he clasped her face again, hard.

"You didn't get knocked up like this, cunt," he rasped in her face.

She didn't know what to do. She stared into his eyes.

"Pete," she said quietly. "If you don't let me go, I'm going to yell."

"Whatta you gonna yell? Rape? That'd be a laugh. Charlotte Morton yell'n rape."

Charlotte sickened. Well, it's that way. At least in this fool's eyes. Her jaws hurt beneath his grasp. But she did not move her eyes from his. *My God, I don't know what to do.*

At last, she said evenly, "Take out your prick, Pete. I dare you."

She kept her eyes on his for the long moment that he took to decide to release her. He didn't know what to make of her dare.

He tried to laugh it away. "Who wants you anyway? You're probably burnt. Who needs you?"

He stood, ran his hands through his hair, swaggered out a couple of steps, struck the hands on hips stance.

Charlotte was trembling as she tried to straighten her hair and clothes. She looked at this empty fool standing before her. Fool who had ruined this night.

She stood and walked unsteadily toward the club. Then fury blinded her. She wheeled.

"Pete!"

He was watching her.

She turned into the moonlight. She fixed her eyes on him, then very slowly, she drew her skirt up the long moonbathed legs. Up. Up above her panties, above her waist. She turned, swaying her hips, stood still for a moment.

Then she dropped her skirt and stalked to the Club.

Outside the terrace, she stopped, leaned against the cool brick wall, and swept her hair. She was panting. She looked out across the lawn. He hadn't moved.

"Bastard," she hissed, and entered the chaos.

"Charlotte, your face!" It was Sybil.

"Yours is a little worn, too. Too many kisses for us both." She smiled wryly and went to the powder room.

His finger prints were red on her face. She needed a drink. She went to Spence and her father. They opened arms to her, put a glass in her hand, were flying too high to notice her red cheeks.

Later, the handsome Lieutenant McCanless entered. He did not meet her eyes, but he could not take his eyes off of her. Not even when Millie Hargrove sat on his lap, offering.

Much later she soaked in a hot bath, washing the heavy lust from her body. Tonight men had touched her. She sobbed. *Oh, Max, please write*.

Her hands trembled as she opened the letter. The return address was United States Naval Hospital, Terminal Island, San Francisco.

Dear Charlotte Morton,

This will be a strange letter, containing strange requests, so let me begin at the beginning. I am the psychiatrist assigned to treat Marine Corps Private Maxwell Compton, who is a severely wounded patient at this hospital. Since, depending on your answer, I may require your confidence to a degree hard to grant, I add that I requested the assignment to Compton. My reasons for requesting this assignment were two. First, his wounds are so unique that my professional interest is engaged. Second, his records suggest that he may be a valuable young man.

Having said these things in an effort to persuade you that I am devoted to helping Compton both professionally and personally, I wish to know your feelings toward him on the chance that you can help me.

I have talked at length with his parents. It was some help, though I must say that they seem to have had a rather formal relationship with him. I asked them about you because of your daily letters, hoping for an approach to the patient. Mrs. Compton said you were a friend of her son, perhaps a childhood sweetheart. Mr. Compton said simply that you lived down the block.

The regularity of your letters suggests to me something deeper—a genuine care for him. If my impression is correct, and if you can find a way to trust me on such meagre evidence, I want you to give me permission to read your letters to him, for I must tell you that he has not even opened them. Miss Morton, I realize what I am asking. I want to convince you that I do not ask this with any interest in mind except Compton's recovery.

Since his entry into the hospital, I have spent several hours with him daily. I talk. Sometimes we walk together on the grounds—yes, he can walk very well. His body is perfect. Nutrition is a problem, because he cannot eat normally. But so far, so good on that score. After nearly a month together, he has made no effort to communicate with me. He sits and listens. He comes, shows no impatience, moves to leave only when I signal that the session is over. There is always a pencil and paper before him—but he has so far refused to use it. Except once, when his parents were here. He did not wish to see them—indeed, he wrote, 'Tell them I am dead.' Otherwise, he will not communicate. I am unable to tell anything about his mental state—though the note suggests to me that his mind is sound. As I talk, his eyes sometimes meet mine. His face is heavily bandaged so I am unable to draw impressions from expression.

So, Miss Morton, I would like to use your unopened letters to try to break the wall of silence around him. If you can give me that permission, I promise to read them only aloud to Compton. And I assure you that though I am in the Service, professional confidence applies. I promise that nothing in the letters will go beyond Compton, myself, and his records. I ask this only in his interest.

Later, Miss Morton, depending on your answer, I may have other requests, or perhaps you can suggest approaches to me. If you care for Private Compton as strongly as your correspondence suggests, please write to me.

I don't want to offer false encouragement, but perhaps working together, we can help this boy.

Sincerely,
David Fried, Lieutenant, USNR

328

Immediately she wrote Dr. Fried a letter urging him to use her letters, promising that her interest in Max was serious, promising anything that would help.

She told him that she had borne a son by Max. That her interest was indeed permanent. She told him that in some of the letters she had spoken candidly of their lovemaking. If he would not be embarrassed, read them, use them, do anything which might help Max.

She thanked him for his unusual interest and compassion. She assured him that Max was valuable indeed. There was no way to express her gratitude.

There wasn't.

She mailed her letter, and ran around the corner from the office to the bank. Mr. Compton saw her immediately.

"Mr. Compton, perhaps you should read this letter."

He read it, re-read it.

"That was very kind of Dr. Fried. Very, very kind. It makes me feel better." He turned around in his chair and looked at the walls of his office. "It seems that I don't know my own son."

He sobbed audibly.

"Charlotte, thank you for writing to him so regularly. That's kind."

"Mr. Compton, I love Max."

This simple declaration seemed to stun him. He lifted his head, turned around to her, started to speak, found no words.

They talked again of plastic surgery. They were both glad that the doctor hoped that there was no brain damage.

"I think this news may help Mrs. Compton," he said at last.

Leaving, she promised to keep him informed when she had information.

At the door, he said abruptly, "Charlotte, you have a child, don't you?"

"Yes, Mr. Compton, I have a son."

"Yes. Is he well?"

"Yes. Very. Too well. He keeps me running."

They parted. She wondered if he was beginning to put two and two together.

Douglas and Spence agreed that this doctor seemed unusual. Max was lucky in him. And in his girl. Maybe. Just maybe.

A week later she had her second letter from Dr. David Fried. He thanked her for her trust. He had spent the last three days with Max reading the stack of unopened letters. He was sorry but he could report no reaction from Max. He had sat, patiently as at all their meetings, and listened. Perhaps that in itself was positive. He couldn't tell yet. However, please keep writing. He planned to use her letters, he said, in many ways. He would work them into the sessions with Max anecdotally. He would speak of the river. Of The Wreck. Of Big Edna. Of Cal, Whit, Billy. He hoped that there might be many ways to use her letters, many approaches.

Again he thanked her and promised to try to be worthy of her trust.

> *And, Charlotte Morton, I must say that yours are the most engaging, humorous, delightful letters I have ever read.*
>
> *You are an interesting, intelligent, charming person. Max is very lucky to have you on his side. But the letters—I feel that I know your town. You have the art of capturing place and person. I feel that I know Cal, Whit, Billy, and your wonderful father. And Blanche— whose P.S.'s make my mouth water.*
>
> *I promise to keep in touch with you—maybe ask for pictures and other things which might awaken Max to what he is rejecting. Incidentally, Alex sounds like a fine son. Maybe some pictures of him.*
>
> *Until next time.*
>
> *Sincerely,*
> *David Fried.*

That letter began a long and treasured friendship, by correspondence, between Charlotte and the doctor.

Two letters later, they became Charlotte and Dave to each other. Though always centered on Max, they became personal also. He was thirty-one. Had been in the Navy four years. Right out of university. He was the only son of a New York garment executive. He wasn't married, but was madly in love with a librarian here in San Francisco. He had a real problem. She was Gentile. They really loved each other, but there were family objections on both sides.

Charlotte wrote:

Marry her. Marry her. Marry her. Dear God (either Christian or Judaic), love is rare enough. Besides objections will go away. Who in their right mind would not want you for a son-in-law? And if you love her, she must be fine.

They were friends.

On August 6, the towering Southern sun fell upon the town. Heat swarmed the stone and concrete streets. No one moved except in necessity. Meeting, no one spoke of it. That would be like saying the lights went out just after the lights had gone out.

On August 6, a man-made sun fell like a great beast on a city in Japan named Hiroshima. Over a hundred thousand people died.

"What the hell can it have been? Spence, they say it was one bomb."

"Christ, I don't know."

On August 9th, a man-made sun fell like a great beast on another city in Japan named Nagasaki. Over sixty thousand people died.

"Well," Spence said, "if the Japanese don't surrender now, there isn't one brain in that nation collectively."

On August 14th, Japan surrendered unconditionally. Not even the Japanese truly understood what those man-made suns implied.

Charlotte declined another victory celebration and sent the jubilant Spence, Sybil and Douglas off to carnival.

She spent the night walking on the gallery listening to the celebration bells, horns and sirens, sitting beside the sleeping Alex, listening to his quiet breathing. She looked at his face, dimly outlined by reflected moon light. She studied his chin—the baby flesh was gone now and the chin was becoming straight and true. *Your father's and mine*, she thought. *May you not have your war, boy.*

Near dawn she heard her father stumble in. She heard him tiptoe into Alex's room. He was there a long time. Perhaps he too was thinking of this baby's time to carry a gun, kill, and be killed.

The next day Amy Winston came by. It was the first time Charlotte had seen her since Amy left for college. She was full of stories about weekends at Chapel Hill, Duke, and

Wake Forest. She was dating Senator Dunham's son. A-OK. She had met that co-lo-sal bore Jennings Hall a couple of times at Chapel Hill. He was such a 'Clyde,' but, of course, he was first in his class academically. He had questioned her about her soul.

"My soul!" Amy sneered.

"Yes. He would do just that," Charlotte said. "He wouldn't ask about mine. He knows. Don't be too hard on him, Amy. And when he becomes a doctor, he will be as good as the best."

"I wish he would change his glasses. He's not that bad looking."

"Looks are not his game, Amy. Salvation is."

Amy asked about Max. Her parents had dined with the Comptons. Elsa was very detached and sad. Her parents were concerned about her.

Then she got to the point. What from Cal?

"I just talked to Mrs. Hendricks. He's fine. He was staging—whatever that means. He's fine. Damn him. I have written every single week for two years and that clown has not even licked a stamp for me. Of course, I understand that stamps are not what Cal likes to lick."

They both laughed.

Amy admired Alex, fondled him.

She took Max's address and promised to write to him.

They kissed and parted. A pleasant interlude. Exactly what Amy was for.

For the next two months letters from Whit came weekly. His outfit had moved up to Japan into the port city of Sasebo. Japan is beautiful, he wrote, mountainous. He and those of his outfit who wanted to go, had been trucked over to Nagasaki. The city was cupped in a valley surrounded by mountains. But the city was not there anymore. He couldn't believe it. They said it was one bomb. Seven and a half square miles were swept clean.

Death must have been hovering, grinning, pleased at this piece of work. No more petty little bullets and shrapnel and bombs. *This* was what he could really do!

Six weeks later, she heard from Cal!—a note attached to another letter from Whit. They had met in Tokyo. Cal was stationed in Yokohama. Whit had seventy-two hours liberty in Tokyo.

We met at the Imperial Hotel. It was built by that American architect Max used to talk about, Frank Lloyd Wright. Tell Max it's really great—and supposed to be earthquake proof because it is built on ball bearings. Is that true?

He and Cal had a great time. A lot of Tokyo was burnt out, but a lot wasn't. Cal, he said, had a *yen* for *geishas* (sorry for the pun). They wished for Max. And her. And Billy.

And at the bottom, in Cal's very own bold, childish script—

Hi Char, the japes arent all bad. Theres sake (white lightning!) and gayshas. And it isn't cross-wise. I'll see you soon. Hi to Billy, Max, Jennings, Amy and youre dad. love, Uncle Calvin. P.S. Save me a feel.

She closed her eyes and pressed the letter to her cheek. Dear Whit. Dear, dear Cal. One loved him for what he was or not at all. She loved him.

Oh God, neither of them realizes how bad it is with Max. Then, cross-wise! That wicked, dear, lovable bastard.

She called Mrs. Hendricks and 'invented' a message—cross-wise, indeed! She didn't have to counterfeit her delight that she had heard from him.

19

THE weekly exchange of letters with David Fried continued. Max, he reported, took each picture that she had sent from his hand, looked at it, then put it down. Dave said that perhaps he lingered over a couple of shots of Alex. He couldn't be sure. Charlotte had sent the high school yearbook. Max glanced at the pages Dave opened for him, but did not turn pages himself. Dave left the book and pictures and letters in Max's room. He did not know whether or not Max looked at them when he was alone. Max wrote nothing on the pad which was always before him. *It will be a long, long road,* he wrote. *I can't encourage, but we, you and I, can't give up.*

Later, he wrote that the preliminary plastic surgery had begun. So far, so good. That too would be a long road. The greatest problem was the muscle which made the jaw mobile.

Still later, he sent a snapshot of him and Shirley. They would be married—devil take both families—sometime around the New Year.

Charlotte wrote best wishes with her whole heart. She enclosed a note to Shirley telling her that she was getting a splendid man.

Just after midnight a week before Christmas, a sea bag thrown from a passenger car thudded to the concrete platform beside the hissing, screaling train. He swung down after it. Charlotte saw him first, and turned Mrs. Hendricks toward him. Then they all, Mr. and Mrs. Hendricks, Douglas and Charlotte Morton, cried, "Cal!"

He was home.

Life changed. For with Cal's presence a room, a field, a building became charged with possibility.

The next day he was at her house in khakis and sweater. Swinging Alex, a new friend and playmate. Sneaking up behind Blanche, goosing her, kissing her, sitting at her table. Feeling up Charlotte. Touching glasses with Douglas, Spence, and Sybil.

The war hadn't happened. Cal didn't remember it. Asked direct questions, he would answer, but he never mentioned it. *That* was last week's game.

Taking the keys to The Wreck from Charlotte that night and heading for The Track was *now*. Sipping beer in the car, he was genuinely touched by Max's disaster. When he came by the office next day, Charlotte made him write a letter to Max for inclusion with hers. He did it. Six sentences. But he did it. And Max would know.

And *she* knew. Cal's midnight was over. He was back. He was whole. He was dear. He was Cal. They were playmates. They were dear friends. They were each other's safety valve. Charlotte knew she owed the stars for this.

He's reading. He's reading! He's reading! Dave's note read. *From the hospital library. It was by his bed. H.G. Wells's History Of Mankind. I brought a pen and note-*

book and left it by his bed. I wrote NOTES on it. More later, Love, D. P.S. Happy Holiday. Tell Blanche I love her. Shirley loves her. The fruitcake was superb. I love it. I'll lose my figure.

Charlotte ran to the bank with the note. Mr. Compton smiled. He actually touched Charlotte's arm as she left.

Spence roared over the phone, "How you say? A-OK."

Billy came home for Christmas and brought Bucky with him. Jessica came. It was wonderful. Blanche cooked and cooked. Alex got a tricycle and bumped into everything. They had a day of snow and Cal took everybody, including Jessica and Sybil, out to the pasture hills. Half the town was there. They slid and skidded, then grouped around a bonfire. Everybody got tired except Alex.

"Come on, Uncle Cal. Let's slide."

Cal wasn't tired either.

Then warm apple juice and vodka, mixed with cinnamon sticks before the open fire. And great chunks of Blanche's fourth fruitcake. And keeping Alex out of the roaring fire.

While Sybil, Charlotte, Jess, and Alex, under Blanche's supervision, prepared the gorgeous banquet to surround the turkey, Billy and Bucky slithered down the icy street in The Wreck to get Bucky's saxaphone. Charlotte had slipped the car keys from Cal's pocket as he dozed spread-eagle before the fire with Alex's tricycle front wheel on his belly.

Having eaten themselves into discomfort, Billy sat at the piano and Bucky's sax moaned and fretted. Billy then moved to the old bass which had stood in the corner for half a century and Charlotte sat at the piano before her Christmas gift from Billy and Bucky, a coveted Fake Book which they had gotten for her on a New York weekend. In a single line the book had every standard jazz song chord-sketched so that an adept pianist could flesh it out. These books were rare and much sought-after. Bucky explained that they were treated like heirlooms or union memberships.

Jack Daniels and a bowl of ice. Cal stretched again on the floor. Alex's head on his belly. The fire fuming.

They played and faked and improvised on old standards for hours. Charlotte and her father were again thrilled. Bucky was an artist. And Billy's bass gave structure, nuance, and articulation in subtle ways that Charlotte had never apprehended before. He had become a pro. He led her, supported her, augmented, and caused her to 'get loose' for improvisation of her own. She had never felt so free and sure at the piano before. What pleasure!

They strayed into *Body and Soul* and worked it for fifteen minutes. Billy then made a long slow, winding bass figure which hung softly. He nodded to her and she sang, Billy holding the tempo back so that she had to yearn to keep the melody line from collapsing. Bucky's horn moaned orgasmically under her voice.

"Again," Bucky said, "back farther in your throat. Breathe one second before you make a sound. Right. Right. Make it husky, make it dusty. Whiskey voice."

Still blowing, he walked behind her and reached for some soft, dissonant, grieving chords.

When Billy's bass trailed it off to nowhere, everybody was awake and silent.

"Terrific!" Bucky said. "Real down in the guts blues."

"Jesus," Cal whistled. "You had me, Morton."

Sybil and Douglas nodded.

"You know, we ought to record that and send it to Max," Billy said.

Charlotte stood. "Oh, Bucky, *could* we? God, that would be great."

"Sure. Sure. When? Where?"

"Dad, the radio station could do it, couldn't it?"

"Yes, they could. It's a great idea. I'll speak to Dan Widmere tomorrow. How long will you be here, Bucky?"

"Till the end of the week. Right. Hey, Char, I'll write out the piano part tomorrow. You can work on it and we'll do it some more tomorrow night."

"I'll call Dan in the morning," Douglas said.

"Jesus," Cal said. "Max will get out of bed and run cross country when he hears that. That's what he needs. Sex on wax."

She memorized the chords in the arrangement Bucky and Billy gave her the next afternoon. They worked at it a couple of nights—sometimes alone, sometimes Cal and Amy, Spence and Sybil made an audience. Cal wanted to be on the recording, so Billy brought an old tambourine stolen years ago from the school and they allowed him a two second shake before Billy began and ended it with slow bass figures.

And they recorded it at the radio station. It was OK, Bucky

decided after nine takes, and they ordered a dozen copies. Sybil, Spence, Cal and all had to have one. Cal supervised Charlotte's typing of the labels to be sure that she did not omit, *Tambourine: Calvin Hendricks*, from any of them. That night Smokey the late night disc jockey, called and asked if he could play it.

They turned all the radios in the house on full blast and waited an hour. Then it came. It sounded wonderful. Even Bucky approved, with engineering reservations. Cal called the station six times requesting repeats. Smokey actually played it twice more that night. They were thrilled.

"Calvin Hendricks, musician. I like it. I like it," this from Cal. "Did you hear? On tambourine, Calvin Hendricks!"

Charlotte packed it carefully and mailed two copies to Dave.

For the next two weeks Smokey played it once a night. On request, he said. Cal swore he was not responsible for the requests. Charlotte decided that it was, in fact, a damned good *Body and Soul*.

She sent one to Whit. Note the musician on tambourine, she instructed.

Dave must have ESP, she thought when his letter arrived the very day after she mailed the records.

Charlotte forgive me for suggesting this and discount it if you think it's foolish. It occurs to me that sex is a powerful motive. Not even Max in his condition can shut that off. What about this? Have you got or could you get, some cheesecake pictures of yourself which really show off your figure. Something that really could make a man look. It's a thought. And I think it's time we really tried anything to shake him loose. Consider and let me know.

"Sex is a powerful impulse," Douglas said, no doubt speaking from experience. "Perhaps the most powerful. Anyone treating mental illness who does not account it has to be foolish."

"Well, of course," said Jessica. "Send some cheesecake."

"Why not. Look, it may waken something in that poor defeated boy that will make him want to rejoin the world.

337

And it may be subtle, even subconscious. Do you have any good pictures in a bathing suit, Charlotte?"

She brought some albums. There was nothing really good and suggestive. They were all too sunlit and healthy.

"Well, it's too cold for bathing suits. That's sure."

"Unless it's indoors," Spence said. "I could get Cooley from the paper. He would come here. The old fool would love it. He's a pretty good photographer, and I'm sure he wouldn't charge too much."

"What about Calvin Hendricks, photographer?"

"Cooley is a pro and we'll need special lights. Sybil and Jess can stay with you," Spence said reassuringly. "Although Cooley would have a stroke if passion reared its lurid head."

Cooley came the next evening after dinner, a plump, balding, bespeckled, little bulldog of a man burdened with a battery of lights and a fixed smile.

"You understand, Mr. Cooley," said Sybil, "This is confidential."

"Sure. Sure. Spence explained."

They decided on Charlotte's bedroom with its lovely, beveled, oval mirror and drapes.

They did two nudes. "You don't have to send them. We'll see," Sybil said.

Charlotte sat on the bed for one, holding a brush discreetly. Then she stood before the mirror which reflected her back. Her arm and a towel barely hid nipples and her triangle. Sybil arranged her hip sway into a classical S.

"Spence will have the prints and negatives tomorrow afternoon. G'night ladies."

"Would we be able to have extra prints if we wished?" Sybil asked.

"Sure. Sure. Just give the negatives to Spence and say how many."

Spence brought the proofs next day at five. Cooley was a good photographer. *She's lovely*, Charlotte murmured, looking at herself. *She's lovely*.

Finally, they picked three to send. Address them to Max, not me, Dave had insisted. Neither of the nudes was picked.

"You know," Charlotte said. "Wouldn't Max wonder who took them? And, well, I don't know."

"Maybe you're right," Jess said. "He is a man. And you never know about them."

"Charlotte, you should have a set for yourself surely," Sybil said. "I certainly want some. They are perfectly lovely. No movie star pin-up is better."

Douglas looked at the pictures in disbelief.

"Daughter. Daughter. How unutterably beautiful you are. Ann-Charlotte would be so proud. These pictures—I think of her. Oh, hell, I'm getting old."

Later, alone in her room, Charlotte pored over the proofs. *She is beautiful*, she thought, as though thinking of another. *Make Max want her. Make Max want her so much he has to come and have her.*

Mr. Compton called her and nearly broke down over the phone. "Mrs. Compton has gone away for a rest. To a hospital, Charlotte."

"Oh, Mr. Compton."

"Yes, I don't know how long it will be. Oh, Charlotte, she wouldn't eat. She wouldn't talk. I—I—simply didn't know what to do."

"Perhaps it won't be so long, Mr. Compton. Poor woman, she probably feels that she has lost all."

"Charlotte, what . . . You haven't given up on Max, have you? His recovery, I mean. He *can* get well, can't he? If that would happen, Elsa, Mrs. Compton, would be all right, I'm sure."

"Of course, I haven't. Of course not. Neither has Dr. Fried and I'm sure that he tells us the truth. It's the surgery. As he says, it must be done tissue by tissue. Grafting cannot be done in quantity. And each graft must heal before the next is made. No, sir. I haven't given up. I can't, Mr. Compton. You see, I love him too."

Oh God, I haven't given up, she thought. *I can't. I'm betting my life on this.*

"Thank you, Charlotte. I . . ." he cleared his throat. "I must say that talking to you these weeks has given me hope and . . . courage. And I thank you for that."

"Mr. Compton, you are going to be lonely. Come down and visit. Come for dinner. Our Blanche is the best cook in North Carolina. And I have a splendid son for you to meet. Mr. Compton, friends of yours come almost every day at five. Mr. Fulton—Spence, Miss Schraeder. And oh, yes, Cal Hendricks, you remember him. He's a friend of Max's. He's out of the Marine Corps now. Please come. You don't have to call. Please. We're only a block away."

"Thank you, Charlotte. Perhaps. Yes, perhaps I will."

She didn't press him for a date. If Elsa were there it would be unthinkable. Her father becoming a notorious drunk. She with an illegitimate child. Sin. Sin. Sin. But maybe. She felt that Mr. Compton was, at last, beginning to comprehend a whole world of human emotion which lay beyond form and propriety.

Perhaps he would come. *He had called her.*

By God, her father had better not be drunk when he did.

Dave loved the recording.

It is for me The Body and Soul. Yes, Bucky and Billy are consummate musicians. But you. Move over Lee Wiley and Lady Day. Shirley loved it too. Thanks for sending us a copy. We treasure it. I play it for Max every day. Nothing yet. Be patient. Always keep in mind the nature of his wound. He is reading. Like crazy. History. Bury's Greece. The Oxford Medieval. Why not? Surely he is contemplating the hardest questions. The meaning of life. The whole human condition. Was he religious? Are you, Charlotte? I am not. This is hard to deal with. Surely this marred boy is wondering why? Why me? Job's question. Was it mere chance? If indeed, as flies to wanton boys are we to the gods. They kill us for their sport.

Was Dave psychic? That was her father's favorite quotation lately. Always. But especially lately. *King Lear.* Poor, foolish, old, hopeless fool.

Every day the papers were filled with separation notices.

Captain Peter McCanless, honorably discharged from the Army Air Force.

Machinist Mate Third Class Coy Trexler, Jr., honorably discharged.

Lieutenant Thomas Kinder, Army, honorably discharged.

Cpl. Rufus Edmond, USMC, honorably discharged.

On and on.

She wrote:

Oh, Whit—when are you coming? Cal and I need you. And Whit, a great favor. A very great favor. When you arrive on the West Coast, telephone me. Call collect. I

*want to beg you, if at all possible to go to San Francisco
and try to see Max. To see if he will see you. I will do
anything in the world for you if you will just call me. I
know that a day or two will be so important for you,
having been away for so long. But, please, promise
nothing more than a telephone call.*

Whit's letters came one after another. One raved about
Body and Soul. He loved it. Tell Billy he *is* great. Calvin
Hendricks will be a star. But, you, Charlotte, were wonderful
in this. One of his fellows had said, "I know about her soul
from this, how about her body?" He had told him terrific.
That is, she looks terrific, sweet Whit had added. It was
playing all day long, he said. I'll soon have to have another
copy.

In the next letter Whit promised that he would call, and
promised that even though it cost him a couple of days, he
would visit Max. Max was too fine to lose. Of course, he
would go. Perhaps he would land in San Francisco anyway.

Whitlow Manson was serious, had been a serious boy.
He came from Mill Hill. He realized that his friends
started with advantages. They talked of things that he had
never heard of. Max and Charlotte's curiosity was continually squirting off in directions he did not know existed. He
could achieve in any of the academic areas at school. But
they made him aware of things, other things. For instance,
that buildings did not simply afford shelter. Max and Charlotte had known that. Music was not background for other
activities. They had known that. Douglas Morton was a
drunkard like his father, but he was a different kind of
drunkard, and Whit listened to Douglas on those long
evenings when he 'lectured,' and read, and played the
piano for them all. Whit learned that Billy was not to be
tolerated, he was to be prized, that if Jennings bored, he
bored out of profound passion. And that black Blanche was
wise and made life pleasant. And he had never before
found life particularly pleasant.

Whit came from redneck. He kept the toughness of redneck. But he discarded the ignorance and bigotry, and he was
still testing.

Of course, he could go and see Max, no matter how many
days it cost him. *We all need Max.*

*   *   *

341

Cal settled easily into the life of the returned veteran. He registered for the weekly stipend which was due anyone who had served in the armed forces. He lived at home, except when he got lucky at night. Most of his days were spent in the poolroom. Each afternoon he was in Charlotte's office. Many nights were spent in the American Legion Club drinking and playing cards. He and Alex took to each other like teddy bears and Cal frequently took him off Charlotte's hands.

Bucky had been discharged and had returned to New York. It had been agreed that Billy would forsake college and join him when he was released. Bucky was to feel the musical air, to get his hand back in.

Dave wrote that the pictures were indeed lovely. He had read the letter and placed the pictures in Max's hand. Max still refused to open any mail, or to signify that he was interested in the least. Dave said that as always he placed the letters and the pictures on the table in Max's room. He did not know whether or not they were touched thereafter. But *he continues to read avidly.*

Yes, Dave said, he would be pleased to meet Whit. Maybe. Maybe a visit from him could penetrate Max's shield. Maybe even prepare the way for a visit from Charlotte.

In September, Whit called from San Francisco. Charlotte told him that it was wonderful that he would soon be home. She gave him Dave's address and number.

And held her breath.

She called Mr. Compton and told him that Whit was going to visit Dr. Fried and try to see Max. Finally he agreed to drop by on his way home from the bank.

Spence, Sybil, and Cal were there and Charlotte insisted that they stick to sherry.

She scrubbed and combed Alex and he promised to be good.

It was fine. Mr. Compton actually drank a glass of sherry, ate from Blanche's tray of appetizers, and after some stiffness, talked amiably. Alex *was* good—and charming. Mr. Compton seemed pleased with him, thought him handsome.

They insisted he stay for dinner. Clearly he had not known so much warmth and laughter and pleasant disorder. Cal talked of the Marine Corps. Sybil and Charlotte took pains to put him at ease.

At the end of the meal, he complimented Blanche, and

finally said that he wished Elsa was here with them. He then loosened enough to tell them that she was on the brink of a breakdown, but that she had seemed brighter last weekend. He spent every weekend now with her at the hospital in the mountains near Asheville.

Douglas's easy charm won him. After dinner he had another glass of sherry and Charlotte played.

At his bedtime, Alex gave him a good night kiss. He was visibly affected.

When he left, everyone considered that it had been successful. They bet he would come back.

And Douglas dove for the bourbon bottle which had been off limits for too long.

Charlotte was sitting on the porch swing. Blanche was puttering in the yard.

"I do declare," she said, "I believe that crepe myrtle by the gate has shot its wad."

From beyond the hedge, Charlotte heard precipitous, full, male laughter. She gasped. He stood in the gate, still laughing. She ran into his arms.

"Welcome, Whit. Welcome with all my heart."

She held him away. Yes. It was Whit. The candid sky-blue eyes looking at her beneath the sandy brows, sandy hair still crew cut. The square, clean featured face. The wonderful smile, tentative until sure that he was welcome, then bursting across his friendly face. The solid form, a few inches taller than she.

She took his arm, leading. "Blanche. Blanche, come. See who's here. Oh, Whit. Cal left ten minutes ago. He'll be back. He's gone to look at a motorcycle. *Motorcycle!* Isn't that Cal? He'll be back soon."

Blanche came. "Oh, Mr. Whit. Welcome back. Oh, welcome. Lawzee."

He went happily into her vast hug. Her smile went to the farthest corners of the yard. Blanche too held him away, inspected him to see that he was all right.

"Y'all go sit down and talk. I'll bring something nice."

Charlotte took Whit's hand and led him to the music parlor.

"Whit, it is so good."

"Yes, it is. So good. I knew I was home when I heard that crepe myrtle declaration. That voice." He laughed again.

Then she saw his eyes narrow. He looked slowly about the room. He was inspecting, seeing that all was as it had been. His hand moved across the back of an easy chair. Charlotte realized that this room had been a pleasant place for Whit too.

Then they sat, turned to each other on the couch. Blanche appeared with a tray. She patted Whit's shoulder as she left.

"Let me tell you about Dave. And Max first. I know you are anxious."

"Yes, please, Whit. How are you here so soon? I thought...."

"Yeah. Dave's commanding officer arranged a Navy flight for me since I would have missed the train ticket they gave me. I actually gained a couple of days. That Dave is great. And Shirley. You know about Shirley?"

"Yes. Yes, of course. Is she pretty? I've seen pictures."

He nodded.

"Yeah. I stayed with them two days. They were just great." He paused, went on deliberately. "Charlotte, I guess it's very bad with Max. Very bad. Dave took me there, to the hospital. Three times. Charlotte, Max wouldn't see me, or anything."

"Oh God."

"Yeah. It was strange." Whit shook his head. "Dave took me to his room and I stood outside the door. It was so strange. Dave said to just stay and talk. You know, keep talking. Dave said really try to break his heart with memories. So I did."

"Oh, my God."

"Yeah. So I did. I told him it was Whit. About what had happened to me. About Iwo, and Japan, and meeting Cal in Tokyo. I told him how we had wished for him there and all. You know, Charlotte, I begged him to see me. I told him I didn't care what he looked like. Jesus. I guess I choked up a couple of times."

"Oh, Whit. Whit."

He had risen, holding the Coke Blanche had brought. He walked slowly about the room touching things.

"Well, Dave said just keep talking and remembering things. I just rambled. You know, The Track, and Billy, and crazy Jennings. And Big Edna—God, I can't believe she's dead."

Charlotte nodded.

"And the river. And returning punts when we were freshmen. I guess you don't know about that. Hudson, Coach Hudson, used to use Max and me in punt return drills. Cal was always ahead of us, bigger. But, I guess that's when I started hanging around with you guys. Max and I came close because we were smaller and getting the stuffing knocked out of us every day and we kinda got a feeling for each other. Well, anyway. I talked about the talent night, the variety show. And Billy. And you. I talked about everything. The Wreck, Lee Creek, Geraldina—oh, I guess you don't know about that."

His eyes flicked to her.

"I even talked about Coy Trexler. Hey, is he back? My folks didn't mention him."

"Yes, Trex is back. Cal says he's working at Owen Machine Shop. He went right to work."

"Well, I talked the first day. Then the next morning, then that afternoon. I just sat and rambled. It was strange—thinking of Max maybe sitting over there listening. Or maybe with his ears stopped. Charlotte, I—I feel so sorry for that guy."

Whit came and sat beside her.

"Charlotte, Max hasn't got a jaw—or not much of one." Whit swallowed. "I promised Dave I'd tell you everything. I saw the X-rays. Eating is—well, getting food is—just simple things are impossible for him."

Tears came to Charlotte's eyes. Whit took her hand. She looked at him. He too was making tears.

"Oh, Charlotte. But they are in the third course of plastic surgery. And it's coming along, Dave says. Max is so healthy. It's taking. You know, the skin is growing. Well, you know I talked about everything. The *Body and Soul*. That is great, Charlotte. Mine is worn out. Can I get another one?"

"Sure, Whit. I have two more. Sure."

"But, anyway, this Dave. What a great guy. And that Shirley. They took me out and showed me San Francisco. You know, we ate at the Wharf, and to the International Settlement and all around. He's killing himself to help Max."

"Yes. I know. We write."

"Yeah, he told me. It was like I was an old friend. He told me that he felt he knew us all, Mr. Douglas—how is he? —Billy, Cal, Blanche—he really liked her fruitcake. But who wouldn't?"

"I bought it! A Harley 74, black as sin," Cal roared. He burst in. Stopped. *"Whitlow. Baby! 42 on 3."*

"Uncle Calvin!"

For a second they were high school kids again. A war dance. Charlotte was swept in. And joy took her for a moment. Alex entered and was amazed. Blanche appeared frowning.

"You'all stop that this instant. You'll knock down every picture in this house and shatter every piece of china." Then, "Don't he look wonderful, Mr. Cal?"

Whit knelt to Alex. They studied each other's face. They would be friends.

"A bike, Whit. I just bought a Harley. A 74. A cannon."

They went out to look.

Alex could not stop touching it.

"Not my son," Charlotte screeched. "Die young if you will. But not my son on that thing."

She was wrong, of course.

Dave wrote of Whit:

> *It was like meeting an old friend, Shirley and I liked him so much. Someday we are going to visit you—and it will be like coming home. No, no change in Max. I'm sure Whit broke his heart. Nothing from him at all. The recording, the pictures, Whit. But don't be too discouraged. Perhaps it will all add up. The surgery is going as well as it can.*
>
> *Why were you so surprised at the* King Lear *quote?* As flies to wanton boys are we to the gods. They kill us for their sport. *No psychiatrist worth his salt can afford not to know Shakespeare.*
>
> *Give regards to Whit, Cal, Blanche and your father.*

Coy Trexler, Jr. spot-welded and smoothed the slight tear in the rear fender of the Harley out at Owen Machine Shop. Whit had ridden back-saddle out there with Cal.

The three had shaken hands, compared service experiences, as Trex worked. He was an apprentice. The government paid half his salary.

"That's mine," he pointed to the glittering Ford parked in the lot. "I got an order in for a new Buick, soon's they start coming through."

He told them that he was also applying for a government loan for a shop of his own when he finished his apprenticeship.

He mentioned with obvious glee that he'd heard Charlotte Morton had gotten knocked up while we were getting shot at.

Cal snuffed that out curtly. "Fuck you, Trex. Shot at. Shit.

346

You were on a ship with a hot shower and hot chow every day. Shut the fuck up."

And that Max had been shot away and was still in a hospital in San Francisco.

"He was a good ole boy," Trex dropped diffidently.

He did a good job on the fender and the unearthly roar of the machine brought Charlotte out of the office when it threatened to jar out the windows on narrow Lawyer's Row.

It was beautiful, she allowed. Sure, she would design a flame or nude painting for the fenders and gas tank.

Whit slipped into Cal's easy life of the returned veteran. He too registered for the stipend, slept late, helped Cal work on the motorcycle. They got the proper paint and Charlotte painted the fenders and tanks with orange and red flames licking up and back as though wind swept it, and Coy Trexler took the gleaming metal to a friend of his who worked at a body shop and had them baked. So that he would be mobile, Whit took The Wreck, except when Cal had a date and might need the back seat. He shot pool a large part of the day, joined Cal each day at Charlotte's office for an hour or so. He hung around the Legion Club playing cards, drinking too much, took Max's place as Cal's partner in looking for women in the bus station and The Track and the roadhouses.

For six weeks.

"I've got to quit this before it becomes too sweet," Whit told Charlotte.

After several days of talking with her and her father, he decided that he would study some kind of engineering or architecture. Charlotte helped him type out the applications for several colleges, and the papers for G.I. Bill college benefits. Whit's high school academic record was excellent. There would be no problem. He and Charlotte assembled transcripts and the multitude of forms and got them into the mail.

Then Whit did that which Cal considered a sin. He took a job.

He took a back-breaking, but relatively good-paying, job with the railroad. But Whit was strong and he was finished at three o'clock each day. That left him with a couple of hours to spend in the public library scouting the books Douglas Morton suggested on architecture.

That also left him free to play in evenings.

Whit gave Charlotte her cue.

First she suggested it to Cal. Then after seeing him drink eighteen bottles of beer in a single sitting at The Track, then beside Whit in The Wreck following him, saw him hit a gravel spot and go down on the bike, turning his left leg into one gleaming painful strawberry, she roared at him as only she would dare.

"Now, you will get the hell out to that school and register for the equivalency course, take the test, and get a high school diploma. For six months you've done nothing but bum around, shoot pool, lift skirts, prove you can out-drink most, and disturb the sleep of the entire town with that goddamn dragon. Hell, you're becoming the typical American male. If you can't eat it, drink it, drive it, or screw it, it's not important. Now, tomorrow at two, you be at the office with the registration form. Mother has spoken."

He was there.

She typed it for him and Cal was at the high school three nights a week for six weeks. He took the equivalency test—and passed.

"OK. Tonight you can get drunk. We'll join you, won't we, Whit? We really ought to celebrate. This is the first test he's ever passed."

On her own, she had gotten G.I. Bill forms and a registration form for Sapona College, the small liberal arts school on a lovely, green, pine-covered campus on the outskirts of town. For a reason later discerned by Charlotte, Cal was accepted.

"How do I know that I want to be a liberal artist?" he demanded. "Calvin Hendricks, liberal artist. It doesn't sound right."

"We all know what you *want* to be. We are trying to turn you into a productive member of society. You just listen to Mother. You will take something harmless like physical education. Which means that you had better make the football team so they won't flunk you out. Right?"

And so it came to pass that in August, Calvin Hendricks, student, again donned pads and cleats and began to sweat his body free of the gallons of alcohol with which he had burdened it in the past months.

And also, it came to pass that Charlotte Morton found herself writing freshman themes, re-learning chemical formulas in order to drill him for tests, happily reading Morrison and Commager's American history in order to drill him for tests, re-reading the Old Testament in order to drill him for tests.

In mid-September, Whit left for Raleigh for four grueling years at North Carolina State. He repeated his first interview with his adviser to Cal and Charlotte. "Welcome, Mr. Manson. We hope that you will be happy and successful. But I would have you know at the outset, this is a place of excellence. And despite the current flood of would-be students the G.I. Bill is sending us, we intend to keep it a place of excellence."

After a semester of finding time to visit home only at Thanksgiving and Christmas, Whit allowed that they were doing just that.

Charlotte could not fight off the bitter feeling that the world was moving past her. Amy was in college—another, more vital, world. Whit also. Billy would soon join Bucky in New York to pursue that which he loved best. Jennings would graduate in another year or so in his accelerated program. Even Cal was moving. Which way, time would tell. But he was moving.

Then she thought of Max.

Oh God! Her whole being clenched. It was so unfair.

She consciously kept her mind alive and inquiring. She read three or four books weekly, mostly history and biography. She sketched daily—something, anything. She practiced fast portraiture and was surprised how it made her look at faces, note which features moved to form certain attitudes, and the wrinkles which she chose to imagine told what the person beneath the face had endured or enjoyed. She continued the habit of writing daily in her journal. And in it she kept accurate records of Alex's development.

Alex consumed her. He was now reading. She was teaching him to draw, as her father had taught her. And the alphabet, those other symbols—numbers. And she would hold him between her legs at the piano. Sometimes guiding his fingers, comparing tones, playing little pieces and causing him to play a few notes in exact time.

And, of course, she wrote letters each day.

And she worried about her father.

20

LONG tradition stood behind the alcoholism of men like Douglas Morton, the storied Southern gentleman drunkard. But many drank heavily and did not become addicted. And many accepted the tradition emptily, as did Marsh Woods. Marsh drank because he was, as Douglas put it, "Baudelaire's king of the rainy country. No ribbon put on or left off could any longer excite Marsh's drowned senses. He is rich, intelligent, intellectually lazy, and undisciplined by responsibility. He has moved from pleasure to sensual pleasure for so long that I doubt if the most extravagant stimulus could touch his senses."

Douglas was different. He called it his Cosmic Depression, and it was cosmic in the high sense, for Douglas Morton's mind had ranged the scope of human knowledge. He had pondered what he had learned.

And nothing answered the final questions.

Religion had failed him. It seemed meretricious, invented hope for those who could not face the Unknown—and *I am one of those*, he admitted. His discussions with the likes of Sid and Father Cary, a passable theologian, had always ended with *I believe*. But belief cannot be founded in desire or fear. He could not believe in resurrection of the dead, life after death, a personal god who was susceptible to importunity, because his brains and senses denied it. Fear and desire without evidence offer fantasy, not credulity.

He knew that every civilization created a deity. He knew that they did this because man wants what he has not: power, ultimate answers, and most of all, immortality for his precious ego. He therefore creates gods which promise these things.

Except the Greeks. *Except the Greeks*, he thought. They somehow created a symbolic religion as if they were more interested in explanation than consolation. Their gods were what man could be. Their gods were men driven to the limits of possibility. They had a deity for every human impulse— even for thievery. They had no traffic with the supernatural, the miraculous, the mystical. We know all we know about Pallas Athene, the goddess in whom thought and action are a single impulse, only through the *Odyssey*. There is no theology for her. Only one person *sees* her in the *Odyssey* and that is the man who embodies her: Odysseus. Homer is very careful about that. Therefore she must be taken as a symbol for this man's capacity to act on assessment. She is one man's revelation.

Just so with natural phenomena. Poseidon's rage is symbol for a storm at sea. Aphrodite's influence causes love's irrationality. The classical religion had no canon for immortality. It had no canon, beyond hospitality, beyond common sense.

Why? Was it the clear, brilliant Aegean light that scholars and poets made so much of? He himself had once suffered sunblindness that had lasted two hours on Delos. The fluent air, the sun reflected and refracted from the white stone and the combing sea overwhelmed his vision. Was it that brilliant clarity that caused, or allowed, the Greeks to see unflinchingly that nature is indifferent to justice and morality and importunity. They understood that death is a consequence of life. In Man as in every organism.

How did they bear it? He shrugged. They didn't very long. Soon came the mystery cults. To answer the soft, sucking whim of the ego.

And why was monotheism considered without question superior to polytheism? Amazing. Look at the extremes to which theologians are driven. Evil is the absence of God. Yet in the next breath they are insisting that God is omnipresent.

Then this Jesus. Petulant, ego-eaten, jealous as an adolescent. Believe me or perish. Forgiving? Merciful? Hardly. Believe or burn.

But I love him, thought Douglas.

Why? After all, excepting the gorgeous poetry, what did he offer? What, ultimately, is Christ's contribution? The common sense of every civilization which had preceded him.

Except. Yes, except that one diamond-hard idea that each of us has cherished as we do our ego, for our ego depends on it. Original? Did it exist before him? No. I can think of nowhere in human history. The gorgeous idea that is the foundation for all modern political and social thought—that *each separate, single man has value*. *Soul*. And each of us—harpooner, hod-carrier, shepherd, prince—has it. Yes, that is his. We need it. He needed it to get us. Well, then, that places him among the great philosophers. Modern society cannot be imagined without it.

I love him. But I do not believe in him.

And man had failed.

Once he had believed in man. But perhaps there were too many options. Man is contained by nothing. Drought, storm, fire were beast damnations. Option is man's damnation. And his glory. The long slippery track to perfectability—the dream of the Nineteenth Century.

Gone now. How to dream perfectability after these wars? And now the fleshed-out news of the concentration camps. Six million dead. Man unto man. And this new bomb. Too many options. Once men realized—and avoided—destiny with dreams. Dreams were once powerful, gorgeous, awesome. Now the dream is an ugly, ignorant, technical competence without wisdom, without awe. Can do.

Can die.

History alternately grieved and consoled. Five thousand years of thought and effort now guttered into narrow nationalism, the blight of the Twentieth Century. Stupid pride, stupid patriotism, fear of diversity. Diversity, perhaps the final joy of life. Small minds fear it. So—nationalism.

But throughout there had been Homer, Leonardo, Galileo, Chaucer, Giotto, Bach, Pasteur, Newton. Yes. The great ones. His saints and heroes. Telling us. Telling us. Telling us. How to look. How to think. How to love. Revising always. Welcoming revision. Welcoming diversity. Hell, we don't know yet in our guts the implications of Galileo. Earth no longer the apple of God's eye. Another incidental planet, its gravity helping to hold the structure together. No more or less important than the rest.

Unless you happen to live on it.

And I? Me? Man? In an accidental, ephemeral, impersonal universe, I am an interchangeable, expendable, atom. I cannot love this vastness in which I am a 'wink of eternity.' I can admire its power and elegance. But I cannot love it, he murmured.

God is the Big Bang and Mary is His mother. How can I live on this earth?

The stars were his symbol. And so in starlight, glass in hand, he paced the gallery, solitary with his fearful vision. Into the room where his grandson slept. Here was a kind of immortality, a blood line, a gene line. Will I die as long as he lives? Sometimes in demi-light, beneath the smooth skin he imagined—or *saw!*—the small skull, the jawbone beneath the straight chin. He jammed his fists into his eyes. Shook it off. Had a drink.

Charlotte felt his eyes on her in a way she had never known.

This splendid woman is my daughter. Look at her. Tall, straight, clear—*Pallas Athene in that straight back and arrogant head*. Quick, and fluent, each movement a new grace thrown carelessly on the air. A mind like a tight bow string. Touch it. It sings. Disgraced because she lay in love. What else to do with that body?

And her boy marred for an island which probably wouldn't sustain an olive tree. But would sustain an air strip.

In twenty years she'll be a crone, bent, gray, gutted to the rind with child bearing. In forty more years, Alex, all her children, ruined stringy muscle and tendon threaded on creaky bones. Is this what it's for?

Oh God, I could dream man's soul sizzling in flight through this gorgeous imperium, singing, free, shedding dross in the pure leap...

Yes, he said. I could dream it.

But I can't believe it.

Whatever is born, dies. Whatever is built, crumbles. What is acquired is dispersed. Those who love are separated. It always ends badly. All flesh is grass.

And the craving took him. God, for that vivid burning in the belly, muscles falling lax, forgetfulness playing around the edges of his brain, the sweet swim to euphoria.

Expect nothing. Be prepared for joy. I can't prepare any longer. Each day, step by step, he was losing shame and he feared that he might one day arrive at the knowledge and damnation that he, and all men, behaved in perfect accordance with their *natures*. That, to this humanist, was unbearable.

He sought the forgetfulness that played at the edges of his brain.

Aunt Elizabeth died just after Thanksgiving. Nelson Summers suddenly appeared at their door at nine o'clock one evening and announced it administratively: "It was a heart attack. It happened about noon today."

He accepted coffee. He said that Elizabeth was with God. And he left.

"Hell, he doesn't even know how to mourn," said Charlotte.

"She was never really alive," her father said.

He called Aunt Jessica, who also found it hard to mourn Elizabeth. But she would come to the funeral.

Aunt Elizabeth left Charlotte ten thousand dollars. Nothing to Douglas or Jessica.

"Why?" asked Charlotte. "Why me?"

"Jealousy," said Douglas wryly.

The day after Elizabeth's funeral Charlotte received the letter that she had anticipated, and dreaded. David Fried was leaving the Navy. He and Shirley would settle in San Francisco. He regretted that he could not say that he had been able to help Max—though it had not been from want of effort. He had, however, been doing research and was considering a plan. There was a large veteran's hospital in Camp Butner, North Carolina. The head psychologist, Dr. Milton Grossman, had been Dave's teacher at university and was famous in the field. He might suggest that Max be transferred there. A move nearer home might be salutary. Charlotte herself might visit. But more. Walter Reed Hospital in Washington had one of the finest surgical teams in the East who specialized in cases of burn and distortion. Anyway, he would remain with Max for about three months more. And he would reach absolute certainty on a proper course of treatment before he left Max. He would of course continue to keep her posted. And, we have become friends. It was a friendship he and Shirley cherished. Someday we will meet. Perhaps she would be on Max's arm. Then the four of them would dine and dance and laugh like loving friends.

She knew something was ending. Aunt Elizabeth's death. Her father's sullen, solicitous watchfulness. Dear David's sense of failure with Max.

Billy came home. He was discharged. He would spend Christmas there, then join Bucky in New York to begin making music.

Christmas was pleasant—even fun with the reunion of Billy, Cal and Whit. But beneath it was a fretting tension that was hard to identify.

Aunt Elizabeth's passing seemed to affect everyone more than her life had. She *had* died without living, Douglas said, half to himself. Maybe not a bad idea. There was nothing to lose. He quoted Sophocles' better never to have been born. Next best to get it over with as soon as possible. He was stirring his memory for quotes to support the conclusions to which he was arriving. Always a great talker, his rhetoric became extravagant.

Three days after Christmas Pal Harrel, owner of one of the road houses on the edge of town, called just before midnight and asked if someone could come and get Mr. Morton who was drunk and causing a disturbance. Luckily Jessica was still in town and drove Charlotte to get him. They found him leaning against the bar berating Pal for having cut him off. Home, he slipped on the staircase and tumbled down the entire first flight. Both Jessica and Charlotte were required to get him upstairs.

"I'm sorry, my darlings," he blubbered. "Ah, God, *tell Isabelle the queen I looked not thus when for her sake I ran at tilts in France and there unhorsed the Duke of Clermont.*"

"Oh, Doug," Jessica pleaded, "someday you are going to kill yourself. We care—if you have stopped caring. Please. And stop excusing yourself with literary quotations. This is no joke. You are too precious to behave like a clown."

Something was ending.

Days moved. She continued to write Max daily, Dave weekly. And there was Alex. Alex. Four years old, he was now reading a book a day—mostly aloud to her as she did other things. And he wrote A L E X with crayon on the hundred-year-old silk wall paper in the small parlor. His bottom told him that he would never do that again. Blanche's hand instructed first. Then Charlotte reinforced the lesson.

Cal came by the office or the house almost every day. He had made the football team, alternating with the senior fullback, and, at last was playing most of the time, though the senior was allowed to start games. And he did the punting.

He allowed that Calvin Hendricks, scholar, was not so bad. College was the happy hunting grounds. There were literally hundreds of coeds localized within an area his lust could cover at a glance.

As far as Charlotte could determine, he had attended most of his classes. However, she knew that he wasn't above lying to her in such matters.

In mid-January his grades arrived. He didn't even open the

envelope. He came straight to the office and laid it on her desk and then held his ears in mock fear. As she hoped, and feared, he passed everything with D's and C's. She hoped because he was Cal. She feared because she knew that if he passed her father's assessment was true—that American education was corrupting itself to allow G.I.'s to pass so that the flow of government money would continue. "And when even the universities put their wares out to bid, your country has become a whorehouse."

But she leaped from the desk and kissed Cal. For him it was an accomplishment.

In March, an exuberant Mr. Compton dropped by to report that his Elsa was coming home. She seemed her old self, he reported. That night he joined Douglas in a Jack Daniel's to celebrate.

And both Sybil and Spence reported that Elsa did seem her old self, as vague, as giddy, as pious as ever. Mr. Compton continued to talk to Charlotte on the telephone, but his visits ended. She guessed that Elsa was, indeed, her old self.

Dave wrote, both to her and the Comptons, that Max would be transferred in late March. To Charlotte he wrote that he had corresponded at length with his old Professor, Dr. Milton Grossman. He had sent all of Max's records, of course, plus her letters, the pictures, and his anecdotal diary. Dr. Grossman was extremely interested and, Dave assured her, would be perfectly diligent. He gave her Dr. Grossman's address and suggested that she begin a correspondence.

He went on to say that the hospital had access to Dr. Joel Rose, a young oral- and maxilla-facial surgeon, who was working with a team at Johns Hopkins. This team had developed some bold new techniques, both procedurally and materially. They had had singular success in using some new plastic compounds in bone graft. He had corresponded with Dr. Rose and had elicited an interested reply. *Charlotte, I am hopeful.*

Cal had seen her cry once or twice before, in pure rage, or in laughter so perfect that tears spilled down her cheeks. He had never seen her body convulsed as now, her face drawn, mouth salivating, eyes streaming—and he did not know what to do.

Then he saw the picture on the desk. It was a crumpled, dog-eared, defaced 8 × 10 print of the standing nude which Cooley had taken of her holding the towel before her. On it were scrawled obscenities. *Put prick here* with arrows drawn to her mouth and crotch. *I wouldn't know whether to eat up the fucking or fuck up the eating. Cunt,* with a line drawn to the crotch, ending with an angry gouge. *Get this cow in the barn. Sip and dip.*

"Jesus!" Cal hissed. He had torn the same picture from the wall in the poolroom toilet just a week ago. How many are there, he wondered.

She sat erect in shock, stood, began trembling, then collapsed in the chair, and dropped her head on the desk, rolled her face on the hard blotter.

Cal jumped behind her and held her shoulders.

"Jesus, Char."

"It was stuck under the door when I opened the office," she moaned. "Oh, how did...? Oh my God. Why?"

Cal finally shook her to calmness.

"Easy, Char. Easy. It doesn't make any difference. Who the hell cares?"

"But how many people have seen this? How many...?"

She broke down again.

Again he calmed her.

"Mr. Cooley," she sobbed. "Oh, why would he do this?"

"Yeah, I guess. That pig. Yeah."

She looked at herself. What she had thought beautiful, suddenly became obscene. The smile was lean and fox-like. Her flesh bland and obvious. Her body's attitude lewd.

"How many of these did that slime print?" she shrieked.

Again she broke down.

Cal snatched it from the desk, and moved toward the door.

"That son of a bitch is gonna eat this."

"Oh, Cal. Wait. There may be a hundred of them floating around. Oh my God, Cal. I'm so ashamed. So ashamed." She sobbed.

He tried to turn it off.

"Look, Char. It's great. Every guy in town will want you. I mean, look. It's all there. Man, no help from clothes and pads and stuff."

"Oh, stop! Don't you realize what they're going to say?"

"Yeah," he said. "I guess you're right."

Again his anger won. "Cooley is gonna eat this. I'm gonna rearrange his face."

"No, Cal. No. Maybe Spence can at least get the negatives. God, why would he do this? He knew what these pictures were for."

Home, her father wanted to get his pistol.

When Spence came in at five, he got his drink to his lips, took the picture from Douglas, listened as he explained where it had come from, threw the drink back, and dashed out the door.

In twenty minutes he was back.

"He claims there were ten prints. He sold them for two dollars each. I told him to use the money to buy a new camera. I threw his out the third floor window and told him that if I ever saw him on *Herald* property again, I'd blow his head from between his ears. Son of a bitch. I told him why you wanted them. Carefully, I explained. He *knows* Maxwell Compton! I told him that he was never to speak of it—much less show them to anybody. Slimy bastard. Well, here are the negatives, at least. I counted. They're all there."

"This makes me ashamed of the whole human species," Douglas growled.

"Yeah, will we never hit bottom?" said Spence.

"Filthy, obscene man," Sybil too was crying at the turn of such loveliness to filth.

Charlotte wept in bed that night, inconsolable before the meanness of her kind.

The next day was disastrous for Douglas Morton throughout. He had agreed to play tennis with Patsy Ramsey's daughter. Mary Ann Ramsey was a very good sixteen-year-old athlete, and the idea was to sharpen her service return and net game.

He was so shaky he had to take a drink before he could get himself going. On the court he tired quickly and toward the end, his service deserted him. When it went in, it had nothing on it. He fell behind in the second set and didn't have enough left to jam her. He finally eked it out from the baseline, relying on cunning rather than his body.

Near the end, Pete McCanless, who had flunked out of Chapel Hill and was now lounging around his father's automobile agency, sauntered by with another young man, waiting for a court to come free.

Douglas overheard Pete say, "Wait a minute. Old man Morton is about to fall on his face."

"Bastard," he growled to himself. "I'd like to wrap this racket around his empty head."

Then after lunch, Blanche wanted him to lug some bricks to the corner of the yard where she and Charlotte had plotted a new flower bed. Normally he would have loved it.

"Women. Women. Women," he muttered. "Everything I do is for a woman."

But he did it, bitching all the way, and when it was over he saw that what they had planned would be pleasant.

Sugar interrupted his nap at three o'clock to ask him to come to dinner. Someone had brought her a gorgeous flounder from the coast. OK. OK.

Then Sybil called. She was having some of the neighbors over for tea at four-thirty. Sort of a welcome home for Elsa who had agreed to come.

"Tea?" he growled.

"Yes, tea," she answered. "However, in concession to your addiction, I promise to sneak some bourbon into your cup. Oh, come, Doug. It'll be unbearable without you."

It was unbearable. Several old friends were there talking of city council plans to revitalize the downtown area, provide parking, and widen streets.

He knew that it had nothing to do with the health of the city. It was self-centered survival of their threatened enterprises that interested them. He said as much.

"Obviously, the future lies in the shopping centers like that one Clayton Swaringen is building out near the college. Hell, you've got to bring the shopping to the new housing. All those fools are going to do is cut down two hundred-year-old oaks, widen streets, and cover large portions of what is a charming town with asphalt. As city planners, they would make good Greek aviators. Builders like Clayton are doing the planning."

They went on talking of moving the Confederate statue several blocks out of center and destroying the mall which provided the statue's grassy setting.

"Godamighty, in a world thickly populated with fools, that council is certainly not the least," he was getting shrill and he knew it.

God, he thought, I am sunk in stupidity. *Get out*, he thought. *Get out quick*.

Abruptly he rose.

"Elsa, my dear, it is so good to have you back. You and Maxwell will have to come for dinner. Welcome back, with all my heart. Now maybe Maxwell will smile again. Good afternoon, everyone. It's been pleasant. Sybil, thank you."

Sybil saw him out.

"Doug, darling, you are a bastard. If I didn't love you I would throw a cup of tea in your face."

He kissed her cheek. "Make it bourbon. See you in faster company, Syb."

He went to better company. Alex.

"Now we call this a pawn. It can move forward only. Like so. And only one space at the time. See. One. However, and, Alex, listen, closely. The very first time it moves, it can move forward two spaces. Do you see? First time only. Now, it too is a warrior. It can capture the enemy. And it does that this way. Watch closely."

With a bourbon on his dressing table he showered. Sugar. Well, all right. The talk would be simpleminded, but the fish would be good and she was in a sexual frenzy as she entered the last lap. Yeah, the last lap.

He looked at himself in the mirror as he toweled. Not too bad. Not too bad yet. He turned. Some loose skin at the elbow point. Two small creases where the arms joined the breast plates. Still hard though. But some wild gray hairs on his chest. Yeah, moustaches, too. And in the ungovernable wavy mass of hair.

He flexed his bicep. Not bad.

But you gave out this morning. You were really tired. You beat that sixteen-year-old girl on sheer guts.

It's going, he thought. *It's going*. This is the short end. That McCanless whelp, standing there in his perfect youth. If he had half a brain he'd be a half-wit. I should hit a few with him sometime. Don't be a fool. He'd pass you like you weren't there.

I hate it, he growled, looking at himself. Loathsome, slow, inch by inch rot of the whole damned organism. *Soul fastened to a dying animal*.

He gulped half his drink. He dressed slowly. "To hell with you." He flung his tie across the room.

He finished the drink and bounded down the stairs. Sail to Byzantium between Sugar's thighs.

"Let's get schnockered," Sugar said, offering a martini. She had on one of the new synthetic fabric jump suits, skin tight from shoulders to spiked heels.

"How do you like it," she whirled. "One zipper and the treasures of the South are yours."

Her flesh jellied as she moved. The wonderful, high-riding ass was slipping. Had slipped. Her panties showed through clearly. Flesh burgeoned past the elastic. No bra. The massive mammary glands had lost, hung loose. *God,* he thought, *her nipples and her naval are on a plane. No, not true. It's me. I'm seeing it that way.* But too close, too close.

Wrong, he thought. *Wrong thing, Sugar. Your belly . . . ah. . . .We're losing, Sugar. Losing. All the ointment, creams, moisturizers, token exercises, eye shade, all. . . .We're losing.*

They got schnockered. She burned the fish. They drank and picked around the charred carcass, and drank, and drank.

"Come, I need the true staff of life, Dougy, baby."

There was a candle burning in the all-but-Persian bedroom. She did the single zipper herself. The treasures of the South looked pillaged. She knelt between his thighs and prepared him. And herself.

"You have the most beautiful bod. Why is your belly so hard and flat?" she slobbered. "Come, ride me over the mountain."

He mounted her, rode, drilled, humped, gored her, on and on. He could not finish. She was all mushy, slick, slippery, formless, slack. Her flesh was uncertain. Everything gave. Was awash. She was moaning, crying out, flopping about. Then she went slack. He raised on his elbows and looked at her. Sweat gleamed on her fallen face. Eye makeup was smeared across her right cheek. Her mouth was a formless, painted hole, lipstick definition gone.

"Are you trying to kill me?" she moaned.

He had no answer.

"I'm blown. God. Did you come? I couldn't feel. God, I was gone."

"Yes," he lied.

In thirty-six seconds, she was asleep.

He left her scattered across the shipwrecked bed. He dressed, blew the candle, then gently pulled a cover over her.

"It's no use," he whispered. "Have good dreams, lady. *Last night's sensuality glittered like a strobe as innocence blurred*

361

to competence. We're beached fish on the bed's backwater strand, white bellies up."

He walked into the small dining nook where they had eaten. The skeleton of the flounder shone in the ugly debris around it. He took the bourbon bottle.

"Yes, Jessica, my blessed, more justification by quotation."

He turned the bottle up, gasped, cut the lights, threw the night latch and stepped out into the cool air.

He drove. And drove. Nowhere. Anywhere. Clear, clean night. Clear moon and stars. He found himself on the quarry road. The great machine purred, responsive to the slightest impulse of the driver. Yes. He pressed down. It leapt. Seventy. Eighty. The wheel lay in his hand. Not a tremor. Ninety. Ninety-five.

It all works. But you're crazy. This road is too narrow. Yourself, all right. But don't kill anyone else. It wound down. He was near the quarry. He braked, swung off down the narrow dirt road that would lead him to the sheer gorgeous cliffs, the spring-fed, granite-bound, crystal water.

To his left now, the sixty foot sheer drop. The road wound it, then fanned out.

"I beat Puss's ass here," he muttered. "Once upon a time."

He swung the car to face the great lake. As he did he noticed an old Ford parked fifty feet away, parallel as he slowed. On a slab of rock jutting out over the water, his eye and the lights caught a boy and girl. They were both naked. As his lights swept by, the girl jumped up and dove for the Ford. She was beautiful and lithe and her breasts lilted with her pace. The boy was slim and agile. They were like spirits of the place, white, gleaming in his lights, young, strong in their embarrassed dance.

"Jesus. Sorry. I didn't mean to interrupt anything that important. And beautiful," he muttered to himself. "Well, boy, she's lovely, and I'm no *voyeur*."

He jammed the car into reverse, backed out and retraced the narrow route around the quarry.

"Take her again, boy. It's a beautiful place. And maybe the only thing under the moon worth doing. At your age anyway."

He leaned on the wheel on the road back. He was suddenly aware of being desperately tired. In town the station lights caught his eye. OK. A quick cup of coffee.

"Wow. You look badly-stayed-with. Are you all right, Doug?"

"Hello, Gloria. Yeah, just tired. How are you?"

"Any use of complaining?"

He looked at her. White blonde. Working class *haut coiffeur*. Under neon her skin looked lifeless, too white, her mouth too red, her blue eyes faded, couldn't carry it, disinterested. Cheeks puffy, then slack, according to whether she pursed her mouth or not.

Her waist was still thin but everything else pressed out, fell away. He winced. God, what a woman, mother earth, she had been! But, tonight... A month ago he hadn't noticed. Well, maybe the light was different.

She brought him coffee. When she leaned toward him the sickening, cheap perfume disgusted him.

She waddled back and forth as customers came in.

"I'm off at three," she said. "He's on the road. Wanta come over?"

He didn't. But she had been there so many nights.

"Sure."

"Twenty more minutes. You can follow me."

He sat on the edge of the bed in her dreary bedroom. The curved lacy lamp shade was kind, allowing small light. She stood before him and drew him to her breasts.

"It's nice. You being here," she leaned and whispered into his mussed hair.

He knew she meant it. He winced. Why can't I return that simple thought.

She stepped back and unzipped her white uniform and stepped out of it and he knew he couldn't. Her flesh seemed massive, sagging over the white cotton panties. She would smother him, absorb him. Suddenly he thought he would vomit if she unsnapped her bra.

She was so white and shapeless and hopeless. Her flesh had no will.

He put his palms to his face.

"Gloria, I..."

"What, baby?"

"I... I just don't think I can tonight. Wiped out. Too much drink."

She pulled his head to her.

"I'll do it all, honey. You can just relax."

"No. I think... I really am..."

"OK. I know. You can sleep here, if you want."

I hope she believes, he thought. *Can't hurt her.*

"No. I'll try to stagger home. Thanks, Glo. Thanks. It's just that I'm out of it."

"Sure," she said. "Sure. Soon?"

"Sure. I'm sorry."

"It's OK." She kissed him and helped him to the door. "Hey, don't have a wreck."

Charlotte heard him come in. She heard him go into Alex's room. He was there a long time. Then she heard him come to her door. Quietly he opened it and stepped in. She listened to him breathe heavily. *What is he doing?* she thought. He stepped out quietly. She heard the stairs creak, the front door open and close, the Packard engine.

She got up and went out on the gallery. *Now, where is he going?*

He went to the river house.

He didn't enter. He walked the path between the pines to the river. Out on the landing. One, two, three frogs plopped before him. He smiled. Suddenly he wasn't tired anymore.

God, the moon was incredible. A million stars.

"Hello, stars. Sorry about that, frogs."

An afterthought. "The boy and girl, too. Tonight I seem to be a general disturbance in the universe."

The current was gentle. The moon was there too. And out in center, where it was calm, the stars.

No use. He couldn't resist. He wanted to wash the woman off of him. He dropped his clothes, slipped in.

Good, good. Wonderful. He swam powerfully out to the center. Yes. This is life. He turned on his back. *Yes, Charlotte, I'm swimming in stars.*

He wasn't tired any longer. *I could swim forever,* he thought. *I'll go up to the bridge. Then cruise the current back. It's only a mile. Me and you, stars. I'll swim to you maybe. I wish it was noon and I had that McCanless bastard on the tennis court. No, don't be small. No, I wouldn't trade this for anything, anything on earth.*

The water feathered past his stroke. He turned again and looked up. The stars! *The stars! Charlotte's right. Sometimes you can't tell up from down.* He swam powerfully.

Charlotte and Blanche were unconcerned when he didn't return the next day. Sugar, maybe. Or some other woman. At his age, he was still one of the most striking men in town. He was always vanishing, to return with that shameless smile, to soak for two hours in the tub, singing.

But the telephone rang at twelve-thirty that night. Charlotte tripped out of bed to answer.

"Hello. Is this Miss Morton? Miss Charlotte Morton?"

"Yes. Who is this?"

"Miss Morton, this is Bill Helms. I'm sheriff over in Harran County."

Oh, my god, she thought. *What's he done now?*

"Yes, sheriff."

"I'm afraid I got some mighty bad news for you. I'm sorry, Miss Morton. I . . . Well, I'll just say it right out. A couple of niggers was frog gigging and they found your father. He was against the bank a couple of hundred yards down from your property. They knowed him and . . ."

"Dead?" she gasped. "Is he d . . . ?"

I know, she thought. *I know.*

"Yessum. I real sorry to say. He, I guess, drownded."

She couldn't speak.

"Miss Morton. I'm sorry. Are you there?"

"Yes. Yes. Where is he?"

"I'm callin' from your place. As I say, the niggers knew him. His clothes was on the landing. They come in and called me. They seem all right. I mean, good boys."

"I'll come," she said.

Her brain stopped. She couldn't accommodate what she had heard. She called a taxi, slipped into slacks and a blouse. She had to go back for money. She forgot Alex.

The sheriff's car was in the drive behind the Packard.

"Miss Morton," he called.

He met her, followed by another officer and two black men.

"I'm sorry."

"Sorry, Miz Morton."

"Ah loved Mistah Douglas," said one of the Negroes softly.

She couldn't speak.

"We put him on the bed in here."

He was covered with a sheet.

She turned to the sheriff. "What . . . ?"

"Well, if you like, I'll call Concordia and have an ambulance come over."

"Yes. Please. Thank you."

He moved to the phone.

"No, could you radio or . . . I'd like fifteen minutes alone. I'll be all right. There's no . . . problem, is there?"

He nodded.

"I'm sorry, Miss Morton."

"Thank you. Thank you all."

He gestured the others out. They nodded to her.

Alone now, she walked to the bed.

She slowly turned the sheet back. The handsome, ravaged features, now as in sleep. The hair water matted—but still, the curls had their way. The body perfectly relaxed, the muscles, not yet gone stringy with age, seemed to wait only the signal to swim, to dance, to fire a backhand cross court. The great machine which had never failed his will had stopped, was finally and fatally flawed.

Face, voice, the mind which had beckoned, chased, teased her to beauty and terror had also depended on the body—and had stopped with it. He was out of nature now. He could not care. *Death is not caring*, she thought. *He is ruined*.

She covered him. There was no *interest* here.

She walked out slowly down the path to the river. An owl hooted. Something darted before her step—a lizard.

The river flowed almost noiselessly. Starlight, moonlight. Oh God, he's so close. How could he *not* now take her hand and lead her into the water to swim to the other side, then beach at Isola Bella, panting, gorgeous with the water and moon defining the lean strong body?

It was crazy that he did not.

He was her great spirit. He was no more.

She looked up. The moon. The great wheel of stars held. The light we see tonight was cast before Christ was born, he had said to her so often. How small we are, our world. We! Yes. A wink in eternity.

A frog plopped into the water at her feet. She was not of its world. It did not know of her. It fled before her in terror.

She looked up again. The Great Wheel. Her father, one of the innumerable organisms beneath the Great Wheel, was gone. The cold indifferent stars did not care. Did not *know* of him.

She moved up the bank. Another frog plopped into the water. That tiny amphibian. Older than he and she. Monument in the long road from the mired sun-struck miraculous moment when the first cell was stricken with life. The frog, the lizard—memories of the cell's pilgrimage from mire to

366

man. The myriads of organisms. To this, the death of her father.

"Swim well, little brother," she murmured to the frog, brother to them both.

What now? The Great Wheel was brilliant, indifferent.

She looked. Fixed her eyes.

"But I can love," she whispered. "*I can love!* He taught me. *I, and mine, can love.*"

Her voice broke. She walked slowly up the path to the house where the beloved lay uncaring.

Expect nothing. Be prepared for joy.

Expect nothing. Be prepared for joy.

Remember.

She sat on the porch, looked at the moon through the pines.

Then a motor's roar. The flashing light. The ambulance.

She locked the house after them. She drove the Packard back. At one stop, an empty bourbon bottle rolled out from under the seat against her feet. She sobbed.

She sat by Alex's bed when she got home. "Well, little boy, you have lost much tonight. Half a world. He would have told you so much, shown you so much. You will never know what you have missed. I will try to tell you. I will try to show you. *His* telling and showing were part of it. But I will try."

Spence, lost—oh lost—took over and made all the arrangements. Cal actually cried. Then he too could be relied on for errands.

A private funeral. No flowers. No clergy.

His absence was everywhere. Earth was listless. A great presence had stalked this house. Charlotte went mechanically about her daily life, but half of it had been ripped away. The absence of an empty Jack Daniels bottle almost daily. Sound of him kicking over his tennis racquet where he always stood it, just inside the parlor door on his way to the decanter. Huge physical presence. The absence of the festive spirit that had been at table every evening of her life. Mornings on the gallery. Firm correction of a tennis stroke, a Mozart passage. Late night, pacing, reading aloud. Ranting about the Puritans, the war parties. Talking, talking, talking. The wonderful exercise of rhetoric.

A great presence had stalked this house. Shedding joy—no, not joy in the small sense. A fierce *aliveness*. Joy, in that large, infectious sense. The talking, touching, feeling. A great presence had stalked this house, and the lives centered there.

The verse he had fashioned from some Malraux sentences came all day every day in her mind—

> *I expect neither joy nor success from you.*
> *I cannot even imagine a world without you.*

She must begin to imagine. Physically she was listless, yet unable to rest. It seemed that his absence sucked her body of vitality, and of repose. She would sit, feel fatigue settle over her limbs, but would somehow have to rise to do . . . nothing. Nights, she walked and walked and walked the gallery. At last, broken down, fell into a joyless sleep. Sometimes waking, she would forget momentarily that he was gone, and then the heavy realization would bore into her consciousness.

I cannot even imagine a world without you.

Neither could Spence or Sybil. Listless both. Gloria came, a tawdry glitter, a pathetic blubbering. She and Charlotte clasped. Charlotte devoutly kissed the slack cheeks, held the flaccid, mushy body. Flesh that had given him so much pleasure. *I love you, poor, simple, humorous soul,* she thought.

Blanche, who had borne and buried—now six of her children, had watched her dear defeated Grover slip away in his sleep after the last of the innumerable terms in state prison farms—seemed, at last, looted of her great store of sympathy. For years, the voracious appetites of Douglas Morton had been her chief reason for being. Charlotte knew, when she walked into the kitchen and found the old woman simply sitting, staring away, that her desolation was perfect. And she knew, past her own grief, that it must be through Alex and herself, that Blanche recover her capacity to care.

In spring, partially working out her own survival, she was at pains to plan new flower beds, new menus for dinners with Sybil, Spence and Florence, Cal, anybody; to send Alex scurrying to Blanche with his latest cut finger, or the first Sweet William for her to sniff. Took pains to come behind the huge bulk standing, staring out the kitchen window, and kiss her cheek and whisper, "Alex and I need you too. Come, walk around the yard with me and let's see what is blooming today."

Gradually, whether because spring moved to broad sun-stalked summer, or because Spence's assessment of Douglas's estate revealed a household in bankruptcy, Blanche began to recover purpose. She went about the task of ordering the big house with verve, and, Charlotte thought, some of the old pleasure which had been her gift to three generations. There were lapses, certainly, when she would be found sitting, weeping. But gradually more time divided these spasms, and if distance remained in the dark eyes, laughter or fury could come from the broad mouth if Alex or Cal or she earned it.

21

DR. Grossman's reply letter also diverted her from grief. He pledged that he would be as diligent as Dave had been, and extended an invitation to drive to the hospital and have lunch with him. He said that he too felt that he knew her through the letters, photos, and files David had forwarded.

Charlotte drove the sixty gently rolling miles to Camp Butner. It was good to get out of the town, away from Spence's everlasting questions about her father's accounts, and even away from Blanche, for a whole day.

She was stunned with a moment of sweet *déjà vu* when she walked into the office and the doctor raced around his desk to take her hand and seat her. For one wild moment, she thought she was seeing dear, dead, Sid Jacobson again. Milton Grossman had the same thick, curly gray hair beyond a high forehead, the wide animated mouth and nostrils, the same forlorn jowls and vivid eyes. He was about the same age as Sid. She gave her heart to him immediately.

They talked easily, like old friends. He *did* know her. He asked about Cal and Whit. He knew loss when she told him of her father's death. Like Dave, he was enthusiastic, scholarly, and absolutely dedicated to his patients. He took her to the room he had ordered for Max. It was comfortable and he had already placed several history books from the library, along with a note pad on the desk. Charlotte was surprised to see her own pictures, two of the cheesecake, along with some of Alex, Cal, Max himself, thumbtacked to the corkboard over the desk.

"Like Dave, I mean to break his heart," Dr. Grossman said. "I mean to make him cry to see you and the others. And I'll have one big advantage—your proximity. I have another weapon. They supply me with a staff car here. I plan to take Max for rides as soon as possible. Make him see his North Carolina countryside again. Then, if possible, actually drive to your hometown. And, of course, if the right moment comes, you will visit. Maybe we can break his heart in so many places that he will have to come out of his exile."

Lunch was pleasant. Dr. Grossman, like Dave, believed Max's recovery hinged largely on the plastic surgery. He refused to allow Charlotte dreamy optimism. "I know Joe Rose personally and I've talked to him about Max already. He has Max's data and X-rays. I taught Joe a couple of courses several years ago. He is as good as the best—with one degree rising: he has boldness. In a case as radical as Max's, boldness must be there if we are to have a chance. I must warn you, Joe has said that Max has lost too much to expect too much. But we'll see. Joe is good and his team has already done a few small miracles."

Charlotte left the doctor's warm handshake with measured hope. *My father would have liked this man,* she thought.

"I will be in touch with you once a week," he promised, leaning on the car door. "Sometimes it will only be one-liners. But every week."

She thanked him and drove. Max would be in that little room in forty-eight hours.

Spence's final report on Douglas Morton's estate completed the portrait of a man who had ceased to concern himself with daily routine. He had simply lost interest long before his death. Including new mortgages on the house and the river property, the debt was just under twenty-five thousand dollars.

He, Jessica, Charlotte, and Sybil considered possibilities. They did not consider selling either of the properties. There were two other small pieces of land with farm houses on them and a tiny house just off the Mill Hill which Spence agreed to sell for them, and, in fact, realized just over ten thousand for the estate. Jessica paid out the mortgages herself and the houses were left in her and Charlotte's names, Nelson Summers having surrendered Aunt Elizabeth's claim. Charlotte reminded Jessica of the ten thousand dollars Aunt Elizabeth had left her, but Jessica reminded her that she had Alex to consider.

Sybil sincerely offered any help that was needed from her considerable wealth. Spence too offered, and when it was settled, Charlotte found herself holding clear titles with Jessica to the two houses and a ten thousand dollar cushion on which to live until Alex was in school and she was free to work. She was never able to get Spence to admit how much help he or Sybil supplied.

Charlotte again went through the accounts at the office, determined to bill outstanding accounts, no matter how old. Three weeks later, after going through Amelia White's meticulous books she had mailed bills for over fourteen thousand dollars. She did not hope to collect many of them. Most were protected by the statute of limitations, however men or firms who could not pay during the Depression, but had since become successful, might feel pressed by honor to remit.

She was amused by some of them. Several firms, now prosperous, chose to ignore her bill: Clayton Swaringen, the builder, for one. A few immediately sent checks. Cardinal Lumber Company was prompt and included a note of apology. *"I remember it. Simply had misplaced the record. Sorry."* said the note from Henry Ballinger, the owner.

Some replies were pathetic. An old grizzled farmer creaked out of his ancient pick-up and came in the office holding his worn felt hat in his hand. "Name's Harold Toms. I come to give ya forty bucks on my account. Sorta forgot it. See, I usta bring Mistah Douglas some corn and tamaters and watermellons once in a while jus' to let him know I ain't fergot it and he tole me that I had paid up with my produce. But if ya think I still owes, count on it, I'll pay. Mistah Douglas done fer me when I needed it."

Charlotte wrote him a paid in full receipt and refused his crumpled money.

"I'm sorry, Mr. Toms. I didn't know that you had given him vegetables. Many did. And we needed them then. Consider it paid. And thank you very much."

But she did realize three thousand two hundred dollars from the old accounts.

Charlotte Morton had never considered earning a living. Like her father, she had considered that there were those who worked at crafts, at business, at waiting tables as Gloria did, because they liked it, or because they were meant to, or because that was the way of the world. She knew about poverty—from a distance. She had seen her father forgive bills, help people with his customary open hand. Blanche had made her aware of it many times. But somehow, it had never occurred to her that there were bills to be paid, taxes on property, food to be purchased, mouths to be fed, and that the vast majority of people on earth worked very hard for these reasons and no other.

Like her father, she considered that there were books to be read, languages to be learned, music to play. There was the grace of tennis, and of dancing, and a beautiful table. Perhaps, somewhere far away, after college there had been in her mind the possibility of a job. It had never seemed quite real to her, the idea of taking money for doing what somebody else wanted her to do. Whit could have told her of work, or Gloria. But both of them seemed to love the Mortons in a way which set them apart. They did not tell them. They were grateful for the friendship which was so freely offered.

"What shall I do?" Charlotte asked. "My God, I do have Alex and this house to care for."

"There is time," Sybil said. "You have money enough now. And you know that I will help as long as you need me."

"Well," Charlotte laughed, "my advertisement is out if I should decide to hit the streets."

"Oh, the picture," and Sybil laughed too. "But Alex will be in school next year. Then you can start thinking seriously."

Amy finished college that spring. She would be a teacher in Raleigh until she married Senator Dunham's son, who had one more year of law school.

Billy wrote that he and Bucky had found their pianist. The trio was playing hotel lounges and was beginning to second group in some jazz clubs. Bucky was hustling for a recording with several companies.

Charlotte could not decide what to do about the law office. The sedate little building had been in the family for a century. Neither she nor Jessica could decide to sell it.

"Besides," said Jess, "what would we do with that bust of Cicero that our grandfather—or great grandfather, lugged home from his grand tour?"

Actually Charlotte had been hanging her umbrella and

purse on its broad shoulders since she had been going to the office. So the office remained the office.

Some of her happiest times, the times when she escaped the sense of loss, were on the back of Cal's motorcycle. They would simply ride the green, rolling countryside, all lovely and free, leaning into the curves, hair flying out straight, under the enormous surge of power and roar of the engine.

"There's a lot of power between your legs," Cal would quip over his shoulder.

"You or the engine?" she would yell back.

No way out. She had to relent and let Alex ride with him, after extracting the usual mother-promises of safe driving.

Coy Trexler was working hard. Often, she and Cal wound up at his Veteran's Body Shop for Coy to bend out a wrinkle in The Wreck, or supply some dressy piece of chrome for the bike. Trex was doing well. His veteran's loan had come through, and Cal said that his work schedule was always backed up.

"C'mon out. I wanta show you something," Coy said one day. A huge gleaming fishlike Buick was the sight.

They admired.

"I'll come by sometime and take you for a ride," Coy said.

"It's beautiful." Charlotte didn't know what else to say.

Several weeks later, she answered the door and there was Coy.

"C'mon, let me take you for a spin."

She thanked God that Spence and Sybil were there and she could plead guests. *I'll never get in that car.* She remembered V-E Day.

I am getting the same reaction that David got—silence, neither hostile nor amiable. However, I am gaining a kind of subliminal communication with Max. You see, Charlotte, I too am a history buff, primarily ancient. Max has similar tastes. Dave told me and I see the books he takes from the library. During our sessions, I rattle on about the speculations that interest me—what if Alexander had lived? That sort of thing. Just rambling. Max reads and re-reads Bury, Gibbon, Hamilton, etc. There are now book marks in them! And, Charlotte, his eyes are alive and moving above that infernal surgeon's mask that he will not remove in my presence.

So, I am certain there is communication. There are times when I am sure he wished to question or argue with me. Oh, if I can only draw him into discussion! Written on his pad, of course.

Incidentally, I suppose you know that the Comptons come each Saturday. He will not see them. But they do come, talk through the door, to the silence.

Dr. Grossman's letters did come once a week.
In October.

Max and I went for a drive three times this week. Monday, I simply handed him a combat jacket, told him the leaves were turning, took his arm and led him outside to the car. It was OK. I take care to see that there is fuel so he doesn't have to face even a gas station attendant, wearing his mask. Incidentally, the men—fellow patients—refer to him as The Freak and Iron Mask, sometimes within his hearing. I can't tell whether or not it disturbs him. And they will do it despite my requests that they stop it. No help for it. Anyway, we ride over the country side. I point, he looks. I talk, he listens. I'm sure, communication and interest are between us. If food wasn't such a problem, I'd head up to Fredericksburg for a day and see if we couldn't get him into Civil War history. I think he enjoys the rides because he never withdraws his arm when I suggest it.

In November.

More surgery. Joel says coming along. A plastic jaw bone may be coming. Waiting for the technology, which Joel says is there.

And ah ha. Grossman scored today. Beside the car, I handed Max the keys, opened the driver's door, and told him to drive—so you don't forget how, I said. I made him take us around the parking lot a couple times, then we were off. Charlotte, maybe, maybe, maybe.

December.

Christmas is coming—perennially sad for invalids. I told you I was an ancient history buff—that encompasses

Semitic history. Racial pride, I guess. We Jews fight hard to protect our identity. So Christmas. Knowing your and Max's wide nature I brought him my copy of Robertson Smith's Religion of the Semites and Frazier's Golden Bough. He's finished the Smith and is plugging through Frazier. Hey, Charlotte, you had better get busy. This boy of yours is going to be a genuine scholar. Anyway, perhaps new interests to divert from Christmas sadness.

Incidentally, he now drives each day. He has favorite routes and places. There is a lovely dairy farm not ten miles from the hospital. He goes there every time. It is indeed beautiful. Thick woods border green pastures where the cows graze. The house and barns are gleaming white—clearly the owner loves it too. Sometimes we pull over, and, Charlotte, Max's eyes devour the scene. Is he dreaming that here is a place that a marred, faceless man might live, read, wander, work without shame or attention? I think so.

Maybe he is beginning to have dreams again. God, help Joel's hands. Part of a face. A working, eating, talking face. Beautiful, no. Merely working. This I pray for.

Charlotte, an important question. Could you live with a truly misshapen face, halting speech, grotesque eating attitudes? Think carefully. Could you kiss, sleep, and live with him? I can't document it, but I sense progress. But I can't bring him to that point and have you fail—through no fault of your own, of course. Think. There is plenty of time. But once decided, it must be irreversible. He could not survive another failure.

I will not fail, she thought. I could not fail.

Riding, we always have the radio going. Do you know, I'm beginning to like country music. Hank Williams. Good lord, a Bronx Jewish psychiatrist! You Southerners! What am I coming to? And at my age.

April.

I pulled a dirty trick on Maxwell today. I told him we were going to have a passenger. If he objected, he

should shake his head. He did nothing. Sooooooo.
When we got to the door, the other rider was waiting
for us.

He was Bessemer Hanks—truth, I swear. He is from
Bluefield, West Virginia. I have worked with him for
several years now and I must tell you that it has been
an experience. First, poor man, he lost both legs just
below the groin, and his left arm at the elbow in the
Italian campaign—terrible wounds. He is an ugly wart
of a man with a neck like a hippo. He is illiterate,
stupid, bigoted—God help me if it ever occurs to him
that Grossman is a Jewish name, if, indeed, he knows
what a Jew is. He is loud, raucous, never shuts his
mouth and has a single obsession—woman's flesh. If a
nurse or female visitor comes within ten feet of the
right side of his wheel chair, the arm goes up her dress.
He has molested every nurse and nine-tenths of the
female visitors in the four years that he has been here.
He is absolutely irrepressible. And—I was going to say,
optimistic, but that is not quite the word. No, Bessemer
is quite simply alive. I, and all the staff, love him. He is
so predictable, and comic, that we wonder what it
would be like here without Bess. Perhaps it is his
enormous, shameless, carnal appetite that makes him
so. He asks every day when he is going to get his legs so
he can get a woman. Perhaps that is a form of hell—
desire so large, without satisfaction.

Anyway, I wheeled the babbling Bess out to the car,
then—Max had to help lift him into the back seat! Now
you see my motive. Bessemer is a bigger freak than
Max. Max actually had to help him. Max had to think—
and think profoundly about this curious bubbling being
who required help from him.

It went well. Max headed for the countryside. Fine.
Bess was reminded of West Virginia. But it wasn't long
before Bess wanted a shopping center where he could
watch the girls walk by. Max did it. We sat in the car
for an hour, Max with his hand over his mask, me
beside him, Bessemer in the back seat saying, "Look at
them boobs." What a scene it was! Come, Charlotte,
it's all right to laugh. I'm sure Bess wouldn't mind at
all.

Now we must see if there is value for both of these

*poor men. I am hoping that Max will see that he is not
so isolated as he had thought.*

In his first year at school Alex was called The Demon by a
sniffing Mrs. Shenniman who, aware of his birth, seemed to
expect bastardly conduct from him. He could read, calculate,
and draw better than anyone in his class. Therefore he read,
calculated and drew everything quickly and then got clay,
crayon, and paint all over everything and everyone.

In his second year, he was called The Vanishing Imp by
Mrs. Klein because, having completed whatever was at hand,
his curiosity led him everywhere, including the ladies' room
once where he surprised his ex-teacher, Mrs. Shenniman, in
a very embarrassing position by peeking under the door of
the booth.

"He is not undisciplined, Mrs. Morton," Mrs. Klein told
Charlotte one day after he had been missing for three hours
to be discovered in the furnace room asking the janitor the
forty-sixth question about the boilers. "He will do what I tell
him to do. It is simply that I have to tell him *not* to do
everything else. If I do not tell him *not* to leave the room he
leaves. If I do not tell him *not* to go behind the screen and
paint, I will find him behind the screen painting."

In the third grade, he was lucky in old creaky Mrs. Hart
who delighted in his energy and swiftness, and who fed his
curiosity and gained his love. He alone did the Christmas
mural for their class and wrote the reindeer names on each of
their collars. When they sang standards like *Twinkle, Twinkle, Little Star,* he could play the piano accompaniment.
When they went to the library, she had to help him carry his
selections back to the room. When they were assigned to
write five sentences so that the class could play at identifying
what was being described, his were so clear and cogent that
identification was immediate.

"Clearly, he is very bright, Mrs. Morton," Mrs. Hart spoke
across her desk to Charlotte one day in conference. "And
clearly, you have spent much time with him."

Alex was a classic case of a child who had grown up
surrounded by adults rather than siblings with childish interests. Like his mother, he had the advantage of being listened
to when he spoke, answered when he questioned. Therefore
he knew he was a person, was important. It was not until

later that he would realize that he was different, that the sins of his father and mother would be visited on him.

Depression sometimes seized Charlotte like a beast, shook her like a prey in its jaws. Amy did not invite her to her wedding, leaving her for Cal to find face down on the desk, sobbing, furious at herself. "Why am I crying over this childishness?"

She read in the paper that Jennings Hall had graduated at the top of his class and was now a doctor and had been commissioned as an ensign in the Navy to serve out his two-year obligation. She wanted to write him a note to tell him how proud she was of him, but dared not.

Pete McCanless and Louise Whitley were married and moved into a handsome house which the two fathers had built for them.

Whit would graduate in spring. He had made the dean's list in all semesters except three. He would be the first member of his family to hold a degree.

Cal would play out his eligibility next year and drop out, she knew. He simply would never pass the French requirement for graduation. He had at last shown a minor interest in math, and had managed to pass everything else.

The album was called *Bucky's Music*. She listened breathlessly the day it arrived. And listened. She called Billy and Bucky. She loved it. It had the first recording of *Cool Drive*. The album got fair reviews and some air time. No big splash, but the trio was launched.

Alex was in school.

Everything was moving—except her. What was she doing? Waiting for Max. Poor wounded, flawed Max. The endless operations. The ceaseless letters from Dr. Grossman, enthusiastic, sometimes hopeful, but never reporting tangible progress. The crazy habit of going to a non-functioning office, sitting, writing the daily letters into the void.

The day Mr. Compton died, Cal found her in the office, simply staring. Mr. Compton's secretary had found him slumped over his desk. He had had a massive stroke and died in the bank.

"It's no use, Cal," she finally spoke through the sobs. "It's no use. Simply no use. What will this do to Max? He'll never recover. What am I doing? Waiting to die? Oh, Cal, it's no use."

"Stop it. Stop it. Max will hardly miss his father. They weren't close at all. You know that. Listen, beautiful, let's go home and tonight we'll dance our brains out."

She knew that what he said about Max's father was true. They had hardly been aware of each other. Mr. Compton had changed over the last two years, but Max could not have known that. God, what will happen to daffy Elsa now, she wondered?

She let Cal lead her out to the bike, bunch her skirt, and ride her home. He gave her to the arms of Blanche and the energy of Alex who had just come from school with three new books to read to her.

Dr. Grossman's letter three days later was her information that Cal had left her and headed for Camp Butner.

I like your Cal so much—fine young man. But I'm afraid that his visit accomplished no more than Max's parents' visits. He would not see him either.

"You didn't tell me that you went to see Max. Oh, Cal," she threw herself into his arms. Cal's sympathies and sentiments, though short-lived, were fierce.

"Yeah, well, I thought I would see for myself. You seemed so broken up. Grossman's a great guy. He left a conference to see me. I told him I had to see Max. It's terrible, Charlotte. I didn't realize that Max moused around in his room all the time. He wears a mask. He never talks—hasn't spoken since the wound. Can't, I guess. Won't write anything. Poor bastard. Anyway, Grossman didn't know what to do with me. You know, I was wild. He didn't know how Max would react. So he sorta set a plan. I left and came back in exactly a half hour. He had Max in his office. Right over the parking field. I was to roar up, gun the motor, he was to go to the window, call Max over to the noisy bike—and me. He did it and Max ran back to his room and shut himself up again. I don't know." Cal ran his hand through his hair.

"So, anyway, Grossman took me up to the room and I called through the door. You know. 'It's me, Cal. Your old buddy.' Football, swimming, drinking, girls. Nothing. God, Charlotte, he must be miserable. I felt so stupid. Then I told him how you loved him and were waiting for him. And about how great Alex was. Nothing. 'It's me, Cal. Uncle Calvin. I don't care what you look like.' Silence. Nothing. I got mad. I said, 'Max, if you don't open that door I'm gonna knock the damned thing down and throw a figure eight on you.' I told him it was unfair. To you. Especially to Alex. I told him everything. 'I got a bike. We'll fly. I don't care if you're messed up.' Oh, Charlotte, I . . . I don't know. And from what Grossman says . . . I don't know. You can't stay on ice forever. Poor guy. Jesus. I just don't know."

"I don't either, Cal. I don't know either." She went into his arms.

On ice, she thought. Yes, on ice. I'm a woman, a damned good woman. I want to go, to do, to love, to . . .

Things moved about her, around her. But she seemed compartmentalized out of it. Time was dates on the calendar. Alex grew like the proverbial bean. Whit would graduate in spring. Amy was expecting a baby. Billy wrote of jam sessions, dates played, the new freedom and growth the trio had gained. Another album in the works. Coy kept driving around in his damned new car. Coy was getting rich, Cal said. He had four workers and still had a waiting list of jobs to do.

But she. Beneath the shroud her father's absence dropped over her, she waited for the next millionth of a millimeter of tissue to be added to Max's flesh, for the next doubtful letter from Dr. Grossman, for the next—nothing. Time stretched out before her like the dunes of Barbary.

There were some peaks. Sybil packed her off to New York and Billy for ten days of freedom and jazz. They reversed night and day. She listened, danced some, sat in some, sang some, never knew what time it was, went happily, freely, drunkenly to bed with two musician friends of Billy's, and came home with ten skinny marijuana cigarettes Billy gave her. She shared them with Sybil and Cal who giggled non-stop for hours.

And three times she went to Raleigh as Whit's guest for football weekends. Whit had never really asked her. He was too shy. But when he was home for a weekend, he spoke of it, and she asked who he was dating. He said no one. She said, "Let me come."

These weekends were fun and touching, for she realized that Whit was deeply in love with her, and had been throughout school. When the dances were over and he took her to her motel near campus, she had wanted to say, come, you can stay with me. But Whit's mythical image of her as some high, beautiful, untouchable priestess prevented her.

At graduation, she kissed him goodbye and saw him off to Cleveland, where he would work for a construction company. After six months' training, he was sent to Dallas where the company was building a new shopping complex. Weekly his letters came. Weekly she answered.

And the time came when she had to explain to Alex about being a bastard. It came at last when the tall, handsome boy was in the fourth grade. The kids had called him a bastard. He knew what it was. He had been to a dictionary. It meant that he had no father. Yet Charlotte had always told him that one day his father would come home and they would be like other families, she hoped.

Now it was time.

"Alex, a bastard is a child who is born to a man and a woman who love but are not married. You are one. Alexander Hamilton was one. It is a thing which happens sometimes because of unusual circumstances. Society, people, always condemn it when it happens. And they do it without even thinking of the circumstances—and, Alex, they usually call it a sin, and rarely, rarely do they forgive it.

"Things were different a few years ago. There was a war. You know about that. The men that we women loved were each day being sent away to fight. Your father was my age and we had been in love all through school. He was a friend of Uncle Cal, of Whit, of your grandfather, of Blanche. He was tall and handsome and bright. I loved him. He loved me. But there was a war. He had to go away. We would have been married, we talked of it, but we thought there would be world enough and time after the war was over. After he was gone into the Marines, you came along. We didn't know until after he had left that we were going to have a baby. I wrote to him and we dreamed together of the fine child you would be and how happy we would be when he returned. I have the letters. Someday soon I will give them to you to read. He gave you your name. As I have told you, after Alexander the Great. But he never came back, has not come back yet. He was wounded in an especially cruel way and he is still in a hospital. You know I write him every day. The doctors tell me that he may yet recover, that he may come home, and if he does, then perhaps we will be married and you will have your father. Like everyone else. And what a father he will be."

Rehearsing her failed hopes nearly caused the mother to

sob. She took her son's hand. He could see that she was moved and gave it gladly.

"Now it is very difficult for you, I know. All your life, people are going to blame, or say things to you because your mother and father were not married. It is unfair. But it will happen. Your father and I made the mistake of thinking that our love and luck were bigger than the war. We were wrong and you must pay for that. I am so sorry, for you and for myself. And for your father. I am sorry that you are deprived of him as a father. He is splendid. And I wanted him for my husband. It did not happen that way.

"Now what can I tell you? I suspect that things will be very hard for you, and cruel, harder and more cruel as you grow older. I cannot tell you I am sorry for what happened, because you would not be here. And that would be to wish away my love. I can't do that. I cannot tell you that I'm ashamed, because I'm not. I loved him truly, and you are my fine son. I am proud that I loved him, and proud of you. In fact, I have been very lucky in many ways. My love was—has been, for now at least, very brief. But many people do not in a whole life have the kind of love that I have had from your father. So I cannot even ask your forgiveness for the cruelties which you are going to suffer because of me, of us.

"I am only going to say that you are you, the son of a fine man who was wounded badly in a ghastly, stupid war. You, like your father, must be as much as you can be. You must try not to hate those who are cruel to you, because they simply don't know any better. They don't know where you came from, and the love that was there when you were made, and the bad luck that came after.

"Come with me. Later, I will tell you all I know of your father. But now I want to show you just one thing which will tell you of his quality."

She led to her bedroom and from her jewel case took a small wooden box. It held a stop watch inside a felt bag.

She held it for him to see.

"Notice the time, son. Four minutes and fourteen seconds. Your father gave this to me, and one day I will give it to you. This is the official time watch that the judges held on the day that your father set a new North Carolina high school record for running the mile. It has not been broken yet. He was—is—very intelligent also. And courageous. He has not yet had a chance to prove those qualities to you. But this I think shows you something of the kind of man he is. Now he is in the greatest struggle of his life. Perhaps one of the greatest struggles any man has ever had. Perhaps it is greater than any man should have. If he wins, he will come to us. If he loses, we know, because of this watch, that the struggle could not be won. And we will not be ashamed. Will we?"

The boy shook his head.

Blanche called them to dinner. They held hands on the way down.

That night before he went to bed, he kissed her more tenderly than usual.

Three months after Cal's abortive visit, Dr. Grossman wrote excitedly.

> The other day I rounded the corner by Max's room and I heard a furious beating on the door, and loud shouts—something like this—"Hey, Freaky, open up. It's me, Bess. Hey, Freaks. C'mon. It's Bess. I got something to show you." He was clutching a copy of Playboy. I ducked back around the corner, and, lo, Max opened the door. I couldn't believe my eyes. Bess rolled himself in. Well, I waited and when Bess came out half an hour later, I collared him. Sure, he went into Max's room whenever he wanted. No, Max didn't talk or write to him. But he listened.
>
> I have to believe that this is progress. I don't know whether Max is sympathetic to Bess—or what. Maybe he likes him, is amused by him. But I'm sure that this is progress.

Three weeks later, he wrote.

> Bessemer has pestered me—pestered is mild, believe me—for weeks to allow Max to take him to a drive-in movie. I have done it. I went with them the first night. A flesh film, but you know Bess—by reputation at least. I really think it is good though. Both of these men are making a first step out of this sheltered atmosphere. Now, I'm taking a real risk. I have taken Max down to the car pool, registered him, and he will be allowed to

take a car out by himself—even at night. It's a risk. But I think it is worth it.

And in April.

> *Yesterday Max drove us all the way to Kernston. We drove around. Max was obviously familiar with the city. I have a plan. On next Wednesday afternoon, I am going to try to have him drive to and around your town. If he will, I am going to try to get him to cruise along Well Street. He may not do it, but I'm going to try. Charlotte, could you arrange to be on your porch in the yard, or out front, with Alex between three and four. I'll try to make it as close to three as possible, if at all. If it does happen we will probably merely ride by. I'd prefer that you don't try to see us. I'd just like for him to glimpse you and his son and his home. It's worth a try. If he won't do it, what have we lost?*

Charlotte was like a school girl preparing for her first date. She selected, rejected, ten dresses. Sybil helped, applying just the correct make-up, combing, praying that there would be no breeze to toss her hair. She kept Alex out of school that day so that there would be no possibility of his being late.

At ten to three, he and she began walking to and fro before the house. They walked until four-fifteen, Alex complaining because he did not understand. His mother had told him simply that it was important, *very important*. She would explain to him at dinner. She did not want to take a chance on his childish curiosity causing him to ogle at every passing car.

Many cars passed during their walk. Several had three men—three figures—in them. She tried to smile, to walk beautifully, and she took Alex's hand whenever a car passed. Alex told her that her hand was hot. It was hard to talk continuously to keep him occupied.

But she talked to herself continuously—talked a prayer. *Let him come. Let him see me. Let him want me. Let him see his fine son. Oh, Max, please. Look at me. I'm beautiful. I'm for you. Come. Take me.*

She was trembling like a girl asking did he like me? Will I see him again? as she dialed Dr. Grossman's number at five-thirty.

"Hello, Dr. Grossman. Yes, this is Charlotte." And she held her breath.

"Yes, Charlotte. We saw you. Yes, we did. And very beautiful you are, indeed. Yes, he saw. No. Not yet, anyway. Don't forget, it's hard for him to express anything. Oh, and Alex. Fine looking boy. Splendid boy. Almost as tall as you. Of course, I'll keep you posted. Oh, Charlotte, Bessemer lusted after you most heartily. Maybe that too will wake Max up. Never discount jealousy. Of course. And, Charlotte, for what it's worth, I admire you very much. Yes. And regards to Alex and Cal."

She was limp when Blanche called them to dinner.

"Alex," she said quietly. "Your father saw you today. Saw us."

Blanche started. She put down the serving dish and leaned to take Charlotte's shoulders over the chair.

Charlotte explained. And explained to Alex more of the nature of Max's wound. The boy was silent.

"You should have told me," he said finally. "I could have had my bike."

"No. I wanted him to see how tall you are, and what long legs you have."

She and her son spent the evening poring over photographs and football and track clippings. Her eyes were vague with distance and memory.

"And there are only four people in the world who know of the treasure buried on Isola Bella. You, me, Cal, and—guess?"

"Max, my father."

"So that's another bond between all of us, isn't it?"

She pledged him not to speak of this to anyone except Blanche, Cal and Sybil. She did not want him telling the children because she did not want their parents gossiping of it over their lunches.

Alex began writing letters to Max that night.

And that night, the beautiful mother, in her bath, before her mirror, and in her bed felt her man's eyes on her, longed in her bones for his hands, his mouth, his body on hers.

Mouth!

22

ALEX had always forced purpose on her. Now Sybil offered purpose.

The new interstate highway had just opened two lanes. The other two were but months away. The nation was truly on wheels. Restaurants already lined both sides of the road. Two new motels, several miles apart were on the verge of opening. Sybil, on advice of several businessmen, had purchased large shares in one of the franchises.

The stockholders had already been received and shown the gleaming new plant. Aside from the rooms, pool, and restaurant, there was a bar which would sell set-ups and beer. A movable partition separated this room from the dining room.

"They are going to feel their way along and see what will be profitable in the way of entertainment," Sybil reported. "What will go. How much tourism—you know, New York to Florida—how many locals. The new restaurant ought to be an event in town. Nick Tambourkis, the manager, was thinking of one of those horrible happy birthday organs in the dining room. And if there is clientele for it, later hiring a small band for dancing. They can't tell whether or not there will be enough local trade to merit the dancing arrangement. I raised my shrill little voice and said that if they had an organ and some goofy smiling fool sponging through dinner hour I would never set foot in the place and would sell my stock. Marsh, bless him, seconded me. And he owns controlling franchise stock. So, we will have a piano. Now we need a pianist, preferably one who can sing. I told Nick that you would be out to see him."

"*What?* Me?"

"He's skeptical. But Marsh seconded me again and he doesn't dare turn you down out of hand. He's to call me when the room is set and the piano installed, which should be by next week."

"Wow," Charlotte said. "Could I do that?"

"Charlotte Morton, saloon pianist. Sounds good. It won't be that good, but you must be running out of money. Right?"

"Right."

"I don't imagine that Nick will pay much, but if you wear low-cut blouses and put a large brandy snifter on the end of the piano, you could retire in six weeks on tips."

"Huh," mused Charlotte.

She called Billy, and also spoke to Bucky.

"Try it," he said. "Hell, yeah. I know you can do it. In Concordia, North Carolina? Hell, I know you can do it. Believe me, in two weeks you'll be a pro. Start preparing. You've got the fake book. Get a fluent left hand first—all the rhythms. Invent a couple of riffs. Will you sing too?"

"I don't know. Yeah, I guess. Nothing's certain. You know, I have to see the manager. Do a couple of numbers for him."

"OK. Play a lot. But listen a lot too. Get some Ella records. Get Peggy Lee for the breathy stuff. But mostly Ella and Lee Wiley for phrasing. They never make mistakes. And, of course, Bessie and Lady Day. They're the main ones. Hey, listen to Sinatra too. He can phrase *Mary Had A Little Lamb* so that people pass out. After a day or so you'll learn to use the mike—you know, like we did on *Body and Soul*. Remember, breathe a split second before you sound. That makes 'em lean forward for the sound. Do it. Do it."

She went to the piano.

"Hello, Mr. Tambourkis. I'm Charlotte Morton."

He was bent over his desk, tie loose, sleeves rolled up. His dark curly hair fell across his forehead, just above the piercing black eyes which he set squarely on her. He was perfectly handsome. He bounced up from the desk. He was tiny.

"Hello, Miss Morton. Right. It *is* three, isn't it. Let's go in and hear you. Miss Schraeder says good things. But, I warn you, I'm looking for a pro."

He spoke like he walked, in bounds. He was a New Yorker.

He led her across the carpeted lobby into the dining room. Beyond the empty tables, two painters were finishing a door jamb.

"Now what the hell is this? Two guys on one door jamb when there are ten rooms that need finishing. Jesus Christ. One of you get the hell over to that south wing. Jesus!"

He wheeled on her and pointed.

"Tuned yesterday." He leaped up on the raised carpeted

platform and struck a couple of keys. "You look terrific. Schraeder said that if you were in a room that's where people would be looking. She was right. But that ain't enough. Play me two minutes of four different tunes. One ricky-ticky hotel music. Like *Blue Birds Over.* One frilly, like Carmen Cavallero. And two like you like."

He bounded to the rear of the room and sat.

She played. *Blue Birds:* one, two, three, four. *Then I Cried for You* with decorations and trills and runs all over. Then she went to *How High The Moon,* jazz, neat, clean. Then a slow, carefully articulated *Who's Sorry Now,* that swung out finally into a fast jazz beat.

"Switch on the mike there in front. At the bulb. Right. Now sing. Sing *Happy Birthday.*"

She did.

"Now something you like."

She did *Body and Soul*—Bucky's chords—breathing a moment first, so slow she had to lean into the melody to keep it from collapsing.

He bounded up front.

"Huh." He put his hand to his chin. He paced back and forth. "Do another one that way."

She did *The Man I Love.* Same way. She had done her homework. The chords fell under her fingers.

Tambourkis got busy pacing, rubbing his chin.

"Roger!" he yelled suddenly. "Roger, where the hell are you?"

"Coming. Coming."

"Let's open this partition." He sprang back across the room and joined the Negro in collapsing the partition behind the last row of tables, revealing the bar with its smaller tables.

"All right. Run and throw number fifteen switch."

In a moment the lights went out.

"Now eighteen."

Little electric candles flared on each table. The little man paced, rubbing his chin.

"Nah. It's too big. Roger!"

He was already closing another sliding partition which cut the dining room by a quarter.

He bounded to the door. Paced back and forth.

"OK. Better. Yeah, not bad. Yeah, could be intimate. Roger, one spot over the piano. Three-foot, no, two-foot shaft. By Thursday night. Got it?"

He wheeled again to Charlotte.

"Play another one. One of those."

She did *I'll Remember April*. Breathy, slow, yearning.

His hand was on his chin.

"You got a repertoire? I mean they ain't gonna listen to repeats."

"Name a tune."

"OK. OK. C'mon. Let's go in here." He stopped her at the door and turned around. "See what I'm gettin' at. It'll be six nights a week. Start at seven. At dinner you play fifty minutes, break ten. OK. Usually that'll go until nine-thirty. If they're tourists, passing through, you'll be making background noise to clattering dishes, jabber, and some crying kids. If Gail, the hostess, has people waiting for tables, keep the tempo fast. People eat fast if the tempo is fast. If the place looks like a morgue, play slow, so those that are here will stay."

His hand was at his chin.

"But you see what I'm gettin' at. They gave me a bar, but they ain't givin' me the dough for a band. Maybe a juke box is enough. We'll see how it goes. Small town and all. But I have a feeling that you could keep people drinking all night with stuff like that *Body and Soul*. Yeah, that face and that body. Anyway, we'll have to feel our way along. See you Thursday night at seven. Fifty and ten. I'll be watchin' the clock. Listen. Low cut dress. Long? I don't know. Nah, I don't guess. We'll see."

They went into the office.

He told her the salary. She almost laughed. But anything would help.

"Charlotte, OK to call you Charlotte? OK. Now, Charlotte, if the bar thing works, you should get tips. It may be horrible. You may get requests. *That Old Gang of Mine*. *Danny Boy*. Who knows. You may have drunks singing along. Traveling salesmen. Hanging all over you. I don't know yet. I think maybe you just could take charge of a room. We'll see."

He looked her up and down. He wanted her. And he would be tough, she knew.

A small article in that evening's paper announced that Lt. Jennings Hall had been separated from the Navy. Dr. Hall, a graduate of the University of North Carolina Medical School, would join Dr. Fred Eason in the practice of general medicine.

Dr. Eason was an old friend of her father. He was contemplating retirement and planned to turn his practice over to Jennings. *I wish that Jennings and I could be friends again, Charlotte thought. I would like to call him. Perhaps I shall.*

And, on the social page, another article announced that someone named Lavelle Campbell was marrying Coy Trexler, Jr.

Cal said that she was plain, silent, plump, and sure to become a punching bag.

She drove back out to the motel the following day. Nick Tambourkis was as she had left him, pacing, rubbing his chin, yelling for Roger.

He glanced at his watch and stepped into his office with her.

He was looking at papers on his desk as she talked.

"Mr. Tambourkis, something you should know."

He didn't look up.

She waited. Thirty seconds.

Then he got it, dropped the papers and looked at her. She looked into his eyes. He dropped his.

"Sorry, Charlotte. There's so much . . . sorry. Sit down."

"No. I only want one moment. But I do want that. You should know that I am from an old family in this town, but we are now in disgrace because I have an illegitimate child. I tell you this because I know that you are counting on local clientele and I don't know whether or not my presence here will hurt your chances."

He rubbed his chin.

"You *are* something, aren't you? Well, I know all that, Charlotte. Nineteen people have told me since yesterday. I know your reputation—I don't know whether or not you deserve it. I don't care. Let me tell you straight out how I viewed it. In a burg like this, I figured that having a Scarlet Lady in the bar might draw people rather than turn them away. You told me. Now I told you. Both of us gamble. Will I see you Thursday night?"

"Yes."

" 'Kay."

"Where are you from Mr. Tambourkis?"

He smiled.

"Nick will do. After all, we're betting on the same horse. The Bronx."

"No. Before."

"Greece. When I was a kid."

"Where?"

"An island. Chios."

"I've been there."

"What?"

"I've been there. I spent three days there."

He stood, hand to chin. She was still looking down to his handsome face.

"Huh. What do you know? I was back there for three weeks two years ago. How do you like it?"

"I loved it. Beautiful. My father and I went to see Homer's grove. Then on over to Turkey by caique."

"Well, I'll be damned." His eyes went up and down her. She turned. "I'll see you Thursday at seven."

"Right, Charlotte. Right."

Scarlet woman! She winked at herself in the rear view mirror.

The first two weeks were just what she needed to break in. Slow. Few tourists. A few locals. She did have to make noise over the clatter of dishes. But it was what she needed. She got the music in her fingers before strangers. The dining room was never crowded enough to open it all the way. By nine, coffee was being served to all the diners—a few salesmen and tourists who had discovered that the interstate was open.

On the second Thursday, Nick told her to cut on the spot after her break. He dampened the lights and opened the bar partition.

"*Body and Soul*," he said. All the touring families with kids were abed. Florida called early in the morning. Some salesmen were ending the week.

She did it and the room fell silent. She went on, singing some, playing some jazz. The drinkers stayed until one. She had five propositions and twenty requests. She had to play some real junk for six drunks who sang along.

As she was leaving, Nick called her into the office.

"That's what we're looking for," he said, pouring two drinks from the bottle in his desk drawer. "Every one of those salesmen will be here next time they're in this area. You had 'em." He raised his glass. "How're you feeling?"

"OK. A little pawed. You look frazzled."

"Yeah. It's always the same. This is the third one I've

391

opened. Always a million problems. Plumbing, heat, air conditioning, can't train and keep help. A million problems. Hey, why don't you come on down to the room and have a drink and relax a while."

"No, Nick. Thanks. I've got a son at home."

"Maybe tomorrow night."

She shook her head.

"I'm not really scarlet, Nick. I had some bad luck. Otherwise I wouldn't be here."

He came around the desk and put his arm around her shoulders. She didn't retreat, but she looked him straight in his dark eyes.

"C'mon, Char. Loosen up. I'll tell you about the clogged plumbing and the cook who quit, and you can tell me your problems and we'll comfort each other."

"No," she said evenly.

"C'mon, we—"

"No."

"All right. All right. But if you ever—"

"I'll tell you. Good night."

"Yeah. Good night, Char."

She left him rubbing his chin.

Sybil came almost every night. Sometimes she brought Alex and they had dinner while his mother played. He was very excited and pleased when he saw the poster in the lobby with his mother's picture and the words

Charlotte
in the *Stag and Doe Lounge*
Tuesday through Sunday

It was the same picture which Nick had run in a quarter-page ad in the newspaper, and would re-run weekly for months. Her white face and shoulders seemed suspended in a black velvet background. Light flared in her dark hair and sparked from the microphone. The photographer had caught her singing and her full lips were parted. The long lashes swept down the high cheekbones. It was a beautiful, deeply sensual picture. Beneath it:

Charlotte sings at the Stag and Doe
Trailblazer Motel, Interstate 85

"Do I really look like that?"

"Yes," said Sybil, "and it's beautiful. Black, Charlotte, under that spot, you'll wear nothing but black."

They went shopping for blouses.

Cal commented on the similarity of the mike to a penis.

"Shut up, you college drop-out. I should be so lucky."

"No. Not you. Me."

But she was pleased with the picture and her own sexuality. *All those years and years ago.*

> *Max was out alone with the car last week twice—indeed, out past midnight. There were hundreds of miles on the car. I have no idea where he went. Neither does Bessemer, who is fuming mad because Max did not take him. Perhaps he is driving around your block, or past your night club. I saw the ad on Max's desk. I haven't told you, but I have stopped reading his mail to him. I just hand it to him as it comes. For two weeks he just let it stack up. Today I see that he is now reading it.*
>
> *I am very nervous about the car. I keep imagining that he will have an accident. But on balance, the possibility of progress outweighs my fears.*
>
> *But the ad. You're very beautiful. I will drive over for dinner one night next week. To dine, and to listen. May I?*

The night Dr. Grossman came, Charlotte telephoned Sybil, who was getting Alex to bed. Sybil came and dined with him. Then Cal, college drop-out, and his new flame, Susan Culbreath, joined them.

She was 'up' that night, felt good, gave. Dr. Grossman seemed to thoroughly enjoy himself and was sincere in his praise of her performance. He and Cal were 'old friends,' and Sybil was charming.

"Charlotte," he said, placing his palms together. "I have a thought. Would you mind if I brought that wicked, strange, distorted Bessemer Hanks over here one night for dinner? It would be so good for him. *And*, he would tell Max—oh, would he tell Max!"

"Of course. Of course. Do it. I'd love to see that creature."

"Let me warn you, he's horrible. If you join us, he will be unable to keep his hand off you—you'll have an advantage, he has only one."

"You think these traveling salesmen sit on their hands?" she winced. "Bring him. I can be very firm. Sybil, maybe you would come and do a diversionary action."

"Of course," Sybil said. "I too can be very firm."

"All right. Wonderful," said the old doctor. "Let's see. Sybil, Charlotte, how about Wednesday night?"

Bessemer didn't know it but he was coming to be seen as well as to see.

He *was* a *blessed sight,* as Sybil said later. He looked like a disreputable frog in his chair, which Dr. Grossman wheeled to the table Charlotte had asked Gail to hold for them. As Sybil observed later, a tie and jacket suited him like a diver's helmet would become Charlotte. And his eating habits were more like feeding and watering.

When she played, his eyes never left her. Between songs he held Sybil's hand, stroked her shoulder, looked down her blouse. When Charlotte joined them at break, he held her hand, stroked her shoulder, looked down her blouse, and when it was clear that it was time to go and last chances were upon him, he put his hand on her thigh beneath the table. She tracked him with hers, but not too firmly. Poor bastard. Those slit eyes glittered with the rawest lust she had ever seen.

At the car, she steeled herself to kiss him on the forehead, and begged him to give Max her love.

"I'll be back, Charlotte. As soon's I git muh legs. I'll be back."

Oh Christ, she thought, *as soon as he gets his face, Max will be back too.*

"I can't get in her pants. What the hell's the matter with the bitch? I mean, has she got one? No, I know that. But what the hell is the matter with her? Does she think it's satin?"

Calvin, bitching about Susan. As he had for six months. Charlotte hooted.

"Marvelous! Marvelous! At last. You're finding out that you too are resistible. Wonderful! Hoorah for Susan!"

"Oh shit," Cal glanced at his watch. "Gotta get back to the office."

When Cal dropped out of school he had taken a job as assistant manager of a small loan company. The motorcycle was now gone and he was in suit and tie. He hated it.

He leaped to his feet. At the door he turned, "Tonight, by God. Tonight. Or she can take a long walk."

He left her laughing. Charlotte could not understand his obsession with the pleasant, silent Susan Culbreath. She was pretty enough and had a figure that was average sexy, but hardly obsession-producing. Susan was sweet and agreeable, but she was not witty or inventive or vivacious, as Cal's women customarily were. In fact, Charlotte thought Susan passive. Either she's insensitive or she's smart, Charlotte thought.

Susan was the only daughter of Sam Culbreath, a builder who had prospered in the post-war housing boom and now headed Culbreath Construction. Seven years younger than Cal, Susan worked in her father's office. It was a business which bid in seven figures. *She must be capable,* Charlotte thought. Diligent, pleasant, capable. Not Cal's customary cup of tea. But Susan had said no, and kept saying it. Cal was confused.

The next day, Charlotte smiled when he entered the office. "Well?"

"She'll exchange her panties for a ring." He sighed deeply. Charlotte howled.

"What are you laughing about? Old Sam's worth a million. Calvin Hendricks, construction coordinator. It doesn't sound bad."

"Bless you, my children," she laughed.

"C'mon, Morton, what do you think?"

"It doesn't matter what I think. I just hope Susan has some inkling of what she is getting into."

"Now what does that mean?"

"Now, Calvin, you leave her half the time and go knocking at the doors of twelve other women five nights a week."

"Yeah, but..."

"But nothing! Do you think a wedding is going to change a virgin into a sex machine?"

"Maybe she's religious."

"Is she?"

"No."

"Cal, look, she's really a nice person. And I'm prepared to bet that she will be a caring wife. If you love her, do it. And you know that you and she will be welcome in my life as you always have been. And I will love her because you do." But Charlotte was thinking, *he's going to marry her because she won't lie down for him. My God!*

Men! Cal! I don't understand sex. I want it. I crave it. I need it. But I sure as hell don't understand it.

How to thank you, wrote Dr. Grossman, and Sybil and Cal? In the two weeks since his visit Bessemer, the ruined little wart hog, had spoken of nothing else.

> *He raved to Max about your—attributes. How can Max not be eating his heart out? It's cruel, but perhaps it must be so, if he is to arrive at longing more powerful than his shame. His lonely nocturnal drives go on. He went out two times last week. He reads all day and exercises. I have found him sweating heavily in his room, but he won't go to the gym. It's good. Everything points to the fact that he has not given up. He hopes.*

Nick Tambourkis stood just inside the dining room entrance. His hand was at his chin. He felt good. He had just showered and had dinner (and Gail). He had slept through the night. Let those Chicago hard-noses read his daily account sheets now. He had every salesman on this route, company affiliation established, discounts set, which meant that every week night at least forty percent of the rooms would be occupied. The fourth lane of the interstate would be opened in two weeks all the way into South Carolina. The tourists were coming. For two weeks now the dining room had been just under breaking even and the bar was showing a profit. Let 'em read 'em. Soon this place will be paying for the opening of two more.

Here it is ten-fifteen, Friday night, and Gail had not had an empty table since seven. *I got the local yokels,* he thought. *Or she's got 'em.* Well, where else you gonna eat in this town? The Country Club for a few. The hotel for a few more. Roadhouses for hicks.

And after ten, this was the place. On weekends even the Country Club bunch was here by midnight. After they had had their three fox trots.

Who needs a band? I got a Scarlet Lady.

"C'mere, Mistah Tambourkis. Looka here. Does she spread it around? She jus' don't seem like she do to me." Clinton the janitor had called him into the men's room ten days ago. "But I scrubs this here wall ever'day."

There it was. *Charlotte is a whore*.

He had smiled. I don't think she does, but let these creeps dream.

Then yesterday Clinton had handed him the picture. Five by eight. Nude except for a touch. Clinton had waved his thumb at the men's room and shambled away. Charlotte nude. Nick had scratched his head.

Well, where in hell...? My God, what a piece she is!

He had stuck the picture in his desk drawer.

Now, he leaned back against the door just inside the dining room. There were no empty tables. Not a one. It was noisy as hell.

But wait, he thought, *just wait*.

In two minutes, the lights dipped. The spot dropped like quicksilver into the dark waterfall of a woman's hair, caught and shone, spilled past a straight forehead, caught again at the points of the cheek bones, skimmed the delicate nostril flare, rimmed the wide mouth, ledged, and dropped from the arrogant chin.

No light could reach the eyes or teeth. It wasn't needed. Her shoulders shone and her breasts yearned above the black blouse.

Suddenly this apparition had appeared in dark. Suddenly the room had hushed.

A single chord softly formed in the air. The woman lifted her head so that the cheek bones narrowed and pointed, the mouth parted, her breath became his and that of the room, and from deep in the long throat which suspended the head and its mantle of midnight hair, came slow, soft words—so slow that he thought she would not make them, so soft he wasn't sure whether she had made them, or he had imagined them.

"This lovely day will lengthen into evening..."

It was the only sound in the room, and you had to strain to hear it. Nick forced his eyes away from the woman. Dimly, adjusting from the sheer light she had become, he could see faces leaning forward, faces turned from the middle of sentences to her. A laugh stopped, the mouth still open.

Gail, slumped against the entrance, immobile, watching and listening. Hardisty, the bartender, looking over his shoulder. Waitresses hovering, trays in hand.

Nick's hand moved to his chin. He had seen this every night for three weeks. And every night for three weeks his hand had gone to his chin. The gleaming white vision at the piano caused, not invited, not attracted, *caused* everyone in the room to look, to be unable to look away.

He broke his revery. Stepped outside. He paced the lobby twice. He went back to the door, drawn.

"I'll remember April and I'll . . ."

Would it *never* come?

". . . smile."

His hand went back to his chin. All the faces, suspended, leaning.

He whirled and went into his office. Applause, whistles followed him.

He lit a cigarette. He sat, poured a drink, opened the drawer and looked down at *the* picture. *Christos,* what flesh. What absolutely gorgeous, curving, generous, velvet, glowing flesh.

He threw the drink back.

His hand went to his chin. *This is something different,* he thought. *I've screwed a hundred women, two hundred, maybe. This is different.*

I've seen 'em just as beautiful. More, in fact. Some. It's an attitude she has. She ain't exactly cold. She ain't icy. Or arrogant. But whenever she moves you watch her. When she tilts that head on that long neck, it does something to you. When she closes her eyes. When she smiles—she don't smile much. Have I ever seen her smile? When she walks you go with her.

I don't know. I don't know. It's the way it is. When she is in a room, she is the place to look. That's all.

At least once every Thursday, Friday, and Saturday night, he heard some woman say, "I'm coming, if I can ever get that

goddam husband of mine away from that bitch at the piano."
Every single night. At least one.

And that guy in the wheelchair, the mill owner with the
chauffeur—here three times a week. Must be rich as hell.
Gail gets ten bucks for the show side table every time.
Thurmond? Thurgood? And every night he is here, Charlotte
gets twenty bucks in her glass.

He went back to the office. Another drink.

If I was a high class Greek, he thought, *I would call that
charisma.*

Charlotte Morton was aware of her aura. For the first
weeks, she had neither seen nor heard those for whom she
played. She had to concentrate on the piano—*had* to. If
Katherine French had lived she would have known more
theory. If Billy were here, he could have worked with her. As
it was, she had to think it out herself. Then do.

But in the last three weeks, it had become like her father
had said it would, as it had been when she was working on a
piece. Think the phrase and your fingers will do it. Think
bells and your fingers will make bells. Think percussion and
your fingers will make drums. The melody was in her head,
and the riff, the *right* riff, came from under her fingers. And
soon she could break the riff, vary it, reverse it, jam it, edit
it. She just listened inside her head and it came. And with it,
freedom, such marvelous free-wheeling freedom. Attacks made
it work. Be on that beat. Get ahead of a few. But in that one
song in fifty—that one when, if you went just behind the
beat, you could break hearts. Listening to Bessie Smith had
taught her that. You had to feel when. And if you were right,
nothing was better.

In six months, I'll be really good, she thought.

With the coming of musical command, she began to be
aware of herself again.

She knew again that she was beautiful. It pleased her, and
pleased her that it pleased others—though here in this bar, it
was both liability and asset.

That first day, Nick had said that she could control a room.
She found that this was true. She could sit at the piano before
a noisy, drunken crowd, switch on the spot, lift her chin, tilt
her head, and command silence. She was a presence. If the
song allowed, she could go to a whisper without a single

person missing a word. Or she could set a junk beat and have them clapping with her.

She could do these things. She knew a power. She liked it.

She noticed the increasing size of the crowds for which she played—and their quality. Week nights there were the salesmen. They listened. They got drunk earlier. They were vulgar, vain, loud, obscene, obvious, and had to try their luck with her each week. Silly to generalize, she cautioned herself. But generally, it was true. Usually they were grouped around the piano at evening's end. Always, at least once, she would simply stop in the middle of whatever she was playing, sit stonily until the hand that was groping her thigh moved—then continue the song.

She noticed that hometown people were coming more and more each week. Many after dinner just to drink. Coming for her. She noticed that on Friday and Saturday nights Country Club habitués were arriving by midnight. Marsh Woods and dear, lost Sugar, Neil and Honey Foster, Bobby and Mary Anne Heitman, and others of her father's old crew.

Her own contemporaries came too: Pete and Louise McCanless—Pete going fast, little pot belly, eyes glazed, lust glittering; Ham and Joanne Beard; Tommy Kinder; Mark Allen Smith, who was engaged to Alice Wilkes (who had aborted, nearly died, and had been forgiven her sin for lack of visible evidence, Charlotte thought bitterly); Claire Lynn still single, becoming shrill and obvious. And others. It was strange playing for these people, strange maintaining the uneasy familiarity, nodding off the automatic 'so glad to see you.'

Coy Trexler was there three or four, sometimes five, nights a week in outrageous, tacky sports jackets, saturnine, drinking heavily, leering from the bar. Cal told her that he had seen and taken a copy of *the* picture from beneath the desk glass in Trex's shop office. Coy was always alone. Cal said that he was keeping Lavelle barefoot and pregnant.

Gorman Neil, the lawyer, was always drunk before he arrived—the swaggering, the feeling of Gail's bottom as he entered. Obscenity was like a duty for him.

And the chauffeur pushed old Dodd Thurmond in several times a week. At first, she did not know who he was. She watched him powerfully lift himself from the wheelchair, steadied by his man, to the chair at his table, then have the chauffeur remove the wheelchair, as if it were a banner of weakness. She was baffled by the twenty-dollar bill she found among the others periodically. Then she realized that they were left on the nights that Mr. Thurmond was in the room. Thereafter, she nodded to him when she went to the piano for her first set. And during the first set she turned and sang one number directly to him. He returned her gaze as directly.

When she learned his name, she knew who he was. He owned a small textile mill in the town of Oak Grove. Indeed, he employed almost the entire town. He would not go public with his mill and he would not tolerate a union. "I am good to my people," he had declared in the press. She recalled several years ago, when his workers approved a vote on whether to organize or not, he closed the mill and went to Florida leaving his foreman with a message: When they wish to return to work without a union, contact me. He left the mill closed eight months. Finally he received the message he wanted and reopened. She had heard no mention of unions related to Thurmond Mills again.

Whenever he was ready to leave, he motioned to Gail who summoned his chauffeur from the lobby. The old man would hoist himself into the wheelchair, the chauffeur would place her tip in the glass and wheel him out. They never spoke.

In her first weeks at the *Stag and Doe* Charlotte took her breaks at a small table in a corner which Gail saved for her. There she could sit and consider the next set, have coffee, or late, a drink.

Soon, however, at every break men came to take their chance with her, and she could not relax. With his and Nick's permission, she began going into Clinton's large janitor pantry with a book and her sketch pad. There she could be alone if she chose.

"You can use my office," Nick offered. "I'm hardly ever there at night."

She preferred the pantry.

At first Nick accused her to being aloof at the piano.

"Talk to the room between numbers. Cozy up to them."

She didn't—it would have been out of nature for her—and he came to realize that she was right. Aloofness fitted the vision that sat at the piano.

Scarlet Lady? Let 'em wonder.

She rarely joined a table other than that of Cal and Susan, and of course, Sybil. Or the Fultons when they came out with Dr. Tom.

She realized that every man in the room wanted her every night.

Lust hung in the air ineluctably. Sometimes it titillated her. Sometimes, usually after she had had a couple of drinks, her groin, the pit of her stomach writhed with it. Her mouth went dry when she realized the magnitude of it. Between sets, when she passed among the tables, she could feel their eyes on her, watching each nuance her fluid waist and stride caused in her hips, each small lilt of her breasts. Those whose lust was refined watched her long fingers fall away from the tiny wrists to bury among the piano keys, watched as her generous mouth parted and closed, her tongue pushing syllables into the air two inches from the crown of the microphone.

Sometimes she got a little crazy. Sometimes, a little drunk, she thought: *I could have many lovers*. She remembered in high school, when she first felt the power of her sensuality, having thought she might take many lovers. Like Catherine the Great, like Julia, Cleopatra. At times she craved.

Other times she was frightened by the lust, or repelled by it. She recognized the cruelty shaded in it. They were there who would use her, pierce her, use Woman. Those who wanted to give pain because their layered desire could not be exhausted. Those times the lust degraded.

One Saturday night late, she stood after a set. Rising amid the crowd around the piano and the pleas of "Don't stop! One more!" she leaned to take her drink from the piano and was stabbed hard, with firm intent to penetrate, to hurt, by a thrust between her legs. She cried out and wheeled, to stare into the half-lidded, blank, slack-mouthed leer of Pete McCanless. Fury swept her, fired by pain. She flung her drink full in his face.

Reacting, he raised a beer bottle but Cal was there. His fist went to McCanless's throat like a projectile and he held the sagging, bleary-eyed, drunken fool like a pelt he could shake apart.

McCanless wavered a split second, then whimpering, tried to laugh it off. That second had told him that he did not want to go against Cal Hendricks. Cal held for a moment, then released. He did not even know what had happened, only that his Charlotte had been a target.

Livid, Charlotte stalked as Pete backed off. She wheeled and faced Louise for a moment, then turned back and hissed into Pete's flaccid face, "If you ever touch me again, I will blow your brains out. That—I swear."

She stood, her chin nearly touching his, glaring into his mindless, blank grin. Then she marched out of the room, into the parking lot, got into the Packard, and drove.

She was trembling when she got home. In the foyer, she saw herself in the huge mirror, tears ruining her face. She covered her image. She wandered into the study. Is this what it was for? Over and over. Is this what it was all for?

She straightened. Don't be stupid. You're hysterical. It's period time. You already cried your eyes out today.

She *had* cried earlier that day. She was in the study licking the stamp on Max's letter. Idly holding it in place she strolled to the window. Blanche was directly below her, hoe in hand, loosening some soil around a flower bed. The old woman placed her hand on her back to straighten. Suddenly tears welled in Charlotte's eyes. Suddenly she realized that Blanche was old. There it was, in the face that she had loved longer than any. Her hair was snow white. When had that happened? Yes. It was there. And there were wrinkles. So many.

The old woman leaned on the hoe, stared at the plants whose health she was tending. The thought, framed out of a hundred impressions, crystallized in Charlotte.

More and more, Blanche fell into a kind of brown study. At the sink, at the stove; Alex, standing with the dish towel, silent, patient, waiting for the next dish, which did not come. *Blanche could die*.

Charlotte sobbed. Then blotted her eyes. In near panic, she ran outside. *Don't die, Blanche!* her heart cried. But she stopped and sobered.

She walked calmly to her friend and kissed her as she stood against the hoe.

"Good morning, chile."

"Good morning, Blanche. Oh, they look nice."

They puttered and walked together for a few minutes.

"Blanche, would you think of moving in with Alex and me? We could have such fun making a room for you. Say that back one, with its own bath. The one looking over the tennis court. You could keep track of the vegetables from your window."

"It would be nice. But, lawzee, no, chile. I got to stay in my house. I wouldn't feel right. That's where I made my chil'ren. Grover lived there. No, I gotta stay there. It would be pretty here, but *that's* my place."

Charlotte dropped it. But this very morning, inside her secret heart, she stored knowledge that Blanche too could die, and it crushed.

"Mother?" Alex's voice called her back.

She closed her eyes, knowing this was what it was for, all of it. Most of it. She clasped her son and shut her eyes against the tears.

"It's OK. I was thinking of grandfather. That's all. What are you doing up at this hour?"

He grinned. "Checking on you."

"OK. Checked? Run to bed. Hey, how about a river jaunt tomorrow. You and me?"

He grinned and nodded.

"Leave your door open. I'll play something sweet for you to go to sleep by."

Cal and Nick arrived one after another. Just checking on her too. They found her playing a Chopin nocturne. She nodded toward the decanter. They made themselves drinks and listened.

"I'm playing Alex back to sleep. I'm OK."

When they finished their drinks, they blew kisses, and started to leave.

"Hey, thanks, you two. You made it all well again."

But the next day she told Nick that she would no longer play at dinner. He read her. She meant it, just as she had meant 'no.' He hired a middle-aged piano teacher to play schlock until nine-thirty.

Now she and Alex could enjoy each other again at long dinners, could talk, and could share their secret bond—his father. She made sure that she was free now by three o'clock when he came home from school, kept up with his homework, and frequently reasoned with him on his conduct at school. Letters continued to come from his teachers. He remained the free spirit his early school years had promised. If he was not engaged, he would get into trouble.

Charlotte began to be concerned that he came home from school every day. She observed that he did not have contemporary friends, that he did not go to the homes of the other kids, and they did not come to his house. He did not complain, and she learned circumspectly of birthday parties to which he was not invited.

She learned from him of school athletic contests, relays, touch football, baseball, in which he was first to be chosen. In academic contests, he was also first chosen because he had learned by growing up in this house.

But it was clear that he was a social loner, and she didn't like it. She prayed that he would meet his own Max and Cal—perhaps *his* Charlotte. And she couldn't resist contempt for the parents who withheld hospitality, or told their children not to play with him, because of circumstances over which he had no control.

But if he was to be a loner, she must make sure that it was not loneliness. She shared with him the richness of the river, of Isola Bella, of swimming, and rambling. They biked out to Lee Creek together, hid their bikes, and followed the creek all the way to the river—tracking, she knew, the route taken by two famous runaways years ago. They collected specimens: rock, fern, bird feathers. Then were breathless as they thumbed books to identify them.

The canoe was still in good shape and they made overnight—Mondays—trips up and down the river. It pleased her that he liked to help Blanche and her in the flower and vegetable gardens. Together they went into the basement and brought up his grandfather's old, slightly rusted barbells, and Alex began a lifting regimen.

They had always read together. Now they told each other of their reading. He was willing to follow her guidance in his selections.

He was diligent about the piano too. She was his exemplar. He admired his mother as she sat at the piano in the bar. And, on the tennis court, she had never allowed him to bend his elbow when he served a ball.

Sybil taught him to ride and was in every way generous with her time, her resources.

Cal was his friend. The bike had made Cal a hero.

Above all, Alex was curious. The early insistence that he finish what he began had developed self-discipline. He had the bearing of a natural athlete. He was serious, but perfectly willing to be joyous, to play practical jokes on her and Blanche. And, Charlotte perceived, he regarded his secret father as marking him with a special destiny, a special purpose.

She frequently found him handling the stop watch which had become a totem to him.

She and her son were friends.

23

CAL and Susan were married. Sam Culbreath took him into the business, gave him and Susan a lovely little home and a company car. The Wreck was retired with eulogies.

As Max and her father had observed, like Achilles, Cal was a perfect sensualist. Charlotte watched him feeding, watering, fighting, playing—all joyously. Reacting to stimuli. Cal ate because it tasted good. He swam because water felt good moving across his fine body. He whored—with me, she cheerfully admitted—because it felt good. His rage, joy, affection were instant, furious, and fleeting, for child-like, Cal's attention was too quickly distracted by each new stimulus to assimilate an emotion as concentrated as hatred, grief—or love.

That he was free made Cal wicked to most. Consciences shaped by Western moralists mistrust the senses. But Cal knew that wickedness is lovely to most men and women—knew instinctively, for philosophical thought was alien to him. Hence his success with women, his grudging pardon by men. He did ignorantly what most men desired, but dared not even after calculating perfect odds for success.

Susan had won him by her fierce pride and sheer obstinance. He didn't love her, but he wanted her and he got her the only way he could. He married as an act of pleasure, without the slightest intimation of the obligation incurred, and he was lucky enough never to realize an obligation. Two children came immediately. He adored them—as a great bear adores his cubs—to tumble with.

Nothing really changed. He was at the bar a couple of nights a week. He walked out of the bar into a motel room with a one night stand as often as usual.

Sometimes Susan locked him out. If he had been especially wicked, two nights in a row. But somehow, a night later, he and Susan would walk into the dining room, eat, drink, and applaud Charlotte's performance. Nothing changed.

Charlotte considered Susan. Perhaps her pride divided her from the knowledge that Cal was untrue, that he regarded her, when he regarded her at all, as a convenience who fed him, gave him children, and made him sleepy with love. Or perhaps, more profound that she indicated (or made profound with child-bearing) she understood her man. Perhaps she loved him, earnestly and wisely, for his wildness, not in spite of it, and knew he would always come home to her simply because nothing could hold his interest long enough to make him stay away. Or perhaps his lovemaking to her when that spindrift energy focused momentarily on her, was enough to satisfy.

The marriage lasted.

Billy had written that the trio was going to Florida to play a six-week gig, then on to Nassau for three weeks—but Charlotte didn't know exactly when.

One Friday night as she was leaving the piano after her first set, she heard a voice behind her say, "She sounds like a frog."

"She looks like a truck driver in drag," another commented.

Those voices! She stopped, turned and opened her arms. Billy and Bucky came to her.

"Bastards," she whispered into their embrace. "Sneaking bastards. I would have laid it out if I'd known there were two pros in the house."

Bucky took both her shoulders. "Lady, you're good. Really good."

"Char, I couldn't believe it. I closed my eyes and couldn't believe what my ears got. My God, you *are* good."

She turned and called toward the bar.

"Cal! Cal. Look who's here."

Cal left the girl he was talking to and threw his great arms around the two.

"Come with me. I've got fifteen minutes." She led the three to her pantry for talk, memories, catching up. And for criticism.

"None," Bucky said. "I'm serious. Wonderful. I couldn't believe it. Hey, you've really learned how to breathe. Right from the gut. You held a couple there as long as I could have.

And you kept them pure. Beautiful. And Charlotte, best of all—taste. You have got taste. You *know.* When and how."

"Can we get off in here?" Bucky asked, brandishing a reefer.

"Sure," she said, "It's an automatic lock."

They passed it, fragrant and lovely.

In moments they were giggling.

"How long are you here for?"

"We'll leave Sunday. We bought a junk station wagon to carry all the equipment. The piano man flew down."

"How is he?"

"Good. We fit. The new album will be released in fall."

"Terrific. Hey, sit in with me tomorrow night. Please. Please. Please."

When her break was over, she caught Nick and introduced him to them. Sure, he said. Great. There were mikes and a standing spot. Easy. Sure. Great.

"Jesus," he said. "All those doctors, the local medical association has the banquet room tomorrow night. Hey, Gail, get those three extra girls for tomorrow night. Hey, make it four if you can."

Billy and Bucky stayed until Charlotte quit. A bit stoned, anxious to please, she laid her heart out. She slipped down the bench and Bucky backed her in a set, including fifteen minutes of *Body and Soul* that wrapped up the room.

Nick's hand was on his chin. Dodd Thurmond didn't summon his chauffeur until closing.

Charlotte spoke to the crowd for the first time.

"Bucky Stafford on piano. Bucky Stafford of *Bucky's Music. Cool Drive* is his song. And tomorrow night will be special at the *Stag and Doe.* Bucky and the trio's bass man, Billy Ennis, will join me here. All night long. Tell your friends. There *will* be music here tomorrow night. Promise."

When the lights went up, she spoke to Mr. Thurmond for the first time.

"Will you come tomorrow night? These two are very good. It really should be special."

He looked up at her.

"Why thank you. I will be here."

The chauffeur told Gail to save a table.

Saturday night she met Dr. Tom in the lobby. He had ducked out on one of the medical association's speakers. He was happy to see Billy again.

"Dr. Tom, come into the bar after your affair. Billy and his friend are going to join me. It'll be special."

"Wouldn't miss it, Char. Billy, I'll be in."

Charlotte nodded to old Dr. Eason, who apparently had ducked out too.

Before they went on Billy collected Cal from his table and the four of them slipped into Clinton's office. He took what looked like a fountain pen from his pocket and shook out eight tiny lines of white powder on the desk. Then he unscrewed a vial from its top.

"Watch."

He stopped one nostril with a finger, inserted the cylindrical vial into the other nostril, and inhaled one line of the powder. Then he stopped the other nostril and repeated the operation. He handed the vial to Bucky who sucked two of the lines of powder.

"Charlotte?"

"What is it?"

"Coke. Cocaine. Try it."

"Will it wreck me?"

"Try it."

She did. Boiiiing! went her brain, like a bell. Again.

"Jesus."

"Yeah. Cal?"

After, she and Cal looked at each other.

"Char. I'm sailing."

"Yeah. I gotta play."

Play they did.

The room was packed. People had told people. Billy had set his electronic bass up to the right. Big bands are finished, he had said that afternoon, when three guys with electric guitars can out-blast a brass section. Wait and see. Something new is beginning. His amplifier could shake the room.

Bucky wandered with his horn.

Before the first number she found Cal's face. She pursed her lips. *I can already hear it and I haven't touched the keyboard*, she thought.

I'll speak, she thought.

"Hello. Great guests tonight. The tenor sax is Bucky Stafford. The bass is Billy Ennis. The song is *Cool Drive*. Bucky wrote it." Her voice dropped to a whisper. "Listen."

They did for fifteen minutes. She couldn't believe it. God,

she couldn't believe it. She listened. Am I doing this? She's doing this. She. Me. It was wonderful.

She had chorded and fallen into a riff with Billy that sounded like they were married, and they ran it out, Bucky taking, handing to her, actually Billy was passing it, then back, then together, then Billy with the bass from all over the room, back to her with Bucky sighing underneath, matching, tangling, then fighting her, and her coming right back at him, smiling at each other, finding Cal's face again. Cal had a halo! He was smiling, angelic. Cal under a halo! She laughed. She pushed them. Only to find that they were leading her. Never end. Never end! And they rode together, with Billy so fast she was remembering and hearing at the same time, and Bucky so fast, so clean, so clear that she knew it couldn't be done.

To the end.

People were screaming. She found Cal again. He didn't have his halo. He had a smile. He was up. Clapping over his smile. Then he reached down and lifted Susan with one hand. She was clapping too. And smiling. *Oh! she has on his halo.*

"Good stuff, cat."

Bucky was speaking into her ear. She wondered if she had a halo. She sure had a smile. Wow. I'm gonna flip inside out, she thought. Nobody can smile like this and stay right side out.

But Bucky had started *How High the Moon* and she had to stay right side out. Suddenly she knew she was going to sing. Everything in the room told her. Billy and Bucky made it clear. She did. What Billy did behind her, and Bucky, told her what she wanted to do, and she could just *do* it.

And they went to a slow *Sophisticated Lady* and she knew she was going to sing again.

And on and on.

Nick's hand was on his chin all night.

She's eatin' that piano, he said to himself. Them two guys are great.

He looked around. Wall to wall people. The lobby was packed. People were sitting on the floor. Gail had given up. Waitresses couldn't move.

After a solid hour and a half, Bucky leaned to the mike and said, "We'll be right back."

And he led her out. Cal grabbed her other hand and followed to Clinton's closet.

"God," she said, kissing Billy, then Bucky. "Oh my God, that was great."

Cal was trying to get his arms around all of them. He must have left his halo with Susan.

"Hey, what about a tambourine man?"

She said, "I can't stop. Let's go back. I don't want to lose this."

"I gotta have something wet," Billy said. "Something delicious and wet."

Charlotte ducked out and told Gail who somehow caught a waitress, who somehow threaded the crowd.

It was beer and it *was* delicious and wet.

On the way back in, she placed her hand on Mr. Thurmond's shoulder.

Take the A Train. Now the music was making little trailing lights about them. She could see them. There were friendly little figures that leaped, fast sprouts of light, lightning flashes. She watched—made some herself.

And Billy's wonderful bass was a blinking glow. On and on.

Then, moaning *Satin Doll*, Bucky's horn called her. Billy took over, under Bucky. He kicked the beat. The horn called her. She had to go. She left the piano. Moved stage center. Everything said *move*. The horn told her how. Not too fast. Just right. Raise your arms, it said. If your waist is fluid, your hips and breasts know the answers. The horn had her. A horn of plenty. It was moaning and shrieking and rippling and fondling at her pelvis. She couldn't stop. It was sexual. Her whole body arced over it. Her vision narrowed. All she could know was the gleaming bell of Bucky's sax. From it gushed the purple flood of sound that poured over her thighs. I'm hung up on it. I'm floating. I'm a fish. A mermaid. Slithering between heaven and earth.

All eyes flashed from her fluent breasts to her hips. To see one was to miss the other. Nick's hands were not on his chin. They were clamped around the back of a chair whose occupant leaned forward across the table.

"*Christos!*" he lapsed into his mother's incantation. *Her head don't move. Look at that chin. But all that swirl below. You could believe her feet were off the ground. She ain't dancing. She's praying.*

*　　*　　*

Wrung out, released by Bucky's horn, she gave herself to Cal who led through the crowd. Faces loomed and melted away. Pete McCanless—intent—burgeoned before her, fell away. Coy Trexler fell away. Sybil's hand fell away from her waist. Claire Lynn soured, fell away. So many. Falling away.

Near the door Dr. Tom took her from Cal. He cupped her hair and face in his hands and kissed her forehead. "My dear. My dear. Douglas would have loved that."

In the glare of the lobby, she flung her hair back—and looked squarely into the stony, thick-lensed eyes of Dr. Jennings Hall.

"Jennings," Cal shouted. "Jennings, baby."

Charlotte stared up into Jennings's impassive face for a moment. He ignored Cal's hand on his shoulder. He stared down into the beautiful face of the Whore of Babylon.

She couldn't speak.

He turned out from under Cal's arm and disappeared into the writhing human mass around her. Shame at *being* cut through her for a moment. Merely *being*.

It didn't last. The music high was high enough. In Clinton's room Billy stuck a reefer between her lips, twice, and she mellowed out and threw her head back across the chair. She and Bucky couldn't look at each other.

Not much talking.

"Baby, baby, you sure showed me something this night," Cal kept muttering quietly. She held Billy's hand.

After some more 'wet and delicious,' they went back. She dreamed through *Stormy Weather*, and Bucky broke hearts, his horn mourning, grieving, keening. In her moment on the piano, she wove in some themes from Billy's *Charlotte's Letters*. They beamed at each other over the arcs of light the music made.

At two-fifteen, they started on *Flying Home*. At two-forty, they quit, hung up, faded out.

Dodd Thurmond grasped her hand as she passed. She squeezed back.

At the Packard, Bucky whispered, "First time I ever had sex with a woman."

"You wore me out, Buck."

They kissed. All of them.

Nick rushed out. He back-slapped. He wanted to pay them.

"Take money for *that*. Don't be vulgar," said Billy.

More handshaking and back-patting.

Home, she fell across the bed. That was how to make music. God, those two. And I wasn't bad. I wasn't bad. I'll never be good if I wasn't good tonight.

For a moment, Jennings's joyless glare cut through her consciousness.

She closed her eyes.

As promised, Billy and Bucky came for Eggs Benedict at ten-thirty. She felt such love and gratitude for her two musicians, her friends who had shared their lives with her momentarily. She understood that, for them, living was playing. It was the heartbeat. Everything else was coming and going to life—music. She could not remember having felt closer to anyone.

"Now we can be together over the miles," he laughed. "Give a couple to Cal." He took her hand and cupped it around some joints. "Char, did you see Jennings last night?"

"Yes," she said. "And he *saw* me. Too much of me. Oh, Billy, he's so God-eaten he can't enjoy the common good of life."

"He was awful to me. We shook hands. You know, said hello, how are you? But he said, I'm not glad to see you here. And as you are. You are dying. Dying! Oh—you know."

"Yes, I know."

"He begged me to—change."

"Yes."

At the station wagon, they embraced and parted.

She joined Sybil at her break that night.

"Well, Charlotte Morton, you are the most famous—and *notorious*—woman in this town today. I went to the tea dance and dinner at the Club for that Dr. Coughlin, the pathologist who spoke to the medical dinner last night. All I heard was—were you at the *Stag and Doe* last night? Charlotte, you are universally desired by men—and hated by women."

Charlotte laughed. "Nick says he has had eighteen calls asking if the same show is on tonight. I have never played or sung like that before in my life. I didn't know I could do it. Sybil, it's so great playing with musicians like that."

"Or danced?"

"Yeah. Was it too much? I was possessed. Making that music, hearing it, you know. I just couldn't help it."

"It was wonderful. But some people couldn't take it. Your

413

old friend Claire Lynn talked about your blouse and the PRO-VOC-A-TIVE way you danced. I told her that I had given you the blouse, that you were an entertainer, and entertain you did. Oh, and Louise Council, the doctor's wife and social arbiter *extraordinaire*, was there for the dinner. Well, she had no *idea* that such things went on at that motel. It should be closed. What if young people should see?"

"My God, Sybil, was it that bad? You're right. I am, I guess, an entertainer. No, by God, after last night, I claim to be a musician."

"Charlotte, you are too beautiful, too confident, too womanly, too alive. Too much."

"And I have sinned grievously. Oh God, Sybil, I wish for Max. I never wanted this. I wanted him and my son and a career for him, and me, maybe, and a rich vital life. I wanted books, a home, music, travel, love—what other people want. It's, well . . ."

"Yes, but you are what you are. Even under those circumstances, you would be that. Therefore, will be hated. And envied. And desired."

"A Scarlet Lady, as Nick says. I don't think I'm cut out for it. I'm a lot like Cal. I too react to stimuli. The dance felt right. I did it." She set her teeth. "To hell with them."

The next day was Monday. She was off. She and Alex went to the river, swam, picnicked. He had his freshman reading list and they read Poe short stories to each other. She gave new orders, for herself, as well as him, that Blanche was to be helped at every opportunity.

"Alex, I suddenly realized it myself the other day. Our Blanche is getting old. All her life she has given us love and help in so many ways. Now it is our turn. Let her garden all she feels like it, but cleaning—from now on the upstairs is yours. And I'll be giving white glove inspections like Uncle Cal told us about in the Marines. The downstairs is mine. And you can give inspections. OK? We won't say anything about this. It would kill her. Besides she'd fuss us both out, and I don't want one of her tongue lashings any more than you do. We'll just do it. But we won't forget that she needs to be needed just as we do. Right?"

He agreed. He understood.

Midnight.

She, in shorty pajamas before her mirror. Sexy. Scarlet

Lady. She winked into her mirror. Right. The aura of Saturday night's music and dance hung on. She spun and arced and threw her hips out of gear for a moment.

She thought music. But tired; the weekend, the sun and river and Alex's pace. Dead tired. She turned her bed back.

Yeah, but that music.

OK. Just for a minute. She wasn't accustomed to bed before three anyway.

She skipped downstairs. Alex, tired from pre-school football practice, could sleep through soft piano anyway. All his life. Even in summer with the windows open.

Two, three chords. Soft pedal. A run.

A little *Satin Doll*. She could see—almost *feel*—the eyes before her still, wide, bright. Bucky's horn was *very* male. *Stormy Weather*. How did I do that? She hummed. From here into Billy's *Charlotte's Letters*. Key change. Bucky knew, and Billy. How? Well, they *felt*. Hey, so did I.

Hummmmm. But those eyes. Funny. All on my belly. I *felt* them. Lust glitters. Softly into *Satin Doll*. The riff had struck. She shifted on the bench with it.

Eyes.

Suddenly she stopped and trembled at the bottom of a chord. *Eyes!* The chord hung softly.

There are eyes on me now!

She lifted her hand. Silence.

She scanned the room. There is no one here.

Silly. She shivered.

Then she sounded the ending chord. Again.

She was chilled. I *feel* it. Eyes. Someone.

She stopped. Memory struck her—a snail of fear on the back of the neck. As a child, from directly behind this piano bench, I watched my father make love to Eleanore Woods years ago. The rose trellis. Even as she had watched, *someone was watching her!* From the rose trellis behind her. *Someone was there!*

Don't move. No. Play. Play six more chords. Calm. What to do?

Stormy Weather. A few soft bars.

Something snapped behind her.

Jesus. Yes. Clear. I heard it.

I *know*. Christ, I've got to stop trembling. Move. Where? How?

The decanter. Yes. Straight across the room. No ducking. You will stand, walk to it. Splash a little bourbon.

Then?

The door? No. That might alarm him. No. Come back. As you come, try to see. Right. Then put the glass on the piano. *No*, sip first. Then put it in clear view on the piano. Then, as if you were going to the bathroom and will return....Right. Yes. Leave the light on. Leave the drink in clear view.

But what then?

Oh, hell, just get out of sight. That's it. That's the main thing.

Oh God, the front door hasn't been locked within memory. Just get out of sight, will you?

Three more chords. Steady. Stand. My God. I'm naked. You can see right through these shorties. Oh my God. But maybe good. Maybe distraction.

Steady. One more chord. Then, stand.

Now.

She dropped one more chord. Stood deliberately. Good. So far. God, what if he shoots? But what else? Do it. Walk straight across the room. On line with the window. Stay in sight. My back to the window. Why would he shoot? I never thought of that. I'm walking. All right. I'm naked. Maybe good.

Just ten steps to the Jackson Press.

She unstoppered the decanter. She dropped the top. Jesus. She poured. Steady. The decanter tinkled against the glass. God, steady. Why would he shoot? She got the glass to her lips, sipped. It burned. She felt it burn. It helped.

Now, get the top. Yes, between her feet. Thank God that was easy. She topped it.

Now. Yes. With both hands I'll hold the glass and sip as I return to the piano. I think I can do that. I'm glad I'm barefooted. So glad.

I know. I'll hold the glass with both hands and sip as I walk. That way I can look at the window. Over the glass, between my fingers.

All right. Now. Do it.

Christ, you could jump for the door from here. No, that would alarm him.

So just do it slowly.

Just ten steps. Back to the piano. Put the glass down. Then slowly, slowly, as if you will return. The light will still be on.

Your drink there. Go to the bathroom. Upstairs. Then from the gallery. Where is Dad's pistol? God, where? I think . . . .

To hell with that. Get upstairs. Then you can find it. Yes, you'll have a few minutes.

She took a deep breath. She glanced at the clock. Twelve-twenty-seven. With both hands she grasped the glass, turned carefully, sipping, looking—oh looking—she walked slowly back to the piano. She could see nothing. Beyond the high window, perfect blackness. She trembled. Steadied. Deliberately she put the tumbler on the piano. She leaned and struck a note. Then, casually, she turned and walked from the room.

She rounded the corner and ran upstairs. At top, she had to stop to breathe. I'm scared. I'm scared. She glanced at Alex's door. Closed.

The pistol!

She ran to her father's room. No lights. I think the second drawer of the large chest. Slowly she opened the drawer, soundlessly.

All these shirts. Must do something with all these shirts. Shirts. To hell with shirts.

Here. Yes. God, it's big. Heavy. Stop trembling. I can't shoot this. She clasped it with both hands.

She took a deep breath. I can do anything. Using both thumbs she drew the hammer back. Two clicks. The first is safety. Yes. Now.

She ran across to her room. Carefully she opened the door and stepped out on the gallery. Clutching the pistol in both hands. She padded along the walls of the house. Past Alex's room and its door. She slipped around the corner and started along the front of the house.

Well Street was silent. Before the gallery door, a board cracked. She flattened against the wall. Careful.

Must hurry. Must move. She clutched the pistol, slid along the wall. Careful. She came to the corner of the house. She leaned. No. Out to the column. Better. Can see better. As she stepped out, the flooring gave a millionth of a millimeter. Merest sigh.

Jesus.

The piano window was just below. Again a deep breath.

She stepped out carefully, and toward the railing. Ah, beside the column. Yes. Beside the column. Pistol in both hands. She set her shoulder against the column. And leaned.

Below, the piano lamp threw a long rectangular block of light, large at the top, through the lattice and rambler rose. She leaned over the railing and scanned the side of the house at a single sweep.

Nothing.

She quickly swept the yard out to the hedge.

Nothing.

Down toward the tennis court garden.

Up to the corner of Well Street. The streetlight helped. But nothing.

Is someone crouching?

She could see nothing. Am I crazy?

Suddenly she panicked. She wheeled.

Was he inside? Had he come in when she was after the pistol?

Alex!

Trembling took her. She pressed her back against the column.

A deep breath. I've got to go inside.

She leaned away from the post. The silence that rings. Took one step.

Then a noise. Perfectly clear. Not inside. Down the street. A two step. A foot. Fifty feet down the street. She froze.

Then clearly. A car door opened. Shut. Quietly. As if someone were being careful.

A moment.

An engine purred. Clearly under the silence. It moved away. Faded.

Silence.

She was panting. Frozen. Two minutes? Five?

Her shoulders slumped. The pistol dangled from her left hand. He's gone. I guess. Yes, he's gone.

Limply she stepped away from the column and started to retrace her steps along the front of the house.

Suddenly car lights flashed among the branches above Well Street. Then the purring of a motor.

She flattened herself against the house. Panting again.

The car passed, too fast for Well Street, without stopping at the corner. She saw it. But not really. Just a car. God, I should have tried to see it.

Maybe he'll come back. Would he? Is that logical? I don't know.

I'll wait. I'll be ready to look. And remember.

He's not the only car. If a car passed, it could be anybody. Even the police cruisers.

Police.

I'll wait a while. Then I'll call the police.

She moved to one of the wicker chairs on the porch and sat down. I'll wait. The chair was cool through the little panties. And cruel. She could feel it making little ridges on her thighs.

I'll wait a while anyway. She leaned over and laid the pistol at her feet. *Don't kick that*, she thought. *It's cocked*.

She sat. She slumped. God, I'm exhausted.

It was chilly now. She cupped her elbows with her hands. Ten minutes? Twenty?

Then car lights. She tensed. Lights playing in the oaks. She crouched and moved to the bannister. The car drifted up. Stopped at the corner. Slowly cruised away.

She couldn't tell. The hedges. The trees.

It could be anyone.

At last, carrying the pistol carefully, she went into the house. She tiptoed to Alex's room, opened the door quietly and looked in. He was breathing evenly, in careless sleep.

She stepped out and went downstairs. She threw the bolt on the front door. At the parlor, she paused, peeped in, ran across the room and cut the light. There was moon. She took the bourbon, threw it back.

Still holding the pistol she went to the study and picked up the phone.

She dialed 0.

Buzz.

"Operator. May I help you?"

She paused. Then placed the receiver in the cradle.

Charlotte Morton. Reporting a Peeping Tom. Yeah. I'll bet. She was flashing him, you know. You work out at the *Stag and Doe*, don't you? What were you wearing, Miss Morton? Oh yeah. Pajamas. Yes. Of course.

Puss Hoffman. Or Weasel Hefner. It would be just her luck. He'd answer the call. He worked all the time. Afraid he'd miss the chance to beat up a nigger. Sure, Miss Charlotte. Now would you show us exactly what you were doing. What makes you think someone was out there? Have you provoked anybody? I mean, well, we seen the picture of you. Naw. Not the one in the papers. The other one. *You know*.

Well, Scarlet Lady. Do you want to call the police?

To hell with them. I pay taxes.

But she didn't call.

She walked into the parlor again. She poured another neat bourbon in the dark. *That's two*, she thought. *That's enough*.

She was exhausted, but she couldn't sleep. She sat in her father's chair facing the piano, the window. She laid the pistol at her feet. She waited.

Blanche found her with a shawl over her, asleep, the pistol at her feet.

"Honey, what you doing? What is this thing doing here?"

Charlotte brushed it off. "Nerves, I guess. I was just thinking I should know how to use the pistol. Just in case."

"In case of what?" Blanche did not believe her.

Alex came down in riding clothes. Oh yes, Sybil was taking him out today.

She yawned over coffee as he told her the plot of Poe's *Black Cat*.

But, suddenly, cup halfway to her lips, she straightened.

"Excuse me a moment, Alex. I'll be right back."

She dashed upstairs and slipped into slacks and T-shirt. She went outside, under the parlor window, beneath the rose trellis. Yes. Blanche had loosened the soil around it too.

There were footprints! Heavy. A man's.

I did not imagine it. She trembled. Then she followed down the side of the house. They disappeared on the grass.

She puzzled. The car! She whirled and looked to the tennis court corner of the property. She walked down to where the hedges met. The tomatoes were there.

You could push through the hedge here. At least, on hands and knees. The Benson's dog, Harlequin, used it all the time.

She leaned and inspected. You couldn't tell. She came back to the house. She finished coffee—and *The Black Cat*. Had another cup with Sybil while Alex brushed his teeth. She told her. Then took her outside and showed her the footprints.

"Well, if you don't call the police, I will."

Charlotte dissuaded her for the time being.

"Maybe when you two come back from riding. Hey, have lunch. Blanche, is there something nice for Sybil at lunch?"

Later, in her bath, she sat erect suddenly. She jumped up, grabbed a towel, then threw on her robe, and ran down to the study.

She snatched the telephone.

"Dr. Grossman. Yes, good morning. I'm fine. Fine. Yes, Alex is fine. In fact, he's out riding right now—with

Sybil.... Oh, played like crazy Saturday night. Should have called you. A friend from New York was in town. In fact, two. They sat in with me.... Huh. Bess would have loved it. Yes...

"Do me a favor, Dr. Grossman. It will sound strange, I know. Listen, do you know, or can you find out, if Max had a car out last night? Sure, I'll hold."

Three minutes later.

"He did." She sighed. "You're sure. At one forty-eight. Oh, wonderful. Listen. This may be important."

She told him. It was important. Yes, he'd check the mileage register for the car. But he was sure she was right. He's breaking, Charlotte. Yes. Goodbye.

She slumped back in the chair. He was watching me. He... Oh, and in those pajamas. He could see through. That light. Oh, baby. Scarlet Lady, OK. Hell, I'll open the hedge. I'll dance. I'll go naked. Max, come back.

Summer moved to Autumn. She made sure that she was home on Monday nights, her only free night. She was motherly, sexy, talented, alluring.

Sybil said she prepared herself for nights at home more than she did for nights at the piano.

"Hell, I'd like to cook for him and leave it on the trellis. Anything to make him come home."

Several times she kept Alex up very late, in the hope that Max would see his son. She loosened the dirt around the ramblers each day. She cut away some branches to make it easier. Each Monday night the footprints were there. But some other nights too.

Dr. Grossman's letters contained two interesting pieces of news. Bessemer Hanks had received his arm, had promptly mastered the goose, and now the nurses had to give wide berth on both sides of his chair. He complained bitterly that *they* could feel it but he couldn't.

Last Monday night, sometime between three and four, the attendants reported a loud crash from Max's room. They entered and found him seated on his bed in the dark, staring into space. His mask was on. The mirror over his lavatory was smashed. He did it with his fist. He required eight stitches on the hand. This is passion, Charlotte. I think it's good. Progress in these cases

*sometimes takes strange forms. However, I am very
nervous about the car now.*

He wrote a week later that he had reviewed Max's case
with the chief of staff and they had decided that Max was to
continue to use the car on his return from three weeks at
Johns Hopkins. The trip was for a delicate phase of the plastic
surgery. He would be back by mid-October.

She herself was gone a week during that period. Aunt
Jessica married her commander, now retired as captain, and
moved to New Orleans where he became an executive with a
marine engineering firm. Charlotte and Alex went to the
wedding.

She found that she had to say no to Nick once a week, but
he was generally amiable, and easy to work for. Since *the*
Saturday night, the police dropped by regularly—clearly they
had had calls from high places—stood at the door of the bar
for a while, then left. Nick always badgered them with "No
luck. She's still got her clothes on."

Dr. Jennings Hall had left practice for a few months of
surgical training in Texas. He had already gained a reputation
for his diagnostic skill and was increasingly consulted by
other doctors. Dr. Tom spoke glowingly of him and Sybil
reported all sorts of praise from bridge club gossip.

"But do you know, he sometimes asks patients to join him
in prayer. Elsa Compton, who goes through doctors at the
rate of one a week, is sold on him because God directs his
every move."

"How is Elsa?" Charlotte asked.

"Nutsy. Vague. Other-worldly. Thank God, Martha, the
maid, is faithful. I really don't know how things would be
without her."

In early November, Blanche Pfeiffer, who had raised four
families for the earth, went herself into the earth.

At eight-thirty one rainy morning, she had not arrived and
did not answer the telephone. Fearful, Charlotte called Elvira,
Blanche's old friend and next door neighbor, and asked her to
run over and check on Blanche.

"She's done gone, Miss Charlotte. You better come."

Charlotte came. Blanche was indeed gone. She had slept
away.

Not only as friend, as mother, not only for her wit and joy

in life, as provider of that most persistent pleasure—good food; not even for the love they shared—not only for these did Charlotte mourn Blanche. It was more elemental. It was as if Earth, the Great Mother, had herself been grievously wounded and would never be whole again.

Charlotte's grief went past tears, and would, she knew, never, never heal. This was loss in a great final sense, beyond sentiment, beyond romance. It was as though part of the life-force was gone.

Four families, Charlotte thought. Her father, herself, Alex, her own children. Four.

She was aware that Blanche had symbolized a dying institution, that Blacks were finally forming a political force to be reckoned with, that the days of Mammyism were numbered. She and Blanche had tracked it, applauded it.

But how can I live without her?

Staring through the window in the November rain, she thought how deep and quiet and secret earth was. Take her, she sobbed. Take her into you. Only you are large and profound enough for her. Oh, Blanche there was so much I wanted to say, to ask.

She yearned for the smell of linen dried by a wood fire which meant Blanche was there and all was well. Alex was inconsolable and lost. For ten days he simply could not speak. He, at his age, went to his mother's bed each night, but sleep would not come.

Billy cried openly over the phone. Sybil and Spence and Cal could find no words. They merely opened their hands to a new emptiness.

Oh Blanche, there was so much I wanted to ask.

She simply could not accommodate the loss. It hurt deep in her breast. She carried on mindlessly—the house, her job. She wandered the house aimlessly.

Until one night—late, after the bar. A thought.

She ran to the study. Her fingers traced the books, caught, held onto a childish, universal book. Her father's voice came to her, a girl before sleep, years ago. Merlyn's advice to the boy who would become Arthur, the king. She seized it, thumbed, found, read, hearing her father's voice.

"The best thing for being sad," said Merlyn, beginning to puff and blow, "is to learn something. That is the only thing that never fails. You may grow old and

*trembling in your anatomies, you may lie awake at
night listening to the disorder of your veins, you may
miss your only love, you may see the world about you
devastated by evil lunatics, or know your honor tram-
pled in the sewers of base minds. There is only one
thing for it then—to learn."*

She raised her chin, snapped the magician's book closed,
replaced it, moved around the corner of the room to the
music shelves. Bent, searching, her fingers moving along the
tall thin volumes. *You will know when you are ready to try it.
You'll never be able to play it. But you will suddenly know
when you are ready to start living with it.* Yes, Father. Her
fingers found it and she carefully slipped the worn folio from
the slot. *Goldberg Variations.*

She went to the piano. Blanche had stood behind her at
this piano many times.

That winter Sybil went away for two months. "I simply
must get away," she said. She would start on the West Coast,
then perhaps Hawaii, then back to New York. Cards came
from Los Angeles. Then in quick succession from Honolulu
and New York, and when Sybil returned, she looked ten
years younger. They never spoke of it, but Charlotte perceived that she had had cosmetic surgery. Once again she was
the beautiful, Nordic queen.

"I needed the change," she said simply.

Charlotte's strange, unearthly Monday night romance continued. Sometimes she would dress elegantly, play Chopin,
Scarlatti, Mozart, Liszt—things Max had heard her preparing. Sometimes in slacks, or in the revealing things she wore
at the *Stag and Doe,* she would play jazz and pop. Always
Body and Soul. And songs that they had danced to, *Stardust,
I Cried for You, Who's Sorry Now.* When she kept Alex up,
she would give him a lesson, hear the things he had been
working on, yell at him—like a mother!—when he violated
time, phrased clumsily, dropped too many notes.

Often, she was seductress. She would stroll before the
window, lean over the piano, and some nights, forget something and dash in wearing only panties. Then sit on the piano
bench, lounge, pose, offer herself to the night.

She was enraged when it rained on Monday nights. *How
awful,* she thought on cold nights. *He could sit in the*

darkness of the study, instead of freezing. If he is there at all. And the footprints testified, he was there many times, not only on Mondays. She was furious that the winter's six-inch snowfall came on 'her' night.

But the snowfall also brought a curious event. That Tuesday morning, she and Alex—sadly, the first time without the help and criticism of Blanche—built their snowman. As she was standing back near the street, watching Alex arrange eyebrows from black shoelaces, a voice piped behind her.

"Charlotte Morton."

She turned and there was Elsa Compton standing at the edge of the plowed street.

"Come here."

Charlotte jumped the drift.

"Good morning, Mrs. Compton. Beautiful—isn't it beautiful? How are you?"

"I am, Charlotte Morton, as God wills." Elsa paused. Then, "Charlotte Morton, is that my grandson there?"

"Yes, Mrs. Compton."

The old woman sniffed. Then without another word, turned and shuffled off down the street.

"Mrs. Compton, do you want to meet him? Alex, come here."

But the old woman did not turn.

Alex ran to his mother.

She stood a moment, then—"I was thinking that our snowman looks a little like Spence, who is also getting a little pot belly."

A Tuesday night. Reams of March rain swung back and forth across the flare of light in the *Stag and Doe* parking lot. Lightning and thunder had flickered the interior lights about ten-thirty and the bar had emptied.

"I'll get some coffee from the kitchen," Gail said. "Maybe it'll let up in a while."

They sat in the dim bar.

"You don't seem to have anybody."

"Yes. Yes, I do," Charlotte said with a sigh. "It's just that it's strange and unlucky."

"Married?"

"No. No. It's a long story. He was wounded terribly in the war and has never recovered."

"Hummm. That's awful. Will he? Will he come back? I

know Nick always had it for you. Still has, I guess. I was jealous. Then it was Sudie. Now that damned new waitress, Carolyn. But I always wondered about you. What do you do?"

"I'm with my son. I come here. That's it, Gail, pretty much. During the days I still go sometimes to my father's old law office. Not for business. I don't really know why."

"What do you do for a man?" Gail asked. "You're sexy as hell. I don't mean to pry."

Charlotte laughed. "Sometimes I go crazy. Sometimes I repress. Sometimes I play it out on the piano. Sometimes I'm numb. And, Gail, sometimes I slip. I'm human."

Charlotte and Gail had nights like this intermittently. Sometimes late. Once in a while early, when the weather was bad, like tonight. These chats began shortly after Nick dropped Gail and she was heartbroken. She had needed. Charlotte liked her and had listened two or three nights. Since Nick there had been three men in Gail's life, but sadly, nothing had lasted for her. Perhaps it was the job—what it must seem to men. And the crazy hours which allowed no normal relationship. *Soon*, Charlotte thought, *Gail will be pitiful*. She wished the pretty, simple girl could have some luck.

We two women! What our lives must seem to others? What they really are! God, if Gail knew about my Monday nights, she would think I'm crazy.

Waiting for the rain to stop seemed useless.

"It's still not eleven-thirty. I'm just around the corner. 'Night, Char. See you tomorrow night."

Gail ducked out and was gone. "'Night, Sudie," she yelled to the desk clerk.

Cowled under her own coat, Charlotte scooted out. "'Night, Sudie."

As she came out to the Packard, a long, sleek white car edged up. In its lights, Charlotte saw at a glance that the Packard was listing. A flat tire.

"Jesus," she snarled into the rain. "Of all nights."

The white car threw its lights full on her.

It tooted.

"Charlotte," someone yelled.

She stepped back under the canopy.

The white car pulled beside her. "Hi. Looks like ya got trouble."

It was Coy Trexler, Jr.

"Oh, Coy. Yeah."

"Kin I help?"

"No. Thanks anyway. I'll just leave it here and get Nick to run me home."

"C'mon. I'll run you. Give you a chance to ride in my new wagon."

"No. Thanks. I'll get Nick." Damn it, Nick's probably on top of Carolyn right now.

"C'mon. I just picked her up yesterday. El Dorado convertible. C'mon. She's a beaut."

Charlotte glanced around. Nobody. Damn it. Damn the tire. Damn Nick and his lust. Damn this night.

"C'mon. I'll take you."

Now, do I dare do this?

"I'll even send one of my boys out tomorrow to change the tire."

She shrugged.

"Straight home, Trex?"

"Straight home. Sware."

She looked around again. All right. She ran around the car and slipped in.

"Some night for this to happen."

"Always does. How do ye like it?"

"Beautiful," she said as the car oozed across the lot and out on the interstate, cruising through the sizzling rain.

"Yeah. Listen," he flicked the radio up. "Some sound, huh?"

He then proceeded to point out all the gadgets. She admired. "And looka here." He reached under the dash. She heard a decisive metallic click, and he palmed a gleaming murderous-looking, sawed-off shotgun which fitted flush beneath the dash.

"Beauty too. Isn't it? That's muh nigger chaser. Mounted it myself today. That baby'll blow away a door. From the shoulder. Or like this." He balanced it in the palm of his hand.

She expressed respect for it.

They rode. She felt the tension building. He was trying to think of a way.

"Maybe we oughta run out to Pal Hardison's fer a drink. You kin always git a drink there. No matter the time."

She stiffened. She had to stop this *now*. Firmly.

"Alex, my son, is waiting up for me. I called just before I left. Thanks—but home. I'm expected."

"Hummm. Too bad. We coulda had a drink and talked over old times. Wadda ya hear from Max?"

"Not much. He's coming along." *His wife*, thought Charlotte. *Yes, remind him of his wife. Put that in for insurance.* "How's your wife?"

"She's a'right. You know. A wife."

"Have you got children, Coy?"

"Two. Two boys. 'N one in the cooker."

"Oh, nice. I didn't know."

They rode. He made the right turns.

"Maybe when the weather clears up, I'll put the top down and take you fer a ride. It'll be like flyin' in this here baby."

At the door, she tried to jump out. He grabbed her and demanded one kiss for the ride. She stonewalled and he smashed a kiss on her cheek. He did not go for a long wrestling match. She thanked him and got out.

Inside, she heaved a sigh, remembering his viciousness on VE-day.

The next morning Nick called early. He had seen the Packard and had it fixed. There was nothing wrong with the tire. Just needed air and was holding now.

She mused. Surely Coy had not let the air out. Not on a night like that, in that rain. And he hadn't been too rough.

Strange.

24

AN accident that spring gave Charlotte Morton a purpose which was to consume her for the rest of her life.

She was drying her hair on the sun-struck gallery when she heard Alex call.

"Mom, come down here for a moment. Something wonderful."

They had both been gardening industriously all spring. That morning, after sharpening his shovel as Blanche had taught him—by standing on the hasp and whirring it in some loose gravel—he had accidentally brought it down against the shaft of an Acuba. The blade had sliced the trunk of the shrub and cut cleanly down the root construction, laying bare the plant in cross-sectioned view. All its intricate root system, its deep, secret struggle under earth, was revealed. Charlotte and Alex crouched and stared. The delicate flesh tones of the riven roots shone against the rich black loam.

"I didn't mean to hit it," Alex said. "But isn't it wonderful?"

Charlotte's eyes traced the deepest tendril of root threads, reaching tentatively, testing the earth, slithering, trying in all directions to find new ways deeper to the life-giving water. From there her eyes raced up the shaft, to the reason—the gorgeous, brilliantly flecked, green and ivory leaves. It was a saga, from the deep, hard-won struggle in the dark earth to the triumph of the radiant foliage.

Immediately she saw it also as a drawing. She had seen many cross-section botanical diagrams—instructional, photographic, without beauty or awe. She saw this from a genuine artistic impulse. The dark loam, the flesh tones of the inner root, the green shaft, and the brilliant leaves drew the colorist in her. But the supreme opportunity lay in the tension of the root struggle below the triumph of the foliage. A painting of classical drama lay before her.

She ran for her sketch pad. Long into the afternoon she sat before the wounded plant. When the loam grayed beneath the sun's sapping rays, she and Alex took a broken pane of glass and set it flush against the scarred shaft and root, pressed, and poured water behind it.

When at last her back was broken with bending, she had thirty-six sketches: the whole drama, detail studies of root, shaft, and leaf. And there was a pallette of tones made in watercolor. Not *the* color, but the color that they *looked* like.

Six days and many versions later, she and Alex stood over an ink and watercolor.

"It's—it's alive, Mother. It seems to be still growing. It *is* still growing."

"Yes," she said quietly. "Yes. It is, isn't it?"

So it was. The drama and tension under earth were realized. The victory above the dark loam shone. The colors were brilliantly untrue, but were perfectly correct. It was not a photograph. It was not realistic. It was real.

It affected Sybil strongly. "There is something slightly frightening about it, Charlotte. Perhaps a little as if its struggle to grow might affect the whole earth."

That remark was precisely what Charlotte had hoped for.

The composition was as daring as the plant itself, especially beneath the earth where its splayed, driving tendrils pierced and wove and drove, giving the entire picture a tension physically as well as tonally. The nakedness of the flesh hues against the dark loam hurt. Above, the leaves were pennants whose green flared victory.

The life long regimen her father had set her—draw a picture a day—had made her line sure, her vision acute. The museums in New York and Europe at her father's side had sharpened her critical judgment. The childish lollypop trees had slowly matured into the skilled portrait of Max painted from the photograph. Nightly in her sketch pad she set and solved problems of perspective and composition between stints at the piano. Now, the lucky garden accident gave her a subject which she began to make her own.

Thereafter, one or more of the botanical drawings was always in progress. She learned as she worked—sometimes remembering Merlyn—developing precise draftsmanship and a glowing coloring modeled on the Flemish painters.

She and Alex were so pleased that they dedicated a whole wall in the study to them, and under sun or brilliant interior light, that wall writhed with life.

When she felt she had perfected product to purpose, she entered four watercolors and eight oils in the annual show to raise money for the Heart Fund. And was heartbroken when a curt note informed her that the committee had found them unsuitable for the exhibition. It was signed Louise Council, Chairman.

As she and Sybil and Alex wandered the exhibit, Charlotte understood that Louise Council's committee extended her 'leper state' beyond the merely social. She was amused by the collection of vacuous, 'pretty' landscapes, hopeless dories on river banks, vapid rosy-cheeked children, saccharine old men and women, the endless, bland still lifes, and the several 'daring' non-objective pieces which had neither humor nor tension, spatial awareness nor sophisticated color, movement nor stasis, restraint nor vigor, problem nor solution—had nothing but the poseur's mindless freedom from technique, discipline and thought.

She could no longer wonder at the town's contempt for art if this was to provide example.

"Your pictures would boil off this wall," Sybil said. "That's another reason they had to reject you."

Charlotte let herself be reminded that the town still held her in contempt, regarded her life as a threat. After all these years.

And my son.

Alex, freshman now, was running punts back, as his father had done. And, quarterbacking the JV team. She and Cal rode out to practice at least once a week. He was marvelous in a broken field.

"Like Max," Cal said. "Just exactly. Christ, look at that change of pace. And you know, Hudson is using him exactly like he did Max. And Whit. If he lives through it, he's gonna be good."

They watched him running the offense against the varsity, cool with freshman blocking in front of him, throwing fast, scrambling, getting buried, getting intercepted, throwing high, low, leading too much. Making mistakes, learning. But cool.

She glowed when the handsome six-foot youth trotted over to her as the drill ended. Unashamed to trot to his mother, smiling.

Can this beautiful young man really be my son? she asked herself.

Two months later she would ask Cal to select an electric razor, a Christmas gift for her man/boy whose upper lip was beginning to look dusty.

His voice cracked every fourth syllable. Embarrassed, he would cock his head and bite his lip.

"When you stop croaking like a bullfrog, I'll tell you about s-e-x," she teased.

"Promise?" he smiled.

Monday night. Gorgeous late Indian Summer. Mild October. Too long. Too long. *I will tell Alex about sex. Indeed!* she thought. Riding with Sybil yesterday, I nearly went mad. I'm wiggly. Twitchy. For no reason I get damp at the thighs. I want to flood. *I want to April.*

> *Every night you don't love*
> *Is a night you won't love.*

My father's voice. Singing. Life goes. Damn it, Max. I'm sexual.

Her mirror told her. It told her each time she turned. Each

change of shadow. So he can't kiss and suck. Christ, his hands can touch. I have nipples, Max. They need to be *touched*.

They have to be touched. In dark he could put his hands over me. He could do that. Her teeth were clenched. He could push my thighs apart. He *could*! Oh, could please me so much. So much.

God damn! She boiled through drawers full of lingerie. Yes! Transparent. Yes! She slipped into it.

Look, man, she hissed at the mirror. *Through this you can see. You can see it all. And nothing promised that is not performed.*

"Oh God, Max, take it," she had actually made the words.

Eleven. Alex abed. She went to the parlor. Curtain cleared of the rose trellis. Light on. And right. I am naked. She touched the wisp of cloth where her legs met. This is the thing *not* taken off. What's it for if no man sees it?

She moved, arced, walked, with the easy swaying gait. She poured herself a drink. Sipped. She stood between the light and the window. Look. If you are there.

She played. And sang. She drank. Sang *Body and Soul*. Drank again. Sang *Love for Sale*.

Is he there? Between music, her ears were quick for sound.

Then?

I don't know.

Or now?—a small night sound. A man is looking at you. Eyes fastened on your breasts, and where your legs meet darkly.

Perhaps.

Turn. Look out the window. Open your legs. Offer. Yes, bring one foot up to the bench. Max. Max, look. I'm dead center. I need. I need a shaft to turn on.

She turned back to the piano. She sipped again. *I'm absolutely feverish*, she thought. She played and sang *How High the Moon*. Then sipped again.

I'm getting a little drunk.

"Max," she whispered. "Max, I know that you are there behind me. Come and take me. Please. *Please*, Max. Max, I know you are there. Give me a signal. Max, give me a signal. For me. Oh, Max—for Charlotte."

Silence. That silence that rings with silence. Then a car went by. Another car.

"Please, a signal. I understand. I know about the wound."

Silence. Cars. A distant siren.

"Max, I . . ."

She sobbed and covered her face with her palms. She stood, cut out the light, and ran from the room.

In her room she smoked the last of Billy's cigarettes. She smoked it all. Inhaling deeply.

In bed and mind, a man had her. Not Max. A man. Just man. Male. Masculine. Had her. Had her. *Had her!*

Cal had found his place. He was interested because there were so many projects going at once, so many areas, so many different problems. Sam Culbreath stayed in the office and was happy. He sent Cal to the field and made *him* happy.

He took Charlotte and Alex to each new site.

"See. Eighteen houses. The whole side of that hill."

Charlotte was happy, with and for him. He'd probably get his brains blown out by some violated husband sooner or later—but that was Cal. For now, he was dear and happy.

He still took Alex fishing and rambling once in a while, beginning the day with his construction rounds, ending at the river with the boy, and sometimes on his own five-year oldest.

Alex, like all, adored this vivid animal.

Whit Manson came in rarely. The Korean War had spurred growth for his company and he had grown with it, helped it to grow. He was moving. Now a vice president. Tailored, confident, that confidence founded on discovered, tested quality. Posture was completely alien to the quietly handsome man who sat across from Charlotte at dinner when he was home, whose blue eyes adored her as she sat piano in the bar. *He still loves me,* she thought. But he never took her, never tried. He was too involved in the tragedy to move it.

The new album, *Bucky's Music II*, was fine. The piano was good. *My God*, she thought. *I* am *an amateur*. The trio was making its way. They had played *Birdland*, as warm up band. They had a long stint at the *Village Door*.

But Nick's periodic trips to New York began to bring alarm.

"Billy's really got the sniffles, Char. I caught 'em at the *Door*. Terrific stuff, but hell, he has to blow after every number now."

"What do you mean?" her dark eyes wide with horrible fascination.

"Honey, he must be doin' a ton of coke. It looks like he has burnt out his nostrils."

She fired off letters. Damn you, you're too important to destroy yourself. This is Mother. See a doctor. *Stop* it!

Another Monday. Two years of Monday nights. Other nights too, she knew. Footprints talk.

Full moon. In June, she sighed, slightly drunk. Sexually poised. Music. Sipping. Listening. Sipping. Listening. Turning. Opening. More music.

Something snapped behind her.

Clearly! She heard. He was there.

She lifted her hands. *Enough!* She sat erect.

"Max," she said clearly and deliberately. "Alex is canoeing with Cal. I am alone. I am going to turn off all the lights. I am going up to my room and lie naked across my bed. Come to me. Max, come in the front door and walk up the stairs. There will be no lights. Me. I'll be there. Max, come. Oh, Max, *please come.*"

She became hoarse with emotion.

"Max, come tonight—or don't come back to this window. Ever."

She sat, listening. Then she rose and cut the light. She walked slowly across the room, up the stairs. She drew off the gown. There was moon, but not so much. Not too much.

She was trembling. God, she was trembling. I can't stop shaking. Please come. Tears welled. Move. Do something. She turned down the bed. I can't stop trembling. He won't come. All these years. He won't come. I should have said I love you. I can't think. He won't come. Maybe he knows best. This is the end. I don't care. I'll look at his face. I'll love him in a mask. Oh God, maybe he *does* know best.

She sat in the middle of the bed, facing the door. Her breath seemed to deafen her. She stopped her ears. Then opened.

And she *heard.* She heard steps crossing the porch. Be still. For godssakes, be still. She was trembling uncontrollably. Her heart actually drowned the sound.

The front door opened, closed.

She gasped. *He is coming!*

She was whimpering as she heard the steps slowly mounting the stairs. At last, my God, at last! I'm winning. He's coming at last.

On the landing, he paused. Continued climbing.

What if he knew best? But no. This *has* to happen. This has to happen. Remember, no matter what, it's Max. Dear, dear Max.

He walked toward the door. One step at a time.

She heard him pause outside the door. He was panting too. She knew they were listening to each other.

"Max," she whispered.

Breathing.

"Oh, Max, please. It's Charlotte. Come." She sobbed. She couldn't control her voice.

In demi-light, she saw him step slowly into the room, brace against the jamb.

"Come," she pleaded.

He stepped forward. Stopped. Turned. Reached for the lamp and turned it on.

She recoiled.

Coy Trexler stood at her bedside table.

"I ain't Max. But I'll do."

His face was slimy with sweat and grease. He had on khakis and a T-shirt stained with grease and paint. His rusty hair was matted down across his forehead. His thin, liver-like lips were curled into a sneer. He dangled a whiskey bottle in his left hand.

"Drink?" He thrust it forward.

She sat up straight. Something snapped behind her eyes. Time and place slipped, wrenched off track. This was not now. Or her bedroom. She looked past him to the door. Where was Max?

"Max," she whimpered.

Then she knew. It was not Max. It had never been Max. *It has never been Max!*

She could not make this real. All those nights! I cannot . . .

But she must know. It has never been Max. Never. Never. *Never.* Knowing struck. She fell forward sobbing. Writhing. Moaning. Wretching.

A hand grasped her hair and cruelly jerked her head up.

"Quit slobbering. I'll do."

Her face was blank. She looked up the arm, to the shoulder, to the face. This was not now. Or ever.

"I'll do," he was leering.

And she knew it *was* now. And her bedroom. Her brain sought a fixed point.

He jerked her head again. Her teeth clicked.

"I . . . ." She began.

My bedroom. My lovely place. Yes. She set her teeth. Swung her eyes. Met his glittering gaze. Stiffened. Repelled.

"Get out of here," she spat.

He popped her head back so violently her eyes lost bearing. She moved to reach her gown. Again popped back. He held her hair and looked down at her.

"Easy. Have a drink."

"Get out of my house!" she hissed.

He looked down, moving his eyes across her body. "I'm gonna get this. Tonight," he drawled. "Been wantin' it a long time. Gonna have it. Tonight. Walking around, showin' it off."

She stiffened. "Like bloody hell, you slime," she snarled, and wrenched toward the door.

He dropped the bottle and slapped her backwards across the bed with such force that she slid off on the other side. Stunned, she scrambled to her feet, slipped, clawed the bed, stood, fell forward and rolled toward the foot. He was on top of her, breathing in her face.

"I seen this too much. I'm gonna git it. I'm gonna eat those big tits. I'm gittin' this now."

She looked up into his greasy face. Glittering slits for eyes. Breath rancid with cigarettes and whiskey.

Stars still fluttered at the sides of her brain from the blow. *Stay up*, she thought. *Stay up*. In the eyes. Look him in the eyes.

He had her hands in crucifixion above her head. He arched his thin frame, drove one knee into her belly, drew it across her groin and bore his weight to drive between her thighs.

The knees had pumped her breath out. But it came back.

His breath stifled her. Don't turn. Stare into his eyes. He can't do it. She tried her hands. His grasp was steel. Oh God, he is strong. This is . . . abomination.

He drew her hands together above her head, clasped them with one hand, bowed his body, tussled with his belt.

She tore her left hand free, grasped the edge of the bed, pulled herself nearly from beneath him, kicked up with her legs, slid off the bed to the floor.

He held her right hand and came on top of her. He released her hand and drove his right fist, glancing across her cheek. His left hand caught her between the eyes. Stars again. His right hit her above the ear.

"Bitch. Cunt. Lie still or I'll beat hell out of you."

My God, she thought. *He means it.* Oh my God, he means it. Oh my God, I can't bear this. Please, I can't bear this. In my own lovely place. I don't want him in me. I don't want his slime in me. He's strong. I hadn't thought he was this strong.

"Coy, for God's sake!"

"I'm gonna screw you.".

"Coy, you're hurting me! Get up!"

"I'm gonna screw you."

"Listen, Alex and Cal will be here in a minute. They just went to the river."

He open-handed her across the cheek. Again.

"Lying cunt. They ain't comin'."

She was hazy. He'd hit her hard. Again, he took both her hands above her head. With his left hand he was at his belt again.

He was staring at her breasts with fascination. He clasped her left breast in his hand, leaving his belt.

"What tits you got, Morton."

Revulsion wrenched her. She tore her left hand free again, raised up on her elbow. He slammed her flat. Moved his right hand to her throat. Pressed her head down. Held, held, pressed. She was choking. There was no air. She flung her head from side to side. His belt buckle hit her belly. Cold. He released her throat. She heaved back for the air.

"Lay there, cunt. Or I'll choke you."

She was panting, taking the lovely oxygen. He was clawing at her breasts again. Hard. Too hard. *You hurt,* she thought. *My throat hurts.* He's strong. Oh God, what to do?

He was unzipping himself with one hand now. She was getting enough air. *Think,* she thought. *Think.* This fool will kill you. Talk. That's it. Talk.

"Coy," she rasped. "Coy, you hurt. You hurt me. I'm Charlotte Morton. Why are you hurting me, Coy?"

"I want your ass. I'm gonna have your high and mighty ass, Miss Charlotte Morton. I been seein' you too long. I ain't Max. Max ain't nowhere. I'm gonna do you."

He was looking down at her. Sweat and spittle dripped down on her. *Oh God,* she thought. *This* is *abomination.*

"Don't think you kin be hurt, bitch. Huh? Do ya?"

He slapped her twice across the cheek.

"Don't think that pussy face can be beat."

He hit her again.

"Oh stop it, Coy. Please. Don't."

He hit again. His eyes glittered in their slits. Again, he hit her. Then he was crushing her breast. Hard. Too hard. Like kneading. Like Blanche kneading a clod in the garden. Hard. She felt his nails bite.

Stay up, she thought. *Stay up!* You have to think. He means it. He's crazy. He'll kill you. Think!

"Stop. Coy, listen. Stop hurting me and I'll give. Stop. I'll give. I'll give you good. Stop. I'll give you heaven. Please. I promise."

Begging this slime! But the pain. God, he'll kill me.

He was listening, struggling with his pants. It was hard for him. He was listening to reason.

"Let me go and I'll give you the best you ever had."

He paused. It was a struggle. He had his pants down to his knees. He was struggling.

"You could. You been flat-backing fer everybody in this here county. That motel. That Nick. Big deal Pete McCanless said you had the best ass in town."

She wanted to vomit. Keep talking, she told herself. Talk.

"I can suck, too, Coy. Look at my mouth. I can suck." She ran her tongue over her lip. Blood. *I taste blood!*

"Listen, let me go. I'll give you heaven. Listen, I'll be good. I'll be so good."

He was considering it. She could tell. It was hard for him to hold her and get his pants off. Maybe pain didn't have to be part of it. Maybe . . . .

"If you make a dumb move I'll beat your brains out. Know it."

"I'll be good. I'll be so good."

He released her hands, sat back on his haunches. Then stood over her. His pants fell to his ankles. His legs were short, skinny, knobby, pale, repulsive.

"Awright. Get up. Get on the bed."

When she tried to rise, a sharp pain drove through her left hand. She held it up. Looked at it, wondering, horrified. Her left index finger was too far back. It didn't respond to orders from her muscles. It was different. The pain was clear and clean.

"My finger. My finger! It's broken! Coy, you broke my finger. I have to play the piano. And paint. My God," a whimper, "you broke my finger."

"They heal quick. Git on the bed. Or I'll spread your

nose." Hands on hips he stood over her like a master. "I'm gonna get that pussy." His teeth were set. His eyes fastened on her belly. He started unbuttoning his shirt.

It's now, she thought. *It's now or never.* He can't run with his pants down. Wait. Yes. Wait until his shirt is behind him, both arms in. Oh God, I'm vague and floppy. Can I run? I have to. I have to run. Where? The pistol. Dad's room. No. No chance. He'd be there before I got it out of the drawer. Downstairs. That's the only chance. Downstairs. The door.

"Coy, I'll get on the bed. My finger..."

She raised herself on her elbow, turned on hands and knees, him still astride her. *My hand hurts,* she thought. *So badly.* She was panting. She looked over her shoulder. Both his hands were behind him pulling at his shirt.

She took a deep breath.

Now.

She crawled two steps, jumped to her feet, fell dizzily to one knee, dove for the door. No good. He leaped across the room, caught her thighs, pulled her down.

He was rasping. "Bitch. Cunt. Whore."

He caught her hair with one hand and pinned her head to the floor with it. With the other he freed one of his pant legs. Drew down his shorts. Kicked out of them.

"Now, bitch, I'm gonna plug you."

Then began the hailstorm of blows. His bony fists across her face, her head flopping, bouncing off the floor. The heel of his hand pounding her skull.

She faded. Lights swam under her closed lids. Things in her face gave. She felt them give, broken, smashed. Pain summoned. She came back.

I don't know what to do. He's killing me. In and out of pain, she flitted. Sweet to sink, to free-fall. Oh Max. Hold me. Only, horribly, to be jerked back to pain. My belly...hurts. What are those rods thudding into my belly? Suddenly there was no air. Wretching. Twisting head, frenzied, left to right, trying to rise. Can't breathe. No air. Screeching sounds. Can't breathe. Don't want to breathe.

Something between my legs. Someone. She was panting, heaving, rasping. But someone is between my legs. I am split like a steak falling open behind the blade. I'm naked.

She faded. Pain recalled her. Someone is kneeling between my thighs. It's Coy Trexler. How...? His hand is under me. His finger...he's lifting me...

Oh God. He's there . . . he's at my opening! I can't move. I don't want him inside me! Max! I don't want his slime in me. This *is* abomination . . . .

Stay. I must stay. I'll move. He can't do it if I can move, just a little.

A sudden smash to her skull . . . .

Sybil found her the next morning.

The police came. Ambulance.

Sergeants Hoffman and Hefner looked. Noted the whiskey bottle. Noted the slip of gown slung across the chaise. Front door open.

Following the ambulance, Hefner muttered, "Wal, she went too fur this time."

"Yeah," said Puss around his Camel.

Pain called her out. She sank again. Was recalled. Brilliant light through her lids. Spinning.

Voices came.

"Nose . . . left index finger . . . Multiple bruises . . ."

Something was in her mouth. Horrible pain. My head . . .

"Call Dr. Heck. Yes, the dentist . . . Ask him if he could run over here."

That voice. Then a woman's. That voice. Not the woman's. The other. It has spoken to me. Sometime . . .

"Sexually penetrated . . ." Yes. "Inclusive X-rays. Immediately, yes. Yes, cranial." Voice. Yes. That voice. It is friendly. Cold but friendly. *Déjà vu*. That's French. I can speak French.

"Miss Gordiner. Joe. Great care. Wait. Let me get around . . ."

Yes. That voice. From memory lane, she giddily thought. *I will do God's will*. Oh, it's Jennings! Oh, thank God. It's Jennings. My friend. My friend Jennings. He will help me. Oh, thank God!

She went away.

Iris Gordiner snapped the film screen.

We were in school together—me and Charlotte Morton. She got knocked up. Boy, someone really worked her over. She probably deserved it, from what I hear. But not this bad. Jesus. She sang real pretty the night me and Tom heard her. But I heard tell she was a whore. Or, at least, free beaver. At that motel. Always was wild. Got knocked up. Yeah, even then. Cal. And that Max Compton. Where is he? Cal, yeah, we had a night. Back then. I liked him. And that Pete McCanless, the car dealer. He was older. God, she is battered, but nothing really broken. Except the nose and finger. Jesus.

She changed the film.

Yeah, looks OK. Hall is funny today. He's funny every day, but I never seen him like this. Steadiest, surest hand with a scalpel—he's trembling like a leaf. Hard to understand his words. Another religious revelation, probably. Up all night praying.

Film change.

Looks OK. Some gorgeous body laying on that table. I wonder if that was what it was. Wonder if Hall had that. At a prayer meeting! They used to hang out together in school. Her and Cal and Max, and that queer Ennis. What's-his-name Ennis. Hall had straightened her nose like it was a jewel. But he had a hard time making himself touch them tits. Even bruised and blue. Yeah, she's a beauty. Well, she went too far this time for sure.

Another film. Nothin's broken. I can tell.

Hall's hands were really shaking like a leaf down in Morton's bush. He was breathing like a horse.

I think even Hall has sex. Even Hall. His fingers actually jumped back from them nail marks over her nipple. Her skin is so smooth. She sure stank of whiskey. It even come from her cunt. Maybe some licking. Maybe there was a couple of 'em.

Lucky. She'll be as good as new in a week.

Sperm from the lab. Well, she was all right to me in school. A little conceited. If I looked like that, I would've been too. Wonder why she never married. Money. Looks. The kid, I guess. Who wants to raise a bastard? Well, she'll be OK. Dr. Heck says the teeth are loose. But OK. None lost. She can't swallow 'em. She'll be OK. Black and blue for a month. But OK. Nose not messed up. Maybe a little scar on the lip. Good luck, Charlotte. But, baby, you'd better change the way you strut your stuff.

"Oh, Dr. Hall. Yes, they're set up."

"Let me study these, Mrs. Gordiner."

Sure. OK. I'll get out. Wants to pray over them, I guess. He's a good man. The best surgeon in this county. I'll testify to that. But, my God, you can go too far with that religious stuff. But that body. Huh, I think even Dr. Jennings Hall wanted some of that.

She lit a cigarette and glanced down the hall—"Cal! Cal Hendricks. Hello!"

"Oh, Iris. Iris. Didn't recognize you. You a nurse?"

"Yeah. Yeah. How're you doin'?"

"Listen, Iris. How is she? Charlotte. Charlotte Morton?"

"Beat up. Wow, beat up. She's OK. But, baby, who got hold of her?"

"I don't know. Are you sure she's OK?"

"The X-rays look clean to me. Dr. Hall is looking at 'em now. She'll be black and blue for a month though. What are you doing now? I hear you got married."

"Jennings Hall?"

"Yeah."

"Sybil," he turned to the blonde woman who was crying. "She's OK. Jennings is taking care of her. It's OK. I guess."

He took her arm.

"C'mon, we'll get coffee."

He turned to the nurse.

"Thanks, Iris. Thanks a lot."

Iris Gordiner pushed the door, glanced in. Dr. Hall was kneeling in the demi-light of the screen. She silently closed the door. Christ, he has to pray before an injection. One cannot be too fanatic in performing God's will, he says. Well, he's good. So, OK.

She stepped out and lit another cigarette.

Dr. Jennings Hall knelt in silence. His chest was heaving. He listened to himself breathe.

All those years. When I danced with her, all those years ago, I could not get enough breath. Now, after all those years, my hand still trembles. *My* hand! Your gift, Lord! Your instrument. *Her* flesh is so smooth. She is so perfectly beautiful. So utterly . . . *O Daughters of Israel, thy beauty* . . . Her flesh is so utterly smooth, even now, wounded. Lord, I have tried to purify. I have tried to perfect myself according to Thy Will, begged to be allowd to be Thy instrument. *If a woman have long hair, it is a glory to her* . . . no hair like hers. She could have been a saint. Ah Lord, a soul is such a little thing. So easily lost. So fragile. It is hard. Thy Will. That which is asked . . . which is *commanded*! A childish hayride. My hands trembled that night. And they tremble now. At this moment. It is hard. What is asked. What is commanded. *To*

442

deliver such an one unto Satan for the destruction of the flesh, that the spirit may be saved in the day of the Lord Jesus. Such an one! Loveliest of all His creatures. *If a man defile the temple of God, him shall God, him shall God destroy...which temple are ye.* I think there is no more grievous temptation in this city than that small flesh that is before me now. My hand trembles before it...trembling now. Dancing. It was the dance...*which temple are ye...* The head of another Baptist could have been taken that night. It is everywhere, isn't it? I could not dream such quivering lust as she created in that room. *Neither let us commit fornication, as some of them committed, and fell in one day three and twenty thousand.* Every soul damned. Damned! Damned all. And the soul, so fragile, so perilous...*which temple are ye!* Every soul of them damned. *Let us cleanse ourselves from all filthiness of the flesh and spirit, perfecting holiness in fear of God.* And now *this*! Some man, some soul, driven to commit this—abomination! Unclean. Unclean vessel. *Wherefore if thy hand or thy foot offend thee, cut them off, and cast them from thee: it is better for thee to enter into life halt or maimed, rather than...be cast into hell fire.* Everlasting. Everlasting.

Dr. Jennings Hall, sworn to Hippocrates, rose.

Fill me, Lord. *Lord, fill me!*

He held out his hand in the demi-light. Steady. As a rock. *The Rock!*

He breathed deeply. He *felt* the strength of his God surge. He was perfected. He closed his eyes.

"Mrs. Gordiner."

Iris entered. "Yes, Dr. Hall."

"Prepare the patient for surgery. Mastectomy. Left Mammary. Simple. Who is the duty anaesthetist?"

"Surgery?" She glanced at the screen.

"Yes. Who is the duty anaesthetist?"

"I just saw Dr. Wambler. Did you say surgery? Mastectomy?"

"Yes. Ask Dr. Wambler to assist me, please."

She paused. Her eyes went back to the screen.

"What is it? Ask Dr. Wambler. I'm scheduled for ten-thirty."

"Yes, Doctor."

She went out. She lit a cigarette as she walked down the corridor to the station. She frowned, touched her hair. She put out the cigarette and retraced her steps. She quietly opened the door. Dr. Hall was kneeling.

He turned. "Yes. Yes, Mrs. Gordiner?"

"Excuse me, Dr. Hall. You said mastectomy, Dr. Hall?"

"Yes, Mrs. Gordiner. Yes."

"Yes. I'm sorry, Doctor. Yes."

Late that afternoon, Cal paced the waiting area. Sybil was lounged in a chair. Cal had taken Alex to Susan and his children.

"Her breast. Jesus!"

"Her beautiful breast. Gone!" Sybil sobbed. "Why would anyone—"

The elevator door opened and Detectives Hoffman and Hefner came out.

"Puss," Cal sprang toward them. "Who did this?"

"We don't know, Cal. Wait a second." He walked to the nurse's station, talked a few minutes, and returned.

"Who did it?" Cal said trembling. "I want his ass. *Boy,* do I want his ass."

"Easy, Cal. We don't know."

"Well, what . . . ?"

"Listen, easy." Puss pulled Cal out of Sybil's hearing. "Listen. I know how you feel about her. But it could have been anyone. You know what she was."

"What do you mean?"

"Look. You know. Everybody knows. C'mon. You seen them pictures of her floating around. You know what happens at that motel. C'mon. Who knows who she brought home?"

"She doesn't work on Mondays."

"I know that. I mean—somebody come back for more. Or something. He got a little rough. Too rough. I don't buy rape though."

"Wha . . . ? Puss, that's a lot of shit. Who did it? Find that bastard."

"Easy, Cal. She was semi-conscious a while ago. She muttered Coy Trexler's name—the auto repair man. She—"

"Coy Trexler!"

"*Easy.* We talked to him. You know him. Got a going business. He admits he's screwed her. Been doing it. But he swears he was home last night."

"Coy Trex . . ." Cal whirled. Turned back. "Coy Trexler.

444

Screwed Charlotte! Puss, if he screwed her, he did it. He raped her. You don't think for a minute she'd—"

"Take it easy, Cal. We're going back over to the house and look around again. They're gonna call us when she comes around. Just take it easy. She's gonna be all right anyway."

"She lost a breast, Puss!" Cal snarled.

"I know. I *know*! We'll be on it."

They left.

Cal paced. Coy. *Coy!* But he wouldn't do *this*. Not even Trex would do this. Screw Coy? Never. This is crazy.

At nine o'clock Jennings beckoned Cal and Sybil.

"She's groggy. Don't stay but a minute."

Cal clasped Jennings's arm. He pulled Sybil up from the couch. They went to the door. Cal walked like a young elephant avoiding tulips.

He smiled down at her. Her eyes were open. Then closed.

"Oh, Cal," she whispered.

"Darling," Sybil leaned over her.

"Sybil. Sybil."

Cal leaned to her ear, whispering. "Oh, Char. You look beautiful. And it's all over. You're all right. You got a broken finger. You're gonna have a black eye. But you're all right. Jennings fixed your nose perfect. I wanta kiss it, in fact. He says I gotta wait a week. You're all right, sweetheart."

"Oh Cal, Cal." She could hardly speak. He strained to listen.

"Don't talk, honey. It's all right."

She swallowed. Tears welled, overflowed down her cheeks. Sybil sponged them.

"I don't want to be pregnant," she whispered. "I don't want that."

"No," Sybil lied. "Of course not. Don't worry about that. Jennings said no."

Charlotte sighed.

"I don't want that. I couldn't bear that."

"No. No. Of course not, darling. Just relax. Rest. Get well."

"He kept hitting me," she choked. "He kept hitting, hitting, hitting."

"Who was it, Char. Who?"

"Oh, it was Coy. He hit and hit and . . ."

Jennings touched Cal's elbow. Cal stepped back.

"Charlotte, this is Jennings. Mr. Burke, the county solicitor, is here. Do you feel like talking to him for a moment?"

"Yes," she managed.

Cal and Sybil stepped outside. He helped her to a chair. He paced.

It begins to make sense, he thought. *A little*. Five nights a week Trex was out at that bar. Drooling. The picture, the nude, on his desk. Christ, would he beat her like that? If he did, I'll kill him. He did. Charlotte said so. Charlotte doesn't lie. Trex did this to her.

Mr. Burke and Puss and Hefner stepped out.

Cal stalked them.

"Trexler swears he was home. His wife says yes," Puss was saying.

"Well, one thing's for sure. You'd never get a rape conviction on Charlotte Morton's word," Burke snapped.

"What do you mean?" Cal spat. "You saw her."

"I mean just that. Not in this county. Assault maybe. Rape, never."

"What do you mean? You saw her. Jennings says she was sexually penetrated."

"I'm talking about a jury. Cal, she's got an illegitimate child. You know her reputation. No jury would ever believe she didn't provoke him—if, indeed, he did it."

"She said he did. He kept hitting her. Charlotte said it," Cal was stalking Burke.

"Hold it, Hendricks. Of course, she said it. That's the point. *She* said it. Trexler says no. Trexler is a business man. A veteran. You know what she is."

"*What is she?* Tell me what she is," Cal was roaring.

Puss stepped between them. Sybil came near, holding her face, horrified.

"Easy, Cal," Puss said.

Cal stepped off.

"Cal," Burke said. "Listen. Listen. We're investigating. All right? As things stand now, it would be Trexler's word against hers. You know what a jury is going to believe. Look, we know someone was there. We know he drove her home sometimes. Tambourkis out at the motel told us that. Now, as things stand I might go for assault if we think Trexler was there. OK? Use that. Now, let's say a jury believes that—rape they'd never believe—but let's say assault. And I doubt if

446

they're going to take her word for that. But let's say assault. He might get..."

Cal had strode away. Was against the wall, his fist pounding his thigh. Trexler drove Charlotte home. Sure. *One* time. That flat tire. *That flat tire!* That son of a bitch. He *did* let the air out.

Sybil came to him, put her head against his shoulder. He looked over her to the room where Charlotte lay. Trex did it. And nothing was going to be done about it. She's in there beaten to a pulp. By that bastard. Lost a breast. And nothing was going to be done about it. Because. Because they don't know her. What do they know? They can't even imagine her. They don't know about Max. About Alex. They don't know she writes every day. They don't know she's been waiting all this time. Those fucking pictures. That Cooley. I'll beat his brains out. Two fucking dollars each. I'll kill him. That stupid talk—none of it true. They don't know her. That pig beat her and raped her. And he's hanging around the Legion hall right now.

Jennings approached.

"Does she know about the breast?" Sybil asked.

"No. I thought tomorrow might be best," he said. "Sybil, if you would like, we can go down to an office. Perhaps you and Cal would join me in a prayer for her. I'm going to stay here tonight."

"Could she be pregnant, Jennings? Could she?"

He sighed. "It is, of course, a possibility."

Cal leaned away. He took three steps, gathered momentum, hit the elevator button, wheeled, entered the stair well, bounded down, dashed across the parking lot, leaped into his car, drove.

I'll know when I look into his face. If it's there, I'm going to beat his brains out. Out! I'm going to ruin him. I'll *know*.

He screeled into the Legion parking lot. Leaped for the door.

Those who were there said afterwards that he burst through the door, eyes darting, searching. He scanned the dining room. Almost empty. Bounded downstairs to the game room. Scanned. Hit the cardroom. Scanned. There were four tables of cards.

Coy Trexler saw him when he entered. Those who were there say Coy started up, lurched toward the door. And they said Cal was across the room, across the table, scattering chips, drinks, cards.

He had seen Coy's face. *He knew.*

Those who were there said his whole body hit Trexler like a projectile, drove him into the wall, didn't allow him to fall. Held him up, drove his fist into the skinny rib cage. There were those who said they heard the ribs crack. Just snap. Then it took five men to rip Cal's hands from Trexler's throat. Then it took two more, seven all told, to press him against the wall, to keep him there for the ten minutes it took to settle it down. They said he couldn't speak. They said spittle came from his mouth like foam. That it truly took all seven men to hold him.

They said also that Coy crawled out the door, choking, his left arm gimpy. And outside, two men who were just entering the place stopped Coy as he stepped away from his white Caddie and took a sawed-off shotgun away from him.

Eddie, the house manager, didn't want to call the police. Would give the place a bad name. They finally persuaded Coy to go home. They examined him. Felt like ribs. That's all. Some tape. That was all a doctor would do anyway.

And all the time, seven men holding Cal, holding, not daring to look into his eyes.

"He was temporarily insane."

When they let him go, Eddie brought him a shot of bourbon. He threw it back, slumped, walked slowly out the door. He hadn't spoken a word.

At three A.M. he called under Sybil's window. She came down and made him coffee.

He kept saying it over and over. "He did it. I know he did it. I saw it in his face. He beat Charlotte. He beat her. I would have killed him. I would have."

And Sybil took his handsome, ravaged, drunken face between her palms. "Look at me, Cal. Please, please promise. She's going to need you now as never before. Please don't do anything foolish that will take you away from her. Please promise. Please, Cal, I beg you. She needs you. So much."

He promised. After he thought it over.

When he got home, Susan listened. Then she said the same thing. "We need you. She needs you. Don't do anything dumb."

He promised her too. Then he leaned on his wife's breast and cried. She held him.

*   *   *

The night nurse was terrorized by the most piteous wail she had ever heard in her young life. It was like all the sadness of the earth gathered into a single utterance. She rushed to call Dr. Hall from the surgeon's office. He was there. He had stayed. She thought, *how good of him*. He stayed. To be with his patient.

He ordered a sedative, and went to her.

She was keening softly now, steadily, in a grieving rhythm that held him at the door for a moment. Then he went to her.

"Charlotte, it's Jennings."

"My breast," she rasped.

"Yes, Charlotte. Yes. I'm sorry. I'm so sorry."

She didn't answer. She stared at the ceiling.

"Charlotte, this will be very hard for you," he spoke gently. "If only this once, please, I beg you, think of this as God's will, submit to it, give over to Him, and begin a new life. Think of it as a new life. A new chance. Charlotte, you are brave. I know that. Please, dear friend, think of it as the Lord's will. It is God's will, I assure you. I know. I *know*. It is, it can be, the beginning of a whole new life, dear friend. Charlotte, I will pray for you every day. I promise that I will pray for you every day."

She did not answer. He took the syringe from the nurse.

"Charlotte, I am going to give you something to make you sleep. I'll stay here with you tonight. Dear Charlotte, I will pray for you. I'll be here beside you. Sleep. Soon you'll be well. Sleep."

The young nurse told everybody he stayed in her room all night.

Iris Gordiner had coffee waiting for her husband Tom when he came in from the third shift.

"Oh, the dynamite chick that played the piano? Sure, I remember. Charlotte, yeah, Morton. Yeah, Charlotte Morton. Right. Hell, what a shame. Wow, what a woman. Jesus, half the guys out at the plant will burst into tears when I tell 'em. But wadda ya mean, Hall is crazy? You been tellin' me he's the best butcher in town."

"Well, it just bothers me. It's just that I looked at them X-rays myself and—well, her tit was bruised and there was nail marks, but it looked OK to me. Sure, Hall is the best. That's what I can't understand. He was strange during the examination. Like he was afraid to touch her. Lying there. And I'll swear he had to force himself to touch her bush. Like he made three starts before he could make himself actually touch her bush. You know, to examine. I don't know. It's like I don't understand the man. I respect him. But I can't like him."

"Look. He's the doctor. Maybe it was so smushed it had to come off. Don't worry about it. She was kinda easy beaver anyway, wasn't she? From what I hear. She probably invited some guy, teased along, then backed off. Like you sometimes."

"Oh, stop it. Get a bath and let's get some sleep. It's just that . . . Anyway, I'm gonna look at those X-rays again. Tomorrow."

The first nights were long, long. The sleeping, waking. The loss. Oh, the loss. Jennings there, always, there, praying. The second night she quietly asked him to leave her alone. He seemed to understand. He would be as near as the nurse's station.

She stared at the ceiling.

It is not a cut. It will not heal and go away. Something, part of me, is gone permanently, forever, for as long as I am. And it isn't a hand, or leg. It's part of womanness, of capacity. I fed my son. I wanted to feed others. It isn't part of humanness. That's there. Its not like an arm. It's . . . gone. Forever and forever . . . .

Then she would choke. The stupidity of it all, the meanness. My beautiful breast is gone. But worst, oh *worst!*—it had never been Max, whom she loved, at that window. This was the final betrayal of her botched, violated love. All those nights I thought I had wooed the man I truly, oh, God, truly loved . . . .

She thought of giving up. She thought of it. Sleep away, whatever is left of me. Just disappear. The first day she stared out the window. She could follow the tall, sun-splintered pines, and beyond, the towering oaks, the endless blue, endless, the great white clouds, sometimes cruelly puffy—like breasts!—could follow beyond beyond. I could go. I could go and go and finally vanish.

But, even wounded, she was Charlotte Morton. She couldn't. She had . . . *life!* In her. Crackling, coiled and fierce to be run out.

Behind her she had her father, Blanche, Alex, the wraith of

Max, Cal boiling between her thighs—oh, she sobbed, would he? Would he be able? Now? Will any man? Oh.

But at that moment Sybil Schraeder was pouring Cal a drink.

"Now listen, I know that you have been her lover. She never said so, nor you. But I know. You must go to her the moment she is able. Do you understand? And, look at these. I bought them to use until we can have some especially made to fit."

Sybil held a bra, lacy, feminine, with a padded left cup.

"See? And you will bury your face here, between them. And, Cal, listen. Take it off. All the way. You take it off, even if she objects. Throw it across the room. And Cal, please, no matter how ugly or strange the scar is, put your mouth to it. Cal, as often as you kiss her whole breast. It will be so important to her. And you make her know that she is desired. Cal, will you? Please."

"Sybil," he said, shaking his handsome head, "you didn't have to tell me. For once, I knew."

25

"SYBIL, I went over to Camp Butner this morning," Cal said the next day.

"What?"

"Yeah. I didn't even ask Grossman. I went straight up to that door. Enough is enough. Crazy Bessemer was around. He said Max was in his room. I laid it on the line. I told him that she needed him. I told him what happened. Coy Trexler, the breast, the works. I said that she had waited for him, had written, had done everything that a woman could do, and if he had any manhood left, to come. She needed him now. I got vicious, I guess, poor bastard. I told him she didn't need his looks, she needed his guts. I told him that if he didn't come now, or at least call or write, he was not worth a hair on her head. Sitting around moping, feeling sorry for himself. Yeah, I said it all. Talking to a door. Grossman came up and pulled me away. Well, I don't know. Maybe I was wrong. But, Jesus, Sybil, Charlotte's so much. And nothing good ever happens to her. Now, to hell with Max. She needs. She's got to forget him if he doesn't make a move now."

"Yes, Cal, I think you are right. Enough is enough."

At the end of the second day, enough was enough for Charlotte Morton. Enough of lying in. She was Charlotte Morton and could not go beyond beyond. Yet.

Jennings had her up for a few minutes before and after dinner. She looked in the mirror.

"I never had a black eye before. Brawler. Scarlet Lady," she said to herself.

Back in bed at night, she wept again. But stiffened, clenching her teeth, which hurt. I'm me. Besides sexuality is not all looks and curves and bulges.

But Coy's face, cruel, livid, loomed in and out of her consciousness. Bringing fear. He hurt me. He defiled me. She trembled.

And there was Alex, brooding, unable to understand why anyone would want to hurt his mother. Listening to Cal. Listening to Sybil. Holding his mother's broken hand. Wanting to do something to help her, who was his mother and his friend. And at last, helping Nick prepare a surprise for her when she came home.

She explained to her young son in her bedroom the first night at home.

"Some people, Alex, believe that the satisfaction of their desires is all there is to life. They believe that their desires are worth sacrificing the health, well-being, even the lives of others. Therefore we have murder, robbery, and, on a larger scale, war. Probably it can be reduced to the human ego. A man wanted thirty seconds of pleasure from me, and was willing to do this to obtain it. This kind of person is very dangerous. They have no vision beyond their own petty desires. Or they are so insecure and insignificant that only by causing pain can they call attention to themselves. Or they feel that they must dominate because they are not secure enough to cooperate. Or they must hurt to feel power because they are unable to become valuable or respected by achievement. They are dangerous, but most people are not like this. We know—most of us—that gratified desire is not all there is to life. There is love, art, beauty, fellowship, trees, knowledge. We know there are these things.

"A bad thing happened to me. But you and I will realize that most people would not hurt others to satisfy their own wants. Therefore we will not become misanthropes—there's a word for you. Where's your vocabulary pad? Notice the prefix. Nor misogynists. Got them? Now, run and look them up and let mother rest. Hey, go down and play something for me. I haven't heard you play in five days."

The surprise came the next day when she came downstairs and entered the study. Alex was dogging her for some reason.

"What . . .?" she cried.

The wall which had been covered with her botanical paintings was empty. There was a little tag stuck to one of the nails. In Alex's graceful calligraphy, she read *This exhibition is on loan to the lobby of the* Stag and Doe. Sybil had brought Nick to the house and suggested the idea.

The next night Cal and Susan drove her, Sybil, and Alex out to the motel for dinner. Nick hugged her. He had been wonderful. He had sent flowers twice, been to the hospital every night, had taken Alex for dinner twice when Sybil had been busy. And now this blazing wall.

"Hey, do you want to sell?" he asked. "People are asking."

Here, outside her home, she saw her pictures anew. Her colors dazzled, but it was the whole—the writhing root structures, the foliage, the tension—held together by the colors. In one corner of the collection, in the same Alex-calligraphy, was a modest little card which held her name.

The evening was good. Gail embraced her. Clinton, who was there to fix a plumbing problem, embraced her, Sudie was warmly solicitous. Several of the bar habitués wanted to know when she would be back. She waved her splinted finger.

Nick joined them, talking a mile a minute about how receipts were way off since she wasn't there. And, "Oh, I almost forgot. I put it in my pocket, and then—well, this is for you from an admirer."

She opened the envelope.

Dear Charlotte Morton,

I hope you recover quickly. The evenings at Stag and Doe are slow without you at the piano.
I offer to pay whatever you ask for one, or as many

of your pictures as you will sell. Remarkable. Indeed, you are a remarkable woman.

Charlotte Morton, I would like to speak to you privately sometime soon after your recovery. I have several proposals to present to you which I hope you will find interesting. Perhaps we can discuss a meeting when you return to the piano. Get well soon. Your public misses you.

With admiration,
Dodd Thurmond

"Nice," she murmured, handing the note to Sybil. "He sent that lovely array of flowers—array is the only word to use. Cal, you saw them. You couldn't miss them."

"What on earth can he be proposing?" Sybil wondered. "Charlotte, I'll tell you this. Dodd Thurmond is one of the richest and most powerful men in the state."

"I know. Interesting."

She leaned back in her seat. She felt good. Tired, for she was still weak. But twice she went to the ladies room just to pass her pictures, to stand alone and appraise them for a moment. She was pleased.

In bed that night she ran her hand over the bandage. *Well,* she thought, *I will not die.* It is a loss and part of life is taking losses. She thought how kind Nick had been. How devoted Jennings had been. Jennings—perhaps it had taken this disaster to recall him to her friendship which at one time, she knew, had been valuable to him. And Sybil, dear, cold, aloof, unapproachable Sybil, immediately searching out the padded bras, thinking of the pictures, protecting, caring in ways that would not occur to others. I am lucky in her. And Cal. Cal. Cal. Dear one. When Susan left the table, he had leaned and whispered wickedly, "Hey, Boob,"—he emphasized *Boob,* not the plural—"You'd better get well. I'm coming to take your panties off."

That night in bed she reviewed the long, sickly, heartbreaking relationship with Max. Her nocturnal seduction scenes and their betrayal revolted her. *It is time,* she thought. *Alex*—but this was not healthy for him either, not this crazy dream-like miasma in which they secretly lived. I too have a life. Suddenly a sense of urgency swept her. I am not Penelope. Keeping your legs crossed beneath weaving hands is not for me. He must come, or not come. I want my life.

Again she considered the pictures. She snuggled her pillow. Perhaps they are really good. Seeing them there as a visitor, she had gained perspective. They were not merely 'pretty.' They did suggest the tension of life. Oh, there were two weak ones in the ten. The Nandina was frivolous. Must do another. Try for genuine gaiety. It's there in the sprays of berries. But she had been newly stunned at the primitive sexuality of several—the Bromeliad. The fountain of fronds above the bold male shaft driven into Mother Earth was, she considered, powerful and savage. Maybe, just maybe, I can become really good.

"Charlotte, I have a present for you," Jennings handed her a small box across his desk.

She smiled and opened it. It was a small, soft rubber ball.

He rose and cut the splint from her finger.

"Carry it with you and squeeze now and then. In a week you'll be able to play again as well as ever."

"Oh, Jennings, thank you."

He turned to the door. "Miss Hinkle, will you step in here please. Now, Charlotte, take off your blouse."

She did. He tenderly removed the dressing.

"All right. All well."

"Oh, Jennings. Thank you so much."

He helped her with the blouse, saw how the midnight hair fell across the pale shoulders, and nodded Miss Hinkle out.

She leaned up to kiss him. He recoiled automatically, involuntarily.

"No, Jennings. *No!*" and she took his hand and kissed it. "Oh, Jennings, I have missed you so these past years. Come back. We were friends, Jennings, such friends once. You meant so much to me, and to Billy and Cal, and poor Max. Please, let me think of you as a friend."

He was flustered, uncomfortable.

"Of course, Charlotte. Charlotte, yes. But please think of the things I have said to you. Think of your soul. Could you give up that place? Give up that place where sin—writhes. There is such beauty in the radiance of Christ's care. Charlotte, would you see Reverend Frye if I brought him to your house? He's very old and feeble now. But he still has the power of God in him. Would you see him if I brought him by one day?"

"Of course. Jennings, I would do anything for you. Oh,

Jennings, we do not have to agree on everything. Only on one—that we both are worthwhile people. Of course, bring him. I will be pleased to see him. And, Jennings, thank you. You could not have been finer to me. I can count you as my good, dear friend Jennings again?"

"Yes. Yes, Charlotte."

"I've got a present for you," Cal leered. Black, transparent, vulgar, lascivious panties which covered neither buttocks nor pubic triangle.

She loved them. She modeled them.

"I can just pull it over my shoulder so you can have one mouthful."

"You can. But I won't let you." He flung the bra across the room.

"Cal!"

He couldn't answer. His mouth was full.

She was radiant the next day.

She could type.

Dear Max,

This will be the last letter that I will write to you, unless you reply in some way. And I cry—I am sitting in Dad's old office crying like a baby.

I have loved you since the possibility of love came into my life. My father, now dead, and Blanche, now dead, grew tired of hearing my childish tales of Max the Terrible. Later, I loved you when you were becoming a man, for helping Billy, for helping Jennings, for being so beautiful on the football field, for The Mile—my heart was so full of pride that day. My boy had done something no one else could do. For your camaraderie with Cal, for your curiosity, for your love of Big Edna, for your sensitivity and tenderness, for growing toward all I could have wanted in a man. All this you know.

I bore you a son. You know this. You have seen him—tall, fine as you.

We loved once. Once, Max, we were two of "many ingenious lovely things." You remember the Yeats' line— my father carrying his drink, pacing, reading the poem? Now we are both marred. Things happened over which

*we had no control. Max, I too am marred. You know.
Cal told you.*

*I beg you to come, or to tell me that you will come—
sometime. I need you and I love you. And I am not
asking you to come and hold my hand and lie down and
die with me. Come live with me. We are not beautiful
any longer. But we are alive. We can learn and love and
grow. We have a fine son. He also needs you—us.
Together.*

*Max, please. It has been too long. And Max, if you do
not answer this letter, I will break the habit of loving
you. I will not write again. I have been true. Devoted.
But this is the end.*

> *With love,*
> *Charlotte*

She was crying as she addressed it, licked, stamped it.
It was the end of something.

Coy Trexler's hand went for the drawer of his desk when he
realized who was standing over him.

Cal jerked him from his chair, hauled him halfway across
the desk, spoke into his face.

"Keep your hands where I can see them or I will tear your
arm off and beat you to death with it. Now listen. I'm going
to tell you about the rest of your short life. I am gonna have
your ass. I promise. Sometime. From now on, Trex, your life
is looking over your shoulder. Cal is coming. Sometime. A
year. Two. But Cal is coming. Remember it every time you
shut your eyes. Look in the back of that slick Caddie, every
time you get in it. Look every night you step out of this shop.
Watch every shadow. Because some day that shadow is going
to be me. Got it, you bastard? And one day they're going to
fish that sleek El Dorado out of the river. And there's gonna
be a body in it. Yours. The neck will be broken from the
crash. Remember it, Trex. One day. Live with it. Sleep with
it. Eat it. Look over your shoulder."

He dragged Coy across the desk, flung him out the door,
grabbed him, and marched him to the Culbreath Construction pick-up with the motor running, dropped him, and drove
away.

The night before Coy had walked into the *Stag and Doe*, placed his bottle on the bar and yelled to Hardisty to mix him one with water, a double.

Hardisty had turned, looked at him, walked away.

Coy had sniffed. Stretched his left arm where the tape across his ribs bound.

He turned and looked straight into the eyes of that squirt Greek Tambourkis.

"Leave," the Greek said.

"Wadda ya mean?"

The Greek's eyes burned into him. His eye tailed to Hardisty who had moved back behind him and was leaning over the bar.

Coy smirked. He reached around with his right hand, took his bottle, and walked out.

Jennings visited her often. Sometimes two or three days in succession. They were short visits between the hospital and house calls. He had become the last doctor in town—and a surgeon!—who still made house calls. He always looked rumpled and haggard.

His visits were short. But they were the most intense moments of Charlotte's day, more intense than those at the piano or when she was nearing the realization of a new painting.

He would hunch in a chair, his hands on his knees. Nothing moved, his expressionless face, stooped shoulders, nothing except the long fluent fingers which coiled and reared and twisted like a nest of serpents.

It seemed that not even the thick slack lips had to move to allow the monotones escape.

"Charlotte, you were elected. You have received a sign from God. Acknowledge it. Such election! You. *You*. Receive it. Open to it. Please, open to it. Others will follow. I know it is a sign. I *know*."

He did bring Reverend Frye one afternoon. The man of God was indeed old. Jennings had to help him from the car and into the house. The merest movement was tentative. Charlotte served tea. It was difficult for him to take it. She prepared it for him and he managed, holding the cup with both hands. But he had not lost a measure of the power which had so moved her that Sunday long ago. Staring straight ahead he spoke as though preaching in his raw-boned

458

church with the old sure rhetoric a command. And she was again spellbound.

He was interrupted when Alex came bounding in from school.

"Alex, please come in," she called. "There is someone special for you to meet. This is Reverend Frye, a man who has been a great force in many lives. I want you to sit and listen as he talks."

Frye, as those years ago, moved past the interruption without seeming to notice it. He too dwelled on the sure sign that she had received. He recited passionately, "'. . . woe to that man by whom offence cometh! Wherefore if thy hand or thy foot offend thee, cut them off, and cast them from thee: it is better for thee to enter into life halt or maimed, rather than having two hands or two feet to be cast into hell fire. And if thine eye offend thee, pluck it out. . . .' Charlotte Morton, to you I say, a sign has been given. Some part of thy flesh hath been cast from thee. It is indeed a sign. Do not betray a sign from God. Come ye in the way of the light."

When Jennings and the ancient preacher left, both Charlotte and Alex were drained.

"A sign? Mother. The loss of your breast?"

"Listen, son, believe him or not, you will have to admit that he is persuasive. He is responsible for Jennings being the religious fanatic that he is—and many others."

Alex needed no convincing. He recognized the power of a great folk art.

When the day came that she was to go back to the bar, she played for Jennings to show that her hand was again perfect. His reaction shocked her, not in effect, but in magnitude. He approached hysteria.

"Charlotte, I beg you, *do not go back there*. You have received a sign. I can testify. I myself was the vehicle. I know. I *know* its truth. It filled me that morning. So that I was shaking. It was to deliver you from the flesh. Do not go back there! To that lust, sick desire, drunkenness, degradation. Please. Please! Do *not* betray this warning."

She was uncomfortable and unstrung when he left. She touched her padded cup. She ran upstairs to her room and exposed the scar to her mirror. Something was strange. The hairs on her neck raised themselves. She sensed something macabre, something too terrible to formulate.

A sign?

*   *   *

She played that night.

Glasses were raised.

Nick was solicitous. "Is everything OK?" The room was packed. He had run a half-page ad.

Mr. Thurmond was there. Gail told Charlotte that Clifford the chauffeur had driven down with an envelope containing twenty-five dollars if she would call the enclosed number on the day Charlotte Morton was to return to the piano.

She nodded to his table when she began her first set. She sang *September Song* directly to him.

When the set was over, she went to his table, held out her hand.

"The flowers were very beautiful. It was so kind of you. And I promise, they helped. Thank you so much."

He waved his hand. "We're so glad to have you back. You have no idea. Please, Charlotte Morton, join me for one drink. I know it is against your policy, but it would please me very much."

She smiled. "I'm glad you asked."

"I can offer Jack Daniels."

"That I can accept. A splash of water."

He poured.

"To your return. How are you feeling?"

She smiled and leaned to him, lowering her head.

"Is my Roman nose straight?"

He laughed. "Perfectly. Elegantly."

"I had a broken finger." She held her hand. "But my good doctor gave me a red rubber ball which I have diligently squeezed and it seems as strong as before. How did the piano sound?"

"Accomplished, as always. And I'm not given to flattery."

"I received your note, Mr. Thurmond. And I thank you for that also. Your kindness certainly earns you an attentive ear, whatever the proposal. But I must tell you that I am reasonably happy here. You see, I have a son. It leaves me free for him, and to dabble at painting and music during the day. And there is enough money—partially, I must say, due to you. However, I will certainly listen attentively. And gratefully."

"Alex?"

"Yes. Did you meet him? He comes out sometimes, usually with Sybil Schraeder, a friend—"

"I know. I know of Miss Schraeder. She is sitting over there with the Hendrickses."

She raised her brows. And nodded.

"He is a fine-looking boy. I'm told he is going to be a fine athlete. And that he is a splendid student."

She raised her brows again and nodded.

"Now, Miss Charlotte Morton—may I call you Charlotte?"

"Of course, Dodd."

He smiled.

"Charlotte—good, I like that—if you will give me an hour I will send Clifford for you. Are you free tomorrow? At any time."

"No, not tomorrow. I have promised myself to drive to Camp Butner tomorrow. It's a matter—well, that I simply must settle in my mind . . . no later than tomorrow. Suggest another day."

"The wounded Marine, Compton?"

She straightened. She was not smiling.

He too stiffened.

"I will collect no more information, Charlotte. I promise it. And apologize for what you may justly call snooping. It is ended, I promise."

"Let's say day after tomorrow then, Dodd. Will you offer lunch? I'll be ready at, say, twelve-thirty? And, Dodd, I hold you to your promise. Absolutely."

"Twelve-thirty. I already have the address. Yes, I consider myself held. I will not violate that promise. I'll even tell you something which will intimate my reasons for snooping. When I heard of your assault, I came very very close to something I have never done, though I've been tempted several times in my life. I came very close to ordering the elimination of Coy Trexler. Almost as close as your Cal did. I . . . well, enough. No more. I will not violate the promise."

Her stare was intent. He met it unflinchingly. *What man is this?* she wondered.

Then, "May I call Clifford? I will not miss my turn to be kind."

Clifford came with the wheel chair.

Charlotte beckoned to Sybil, Cal, and Susan to follow Clifford into the lobby.

"Some special people, Dodd. Sybil Schraeder, Susan and Cal Hendricks."

She turned the chair to the wall which held the paintings.

"Which do you like best?" she asked him.

He considered, but quickly selected the Bromeliad.

"Oh," she gasped and dropped to her knees beside him. "Do you? Truly. Well, yes, why not? It *is* the very best, you know."

She stood smiling, turned to the wall, took the picture down and handed it to Clifford.

"Clifford, don't let that get broken. It's my favorite too."

Dodd Thurmond smiled, and took her hand.

"Now, c'mon, all of you," she said, "I'm gonna tear up *Cool Drive*."

She was trembling as Dr. Grossman touched her shoulder, smiled encouragement, and left her outside the alien door in the alien hall. Here was where the man she had loved—out of habit, perhaps—for all these years, lived.

She tapped the closed door.

"Max," she spoke softly. "This is Charlotte. Max, I know you got my letter. I wanted you to hear my voice. Max, I love you. I want you. I know that you are . . . Max, I *too* am maimed, marred. You know about that. Cal told you. We could help each other, Max. There would be no shame or uneasiness between us. Max, our son is so fine. Max, he's running punts back. Can you believe that? He's running punts . . ." Her voice broke, went coarse, throaty. "Max, I will stand here two minutes. Give me a signal. Tap. Just tap. Two minutes. If you don't signal—oh God, just a tap, *one*—I am going. Forever."

She folded her hands at her waist, took a deep breath, lifted her chin and fixed her eyes on the hall clock. With but thirty seconds left, she could not keep her lips from trembling. Max, *please*.

Two minutes.

She leaned against the door. "Goodbye, Max," she whispered.

She felt her way around the corner of the hall and slumped against the wall. She sobbed softly for a moment. Dr. Grossman's hand took her arm.

Relief gradually came. Slowly, a lifting. The steam from the coffee Dr. Grossman gave her in his office, went to her brain. Something fell away. Huge fragments melted, fell. Evaporat-

462

ed. She became almost lightheaded. It was coming like a wind. It. *It!*

It was called freedom.

"Write to me personally, because we are freinds. Come to the bar. Bring Bess. But no more reports. It's over."

He understood. He kissed her on the cheek beside the Packard.

On the way home the sun was blinding. I can't even remember it—all those years. She flicked the radio to full blast. She sang along. *Hound Dog*. Marvelous! Elvis. A new primitive, boiling energy barreling into American music. So long Doris Day.

I could do one hellava Twist. I got hips, baby.

The next day she got her period and found her first gray hair. The joy of the first overwhelmed the shock of the second.

She was almost giddy at lunch.

"You are very animated," Dodd Thurmond smiled. "Is this the daylight Charlotte?"

They lunched in a small breakfast room which was walled on three sides with French doors and floor to ceiling windows. It was a forest of plants and vines.

"The plants? Only recently since my stroke," he said. "Much has happened to me since then. I have been forced to seek more sedentary pleasures—and I have been totally changed by what I have found."

His house was huge, imposing, enormously ugly, blocky. It was secluded from the small town and his mills by distance, trees, rolling meadowland. Inside it was formal, elegance without comfort.

"The house is changing," he said, "as I change. Actually, I have a place at the river which is liveable, and was my favorite place until I could no longer be active. This room is a new addition. And my so-called study, which I will show you later. The rest is a designer's nightmare of what a rich mill owner would want. And, of course, he was exactly right. Only the mill owner had a stroke, spends more time in his home, has begun to read books, hear music, look at flowers, and consider his largely wasted life. It no longer satisfies. You must help me."

She had had two glasses of wine. "For Godsakes, trim down those Stonehenge pillars that support the porch. Something slimmer, lighter will change this house from a fortress to a sedate home that will deserve your magnificent oaks."

He lifted his chin, smiling broadly. "Precisely. *Precisely!* Ah. You see, those are the things that I am not equipped to imagine. Yes."

"No life histories," he promised. But . . . as a young man he had worked four manual jobs for five years to buy his first loom. Theoretically there had not been time even for sleep, he smiled. End of life history. He vaguely remembered having married, purchased the house, buried her childless. The rest had been production, costs, quality control, logistics, *etc.* In the hospital after the stroke, he had read a book called *A Tale of Two Cities.* It had diverted, confused. In fact, it had given a lot of pleasure.

"And only six weeks ago, I did that which I would never have dreamed Dodd Thurmond would do: I read a whole Shakespeare play."

"Which one?"

"*King Lear.*"

"Ah, my father's very favorite Shakespeare. I can hear him now. 'Like flies to wanton boys are we to the gods. They kill us for their sport.'"

"Ah, but also, 'Her voice was ever soft, gentle and low—an excellent thing in woman.'"

"*Wonderful!*" she beamed. "Lovely."

"This play has been here four hundred years. And I had always considered Las Vegas and Miami the pinnacle of experience. After I was able to return to the office, a young executive trainee, who hated mills and textiles, and the whole picture—and whom I was going to fire immediately—passed me in the hall carrying a couple of record albums. I can't remember what they were now, but I called him into my office and told him to write out the names of three pieces that would be a good place for a child to begin listening to classical music.

"For the first time since he had been there he showed interest in something that was going on inside the mill. He asked for fifteen minutes personal time. When he came back, he handed me recordings of Tschaikovsky's Fifth Symphony, Rachmaninoff's Second piano Concerto, and Beethoven's Fifth Symphony—'Save that till last,' he said. I now have, I suppose, several hundred recordings. He still hangs around the office, of course. He still has no interest. But I could never fire him."

"Oh, what a great story," she said.

"I now also look at pictures. And tomorrow, after that perceptive remark about columns, I will order several books on architecture."

They laughed.

"Did your trip to Camp Butner end as you wished? You may tell me to mind my own business. I am holding to my promise," he said quietly.

"Yes. It's all right. Yes. I feel a little lightheaded. Suddenly—freedom. It will take weeks for it to sink in. He is my son's father as you have surmised. I may be very happy and free. It will take a little time to decide."

"Well, then, no proposals today. One should be gloomy when making decisions. If you make them when you are happy, you project sunny results. Except one, because of the time element. Annually, I host all my suppliers, my markets, my transports, *etc.*, all the executives, for a few days. You see, I must woo ardently, because although I am very rich, my operation is relatively small, and since I am not public, my establishment is, by some standards, medieval. In any event they come for a few days, tour the mills, use the river house, for tennis, water sports, drunkenness—and leave with handsome gifts. Mostly they are mean, narrow, ambitious, dull men—just as I was—but, as I say, I must woo them.

"So a proposal. I will pay you a hundred dollars for two hours of music, here—say from five to seven on Friday two weeks from now. Before I serve them dinner. I think that you could charm them, and therefore help my cause."

"Of course I will. On condition that there be no further talk of payment. I would enjoy it. No, if you mention payment, I'll refuse."

"A deal, Charlotte Morton. The piano is a Steinway—the decorator thought it essential. Want to try it? I had it tuned yesterday."

It was a gorgeous instrument, still new and tough, to be mastered, broken.

"Ah, marvelous. Dodd, I will play you a Schubert Impromptu, and then perhaps you will call Clifford. Alex will be coming home soon. They have a skull drill—tactics and plays—today. A game tonight."

"Of course."

She played.

"Charlotte, how to thank you? I haven't enjoyed anything so much within memory. I'll be over to listen. But Clifford will pick you up—four-thirty?—on the second Friday."

It was *pleasant*, she thought on the way home. Very. And I'll bet *he* was a bastard.

Charlotte Morton was charming at the piano for Dodd Thurmond's executives. The great Steinway was a honeycomb to gray suits and dark ties. She was sexual, then gay, then animated. Every man in the room lusted after her. Every wife in the room wished her a hasty and painful death. When the lust became aggressive, she parried it with deft subtlety by deferring to Mr. Thurmond. She knew that he would be pleased that they thought she was his property. She gave that impression. He watched her with perfect admiration. He clearly adored her.

When Clifford saw her to the door at home, he handed her a small package.

"For you, Miss Morton."

Sybil held the delicate diamond bracelet beneath the light.

"Whew! This is worth ten thousand dollars, if it's worth a dime."

The card read, *No payment. Simple reciprocity. One gift deserves another. With admiration, Dodd.*

"I can't keep this," Charlotte said.

"Wow. Well, I'd at least listen to his arguments."

When she called Billy the next day to fill him in on events, she knew something was wrong instantly. His speech was lazy, he could not put two thoughts together. He cried easily at her account of her attack.

"Ennis," she snarled, "what are you on?"

"Nothing. Nothing. I'm a little smoked up. That's all."

"Put Bucky on."

He was worse, rambling about what a gig they did last night. Never such a session. Yeah, they were smoking. Down from last night.

"Put Billy back on."

No use.

Cal and Susan were going to New York for vacation in six weeks. What would they find?

"Of course, you will keep it. Listen, Charlotte, I am very very rich. Which is why you are sitting across from me now.

If I were an old paralyzed druggist, or lawyer, or dentist, or anything, do you think you would be here now? Hardly. My money allows me, even in my condition, to make an impression. An impression unavailable to men of average circumstances. The bracelet." He waved his hand. "It's as if a dentist had sent you a dozen roses, if I may make a crude analogy. But that is not all. The bracelet is exquisite. And exquisite on your wrist. I selected myself from Thaler's. I made them send a man to New York and bring fifteen to choose from. Myself! And I am so pleased with it because I see that I am beginning to develop taste."

He was holding her hand across the luncheon table three days after she had played for his guests.

"And that pleases me. So, no argument. I am pleased with my discovery of my taste, with the woman who wears it. Few pleasures remain for me. Allow me those that do. And also join me in giving thanks that I do have the money to indulge them."

"Dodd, I accept with a little reluctance and a load of pleasure. These are the first diamonds a man has ever given me. Actually, I am not sure I have even a little reluctance. In fact, I don't. I love it shamelessly."

"Good. Good. Then we are both happy. Listen, let's have coffee over by the window. I want to offer another proposal."

She brought the coffee over and they sat looking out over the coiffed lawn and oaks.

"So many things have opened to me since that damned stroke, I feel like a child. The stroke was a horror—look at me—but dammit, it forced some things on me that I would never have experienced without it. For instance, what do you want to know about Gothic Architecture?"

She laughed, "I've been to Rheims and Chartres. You got the books I sent?"

"I did. I read a survey of Gothic in a day. Next the book on Romanesque. Incidentally, by the end of the week there will be new columns on the porch. I wheel myself out on the drive five times a day and imagine them. And wonder how I could not have realized it? All those years of living in this house. I simply can't wait for them to come."

"I'm excited too. Truly. Don't tell me—I want to *see* them! Call me the minute they are up. I'll run over."

"Ah, Charlotte, I almost believe you."

"Try me."

"I am. Right now a proposal. More coffee? Fine. I now wish to talk four minutes without interruption. All right?

"I don't expect a decision now, or in the next months. Take as long as you wish. Five years even. I want you to marry me. Wait. Obviously an outrageous idea. However, I wish to make it as reasonable as I can. Of course, I am trying to buy you. My money again. But that's ultimately the reason you are here. What else could I offer a woman like you? But the proposal.

"Clearly, it would not be the conventional marriage. I am much too old for you. Though sex is still very much in my head, the stroke took it from my body. So. It would be a—I gag to say it—a companionship arrangement. I love looking at you. Your face, your movements, and . . . well, your *presence*, are thrilling to me. So that is what I would ask. Your presence, some of the time. Despite appearances, I am still vital enough to have too many interests to be possessive. You would have freedom to come and go as you wish. You could have other homes—a Paris or Rome, or New York apartment. Clearly, you would have a lover—lovers. You should. That marvelous femininity and body should not be wasted. I would not like to know of them. I would ask only that you not embarrass me. And I don't believe *that* is in you anyway. And I will give you a safety valve, in case those minimum requirements become too heavy. On the day that you marry me I will place in an account, in your name only, three hundred thousand dollars—so that if you found the burden too confining, you could leave with resources of your own. And I suspect that the day might come. I come from longevity. I could live a very long time. I could become a doddering old fool.

"Well, that's my proposal. Your presence some of the time, a relationship founded on respect, and a handsome safety valve for quick escape. Think about it. There's no time limit. If it ever becomes attractive to you, say so. I will not ever mention it again.

"My four minutes are up. All right, let's go down the drive. Now, I nearly can't resist telling you about the columns I have selected. Did you want more coffee? Good. Let's go see if you can imagine them."

26

"WHAT do you want to know about sex?"

She and Alex were walking by the river, looking across the chilly sun-struck water to *Isola Bella*.

"Everything," the boy leered, laughing.

She told him everything she knew. She was explicit about female anatomy. And contraception. And gentleness.

"Alex, this too about women: I don't quite know what to make of it, or what you, a man, should make of it. I suspect that simply being aware of it is enough. A woman deals in body fluids. We lactate—make milk, we menstruate, and we must cause your oil to flow into us. And this—woman is the receiver. I imagine it is one thing to place yourself into someone's body, but it is quite a different thing to take another deeply into your body, receive fluid, keep it inside you. And woman does this. This is strange and wonderful to me. I don't know what to make of it. But I think that you should know it and puzzle over it yourself."

She looked at him. The fine young man he had become.

"Any questions?"

"Nope. Sounds great."

"It is. Enjoy it. Those who don't are invariably small and mean."

He has no girl, she thought. *This loner of a son I've made*.

She knew her son and was, perhaps, his best friend. Yet, she did not know him. He opened to her, yet held back. He never asked for things. She bought his guitar, and saw that, yes, he was pleased. But he didn't ask for things. Things. He had been trooping to the public library on his own since he could walk. He had started his own vocabulary lists. His grammar school habit of disappearing extended to the woods, the streets, the river. He went alone. She did not know whether it was because of her social sin, or whether it was his nature, or if one shaped the other.

He had begun running. He sometimes looked at the stop watch, and she realized that a goal was shaping in his mind.

His father was a miler. Cal had told of the football days when he and Max and Whit and even stodgy Dr. Hall had gotten hit and won and lost.

In September, he had simply told her that he was going out for football and would be home later from school. It was then that the punt returning drills began. He was already six feet tall and his flesh was trying to catch up with the wild running growth of his frame.

But the running was an obsession. According to Cal, his father ran ten miles a day. Alex was going cross-country, along the river banks, down secondary roads. Once Charlotte had driven with him up to Oak Grove, Dodd Thurmond's village fourteen miles away, to see a cabinet maker to repair a fine old chair.

"I run up here sometimes," he said.

At night, she would hear him go out. He ran the street, he said. He told her of the fight between two drunks he had seen below the railroad station. He told her of the woman on South Street who cut on every light in the room and undressed directly in front of the window and of the two car loads of men who sat out there almost every night watching.

Sometimes before dawn she would hear him get up and leave for his run. Sometimes in the middle of the night she would hear him—the pad of his sneakers striking a muffled echo down Well Street after she had returned from the bar. That sound loaded her with memories—herself at his age, standing on the gallery, listening to the pad of the lean boy from up the street, running, preparing to break a mile record—a hoard of memories which broke her down into tears, or lifted her chin in pride. *Well*, she thought, *I chose it*.

Zen and other Eastern thought had begun to make their way into Western consciousness. Alex, young and solitary, pondered the possibility of causing his body to yield to direction of the mind. A girl in his Latin class whose father taught at the local college had loaned him a couple of books.

"You see, Mom, if I could train myself to sleep only four hours a day, how much more time I would have to do other things."

"Alex, you are growing. You run miles a day, plus football, plus studying, and the piano. And—at highly irregular intervals, I must say—clean your room. You need eight hours of sleep."

"Mom, Fran Viscounti's father has conditioned himself to

four hours of sleep. And she says he is in perfect health and has done this for two years. He's a scholar and says he can't waste time sleeping."

"Who? Viscounti?" Such a name in this town.

"They just moved here from New Jersey. Dr. Viscounti teaches at the college."

It turned out that Fran Viscounti was Francesca Viscounti and that her father was Dr. Buonocorso Viscounti, new to the political science department at the college. If Alex did not find his Max or Cal, Francesca Viscounti was to become his Charlotte.

"She sits beside me in Latin. We talk sometimes."

Later Charlotte would learn that Buonocorso Viscounti *was* a scholar. That he was doing a massive—"definitive, I hope," he would say to her when they met and became friends— work on the *Condottieri* in Medieval and Renaissance Italy, from an incipient institution to the decisive military and political force that they became. He had a contract with a Northeastern university press for the work and was laboring under a deadline that made this dynamo of a man think of reducing his sleeping hours to three.

Eileen Viscounti was Irish. Her eyes and complexion announced it immediately.

The Viscountis became a godsend to Charlotte. He played cello, Eileen played violin, Clement, their eight-year-old son, was squeaking away at clarinet, and Fran was begging Alex to learn some violin sonatas so they could play together. They were an enormously interesting family. Their house, on the surface, was chaotic. But Charlotte saw, as she came to know them better, that curiosity and activity were the only order that they recognized, that the cross currents which shook the house were not haphazard. The Viscountis were keenly conscious of the social and political mores of their new home. This, combined with music, helped to form the bond which grew between Charlotte and her son and the boisterous new arrivals.

"How about six hours' sleep, son?"

"Momma know best," he sighed, kissing her cheek. "Wait'll I'm eighteen. I'm gonna grab my toothbrush and loin cloth and camp on the river."

"I will not come out and wash your loin cloth nor make your bed of leaves, ingrate."

"I'll stay. I'll stay."

One spring night when they sat on the gallery after she had returned from the bar and he from running, he made a shy but primal announcement.

"Mother, I . . . ah . . . had a woman, was with a girl . . . last week."

"Oh," she said, thinking, *at last*! Well, I will not pry. I will not ask. *I will not ask one question*.

She's not going to ask, he thought, after the silence began to have mass.

"Well, it was down on the South River," he said. "I was running."

"Oh."

Long silence.

I will not ask, she thought.

She's not going to ask, he thought.

"I had seen her lots of times. We waved when I ran by."

"Oh."

Long silence.

"This time she ran down and flagged me. She asked if I wanted some lemonade."

"Oh."

"Yes. I thought that was nice."

"Yes, it was. Very nice."

Long silence.

"It was just what I needed that day. The lemonade."

"Of course."

Long silence.

"Her name is Luella."

"Oh."

"Yeah."

Long silence.

"She had on shorts and a halter."

"Oh."

"Yeah."

After a moment, he said, "Well, I guess I'd better go to bed."

"All right. Good night."

Short silence.

"She was great, Mom. She asked if I wanted more. More lemonade. I said it would be nice. She went in the house—a little house. She called me. I went in. She said 'come in here.' It was a bedroom, I guess, sorta. Yeah, it was a bedroom. The shades were down. She . . . ah . . ."

Charlotte finally said, "She what?"

"She was naked."

"Oh."

"Yeah."

He went on after a moment. "She was very pretty. That way. I . . . ah . . . She's a senior at the county high school. Her mother works second shift at Thurmond Mills at Oak Grove. Mom, you were right. I like it a lot. I've been running out there every day since then."

"Oh."

Silence.

"Yeah. Mother, she goes crazy. It scared me the first time. But I see it's just the way she is."

"*We* are," Charlotte said.

"Yeah? It's a very strong feeling, isn't it?"

So he *had* learned the enormous power of the senses.

"Yes, Alex. So it is."

"Hummmm. Her father's a drunkard. Her mother ran him off."

"Oh."

"Yeah, I like it a lot. She's different from you. From us. But I like it a lot."

"Alex, if she is good to you, be good to her."

"Oh, sure. I like it so much."

Long silence.

"Alex, contraception?"

"She had one. Some. I think they were her mother's. Or something."

"Oh."

"Yeah."

"Alex."

"Yes."

"Venus's disease."

"What?"

"The goddess. Venus. Venus's disease. Venereal disease. You know about it?"

"Oh yeah. Venus. Yeah. Right. Well, she's really clean and smooth and neat. I . . ."

"You'll take your chances like the rest of the world?"

"I guess so."

They rose together. She kissed him. "I'm glad, Alex. Good night."

"I'm glad too. You were right. Good night, Mom."

Two weeks later. Same time, same place.

"Luella's sister caught us."

"Oh."

"Yeah."

Long silence.

"She was barefooted. She just walked in."

"And?"

"Well," he burst out laughing. "I had to do her too."

She burst out laughing. They laughed and laughed. And laughed.

"I liked that too," he gasped.

Their laughter echoed down Well Street.

During his sophomore year, in the close, bruising game with Kernston, with a fourth quarter score of 0-0, Joe Hudson gambled to try to break it and sent Alex in to return a punt. He set up a return to the left side, and who knows? The kid might fumble, but he's the kind who could get away.

Alex got away. Eighty-two yards he sped, cut back, changed up, turned with the tackling, picked up two blockers and crossed the goal with ten yards' lead on the pursuit. By the time the boy had trotted back to the bench, he had to shed half the grandstand, but most difficult, his beautiful mother and outrageous Uncle Cal. The game ended at 7-0. It was the first victory over the strong Kernston in twelve years.

Thereafter, Charlotte noticed that the telephone became unusually busy. It was always for Alex, football star.

Once, "Alex, was that Fran? She called just before you came in. I'm sorry, dear, I forgot to tell you."

"Oh, I'll call her. No, that was Lou Council. She wanted the history assignment."

"Lou Council?"

"Yeah. Her father's Dr. Council."

Hummm, thought Charlotte.

"Alex, I don't wish to pry, but may I ask one question? Does Mrs. Council know that you and Lou are friends, that she calls you?"

"I don't know. Why?"

"Between you and me?"

"Sure."

"I don't want to taint your opinion of young Louise. I won't will I? It's just that her mother is self-proclaimed social arbiter of this town and has been especially malicious concerning me. I...Look, Alex, I'm a little ashamed for mentioning it. Young Louise is probably a fine young lady. Just forget it, can you?"

"Forgotten. Yeah, Louise seems OK. Like the rest anyway. Forget it. I couldn't be that way."

The hell you couldn't, Charlotte thought. Oh, what exquisite irony. Knock her up, Alex. Knock her up. Charlotte Morton! How easily you slip into bitchiness. Shame. The finest irony would be for Lou to become a really good person.

Alex accepted earned homage with the same detachment that he had accepted gratuitous cruelty. By the end of his sophomore season he was punt and kick-off return man, and he was quarterbacking at least half of each game. He had become a star. Joe Hudson, conservative to the end, had been slow to go to the T-formation, finally had been forced by statistics to the change and with it to the attendant wide-open game. He had to have a quarterback who could move and throw. This six-foot sophomore could do that, could handle the ball as if it were an egg, recognized that he was in charge of the team when he was on the field, and gave orders like they were from Above. *Next year*, Hudson thought, *next year that kid is going to throw on first down*.

A new young track coach had instituted the three mile cross-country high school track program. It was tailor made for the tall, long-legged youth. He and his mother looked at the treasured stop watch. Splendid. But he would fly over hills and creeks, and who would try to beat him had better be as good as the best.

But he also set his sights on a higher goal, the Whitehead Scholarship, the highest academic award offered in the state. Its presentation was based on academic average, interviews, and a senior essay. He finished his second year with an average of ninety-seven, and entered his junior year determined to raise it.

"Oh, c'mon," his mother said. "Both of us know that anything above eighty-five is time wasted which could have been spent at the piano or reading a good book. No teacher is capable of refining an average to within ten points of what you know anyway."

He grinned. "I know. But I'm going to do both."

Ironically, his closest local competitor was Fran Visconti, who shared their cynicism about academic averages, but who nonetheless read throughout the Civil Rights Demonstrations on which she accompanied her father and mother, bringing her body to bear witness while studying Latin verbs with her mind. The rivalry between the two was fierce—contested to the finest detail of petty memorization—and warmly affectionate.

So Alex slept his six hours, read everything in sight, ran, memorized, and—Charlotte suspected—slipped several cheerleaders and other Populars out of their panties while she sat at the piano in the *Stag and Doe*.

He still received no invitations to the homes of the Elect of the town, and snatches of telephone conversations told Charlotte that certain young ladies were deceiving their parents after sundown to be with her son, who took them, enjoyed them—but gave his heart to Francesca, who combined substance with sexuality.

War is not Death's sole employer, only his most sensational. Death will work for anyone: greed, disease, old age, chance—even, some would say, perversion.

Spence was Death's messenger to Charlotte. Suddenly old, bent over a cane, drawn—looking like a caricature of a squirrel, moving in sudden starts—he came in the office. She offered coffee, or a drink.

"Drink," he said.

He took it, holding out the day's newspaper.

"I wanted to tell you so you wouldn't just pick up the paper and read it."

He dropped the paper and took her hand across the desk.

"My dear, your friend Billy is dead. I just noticed it before the issue went out. I'm so sorry."

It was there. Local musician found dead in New York. William Ennis, son of Mr. and Mrs. Howard Ennis of such and such street was found dead last night in the alley behind the *Kings and Queens Club* on such and such street in New York City.

She remembered the *Kings and Queens Club* from her visit with Billy and Bucky. It was a gay bar in the Village. They had taken her there several times, to meet friends and musicians.

The cause of death was thought to be an overdose of drugs. Mr. Ennis was seen leaving the performer's entrance with an

476

unidentified sailor in the U.S. Navy at about two-thirty A.M. The body was found by a sanitation worker at six-forty A.M.

Mr. Ennis was a graduate of the local high school, a veteran, and was a member of the *Bucky's Music* jazz trio, a group which was gaining recognition in the jazz world. The group had recorded such and such albums.

Such and such.

She leaned back in the chair and folded her hands under her chin.

"I'm sorry. Charlotte, I'm so sorry. I know you loved him so."

"Yes," she sighed.

"Drugs, they guess."

"Sure. Why not? He was never at home in earth. Except playing."

"I remember. In your parlor."

She sighed again.

"Oh, Spence. He was so dear and sweet and gifted. And so fragile. Now that it's happened, it seemed foreordained. Where was Billy's place on earth?"

"I'm sorry, Charlotte."

"Thanks, Spence. Thanks so much for coming around to tell me. It was easier coming from you."

She could not reach Bucky. With the aid of a kind New York operator, she finally located Johnny Barbato, a trumpet man with whom she had had a casual affair in New York long ago.

Yes, Johnny said, terrible. But Billy and Bucky had been doing heroin for a year or so now. Lately it had gotten bad. They were living between fixes and gigs. In performance, they were better than ever. Offstage, just drifting. Bucky was in the hospital. Had been for about three weeks. Drying out. He'd go over and see him tonight. Yeah, what a loss. Billy was as good as anybody around. Terrible loss. I'll miss him. Keep in touch, Charlotte. Right. Goodbye.

She called Cal. He was in the field. Susan said she would break it to him and have him call her.

That evening she and Alex and Sybil listened quietly to *Bucky's Music II*. *Cool Drive* was on it too. It was a tighter version than on the first album. They were so good. Billy was so free. Now, so free.

Cal came in and took her in his arms. Sat and listened. He understood. She had taught him to understand.

Oh, Max, she wrote late that night for the first time since her withdrawal, *he was so fragile and dear.* Max understood. *Now he can't be hurt.*

Death wasn't finished. Spence died three weeks later in his bed. She wondered if it wasn't just as well. He had become feeble: even the sharp mind which had wrestled so often with her father, had gone vague.

"Alex, my son, what conversations have been in this room. Oh, Spence, old guardian angel, how to say goodbye to you?"

Death did something easy next. Six weeks later, without even pausing, Death snatched quaint, whimsical, bird-like Elsa Compton. She had been in the hospital making the nurses giggle for three weeks. Death took her, almost as an afterthought, as though he should have done it years ago.

Max's family is gone, Charlotte thought. She walked by the great white house sometimes. Sybil said that Hal Link, Compton's attorney, was paying Martha's salary and that she continued to care for the house. Max was a very rich recluse. Sybil wondered if Max were making decisions or if Hal had provisional instructions. The house looked as it always had, formal, well-kept, uninhabited.

A short stocky man with a powerful Negroid face and a ridiculous moustache had a dream and had begun to tell the nation about it. Some resented his dream, felt threatened, became violent. Some grew into it, up to it. But even after the dull, prosperous years of the bald, smiling, insipid general, nobody could ignore this dream.

Least of all, Dr. Viscounti. His father had been active in the labor movement early in the century, and had tempered his son's social conscience. Dr. Viscounti's radicalism was an informed radicalism. He knew his social and political history. He had established friendships with the faculty at Bascombe College, the underendowed Negro college, and had got himself talked about by teaching one course there. He was a compelling lecturer, a successful organizer. Blacks and long hairs were constantly coming and going from the little house in the college section of the town.

Quickly Dr. Viscounti was labeled a Communist. He was not. Nowhere in the nation was there a man with greater commitment to the Constitution of the United States and Bill of Rights.

"How did they do it?" he would ask rhetorically as Charlotte and Alex and others sat at the modest but delicious Italian table his Irish wife laid before them. "Our ancestors were the refuse of Europe. The undesirables. Criminals, fanatics, opportunists with nothing to lose. How did they do it? Two enormous pieces of luck. They had the great good fortune to feel oppressed. And they found that they had landed in a place endowed like no other with natural resources. The one forced them to action. The other gave them the tools. But those two documents! My God, they may yet work the salvation of mankind!"

To Visconti, America was a rough template of the social masterpiece toward which man had struggled since Egypt developed the first organized state. With intelligence, energy, and compassion it could lead the underdeveloped, oppressed, and misguided peoples of earth into that ultimate masterpiece which would embrace, not despise, the diversity of mankind, would nurture justice and charity, would lead them past narrow nationalism to love of all creation.

The vision he held was fierce and frightening. He had flung himself and his family into the Civil Rights Movement aware that it promised dreadful consequences. Public education would be crippled for years. Incompetents and charlatans would rise to power in the name of equality. There would surely be violence. But he knew that every gain had its cost, and that the American masterpiece would never be realized so long as one segment of the population was excluded.

Alex was a ready disciple. He knew already that the circumstance of one's birth was not a personal achievement. He was a bastard. He had suffered exclusion because of it. He would not have changed his genes, his mother, his circumstances for Savoy or Windsor lineage, but he understood that certain pleasures and opportunities were denied him because of it.

He understood also that skin pigmentation made life a totally different proposition in America.

With his mother's blessing he began to accompany the Viscountis to demonstrations. He was a willing messenger when Dr. Visconti had pamphlets to be distributed. He had a passion for justice.

And a passion for Fran Visconti.

*   *   *

When Alexander Morton, who was to be quarterback for Joe Hudson's championship contending team, reported for practice in his junior year, he was in blue jeans and wearing his hair, his mother's dark cascade of waves, down to his shoulders.

"Have it cut by the time we start heavy equipment drills," Hudson snapped.

"Coach, I'm not going to cut my hair," Alex said calmly.

The hair had become a symbol of allegiance already, as jeans and guitars and pot would become in a year. Alex, full of admiration for Dr. Viscounti and others, was anxious to test his own convictions.

A week later, under the blazing August sun, the team, in pads and helmets, gathered around Hudson. The coach glared around him, spotted Alex. *Now*, he thought. *Cut this down now.* Else you're gonna have a bunch of hippy, Communist reds playing for this high school. Discipline gets tougher enough each year without this!

"Morton, I thought I told you to get your hair cut."

"You did, sir. But I told you that I wasn't going to get it cut."

"What if I told you to either cut it or get cut from the team?"

Alex stood up.

"Coach, I don't want to be a pain. I certainly don't want to be dropped from the team. But I don't believe that you would do that, because the length of my hair doesn't have anything to do with playing football any more than the length of my nose or the color of my eyes. I'm not going to cut my hair. I want to play football, but I'm not going to cut my hair."

"Alex, what if the school board passes a rule saying that no student will be allowed to have hair longer than, say two inches."

"Well, I don't know..." (Actually, Alex *did* know that, at the moment, there were several test cases before the courts. He knew this because Dr. Viscounti tracked every move in the civil rights cause.) "But I doubt if the school board would be so unreasonable as to command students to cut their hair. And I don't think that the courts would allow them to deny a person the right to public education because of long hair. There sure would be a lot of angry girls."

"Not funny." Behind his glare, Hudson was thinking, *I need this kid, and he is not going to back down.* This is the son of Charlotte Morton—and I remember her night on the stage at the variety show. He is her son and he is not going to back down.

"I'm sorry, Mr. Hudson. I don't mean to be wise."

"Well, what if?"

"I'd drop out of school. Coach, I am not going to cut my hair."

"Why?"

"Coach, please. I'm not setting out to be a pain. I want to play football for you. I will do anything you tell me on the field and anything you tell me to do to prepare myself to play. I promise. It's just that this doesn't make any difference. I'll throw, kick, run my heart out for this team. But I'm not going to cut my hair. My reasons are personal. They'd be as . . . curious . . . to you as—as your reasons for wanting me to cut my hair are to me."

"What are those reasons?" Hudson snapped.

"My girl friend likes it long," Alex snapped back. Then, hesitantly, "Some friends and I have agreed to wear our hair long as a symbol—"

"Oh, your girl friend likes it!" Hudson interrupted.

"Yes, sir."

"What about this—symbol business?"

Alex glanced around the faces of the players. No help. His chin came out farther.

"Mr. Hudson, you're not going to embarrass me—and I am not going to cut my hair. I will play the best football I can for you if you want me to. But I am not going to cut my hair."

He sat down again. He was through talking.

"We'll see."

Hudson went to the new, crew cut principal, explaining that there was great danger to the American way of life if kids were to wear their hair long and become radicals. He asked the principal to suggest to the Board of Education that they pass some sort of rule against long hair.

The principal agreed and did as Hudson suggested. The Board of Education agreed. But conservative zeal and gut fear worked at opposites. There *were* cases in the courts. They did not wish to start a 'tempest in a teapot' as one member wittily put it. Besides—perhaps young Morton would be the only one. Perhaps peer pressure would lead him to cut it of his own volition. Several of them remembered Charlotte Morton, his mother, who now played at that motel bar.

Besides—as the assistant principal pointed out—the young student was carrying a 97 plus average and bid fair to be one of the strong hopes for bringing the Whitehead Scholarship to the school.

Better wait and watch was the consensus.

So they waited and watched some two dozen heads of hair grow longer and longer and longer as the school year wore on. Alex Morton ignored criticism and adulation, but he couldn't prevent imitation.

27

DR. Hall continued to drop by the Well Street house at least once a week. He was extremely solicitous.

"Jennings, I'm fine. I'm working. I'm painting as never before. I'm fine. C'mon. Sit. I'll make tea."

"I really haven't got time, Charlotte. Must get back to the office. Charlotte, what about what Reverend Frye said? Have you thought . . . considered? Charlotte, I beg you. Don't disregard this clear message."

"Jennings, please don't press like this. Yes, I promised I would think—and consider. Oh, Jennings, please. We don't have to agree on that to be friends. Come, have tea with me and let me show you my last picture. Will you?"

"Charlotte, please don't work at that place any more. Listen, if it's a matter of money, I can use an office manager. My present manager, mine and Dr. Eason's, is pregnant. We will pay you exactly what you earn there. More! Would you? Would you think about it? It will be so much better, for you and for Alex. Please."

She studied his face. He was her age, but he looked twenty years older. His face was cross-hatched with wrinkles, which looked like dry-point on skin gone so gaunt across the cheeks that the bones shone through. His high forehead bore the same thin markings. The thatch of straw hair was dead with gray. His clothes sagged like last leaves from his limbs, but Charlotte noticed that the knees of his pants were worn shiny. Tall, he had always stooped; now he bent. But his eyes, his eyes blazed like sun-struck crystals from beneath the pouches of dead skin.

"Charlotte, I am concerned with all souls. But your sign was delivered through *me*. It was *my* hand which cast your flesh from you. On that morning, I *felt* God's will in this hand." He thrust his right hand forward, looked at it closely himself, stared at it, touched it with his left hand. "The surge of the Holy Spirit ran in these fingers. Oh Charlotte, at that moment, I knew I was truly His servant, His instrument. Please, let that spirit guide you. Please, I beg you."

For a moment she was horrified. *He looks slightly mad*, she thought. She felt the hairs rise on her neck. *He is killing himself*.

She retreated involuntarily.

"Jennings, have you had lunch? Jennings!—answer me!"

"Well, I... Well, no... But Charlotte..."

"Sit down." It was an order.

Five minutes later, when she returned with tea and a sandwich, she found him in a dead sleep on her couch. She sat for a moment and watched him breathe. *Old friend*, she thought, *your mission is killing you*. She studied his face. She felt again an amazing sensation she had known before. Suddenly, she identified the sensation: *Jennings, I am afraid of you. I love you. I respect you. But I fear you. You are possessed.*

She shook herself out of it, tiptoed to the study and dialed his office. She asked his secretary if his next appointment was critical.

"No, he has to remove stitches from a cut arm. Kid fell off his bicycle."

Charlotte explained that he was asleep, clearly exhausted.

"Oh, yes." the voice said. "I understand completely. Yes. Don't disturb him. Dr. Eason is here and can remove the stitches. Dr. Hall is going to collapse some day. Yes, do let him sleep."

Three hours later she woke him with hot tea, then led him bodily to her table.

"You are going to dine with Alex and me. Hush!—I won't hear of it! You're not going to kill yourself if I can help it. Sit down."

Two days later she made quiche and veal and brilliant salad for Sybil and herself. There was a generous portion left over. She called his office and asked if he were there. He was, he

483

had two more patients to see. She wrapped the food carefully and drove out to the office.

"Oh, Charlotte, how kind. How thoughtful. Bless you."

She ran out. "Sybil's waiting," she lied.

"Dodd Thurmond, you bought this! You paid her to do this."

Charlotte was bristling.

"Of course, my money got the viewing. You don't think Sheila would take you in off the street, do you? But the pictures will hang on their own merit. She swears it—and she had better not lie to me! I give her too much money. I have bought several thousand dollars' worth of paintings from her in the past. And she purchases for me in New York. She is not going to be less than truthful with me—she wouldn't risk it."

Sheila Martin Gallery of Kernston, the only true art gallery in that section of the state, had agreed to exhibit twenty of her paintings and watercolors.

"Look," he said, "Sheila came out and I showed her my *Bromeliad*. In fact, she is going to borrow it to hang in the exhibition—with a tag saying *sold to Mr. Dodd Thurmond*. She was truly taken by it. Then Clifford drove us to the motel and she saw the ones there. We had lunch and she asked me—repeat, she asked me—if you showed and sold. That's the truth."

"Dodd, I'll never lie to you and—"

"Nor I to you. A pact! Never anything but the bare truth." He raised his glass. "To opening day."

"Well, my truthful friend, I, Charlotte Morton...artist...oh yes, Dodd! To opening day!"

Opening day was to be a Monday. Sheila Martin took quarter page ads in the Greensboro, Raleigh, Kernston, and local papers on the preceding Sunday. They reproduced a photograph of *Bromeliad*.

"You bought these ads," Charlotte growled.

"No, I did not," Dodd Thurmond said serenely. "I merely guaranteed. The truth. I swear. Hey, we have a pact! Am I a double-crosser? No. I told Sheila that if she didn't make them on sales, I'd pay for them. Surely that's OK."

On the Sunday afternoon there was a preview party for most-favored customers and the art critics from the three large newspapers.

The reviews were favorable. One read: *Anyone who visits*

Miss Morton's exhibit expecting to see merely pretty flowers is in for a jolt.

All hinted at the 'elemental quality of the paintings.'

The Raleigh review said, *I was forced to ask the silly question of myself if a man, any man, would be capable of these pictures? There is such a primitive aura of fertility, of the concept of Mother Earth, of a universal womb present in them that they seem to contain special knowledge available only to a woman.*

The *Herald* printed all the reviews and photographs of the exhibit.

Dodd Thurmond did not have to make good his guarantee to Sheila Martin. At four hundred dollars an oil, two-hundred-fifty dollars a watercolor, twelve of the pictures had been sold in the first week—and Sheila Martin was telephoning for more.

Charlotte Morton was exultant.

Death had his eye on Calvin Hendricks for years. A hundred times, it would have been easy—Cal did such dumb things, *life* things.

Just the other night Pete McCanless could have shot him, having pulled into the motel parking lot just thirty seconds after said Calvin Hendricks stepped out of a room with Louise Whitley McCanless. It would have been easy for Death then.

There had been thirty-seven times when Cal had been on the motorcycle, knee-walking drunk, flying. It would have been so easy.

Or when the damned fool plunged into Lee Creek after the flood-producing rains only a month ago.

Or it would have been easy to have Coy Trexler blow his brains out. Death could have found a way for that because Coy was scared out of his mind that Cal would carry out the threat he had made. And because Coy, in circling Charlotte Morton's house at night, would frequently find Cal's car there. It wouldn't have been anything at all.

Now, at last, Death set a date. He would cause Cal to approach old Carl Sebastian just when Carl had his shotgun nearby. Right at that moment. It would be easy.

Cal appeared at Charlotte's breakfast table. Over coffee he asked her to drive out to South River with him.

"I've got to talk to old Carl Sebastian again. Stubborn mule. Where's my wallet? Yeah. Look." He handed her a check for eight thousand dollars made out to Sebastian and signed by Sam Culbreath. "For two years right-of-way on his damned cowpath of a road out to the Ferry spit."

He had been raving to her for months about the new summer home development they were building out on the neck that formed Lingle's Ferry. One could reach the site from the end of the Ferry spit by bridge. But in the two years they anticipated for construction, Sam and Cal figured that it would cost them thousands of dollars to take that route with the caravan of trucks that would be going out there daily. They wanted to buy right-of-way from Sebastian, who owned the land completely surrounding the Ferry spit from the direction of the town. Cal said they had been negotiating with Sebastian for six months. They had offered to asphalt the road. Had offered four thousand, then five, then six thousand dollars for right-of-way. Old Sebastian steadfastly refused.

"He don' want them trucks disturbing his cows or hisself," Cal mimicked the river drawl of Sebastian. "Stubborn bastard. I've got to drive out and try to talk him into taking this for use of his lousy road."

"Huh," she chuckled. "I know Carl. He and my father were fishing buddies."

"Listen," Cal said, "grab your bathing suit. Maybe we can take a dip while we're out there. By noon it will be warm enough."

On the way out he muttered. "I think there must be some bad blood between Sam and old Sebastian. Sam won't come out himself. It's crazy as hell that Sebastian won't take money for right-of-way."

"Sebastian doesn't need money, Cal. He's rich as cream. He owned half the South River bank. He and his father before him."

"I know, but Jesus, it'll cost us a fortune to run the trucks out and back over the bridge for two years . . . ah, I'll talk him into this."

The day was warm and brilliant. Deep Indian Summer. She lay her head back in the jouncing pick-up and let the breeze play her hair.

"What's Alex talking these days—state championship? Wow, they're having some season!"

"I hope so. If they can beat Kernston. It's Thomaston this

Friday. He seems to think they can do it. Kernston is the only undefeated team in the Conference."

"Yeah—nobody's come within twenty-one points of them. Alex has really come along. He's a real natural quarterback. He's got the moves, the deception, and a sling shot arm. Hudson laid off the hair, huh? Guess he had to. Alex's picture is all over the sports page."

"Well, he hasn't exactly laid off. He calls Alex a hippie—meaning Commie. Can you imagine the creep? But he's tolerating it."

"Yeah. Good coach—but a creepy man. Hey, you remember swiping the boxing gloves?"

Charlotte laughed.

"Sure. Hudson let us do that. Hey, did you ever take them back?"

"Yeah. He rode me until I did. See?—here's where Sebastian's land begins. Right there along the barbed wire."

It was lovely, green with river growth, and patches of tall loblollies.

"Oh hell. There he is now."

She saw a pick-up truck just inside a gate a hundred yards down the easy road. About twenty yards inside the barbed wire, two men in overalls seemed to wander aimlessly.

Cal pulled up beside the fence, ten yards from the open gate. Sebastian waved his hand in anger, as if telling them to be quiet. He glanced up and saw Culbreath Construction on the side of the truck, then hesitated between following the wanderings of the other men and heading for his own truck.

"That's old Gramp Kern. Sebastian must be planning a well out here."

Gramp Kern was the oldest man in the county. He looked like an ancient, weathered, riverside mimosa, life looted, bending each day closer to the ground and flowing water. Gramp was a dowser. He made his living 'hearing the water' under the ground and 'talking warts and other unnatural growths off' the country people. He was a county institution. At this moment he was wandering about in an ever smaller circle, a two-foot prong from a cherry tree grasped in both hands before him. He was mumbling words that Charlotte and Cal could not hear. Periodically, it appeared that the two prongs would shudder in his hands, sending vibrations throughout his reed-thin frame. He was walking slower and slower.

Sebastian's eyes were darting between the old man, Cal's

truck, and his own truck. He was frantically waving his hand, waving Cal and his truck away, waving him to silence. He hesitated a long time, then he decided. He made a dart for his own pick-up.

"Cal, he's got a shotgun rack in the back of his truck."

"Yeah, I see."

The shotgun was Sebastian's purpose. He grabbed it and scuttled back to Gramp, still waving his warning at Cal.

He and Charlotte sat in the truck waiting.

Finally, the cherry prong took hold of old Gramp and shook him like a sandy towel.

"'Ere," he croaked. "Carl. Right 'ere. Seems she'll be eight to twelve foot under."

He got control of the prong and drove it into the earth.

"Right 'ere," he cackled. "Eight or twelve foot under."

Sebastian shook his head. Then he turned to the fence and Cal's truck.

"Thuh answer's no, Hendricks. Final as death. And I done tole yuh that if'n eny of Culbreath's boys set foot on muh property agin, I'd blow 'em away. I ain't speakin' agin. I'm shootin'."

He turned back to Gramp.

Cal got out of the truck. He took out the check.

"Hey, Carl, just look at this. Just read it. It's yours. Just for right-of-way."

Sebastian didn't even turn.

Cal sidled down to the gate.

"C'mon, Carl. Just look at it. Be reasonable."

He kept moving toward the gate.

Now Sebastian turned toward him. As Cal approached the gate, he put his other hand on the gun.

"Cal," Charlotte breathed.

Cal rounded the gate, still talking.

Charlotte saw Sebastian's thumb draw the hammer.

Cal was still talking, still walking toward the gun, grinning, talking.

She heard, "Oh, cut it, Carl. Eight grand. Yours. To let a few trucks pass."

He was flourishing the check.

"Cal!" Charlotte screamed.

Everything went slow motion. Cal walking, talking, smiling. Sebastian lifting the gun waist high. Cal walking. Not taking it seriously. Talking. Grinning.

"Cal!" she screamed again.

Then the flame dart from the barrels, the tremendous, dull wham! that went the two hundred yards to the river, crossed and came back for many seconds. Echoing.

Both men jerked. Sebastian swayed backward suddenly, a child on a rocking horse. It seemed that Cal was hit at the belt line with a pile driver which could have driven a shaft to the center of earth. His arms and feet flung out in front of him. The eight thousand dollar check fluttered, an aimless butterfly. Surprise flared across his face. He was dead before he hit the ground.

It had been easy for Death. A little time/space manipulation. That's all. Gramp Kern wasn't even needed. Noisy. But easy. Two minutes. Easy.

Neither Alex, her son, nor Sybil, her friend, had ever seen or dreamed the Charlotte Morton before them. They feared for her. Feared her. Feared for Creation. Feared Creation. They wished to believe hysteria. Could not. She had reason. She was alone, as on a tower. Unapproachable. Solitary on that height she had heard a primal whisper that had spiraled among the stars from before Always.

She lay on the couch moaning, keening. Then on her feet, moving to and fro, crouched, sleek and lithe as a splendid leopard, hurling her glass into the fireplace, sweeping a limoges demitasse from the side board, shrieking.

"Stupid, mindless, obscene, brainless waste. I can't bear it—this insane joke, this disgusting, filthy, brainless existence. I don't *want* it! I won't *bear* it! I choose! I won't bear it, another breath! God damned . . . it's God damned! Hell damned! Man damned. Over and over again. Century after century after century. Birth slime. Death slime. Senseless. Mindless!"

She wheeled on a terrified Sybil.

"Shall I wear a new dress for tea this afternoon? Plant some cowslips? Cook a meal? Lie under a man? Write a sonata? Have a son. Earn a living. Build a cathedral!"

She was shrieking.

"Tell me the difference. Tell me. Can you? Shall I get raped! Or get crowned!"

Her voice suddenly dropped to a guttural, coarse rasp that struggled from her chest cavity.

"Listen. Shhhh. Listen, Sybil, can you hear? It comes from far. From beyond the vast blue? Shhh. Can you, Sybil? Hear?

Can you hear ever so softly the mindless, empty, vacant, cackling laughter? Listen, you'll hear. It began before the beginning. Oh, my God and all the blessed angels, what a joke!"

She shrieked again.

"I can't bear it!"

Her tower collapsed, flinging her down to the merely human. To break down sobbing, crumple on the couch, moaning like a wounded animal. Lost. Lost. Face down. Writhing.

To rise, seeking humanity, going to Alex's arms. Sobbing. To Sybil's breast. Sobbing.

Dr. Jennings Hall came in, himself stricken at Cal's loss. He was appalled and frightened at her condition. He tried to comfort. Babbled of God's Will. Begged her to pray.

She turned on him, a fury-ridden bitch.

"Jennings, get out of here with that God damned *offal*," she hissed in his face. "I won't hear it. Any of it. Half the life in this obscene town is gone and you want me to thank God. Never! Damn him. Damn your God. And his mother. And his planet. And his universe. Damn his obscene Creation."

She collapsed again.

He turned to run to his car for a sedative. She leaped from the couch, ran down the walk after him, flung herself into his arms, trembling, her whole frame wracked.

He helped her into the house.

She rolled her head back on the couch.

"Senseless," she moaned. "There's no meaning. It's senseless. Stupid. I'm through with it."

Later, exhausted, she lay on the couch. Alex bent over her, comforting—and comforting himself, for Cal had been his dear friend.

"Mother, he was your lover, wasn't he? I hope he was your lover. You were lover to him, weren't you?"

She was whispering now. "Lover? Yes, lover. He was . . . my playmate, my teddy bear. He was my hero. My strange one. My life force. He was . . . my fast one. Slippery, unaccountable one. My bad boy. My smiling, handsome, perilous, fluent one. I . . ." She laughed softly now. "If there was a . . . he'd laugh his head off at me. He is laughing! At me! Hey, Boobs, what the hell are you doing? Oh, Cal . . . *Cal!*"

By nightfall she was catatonic. Drained, dazed, she spooned Sybil's soup to her mouth. Then she sat.

Later Alex went to her where she sat on the gallery in the moonlight.

"Mother. . . ."

"I'm all right now, Precious. I'm sorry. Don't worry."

"Mother, you won't . . . you won't leave me. Or anything, will you?"

She took his hand.

"Oh. No, son. No. You mean? . . . No. I couldn't leave you. How could I leave you? No. I'm just sitting here, thinking of him. No. I promise. With all my heart. Go to bed. I'm all right. I'm just loving him for the last time."

He went in. To tiptoe and look at her all night.

Incidental. Gratuitous. The same shotgun had killed squirrel, coon, rabbit, partridge.

Yet it was foretold. Achilles, Max and her father had called him.

Achilles, thou shalt . . . a short, but glorious life.

Foretold. You should have been prepared. Cassandra, heed yourself.

But how to prepare for the like of this? She sat and sat and sat. Attending night sounds. Cars going to and fro. A siren in the distance. The moon moved past her.

Oh, Cal!

Immense, towering grief had drained her. She slipped in and out from under thin sleep. Woke shivering. Under sleep again.

Several cars breathed by. She caught the play of lights on the trees. The driver of the white El Dorado murmured to himself in front of the house, *Son of a bitch Hendricks is gone, you cunt.*

Once she felt, half felt, Alex spread a comforter over her. Alex, heir to all this hell.

She could dream Cal free.

Pelean fields are green. Cliffs sheer and white. The sun brilliant unto blinding, quintessentially Grecian. She had to squint. Her father had warned of sunblindness. Take care. Past a lunge of cliff, not far, where the breeze flicked silver through the olive trees, light-vague, unsubstantial—Achilles the Hero? Or Cal? Cal, the careless satyr? Oh, it is Cal! Yes, now he's clear. Naked and gleaming. Oh, how he moves! Running, ah, wrestling with someone. Throwing. Watch! He's throwing something! All grace and power. Effortless. Oh, man. Beautiful man! Sheer delight in motion. Brilliant green the fields. Flanked by olives, ancient, silver-sown, gnarled, like old men! He would never be old. Look at him move. How be old? This man! How he moves! Come to me. Oh, Cal, come to me! Running just . . . to run—running, plunging into clear, sweet water. Breaking, swift and sleek as a dolphin. Heaving clear, breast plates taut, roped belly, coiling thighs, great fluent penis. Now, yes, now flinging himself down to green grass, his head on a girl's breast—Oh, Cal, I have lost my breast!—slipping carelessly into careless sleep, the breeze softly turning his hair. The collonades of the sun on his shining, clean-limbed body. All repose now. One could get sunblindness. I must squint. My father warned me.

Alex's hand was on her hair, her cheek. The morning sun bore through the oaks full on her face, blinding.

"You're very beautiful, Mother," he whispered.

She did not move from under his palm. A rich coffee odor rose to her.

Blanche used to bring me coffee, she thought. *My lost Blanche.*

She kissed her son's fingertips.

"I'm all right, darling. I'm all right."

She was purged. But as long as she lived, she would remember the whisper that she had heard in that moment on grief's tower. She understood that she would never *understand*. Therefore, she would never again fear. And she heard her father's voice over and over: *Expect nothing. Be prepared for joy.*

"You miss him horribly." It was not a question.

"Oh, Dodd, you can't imagine. There are no words. The days are settled now. When Cal was here nothing was ever settled. He was mercurial. He was . . . was possibility."

"You could travel. Take a couple of months off. Go back to Europe."

"No. No, I can't. In two weeks Alex plays Kernston. Both are undefeated. This game will decide. I'm sure the winner will get the votes for State Champion. Imagine . . . our little town the state champion. It's too important to him."

"I know. Dammit, I'm coming to that game."

"Wonderful, Dodd. Do it. Listen, come for dinner. We'll have to eat early. It has to be steak—my football player, you know. And, of course, I have to run to the bar after. You could come too. And, at last, you'll meet the famous Francesca Viscounti. She'll come to dinner too."

"Sounds wonderful."

Dinner was exciting that night. Alex alone remained calm. He left early for the school. Fran was charming, but giddy. Dodd drew spirit from the young people.

"You're different tonight," Charlotte told him on the way to the game.

"Maybe so. I guess it's the kids. I love Fran. Hey, does Alex ever get excited?"

"Sure. He's excited now. But he's got self-control, Dodd. Has to have it. He's had a tough time . . . you know . . . his background thrown in his face. . . ."

Dodd got *into* the game too. And it *was* a game. At half it was 21-21. Alex had thrown for one touchdown and run for one. Both teams scored in the third quarter. The crowd was frenzied. Score tied with four minutes to play, Alex marched them sixty yards, mixing plays expertly. Then on the Kernston sixteen yard line, he threw a down and out pattern, thinking that he had worked that side on the ground enough to draw the defensive back two steps in. But the Kernston back stayed home, intercepted, picked up blocking, and went ninety-six yards for a touchdown.

"Why the hell did you throw that?" Hudson screeched as he trotted off the field.

Alex just shook his head. It had cost them the championship. He looked up into the stands, located his mother, and shrugged.

They got one more series offensively, but Kernston was not about to give.

The night was filled with tears and curses. Hudson was broken. Alex went to him. "I'm sorry, coach. I thought I had run that way enough to draw him in. In fact, he was in for two straight plays. I guess it was dumb. And underthrown. I'm sorry, Mr. Hudson. So sorry. We'll try to get it for you next year."

Charlotte and Dodd waited for him to come home before leaving for the bar. Fran came with them, and she sobbed as they waited.

When he walked in, he was smiling. "Well, here's the goat. Boy, of all times to do it. Any other game we would have had a margin. Oh well."

He comforted Fran. When she wouldn't stop sniffling, he

became firm. "Stop it. It's only a game. Who'll remember in two weeks?"

Shrugging, he went to the piano and started her favorite song, Bob Dylan's *Blowin' in the Wind*.

"Stop sniffling. Come sing to me. Hey, stop it. I love you."

On the way to the bar, Dodd said, "Well, he certainly has perspective."

Football over, Alex ran like a madman. And pored over books on Zen, most of which came from the Viscounti library. He was profoundly interested in mind/control, mind/surrender concepts. And he was not interested in a childish way. He knew there was no magic. But he had made a bad mistake. He had known the moment he had thrown that pass that it was an error: he wanted to know error the moment *before* he threw.

He had his mother on the tennis court as often as the weather allowed, in sweat suits. He wanted the net. He had her fire her best shots at him. He wanted the union of thought and action, not cause then reaction.

"Pallas Athene, be with me," he chanted.

She smiled and fired away. Top spin, cross court, down the lines, handcuffs straight at him, lobs he had to take on the dead run.

He was also experimenting with sleep. A few hours after dinner. Up to run at midnight, to be found sipping milk when she came in from the bar.

And one night when she came in, he handed her a Jack Daniel's and ice.

"Hey, beautiful," he leered. "Are you leading a secret life?"

"What do you mean, handsome?"

"Do you have a lover?"

"No, dammit. I have a son who watches me like a maiden aunt. What do you mean?"

"Well, you see. At least once a week, there's this cat in a long, sleek, white El Dorado convertible who pulls away just when I end run here. For a while I thought he belonged over at the Bensons. But now it seems that he doesn't want me to see him. Soooooo, I think you have a lover."

Her drink was almost to her lips. It stopped there and the ice tinkled her shock. She felt the hair rise electrically at the back of her neck. Then the impulse to nausea.

"Hey," he said. "It's OK—you ought to have a lover."

"No," she forced a smile. "No such luck. El Do convertible? Well, not for me. Do you see him often?"

"At least once a week lately. Like I said, I thought he was at the Bensons. But he's getting fairly obvious. He doesn't want me to see him. Or run up on him."

"I don't know who he is. Listen, Alex, let me know each time you see him, will you? I . . . ah, maybe I should run up to the gallery and flash him, huh? Maybe he's rich and handsome."

Again the impulse to nausea. The demeaning memory of all those Monday nights. The abomination. And she did not want Alex to run up on the car. She remembered the sawed-off shotgun under the dash. She knew Coy's viciousness.

No. She did not want him to run up on Coy Trexler. She did not want her boy to confront him.

"Sure," he said. He rose and kissed her. "Beddy-bye. Have good dreams."

She didn't.

The next day the paper announced that Charlotte Morton's *Nandina*—the new *Nandina*, infested with gaiety—had won best-in-show for watercolors in the Southeastern Art Guild's Annual Contest in Atlanta. Dodd Thurmond had dispatched Clifford to deliver the picture and make the entry.

It was becoming hard for all but the most narrow snob to ignore the Scarlet Lady and her bastard son.

For several weeks after winning the award, Charlotte could not go near paints or brushes or paper. It was as if she feared. The prize signaled to her that she was attempting art, that she was no longer sketching, as her father had tutored her, merely to learn to really *see* things.

Now suddenly her attitude toward painting became different in a way that frightened and attracted at the same time. She realized that if she picked up her brush, she would be attempting to enter a place inhabited by those she revered. "If you have any perspective at all, the arts are the only thing in the world which lasts longer than the blink of an eye," Douglas Morton had drilled into her. "Therefore they are the only thing worth more than a passing notice. What's older than the *Iliad*, the *Odyssey*, the *Book of Job*? Poetry, painting, music, and architecture are where mankind invests his highest gifts. Everything else, politics, religion, finance—and

that pack of fools—are ephermeral trivia, changed
tion every couple of generations. And I include
mere gadgetry—in the arts."

was that she feared to go where she was not worthy.
Keep your head, she thought. *You paint for diversion*. Or *is it*
compulsion? You *had* to paint that Acuba.

And you *are* a woman.

She pondered this. Why were there no women among the
highest rank of writers, painters, sculptors, musicians? No
female Homer, Shakespeare, Rembrandt, Michelangelo, Mozart,
Wren? Strange. Perhaps.

There was talk now of repression, exploitation, role definition. But if genius will out—and, at least, sometimes it will
(Villon writing in such cold that his ink froze, Mozart hurrying through compositions to pay his bills), why haven't *some*
women created great art? Perhaps that other creative force
which guaranteed the race sapped them. Women were different from men. Different. It has nothing to do with equality.
It's *difference*. Both were humans—different capacities? Same
species—but different assignments? The plum and cherry
were both trees. Should the plum be blamed for not bearing
cherries?

Well, this was the Twentieth Century. Woolf, Porter, Wylie,
Welty, McCullers, Rich, Moore had been, or were.

The season moved.

Charlotte's mind moved, searching for new direction, a
new way to grow. She did hundreds of quick-sketch portraits
of everyone who would pause for a moment. She searched for
the 'quality' of Sybil's icy beauty, that aloofness which was
forbidding but could collapse before a surge of generosity.
Dodd, the young man ego-driven to create, populate,
tyrannically dominate an entire town, only to become a child
for the first time, discovering a world he had never known
after the stroke had marred him. God, what he might have
been if... Doc, the keenly tuned intelligence, hung, writhing on his livid social consciousness as surely as if he had run
on a high voltage wire. Alex sat and his finely modeled face
came, but when she attempted to capture the essential
sweetness and sympathy which caused her son to act in
behalf of others, the drawings came out sentimental. She
longed for a chance to try the passion she saw in the face of
Dr. Jennings Hall. Ah, to catch him in a moment of prayer.

But that would require a...

Rembrandt. She returned daily to the folios of his reductions with almost religious awe. If creation required god, surely this man was a god. Or an interpreter of God.

She looked at Cassatt's pictures closely. Fine indeed, but there was nothing to learn that she couldn't learn better elsewhere. But when Dodd presented her with a folio of Georgia O'Keefe reproductions, she was stunned. Dodd had bought them for the massive flowers, thinking that they might give her a new way of looking at them. They did, a powerful new way. But she was struck more by the stark crosses and landscapes—the *Evening Star* series overwhelmed her. This was truly elemental and powerful. What was this Georgia O'Keefe?

Very well. Let's go on the line. It's time to grow. There would be only one more of the botanical series, that would make forty, even. This was to be the last, the one all the others pointed to. And it was a debt she owed.

And the season was right. She did many false starts of the Trailing Arbutus without realizing her purpose. Her purpose was quite simply the flower, the tiny plant which had caused her and Blanche to drop to their knees in wonder and joy. As much as anything else in earth it was symbolic to her of the small, stunning little goodnesses that life sometimes flings in our path—*if one is prepared for joy*. This picture must be surprising—dear, welcome, and durable as life itself.

It seemed that every bird in the planet had come to her yard to sing, chatter, and mate. She listened, and struggled. She sat hours in the yard, sketch pad on her lap, remembering the day Blanche had brought her to this place—brought her to joy.

Alex stretched out beside her, a physics book in his hand. Man had been into space. He was excited.

Summer wore on. She could not quite win. The Arbutus was to be the culmination, the perfection of her botanical effort. It must be *Art!* Form and shading were hers. But the surprise and delight she needed eluded her. I don't *smell it!* She decided to put it aside for a few weeks, then return to it refreshed, using sketches and memory for model. Pondering a new direction to attempt after the Arbutus, she studied the O'Keefe folio daily. She and Alex talked about the pictures. At dinner, they would prop one or another up and look at it as they ate.

*   *   *

...astian's trial for Cal's murder came to court. Along
... Gramp Kern, Charlotte was a principal witness.
... olutely no interest in the proceedings. Whether
...bastian was found guilty made no difference to her.
Cal was dead.

The courtroom was jammed throughout the two-day trial.
Cal had been popular—or, at least, notorious. And it was a
shooting. Hal Link was defense. His course was to discredit
old Gramp Kern and Charlotte in an effort to prove that Cal
had threatened, that Sebastian had acted in self-defense.

He ripped poor Kern apart. When Link finished, the
fabled old dowser was reduced to a senile, superstitious fool
who actually thought he could conjure water from earth and
would soon fill the unemployment lines with doctors because
of his miracle cures of warts, growths, and other disorders.

When Charlotte took the stand she knew that Link was
going to attack her reputation; he had to in order to discredit
her version that Cal had merely approached Sebastian with a
check.

"Miss Morton, you are not married. Is that correct?"

"I am not and never have been."

"You . . . ah . . . you have a son, do you not?"

"I do. Alexander Morton. He is seventeen years old."

"I see."

He cleared his throat. Effect. He straightened his tie.

"Now, Miss Morton, I understand that you work at the
Stag and Doe bar at the *Trailblazer Motel* on the interstate."

"I do."

"Will you describe your duties there."

"I play the piano and sing from nine-thirty until closing."

"And, I believe, dance."

"My duties are to play the piano and sing."

"And dance. At least, according to my information."

"I have danced once."

"*Once*, Miss Morton?"

"Once."

Her answers were rapid and crisp.

"But dancing is not among your regular duties?"

"No."

"Are there other little—how shall I say—chores that you
sometimes perform which are not part of your regular duties?
As the dance was?"

She smiled.

"I cut on my own spotlight when I go to the piano."

"Ah. Now Miss Morton, when you are not at the piano, performing your duties—I assume you take a break periodically—where and how do you spend your time?"

"Clinton, my friend and the head custodian of the motel, has been kind enough to give me a key to his pantry and storeroom. I usually sit in there at his desk and read or sketch. Sometimes I have coffee. Sometimes I have a drink. Sometimes I merely put my feet up on the desk and contemplate the human condition. I have done my nails there. Oh—and I have stopped by the ladies' room on the way to and from the pantry."

"Ah. That seems a complete enough description. Now, Miss Morton, is it true that you sometimes spend all, or part of a night, there at your place of employment, the *Trailblazer Motel*?"

"It is untrue. My back has never touched a bed at the *Trailblazer Motel*."

"Ah. Then I am misinformed."

"You are, Counsel. And I remind you that I am under oath."

"Ah, so you are."

She began to enjoy sparring with Link. She had nothing to lose. Those who relied on hearsay would think the worst of her anyway because it pleased their tiny minds. She scanned the courtroom. It was obviously an event of high drama. Most of the viewers were leaning forward on their seats.

Suddenly she too leaned forward, smiling broadly, and said crisply, "Am I speaking loud enough to be heard in the rear?"

Hal Link laughed. She realized that he too was enjoying it, and that he was so cynical there was no personal malice.

She saw Sybil smile. And there was Pete McCanless, lounging against the wall in the rear. He wouldn't miss this for anything. Then her eyes caught a face which riveted her. Coy Trexler slumped against the wall up close to the bench. She met his eyes directly and held. Cal was dead. She felt a chill. This was the first time she had seen Coy since the abomination.

"Let's return for a moment, Miss Morton, if we may, to the one night that you did dance at the *Stag and Doe*."

"Let's," replied Charlotte, "if it bears on the case and is of interest to our audience."

"I regret to say, Miss Morton, that I was not present that night. However, I have heard several descriptions of your performance. Eyewitness, mind you. All of them agree that it was extremely suggestive."

"Suggestive. Counsel, I'm afraid I will have to ask you to use the language more precisely. Suggestive of what? Lilacs? A flowing brook? Sunset at Cape Sounion? I'm afraid I don't know how to respond."

"Ah, perhaps you are correct. Precision. However, I think that I can come no closer than saying that it was sexually suggestive. Perhaps a dance designed to arouse the libidinous desire of your audience. Perhaps your own description of the dance would be fruitful."

"Ah," she mimicked. "I'm afraid that you have set me a task beyond my poor rhetorical talents. As you must know, Counsel, since you are a cultivated gentleman, not even the most acute dance critic or commentator will attempt to *describe* a dance. It is one of those elusive experiences which must be seen, which can be described only in the most general terms, such as graceful, or clumsy, or sexy. There are many such experiences in life. Words are simply not equal. For instance, Counsel, could you describe the taste of cherry pie in a way that I could never mistake it for anything else? Or the odor of a rose? Of a Rembrandt painting? Or the sensation of an orgasm? Could you, Counsel? That would require a poet of the very first order."

Link smiled in admiration.

"Perhaps," she went on, "I could better demonstrate my dance that night. If the court truly regards this as crucial to the argument, perhaps it will supply music with a driving beat and I will reasonably recreate my dance. A spotlight would help too, of course." She stood in the box and raised her arms on level with her shoulders. "I was a girl—a woman—dancing, probably much as any other woman would dance. One moves ones feet and hips to the rhythm of the music—just so. Perhaps weaves and arcs her body. Turns, as the music dictates. Could you clap a beat, Mr. Link? It would be helpful. No, well. Just so did I dance. Probably using my modest female endowments to whatever advantage the music called out of me." She sat again, half smiling. "Certainly there are those who would, because of a certain mental set, call that sexual. But there are always those. Why, would you believe, Counsel, on occasion I have heard whistles and cat calls issue from certain persons when a girl merely walked down the street, or appeared in a bathing suit? I have heard this. And I declare it fully aware of the burden of the oath I am under."

"Touché, Miss Morton, bravo."

The bench ordered Mr. Link to restrain his questioning to the pertinent.

"You had a close relationship with the deceased, Calvin Hendricks, did you not?"

"I cannot think of a relationship which I have treasured more in my entire life."

"Miss Morton, I am bound to ask this. Were you and Calvin Hendricks lovers?"

She looked him straight in the eye. "We were lovers—of life, of good food, of music, of beauty, of honesty, of many things."

"Ah. Carnal lovers, Miss Morton?"

"Hmmmm, yes. However, we also enjoyed fish."

"Miss Morton, were you and Mr. Hendricks sexual lovers?" asked Link with patient admiration.

"That is none of your business, nor the business of this court." Susan Culbreath Hendricks's face passed through Charlotte's mind. *Fuck you, Link,* she thought.

"Miss Morton, I must remind you that refusal to answer a question could result in a contempt of court citation."

"I do not have contempt for this court. Only for those who measure all human activity, good and evil, in sexual terms. Be that as it may, my answer is and will remain unalterable."

Link nodded. She is Douglas Morton's daughter and she is splendid.

He dropped it. He led her into a description of the shooting.

No, she had never heard Cal say that he intended to hurt or threaten Sebastian. She had heard him refer to Sebastian as an old fool, scarcely an indication that he intended violence to his person. Cal had driven out that morning to offer him a check for right-of-way across his property. She had seen the check. Cal had approached Sebastian with both hands clearly visible, one clasping the check, the other empty. She agreed in every way with the testimony of old Gramp Kern.

She ended with, "It is not my place to decide the guilt or innocence of Mr. Sebastian of murder. But I have decided that like half the mean-minded, bigoted population of this county, he is guilty of the sublime stupidity of riding about a civilized community with a loaded shotgun in case he gets a chance to shoot a squirrel or rabbit or Negro or long hair or anyone else he regards as different and therefore wrongheaded and a threat to his fragile ego."

Link dismissed her. He extended his hand to help her down. She took it and met his eyes.

"You are indeed Doug's daughter," he said.

She nodded.

Sybil joined her in the aisle. She lifted her chin and began the long walk to the door. Coy Trexler had moved to the door.

Her chin went farther out. She fixed her eyes firmly on his. When she drew near, he dropped his eyes. She walked.

Indifferently, she received the news that Carl Sebastian had received eight to fourteen years for manslaughter.

28

AT the piano that night it occurred to her that the Arbutus was a small surprising delight, that its scent was so subtle that one had to bend to it. It was a miniature pleasantry. Miniature? Perhaps that was the word and the key. Perhaps the last of her series should be a miniature. Perhaps there was something in smallness which would dictate to her the meaning she wanted from the composition. Let the subject choose the medium, she thought.

She was impatient throughout the remainder of the evening. Go home, she kept muttering under her breath to the drinkers.

She raced home at closing and worked feverishly throughout the night, bent over her pad. And when she finally went to bed, she thought that she had drafted what she wanted. It was a six-inch by six-inch detailed miniature.

When Sybil woke her at eleven with coffee, she dashed to her 'office' to look at last night's effort. But though it was the best yet, it did not satisfy.

Sybil's chatter intruded as she pondered her problem.

"Charlotte Morton, you are a wonder. You are beginning to win, do you know that?"

"Win? What, Sybil?"

"To win. You are beating this town to its knees. Believe me when I say that there is never a luncheon conversation that does not include at least one allusion to you. And I would bet my life that no family sits at dinner without some mention of you or Alex."

"Win," Charlotte smiled. "Win what? Notice from ninnies who were willing to condemn me and my son, because at seventeen I got pregnant by a boy I loved who was leaving for that insane war. What's to win?"

"Well, in any event, when they speak of you now, it is not with the old self-righteous sneer. It is with genuine respect. Also, they are beginning to link your name with Dodd Thurmond's. Even they are beginning to glimpse the fine irony of one of the richest men in the state patronizing you. Also, the prize. Some are afraid that you will turn out to be a famous artist and they will have missed a chance to name drop."

"Nonsense," Charlotte sniffed, still holding her draft at angles.

"Oh yes. Others fear you. Nothing hurts so much as to realize that someone considers you inconsiderable. But, darling, with some I think you have truly become a sort of alter-conscience. Your values are not theirs, and you are truer to yours than they are to theirs. Well, I think that you have pricked their conscience, at least. And of course, Alex has helped. He is so unique."

"Ah, my boy. He is a true work of art. Well, I hope that Saturday he and I can indeed prick a few consciences. You'll come, won't you Sybil?"

"Of course. Of course."

During the past week, five black children had been killed in a small Alabama town as a result of efforts to integrate the schools. Dr. Viscounti and his colleagues at the Negro college along with some of his students had organized a four-hour vigil beneath the Confederate statue for Saturday afternoon. Charlotte and Alex Morton would be there.

The demonstration was a mild success, and a long bore. Roughly a hundred people, mostly black and white students, participated. They simply gathered, carried placards, sang to a student's guitar. Police were everywhere but there was no trouble beyond a couple of minor traffic jams. Once or twice shouts of "Freaks," "Nigger-lovers," and "Commies" came from passing cars.

In the third hour of the vigil, Charlotte had a revelation. She lay on the grass at the base of the statue. Alex sat beside her, reading aloud passages from a book of physics that was currently always in his hip pocket. He was fascinated by the idea that space was curved, therefore the shortest distance between two points was *not* a straight line. She was half-dozing in the sunlight, when a horn woke her. She looked skyward straight up from the base of the statue. It appeared to her in that moment, that the statue leaned back from her. The base was gigantic, but as her eyes followed it, the whole figure leaned away from her so that the tips of the angel's wings almost bent backward. She swept her eyes over to the Baptist Church tower. The same thing happened. The top of the tower seemed to lean back away from her. She sat upright.

"I'm going over under the trees," she said to Alex.

"I'll come with you."

They walked over to another group of demonstrators sitting on the green under giant oaks and elms. She flopped down near the base of an enormous oak. It too bent away from her, but still flung its canopy of branches over her.

She had it.

"Alex, baby, space is curved. Hooray for space!"

"What?"

"I'll show you when we get home."

When the demonstration broke up, she fairly jogged the three blocks home.

"Hey," Alex protested, "Do you want to race me and Sybil? Or is there a fire?"

"There is a fire. *Inside me!*"

At home she rounded the entrance between the hedge, raced to the triptich of long leaf pines which sheltered the Trailing Arbutus, and flung herself on the ground beneath them.

"Alex," she yelled. "Sybil. Space is curved. I've got my picture."

She bounded into the house.

"Sybil, be a darling and make us dinner. There's chicken. Alex will help, won't you, darling? Please. I don't want this to get away from me. It will be gigantic."

She ran upstairs.

An hour and a half later she yelled down to them, "Come and see. The sketch is made."

Pinned to the wall was a piece of the brown wrapping paper she and her father and Alex had used for the chronological tables, thirty-six inches wide and nearly four feet long. Sketched in black charcoal, it was overpowering.

The right two-thirds of the paper were blocked by the massive trunk of the long-leaf pine which extended straight up for three feet, then bent left and thinned out of sight in the huge, space-covering canopy of branches with their sprays of long needles. The leprous bark of the trunk was detailed almost photographically, to fade at the curve into darkness where the branches broke out against the sky. At bottom the trunk dominated. But there, beneath this mass which churned to heaven, was the gleaming pink chalk she had used on the blossom. In exquisite detail of leaf, flower and cross-section root structure, the tiny, fragile Trailing Arbutus . . . *surprised!*

"My God!" Sybil murmured.

Alex went close, backed up, went close again. Then he seized his mother and swung her around in a giant, mobile bearhug.

He released her.

"Oils," he cried. "This has got to be in oils."

He turned to the other side of the room, grabbed one of the huge strips of prepared canvas.

"This is big enough and it's treated and ready. I'll make the frame tonight and stretch it. You can start tomorrow."

Then he noticed the open O'Keefe folio on the work table. Her massive *Lawrence Tree* was on the top.

He took her hand and they looked at it.

"Yeah," she said.

For the next three weeks she was obsessed with it. She rushed to it first thing when she woke up. Stayed with it most of the day. When her concentration was worn thin she walked in the yard beneath the pines, amid the tiny flowers. Or played the piano. She came home to it from the bar late at night.

When she left the work—the 'office'—she locked the door.

"You're like a squirrel hiding nuts," Alex said. "Why can't I see it?"

"In time, Precious. In time."

Meals were never made.

"Starving your own son is not in keeping with the noble cause of art," he twitted. "I may run away."

Dodd called four times a week, sometimes he had to be content with speaking to Alex.

"She looked tired at the bar last night," he would say.

"I know," Alex said. "Soon, I hope, Mr. Thurmond. I'm getting tired of cooking."

She was not sleeping enough, but she was serene and, strangely, *not* tired. Late at night, after working at the picture, she would stand on the gallery with the stars. The detail work sometimes caused her to seek darkness, but she was determined that every pine needle have its proper track of silver where the sun struck.

One night, leaning against a pillar, breathing the night air before returning to the picture, she heard the steady pad of running footsteps.

She glanced at her watch, illumined by the moon. Three twenty-five!

"That scoundrel," she murmured.

She waited until the steps had padded to the house walk. She could hear the rasping breath and she prepared to bristle and give him hell for running at that hour. But to her surprise, the steps went past the house, turned at the corner and went on.

"Damn him," she said. "It's three-thirty."

She marched huffily into the house, stopped short. Alex's door was closed. Puzzled she tiptoed to the door, silently opened it, and saw that he was in bed, fast asleep.

"Huh," she said softly. "So my son is not the only mad runner in the town."

She didn't know whether to be comforted or alarmed by this fact.

When she told him of it at breakfast, he mused. "Wow, you mean there are two of us. Wonder who it is? Am I in for a surprise next season?"

Twice more that week, late at night she heard the pad of the other runner.

At the height of her obsession, driving herself three, perhaps four days from completion of the picture that she now *knew* was the realization for which she had searched so long, she rushed into the ladies' room at the bar.

"Go home, go home, go home," she muttered aloud to

herself—to her audience—as she stepped out of the way of the closing door. Then stopped short and froze.

From one of the booths she heard sobbing, then a short moan, then more sobbing.

She stood for a moment. The sadness continued.

She stepped to the booth and said quietly, "Are you all right? Can I help in any way?"

A sniff. Then silence.

"Is there anything I can do?" Charlotte said.

"No. I'm all right. Thanks," weakly. Then, "Oh God all mighty, I'll never be all right again."

Charlotte waited a moment, then said, "Easy, dear. Is there any way I can help?"

"Nobody can help. Ever. Ever."

"Now . . . Nothing is that bad. Come out and let me help you straighten up. That will help."

"What do you know?" It was a snarl. "They've found a lump in my breast. They're going to remove my breast. Nobody can help. Oh . . ."

Charlotte stiffened.

She paused a moment. Then spoke softly, "Listen, dear. This is Charlotte. Charlotte Morton, the girl who plays the piano. Listen, because I speak true. It's not the end of the world. I know. I too have lost a breast. I promise. It's not so serious as you think now. I promise."

"Charlotte?"

"Yes."

She heard the latch slide and a distraught woman stepped out and slumped against the door frame.

"Iris. Why, Iris," Charlotte remembered her from school. "Oh, my dear. Come."

She opened her arms and held the sobbing Iris Gordiner.

"They just told me this morning. The biopsy is . . . Oh!"

"Now. Now. It may not be as bad as you think. Iris, don't worry too much about the breast. I have lost one. It's—"

"I know Charlotte," the lost girl wept. "I know about you. I'm a nurse. Operating room. I was there the day you . . . Dr. Hall and I . . ."

"Well, see? It isn't so bad. Truly. I've adjusted. It's—"

"I know. I was there. I didn't think yours needed to be removed. I saw the X-rays. Oh God, I'm so scared. . . . So scared. But, you. Well, Dr. Hall wouldn't talk about it. I said to Tom. That's my husband. There was nothing wrong with you. Bruises. But, Dr. Hall..."

Charlotte stiffened. She lifted Iris's swollen face and stared into her eyes. What...?

Iris's eyes couldn't stay on hers. Tears streamed down her cheeks.

"I told Tom... I tried to find the X-rays the next day, but they weren't there. But I guess... Tom says Dr. Hall knows best. Oh God, I'm so scared. Oh Charlotte..."

She began sobbing again. Charlotte clasped her. Held for dear life.

I don't want to know this, she thought. *Jennings?* I don't want to know.

The two women held.

Finally, Charlotte held her away. "Listen, I've a bottle of Jack Daniel's in the janitor's pantry just across the hall. Fix your face and come over. We'll both take a big slug. Maybe it will help. Will you do that?"

"Yes. Tom's so sweet. He thought a night out would... Yes," she sniffed. "Let me do something to my face."

"The door will be open. Come in. I'm going to pour. So come."

In the lobby hall Charlotte slumped against the door. *Oh Jennings. You did do that, didn't you? Oh my God. A sign. And you were its instrument.*

She staggered into the pantry, poured two shots. Iris came, somewhat collected.

Charlotte raised her glass. "Iris, to being lopsided."

They both forced smiles.

"Oh, Charlotte, thank you so much. I really need it."

"Iris, listen. It's going to be hard. But it really is not the end. My number is listed. If you ever need just to talk, or another shot, call me. Please do. Sometimes it helps just to talk."

"Thank you, Charlotte. Thank you so much. You're not like I thought. You're... well, thanks. I'll go back to poor Tom now."

She forced another smile and left.

Charlotte sat in the little, silent room. Oh Jennings. Jennings, you *are* mad! She rested her head back against the wall, saw the ceiling. Softly heard the whisper she had heard that day when grief had made her see earth as from a solitary tower.

When she went to the piano her fingers were steel. *Cool Drive* leaped from under them.

At home, she went to her room, undressed and looked in the mirror. The great scar.

I've known all along. I felt it. He's crazy, god-eaten. Jennings, the flesh is not evil. Poor Jennings.

She ran her hand across the cavity where her beautiful breast had been, then drew on a sweat shirt and walked out on the gallery. The stars. The other runner padded past in the street. Her hand under the sweat shirt returned to the scar, searching, grieving.

Finally she went to the 'office,' adjusted the flood lights. Looked, her hand still searching, feeling the truncated nerve ends, at the canvas. A shading of the bark just above the tiny flower drew her eye. She backed up. Went close. Leaned. Her hand still pressed to her breast place.

Still looking intently, her free hand darted, fumbling for a palette knife, touched it, took it. Her other hand left grieving, the fingers needed urgently. She leaned over the canvas.

When the sun's shifts fell across the room, she dropped the brush she held, went into her room and fell across the bed.

Two days later, she had Dodd, Sybil and the Viscountis for dinner.

All were deeply affected by the picture. Charlotte was triumphant.

She talked a mile a minute.

"I was tempted to detail only the flower, none of the tree and its foliage. But I thought that would be a cheap way to point up the surprise of the flower beneath all that bulk. As it is, if the surprise is there and delightful, it is also honest."

At bottom she had chosen deep greens which gradually faded into blue at horizon level and finally passed to egg shell at canvas top. The delicate flowers glowed at the pocked, massive tree trunk which drew the eye up to the sky-blotting mass of branches and singing sprays of needles. The tree dominated. The flower surprised.

She drew them all up close and handed Alex a magnifying glass.

"I was a little corny here."

On a tiny, waxen, forest-green leaf, she had stretched one

of the ivory colored veins out into needle fine script which read *blanche*.

"Mother." He hugged her.

"Charlotte, if you can ever bear to sell it, I'll pay you anything you ask for it."

"Dodd, I'll give it to you one day, but I do want to keep it for a while. Though I don't deny I'm glad it's finished."

"I'm very proud of you, Mother, but I'm bound to ask if this means that I can resume eating regularly again?"

"It does, wretched boy."

Three nights later when she got home from the bar, Alex was lounged in a chair in the parlor still wearing his running shorts, sneakers, and sweat shirt. He was drinking a glass of milk.

"Hi," he said. "Hey, I met the other runner tonight."

"Oh yeah?"

"Yeah. He's pretty good. I had run down to the high school track—it's kinda spooky and silent and great at night. I go there sometimes. Anyway he picked me up on the last lap and followed me into the street. Kinda dogged me for half a mile. Then I decided to turn it on for the last mile and he stayed with me."

"Who is he?"

"I don't know. It's kind of a thing with runners. You might nod. But you don't speak. You're too busy breathing. I don't know who he is. He had on some kind of mask thing across his mouth. I wonder if it is some kind of breathing device. I never saw anything like it before. And his breathing was really loud and husky, maybe a little whistle. But he was pretty good."

"Mask? Alex, did you say mask?" She was standing.

"Yeah. Like a surgeon's mask. I just glimpsed it once under a street light."

She stood frozen for a moment, then turned and ran out the door and onto the porch.

"Hey, Mom."

She stood on the porch for a moment. Then she skipped down the steps and out to the sidewalk. She turned up the street and ran all the way down the block.

She stopped suddenly. There was a light on upstairs in the Compton house.

* * *

"Charlotte, guess what?" Sybil panted as she raced into the dining room where Charlotte sat over morning coffee.

"Max is home."

"Yes, how did you know? Has he...?"

"Alex and he are already old running buddies."

"What?"

Charlotte told her about last night.

"I met Martha this morning. He's been back ten days. She saw him once. Just once. He had on a mask. He can talk, but she says it's difficult to understand. He leaves her notes each morning. Things to do. Then stays in his room all day. Poor man."

"Yes. Yes! I don't know whether to try to contact him or not."

"Hum. How do you feel, Charlotte? Now?"

"It's dead, Sybil. I think. No, I don't think of him any more. That way."

When Alex came down, she took his arm and led him out into the yard under the great long leaf pines, and softly told him that his father was one hundred yards away, that he was the 'other runner.' He turned his eyes in the direction of the Compton house.

"No," she said. "We must wait for him. He will come to us—if he can."

Alex and his father met, ran together, half a dozen times that summer.

"I'd like to speak to him, or something," he said. "Gee, it's really strange. Mom, are you absolutely sure he knows who I am?"

"Yes, Alex, I'm sure. Son, I don't suppose we can imagine how dreadful his life has been. Listen, I lost a breast years ago. Yet I still find that I am very self-conscious when I select a blouse, or a sweater. Especially in summer. Can you imagine what it must be like having lost part of your face? Think! What must eating be like for him?"

"It's so cruel, isn't it, Mom?"

"Yes, darling. It is so cruel. So strange—for a place called Iwo Jima. Who even remembers that place now?"

"From now on I'm going to nod to him. Or wave."

"Do, son. Do."

After a few weeks of the new school year, Alex reported to his mother that the kids were talking about The Freak of Well Street.

*   *   *

For Alex the new school year began triumphantly both on the football field and academically. As Cal and Coach Hudson had foreseen, he developed into the consummate high school quarterback. He could throw, kick, scramble, command a team, and utilize the whole field. The opposition was not within fourteen points of them in the first games. Hudson could smell the championship banquet.

He never tasted it. He had the team, but the crown was sacrificed to bigotry. Local Black action groups began to agitate for use of the high school mini-stadium for their games on Saturday afternoons—instead of the poorly kept, unbleachered field at their own high school. By the sixth scheduled game, their petition was before the school board. It became a *cause celebre*.

Hudson's passion drove him to rave.

". . . and they want us to let a bunch of niggers use our field, chewing up the turf, which is in bad enough condition, for that kind of back-lot football. Next thing, they'll want to use our showers and dressing rooms."

Alex, tutored and infected by Dr. Viscounti, driven by his passion, rose and objected:

"Coach, we play on Friday nights. What difference does it make if they play on Saturday afternoons? Have you seen that field they play on? It's like bald granite. My gosh, I wouldn't want to get tackled on that packed red clay. What difference does it make?"

His shoulder-long hair shone in the autumn sunlight as he spoke. Hudson should have realized that the symbol had substance under it.

Alex and Fran Viscounti sought and obtained permission to address the Student Council to urge a petition to the school board to grant the black high school permission to play on the field.

Both were eloquent and passionate. Their request was voted down.

Letters to the editor appeared daily in the paper. Two were by Dr. Buonocorso Viscounti, Yankee *émigré* to the college. No one in the city was ignorant of the conflict over the one hundred by fifty-yard piece of city-owned property for which all citizens paid taxes.

On the Wednesday night before the Thomaston game, the school board, in closed session, voted unanimously to deny the black request—and allocated funds to build a grandstand and refurbish the athletic field at the black high school over the coming summer.

Fran called the next morning. "You heard the board decision?"

"Yes."

For Alex, that night was a moment of truth. As Charlotte was about to leave for the bar, he said, "Could I use the Packard tonight? Would you mind taking a taxi to and from the bar. It's important. I want to ride out and talk to Doc Viscounti for a while. Hey, Mom, when are we going to get a new car anyway? We've got the money, haven't we? Hey, how old is the Packard anyway?"

Car? she thought. *He isn't thinking about cars.*

"We'll get a new car when you can find a new one with leather upholstery and a wood interior as beautiful as the Packard. Are you going to do what I think you're going to do?"

When he didn't answer, she took his hand. "You're going to do it, aren't you?"

"I think so. I'm sorry for you—you don't need this. And, Mom, it could get rough. You know how seriously this town takes their football team."

"I need you—and this is entirely you. I love you, son."

He called the bar at eleven and asked that she phone him at her break.

"I called Hudson from Doc Viscounti's. That way he can at least call Jerry and have him ready to play. He said a lot of bad things. Traitor, and all that. He even slipped and called me a nigger-lover. But I did it."

"I love you, son."

"I counted on that. Wow, I'm scared for tomorrow to come. Listen, I'll pick you up at one-thirty. I can't sleep anyway."

"I do love you, son."

Standing together on the gallery at two o'clock, they heard the other runner pad by in the silence.

Before classes that Friday morning, Alex walked into the athletic office carrying his equipment. Hudson was sitting at the desk. Neither spoke. It had all been said the night before. Alex placed the equipment on the desk and walked out.

Before the first period was over, everyone in the school

knew. All that day, not a single student or teacher spoke to him. Fran held his hand as they walked between classes.

Home, he answered the telephone all afternoon, heard threats, hatred, and a few pleas. Between them he got a call he would remember the rest of his life.

"Hello, Mr. Morton? Mr. Alexander Morton?" the voice had a broad Negro intonation.

"Yes."

"This is Donald Cleveland. I'm the captain of the *other* high school football team."

"Oh, sure, Cleveland. Yeah."

"Listen, I'm calling for all the guys on our team. We want to just say thanks and, man, you sure got a set of balls."

"Thanks, Cleveland. Thanks, Donald. A lot."

"Whatever it's worth, you sure got our respect."

"Thanks. Donald, I've just got to live with myself. Hey. I'm putting this phone call in the bank. To use when I need it."

"You're a good man, Alex. A good man."

The afternoon paper reported that the team would go on the field with the second-string quarterback leading them. Alex Morton, first-string quarterback, gave as his reason for quitting the team the recent school board decision to deny the Prince High School team the use of the stadium for their games.

The game was a disaster. They lost 24-0. They simply had no offense without him.

All night the telephone rang hatred. All night cars rode by blowing horns, occupants yelling hatred. "Traitor. Nigger-lover. Bastard. Bastard traitor."

Beer bottles were thrown. Eggs peppered the house.

Alex and Fran stood on the gallery, listening.

In deep night the pad of a runner's shoes caused them to clasp hands.

His mother remembered her nights of shouts, taunts, beer bottles, fear. The next morning at breakfast she lifted his chin with her palm.

"C'mon, let's take it together. You've got five minutes to dress and help me select a new car."

She and he strode into the showroom, walked around the gleaming Thunderbird that was the centerpiece.

"Like it?" she asked.

"Yeah."

Pete McCanless looked up from his coffee, saw the two, went blank and slack-jawed.

"Mr. McCanless, is that car sold?"

She pointed out into the showroom.

"Huh? No. No, it isn't!"

She took out her checkbook.

"How much?"

He told her and she wrote out the check.

"Road ready before closing this afternoon?"

"Huh? Yeah, I guess. Sure."

"My son here, Alexander, will pick it up—five o'clock?"

"Yeah," he controlled his astonishment enough to rise. "Sure. Yeah, you'll love it. It's—"

"It's paid for."

They walked out.

In a week, both doors of the beautiful machine had *nigger lover* scratched on them. Charlotte thought of filling in the scratches with silver paint. But she knew that with Alex driving it, that could be dangerous. Instead, she cut down twenty feet of the beautiful hedge around the tennis court and built a two-car garage. The grand old Packard would have a proper nest too.

She had the Thunderbird doors repainted—not by Coy Trexler.

The paper was filled with letters to the editor damning the quarterback who had deserted his team and cost them the championship. Spence's old paper took no editorial position.

Dodd read the letters and warned, "Listen, take this seriously. Somebody could take a shot at him. Remember the car."

"I know, Dodd. I know. But he's in the house before dark. He drives nowhere but to the Viscountis and back."

"Listen, maybe I'll pull one of the mill guards off the third shift and send him up to your house."

"Oh, Dodd, really. Do you think it's that bad? He's still a boy. It was only a damned football game."

"It's games. Plural. And a championship. I tell you, someone could take a shot at him. Some of these people simply cannot let him go on. Can't let him live. He's walking evidence of their meanness."

"Oh God, you frighten me. But I cannot put him in a cage." Time passed. Hatred did not.

She wasn't surprised, but she was furious when in January

Alex told her casually, "Mom, I wasn't nominated for the Whitehead Scholarship. Neither was Fran."

Her rage began to mount. She had read his essay and it was splendid. As was Fran's. Alex had written a local history of slavery; Fran had written about the American labor movement. Charlotte knew that both of them had had good interviews with the faculty scholarship committees. Both were confident, intelligent, articulate. But the only part of the competition which was documented was the academic average. And he and Fran were the only students in the school carrying an average of over 97 for the four years.

"I will go to that school and raise holy hell," Charlotte snarled.

"No," he shrugged. "It wouldn't do any good, Mom. Our averages stand for themselves. But the rest is subjective. How could you attack the interview or essay judgment? Let it go."

"But you worked so hard, darling. God, it is so clearly political. Especially, since neither you nor Fran was nominated."

She talked to Dr. Visconti about it. He was in a towering Mediterannean rage. She knew that Doc and his family could have used the financial aid the scholarship would have brought Fran. But he agreed with Alex that nothing could be done.

"The dwarfs win again," he said philosophically.

29

THE same people, in a different place, wearing different faces, broke his skull that spring in an Alabama town she had never heard of.

It was to have been a one-week demonstration, following the burning of a Negro church in Denton, Alabama. A massive group of activitists, including engineers and carpenters, was assembled for the reconstruction of the destroyed building. Organizers hoped that, with a large work force, the simple architectural plan could be completed in a single week. All the material and equipment had been stockpiled.

Alex and Fran stayed out of school that Friday and Dr.

Viscounti drove the whole family, with tent, clothing and food, the several hundred miles on Thursday night.

Charlotte was called from the piano at eleven-thirty Friday night. Fran tried to tell her, became hysterical. Doc took the phone.

"Charlotte—oh, Charlotte! He had run into town to get Eileen some cigarettes. She had either forgotten to pack them or someone hooked them. He left about sundown. We know he bought the cigarettes in the local poolroom—Spratt's Poolroom. When he didn't return and didn't return, a group of us went looking for him. A couple of hours ago we found him in an alley about a block from the poolroom there—in Denton. He's badly beaten. Char, he's badly beaten. Char, he's unconscious. No . . . no, we don't know yet. They haven't completed the examination. Yes, we are in the hospital in Vadelia—about eighteen miles from Denton. Oh, Charlotte, I'm . . . Yes . . . we'll be here. Yes, we'll wait."

It didn't register. She walked calmly to Dodd's table and told him. He summoned Clifford. He ordered him to drive her to Vadelia, Alabama. To stay with her every moment.

Nothing registered.

"Clifford, if you let her out of your sight for one moment, you'll never work again. Ah, forgive me, Clifford. I'm . . . I trust you perfectly. Care for her, Clifford." He called him back. "Clifford, take the revolver from the compartment. Keep it with you."

Charlottte did not speak during the four-hour drive. The hospital, a sprawling single story clapboard building in a pine grove, seemed a white ship cruising the dark night of Vadelia, Alabama. Two state patrol cars, colored lights twirling importantly, were in the parking lot.

Fran and Doc ran across the lobby to her. She searched Doc's face.

He simply shook his head. "He's still unconscious."

"I'm Dr. Sykes." The young man in white extended his hand and looked at her over his glasses.

Her eyes went to him. He was the one.

He led her into a small office, passed his hand lightly over her shoulder as he took the chair opposite her.

"I simply cannot tell yet, Mrs. Morton." He spoke gently. "Let me explain. His whole body has been severely traumatized. Every area is bruised. There are two broken ribs. I suppose every organ is at least bruised. However, insofar as we can tell now, there's no serious injury there. Insofar as we can tell now—no hemorrhage, or . . . yet . . ."

The intensity of her eyes distracted him. He moved from under her gaze and poured coffee. Returned.

"Mrs. Morton, it is the head that troubles me."

Her gaze narrowed, became steel. *The head!*

He dropped his eyes.

"He is unconscious. There are multiple fractures. We know this. We are capable of excellent X-Rays here—unlikely as it may appear. Our new machine was placed only last month. Government grant."

Christ, he thought. *Is she in shock? Those eyes are . . .*

"This is not crucial, however," he was talking compulsively under her gaze. "The brain, Mrs. Morton, is—you may know this—is not fastened securely to the skull. It is suspended in tissue—for protection. The skull can be fractured without serious damage to the brain. We call that tissue meninges. It's soft and spongy. It protects. Have I made myself clear?"

She's in shock. Or mad, he thought. He turned his eyes away. Took his coffee.

"More coffee, Mrs. . . . ?" *She hasn't touched it*, he thought.

"Fracture does not necessarily indicate serious trauma. Or permanent damage. The brain can—in a sense—bounce back and forth inside the skull. Frequently without damage. Without serious damage. Do you understand, Mrs. Morton?"

She did not answer. She took his hand. Her grip had the strength of possession. *Jesus*, he thought.

"Are you all right, Mrs. Morton?"

"May I see him?"

"Yes. Of course." He placed his other hand where hers was burning him. "Let me tell you about it, so you will understand what you see—and not be alarmed. Mrs. Morton—if it will help you to know—I contributed to the Denton church reconstruction fund. I . . . ."

Her face loosened for a moment. She nodded—once. She pressed his hand.

"They clearly left him for dead. He was severely beaten. There must have been several of them."

The steel returned to her gaze.

"His nose is broken. That's nothing. There's a bandage over the left side of the face. Someone apparently struck at him and nearly missed. The tip, or end, of the weapon caught his forehead and cut from the hair line down to the corner of the mouth—it snagged the eyelid, and tore it on the way. So—the bandage. And the nose—the swelling and discoloration. But these things are not serious, Mrs. Morton. I closed the wound quite successfully, I think. There will be a scar, but nothing terrible, nothing that can't be virtually erased by plastic surgery later—you know the capabilities of cosmetic surgery?"

Charlotte sighed. Her first truly human reaction. Yes, she did know about plastic surgery.

"So none of this is important really. Don't be alarmed by all the paraphernalia."

She nodded.

"The continuing coma is troublesome. Troublesome because it is difficult to assess damage. Now we have the scans. We have begun a cold pack series hoping to arrest, or even prevent, damage. There is a tube. It's only glucose to assure sufficient nutrition to the brain. Don't be alarmed by these things."

She nodded.

She was not alarmed. The doctor watched as she entered the room, stood for a moment beside the bed. Then she leaned over her son's battered and bandaged face and kissed the cheek which was exposed, sat beside the bed, held his hand, waited. She was not alarmed. For six days thereafter the young doctor watched the profound patience with which this mother sat beside her son, waiting.

Next morning Sybil drove down and joined her, tried to force feed, force her to rest in the motel rooms Clifford had taken. Sybil, like the young doctor, began to realize that Charlotte seemed no longer to depend on food—or drink or sun. Could perhaps have gone without. Showed neither love, nor grief, nor hate, nor sympathy. She was patience. She was awaiting a decision which emotion could not alter.

To be near her was unbearable. Fran and Doc came each evening from the church construction site. Came for hope and sympathy. Left soon. Left, unable to give or take comfort.

Sybil came, left in moments, was drawn back, driven away, brought food, pulled her to the motel for a bath and nap, followed her back to the room where the decision was being made.

The young doctor hovered in his duty, could not take his eyes from her, could not bear to look into her eyes.

For six days, Charlotte Morton was like clasped hands resting on a lap.

And six nights.

In deep night, her own breathing set by the rhythms of her son's breathing, she would silently move past Clifford dozing on a chair in the corridor, walk across the deserted hospital lobby, across the white-lined parking lot, into the moonlit pine grove which surrounded the white building, and stand. Merely stand. Breathing. Under moon and stars.

For six days, Charlotte Morton knew what God knows, was splayed on the Great Wheel, suspended above action, listening to the Great Silence. Neither expecting, nor—it seemed—desiring. Waiting. She touched her palms to the trunk of the tall pines and felt life throb in them, felt the press of centuries against their fall, the earth-change beneath her palm, felt the thread-like fossil of the tiny spider in the crystals, the filigree leaf the thousand thousand years petrified into the flood-tempered, ice-tempered, heat-tempered trunk of the great tree.

Knew that many ingenious lovely things had been. That many more would come. Or would not.

Knew that all was foretold and unknowable. Knew patience. *The* Patience.

The sixth night broke her down to human. Standing among the pines, she began to tremble. Tears streaked her cheeks.

"I love him so much," she said. "He is what I have. I love him so much. I, and my kind, *can love.*"

She was speaking to the stars which did not know of him. Or her.

Powerful trembling took her. Clifford, who had followed, rushed from the edge of the parking lot into the pines and led her back to the hospital.

He drove her to the motel where she sobbed in Sybil's arms for an hour, and, at last, slept.

The next morning she asked Clifford to drive her to Denton, Alabama. He glanced at Sybil, who rose to join them. Charlotte pressed her back into the chair beside the bed, walked from the room to the car, waited for Clifford.

She told him to park at the edge of the tiny, four-block-square town. He pulled the Mercedes into a slot in front of a shabby service station and held the door for her. Then he followed her as she walked the streets of the heat-tormented, dusty, depressed town. Up and down the street he followed her, walking through the dead air, looking into the lifeless eyes of the townspeople as they went about the business of shopping, trading, loitering.

She was beautiful and otherworldly as she walked with her stately gait beneath the rickety tin canopy which shielded the walk of the main street from the towering sun. She paused, turned, watched as a flat bed wagon pulled by a dead-tired mule shambled down the street, holding up the few dusty automobiles and pick-up trucks. People, the dead-eyed passersby and loiterers, looked at her. Did not meet her eye.

These were the humans who had beaten her son.

Clifford followed her, stiff in his black uniform.

She looked out the end of the street, to shacks, past them to cleared bull tallow fields, past them to loblolly pines, past them to the vast blue.

She retraced her steps. She entered the hardware store.

"Give me some money," she said to her guardian.

He nervously gave her some bills.

She bought a small .32 calibre revolver, some ammunition, stood before the sullen store owner and customers, loaded it, and dropped it into her purse.

Outside, "Miss Charlotte, what . . .?" Clifford began.

Then he fell in behind her as she crossed the street and entered Spratt's Poolroom. Three soda drinkers and the old bent rack boy looked up expressionless, motionless as this tall apparition entered the door. Clifford stood close behind her. He feared her.

After a minute of absolute silence, the ancient rack boy croaked, "Ladies don' usually come in 'ere."

She didn't even look at him. Finally she walked to one of the high stools which lined the walls, stepped up on it and sat, expressionless. Clifford took up a position ten feet away, standing, arms crossed, leaning against the wall.

She did not speak or move all day. Men began to come in, men in overalls, jeans, khakis, men in old plaid shirts; dirty, sweat-stained, old white shirts; dirty, sweat-browned, t-shirts. Men lean and hungry looking with dirty nails; men with short stubby legs and no waists and darting piggy eyes set too close together; red-faced men, some lame, several using canes, some in sweat-stained felt hats, brown mostly, or gray, or straw hats pulled down over their eyes, or pushed high on their sunburned foreheads; unshaven, many with tobacco juice clotted at the corners of their mouths, drooling; one with six fingers on each hand; all with greasy faces, a few already drunk; slack-jawed, aimless men wanting to shoot a little pool and talk of them yankee sons of bitches camped outside their town helping the niggers, and the yankee son of a bitch who got his brains beat out t'other night; wanting to boast how they'd kill them sons of bitches, how one or six of them had near kilt one of them sons of bitches. They wanted this, while their women bought the grits, and coffee, and dry goods.

But there was this noble, elegant, expressionless vision sitting perfectly erect against the wall in their poolroom and her eyes bored into them and they couldn't very well have their say in her presence. Not very well. Now and then a couple of young mean-looking swaggerers ventured a couple of games of pool, but they found that for all their swagger they could not play very well beneath the glare of the coals that were her eyes. And it was too silent, too quiet. Her eyes caused that. A couple of them laughed too loud, and cursed some, but it didn't work. Each time some of them tried to shoot pool or get a conversation going over beer, it faded. This woman's face, the enormous distance in her eyes, would not abide their lives. She looked like the marble-face of Justice in front of the Federal Court House in Montgomery. Two or three of them had been there. They had seen the statue. She reminded them of that statue.

Business was terrible that day in the poolroom. It should have been a good day, all the excitement, niggers and yankees in town, but it was terrible. Many people came in, tried to stay, drink a coke or beer, swap things, get some kerosene which was sold in the back, but the awful presence sitting high against the wall in their poolroom ruined it, ruined the week which always ended here. They came and stopped five feet inside the door. Her eyes met theirs, burned them out, caused them to drop their gaze to their scuffed brogans there on the tobacco-stained floor. They were like a pack of hounds. Something was strange here in an accustomed place. They could not get used to her smell.

Eight times that day the sheriff came into the poolroom wearing his sweat-stained khakis and sweat-stained felt, broad-brimmed hat, wearing his five pointed star, wearing his brutal, big-belted holster and huge revolver with which he had shot dead two niggers.

"Look, mam, this here ain't no place fer. . . ."

She didn't acknowledge his existence.

Three times, lean young state troopers came with him. They would just step inside the door, look at her for a moment. Then met by her eyes, look around the room, saunter out.

Clifford quietly suggested food to her several times that day. She did not even look at him.

At four-thirty, Fran's slight figure wavered in the doorway, silhouetted by the brilliant sun. She hung there for a moment, searching, accustoming her eyes. She saw Clifford, ran to him, clasped his arm. Then Charlotte. Ran to her. Embraced her, whispered between sobs, "He's come out of it. Sybil just called. He'll be all right."

Charlotte closed her eyes, lifted her head, held her breath for a moment, then sighed. She and Fran held and held and held. Tears came. Her hand went out behind Fran to Clifford, who took it.

The decision had been made. It was in her favor. She thought of tall pines in deep night.

At last, elected, blesséd, she rose and, followed by Clifford and Fran, walked, with that way of walking, out into the glare of the merciless sun.

At least fifty people were gathered outside the entrance. Some had been there for hours for this event, chewing tobacco, speaking in low tones. They fell away when this hard, brilliant, fearful presence walked through them, fell away, stealing glances at that face which held neither pity, nor grief, nor anger, which held nothing—a terrible nothingness.

Clifford followed her, opened the car door and stood beside it. She turned and faced the crowd, slowly traversed the feral-eyed, mangy faces that surrounded her from a respectable distance. Then she reached into her bag, with thumb and forefinger took the small revolver and dropped it into the dust at her feet, and entered the huge automobile. None of the crowd moved until the great shining machine had passed out of their town and sight and lives.

Alex smiled up at her weakly.

"It hurts," he whispered. "Even smiling hurts."

"Do nothing. Lie. Rest. Sleep. Darling, I love you so much. Live. Live. My darling."

He slipped in and out of sleep for two days. She sat by him. On orders, she wakened him every hour to be sure it was sleep, not coma. It was sleep.

She went slack. She cried. Tears simply came. Sitting by his bed. In Sybil's arms, or Fran's. With Dr. Sykes, who didn't know what to do. Twice at a table in the Vadelia Motel restaurant where she, Sybil, Fran, Doc, Eileen, Clifford, and Dr. Sykes held a celebration banquet—a near-normal meal—on the second night after the decision.

In late night, she walked out among the pines she knew from her vigil.

"I don't understand," she said, again to the stars, to nothingness. "I don't understand. But I'm so glad I cry half the time."

By day she sat smiling at her son.

Alex recovered rapidly. Splitting headaches almost out of reach of the pills. Aching ribs. Every province of his body flashed a charge of pain when he moved, but he had slept through the worst.

Vertigo made the first steps hazardous. When it persisted Dr. Sykes was concerned. There was an inner ear clinic at the University Hospital at Kernston, only forty miles from home. The Cawthorne-Cooksey muscle and balance exercises should begin as soon as possible, in case the condition was lasting. Dr. Sykes insisted on the transfer.

A day later, the vertigo diminished. Another day and it passed completely. However, a week's observation at University Hospital was advisable.

Dodd Thurmond made ambulance and accommodation arrangements. On Friday, Alex and Charlotte made the trip under the flashing alarm lights of the ambulance.

As they pulled away from the Vadelia hospital, she kissed her hand to young Dr. Sykes. And looked past him to the pine grove where one could stand in silence at night.

When she returned to the bar the next night, Saturday night, her beauty was stirring. She was woman perfected: Pallas Athene. Her smile was surely touched with a Gioconda elusiveness.

Piano, song, vision were inseparable. Her first set was starkly edited, spare, the bone beneath the flesh of *Down*

524

and Out gleamed. *Body and Soul* was sexual unto sin. *Cool Drive* vivid. *Take the A Train* joyous.

After the first set she walked around the room, took hands and welcomes. Met Pete McCanless eye to eye with an oriental smile, passed as his leer moved to awe.

She sat at Dodd's table, took a Jack Daniel's, leaned and whispered to his ear, "I could not love you more if we were children playing on a beach."

She kissed Sybil and clasped her hand.

Nick hopped around, wanting to do something for her. There was nothing. All manner of thing was well.

At two-thirty when the room finally emptied, she and Gail sat alone and shared coffee. Gail told her of the new man in her life.

When she stepped out into the misty soft summer rain of the night, Charlotte embraced the slight girl. "Have luck, Gail. Good night."

When she walked around the corner of the motel office and into the parking lot glare, she saw the long sleek gleaming nose of a white Eldorado sticking out of a slip between two other cars. She stopped dead in her tracks in the middle of the parking lot. She stood for a moment with her hands folded across her breasts. Only the small sounds of the soft rain.

Slowly, with that way of walking, she moved out. She came before the car and wheeled, facing the wide hood and rain dappled windshield. She folded her hands across her breasts and stood motionless.

Sixty second tableau. Rain. Car. Erect woman.

Suddenly, the lights of the Eldorado flashed on, blinding. She stood. The engine snarled. She stood. The gears snapped in. She stood, staring across the gleaming white hood. The tableau. Her long shadow flung back, lost in the rain. Erect. Daring.

The dare was not taken.

She threw her head back, hair to the rain, and laughed.

Then she turned her back slowly on the glaring lights, struck the stately gait across the parking lot, opened her car door, got in, drove.

She drove out of the rain by the time she reached Well Street. Mist hung in insubstantial dragon's breath about the street lamps. She swung the Packard into the garage, swept her hand along the Thunderbird flank, walked across the damp lawn to the front of the house.

She had climbed two steps when a lovely sin tempted her. She put her purse on the step and walked to the stand of long leaf pines at the corner of the yard. She kicked off her shoes. She walked lightly, bending over, nostrils quivering. The scent rose to her. She knelt.

She plucked one Arbutus blossom, carried it to her nose, and walked dreamily to the house. Upstairs, she wandered the gallery, holding the precious flower, then stood in the silent mist.

Small water dripped from the roof, fell softly to the bannister, the floor, the ground below. *I can live*, she whispered. *I can live*. She drew from the flower's scent.

Then a heartbeat sound from deep quiet night. Barely perceptible. Steady. Then clear. The pad of a runner's shoes on the pavement. She leaned against the gallery column. Clearer. Steadily growing louder. Louder. The runner drew abreast of the corner hedge. She could hear his breathing now, clear in the quiet night, and the pad of his shoes.

"Max," she whispered. "He will live. He will live, Max."

He moved past the entrance, down the hedge, rounded the corner, steadily the pad, growing softer, more distant, fading, gone.

Bless you, Max. Bless you, lost one.

She tossed the flower into the night.

She went inside. She dropped her clothes and stood before the huge standing mirror. She turned.

Jennings took my breast, but I am still beautiful. He took my breast to save my soul. Poor Iris Gordiner told me. I think I knew. I think I knew he did it. I feared to think it. He took her breast to save her life. He took my breast to save my soul. Poor demented, god-eaten Jennings. It is sad that his god needed my beautiful breast in fee for my soul. It is very sad.

But I am still beautiful. And now, I want. I want what I have never had. I want love, love shared, and I am ready to give love. I am thirty-seven years old and I am beautiful and perfectly prepared. I want a man, my man. I want to meet him, be taken by him, held by him, to take him, hold him. I want to eat with him, laugh with him, play in bed with him, sleep each night beside him. I want this. So much. I am going to have this. I will give him such luck as he could not dream. I want this. Tomorrow I will begin looking for him. And I will find him. All my flags will be out.

She slipped into a nightgown and cut out the light.

Rain dripping. A sound on the gallery? Another? Sound? or merely the rain? She moved toward the screen door. She reached for it.

It flung open, driving her backward.

Coy Trexler stepped into the room.

She was too amazed to react. In the demi-light, she thought for a moment she had imagined it. Wanted to have imagined it.

It was he. They stood like two animals engaged, glaring at each other. At last she took two steps backward.

"Wha...?" her voice failed.

He was panting. He had climbed the ivy strong column.

"You shouldn' a done that tonight. I nearly floored her. I nearly smushed you. You don't know how close I come to it."

He spoke under his breath. "Sonova bitch Hendricks is gone. Yer whelp ain't here. I figgered you need some company."

She couldn't make a sentence, a thought. Belief would not come so that she could react.

He lounged against the door. "I wuz...I figgered since you wuz all alone in this here big house I'd come an take a little of you."

She shook her head violently from left to right. "But...But you have..."

"Yeah. I figgered I'd git some more. It ain't used up, is it?"

She calmed now.

"Coy, you ruined me. You hurt me. You beat me up. My nose was broken. My finger... For God's sakes, leave me alone."

"Wal, I figgered you'd remember. An' take it easy this time."

She gathered herself. She made a move for the door. He caught her arm, spun her and open-handed her across the face so hard that her head snapped to the side and she reeled.

She slumped against the door. *No,* she thought. *Not this. Not this again. As long as I breathe.*

He dropped her hand.

"Gonna be good now? I shoulda run you over down at the motel. You gonna be good?"

"Listen, Coy. You don't want me. Listen, I'm ruined. I lost a breast. Listen. Look."

She reached across and tore the left strap of her gown, ripped it down the side and showed her scar.

"You don't want me. Look."

He put his hands on his hips, swaggering.

"I knowed you wuz a gimp. I heard. Ain't nuthing wrong between yer legs, is it?"

He reached for her gown. She sidestepped, again moved for the door. Again he caught her wrist, slapped her, circled her and caught her hair and popped her head back, snarled into her face, "Know it, cunt. Know it."

She tasted blood. Her blood. *My lip is cut.* She looked into his eyes and she knew. *But, I won't go through that again. I won't. I will not endure that again. Why didn't I bring that pistol in here? But, by God, this slime will not use me again. I am not going to endure that abomination again.* Her eyes darted the room for a way—a weapon.

He saw. "Sonova bitch Hendricks is dead. Lie down, cunt. It's gonna be."

Stall, she thought, *stall.* She relaxed her hand in his.

"All right, Coy. All right. You win. Listen, I've got to go to the bathroom. I've got to go. I just got in the house. You know that."

His weasel eyes searched her face.

"Let me run into the bathroom. I have to go. One minute."

"How do I know . . . ?"

"Listen. One minute. I have to go."

He was giving. She saw.

"I just got here. You know that."

Finally, still holding her hair, he walked her, head bent backward, toward the bathroom.

"You got sixty seconds."

He entered with her, switched on the light, looked around. He released her.

"Sixty seconds. I'll be at the porch door watching the window. Sixty seconds."

He jerked the key from the door, flung it across the bedroom, and backed out.

She closed the door. Her eyes swept the room. In the shower. Nothing. Her bath brush. The little boudoir chair. It was too short to barricade the door. She opened the pantry door. Some bottles. She grasped the alcohol. What? Hit him

528

with it? Stupid. Break it? An edge? He'd hear and be ready. She opened the medicine cabinet. Not even a nail file or scissors. Outside on her dressing table. Oh God.

Her hands went in frustration to her temples. She turned and flushed the toilet. Noise.

She leaned back to the lavatory. She glanced up into the mirror. There was a drop of blood at the corner of her mouth. *That slime hit me! He'll beat me again.* She cupped water in her hand and splashed her mouth. Toweled. The blood had stopped.

She took the water tumbler, filled it, and rinsed.

He struck the door. "Awright."

She straightened.

"A minute. I'm coming."

Oh God! She emptied the tumbler and reached to replace it in its holder. Her arm froze in half gesture. Still holding the glass, she wheeled to the pantry, opened the door, grasped the alcohol.

Yes. She uncapped the bottle and splashed the tumbler full.

I don't know.

She leaned against the door.

"Coy. Coy, listen. Please, please go away. Please."

"Time's up. Come out or I'm comin' in."

"Oh, Coy. Coy, listen, I'm getting my period. Please. Please, Coy.

Her voice broke, but she held the tumbler steady.

"I'm comin'."

Her head fell forward. The fumes of the alcohol stung her nostrils.

"All right. All right. Three seconds. I'll come out."

She went to the mirror. Stared. Set her chin. Breathed deeply. Once. Turned and reached for the door.

No. With her left hand she ripped the gown away. It fell at her feet. She was naked. She stepped to the door, grasped the tumbler, curved her wrist and it behind her hip. Pressed it firmly to her hip. Took breath.

She opened the door with her left hand and stepped into the shaft of light. She could dimly see him crouched over the bed. She leaned back against the jamb, arced her hip, and stood. Then she raised her left arm, welcoming.

For a moment, he didn't move. This was a vision he could

529

not have dreamed. Live a thousand years, he could not have dreamed this.

"Gargh," he growled and sprang toward her, arms reaching.

Her right hand flashed from her hip. The quicksilver glitter of the alcohol leapt full in his face.

He snarled surprise. Fell back. Coughed. Spat. Covered his face with his hands.

Charlotte dropped the tumbler, leapt past him to the bed, skittered across it, whipped her feet to the floor, hit the door jamb, spun, grabbed the ladderback chair there and jerked it across the doorway. She dashed for the stair. Using the bannister post for pivot, she flung herself down.

She heard him shriek a curse as he kicked the chair aside. Then he was behind her on the stairs.

She bounded the landing and sprang for the door, wrenched it open, and jumped, breaking the screen door open. She leaned into the night.

But her body flew out from under her head. Her neck jerked back. He had caught her hair. Momentum flung them both out onto the porch.

He tumbled across her. He turned on her, spitting and coughing. He flung a hailstorm of aimless blows, missing, hitting, grasping, hitting, hitting.

She rolled and bridged, slithered from under him, made it to her knees, then feet. But he drove himself against her, slamming her back against the porch wall. With both hands he pinned her shoulders against the wall.

They glared at each other for a moment. He was squinting, cockeyed.

Tears streamed his face. His breath was clotted.

From her shoulder to her face, his open hand whacked her across the ear, drove her head against the wall.

Stars and spangles swam her vision. Another blow, close-fisted, jolted her head against the wall.

Another. She felt a sinking, a going away. *Stay up*, she thought.

But he had stopped. One hand released. She looked. He was wiping his eyes. Panting.

Then a sound thudded against the night. He heard it too. He cocked his head. Stopped rubbing his eyes.

Over her heart beat, another beat. The pad of a runner in the street. Clearly. Persistently. Gently echoed in the cavern the great oaks and elms flung over Well Street. Coming. The slow distance pace. She gasped.

She took breath, screamed, *"Max! Help! Hel—!"*

Coy's balled fist smashed across her face, drove her head murderously against the wall. Again.

She lost, faded momentarily, came back, went slack. He released her and she crumpled.

She vaguely registered his dash to the end of the porch. His vault of the bannister. She sank down, her head listed to her knee.

Then, most gently, she felt hands cup and lift her face. She looked momently into eyes above a white mask that dampened the rasping breath. She was aware of those hands sweeping her hair back, the eyes staring intently into hers, reading her. The hands, gently but firmly, pressed her shoulders back against the wall. Then they left her.

She heard the feet leap to the end of the porch, vault the bannister. Then she released again and let her head fall forward to her knee.

As he reached the end of the hedge, rubbing and clawing his seared eyes, Coy Trexler heard those steps pound the wooden floor of the porch. He heard the thud as the vault ended on the ground. Coy dropped to hands and knees and dogged through the hedge.

Lights went on in the house across the street. Then the porch lights. A yard lamp. He raced for the shimmering El Dorado.

As he closed the door, he heard the runner's feet pounding the pavement behind the car. He jammed the key into the ignition, turned it. The engine roared. He snapped it into gear just as the runner leaped on the trunk. As he touched the accelerator, a fist smashed through the plastic rear window of the convertible. In the mirror he saw a man's arm, then shoulder, then face—a face half covered with some crazy kind of mask—heave through the opening.

Coy reached under the dash, sprung the shotgun just as the runner's arms closed around his throat, sliding easily on the grease of his own tears and sweat. Breath stopped. His throat shut down. He dropped the shotgun to his lap. Clawed at his throat. As the arm tightened, he saw in the mirror the face of the man who was killing him. The mask had slipped away. In the moment before his eyes popped, Coy Trexler fastened on a horrible distortion of a memory. The face was layered scars, the mouth pulled aslant, almost into his cheek. But vaguely familiar, suggestive. The man whistled and rasped in his ear as he killed him.

Oh yeah, Coy thought. *Oh yeah, it's Max Compton. I wouldna' recognized him.*

Then kicking and scratching, he died.

The car, adrift, rolled, lurched, jumped the curb, rammed a telephone pole and stopped.

Mr. Benson and Mrs. Summersett, standing in robes and pajamas on their lighted porches, saw a man in shorts and sweat shirt carrying a strange looking gun dash away from the car, turn the corner, head down Well Street.

By the time they reached the grounded El Dorado, a loud explosion tunneled down beneath the great oak and elm canopy.

When Sybil, robed, made her way across the lawn and street, she saw Mr. Summersett standing on the lighted porch of the Compton house.

"What—?"

"It's horrible. Awful. Young Max has committed suicide. He put a shot-gun in his mouth. It's horrible. And down there . . . We must get the police."

Sybil ran to Charlotte.

Six weeks later, Charlotte and Alex turned in to the walk of the Compton house. Hal Link stood on the porch waiting for them. He gave her his hand.

"Charlotte Morton. And Alexander."

"Hello, Counsel."

"Mr. Link."

He extended a set of keys.

"The probate is completed and registered. The house and all other holdings are yours."

"Thank you, Counsel. Thank you for being so efficient."

"Glad to help. Ah, Charlotte. One thing. Martha, the old maid. Max provided for her, of course. Handsomely. She was in my office this morning. She, I think, sort of feels she belongs with the house. I don't know what arrangements you are considering, but perhaps you can find a place for her. I mean . . ."

"Of course, she can stay. She can have anything she wants."

"Good. Good. I hoped that would be your attitude. It will make her happy. She's old and . . ."

"Yes. I know Martha. I'll want her and need her. Of course."

"Well, that's all I guess. If anything comes up, I'll contact you. And if I can help in any way . . ." He opened his hands.

"Thank you again, Counsel."

Link turned to go. But on the first step he paused.

"Charlotte, I . . . Well, many things have . . . have come to light because of this horror. There were many misconceptions. This town was . . . well, anyway, Charlotte Morton, respected daughter of my old respected adversary, I wish you well with all my heart."

It was nearly dusk when, hand in hand, Charlotte Morton and her son left the house and walked slowly down Well Street. Alex carried under his arm a large mahogany stationery box.

They had lingered in only one room of the formal house, the rear upstairs morning room, the room from which Charlotte had so often seen light burning all night. The shades were still drawn when they entered.

They had found the stationery box open on the coffee table. In it were letters. Many. Old. From Whitlow Manson, from Billy, from Jennings, from David Fried and his Shirley, recent letters from Dr. Grossman. And there were photographs, old and many. Of a tall handsome youth with his friends. And his girl. And her smiling father. And the great black woman who cared for them. And a car called The Wreck. And his French teacher. Some were by a river which had little islands.

Cached in a corner of the box was a little stoppered Turkish jar holding a handful of sand from the plain of Troy—sand the youth and his girl dreamed had ground through the sandals of Achilles. And in a tiny felt pouch, a silver coin bearing the head of Alexander the Great.

There were some sepia-colored newspaper clippings. One told how a local high school athlete had broken the state record for the mile. One told of an automobile accident which had claimed a young man named Blaine Watkins. Another told of the death of a local musician in New York. There were two letters in outrageous script, distinguished by original spelling and amusing obscenities, from someone named Bessemer Hanks.

But mostly there were letters from his girl—hundreds of them. Some were very old. From Rome. From Greece. One from Troy. Some, many, were addressed to the Fleet Post Office, San Francisco, and Terminal Island, and to Camp Butner. They were letters, these last, to a phantom love. Clearly, they had been treasured most humanly.

Several times that afternoon, Alex watched his mother stare aimlessly away, distance in her eyes, or cover her face with her hands and sob, and he leaned to her. Once she murmured softly, "*Many ingenious lovely things are gone that seemed sheer miracle* . . . sheer miracle . . . oh God—they *were* sheer miracle!"

"What?"

"Oh, dear. I was remembering your grandfather. The poem he loved so. Remember? The Yeats. You know it."

When the boy and his mother turned into their walk, she pulled him across the lawn to the stand of long leaf pines. Walking carefully, they looked down at the sturdy miniature grove of Trailing Arbutus which she—they, and another—had guarded so long.

They stood quietly breathing, until suddenly she gasped, "Alex, look! Over there! And here! Careful. It's hard to see."

Trailing Arbutus spreads—trails—so slowly. Only an inch a year, it seems. And yet sometimes, you can walk out and suddenly find yourself surrounded by small dark green plants. Trapped, you'll fear to step. Ambushed! And on familiar ground too.

Charlotte and Alex were trapped. They knelt in wonder.

Finally they stood. Charlotte threw her head back. Dusk had deepened. The stars were there. The Great Wheel. She gasped. *They do not know we are here*, she thought. *They do not know of us. But we can love*, she thought. *We can love, stars. I, and my son, and my kind can love.*

Suddenly she took her son's hand and tugged him toward the house.

"Come, Alex. I'm starved. Aren't you starved? Come on. Let's have dinner at the bar. Hey, I'll run and change. You call Sybil and grab a bottle of Jack. Tonight I'm gonna play and sing like a coven of angels. Hurry! Let's get prepared for joy. Just in case."

APPENDIX

No rational argument exists for nuclear armament. The rhetoric of deterrence, parity, and limited warfare is perfect stupidity or perfect charlatanism. Only the senseless or suicidal would amass enough weapons to incinerate the planet, weapons which may be activated at the whim of fool, fanatic or mechanical failure. There is no defense for striker or victim. Who can protect or evacuate the botanical forms and their auxiliaries, insects and birds, on whom earth and life depend? Who can defend or evacuate earth's ozone layer? Who, no matter how devoted, can construe value for any sovereign state, art, science, political or spiritual form after extermination? Political, economic and spiritual conventions change or pass. Extermination, the 'death of death', is everlasting and unchanging. I claim the highest moral duty of every human is to demand the disarmament and destruction of all nuclear weapons. Now.

—F. Y.

"POWERFUL ... SUPERB ... NEVER FAILS
TO TOUCH THE READER ON EVERY PAGE"
—Barbara Taylor Bradford,
author of VOICE OF THE HEART

The Days
of Eternity

by

Gordon Glasco

Here is a breathtaking saga of a passionate love so overwhelming that it
defies war, betrayal, conscience—and time itself. One Sunday morning,
Anna Miceli, a successful American lawyer, sits in church and sees a
man—and her heart stands still. At that moment, time melts away. Once
again Anna is the innocent girl of an Italian country village. It is wartime,
and the time of her first consuming love—for the young German lieutenant
who commands the occupying forces. But when he commits an unspeakable
act, Anna's world is shattered, her life changed forever. Now, twenty-
eight years later, he stands before her—a priest. And now, Anna knows
the time has come to face an agonizing choice. For here is the man whose
memory has been a cold cinder of hatred inside her, the man she has vowed
someday to destroy—and the man her turbulent heart can never surrender.

Read THE DAYS OF ETERNITY, on sale September 1, 1984,
wherever Bantam paperbacks are sold, or use the handy coupon below
for ordering:

SPECIAL MONEY SAVING OFFER

Now you can have an up-to-date listing of Bantam's hundreds of titles plus take advantage of our unique and exciting bonus book offer. A special offer which gives you the opportunity to purchase a Bantam book for only 50¢. Here's how!

By ordering any five books at the regular price per order, you can also choose any other single book listed (up to a $4.95 value) for just 50¢. Some restrictions do apply, but for further details why not send for Bantam's listing of titles today!

Just send us your name and address plus 50¢ to defray the postage and handling costs.

SPECIAL
MONEY SAVING
OFFER

Now you can have an up-to-date listing of Bantam's hundreds of titles plus take advantage of our unique and exciting bonus book offer. A special offer which gives you the opportunity to purchase a Bantam book for only 50¢. Here's how!

By ordering any five books at the regular price per order, you can also choose any other single book listed (up to a $4.95 value) for just 50¢. Some restrictions do apply, but for further details why not send for Bantam's listing of titles today!

Just send us your name and address plus 50¢ to defray the postage and handling costs.

"POWERFUL ... SUPERB ... NEVER FAILS
TO TOUCH THE READER ON EVERY PAGE"
—Barbara Taylor Bradford,
author of VOICE OF THE HEART

The Days
of Eternity

by

Gordon Glasco

Here is a breathtaking saga of a passionate love so overwhelming that it
defies war, betrayal, conscience—and time itself. One Sunday morning,
Anna Miceli, a successful American lawyer, sits in church and sees a
man—and her heart stands still. At that moment, time melts away. Once
again Anna is the innocent girl of an Italian country village. It is wartime,
and the time of her first consuming love—for the young German lieutenant
who commands the occupying forces. But when he commits an unspeakable
act, Anna's world is shattered, her life changed forever. Now, twenty-
eight years later, he stands before her—a priest. And now, Anna knows
the time has come to face an agonizing choice. For here is the man whose
memory has been a cold cinder of hatred inside her, the man she has vowed
someday to destroy—and the man her turbulent heart can never surrender.